LOVE GRACE

FUNDRAISER

GRACEPOINT School

A school for the dyslexic learner.

LOVE & GRACE

Cover by Airicka's Mystical Creations
www.airickaphoenix.com

Formatting by Rene Folsom
www.renefoslom.com

ISBN: 978-1-939081-53-7
First Paperback Edition | Printed in the United States of America

DEDICATION

To all those who are gifted with dyslexia, we dedicate these stories to you and your family.

If you'd like to give to Gracepoint – A school for dyslexic learners, please visit http://www.gracepointschool.org/donate-online/.

TABLE OF CONTENTS

INTRODUCTION

Romance for the soul, a gift from the heart.

This collection of sweet and inspirational novellas has an uplifting love story for everyone. These stories bring a touch of grace to romance, and a touch of romance to your heart.

Our twelve authors have collaborated to bring together this collection. Each story relates to dyslexia in some way, and the full proceeds from all the stories benefit Gracepoint – A School for Dyslexia. This box set is our collective gift of love and support to you and the children Gracepoint serves.

Can a town save a marriage? Will a high school reunion offer a second chance at love? Can a man with a secret and a woman afraid of being hurt learn to trust? Can a girl running from her past escape her heart? Will a woman trapped in the past discover the true importance of family? Can unexpected love become the best present ever?

You'll find hours of enjoyment as well as a satisfying ending to each story. No cliffhangers and no partial novels are offered here, just an escape into worlds of love, families, and grace.

FOREWORD
By Sherrilyn Kenyon

Dyslexia is one of the few learning disabilities that everyone likes to joke that they have, without ever truly realizing just what a challenge it poses to those of us who struggle with it every day of our lives. Yeah, it can be hilarious when someone mispronounces a word or sentence when they're in a hurry, or they transpose numbers either (or both) verbally and on paper because they're in a rush or not paying attention. But that is not the same as being physically incapable of pronouncing a compound word such as lab rat, hay bale or stereotypical (and not being able to recognize that it's wrong because we literally cannot see or hear that it's wrong). Of living through that horrible moment when everyone around you laughs at what you just said, and you don't even know why because you're unaware of the fact that you just said it backwards without intent. And when you ask what you said to prompt the laughter, they still think you're in on the joke, and you're not. You're really trying to understand what you said that was wrong.

Of trying to play a videogame, but your dyslexia refuses to orient with the screen to such an extent that you not only slam into walls, you can't even pick items in the game. And don't get me started on trying to follow a diagram or instructions. Oh the things I've misassembled over the years. Pretty sure I've created a diabolical robot or two, completely by accident. If only they could have stood up with one crooked leg, they would have taken over the world!

I know all this, because I am that person who struggles in a misaligned world every day of my life. As a girl in school, I was called stupid, and even stubborn by teachers who didn't know what dyslexia was (back then, they didn't diagnose it). They thought I was being difficult because I mirror-wrote. Or because in math, I wouldn't write down my work, only the answers– I was even accused of cheating because of it. I could solve the problems in my head, but if I wrote down the steps or all those numbers, I got confused by the chaos, transposed the numbers, and became so frustrated that I would burst into tears in the middle of class. I just could not write out the work, no matter how hard I tried, especially in trig or algebra.

Nwod ti etorw I revenehw siht ekil dekool ginhtyreve nehw deen on saw ereht— There was no need when everything looked like this whenever I wrote it down.

Only picture all the letters backwards, to boot.

That really is how I see the world. If you tell me to go right, I go left because that is my right. Same for clicking on things for accept and cancel. I can see them, but my hand goes in the wrong direction. It's like an alien beast has control of my body at times, and I can't make it obey me.

Whenever I handwrite, everything is backwards, left to right. My dyslexia is so bad that on the day I sold my first novel, it took me twenty minutes to dial my mother's phone number (same number we had that I grew up with). I was so excited I couldn't punch the numbers in for it, in their correct sequence. I wish I were making that up, but stress or excitement worsens the condition.

Even more embarrassing, I wrote down my editor's number incorrectly and had to call the publisher and ask them for her correct number and extension because, even though I'd called it out to her, I somehow wrote it down incorrectly. And multiple attempts before I had all the numbers on the paper in their proper sequential order.

Yeah, it is *that* bad. It's why my autograph looks the way it does, and why I sign things in Latin. No one can tell that my letters aren't in their proper places.

What's bad is that I still have trouble talking about it in public, because of the childhood trauma and stigma. I remember after it was finally diagnosed in high school and I was having trouble filling out financial aid forms for college, telling a loan officer I had it. My sister who was with me hissed at me. "Sherri! Don't tell people you have that. They'll think you're stupid!"

My reponse? "Well, sis. It's not like I can hide it. Better they know there's a reason than think I'm idiot just because I can't get my name on the correct line."

It's why you'll never hear me read a passage from one of my books out loud in public— and as an author, we are asked to do this constantly. But I can't do it. Physically or mentally. The trauma of being mocked, of knowing that even though I wrote it, I will read some of it backwards and not even know I'm doing it hangs in my mind and paralyzes me with absolute terror. That is the reality of dyslexia.

No, it's not the worst thing a human can face. There are far, far worse boogie men and traumas in the world. My eldest sister has severe Cerebral Palsy. She can't bathe or dress herself, and something as innocuous as eating is almost impossible for her. So I'm well aware that as far as irritating brain quirks go I'm fortunate that I only have a mild paralysis in one hand and dyslexia to cope with.

Yet that being said, just because letters, words and numbers dance in our heads does not make us stupid. It just makes us human.

If I could say one thing to someone with dyslexia it is to stop beating yourself up for it. Yes, it's frustrating and sometimes it feels debilitating when you can't even dial a phone that's preset with numbers and people faces (remember what I said about not being able to choose the correct line), but hey those accidental dials have led to some fun conversations.

I think because I grew up with an older sister who can't speak or hear and yet I saw her do tremendous things in spite of the doctors and what they told my family would be impossible for Patricia, I know that in life, the only limitations we have are those we accept.

What I tell my sons (two have autism and one has Aspergers) is that over, under, around or through— there's always a way to get your desires. To be who and what you want to be. Don't let anything stop you!

Remember that three-year-old we all used to be? The kid who knew nothing about gravity and thought they could fly? Even though everyone said you couldn't, you tried any way, because you were convinced you could do it. No one could talk sense into you. And when they gave you all those reasons why you couldn't fly, you stuck your tongue out at them and said, "Oh yeah? Watch me!"

The worst part of life is when that three-year-old perishes inside us and we begin telling ourselves why we can't do something. Well, I have . . .

Stop it! Don't ever do it again. Don't become one of those nay-sayers who is too afraid to try. Because you know what, we can fly. Okay, granted we have to be in a jet or glider, but people can and do fly. There is absolutely nothing you can't do if you set your heart and mind to it.

My grandfather showed me that. He was a faith-healer and a Baptist minister. And I saw many a miracle delivered at his hands. Because people believed. The human mind is an incredible thing. The human spirit even more so. You might judge a dog based on his size, but you can never limit the strength of his raw determination.

Live life without boundaries! Never let anyone, especially yourself, tell you what you can and can't do. The only time we fail is when we stop trying. As I like to quote to my boys, Thomas Edison once said, "I have not failed seven hundred times. I have not failed once. I have succeeded in proving that those seven hundred ways will not work. When I have eliminated the ways that will not work, I will find the way that will work."

Or in the words of my older brother when he was teaching me to bat because I was scared of the balls he pitched at me, "Baby, you will never hit the balls you don't swing at. And if you don't hit the ball, you'll never make your home run. You gotta try."

And everyone, no matter who they are or where they come from; no matter what quirks their minds or bodies might have, can try. I know you can achieve whatever dream you hold. God knows if a girl with dyslexia as bad as mine can actually write a correct sentence— never mind becoming a

#1 international bestselling author, and humans can walk on the moon, then there is nothing standing in the way of anyone else. Go make your dream happen!

— **Sherrilyn Kenyon**

GRACE IN SWEETWATER COUNTY

Ciara Knight

It takes a town to save a marriage.
Carter Davidson suffered humiliating torment as a child for his learning difficulties and has spent his entire life overcoming the stereotype of being stupid. As an adult he's achieved a corporate title, lives a perfect life, until tragedy strikes in threes; loss of a baby, his wife disappearing behind a cloud of depression, and his son facing the same bullying he did as a child.

After the loss of her baby girl, Emily Davidson sinks into a world of despair. When she awakens from her life hiatus she must face her neglect of her only son. A third grader who's unable to read or write. Emily focuses all her energy on helping her son, but with her husband's inexplicable aversion to her son receiving help, Emily is forced to choose between the love of her husband, or the well-being of her only surviving child.

*****

Although this is designed to be a standalone book, it is book IX in the Sweetwater County series. Some secondary characters will make cameo appearance in this book. For this reason, I've included a character list at the end of the story to make your reading experience as flawless as possible.

Chapter One

Welcome to Sweetwater County, Tennessee. Population 5,000. Where your heart and home belong. Those simple old words on a newly-crafted sign caused memories of Emily Davidson's youth to flood her mind and incite her emotions. *Home.* After seventeen years of looking for the next adventure, experiencing life beyond the small town of Creekside, she now reluctantly returned.

An open field came into view out the passenger window. It was once her playground, where friends would meet on their bikes and play hide and seek, or sit in the tall grass and watch the clouds go by. *Simpler times.*

She glanced at Carter, his hands on the steering wheel at the ten-and-two positions and his eyes forward. Did he not want to look at her? Touch her? How long had it been? Her hand slipped to her belly and she rubbed the emptiness away. *Months.* It had been months, almost a year, since they'd touched each other in a loving, marital way. A marriage that had once been full of love had withered and faded.

Carter's hand slipped over hers and her pulse baby-stepped toward hope. "It'll be different here. I promise. We're moving forward, not looking back, right? We've left everything behind for a new start. New school for Jacob. You'll be staying home to help. We'll be closer to my mother and your aunt. It's going to be good."

Good? With a mother-in-law who hated her? Her days spent stuck in an empty, lonely house while Carter traveled to avoid her? And her son, Jacob, fighting every moment not to attend school? Carter was right about one thing, though. Her Aunt Sue would be a beacon of light in her loneliness. Perhaps she could hang out at Café Bliss on occasion and chat while Aunt Sue worked. Emily squeezed his hand in response and forced a smile, trying to show him she was on board, even though she knew their troubles would follow no matter where they lived.

Carter pulled his hand away and hope crawled back into its vault. He pointed out the windshield. "Look, Jacob. That'll be your new school."

Emily turned in her seat to find her nine-year-old son slouching in the back seat, with his arms crossed over his chest. The idea of school—any school—terrified him. Third grade shouldn't make her child feel like he was facing a firing squad every day.

"Don't worry, buddy," Carter said. "It's a great school. Much better teachers than your old one. You'll do great here." Her husband's voice was a touch lighter than it should be. "When we moved here in elementary school, my life changed. I know yours will, too.

Tears welled up in her son's eyes, but she knew better than to push the subject. Carter refused to discuss their son's issues in school, and now wasn't the time to try broaching the subject again, not in front of Jacob. She settled back into her seat and kept her mouth shut. It was the way of their marriage and it worked, for now.

The car dipped, leaving Emily's stomach behind as they drove down a hill then up the next into town. "Wow, I can't believe Main Street hasn't changed much," Emily mumbled, eyeing the potted flowers, old-fashioned street lights, and shop windows full of antiques, yarn, and other items. They drove further and she spotted her aunt's coffee shop, Café Bliss. A shutter of regret surged through her. "But that's changed." The once quaint shop looked modern now, remodeled after a tornado had struck the town a year or so ago.

Carter leaned over the steering wheel and eyed the large front windows. "It's better than I imagined. I guess the insurance money came through and then some. Do you want to stop and say hi? I could drop you and Jacob off, and you can show him around town while I go pick up the keys to the rental house."

Jacob shot forward, gripping the back of her seat. "Can we, Mom?"

It was the first smile she'd seen from him all day. How could she say no? "Sure. We can go check out the town."

Carter veered into a parking spot out front of J & L Antiques. That was also new. She caught a glimpse of Judy Gaylord through the large display window. Wait, her aunt had told her Judy had gotten married. What was her last name again? Benjamin? She'd have to ask Aunt Sue.

"Okay, you two have fun." Carter held up his fist to Jacob, and they did the fist bump and explosion thing they'd perfected over the last few months. Something she'd tried once, but Jacob begged her to never, ever do it again, especially in public. Apparently, it was a father-son thing. If she had a daughter, perhaps…

She straightened, pushing the thought of having another child out of her mind. She grabbed the door handle, but Carter snagged her arm before she could get out of the car. Jacob already stood, hopping up and down on the sidewalk in front of the car with eager anticipation.

"Hey, new start, remember?" Carter leaned in, and her breath swooshed from her lungs. Even after all this time, the littlest touch still made her heart flutter. His lips pressed to her cheek, sending warmth down her neck. He gave her shoulder an awkward squeeze then sat back. It was an effort, she knew. Perhaps someday it wouldn't be work to remain married. Perhaps they could go back to how things were in the old days and they'd laugh and enjoy each other's company again. Perhaps, he'd forgive her for not being able to have more children, forgive her for losing their daughter.

She climbed out of the car and made her way to the sidewalk, taking deep breaths on the way. Her heart ached as she watched him drive away, even though the distance remained between them, regardless of their proximity.

"Come on, Mom." Jacob tugged her toward Café Bliss. Ever since Aunt Sue had sent him a teen-rated video game for Christmas, she'd become the coolest aunt to ever walk the cosmos.

A man held open the door for them with a knowing smile, one that suggested he recognized her. She only nodded and returned the smile, unable to place him until she looked back and saw him climb into a fancy town car. That had to be Mr. Burton, the man who owned most of the town.

The café was bustling with people, their faces familiar yet foreign. The feeling of being an outsider in her hometown scraped at her determination to make Creekside her home once again. Would she ever belong here? How would she handle the questions and subsequent pity that were bound to come up?

"Emily! Jacob!" Aunt Sue raced from behind the counter with open arms. She looked almost the same, her usually dark hair a light honey wheat now. She had a few more lines on her forehead and around her eyes, but nothing about her warm smile had changed. Soft, yet strong arms wrapped around Emily, an embrace she remembered from her childhood that had always made everything better. After a second, she relaxed into the physical contact. Something she wasn't so good at accepting anymore.

Aunt Sue rubbed her back and held her tight. "It's so good to see you. I've missed you forever. I'm so glad you're here."

Emily hugged her back. She felt awkward and stiff, but she was grateful all the same. Grateful her aunt was just as welcoming as she remembered.

Aunt Sue released her and looked at Jacob. "I don't know if you remember me. You were only a little guy when I saw you last. I can't believe how big you are now. Are you in college yet?"

Jacob laughed for the first time in weeks. A beautiful sound that Emily had missed, had feared she'd never hear again. "Nooooo. I'm only in third grade." He quirked a you're-a-crazy-lady brow at her.

Emily leaned against a wrought iron bistro chair with a leather seat and eyed the hardwood floors and marble-top tables. "The place looks awesome. I'm so sorry I wasn't able to be here to help after the tornado. It was a difficult time for me to travel." Emily stopped her hand from reaching for her belly once more and dropped it to her side. Guilt at the thought of abandoning her beloved aunt when she needed her most conflicted with her own needs. In the end, it didn't matter. The baby hadn't made it...again.

Aunt Sue wrapped an arm around her shoulder and pulled her into a half hug. "Hey, no need to fret. All's well. I totally understand. Besides, you're here now, and you did call to check on me daily, remember? That's more than I can say for your dad. I haven't heard from him in almost a year, and he's my only brother, for goodness sake. Where is he, anyway? South Africa? Europe? Taiwan?"

Emily shrugged. "I called him and Mom a few weeks ago to tell them I was returning to Sweetwater County. They were in Ireland at the time, but they can't seem to stay in one place for long."

"Oh, I bet that went over well. They hightailed it out of here the second you went to college. He believed you all were meant for bigger and better things than small town living."

Emily patted Jacob's soft, dark hair. "I thought so, too, but things change."

"Mrs. Fletcher, I need the key for the register," a girl behind the counter called.

Aunt Sue pulled a lanyard with keys from her pocket and twirled it around her hand. "Don't go anywhere. I'll be right back. Hey, little man. You want the Jacob Freeze?"

Jacob tilted his head to the side. "What's that?"

Aunt Sue backed toward the counter, the register key in hand. "Look at the board."

Emily stiffened, knowing her son wouldn't be able to read it out loud, if at all. She quickly spotted Jacob's name in stark white writing and swooped in to cover for him. "Oh my goodness! Can you believe that? Aunt Sue created a drink with all your favorite things and named it after you! It's got caramel, whipped cream, sea salt, and ice cream."

"Wow, awesome!" Jacob danced with joy but his hands twisted in panic, a gesture she'd learned meant he was becoming anxious. Emily placed a reassuring hand on the back of his head and scratched. He melted into her palm and relaxed. How many boys his age struggled with reading? He was smart, not just average smart, but he excelled at math and had tremendous common sense for his age. Of course, he could read, but not under pressure and certainly not from a board covered in so much information. He'd made great progress, though. Hopefully, Carter was right, that Creekside Elementary would be the answer. That having great teachers in a small town who cared would allow her son to not just be another nameless face roaming the overcrowded halls.

Aunt Sue waved her hand in front of Emily's face. "Whatcha so deep in thought about, Emmy?"

"Oh my dear lord in heaven! Is that little Emily? Emily Davidson?" The voice that called out left no doubt as to who stood behind Emily. She turned on her heels, thankful for the distraction, but her relief was short lived.

"Cathy Mitchell?" Emily forced a friendly smile, not sure she was ready for the town gossip.

"Cathy West now." Cathy held up her left hand, displaying a pretty engagement ring and wedding band. She'd lost weight and had ditched the crazy cat sweaters for a more sophisticated style. Emily felt like she'd been dropped into a *Twilight Zone* movie, where she'd returned to her hometown only to find her friends and family had been replaced by aliens.

Cathy's ring dazzled under the lights. Emily's hadn't been as fancy, but it was special. Carter had given it to her when they were just eighteen years old. It was either get married or move away with her parents, so they got married. The whole thing was against his mother's wishes—still was—and she'd kept her mother's ring in protest. Not that Emily would have exchanged it if given the chance, though. The ring Carter gave her was perfect. Until they had to cut it off with her wedding ring in the hospital when her hands swelled during delivery. Rings they'd yet to fix or replace. They'd tarnished with loss.

"You look shell-shocked, hon. I know, I know, I cleaned myself up a little." Cathy twirled, an actual twirl in the middle of the coffee shop.

Emily leaned against the chair to remain upright, fightening the after-shocks of bad memories. "You look amazing. It's great to see you."

"Good to see you, too, hon. How's everything going? Oh, and who's this dashing young man?"

Jacob stepped back into Aunt Sue. "It's okay, honey. She's a lot to take in, but she never hurts anyone. Promise." Aunt Sue patted his shoulder.

He nodded and offered his hand like a little gentleman. "I'm Jacob. Nice to meet you."

"So, you're the famous Jacob. Well, I hear I have you to thank for that terrific drink." Cathy tipped her head toward the counter where the espresso machine growled, gurgled, and ground coffee while staff raced about making concoctions. The place began to sound more like a school cafeteria than a coffee shop. "I have to admit, it's my weekly cheat." Cathy shook Jacob's hand and sat down at a table nearby.

"Jacob Freeze," the girl behind the counter called.

Cathy set her purse down on the table top and sighed. "Ah, I see you get to have one. I'm afraid I have to wait until Friday. Oh well, it makes it that much tastier. Kids always have the best taste and ideas." Cathy's eyes twinkled at Jacob then she swiveled to face Emily as her son stepped toward the counter with Aunt Sue to retrieve his drink. "Special boy you've got there. You and Carter planning on having more? Is that what brought you back to Creekside?"

Emily fought the rising grief, her insides twisting and turning with anxiety, darkening her mood.

Jacob returned to her side, ignoring the drink Aunt Sue had in her hand. "Nope, I'm all she can handle. I'm a total handful." He laughed while his hand scratched the middle of her back, the way he always did if she was upset or tired. Did he know? Had he figured out why they left their home up north to move back here? He looked up with a wide smile, his gray eyes bright, and she knew that her son was too smart to keep anything from him. He'd figured it out, and it broke her heart that he'd carried the knowledge without speaking about it. He'd begged for a little sister for so long, yet she'd disappointed him, too.

Chapter Two

Carter stood on the front porch of his childhood home and waited. Waited for memories to flood into him like a dam giving way. Waited for the nostalgia of youth to fill him with butterflies and puffy clouds. Waited for his mother to make her way down the stairs to open the door before he collapsed from old age himself. Why she still lived in such a large house was beyond him.

"Coming!" his mother yelled, her voice as commanding as ever. It had been two years since he'd last seen her. Way too long to be away, but it couldn't have been helped. He'd had to stay with Emily. The last two pregnancies were hard…the most recent loss of their daughter even more so. He shivered at the memory of Emily lying in a hospital bed, her skin pale, her eyes swollen, and her nose red from crying. She'd been so distraught she couldn't even speak for days.

The door creaked open, and he saw Judith Davidson's loving, yet stern, blue eyes. Dressed in polyester pants, she popped a hip out and clutched her waist with a boney, gnarled hand. She was too young, too look so old, her rheumatoid arthritis had eaten away at joints. Guilt for not staying around to help her ate away at his heart. "It's about time you got here. I've been waiting." She peered around him and looked toward the driveway. "Where's that grandson of mine?"

"He's with Emily. I thought I'd come see you alone first." Always a good idea since he knew how she still felt about his wife. He glanced at his watch then back at her. "I'm only five minutes late."

"Try two years late. That wife of yours refused to let you come visit your old mother, didn't she? I knew she was bad news. Told ya she'd emasculate you with her wild ideas of working and careers."

He sighed inwardly, but opened his arms and wrapped them around her shoulders, careful not to squeeze too hard for fear he'd break her bones. A skeleton weighed more than she did. He wanted to tell her the truth about why he'd stayed away but knew it would just bring more animosity between the two women he loved most in the world. "I'm here now, and I'll be around for a long time. You won't have to be alone anymore, and I can make sure you're eating."

"Alone? Who ever said I was alone? I've got friends. I'm no charity case, you know. And I eat plenty. Not my fault it don't stick." She hugged back, a mama bear hug with crushing strength that told him how much she truly missed him, though she'd never admit it.

He let her go and stepped inside, closing the door behind him. The fresh scent of spring flowers from outside faded, replaced by the strong, chemical odor of muscle and joint ointment. Seeing the dark wood molding of the old Victorian home covered in dust surprised him. His mother had always taken such pride in her home. She was a Mrs. Cleaver kind of woman, always the perfect housewife. There had been no such thing as feminism in his house growing up. Perhaps that was what attracted him the most when he met Emily. She was so strong, so independent, and she was a dreamer. She used to be so full of life, until loss extinguished the fire that once burned in her eyes.

"You want something to eat? I can make you a sandwich," his mother offered as she hobbled toward the kitchen.

"No, I'm not hungry, but thanks. We ate an hour or so before we reached Creekside. I figured we'd want some food in our stomachs before we tackled hauling everything into the rental house."

She whirled around with that feisty glare he remembered so well. "You'd rather stay in some rental than your own place? Thought you were coming home. That's what you said."

He took a long breath and leaned against the wall. "Mama, you don't want Emily living here. You two would fight all the time, and you know it. You never liked her. The rental isn't much, but it's only temporary."

"That ain't true. She's my daughter-in-law. I like her just fine."

"Then why haven't you asked about her?"

She smooshed her lips back and forth then huffed and waved him toward the living room. "Come sit."

He followed her into the dimly lit room, the 1980s recliners and couch exactly as he remembered them. An old afghan rested over the back of the couch, the same blanket he used to use anytime he was ill. He couldn't believe she still had it. The feeling of snuggly, childhood safety warmed his insides. "You okay?"

She collapsed into one of the recliners and leaned on the armrest as if her hip was bothering her. "I'm feeling just fine. You're the one who just drove for two days. How you holding up?"

"I'm good." He fought the rising desire to tell his mother about the hell he'd been through the last two years. To lean on her the way he had in his youth, but he knew it was time for the parent-child switch. It was his turn to be her support. Besides, it would only give his mother ammunition to use against Emily. She'd probably tell Emily that she wasn't a woman, that she wasn't fulfilling her duty as a wife if she couldn't have four boys like she had given his father. He never judged a woman's worth the way his mama did but knew she was a great woman all the same. His mother had to be a little tough. She'd raised four boys on her own, her husband being the hands-off type. Not to mention her fight against that horrible, crippling disease.

"Whatcha thinking about? You've got that pensive, constipated look on your face," his mother asked. The old grandfather clock chimed in the hallway, a sound straight from his youth.

He knew better than to mention her condition, she'd go off like firecrackers at the turn of the century. "Just how remarkable you are. You raised us boys practically on your own. You never missed a meal, or a baseball game, not one moment in our lives. How did you keep up with the four of us? I can barely keep up with one?"

She rocked in the recliner and smiled. "There was never a dull moment, but you boys were good."

"Good?" Carter laughed harder than he had in over a year. "What about when we burned the tree house to the ground? Or when Mark and Donald were caught shoplifting? Or when all four of us were arrested for drinking?"

She waved her hand in front of her face. "Growin' pains, that's all. Boys will be boys."

He shrugged. "I guess. You always did believe in us, though. Told us we could do anything if we worked hard and stayed focused."

"Yep, but you didn't listen. You had to go and marry that girl before you even went to college. You didn't believe you'd make it through college, so you used her as a crutch."

Anger stirred within him at her old criticisms. "We put each other through college. It worked for us."

"If it worked so well, and you two are so happy, why do you look like someone died?"

Emotions swirled inside him like a rising cyclone. Loss, grief, loneliness, anger. He swallowed and eyed his watch. He couldn't tell her. As much as he wanted his mother to understand, he knew it would betray his wife's trust. For some reason, she didn't want anyone to know. Their marriage might be rocky, but no matter what, he'd never intentionally harm Emily. She was and always would be the love of his life. Even if their marriage didn't make the long-term commitment train, his heart would never belong to another.

"You're right. It's been a long drive. I'm pretty tired and thirsty. Can I grab some water?" He stood and headed for the kitchen. "You want anything?" he asked over his shoulder, keeping his voice calm.

"Nope."

He stumbled into the kitchen, his knees threatening to collapse from the weight of his grief. He rested his palms against the old Formica counters and breathed. Breathed through the loss of two babies. Breathed through the terror that his wife would be next. He desperately tried to reach out to her, to find some way to keep her tethered to him, but he could feel her slipping away.

The hum of the old refrigerator gave him something to focus on as he breathed, but the harsh fluorescent lighting did nothing for his nerves. It reminded him of the hospital, of the night they held their newborn daughter for two hours before she was taken from them.

"You getting water or making a pie in there?" his mother called from the living room.

He grabbed a glass from the cabinet and turned on the tap. It sputtered and balked, but managed to dispense clear liquid after a moment of protest. "Don't you think it's time to consider moving out of this old place? I mean, it's a great house, but it's just too big for you now."

"Maybe I hope to leave it to one of my boys some day."

He thought for a moment about how their grand house had once stood as the pride of the old neighborhood. They'd done a complete remodel back in the 1980s, but not much had been updated in the poor old home since. It probably needed new everything, inside and out. Still, a lot of memories lived here. "These old homes are mostly being turned into office spaces now."

"Plenty of people still live here. Cathy West lives right around the corner with her new husband."

"Cathy West?"

"Yeah, you know, the Mitchells? You used to play with her daughter, Jenna. Cathy remarried a man named Devon West last Christmas."

"That's right. You wrote me about that." He took a sip of water and returned to the living room, sitting on the edge of the sofa. "Not much has changed around here, yet people have moved on. I saw some new shops on Main Street, and there are actual apartment buildings on the other side of town. Not to mention that big building on the outskirts of Creekside."

"That's the new VA center where they help injured vets reintegrate into society. It's a good cause, I guess." She shrugged. "I haven't been over there. I don't go out much besides to get my hair done and for groceries. Usually, the Red Hat ladies come here to play cards."

How could all four of her sons have left her here, forgotten and alone? When had they all turned their backs on the woman who raised them? He set his glass down on the side table and took his mother's crooked fingers in his hand. "Well, Friday night you're going out. I'm taking you to dinner, so make sure you keep your calendar clear. You pick the best place in town, and I'll take you on a date."

She giggled girlishly, not a sound he thought he'd ever hear from her. "Oh, you're just being silly now."

He squeezed her hand careful not to cause her undue pain, seeing the loneliness in her eyes. That was why she'd wasted away so quickly. She was withering from lack of love. He would change that. Between Emily, Jacob, and himself, she'd feel loved again. "I'll pick you up at five."

"Best make that four. I tend to fall asleep by six or so these days." She winked. "It's nice to have you back home."

He kissed her cheek and helped her from the chair, almost wishing he could just bring his family to her home tonight, but he knew it wouldn't work. He couldn't expect his wife and mother to remain in the same house together for too long without bloodshed being involved.

On the once quiet street out front, where kids would play ball and street hockey, cars now raced by. The oak tree they used to climb now towered over the roof of the second story, its lower branches scraping at the living room window. "As soon as I get settled in the rental, I'll come over and help clean up the yard a bit, trim those branches. I'll do some work on the plumbing also and anything else you might need some help on. Jacob and Emily can work on your garden. I know how much you love flowers."

"That's kind of you, son. Real kind. But first, you need to work in your own garden. Your family garden. You need to mend that broken fence and feed the plants with lots of love."

He quirked his head, wondering if the arthritis attacked her mind as well as her body, or if the pain drove her mad.

She smacked him on the shoulder. "You fool. You never did understand hidden meanings. You need to work out whatever's going on between you and your wife. Marriage is for life, you know. You chose her, so you're stuck with her. Figure out how to make it work."

He grabbed the doorknob, wanting to flee before she dug any deeper into her wellspring of proverbs and phrases and confused him further. "How did you know?"

"Please, the only way you got Emily to move within a hundred miles of me was if your marriage was in trouble."

Chapter Three

Emily slid the last plate into the cabinet and let out a long sigh of relief. The tiny rental was quaint and homey. She liked the smaller space, hoping it would force them to interact more than their grand home back in Washington D.C.

Two arms slipped around her waist, Carter's intimate touch startling her. The familiar heat radiating from him steadied her. Then fingers brushed her bare shoulder, swiping her hair to the side. Warm lips pressed to the nape of her neck, sending a tremor of excitement down her arms and legs. She leaned into Carter. Even now, his strength promised protection. To this day, she knew the man would die for her. It had always been that way. Their love was epic, even back in high school. No one could split them up, not even the head cheerleader who'd tried her best wiles on Carter at the senior homecoming game. It had looked like Tina Townsend had won for a minute, but in the end, Emily had come out the victor. When Tina wrapped her arms around Carter at the homecoming game, she'd thought she'd lost. Yet he pulled free, then crossed the football field and planted a kiss on her lips in front of the entire school.

"I hate that I have to fly out in the morning," Carter whispered in her ear, his warm breath teasing her senses. It had been nearly a year since she'd felt his touch, his love.

Could she dare hope he found her attractive again? The last two years had left her feeling defective and his being distant for so long hadn't helped. What if he decided to never come home again?

His hands slipped to her hips, but she grabbed them. With a breath and a leap of hope, she said, "We have today." She turned in his arms and clasped her fingers together behind his neck, looking up at his gray eyes, their golden-yellow spirals drawing her into their depths. The same eyes she saw in Jacob. The same hair and skin tone. He was a mini replica of her husband.

The sound of toys clattered in the other room reminded her that Jacob was close by, unpacking his bedroom. She tried to read Carter's face. If she offered to spend some alone time with him, would he reject her? "Why don't I check on our boy while you go shower? We have a couple hours until dinner. We can have some quiet time together." Her words felt forced, like she was speaking to a stranger instead of her husband. He went stiff in her arms and her heart sank. Maybe he just needed some more encouragement. It could be he didn't quite get her meaning, so she offered a playful wink.

He rested his forehead on hers and smiled. "That sounds like a great idea." His arms relaxed and he leaned into her. The mingling scents of his aftershave and hard work created an intoxicating aroma that made her snuggle closer to him.

His nose raked down her cheek to her collar bone. "I think you should shower, too, though."

She slipped from his arms and slapped him playfully on the arm. "Hey, now. I just unpacked half a house. I can't always be perfect like your mom."

He sighed and stepped from her, heading for their bedroom. She chased him, knowing she'd screwed up. Why did she have to make a comment about his mother, especially now? "Hey, I didn't mean that the way it came out. Listen, I promise to try my best to make things work with Judith. She's family and if I were to confess the truth to you, I…I admire her. My issues with her are less about how she is, and more about how I don't live up to her image in your eyes."

More boxes shuffled in Jacob's room and she moved to help him, but Carter grabbed her. Pulling her close, he dipped her, planting a kiss on her lips. The air whooshed from her lungs, but she didn't care. She only wanted Carter.

"Mom! What do I do with my towels?" Jacob yelled, shattering their moment.

Carter broke the kiss and lifted her back to standing, but the room continued to spin. He held her upright until she caught her breath. "You're perfect just the way you are," he breathed into her ear. "I don't want anyone else but you as my wife. You're special in so many ways."

Heat flooded up her neck to her cheeks. "Thank you. I wasn't trying to… I know the counselor said—"

"I didn't say that because the counselor advised me to. I said it because I truly believe you're an amazing wife and mother, and I'm lucky to have you." He kissed her check then swatted her bottom. "Now, go help Jacob while I shower so we can have some of that quiet time you promised."

She nodded then sashayed toward Jacob's room, swaying her hips with extra emphasis

"Hurry back."

Carter's words trailed after her. Maybe moving to Creekside *would* be better than she'd thought. During their visit to Café Bliss that afternoon, Aunt Sue had promised to let her work a few hours a week while Jacob was in school. Cathy West seemed almost human compared to the woman full of gossip she once knew, easing some of her anxiety about the town learning things she'd rather keep secret. And Aunt Sue had assured her the schools really were better here.

She spotted Jacob on the floor in the corner, looking at an old picture book. She quickly glanced back to make sure Carter had gone to their room, knowing he wouldn't approve of his nine-year-old son reading baby books.

She slipped through the doorway then closed it behind her. "Whatcha doing?"

Jacob shoved the book under his leg, his glance swaying guiltily between the book and her. His expression was like a squirrel debating whether to flee or freeze and hope she hadn't seen him.

"It's okay." Emily sat down beside him and crossed her legs, easing the book from beneath his leg. "Ah, it's your favorite adventure story. Would you like to read it together?"

He sat stone still and she knew he contemplated his answer carefully. She opened the book to the page where the boy finds his way through the woods and discovers the lion. "Oh, this is my favorite part." She pointed to the lion. "When he eats the boy's lunch, right?"

Jacob cracked a smile and shook his head. "No, that's not what happens. He sits with the lion and the lion gets the monkeys to bring fruit for them to share."

"Really?" She gave him a skeptical look and shook her head for added emphasis. "You sure?"

He snuggled up to her side. "Yep, see? It says right there that *the monkeys got bananas and coconuts*." His little fingers pointed to each of the words. "Then on the next page," he quickly turned the page and pointed to the words, "the lion tells the boy that the hunters are coming and that they have to leave before they *construct their city*."

"Wow, that's a big word. You can read *construct*?"

Jacob nodded double time. "Ah-ha. Oh, and here," he flipped the pages, "the animals form an army to start a revolution against the land owners."

Pride surged through her at his determination to not only read the book, but understand what he read. If only Carter could see his son's accomplishment, but he wouldn't. He'd only see Jacob holding a baby book. "Oh, no. Do they fight a big battle? What happens at the end?"

Jacob gave her his familiar head tilt and eye roll, informing her he'd caught onto her reading game. Still, he shrugged and flipped to the end. "The animals sign a peace treatment."

"You mean treaty?"

Jacob's skin flushed. He slammed the book shut and threw it across the room. "I'm so stupid!"

She wanted to chastise herself for correcting him, but what was she supposed to do? If she didn't correct him, he wouldn't learn, yet when she did he shut down.

Jacob retreated to the corner and faced the wall with his arms crossed over his chest. The sound of soft sniffles told her he was crying, but she knew he hated crying in front of anyone. Should she leave? Hold him? Get the book and tell him to keep practicing? She searched the room for answers. Lego sets designed for children twice his age that he'd constructed in a matter of hours rested on a bookshelf. The electronic keyboard that he'd taught himself to play by watching YouTube videos sat in the opposite corner. He was smart, probably smarter than most.

She sat there for a moment, praying for guidance. "I know this is frustrating, but there are a lot of people who have struggled with reading." She inched closer. "You know, I saw somewhere that Albert Einstein had trouble learning to read, and he was one of the smartest men who ever lived."

Shoulders slumped, Jacob rested his head against the wall. The sniffles had stopped, but he didn't respond, so she scooted a little closer. "Sometimes people are smart in different ways. History is full of stories of people like that, those who excelled in some areas but struggled in others. No one is perfect at everything. Just think about all the things you can do. One day, you could be a famous musician, or a world-renowned architect or engineer who designs airships."

He angled to the side, and she could see the tears running down his cheeks before he swiped them away. She wanted to pull him into her arms and promise it would get better. That she would be there to help him and protect him from the world, but she couldn't learn to read for him. There were some things only he could do.

"Are you just saying that?" Jacob stuttered between short breaths.

"No, it's true. Sometimes people have a weakness because their strengths are so superior. It's like a superhero."

"Superhero?" He turned to face her.

"Yes, you know, like kryptonite is Superman's weakness. Every superhero has some sort of weakness they have to overcome."

"So, reading's my kryptonite," he murmured. "I think it's gonna kill me."

She stifled a laugh. "You're not going to die from reading. Unlike Superman, you can learn to conquer your weakness."

"You really think so?" Jacob looked up at her with the most hopeful eyes she'd ever seen, and she pulled him into her arms, snuggling him in her lap.

"Yes, I really think so. In fact, I know you will. Just a week ago you couldn't read the word *construct*, yet now you can. It may take time and you have to be patient, but if you keep at it you will get better."

He wiggled into her for a moment and she loved the feel of him in her arms. As big as he was, he was still her baby, the only one she was likely to have according to the doctors.

"Mom? Do I have to go to school? Can't you teach me?" he asked.

She squeezed him against her and kissed the top of his head. "I'm afraid not. A superhero needs a sidekick, right? Real teachers are like sidekicks, there to help you overcome your weakness. So, you'll have to be brave and go to school so you can learn."

"Brave like a superhero?"

"Yes, just like a superhero."

He pushed from her arms and stood, lifting his chin high, then walked across the room to retrieve the book. "Let's start at the beginning."

The door opened and Carter stuck his head inside the room. "Hey, what's going on in here? I thought you were going to shower."

Emily held her breath as Jacob hid the book behind his back. No one said anything for a moment.

"I thought I told you to throw that book out before we moved. You don't need baby books anymore." His words cut through her like a bulldozer tearing through a forest and chasing the animals from their homes.

"Carter, it's not a big deal."

"Not a big deal? You think it won't be a big deal when the kids tease him for having a book like that? We moved here so he could do well in school, and to get away from those bullies."

Emily stood and placed herself between them, a protective shield for Jacob, and a calming voice for Carter. "I've got it covered. I'm enrolling him in school tomorrow. Don't worry."

She heard Jacob's sniffles behind her and so did Carter. He stepped toward them, but Emily shook her head. Carter's jaw twitched and his eyes narrowed. "He better not be placed in any remedial classes. He's smart. He needs to be in regular classes." He turned on his heel and headed out the bedroom door. Without looking back, he said, "I'm gonna go check on my mother. I'll be back by dinner." He disappeared, taking his promise to spend time together with him.

The same pattern again. Things got tough and he left, too disappointed in them to stay.

Chapter Four

Birds chirped a calming tune outside as Carter stood by his mother's open family room window, enjoying the chill of the spring air. Behind him, his mother's chair squeaked with each rock. "You gonna stew all night or tell me what's gotcha so upset? Not that I'm not happy to see you twice in as many days."

He shook the haze from his mind and straightened. "Nothing's bothering me."

"Sure. That's why you're here instead of at your own house helping get things unpacked. I didn't raise no son of mine to shirk his responsibilities and abandon his family when there's work to be done."

"I didn't abandon anyone. We're done unpacking." He fought his rising temper, barely managing to keep his voice calm.

"How can you be done unpacking already? The moving truck only arrived this morning, right?"

He dropped into a chair and gripped the armrest. "There wasn't much to unpack because we sold or donated all our furniture. The rental house comes furnished, too, so we didn't need much. So, I'm telling you it's done. They delivered Emily's car and boxes, that's about all we brought."

"Don't take that tone of voice with me. I'll send you out to find a switch then use it on your backside," she said in her thick, country accent.

He shook his head. It was supposed to be different here. Happier, more time together, better schools. Yet, they'd just arrived and already they were fighting. Counseling hadn't helped. Why did he think a move would? "Sorry, I just…" His words trailed off with a heavy sigh.

"Son, I love you, but I can't help you if you don't talk to me." The squeaking of her chair stopped. The old clock chimed as if counting down the seconds he had left before his marriage ended.

How could he tell his mother that his marriage was falling apart? The marriage she told him wouldn't work out because they were too different. He rubbed his forehead in a vain attempt to relieve the pressure building behind his eyes. He swore one of these days his head would explode if he didn't find relief. "Moving is stressful, that's all."

"What's so stressful about it? You load everything up, drive it to a new location then unload it again. It's simple, so whatcha really worried about? You have that game-day expression on your face."

"Game-day expression?" He quirked a brow at her.

She nodded. "You used to become a bear anytime you were pitching in a big game. You'd mope all over the house barking at everyone until the game. Of course, when you did good, you'd come home flying around the place."

"Yeah, well, I wish it was a ball game, but it's nothing as trivial as that." He shut his mouth before he said too much and headed to the kitchen. "I should go work on that faucet."

It only took two minutes for him to drop his wallet, money clip, and keys on the counter, and slide under the sink with a wrench before he spotted his mother's tapping slipper next to his outstretched legs. "You can't hide from me. I know there's something wrong."

"Nothing." But he knew he couldn't keep sidestepping the issue. She'd weasel it out of him eventually, unless he could placate her. "Just worried about Jacob starting a new school tomorrow is all. Meeting new friends and all that."

"Oh." Her foot tapping stopped, and she dragged a chair from the table to sit by his side. "You think your son's gonna be teased like you were in grade school? He got reading problems, too?"

The hurtful words of his youth echoed in his head and fury bubbled to the surface. He turned the wrench too hard, loosening the valve and sending water spraying into his face. "Ugh!" He quickly tightened it again and sat up to a hand towel waiting for him. "Thanks," he grumbled.

"What does Emily say about all this? Does she think he has some learning difficulties?" his mother asked.

Learning difficulties. Those words were like Freddy Krueger nails stabbing his ten-year-old heart over and over again. He knew first hand that kids were cruel, and Jacob deserved better than that. "I don't know. She wants him to get help, but we both know those kind of classes don't work."

"Says who?"

"I say. I sat in a portable behind the school for two years, remember? I had to make that walk of shame daily, where kids shouted things like *retard* and *drool much* at me until I reached that darn classroom. And then I had to sit day after day for hours with the kids who did drool. We were segregated and made to feel like outsiders. No, they don't work."

"You can read, can't ya?"

He paced the floor around the kitchen table and eyed the thin stack of business cards he kept in his money clip. *BSMA, Business Solutions Mergers and Acquisitions, CEO.* He'd done something with his life, despite what the teachers in elementary school had told him. "Yeah, self-taught. When we moved here when I was in fifth grade, it all changed for me. I left that lonely, scared little boy behind by teaching myself to overcome my issues. And so can Jacob. He doesn't need to be put through that kind of cruelty."

His mother rose from the chair to block his path. "Jacob isn't you, and things are different now. I'm not trying to be mean, but you still can barely handwrite a check. You're great with computers, which is how you got to where you are, but you still have difficulties. Don't think I don't know. I'm your mother."

He tossed the towel on the table. "No, you don't know what you're talking about." Not wanting to argue, he sighed. "I've got to go. It's almost time for dinner."

"Oh no, you don't. You're not going anywhere. That pipe is dripping now. You want to pay my water bill?"

Carter spotted the puddle of water at the base of the cabinet. "Geesh, why didn't you say something?" He retrieved the rag and knelt at the counter again.

"Who has a chance to speak when you're on a rampage? I don't know how Emily handles it."

"That's right, because we're so different. She's the smart one."

"That's what you think? That I didn't want you marrying Emily because she was too smart for you?"

Carter took the wrench and loosened the valve on the cold water line once more. "The minute I told you she was the valedictorian you started warning me not to marry her. You think I'm stupid, don't you? Even now that I'm the CEO of a successful company, you still think I'm that dumb little boy that won't amount to anything."

"Listen here," she said, her voice surprisingly stern for such a small body. "You need to mind yourself. You and I both know that's not true. I didn't want you two getting married because I saw how hard you'd worked and I didn't want you to skip going to college. I was worried you'd decide college was too much to handle with a wife and possible kids. I wanted you to have a life before you settled down since I never had that chance."

He nudged the pipe back into perfect alignment and tightened it. "What are you talking about? You've always wanted to be a housewife and take care of a family. It's what women are supposed to do. At least that's what you always said." He sat up and glanced at her. Something in the way she lowered to the chair and clasped her hands in her lap frightened him. "Mother?"

"Times change. I just wanted more for you than what your father and I had. You were a dreamer. You were going to see the world, and you couldn't do that if you had a family to support."

"Maybe I didn't want to see the world alone. Maybe I just wanted to be with Emily and have a family. Someone to share those moments with. Maybe I wanted what you and dad had. The perfect marriage."

She laughed aloud, the kind that explodes from the gut. "Oh, honey. Marriage is never perfect. Just 'cause we didn't fight in front of you kids didn't mean we never fought."

"We would've heard you. You two agreed on everything. There was never a cross word between you two." The clock out in the hall chimed again and for a moment, he thought about throwing his wrench at it.

"Well, believe it or not, even we had some knock-down, drag-out fights. I even sent him to the hospital once because I stabbed a fork in his leg."

"Wait—what? I remember Dad having a bandage on his thigh once, said some guy at work had stabbed him. We all thought it was so cool that he'd gotten in a fight at work and won."

She chuckled. "No, he got in a fight at home and lost. We'd table any discussion until you boys were at school or out with your friends. Sometimes we kept our disagreements bottled up for so long that we'd burst when we finally found an opportunity to talk." She smiled and shook her head at the memories, as if telling a joke instead of shattering his lifelong image of his parents' perfect marriage.

"What about the time Dad had a black eye? He said a machine busted and a part caught him in the face at work."

She toyed with the hem of her shirt. "Me."

"And when he left to visit a sick cousin for a week and came back with a limp?"

"Um, yeah, that was really a hospital visit. But that wasn't my fault. He told me he was going to leave, so I told him *fine, go*. He stepped toward me and I shoved him, but I didn't realize he'd fall down the stairs."

"Geesh, Mom. You could've killed him. You sure he died of a heart attack and not assault?"

She snapped her gaze to him, her lips pursed tightly, and all humor vanished.

He held up both hands in apology. "Sorry, bad joke." He tapped the wrench against his other palm. "Why'd you two stay together if you were always at each other's throats? How did you work it out? I know you two loved each other, but if you were fighting that much you had to be miserable."

"We did love each other, but sometimes love can't make up for inexperience. We were too young when we got married. Add four boys and a husband who worked overtime at a blue-collar job just to keep food on the table and you have the makings for trouble." She stood, snatched the rag from his hand and dropped it to the floor. Using her slipper, she mopped up some of the water that had pooled on the linoleum. "We managed. Looking back, it's kind of a miracle we made it work. Knowing what I did when you were ready for college, I just wanted more for you out of life. I wanted you to experience things, do things before you settled down. You had a love for photography and I knew you could do great things, like go off and be some world-renowned photographer for *National Geographic*. I always believed in you, Carter. I still do."

Warmth settled over him. "I know. I'm sorry I said that." He bent down and picked up the rag before his mother could, not wanting her to strain herself. "Just answer one question for me. Why did you get married so young if you didn't want to?" He placed the soiled rag on the counter then cleaned up the tools and closed the cabinet door.

"Things were different back then. Women were expected to get married, be great wives and mothers. But Emily had choices. You had choices."

Carter chuckled at the thought of his mother being submissive. Sure, she wasn't a feminist, but she was strong and independent. No one told her what to do, as evidenced by the apparent injuries his father suffered. "I don't know. There may have been fewer options for women back then but you still had choices. You chose to be a perfect wife and mother. Well, except for the spousal abuse. Remind me never to make you angry. I don't want to end up in traction."

She busied herself with washing the few glasses sitting in the sink. "It wasn't like that. We were passionate people. I didn't abuse him. We just got carried away at times."

"Look, all I'm saying is you could've told Dad to wait. I bet he would've waited for you to do whatever you wanted in life before you two married. He wasn't an unreasonable man. If I remember correctly, he always told you to pursue whatever you wanted. He even enrolled you in night classes at Riverbend University, but you didn't go."

"Those weren't college classes, hon. They were to get my GED. I never finished high school. You boys never knew this, but I married your father before I could graduate."

A strange prickling sensation, one of too much information, covered his skin and threatened to topple his perfect mother image. "What are you saying?"

"Mark wasn't a preemie. He was born right on time."

Chapter Five

Night faded into morning and the fleeting intimacy they'd shared remained only an echo of a once great marriage. Emily stuck the breakfast dishes in the dishwasher and struggled to find her smile. The happy face she'd need while registering Jacob at his new school in an attempt to show him the world really was bright and cheerful, and not full of disappointments.

"Do you know where my blue tie with silver stripes is?" Carter called from the master bedroom.

Emily dried her hands then padded to the room to find Carter in a tizzy, his neckties tossed all over the bed as he raced about with his collar half turned up. "Relax, you won't be late."

"It's going to take a while to get to the airport from here. If I miss my flight, I'll be late for the client meeting. And I can't be late, not with this client."

Emily searched through the pile of ties and found the blue one buried under a black one with pink dots. "It's right here." How a man who could run a company so efficiently, yet couldn't find a sock in a drawer was beyond her.

"Mom, I can't find my green shirt," Jacob called from the other room.

She handed the tie to Carter then hurried to Jacob. With one glance, she spotted the green shirt in his T-shirt drawer next to a red one. She shook her head. Like father like son. "Here you go, sweetie."

"Emily, where's my gold watch?"

"In the box on your dresser."

"No, not the solid gold one. The silver with the gold rim and band."

She patted Jacob on the head and trotted back to the master bedroom, thankful they lived in a smaller house now. "I don't know who's more stressed out today. You going to meet your new client or Jacob headed to school for the first time." She retrieved the watch, set it on the bathroom vanity by his side, scooped up the pile of ties, and started arranging them on the tie rack in the closet. "Next time, call me so there won't be such a mess."

Bang. Bam.

Startled, Emily dropped the ties on the floor then rushed to the bathroom. "Are you okay?"

Carter leaned over the sink, his electric razor in hand, his face red with anger. "I get it. I'm a slob. You have to clean up after me all the time. I can't find anything and I can't...can't... Never mind." He abandoned the razor and wiped his hands on the towel.

Emily backed out the door at the sudden rise of tension but she remained facing him. "I don't want to fight. Not today." She stood in their master bedroom, wishing the small house had squished them together into the perfect mold they once were. They'd had the happily-ever-after, perfect relationship everyone envied. She longed for that again.

She opened her mouth to tell him she didn't want to fight ever again, that she loved him and always would. But something kept the words trapped in her throat. After being married for almost seventeen years, why did she fear rejection now more than ever?

"Mom, I'm ready," Jacob called from the living room.

Carter leaned out the bathroom door, his brows pinching his nose and his eyes narrowed. "Don't forget, normal classes. I don't want him in any of those special ones."

Anger grabbed hold of her and her resolve crumbled. She crossed her arms over her chest. "You don't even trust me to take care of registering him for school? You micromanage everything. Do you want to do the grocery shopping, too?" The clock on the bedside table clicked away the seconds until she wavered and eventually caved. Defeated, she nodded then left the room and her husband behind before she really lost her temper.

Jacob stood at the door holding his iPad tight and staring out the window. "I know I have to go to school, but…"

Emily scooted closer and placed one hand on the back of his head. "But what?"

Carter marched from the bedroom into the kitchen and grabbed his suitcase. Jacob slid away from Emily. "Never mind. Let's go."

"Have a great day, buddy. You'll do awesome." Carter messed his hair but brushed past her without a glance. "I'll be home by dinner" Without another word, he left their new home, and she felt another bond snap. The bonds tying their marriage together were becoming fewer, weaker. One day soon, there'd be nothing left of them.

Emily reached for Jacob, but he escaped from her arms and stood at the front door. She wanted to pull him to her, keep him home, protect him from the teasing, from the teachers who told him he was slow or lazy, but it wasn't an option. Jacob had to go to school. Running from his problems wouldn't solve anything. She only hoped she could get him into a normal class, or keep it from Carter if she couldn't. She'd never lied to him before, not in all the years they'd been together, but what else could she do?"

The drive to school, although short, felt long on her nerves. She glanced at her son repeatedly and silently prayed. Prayed for the school to ignore the comments on his records and put him in normal classes. Then he'd have lots of friends, and Carter would be happy, and everything would be better.

She pulled into the parking lot and they both sat in the car, eyeing the large red brick building with white trim. It looked friendly and well maintained despite its age. Jacob gripped his iPad so tight his little fingers blanched. She covered his hand with hers and squeezed. "I bet you'll have a ton of friends by the end of the week. This is a small town school. People are much nicer here." Empty words, but she had to say something if she wanted him to get out of the car.

Jacob quirked his head. "There are nice people and mean people everywhere. Moving here won't change that."

He was so smart, too smart. "I know, buddy. But let's give it a chance, okay? It could be great. We won't know until we try."

He nodded and opened his door, slipping his hand away from hers. She knew he had to ready himself, that he couldn't keep leaning on her. He really was a mini-version of his father. Carter always had to stand on his own two feet, prove he could handle anything without help. And he could. He always had.

She climbed out of the car and took a deep breath, readying to fight for her son. Then she marched to the admissions office with Jacob's school folder in hand.

A friendly woman greeted them. Her smile looked familiar, but Emily couldn't place it. "Oh my Gawd, is that Emily? Emily who married Carter Davidson? What are you doing here?"

Emily analyzed the dark hair, pretty smile, and bright eyes. "Meredith? We were in homeroom together, right?"

"Yep, that's me. Okay, I've lost a few pounds and got my teeth fixed, so that's probably why you didn't recognize me." Meredith spun, showing off her new figure, half the size she was in high school. *Good for her*, Emily thought. Meredith had always been nice and Emily felt relieved to see a friendly face.

"It's good to see you. You look fantastic."

Meredith pulled her into a Southern hug, the warm, rib-crushing kind, then bent toward Jacob. "This must be your son I've heard so much about. Mrs. Fletcher always talks about how awesome you are to everyone. You're kind of a hero in our town."

Jacob placed a hand on his chest. "Me?"

"Yep, as a matter of fact, you'll be in my son's class and he already knows all about you. He's thrilled to have another boy around who's musical. I heard you can play the piano exceptionally well."

"Not well, but I play."

"My son, Matt, plays the guitar. He'd love to jam with you sometime." Meredith stood and took the file from Emily. "We already have the electronic records sent over from his old school, but I'll take this and copy anything we might need while you meet with the principal. She's ready for you now. Maybe Jacob would like to come help me make these copies."

"Can I?" Jacob smiled and handed Emily his iPad.

"You bet."

Emily mouthed a silent *thank you* then followed Meredith to the principal's office. Emily never liked to discuss Jacob's challenges in front of him. Besides, she had to ready for a fight.

The door to the principal's office stood open and an older woman with glasses, her hair pulled back in a bun, offered her hand. "Welcome to Creekside Elementary, Mrs. Davidson. It's a pleasure to have you and Jacob here with us. I'm Dr. Kelner, the principal."

Emily shook Dr. Kelner's hand then sat in the chair across the desk from her. Framed certificates and degrees hung on the wall next to a solid, dark wood bookshelf. The large desk was old and worn, covered in papers, files, a phone and a ceramic mug on a coaster. The smell of papers and old musty carpeting filled the room.

"I was going to take Jacob here to help me make copies. We'll be back in a bit." Meredith headed out the door with Jacob bouncing at her side.

Emily scooched forward to the edge of her chair. "Thank you for meeting with me. We're anxious to get Jacob into school as soon as possible."

"Yes, I understand. Have you moved into town yet?"

"Yes, I don't have any bills verifying our address yet, but a copy of my rental agreement is in the file I gave Meredith. Hopefully that will suffice as proof of residency."

Dr. Kelner opened a file on her desk and scanned several sheets of paper. "I see that Jacob was pulled out for special classes last year."

Emily stiffened and took a long breath, hoping to fill her lungs with courage. "Yes, ma'am, but we'd prefer him to be in a regular classroom setting. He's extremely smart, just a little slow on reading. I've been working with him at home, though."

"I'm glad to hear that. At this school, we don't have the funding to hire a ton of special teachers, although we do offer an inclusion program. Each grade has a classroom with one extra teacher who helps children with unique learning needs. This allows them more individualized attention. It also keeps them from missing normal classroom time, or feeling shame for being pulled from class to go to another room."

Emily's heart soared, yet she knew it couldn't be that easy. Would Jacob really be able to receive extra help while remaining in a regular classroom? It would be a win for both Jacob and Carter. Not to mention she wouldn't have to explain to Carter again that his son was just different. She wouldn't have to lie. "I think that sounds perfect."

"It's a great compromise for many students. However, there's limited space in the integrated classrooms. Since there isn't an IEP in his file, we'll place him in a classroom as a regular student. I think we can still squeeze in some extra help for Jacob if it seems necessary, though."

A chill shot through Emily. "What's an IEP?" Would they remove Jacob from the integrated class if he didn't have one?

Dr. Kelner tapped her pen against her hand several times then placed it on the desk and closed the file. "An IEP is an Individualized Education Plan. If it becomes apparent that a student needs special help to succeed within the school environment, we write up an IEP which allows us to make those accommodations. To guarantee Jacob's placement in the integrated class, we'll need to start the process for an evaluation. It can take a bit of time, but it will give us a better understanding of how we can best help Jacob be successful."

Her heart sank. She knew all about evaluations. "I was told it could take a year and a half at our old school. The process was started, but then his first-grade teacher retired and there was no record of the testing. How much time will it take here? And is it possible I could expedite the testing?"

Dr. Kelner laced her hands under her chin. "If you want it expedited, you'd have to have a private evaluation done. It's expensive, though."

Great, she couldn't pay for it without Carter knowing and she'd never get her husband to agree to any more tests. When Jacob's first-grade teacher started testing him, she'd decided he was lazy and slow since she hadn't found any sort of issues. How would Emily get Carter to agree to another evaluation? Maybe she could earn enough working at the coffee shop to pay for it without Carter knowing? "I'll look into the private evaluation. Thank you."

Dr. Kelner nodded. "I understand your concerns, Mrs. Davidson, but we must accommodate all children in this class. We have an eclectic population which creates some challenges. There may be a child or two in need of more significant assistance than Jacob, or there might be a few who have emotional issues that pose a challenge, but I assure you that we do everything in our power to make each classroom as suitable as possible for everyone. Federal funding has been cut to the point of pennies per student, but having an evaluation on file will allow us to get some additional, much-needed funding for Jacob's specific needs. That being said, I'm sure Jacob will fit right in here at Creekside and have a great time."

Despite Dr. Kelner's reassurance, anxiety still plagued Emily. "What happens if he doesn't fit into the classroom? Will you move him to another one?"

Dr. Kelner sighed and shook her head. "I'm afraid with our current capacity and funding, there's no wiggle room for any alternatives. We'd like to hire another teacher, but it's just not possible right now."

The last glimmer of hope faded. Even if Emily managed to get Jacob evaluated, if they found a significant issue or the integrated class was already full, she'd never get Jacob the help he needed while keeping him in a regular classroom setting.

Chapter Six

The airport security line, packed with business travelers and screaming toddlers, moved slower than a government contract negotiation. Carter plopped down into a chair and eyed the picture of Emily and Jacob he'd taken two years ago and set as his cell phone's wallpaper. The image reflected their true happiness at the time, one of her arms wrapped around Jacob's shoulders while the other hand rested on her rounded belly.

Two women giggled across the aisle, probably on their way to a girls' trip based on their casual dress and smiling faces. He wanted to hear Emily's laugh again. She used to laugh like an angel with the pure joy of having just earned her wings.

He entered his pass code to unlock the screen then held his thumb over the image of her face, willing himself to press the icon to call her. It would be quick, just to check in on how Jacob's registration at school went. Would she think he didn't trust her to handle it? Was his mother right and schools really had changed?

All he really wanted to do was hear Emily's voice before he boarded the plane. He'd left so abruptly when things were still awkward between them.

A man sat next to Carter with a friendly nod then he dug into his briefcase. His face looked familiar but Carter couldn't seem to place it. "I don't want to leave either," the man said. At first, Carter thought he was talking to him until he realized the man had his cell phone on his lap with a thin cord attached to an earpiece. "I miss my girls already. Tell Mom that we'll meet them for dinner Friday night at Francisco's. I made a reservation this morning."

Reservation? Shoot, he'd forgotten about taking his mother to dinner Friday night. Since he knew his mother would just leave the location up to him, he quickly did a search on his phone and found Francisco's was rated the best in the area. He dialed and after several rings it went to voicemail. Checking his watch, he realized the restaurant wasn't open for another few hours. He'd have to settle for leaving a message. "Yes, this is Carter Davidson. I'd like to make a reservation for two this Friday at four p.m. I'm about to get on a flight, so you can leave a message to confirm on my home phone, or call me back on my cell." He gave both numbers then hit *end*.

"You'll love that place," the man at his side said.

Carter straightened and angled toward him. He was tall, and a little bit older than Carter, with broad shoulders and dimples which gave a boyish look to his face. He smiled. "Sorry, I overheard the name of the restaurant and thought I'd take my mother there as well. I didn't mean to eavesdrop."

"If it was a private conversation, I wouldn't have it at the airport." The man smiled back and offered his hand. "I'm Eric Gaylord. Nice to meet you."

"Carter Davidson."

Eric quirked an eyebrow. "Wait, did you just move back to Creekside? Your wife's related to Mrs. Fletcher from Café Bliss, right? And if I remember correctly, you were in high school a few years behind me. In Jenna Mitchell's class, right?"

The defensive shield he'd perfected while living in a big city rose instinctively before he remembered he was now in small town USA. Forcing himself to relax, he said, "Yep, just moved in yesterday. My wife, Emily, is at Creekside Elementary right now registering our son. Unfortunately, I have a meeting in D.C. I have to get to this morning."

"Ah, the family man traveling dilemma," Eric said with a nod. "I usually don't travel much myself, but a friend of mine is having some legal difficulties so I'm flying out to meet with him. I really didn't want to leave my girls, though."

The man's love for his family shined brightly in his eyes. A happily married man with children—an endangered species in this day and age. Or at least that was how it seemed. Most of Carter's friends were divorced or already on wife number three or four. And if things didn't improve soon, he'd find himself amongst their ranks. He was sure Emily would give up on him. "How do you do it?" he asked quietly. "Balance work and family, I mean."

Eric removed the earpiece and wrapped the cord around his hand before he shoved it in his briefcase. One of the airline's employees made an announcement over the loudspeaker that their inbound flight had arrived and they planned to deplane and turn the flight around quickly. Eric waited for the announcement to finish before he spoke. "I'm not sure there's really a secret or trick to it. I give my family a hundred and ten percent, and my wife does the same. We're a team in everything."

Carter opened his mouth, but closed it again and sat back in his chair, waiting for boarding to begin.

Eric quirked his head and eyed him. "Of course, it isn't always easy. Our little girl had some health problems after she was born, and we struggled a lot during that time. But in the end, it only made us closer."

Carter clung to the words as if they were a lifeline. "So, once you made it through that rough patch you were closer? How's your little girl now?"

"Great! Crazy little bundle of energy toddling about. We hope to have another one soon, despite the chances that the same health issues could affect our next one."

Darkness covered Carter, fogging up his vision until the lifeline disappeared into a cloudy abyss. They sat silent for a moment as emotions from the last year tumbled through Carter. All this time he believed having another child would cure Emily's unhappiness. But if they could never have another child, would she ever truly get better? Would she ever find happiness again? "Doesn't it scare you? What if she can't have any more children?" he mumbled before realizing Eric had heard him. "Sorry, I didn't mean—"

"Don't worry about it." Eric gave him a sympathetic smile. "To be honest, whether we have more or not, we feel blessed that our Amelia is healthy now. I couldn't ask for more. I have a beautiful daughter and a wife who's perfect. If having another proves to not be in the cards, we'd consider adoption. Blood doesn't make family, after all."

Carter decided digging any deeper would be pushing it, especially considering they were practically strangers. "Well, thanks again for the restaurant recommendation. My mother will be ecstatic."

"No problem. What are neighbors for? By the way, isn't your mother Judith Davidson?"

"Yeah, that's her. And you're the son of Judy Gaylord. Weren't you top of your class or something? A real brainiac?"

Eric chuckled. "That's me."

"I remember all the trophies you had at school for being the debate team champion." Carter relaxed back into his chair.

"Yep, even back then I loved to argue. Now, I get paid for it." He laughed.

"We'd like to begin boarding flight 1951 to Washington, D.C. with those passengers who require assistance and families traveling with small children," a voice blared overhead.

"I confess it's nice to meet a friendly face," Carter said. "Funny how it's at the airport instead of in Creekside. I expected to walk into town and see a ton of people from high school, but you're the first blast from the past I've run into." Carter scooted to the edge of his seat, knowing first class would be the next group to board.

"It's great to have you back here. There's comfort in knowing I'm not the only traveling family man. We'll have to get the families together soon."

The loudspeaker clicked overhead. "Now boarding first class."

Carter and Eric both stood, joining the line of people waiting to board. After scanning their boarding passes, they headed down the gangway and soon discovered their seats were next to each other. "I'm glad we don't have to cut our conversation short," Eric said.

Carter slid his briefcase under the seat in front of him then settled next to the window. "You mentioned you were going to D.C. for legal issues and that you get paid to debate now, so I take it you're a lawyer?"

A long line of people shuffled past, waiting to fill the rows of seats behind them. With it came the clash of perfumes, colognes, and the mustiness of stale airplane air. "Yep." Eric tucked his own bag under the seat then reached up to adjust the air vent. "Don't judge me based on my career, though. Us small-town lawyers are a different breed than the ones from D.C."

"I won't, as long as you don't judge me for being the CEO of a major mergers and acquisitions company. Since I landed the CEO job a few years back people started treating me differently. It's funny how people assume you're a certain way because of your profession. I've heard it all, everything from being bred to take over Daddy's company, being valedictorian and raised with a silver spoon in my mouth." He shook his head. "Couldn't be further from the truth. I struggled with school, worked for every dime I've ever made, and my dad worked a blue-collar job all his life."

Eric loosened his tie. "I know what you mean. My favorite is how I must be a womanizing creep who thrives on power. My wife laughed so hard the first time she heard that she fell off a chair. Power never had any appeal to me. I'm in family law because I've seen the destruction divorce can do in the lives of children. I'm probably the only family lawyer who actually encourages couples to work it out instead of divorcing."

Carter nodded. "I talked a business owner into not selling his company that had been in his family for four generations. His son had died in combat, but he offered the company to his nephew. Granted, the deal wasn't right for our company, but I still could lose my job over that one."

A flight attendant came by and offered beverages, a perk to traveling first class. Everyone in coach had to wait until they were in the air. As the doors were shut and secured, Eric fastened his seatbelt. "I'm already looking forward to getting home and we haven't even taken off yet. But I have to wait until Saturday night. We have a family fun night planned."

"A family fun night? What's that?"

"We have a picnic on the living room floor and eat pizza while we play with Amelia. As she gets older we'll probably watch movies or play board games, but it's a weekly tradition we hope to keep going for years."

A family fun night sounded like a better idea to Carter than anything the counselor had suggested. Perhaps doing something as a family every week would make them closer. Before the pilot could tell them to turn off their devices, he texted Emily. *No need to cook dinner tonight. I'll pick up a pizza on the way. Taking off, I'll call from D.C.* He turned his phone to flight mode and set it on his armrest.

"When do you head back?" Eric asked.

The plane taxied away from the gate and he regretted not calling to check on Emily and Jacob, but there was nothing he could do about it now. "Tonight. It's just a day trip to meet a potential new client." He contemplated telling Emily about them playing a game together when he called her from D.C. That way he could casually find out how things went at school without making Emily angry for meddling too much. He couldn't seem to do anything right lately. If only he could communicate with her better, if he could find a way to get her to understand him better.

"You're a lucky man." Eric leaned back as the jets revved and the plane shot forward at full speed then lifted into the air. "Does your wife work?"

"No, she had to give up her job to stay home with our son." The words slipped out before he could stop them, and he tried to think of an excuse to explain why she had to stay home without revealing his son's learning issues. The ones he'd passed onto his only child. Guilt knotted his chest and he rubbed at the pain to make it go away.

Eric pushed his seat back and relaxed. "That's great. Lots of moms are choosing to stay home nowadays."

"The hours were long, who knew accountants had to work so much? I don't think she ever really enjoyed her job, anyway," Carter added.

"My wife, Lisa, gets to stay home sometimes, but even when she doesn't, Amelia is either with her at the shop, or with my mom. It works well for us."

He was relieved that Eric didn't ask any further questions. He liked the man. Eric was nice, personable, and didn't pry too much. If only more people were like that.

Carter settled back in his chair, hoping for Jacob to get into a normal class. He couldn't bear to watch his son being tortured by mean kids again, by kids who would never let him forget about his issues. He silently prayed that moving to Creekside wouldn't be the disaster he feared it would be and that his family would finally begin to heal.

Although a short flight, it still allowed time for some conversation. It was relaxing to talk with someone who didn't want anything from him, someone he didn't have to worry about letting down.

When the plane landed, Carter checked his phone and discovered two missed calls and a couple of texts from Emily. Unable to reply with the hustle and bustle of people disembarking, he pocketed his cell and collected his briefcase. Everyone funneled out the gangway to the terminal. Carter offered his hand to Eric. "Have a safe trip. I'm sure I'll run into you again soon."

Eric shook his hand. "Give me a call next weekend, and we'll arrange a time to get the families together."

The loudspeaker announced the next departure, reminding Carter of the passage of time. He only had a few hours to make this new deal work before the board of directors caught wind of him letting the last deal go. Although he knew it wasn't the right deal for the company, the board likely wouldn't see it that way. However, he'd stand by his decision.

Eric headed off to get his checked bag from baggage claim while Carter located the man holding a sign with his name on it. Settled in the town car, he checked his text and a smile tugged his cheeks high, almost reaching his eyes.

Sounds like an amazing idea. Be safe.

Love You.

The second text came through two minutes after the first, but still, she'd taken the time to send it. That meant something. He quickly typed a reply. *Arrived in D.C. and headed to my meeting. I'll call this afternoon when I'm headed to the airport. Love you, too.*

It had been so long since they'd texted that phrase to each other. Almost a year since they'd even said the words. It was time to heal and move on. He felt like Emily was finally getting better, overcoming her grief and returning to him. At least, he hoped she was.

With his heart lighter than it had been in months, he checked his two missed calls. The sight of David Aguero's name on the screen clenched his heart and yanked it to his gut. The chairman of the board had it in for Carter, ever since Carter had called him out on an inappropriate business deal.

The second missed call was from a board member and friend, Jim Stallman. Carter listened to his voicemail, but there was only one message. To his relieve, it was from Jim. "Hey, man. I wanted to talk to you in person, but I'm not sure when you're arriving in D.C. Listen, um, there's something going down. The board's meeting suddenly today, and it seems like David is up to something. There are rumors going around about you blowing a big deal for the company. I don't want to worry you for no reason, but you might want to make an appearance at the office today. I think he's trying to oust you, man. Rumor is he's going to try to get the board to vote on replacing you. Call me if you can. I've got your back, but you'll need the majority vote if that's what it comes down to."

The last bit of peace in his world crumbled around him. He felt like Sisyphus, rolling the proverbial rock up the side of the *life sucks* mountain only to watch it roll down again. Heat spread across his skin. The sound of car honks faded beyond the rush of blood pumping through his ears. Layers of cotton invaded his mouth and seemed to soak up any moisture left in his body. Heart-pounding, head-thumping, chest-constricting pain stole his breath and his last hope that life didn't have it out for him.

Chapter Seven

White clouds from the milk steamer billowed high above the counter. "That's it. You've got it," Aunt Sue said in an encouraging tone.

Sweat trickled down from Emily's forehead and she swiped it away with the back of her hand, keeping her attention on the bubbling concoction.

Jacob laughed from the other side of the counter. "Mom, you look like you're scared. It's just a coffee maker."

"Hey, now. I don't want to get burned." Emily moved the metal cup to the side and dumped the shot of espresso into a paper cup then poured the steamed milk over the top. How could making a simple cup of coffee be so complicated? And she even had a perfect GPA in high school and graduated top of her class in college. Heck she'd tested out of a third of her undergrad classes.

"Don't forget to wipe that down." Aunt Sue pointed to the metal nozzle protruding from the steamer machine.

Emily spooned frothed milk on the top of the finished drink then grabbed the rag and wiped down the nozzle. After a final stir with the long metal spoon, she slid the drink across the counter to Cathy West seated next to Jacob. The rich aroma of espresso promised Emily hadn't burned the beans this time.

They all sat in silence, awaiting Cathy's verdict. The older woman sipped then pulled the cup back as if it were poison. "Hot."

Emily exhaled and they all chuckled. "You'd think I'd just performed brain surgery on the president of the United States instead of making a latte."

Cathy set the paper cup on the counter. "Hon, these folks care more about their frou-frou caffeine drinks than any politician. Trust me, you don't want to give someone bad coffee, or you might end up on Sweetwater County's most wanted list."

Jacob pointed up at the sign. "Hey, if Mom creates a new drink, will her name go up on the board, too?"

Aunt Sue tossed a hand towel over her shoulder and leaned against the counter to eye the board overhead. "You know what? I think it's time for a new drink. Where do you think I should put it?"

Jacob shifted in his chair and eyed the sign. "Um, near mine." He bit his bottom lip and squinted. "Maybe above the sweet camel?"

Aunt Sue quirked an eyebrow at him. "You mean salted caramel?"

Jacob bowed his head and nervously turned his stool left and right. "Yeah, that's what I meant."

"I noticed you were squinting. Were you having trouble seeing the board?" Aunt Sue asked in a soft, caring tone.

Emily eyed both Cathy and Aunt Sue and shook her head. They both sat silently, just long enough for Jacob to catch on that he'd been busted for not being able to read. He swirled his chair around. "No, I see fine. I'm just stupid." He bolted for the front door and raced outside. Emily untied her apron and started after him, but Cathy stepped in front of her. "I've got him. You stay here. I think I know what's going on."

"You sure?" Emily wanted to go take care of her son herself, afraid anymore interference would only make the issue worse. "He needs me. I should go."

Aunt Sue touched her shoulder. "Let Cathy try. She's awesome with kids, probably because she acts like one most of the time."

"Hey, now. Be nice or I'll make you drink that concoction Emily made."

Emily sighed. "That bad, huh?"

"Oh, hon. I'm sorry, but I wouldn't give that to a varmint." Cathy stepped backward. "You stay here and practice. I'll have Jacob back in two shakes of a lamb's tail."

Emily reluctantly nodded her consent to let the woman go after her son, but everything in her screamed she should be the one to wrap her arms around him and protect him from harm.

Aunt Sue nudged her toward a table, and they both sat. Emily was thankful it was late afternoon, so there were no customers in the café to witness Jacob's outburst. "How long have you known about Jacob's struggle to read?" Aunt Sue asked.

Emily rubbed her forehead, trying to erase the scars of failure from her mind. "Since kindergarten. He had difficulties learning his alphabet. I didn't know until the end of the year when I visited the classroom. The teacher had listed each of the kids' names on the board of accomplishments for the alphabet and sight words, except for Jacob. Instead of having him participate in the reading and alphabet lessons, she said she'd allowed him to go to the playhouse and the music area. She said it stressed him out too much and he was just a slow learner. She recommended he get some extra help in first grade. I'm still frustrated she never mentioned anything to me during our parent-teacher conference. If I'd known, I could have tried to do something sooner. In first grade, I requested him to be evaluated for a learning issue, which didn't go over well with Carter. He doesn't believe his only son could have a learning disability."

Aunt Sue covered her hand with her own. "I think most parents feel that way, hon. Particularly men. Don't be too hard on him."

Emily sighed. "I'm not. It's just frustrating. The entire situation has been a nightmare. I feel like everything I suggest we try to help Jacob just upsets Carter more. When Jacob reached second grade, I discovered the evaluation had never been done. There was no record of it at all. You see..."

Emily struggled with the words. How could she explain that she'd failed one child while trying to save another?

"It's okay, Emily. I'm family. I won't judge, and I'll always be here if you need me. Let me help." Aunt Sue was so kind and gentle, the way she'd always been. The woman was truly special.

"I…I had a miscarriage when Jacob was starting first grade, so I didn't pay close enough attention. I was sure they'd give him the help he needed. It was early in the pregnancy, but it still shocked us."

"Oh, honey. I'm so sorry. I wish I would've known."

Emily shook her head. "I didn't want to bother you. You had the remodel to deal with, and we ended up pregnant again at the end of his first-grade year. I thought all would be great again, but then the complications started at the beginning of my third trimester. I tried everything to keep my baby girl. I was on bed rest for months, and I ate exactly as my doctor instructed. I was so afraid of having another miscarriage that I neglected what Jacob needed. It's my fault he's having so much difficulty now. And then…I fell apart. The baby made it to seven months, but then they couldn't find a heartbeat, and…" She gulped in a breath. "They induced labor, but she was stillborn." Emily sat back, away from Aunt Sue, and rubbed her chest, trying to ease the tearing pain of loss. "I was a wreck." She picked at a broken nail and forced the last few words out. "I was consumed with grief and neglected to take care of my family. And now my family's falling apart." Tears rolled down her cheeks and her shoulders shook. She'd managed not to cry for months. It had been tough, but she was getting better. Now the floodgates were open and she wept. Wept for the loss of her child, for the distance growing like a chasm between her and her husband, and the failure to take care of her only son.

Aunt Sue moved to her side and held her tight. "You should've told me. I would've been there in a heartbeat to help you. You shouldn't have had to go through that alone."

Emily shook her head. "You couldn't. You were in the middle of rebuilding after the tornado hit. I felt awful that I couldn't be here for you, and that I couldn't tell you. But I didn't want to stress you out anymore. I hated myself for letting so many people down."

Aunt Sue stroked her hair. "You didn't let anyone down, hon. Both the tornado and your baby were beyond your control, beyond anyone's control."

Emily fought to regain control of her emotions before Jacob returned. She knew it would only upset him more. She sat up and wiped the tears from her eyes. "Aunt Sue, you don't understand. I let my entire family down. Now, Jacob's paying the price in school, getting teased for having to go to special classes. And my husband and I are practically strangers. He doesn't look at me the same way he used to, not since I lost the last baby. She was beautiful, our daughter. The nurse let us hold her for a couple of hours. Now, Carter won't even touch me." Her hands shook, but she managed to keep the tears from falling again.

"Maybe Carter's still dealing with his own grief. I've seen the love in his eyes. Trust me, darling. That man worships you. Marriage is complicated and tough. Sometimes we just deal with things differently than men do."

"No, he hates me. He wanted another child so bad, and I couldn't give it to him. I failed him."

"You stop that, right now. You didn't fail anyone. And if that's how Carter truly feels then I'll box his ears. But I don't believe that's true. Listen, God only gives us what we can handle."

"Then tell Him to stop, 'cause I can't handle anymore!" Emily shouted at Aunt Sue, the world, God.

"Oh, honey. What I meant is perhaps having another child isn't what you should focus on right now. You need to work on mending your existing family, and when you're ready then you can try again. Take time to heal, to strengthen what you have. Trust me, I know. Donnie and I went through something similar in our marriage. For a while, I thought we'd never make it through, but we did. You and Carter will, too. Give it time."

Emily knew Aunt Sue spoke from the heart and only wanted to help. She had always been more of a mother in her life than her own mom was. She respected Aunt Sue. Emily wanted to believe, but she felt like her heart had been glued back together with paste that had been left out in the sun too long. Layer after layer had flaked off each time Carter rejected her. How much still remained before she'd be dead inside? "I want to believe."

Aunt Sue snagged a napkin from the counter and handed it to Emily. "Do you want to make your family work? To keep it together?"

Emily thought about all the times she'd wanted to walk away from it all. Heck, she'd practically had one foot out the door, ready to bolt, since she lost the baby. Yet something kept her from pushing that door all the way open. "Yes."

"Then give it your best effort. It'll take more than you know, and you'll have to give and give to make it work, but when your family mends, it'll heal even stronger than it was before."

Emily dabbed at her eyes then blew her nose and straightened tall in the chair. "I'll try."

Aunt Sue stroked her cheek. "That's my girl. I know you can do it. You're strong. I remember when you won that spelling bee in the fourth grade. I knew then and there that you possessed an inner strength like no other."

Emily thought back but couldn't recall much from her elementary school years. "What do you mean?"

"After one of the boys told you a girl couldn't win because they weren't smart enough, you went straight home and studied all night."

"Oh, yeah. Now, I remember. But I lost." A hint of aggravation nipped at her.

"That was just the starting point. Remember, honey? You went home after that spelling bee and studied all year. And in fifth grade?"

"I made it to state."

"And sixth grade?" Aunt Sue asked.

"Nationals."

Aunt Sue smiled then got up and went over to the counter. "And then you graduated top of your class from high school. You've never stopped. That one naysayer spurred you into learning and achieving your goals. And you did it. You proved to that boy how strong you could be." Aunt Sue snagged the cup of toxic liquid Emily had made for Cathy and dumped it into the sink.

"I know one goal I'm never going to achieve," Emily said.

"What's that?"

"A decent cup of coffee." Emily stood and went to the front windows, spotting Jacob and Cathy across the street sitting on a brick-lined step in the courtyard. His eyes were wide as he looked up at Cathy, and his mouth hung open. Whatever she was saying, she seemed to have Jacob's full attention.

"Do you know why Jacob's having difficulty reading?" Aunt Sue asked.

Other than his mother's neglect? "No, he's so smart. He's gifted in both math and science, not to mention he taught himself how to play the piano. I mean, he's like a sponge, soaking up knowledge on anything else. The school said they'd put him in an integrated class, where he'll get to be with regular children but still get the assistance he needs."

"How do you feel about that?"

"I know Carter will be pleased." Emily grasped the door handle and contemplated pushing it open to go find out what topic of conversation Jacob and Cathy were so engrossed in, but she stayed in the café watching from the sidelines. "He doesn't like Jacob being pulled out of class. Actually, he demanded that Jacob remain in a regular classroom at Creekside Elementary." Emily returned to the counter, unable to watch her son confiding in Cathy any longer. She sat on a stool and rested her head in her hands, attempting to steady her spinning thoughts and emotions.

Aunt Sue scrubbed the silver steamer cup and spoon clean then wiped down the counters. "Do you think it's the right thing for Jacob?"

"I don't know. I'm not sure I'm capable of deciding what's best for him. I've failed so far."

"All right. That's enough. You can sit there and feel sorry for yourself, or you can brush yourself off and start fighting for what you want. This woman sitting here isn't my Emmy. I want to see that fourth-grader who lost the spelling bee, but brushed herself off and went on to beat the entire darn nation. That's the mother Jacob needs right now."

Emily inhaled at the possibility of her words. "How can I be the support he needs when I feel so lost myself? I'm not sure how to figure out where I went, or who I am now. You're right, though. Jacob deserves the best I can give him. I'm all he has, besides Carter. And Carter can't face the fact that his son might have difficulties. I mean, Carter's always succeeded in everything he's ever tried. Well, his grades in high school weren't stellar, but he cared more about baseball and me than grades. And in college he had some difficulties with a few classes, but he was working full-time. Now he's the CEO of a large company. He can't imagine how much his son struggles because he's never been through it. How does a man so capable understand a child that can't read?"

"Perhaps you just need to put it in perspective for him. You help him understand all the things that Jacob is gifted at, and then gently guide him to the conclusion that Jacob can learn with some extra help. Some men are more accepting when they think it was their idea. Until you can get an evaluation done, we won't know why Jacob is having difficulty reading. It could be a vision problem. Or maybe it's a language issue. It's hard to say. All I know is that if he's as determined as his mother then he'll conquer this eventually. It may take some time, just like it did with your spelling bee, but he'll get there."

Emily wished she could turn the clock back and do things differently. "Maybe if I had studied early education like I'd planned, I'd be able to figure out what he needs. I'd be better equipped to help him. But when the company I worked for offered to pay for my accounting degree I couldn't pass it up. Carter and I were scraping by at that point."

The bell above the door jingled behind Emily, so she turned around. A man stood outside, but then let the door shut as he continued to speak with the woman beside him. Aunt Sue looked up with a smile and waved before turning her attention back to Emily. "You never enjoyed that job did you? Why didn't you go back to school to change careers, or do something different?"

Emily shrugged. "I didn't do it for that long. About the time I finished the years I owed the company for paying for my education, I got pregnant with Jacob." Emily paced around a table, needing to keep busy, but the torn napkin at the foot of a chair and the droplets of spilled coffee didn't offer much of a distraction. "I can get a private evaluation, which would provide some answers if nothing else, but it'll cost a lot of money. I'd have to tell Carter about it, and considering his resistance so far, I don't know how that's going to go over."

The door jingled again and this time the man, Mr. Burton, entered with a determined stride. He ordered a regular coffee, his stern expression never changing. Emily returned to the window to see Jacob hugging Cathy. When he let go, a bright smile lit his face. What had she said?

Mr. Burton collected his order then raced out the door without a word.

"Even if you don't think it will go well, you should still discuss it with him and soon," Aunt Sue urged.

"I will. Tonight. He's bringing pizza home, so hopefully that means he's in a good mood. I'll talk to him after I put Jacob to bed. Thanks, Aunt Sue. It's time for Carter and me to deal with our problems, and not make Jacob suffer for our issues."

Chapter Eight

Carter fought his rising blood pressure at the sight of David. The weasel stood next to two board members slapping them on the back as they discussed plans to play golf that weekend. He loved playing the golf card, pulling it out whenever he wanted to win someone over. "Carter? What are you doing here? I thought you'd moved to small town USA?" His words were clipped and his jaw tight, giving Carter a little jolt of satisfaction.

The setting sun filtered through the floor-to-ceiling windows and covered the room in an ominous orange hue. "I did, but I'm still available anytime. Thought I'd pop into the office while I was in town. I finished working up the details on a major deal here in town, something I'd like the board to consider."

David's right nostril flared, making him resemble a bull ready to charge. "Really? I thought you'd be too busy with the move and all." He stepped toward Carter and turned sideways with a clap on Carter's shoulder. "I was sorry to hear about your marital problems. We're glad you've decided to spend more time with your family. What with your ailing mother and all."

Carter fisted his hands at his sides but managed to keep his composure. He'd never wanted to knock someone out more in his life, but he didn't make it to the top of a major acquisitions company by losing control. "I'm not sure where you got your information, but my mother is anything but ailing. She might have arthritis, but that woman could take down this entire company with nothing more than a stern look. And losing a child isn't the same as having marital issues. But Emily and I are doing fine. Thanks for asking."

Phillip Grant, a member of the board with a perpetually shiny forehead, winced at Carter's words, but David only slapped him on the shoulder again. "Gotta love those good old Southern ladies and their strength. Reminds me of my grandmother when I was growing up. She'd give great hugs, but no one ever crossed her. That woman didn't go anywhere without a demanding presence and a stick in her hand."

Chuck Morgan, a board member who'd been around the world a few times and had the scars to prove it, crossed the room and shook Carter's hand. "Good to see you, Carter. I'm glad to see the move hasn't kept you away too long."

Carter stepped past David, anchoring himself in the center of the room. "That's right, I forgot you were originally from Tennessee, Chuck. I moved to Creekside. It's small, so you've probably never heard of it."

Chuck leaned against the conference table with relaxed shoulders, and his eyes grew wider than his smile. "Are you kidding? My uncle lives in Riverbend, not too far from there. I used to love going to the Sweetwater

County Fair as a kid. Heck, I've always wanted to take my own son there. You have a boy around my son's age, right? Ten or so?"

"That's right. You know, that fair's coming up in June. You should fly down and join us. Bring the family and we'll all go."

"You know what? I think I'll do that. I can't remember the last time I took a minute out to spend with my family. It's something we should all try to do more often. I'm glad it's working out for you, Carter."

"This June we'll be having our annual golf tournament, so you'll be busy, Chuck. You don't want to allow Phillip a chance to win the championship, do you?" David eyed Phillip who stood nearby watching their conversation, then clapped Chuck on the back.

"I win every year. I think it's time to let the poor guy have a turn," Chuck said.

As if on cue, Phillip crossed the room waving his hands in front of him. "Oh no, you don't. I didn't pay all that money for a professional instructor this past year for you to walk away now."

Chuck laughed a hearty good ol' boy laugh. "Okay, okay."

Carter thought fast, not wanting to lose this new connection. He'd always liked Chuck, but they'd never been close. "Tell you what. It's a quick flight down. Why don't we arrange to do the golf tournament there and hit the fair at the same time? They have a stellar golf course just outside of town. That way no one misses out on family time or guy time."

Jim Stallman entered the conference room, holding a Styrofoam cup. "Sounds like a plan. My kid's been hounding me to take him places. He'd get a kick out of a small town fair. I'm sure my wife would love to get out of D.C. for a bit, too. They got any antique shops in Creekside? She's into collecting antiques lately. Sorry, not collecting, antiquing." Jim air quoted. "I don't know what the appeal is, but she's been wanting to go down south to shop. She's into vintage, not designer. Both are expensive if you ask me."

"What about you, David? You up for some family time at the fair?" Chuck asked.

David's mouth curved into a smile worthy of any super villain. "Yes, that sounds like a great time. You know, as long as it doesn't conflict with the golf tournament."

"I'm in," Phillip agreed eagerly.

"And of course, if we're able to dig ourselves out of this most recent loss we've suffered and start making some money," David added.

"Ah, yes, there's that." Jim nodded. His expression went from child-like happy to businessman serious in an instant. "We need to get to our meeting. Since Carter's here, he can join us."

"This is an executive board meeting. Shouldn't we discuss our options amongst the board members before having the CEO join us?" David's mouth curled at the edges, only a smidgen, but enough that Carter caught it.

Phillip spun one of the leather chairs and plopped down in it, rotating back with his feet to face the table. "I'd like to have all the facts before discussing our options."

"Yes, I agree, but I'm sure Carter's flight will be leaving to get him home soon. We promised him some additional family time when he moved and we'd be breaking that promise by extending his stay," David offered, in a Hannibal Lector tone.

Chuck pulled out his seat and waved for the other board members loitering outside the conference room to join them. "We can call another meeting next week, once you've had a chance to get settled."

Carter dropped his briefcase on the table with a commanding thump. "No need to inconvenience everyone by scheduling another meeting when I'm already here. I'm happy to stay. I may have moved, but I'm still just as dedicated to this company. My family will understand." Or would they? He couldn't even spare a moment to call Emily to tell her he wouldn't make it home tonight. And he still hadn't texted her. He pulled his phone from his pocket and glanced at the door, but the rest of the board members had already begun to flood into the room. Tom Cliver, an ex-vet from Vietnam with quiet commanding power, sat to his right, next to Phillip with Jim at the head of the table, Chuck and David on the other side facing them. The five other members; Scott Waterman, Shawn Palmer, Nicholas Smith, Daniel Reed, and Aidan Stevenson, all settled in for the meeting.

David swiveled his chair and held a hand toward the door. "Do you need to make a call?"

"No, just making sure my cell is off. I wouldn't want to be interrupted during the meeting." He switched his phone off and slipped it into his briefcase at his side, feeling like he'd just severed the last thread holding his marriage together.

Chapter Nine

The setting sun left their small home dark and empty. Emily eyed her cell phone one more time, checked the landline for messages, then her cell again. Nothing. Not so much as a word from Carter. Worry and anger swirled inside her mind, filling her with anxiety. Worry at all the possible things that might have happened to him, and anger that there was nothing.

"Mom, I'm hungry," Jacob said, holding a hand over his belly.

She bit her lip for a moment, keeping the words that threatened to spill from her mouth, a diatribe of worthless husbands and broken promises, at bay. Then she stood, plastered her best attempt at a happy smile on her face and headed for the kitchen. "Let's make tacos and chocolate chip cookies."

"Really? Tonight?" Jacob squealed.

"Sure, why not. Help me get the stuff out of the fridge? You can start on the cookie dough while I brown the ground beef."

Jacob raced around the kitchen, snagging ingredients from the refrigerator and the pantry then set everything down on the counter. For a long moment, he stood there with his head down. "Are you and Dad going to get a divorce?" he asked quietly.

Her skin burned hotter than the gas flame flickering beneath the skillet. There it was, the very question she'd asked herself so often, yet hearing it from her son's mouth made it feel more real. How had their marital issues reached such a stage that her nine-year-old was aware of them? One glance at Jacob and she knew she couldn't placate him with some random answer. She'd have to dig deep to find the right way to handle this, the right way to explain the complicated relationships between men and woman and how marriage could be rocky. But her courage faltered. Instead, she said, "Of course not, honey. Why would you think that?" Lies. It broke her heart to tell her precious child lies, but what else could she do?

"You and Daddy don't talk much anymore. And when you do, you fight." Jacob's words seared her heart.

She put down her spatula and chose her words carefully. So much for ignoring the issue and lying. He was too smart for that. "Sometimes parents go through things that are tough, but Mommy and Daddy love each other very much. And we love you. I'm sorry that you saw us fight. We try not to, but we're not perfect. And it wasn't right that you had to suffer for our anger."

"Are you angry about my baby sister? Or are you angry at each other?" Jacob traced the letter *C* on the front of the chocolate chip bag. "I'm angry, too. I'm angry at God."

Emily fought the tears welling in her eyes and the acid boiling up into her throat. She turned off the stove and sat down on the barstool then pulled him into her arms. "Oh, honey. I'm not angry, and you shouldn't be either." She rested her chin on top of his head and stroked his hair, trying to swallow the melon-sized lump in her throat. "How did you know it was a baby girl?"

"I heard you crying out in your sleep one night. In the beginning, after she died, you cried a lot and Daddy held you. Now, you stopped crying, but Daddy stopped holding you, too."

Her memories flashed and shame filled her. "I'm so sorry." She squeezed him tighter. "I should've handled things better. I'm not perfect, but I'm here now."

"But Daddy isn't and that makes you sad. I don't want you to go back to crying in bed." Jacob burst into tears and she held him to her, rocking him gently.

"It's going to be okay. Trust me. Everything's going to be fine. Your baby sister's in Heaven where she's happy and safe."

"I wish I was in Heaven, too. Why won't God take me?"

A rib-crunching, lung-piercing pain skewered her, and she gasped but recovered quickly. "Don't say that. You belong here with Daddy and me. We love you very, very much. We're trying to make things better, to be better parents. I promise it won't be like it was back then. No matter what happens, I'm stronger now. But I still need you here with me. Daddy and I both need you with us." She pulled away and cupped his small face in her hands. "I'm sorry. I'm sorry I wasn't there for you when you lost your sister."

Jacob wiped his eyes and stepped back. "It's okay, Mommy. I've prayed for Baby Grace every night."

Emily struggled to force words through the constriction of loss choking her. No one had said her daughter's name aloud since the day Carter and she had said goodbye at the hospital. How did Jacob know? "You know her name?"

"Yeah. Her name was perfect, Mom, because she wasn't meant to live with us. She was meant to grace us with her light for a moment and then return to God." Jacob's smile was innocent. A tingle of something beyond her explanation coated her skin, his words creating a cocoon of faith that surrounded her, telling her it would get better.

Emily's cell phone buzzed in her pocket. Grateful for the distraction, she glanced over. To her relief, it was Carter. *I'm sorry. Something happened at work and I've been in meetings all afternoon. They're still going strong. Couldn't get a flight out tonight, so I'm headed back first thing tomorrow. I'll make it up to you and Jacob. I'll plan something special. I promise. I love you, Emily.*

The constriction around her throat eased, her chest relaxed, and her fear subsided. "Daddy'll be home in the morning. He's planning something special for us. He's sorry he couldn't make it home tonight."

Jacob jumped up, snapping back to his usually happy self. "Let's get the cookies made so he can have some with his coffee in the morning! He loves sweets with his coffee."

"That's a great idea." Emily messed his hair like Carter usually did and was rewarded with an excited smile.

They cooked side by side, shredding cheese and creaming butter and sugar. Emily enjoyed her son, really enjoyed listening to his chatter and seeing his many expressions. Aunt Sue was right. She needed to focus on her family, the one she was blessed with now and not the one she wished she had. Jacob was a gift, and she should cherish every moment with him.

Once they'd eaten, she sent Jacob off to shower when the phone rang. She grabbed it anxiously, in anticipation that Carter had managed to get away long enough to call her.

"Hello, this is Andre from Francisco's. I wanted to confirm Mr. Davidson's dinner reservation for two, Friday night."

Dinner reservation? Carter had made reservations? It had been forever since they'd been on a date.

"Um, okay."

"I'm sorry. Do I have the right number? Mr. Davidson left me two numbers. I can text or call his cell as well."

Emily scraped the leftover taco fixings into a container, resting the phone between her ear and shoulder. "Actually, I think this might be a surprise. Could you text him to confirm? Let's not tell him I know."

"Oh, absolutely. I'm so sorry to ruin the surprise. I'll text him now." Andre hung up and she danced around the room, feeling like the girl he'd asked to prom their senior year again. Then she froze. She had nothing to wear. She'd have to go shopping, maybe get her hair done. He was making an effort. She had to, too. She wanted to look like the woman he'd married.

"Mom?"

Emily halted mid-spin and took Jacob's little hands, guiding him to twirl with her around the room. "I think it's going to be a great new start for us here. Sweetwater County is definitely turning out better than D.C. You'll be in regular classes at a school like you and your dad wanted, and I'm going to have family around. And I know you'll have tons of friends." She collapsed on the couch with Jacob by her side and sighed with happiness. The first hint of happiness she'd felt in a long time.

Jacob copied her movements and rested his arms by his side. "And Ms. Cathy. She's amazing. One of her kids couldn't read for a long time, and he's some big wig now. Says it happens to lots of people. She said some of the smartest people she knows had reading problems when they were kids.

Albert Einstein, some writer named Agatha something. I can't remember. Oh, and even Tom Cruise, that actor from the *Mission Impossible* movies."

She'd been trying to tell Jacob just that, that he was smart, smarter than most, and even smart people have difficulties. But it turned out hearing it from a stranger carried more weight. "I didn't know that about Tom Cruise. Those are all smart and successful people, and you'll be just like them one day. I know you will. Heck, how many five-year-olds could bake perfect chocolate chip cookies their first time, without even reading the directions?"

Jacob shrugged. "You showed me how."

"Yes, but you did it from memory after only one time and now, four years later, you're still making them with perfection. That's like a genius. I bet you'll be the next Albert Einstein."

Jacob laughed. "Cooking isn't science."

She shook her head. "You bet it is. Every time you bake, you're doing chemistry. And the results are always so delicious!" She squeezed him to her. "Maybe we should conduct another experiment tomorrow."

He smiled and nodded then pushed from the couch. "I better go to bed. Ms. Cathy says I should always make sure I get plenty of sleep so I can do my best at school."

Emily wanted to hug that woman. Not only had Cathy turned Jacob's attitude about attending school around, but she also had him going to bed without complaint. "I'll tuck you in, and you can text Daddy goodnight. I'm not sure if he can respond, but you can try."

For the first time, he snagged the phone without trying to convince her to text for him. "How do you spell *starting*?"

"S-T-A-R-T-I-N-G," she said, not wanting to rock the boat by telling him to sound it out.

"Is *goodnight* one word?"

"Yes."

His little thumbs tapped at the screen then he handed it back to her. She slipped the phone into her pocket as Jacob crawled into bed. She pulled the covers up to his chin. "I love you more than all the stars in the sky."

Jacob tugged his arms free from the covers and wrapped them around her neck. "I love you more than all the grains of sand in the world."

Her phone buzzed so she pulled it out and read Carter's reply aloud. *"Good luck tomorrow. I know you'll do great, buddy. Love you more than all the leaves on all the trees."*

"I think you're right, Mom. We're going to be okay." He huddled down into the covers and closed his eyes.

Emily tip-toed out of the room, leaving the door ajar so a little light from the hallway could seep in. While the nightly text exchange was heartwarming, the fact her family felt more connected through a cell phone than in person saddened her. It was a start, though. They were making progress. And after Friday night, Carter would fall in love with her all over again.

She texted Aunt Sue. *Do you have recommendations on hair and dress? I need to be pretty for Friday night.* Then she relaxed in her new favorite chair, rested her feet on the ottoman, and grabbed her book off the end table to read for a few minutes before she tackled the laundry.

Her phone buzzed. *Text Cathy. She's a seamstress guru and can make a dress overnight that would fit to perfection. Trust me. I'll take you to my girl for hair on Friday. Need a babysitter? I'm your gal.*

Emily had been so excited she hadn't even thought about a babysitter, figuring Carter had it covered, but just in case. *If you don't mind. I don't want to impose.*

Impose? I'm excited to spend time with Jacob. He's my little man. Why don't you make an all-nighter out of it? Jacob can have a sleepover at my place.

Did she dare? Why not? She wanted to put some spice back into their marriage. What better way than to book a room at the inn for the night?

Thank you. That would be incredible. I owe you big time.

You don't owe me anything. It's my pleasure. I'll see you tomorrow for Frappuccino training.

It had taken her all day to get the latte right. Maybe now that she had the basics she'd catch on quicker. That machine was intimidating, but she'd conquer it. She could conquer anything.

Chapter Ten

The meeting continued well past dinner and late into the night. He didn't even have a hotel room reserved. At this rate, he'd have to just go to the airport and sleep in the terminal. The odor of four-hour-old deli sandwiches tossed in a nearby garbage can made his stomach gurgle in protest. His legs and back ached from sitting still for that long. Meetings were always torture for him.

David leaned forward and cupped his hands, resting them on the table. "It's time to stop wasting our time on small investments. The import and export industry is what we should concentrate on. This company, Martark, is a large enough shipping company that we can make a run at the Chinese import market. It's a huge move. If we purchase it now, once the China deal goes through, we can sell for a major instant profit."

Carter shook his head at the lunacy of that statement.

"You have something to add?" Jim asked.

"I do believe the China deal is a great investment, but there's never an instant profit. Buying a large shipping company with no current import agreement with China isn't the right way to go. With the shipping alliance and China's laws changing all the time, it would be better to acquire a Chinese shipping company that already has their documentation in order and then sell it to a larger import/export company that wants into the Chinese market."

David half-snorted, half-hissed, the sound drawing all ten members' attention to him. "You believe regulations are changing? Please. They're never going to give up their trade agreements with the U.S. It's big money for them. Without us, their economy would crumble."

Carter bit his tongue to keep from accusing David of making an ignorant, prejudice comment. Instead, he focused on the facts, not emotion. "The new CMA/CGM partnership with UASC and CSCL makes the shipping market a dangerous place to invest. That Ocean Three program, with 239 weekly stopovers, twenty-one weekly services, a hundred-and-one ports with a hundred-ninety-five ships, makes competition fierce right now. Their speed, flexibility, and reliability will be difficult to match."

Phillip leaned forward, matching David's posture. "How do you know all that? Did you already research that market?"

"I'm always doing research. It's my job to know what's going on in the markets we invest in. When I research a deal, I want to make sure it'll make this company money, not bankrupt us. We can't dump a bunch of capital into one company and hope for the best." Carter loosened his tie a little further, relaxing into the details. "Once more, deals that will only produce a little return in relation to the manpower required to execute them aren't worth our time. Strategy is everything. One missed step and we could all be out of a job."

David tapped his pencil against the table in an annoying cadence. "Doom and gloom are all I hear, but we can't always be cautious. We need to make money, and we can't do that if we're sitting on our hands unwilling to take some risks."

Jim cleared his throat. His friend's reputation and soft-spoken, yet commanding, nature demanded respect. All the board members, even David, turned their attention on him. "There needs to be a balance between risk and reward."

"I agree," Carter said, "and I believe risk can be minimized through solid research and planning. That's why I recommend we go after SELCM. It's a smaller operation in China, with a logistics department that has them already set up for endless possibilities, but they lack the capital to produce ships at the rate they need them. If we acquire them, invest in leasing ships, we can sell them for a substantial profit to a major player here in the United States. Stability is key when it comes to markets that are constantly changing, like the import/export industry. We prove SELCM is consistently stable, and it will sell for top dollar."

Carter could see David was itching to refute him, but he plowed ahead, not giving him the opportunity. "Currently eBay has a deal with shipping companies in the export industry to reduce the cost of smaller shipments. Due to the overall weight of cargo on each shipment, a few smaller items added on won't affect the fuel efficiency or timeline and reduces the cost for eBay shipping. There are two major online stores in China that have a potential to compete with eBay. If we acquire SELCM, we can sign an agreement with the online retailers to be their exclusive shipping company, allowing us to drop our rates lower than eBay. That will eventually draw business from the other larger existing companies."

David laughed in that manic Joker tone he'd perfected. "You think you can handle a multi-company takeover when you failed to close a simple deal last week?"

Carter straightened and yanked the tie from around his neck, setting it on the table. "As I said, working for small profit and spending too much on manpower is a poor investment. The company you're referring to had no place to go. They'd reached their full potential. I'm not willing to put that much money into a deal when the return is null."

"It was guaranteed income," David replied, "yet, you told them how to save their own company instead of closing the deal."

Carter stiffened. How did David know what happened in that meeting?

"You did what?" Phillip slammed his fists on the table. "You helped a company we'd planned to acquire, handing them a silver spoon to feed themselves with while we starve?"

Carter understood Phillip's limited vision. Money, any amount made, was beneficial to the company. But he didn't understand the business side of things, how the amount made had to be more than the amount spent. Not just on the initial investment, but in terms of the company's overhead. There was the cost of their building's maintenance, their employees' salaries, and utilities to consider.

The AC overhead cut on, cooling the fire blazing up the back of Carter's neck. He took a long breath and chose his words carefully. "We would've lost money in that deal. The plan was to make a quick profit in order to invest in a bigger deal. That would not have been possible. It would've taken more resources, manpower, and money from BSMA in order to sell Martark for a profit. The time frame would've also been extended due to planning and zoning issues."

Jim swiveled his chair to face Carter. "What planning and zoning issues?"

Carter flipped through the stack of documents in front of him until he found the information he needed. "The city won't approve the expansion. That area isn't zoned for businesses of that size, so the water and sewer systems wouldn't be able to accommodate it. Without the expansion, doing a quick turnaround for profit would be impossible." He tried to explain the business side of the deal using as simple terms as he could, without sounding like he was patronizing the man. "Not only that. but the expansion would've created a bidding war over the adjoining land as another company had their eye on it. This would've cut into our profit margin even more."

David waved his hands about. "That's all speculation. We get deals like this pushed through all the time. If you ask me, it sounds like a bunch of excuses. And I know for a fact you were fond of Mr. Martark."

Carter clutched his thighs under the table to keep from slugging the man. "If you're implying that I chose to not continue with the deal for personal reasons then you're gravely mistaken. I'm a businessman. I've generated a lot of money for this company and have never let my emotions play a part in it. I'm in this business to make money for our investors, as well as this board."

"It's getting late, gentleman." Tom pushed from the table and stood. "Carter, we'd like to see your research on Mr. Martark's business, including the planning and zoning issues you mentioned. We'll be discussing the direction this company will be taking in the future over the next few weeks. It's a critical time for us as we determine the next phase of our growth. I believe we should proceed, but with caution and a plan for success."

David stood as well, and Carter had no choice but to let the meeting adjourn. He wanted to demand an explanation. Tom had never requested to see documentation to back his decisions before. Carter had always been given freedom, since the board trusted him to execute the right deals. He'd proven himself to them repeatedly over the years, which is how he even got to this position. Securing an entry level position after college and working his way through the ranks to management and eventually CEO.

David must have gotten to them, planting doubt of his abilities in their minds. The man would do anything to have him fired, but Carter wouldn't let that happen. If David gained control, this company would be bankrupt inside a month. He couldn't let all his employees, who'd worked tirelessly to help him build this company up to what it was today, lose their jobs.

"I'd be glad to. I'll send my current data to each board member directly now, and then send a full report tomorrow morning." Carter shook each of their hands, even David's, trying not to crush the cockroach under the weight of his anger. If this had been high school instead of a boardroom, he'd love to deck the guy just once and knock some sense into him.

The room emptied out, leaving Carter alone to strategize and plan his next moves. He'd have to be careful. One mistake could cause the majority of the board to vote in David's favor.

His phone buzzed and he glanced at it to see a text from Emily. *In bed, thinking about you. Can't wait for you to get home.*

He'd moved his family to Creekside in the hopes of spending more quality time together, to be near his mother and have more family around for Jacob. If he had his way, he'd rent a car and drive all night to get home to his family. He missed them. He wanted to be there for Jacob's first day at his new school, but he couldn't. He had to stay focused and work if he was going to save his job. He'd already let his family down once. The guilt of not being there to help Emily when she collapsed still weighed heavily on him. He couldn't help wondering if their little girl, their little Grace, would've lived if he'd been home that day.

He slammed his fist against the conference room table. Being away was the worst thing for their marriage right now. With the way things were going, he'd soon find himself forced to choose between saving his marriage and saving his job.

Chapter Eleven

The red brick school building looked larger than it had the day before. A spring breeze carried the scent of magnolia and honeysuckle, the fragrance soothing Emily for a moment. Her eyes remained on Jacob, visible through the row of windows as he walked down the hallway toward his new classroom with his teacher. She would've walked him to class herself but left at the urging of the vice principal. Still, she hadn't promised not to watch through the windows.

What if the kids made fun of him? Being the new kid in school was hard enough without having difficulties with reading and writing. She climbed the front steps again and reached for the door, ready to rescue him. If only she possessed the skills to home-school him then none of this would even matter. If she'd gone to college...

No. She shook her head. There was no more time for regrets. Besides, there were plenty of moms out there who home-schooled their children with no formal teacher training. She shouldn't let that stop her either. She was smart and learned quickly. Maybe she could look into attending college to study early childhood education now that they were settled into their new home. If she got her teaching certificate, it would allow her to work and still be home with Jacob after school.

She watched until her only child turned the corner and disappeared from sight then she stepped down to the walkway. Carter shouldn't mind if she attended classes during the day while Jacob was in school, as long as she still took care of the house and Jacob. She would need to schedule in time to work as well, so she could pay for Jacob's evaluation. Could she really manage all of that?

With a sigh, she walked to her car and opened the door. She probably could, but would Carter agree to it? His attitude always seemed to take a turn whenever returning to school were mentioned.

Behind the school, kids ran around the playground, screaming and laughing. She'd always loved kids. If she couldn't have anymore, maybe she could make a difference in other children's lives as a teacher. A job with meaning instead of crunching numbers all day. Not that there was anything wrong with accounting, it wasn't the right job for her.

Emily drove to Café Bliss, where she was meeting Cathy to discuss making a dress, but the short drive allowed her more than enough time to reflect on her plan. There was no parking on Main Street so she turned down a side road past the café and parked on the shoulder. The café bustled with people. She was beginning to think Cathy was right, that you didn't mess with small town folk and their caffeine.

She hurried inside and grabbed an apron then ran over to where Cathy sat near the wall. "Let me help with the rush and then we can talk. Is that okay?"

"Sure, so long as you're not making my drink." Cathy winked and lifted her coffee cup in a toast.

"Promise. I'll be back as soon as I can." Emily went to work wiping down tables, cleaning dishes, and refilling creamer and sugar containers. Within thirty minutes, the morning rush had dwindled to around ten customers, lingering as they chatted over their special brews.

Aunt Sue rested her hip against the counter. "Thanks for the help. I had a call in, and all the high school part-timers are at school, and the college kids have gone home for spring break. It's tough to get help around here."

"No worries. I don't mind helping out as long as you don't ask me to make drinks anymore. Maybe if I drank coffee, I'd be better at it."

Aunt Sue wiped down the machine, tossed some more dishes in the sink and grabbed a water bottle. "Let's sit for a bit. I'll get this cleaned up before the lunch rush."

Cathy pushed a chair out from under the table with her foot for Aunt Sue. "Bless your heart, you're gonna fall over one of these days. You really need to get some help in here."

"I've got some now," Aunt Sue said, patting Emily on the hand.

"You need someone that can actually make coffee. Besides, things might be changing soon." Emily tapped her foot, trying to keep her excitement under control. For the first time in years, she had something to focus on besides loss.

Cathy clicked her fingernails against the surface of the table. "Well, you gonna make us get down on our knees and beg? Or are ya gonna tell us? Whatever it is sure has you glowing like a firefly plugged into the sun."

The door opened as another straggler came in for their morning fix. "You should go. I can tell you after you get her order."

"Oh no, you don't. I'm with Cathy. You've got us on the edge of our stools waiting to find out what you're planning. Besides, Trianna there doesn't mind waiting a few minutes."

"You're gonna think it's crazy." Emily's foot tapped faster.

"Crazier than those concoctions you make?" Cathy lifted her cup and her nose crinkled.

Emily fought to find the words, to actually say them aloud. Would that make it more real? "I'm, uh, thinking about taking some classes to get certified to be a teacher. Maybe even in special education. That way I can work while Jacob's in school, and help him with his reading at home. I'll be able to understand better what he needs." She held her breath, waiting for the laughs she was sure were coming. It even sounded a little ridiculous to her, yet she couldn't help feeling excited at the possibilities.

"I think that's a stupendous idea." Aunt Sue stood and waved at the customer to let her know she'd be right there.

Cathy reached into her purse and pulled out her cell. "Seconded, and I know just the person you should speak to. My friend Rose is studying special education at the University of Tennessee. That girl's so smart she tested out of half her freshman classes. And she's been volunteering at the Center for Autism over on the other side of town. She'd be a great person to chat with."

Prickles of excitement tickled Emily's stomach. "You think she'd mind talking to me next time she's in town?"

Cathy smiled. "I'll do you one better. She can talk to you today. She just so happens to be home for her dad's birthday. Devon, my husband, went over to help with something at the factory and phoned a little while ago to tell me she was back in town. Even Marcus came with her." The left side of Cathy's mouth curved up. "Guess you don't know 'bout all that. Um, Rose's dad didn't exactly approve of her choice, so she and Marcus ran off to college together. Rose even graduated high school early. From what Sue says, she's like a mini version of you."

"Ha, that does sound familiar, but Carter and I didn't run off."

Cathy's lips pressed together and her forehead wrinkled as she raised her eyebrows high. "You kidding? I know you and Carter hightailed it out of here the minute you could. From what I hear you and his mama didn't exactly have a lot in common. Must make you feel good he chose you over his mama."

Had he? It was so long ago. They were young and stupid for sure, but did she really make him choose between them? Is that why the woman hated her?

"What's wrong?" Cathy scrolled through her phone with a few swipes of her finger then tapped the screen and held the phone to her ear.

"Nothing. Just never thought of it that way before."

Cathy tilted the phone to her mouth. "Hey there, Rose. How ya doin'?" Emily held her breath and listened. "You think you can stop over at Café Bliss? Got someone here that would like to chat with you about special education." Cathy nodded and smiled, giving Emily a thumbs up. "Great. See you in a few." She touched the screen once more then dropped her phone into her bag hanging off the back of her chair. "Done. She and Marcus are headed into town anyway. Marcus wanted to visit Sue. He used to work here."

"Work here? He was the best employee I've ever had. Sorry, Emily." Aunt Sue rounded the counter and joined them again. The customer waved goodbye then made a speedy exit.

"No offense taken, really. Coffee isn't my thing, but I've always been good at school. I know I can do this."

"Of course you can. You were Miss Smarty Pants in high school after all. Not to mention how quickly you graduated college." Cathy rubbed Emily's back with a reassuring hand, and Emily felt guilty for all the years she'd thought Cathy was nothing but a bossy, gossipy woman who caused trouble in town. That was what her mother had said anyway. Especially after a rumor of her dad's affairs made the rounds in town. That was when her parents took off, and Emily had to choose between college, going with them, or marrying Carter. It wasn't much of a choice, though. She knew in her heart what she wanted from the moment he asked her to marry him.

"Thank you, Cathy. That means a lot. It's been so long, and I'm much older now. I'll probably be the oldest person on campus."

"Hogwash. A friend of mine in her sixties is working on a master's degree in history just for the fun of it." She shook her head. "Something I can't understand. Why would anyone go to school for fun?" Cathy fluffed her hair and crossed her legs with a harrumph.

"I would," Emily confessed. "I don't know why, but I love to learn."

"Then you were probably meant to teach," Aunt Sue said. "You go for it. I'll pick up Jacob after school if you end up running late talking to Rose. Once I get help in here, I'll have more time for my nephew."

"I can't ask you to do that," Emily said.

Aunt Sue grabbed her wrist and leaned into her. "Listen, you're the closest thing to a daughter I ever had, and Jacob is the closest thing to a grandchild I'll ever have. My brother might have taken off, but I'm here and I want to be a part of your family if you'll have me."

"Yes, of course. You're the only reason I agreed to return to Creekside."

"Gee, thanks," Cathy grumbled. She pushed from the table as if to escape the offensive words.

"I didn't know this Cathy." Emily moved her hand to encompass Cathy from head to toe.

"A girl loses a few pounds and puts on some lipstick and you'd think she'd had a personality transplant. Of course, Rose is to thank for me looking like this. She was originally planning on studying nutrition, but I think after working with nutrition related to children with special needs, she switched her major. She's fantastic."

"I don't think it was only Rose," Aunt Sue said. "While her great nutrition and motivation helped, you did all the hard work. Besides, I think that man of yours had something to do with it, too. He's good for you."

Emily dropped her gaze to her hands, her fingers nervously working at a chipped nail. If only she had a man who lifted her up. While she loved Carter, he hadn't always been the most understanding. Would he even agree to let her go back to school? He'd probably spout something about it being a waste of money, or how it was her job to be home with Jacob working on his reading instead of ignoring him so she could go to school.

"What is it, hon?" Aunt Sue leaned into her.

"It's nothing. I'm just nervous about telling Carter my idea. He's worried about Jacob, and he's right. I should stay home and concentrate on helping my son, instead of being selfish."

Cathy slapped her thigh with a resounding smack. "Don't let that man guilt you. I lived over half my life doing what people expected of me, and it didn't make me happy. Now, I run my own sewing business. I work when I want, and I have fun when I want. I'm happier and healthier than I've ever been. Don't get me wrong. I don't blame my late husband, God rest his soul, for what happened in the past. I blame myself for letting it happen. Don't let it happen, Emily."

Emily searched her soul and knew she needed this. Some might view it as selfish, latching onto something to help her move past her grief, but what she could give back mattered so much more. Becoming a teacher meant she could help Jacob. She could give back to her hometown by helping other children with special issues.

With a small nod, she decided she'd have to stand up to Carter for this one. Or do it behind his back. No, that wasn't the answer. Lying would only put more strain on their already weak marriage. They needed to learn to work together, needed to learn to lean on each other instead of dealing with their grief separately. Not that things were perfect before they'd lost Grace, but it was time to start healing.

"Now that that's decided, let's get down to our original reason for meeting," Cathy said.

"Oh, yes. Are you still up for designing a dress for me? I hear you can make me look beautiful."

"Darling, you don't need any help with that, but I'd be honored to make you something so you don't go to dinner naked. I'm no fashionista, though. I'm just a seamstress. What were you thinking? If you ask me, you should show off those thin shoulders and pretty collar bone with some spaghetti straps or a strapless dress." Cathy's eyes lit up with a passion for fashion despite her claims she had no design skills.

"Carter does like my neck and shoulders. He used to say I looked like Audrey Hepburn when I'd get dressed up. I don't want anything too fancy, though. Just something eye-catching and dressy, but not formal."

Cathy retrieved a little notebook from her purse and opened it up. "As I said, I'm not a designer, but I've learned a lot from Rebecca, my stepdaughter. I think we'll use a casual fabric, something that drapes nicely but is easy to clean. How about a simple design like this, with a pop of color?" Cathy drew a strapless dress with some sort of band around the top of the bodice and another around the waist then shaded it in. The skirt was fitted to just above the knee. "It's a little retro, as Becca would say. You can pick an accent color, and I'll put it here and here." She pointed to the bands at the top of the bodice and waistline. "The rest of the dress can be one solid color or have a simple pattern."

Aunt Sue clapped her hands together. "Wow. That would be gorgeous on you, Emmy."

The café door opened, bringing a spring perfumed breeze inside. A young girl with reddish hair and pale skin entered on the arm of a handsome, young Enrique Iglesias look-alike. "Hi!" the young girl said, her voice full of life and energy. She reminded Emily of herself at nineteen or twenty.

The young man embraced Aunt Sue and twirled her around while the girl rushed over to hug Cathy.

"It's so good to see you, darlin'. Rose, this is my friend Emily. She's the one Devon was telling you about. I thought maybe you two could chat about school and what you know about special education."

"I'd be happy to." Rose smiled, a sweet smile that hinted at inner strength. Emily had no doubt this young girl would take on the world someday.

"Hello, I'm Marcus Vega." His thick Spanish accent and deep voice made him ooze with movie star charm.

"It's a pleasure."

Marcus kissed her knuckles and squeezed her hand. "I've heard much about you. Welcome back to Creekside. If you ladies will excuse us, I need to go take a look at a computer issue my favorite person here seems to be having." He squeezed Aunt Sue to his side. From what Emily knew, Marcus was the son Aunt Sue never had, and Aunt Sue was a surrogate mother for the one he'd lost as a child. "Ladies." He bowed his head then draped his arm over Aunt Sue's shoulder before steering them toward the back of the café.

"Get cozy, ladies," Cathy said. "I need to head out to pick fabrics for a new dress for our lovely Ms. Emily here. I'll see you later. In a few days at your dad's surprise party."

"You don't have to come, you know. I know you two don't exactly get along." Rose sat down with the grace of a ballerina.

"Don't be silly. I believe there's hope for him yet. Besides, he actually lets Marcus enter the factory now when you come home to visit. That's progress." Cathy slipped the notebook in her bag then slung the bag over her shoulder and headed for the door. "There's always hope," Cathy added, her eyes fixed on Emily, before she turned and walked out the door.

Rose's gaze searched the back of the café for a second before returning to rest on Emily. That girl was completely in love with that boy. Emily remembered feeling the same way about Carter when she was young. "So, you're interested in SPED?"

"Yeah, I'm considering returning to school to study Special Education. My son's had some struggles, and I believe pursuing that profession would be a good fit for me, and help me understand my son better."

Rose bounced in her seat with enthusiasm. "It's an amazing field. I started out studying nutrition, but the more I work with children with special needs, the more my heart feels like it belongs there with them. I volunteer at the Autism Center here and at the schools in Nashville, and I love what I do every day." Her demeanor changed in an instance, from bubbly to calm and reserved. "Cathy reached out to me yesterday about Jacob. I hope you don't mind. I'm not a professional, but I do work with kids with learning disabilities on a regular basis and it sounds like he might have some sort of expressive or receptive language issue."

A hint of intrigue drew Emily's undivided attention. "Really?"

"Again, I'm not a professional, yet, so that's only my best guess. But I do have the name of a psycho-educational psychiatrist who does testing to determine what the underlying issue is for these kids. After speaking with Cathy and consulting with someone at the school I volunteer for in Nashville, I definitely recommend you have him tested."

Emily nodded. "He was supposed to be tested back at his previous school, but unfortunately, the test never happened. They mentioned a language disorder but didn't seem too concerned. They claimed he was just lazy and didn't want to participate in the classroom."

Rose huffed. "I hear that a lot from public schools. Don't get me wrong, they do the best they can with the resources they're given. Did you know that in some states, despite the federal laws, they don't recognize dyslexia as a disability? It's crazy, and even those that do recognize it are unable to help due to the lack of training or resources."

"Jacob isn't dyslexic. He doesn't read things backward or write words backward. Well, he'll often write his letters backward."

Rose's mouth tightened and she took a breath before she spoke again. "One of the early signs for dyslexia and dysgraphia is trouble reading and writing, specifically writing letters backward. There are many other indicators as well."

Emily shook her head, anxiety and anger sending a sting through her chest. "Certainly if he was dyslexic or dys-dys—"

"Dysgraphic," Rose supplied.

"…dysgraphic, they would've determined that when I requested he be tested before. Of course, they never completed the testing. His teacher in first grade retired, and the teacher in second grade said nothing so the testing was never completed."

Rose glanced toward the back of the café again then back at Emily. "The only real way to know for sure is to have him tested. I really recommend you speak to a psycho-educational psychiatrist and soon. Early intervention is so important, and if the public school isn't equipped to help, you'll need to look into Orton-Gilliam tutoring or a special school for dyslexia. It's important he receives the help he needs now."

Emily wrung her hands. The guilt of not discovering this sooner, the anger at teachers for not listening to her, the fear that her husband would never understand all churned inside her like a brewing storm. A storm that spun out of control and threatened to tear down the patch job they'd been doing on their lives.

Chapter Twelve

The steaming water from the shower eased the ache in Carter's neck and back. Maybe sleeping in an uncomfortable chair at the airport hadn't been the best idea. He'd wanted to catch Emily and Jacob before they left for school, but the house was empty when he finally made it home.

Carter reluctantly turned off the water, ending his moment of bliss, and toweled off. His mind cleared of its travel haze, his thoughts returned to the problem at hand. There had to be a reason David was going after his job so hard. Sure, the guy had always been a jerk, but this was different, almost personal.

Carter finished shaving and brushing his teeth before entering the small master bedroom. It might only be a rental home, but the bed looked heavenly. The plush comforter, large pillows, and soft sheets called to him. Instead of giving into temptation, he snagged his laptop from his briefcase, made some coffee and settled in a chair in the front room to work.

A hummingbird hovered over a large bush with blooming flowers outside the window. His favorite bird from childhood, he used to watch hummingbirds for hours whenever his parents took them on picnics.

"We have a picnic on the living room floor and eat pizza while we play with Amelia." Eric's words, and devotion to his family gnawed at Carter. He wanted that, to be a family man, a good father and husband. Maybe he'd take them on a picnic after school, go to the park and play catch. If he could just finish up some work, he could take the afternoon off.

He took a sip of his coffee, waiting for the promised caffeine jolt to help wake him up. It worked for a few hours, and he managed to finish the research and documentation he needed for his report to the board about the failed deal with Martark. Once he had his secretary proofread it for the homophone issues, spelling, and grammar mistakes he typically made, he'd send it on. Good thing he was good at mergers and acquisitions and had a secretary who somehow managed to translate his gibberish, or he'd never make any money.

With the documentation out of the way, he immersed himself in searching for information on David, hoping to find some indication as to the reason behind his new hatred for Carter. There wasn't much on his personal life, just that he had a couple kids and had divorced a year ago. Was the man bitter? Maybe, but Carter had a hunch there was more to it than that, something he wasn't seeing.

After a few more clicks, he found out the man was an avid investor. He'd made lots of money over the years and seemed to have an ideal life. Carter couldn't find anything to indicate why David would want him out of the company.

He spotted the hummingbird outside the window again, working hard as it flapped its wings at an invisible speed. Despite being a cockroach, David was a hard worker, seemingly spending all of his spare time on investments. A man so dedicated to making money, he loved his status symbols. He drove an expensive car, lived in an expensive house, and even owned an expensive boat. Had the deal Carter decided to pass on cost him something? It didn't seem likely. Why would David invest in a company like Martark?

Carter sat up abruptly. Because he planned on selling it. If he was right, David had some sort of investment in that company, and he'd been counting on Mr. Martark selling to BSMA. Since David was chairman of the board, he could push the deal through and if successful, he'd not only earn money for the company but a substantial amount for himself.

Carter shook his head at the man's apparent greed. If David stood to make money off the sale, had he even intended on staying on as chairman of the board, knowing the fallout of such a bad investment was inevitable? Carter couldn't see all the pieces, but he knew someone who might. A twinge of anger fueled his desire to get to the truth. Not just for the way David tried to have Carter pushed out of the company, but for putting his personal gain above the company's best interest. If it was true, it was something the board needed to be made aware of, and soon.

Carter pulled out his cell and phoned Mr. Martark. It rang several times until the voicemail picked up. "Mr. Martark? It's Carter Davidson. I have an odd question for you. Do you know a David Aguero? He works for BSMA, and I was wondering if he's contacted you recently. If you could call me back at your earliest convenience, I'd appreciate it. I hope your nephew is working out well, and you've been able to look forward to retirement. Talk to you soon."

Carter hung up the phone. As much as it was risky getting outsiders involved, he trusted Martark. The older man was an honest, old-school kind of person, but it was still a gamble. Carter would have to be cautious or he'd be out of a job come morning.

Caught up on work, and with a moment to breathe, he thought about taking a nap, but with the David issue racing through his head, he knew he'd never be able to sleep. Instead, he headed to his mom's house to check on her and that sink. That was one of the main reasons he'd moved back to Creekside after all, to spend more time with her and help with some of the household chores.

On the way, he called Emily, longing to hear her voice.

"Hi, hon. Where are you?" Emily asked.

"I've been at home for the past few hours. How did it go dropping Jacob off at school this morning?"

"It went okay. I was proud of him. He was a champ."

Carter fist-bumped the air. "That's great. I knew this move would be good for all of us. Hey, what do you think about taking Jacob on a picnic after school?" A long pause of silence deflated his excitement. "I mean, it's not a big deal if you two already made other plans."

"No. I just thought you'd be working. That sounds perfect. We'll be home in an hour or so if you'd like to go then."

"Sounds perfect. I'm heading to Mom's for a few minutes then I'll be home. Why don't we get subs for dinner and go play ball at the park?"

"Good idea. We'll see you soon. And Carter?"

"Yes."

"You might be right. This move might've been just what we needed. I love you."

Carter's heart soared to the white puffy clouds overhead at her words. "I love you, too."

"See you soon." Emily hung up, a happy tone to her voice for once.

He wanted to pat himself on the back for deciding to move his family here. It was one of the best places to raise children…or a child. He shook off the memory of watching his wife nearly die, of holding his lifeless little girl for two hours before they took her away. This wasn't the time or place for sorrow. It was time to heal and rebuild his family.

His mother was kneeling at the front flowerbed when he pulled into the driveway. He quickly hopped out of the car. "Mom, why are you out here? I told you I'd do some of the gardening, or pay someone to help."

"Listen here, I like gardening. I like the dirt. Someday I'll be buried in it, so even if I die on this spot, it don't make no difference."

Carter huffed. "Don't talk like that. You're still young. Besides, the stubborn ones always live the longest." He didn't want to acknowledge that her body looked older than her years with the RA attacking her joints. It saddened him to see her in such a weakened, pained state.

His mother wiped her hands down the front of her old-fashioned gardening apron, tipped up her yellow hat tied beneath her chin with a white bow then pulled it back over her eyes. "You're probably right. What'cha doin' here?"

"I thought I'd come help you with some house stuff. I have about an hour and then I'm going to pick up Emily and Jacob, and we're going to the park."

"Good for you. You work too darn hard, and that woman isn't going to stick around much longer if you keep ignoring her all the time. Fancy jobs mean more to men than they do to their wives. They just want you around."

"That woman is Emily. And why don't you tell me how you really feel?"

She stood, cocked one hip out and dropped the gardening shovel onto the ground. "You best listen to your mama if you want to work things out with that wife of yours. I might not have jumped for joy when you two got hitched, but I certainly don't want to see you alone, taking care of me because you screwed up. Now, give your mama a kiss." She stuck her cheek out so he obliged, not sure where the sudden need for affection came from. His mother was many things—strong, opinionated, smart—but affectionate wasn't on that list.

"Let's go inside and get out of the sun for a bit." Carter took her by the arm, but she snatched it away.

"I'm not no invalid, you know. I plan on walking to my tombstone, digging my own grave, and then lying down. You can put the dirt over me. Otherwise, I don't need your help. That being said, I do need a working kitchen sink," she huffed and gave him that stern look that always struck fear into him as a child.

"Then let me get to it. If I can't fix it, I'll hire a plumber." Carter followed her closely up the front stairs, making sure she didn't fall, but ended up tripping over the top step and nearly taking her down.

"If you'd stop hovering over me, old man, you wouldn't end up in the hospital with a broken hip." She held her nose higher than Scarlett O'Hara and marched inside. "Now, you tell me what's going on in your life. Why do you look like you've got the weight of a civil war on your shoulders?"

The house looked brighter, and more homey with bright sunlight streaming in through the large windows. Memories of sliding down the banister, racing his brothers floated into his mind.

"Hey, you listening to me?"

"Yes, sorry," he said. "Work is complicated right now. I think my job's in danger." His mother pointed at the sink and pulled out a chair where all the tools were laid out on a towel. To his surprise, the water was already shut off. "Were you expecting me?"

She shrugged, pulled out another chair and plopped down on it. "If not, I was gonna fix it. Either way, it was gonna get done. Now, have you told Emily you think your job's in jeopardy?"

"Not yet."

"Don't. Tell me instead of puttin' everything on Emily's shoulders. Sometimes marriage can be stressful 'cause of money and jobs."

"Emily's tougher than you think. She's been through a lot." He quickly slid under the sink to analyze the leak.

"I have no doubt, or she wouldn't have made it this long being married to you. I'm afraid you got my stubborn streak. Of course, I think it's served you well when you needed it most. If I remember correctly, anytime anyone said you couldn't do something you had to prove them wrong. That teacher said you'd never read, and you up and taught yourself. The counselor said you'd never get into college, and you made him eat his words. I told you

you'd never be able to make your marriage work, and here you are still married. Yep, stubbornness can be a gift."

He put the small bucket she'd set out for him under the cold water valve and loosened the washer. "You have a point. I guess I never thought of it that way before. I'm gonna need that stubbornness if I'm going to fight to keep my job. The chairman of the board wants me out, but I'm not giving up that easily."

"Good for you." She patted his leg as if he were a dog. "There's only one problem with being so stubborn."

Carter analyzed the valve, but everything looked fine. No corrosion or rust. The gasket still looked in good shape. It had to be something else. "What's that?"

She handed him a rag to clean up under the cabinet where some water had dripped off the side of the bucket. "You don't know when you should walk away."

He bolted upright, hitting his head on the counter above. "I'm not giving up on my marriage."

"I wasn't referrin' to your marriage." She pointed at his phone where he'd set it on the floor next to him. Two missed calls and a text from Jim. *Get back here now, or you won't have a job by tomorrow. David waited until you returned to Creekside before he called an emergency meeting, knowing you couldn't make it. I've managed to postpone it until tomorrow morning though.*

Rage heated his skin. That man had played too many games. He might not make it in time for the meeting, but he'd figure out what the cockroach had up his sleeves and expose him. He'd show the board what kind of man their chairman of the board really was.

"You've got to go?" His mother stood and pushed the chair back under the table. "What about your picnic?"

He cursed under his breath.

"Not gonna have that kind of talk in my house, young man, or I'll put Tabasco sauce on your tongue and make you stand there until I give you permission to swallow it."

"I'm not a kid anymore, you know. I'm sorry. I really am. I'll finish this Friday night."

"Before or after our date?"

Shoot. That was right. "Don't worry. I'll be here. We already have reservations. You just put on your prettiest dress."

"Can you pick up my meds on your way, please? I'm almost out. The doctor already called it into the pharmacy. If not, I can get Cathy to bring them to me. I'd hate to not take them since they help with the pain" She rubbed her swollen knuckles.

"No need. I've got it. Listen, you just be dressed and ready to go by three-thirty." He kissed her cheek once more and bolted for his car. There was one more flight he could catch tonight, but that would mean canceling his plans with Emily and Jacob. He hated himself for it, but what choice did he have?

Chapter Thirteen

The next two days dragged by as Emily waited for her dress fitting with Cathy. Two days she waited for the psycho-educational evaluation for Jacob. Two days she waited for Carter to return for their epic surprise date. Two days she sat on the information about Jacob's testing, not breathing a word of it to Carter. She knew it was wrong to keep it from him, but she'd chosen to help her son and face her husband's wrath later.

Turning into the parking lot of the Riverbend Therapy Center, she glanced at Jacob in the passenger seat twisting his T-shirt into a worm shape. "It's going to be okay. I heard Dr. Parker is really nice."

Jacob bowed his head, and she could feel the apprehension in the air. "It's not the test I'm scared of."

"What is it then?" Emily nudged.

Jacob released his shirt and grabbed the door handle. "It's stupid. Never mind."

She snagged his arm before he could escape. "It's not stupid. Nothing you have to say could be stupid. You can tell me anything."

He sighed. "What if I'm just stupid? You can't help that."

"Jacob Anthony Davidson, you listen to me. There's nothing stupid about you. Would a stupid person try as hard as you have? I think Ms. Cathy and Rose are right. I think you're just wired a little differently, but that's something we can help you with once we know what's going on. Do you know what kind of gift that is?"

"Gift? Being stupid is a gift?" Jacob rolled his eyes and fiddled with his seatbelt.

"No. Being wired a little differently means you're unique and special. Your brain may not be wired right for reading but it's wired perfectly for something else. It's God's way of giving you a boost without making everyone else jealous. It's a gift He gave especially to you. You know how you mentioned the other day that Einstein and Tom Cruise and a few others had reading difficulties? They're all dyslexic."

"What's that?"

"It's when your brain is wired differently so it makes it hard to see words and letters the way they appear to everyone else. I'm not saying that you're dyslexic. I'm not an expert. I'm just saying that sometimes we have challenges that we have to face in order to reach our full potential. Reading may be a struggle, but you're so gifted at math and many other things."

He straightened a smidgen in his seat and shoved the door open. "I guess."

They entered the building situated at the edge of Riverbend University. It was full of people, and they had to weave through the crowds to the corridor that led to the last office on the right. Inside, the office was tranquil and quiet. A babbling rock garden, soft plush chairs, and a warm cinnamon aroma relaxed her instantly. Jacob raced to the kid area at the back of the waiting room to play video games while she signed him in at the front desk.

"I see our little man likes video games. Wow, look at his thumbs fly." A tall woman with a bright smile and warm voice walked from around the desk and stood by Emily.

"Yeah, he's amazing at that kind of stuff. I can't even figure out how to get the characters to move, let alone keep up with him. He's too fast for me. Always flipping screens and shooting things. I do limit his gaming time, though." Emily thought she should clarify, knowing that too much of any kind of screen time wasn't good for growing children.

"If you let him, could he beat a game in a single day."

"Some take him just a few hours. The last one he wanted to return to the store after only two hours because he'd already beaten the last level."

"I see. Interesting."

All the sudden, Emily realized the woman was analyzing her son. "Um, are you Dr. Parker?"

The woman angled toward her on her stiletto heels and offered her hand. "Yes, I am. Sorry for the late introduction. I was just so impressed I had to observe for a moment. Are you guys ready to get started?" Emily swallowed her anxiety and nodded. "Okay, I'll take Jacob with me while you fill out some paperwork for me."

"I'm not going back with him?" Emily's nerves spiked.

"No. It's best that you don't, but you can watch us through a one-way mirror." Dr. Parker pointed to a window at the end of the room across from the video game area. "We find that having the parents present during the evaluation can skew the results."

"Good luck getting Jacob away from that game anytime soon," Emily chuckled under her breath, but she wasn't joking.

"Here." Dr. Parker handed her a clipboard with about twenty pages of scantron sheets and packets of questions. "I already received the records from his previous school, so we should be good there. If we're able to get through all the testing today, I'll be able to score it for you by Monday."

"Um, okay. Sounds good." Emily lowered into one of the plush red chairs and watched Dr. Parker walk over to talk to her son. To Emily's amazement, Jacob set the controller down and followed Dr. Parker through the doorway. Man, she was good.

Emily still couldn't believe she'd gotten Jacob in for the evaluation so quickly, but apparently Cathy knew someone, who knew someone. That seemed to be the way things worked in small towns. Her phone buzzed with a text from Carter. A zap of excitement electrified her insides, sending her back to their dating years. She remembered sitting by the phone in her kitchen, staring at it as she waited for his call. When it finally came, she'd be flying around the house getting ready to see him.

She swiped her finger across the screen to unlock it and read the message. *Can you do me a favor? Can you take Mom her medicine? Pharmacy called and said I should've picked it up Wednesday, but she told me Friday was fine. According to the pharmacist, she should already be out.*

The happy energy dulled into a heated warning deep inside her. She knew she couldn't ignore it. This was family, and she had to face her mother-in-law and her criticism about how wrong she was for her son at some point.

Yes, I'll take care of it after lunch. No worries.

How is Jacob? Is school going well? Are you having a good day? Miss you bunches.

Her breath caught somewhere between her stomach and her lungs. She couldn't tell him that she'd gone behind his back and done the one thing he never wanted for his son, especially not via text. With a thousand pounds of guilt weighing down her shoulders, she swiped her shaking finger across the screen and typed out a response. *All is good. Love you and can't wait to see you.*

There. That wasn't a lie. She counted on the fact he was probably texting between meetings and wouldn't be able to ask any more prying questions. She needed time to formulate her thoughts, to find the best way to tell him what was going on, but in person, not through their brief phone calls or text messages. She stared at the screen, willing him to say something. The large decorative clock on the wall, which reminded her of the Hugo Cabret clock from the graphic novel Jacob loved so much, ticked several times. Finally, her phone buzzed.

I will make this up to you. Thank you for being such a good mom and wife. I don't tell you that enough. I can't wait to spend time with you. Special time.

As if she'd been given a shot of adrenaline straight to the heart, she nearly jumped up and ran out of the room, heading straight to the hair salon then to Cathy's for her dress. But she'd only end up sitting and waiting on Carter for hours, just like she had on prom night.

I look forward to it.

She stared at the screen a few more seconds, but no more bubbles of words popped up. He'd returned to the business world. Her nervous energy faded and the pile of papers on the clipboard called for her attention. She abandoned her phone to focus on the long list of questions about Jacob from the time he was born until today. Some questions she couldn't answer, or had to guess because she couldn't recall the exact date he started crawling, walking, or talking. Maybe she *was* a bad mother. She knew about how many months old he had been, but should she have remembered the exact date?

Movement beyond the window caught her eye and she looked up. Jacob was standing then reaching, bending, and twisting. Was it part of the test, or a stretch break? She wanted to be in there with him, holding his hand, protecting him, but it was time to let him face things on his own. She couldn't protect him forever.

The clock continued to tick overhead. She concentrated on the repetitive sound, on the cinnamon aroma, hoping they would calm her nerves and her desire to break down the door. More papers asked the same questions in different ways. Her head throbbed from all the small print and little bubbles she had to fill in. She began to see a pattern of language issues based on her answers, which she'd expected. What she hadn't expected were some fine and gross motor issues. She'd been so busy with her pregnancies, and wallowing in grief after the loss of Grace, that she hadn't realized Jacob never learned to ride a bike. He hated anything that required full body coordination. And while he had no problem typing on a computer or tablet, he would cringe from just looking at a pencil or pen. How had she missed these things? She was a horrible mother to have let this go on for so long. But not anymore. Jacob deserved her full attention. He deserved a mom who wouldn't check out on him. She fought the feelings of inadequacy worming their way through her and forced herself to look toward the future. She may have not done anything back then but she was doing it now. She'd do anything to help Jacob overcome his challenges.

Hours passed and she finally finished the last page. She wasn't sure she'd filled them out correctly, or how accurate the information was since a lot of it was based on her memories. But if her responses could help, she'd provide everything Jacob needed, everything Dr. Parker needed to research and evaluate her son.

A moment later, Dr. Parker opened the door and Jacob stepped out. To her relief, she only saw a smile, with no bruises or marks. "You have an extremely bright young man here," Dr. Parker said. "He's full of energy and one of the politest young men I've ever had the pleasure of working with. You've done an excellent job raising him."

Emily clung to those words, pulling them close to her heart even as she feared they were mere flattery. Had she done something right as a mother? "Thank you. Jacob is such a gift. I'm so proud of him."

Jacob vanished to the video game corner without a word as Dr. Parker took a seat beside her in a red plush chair. "Mrs. Davidson, you have an extremely bright boy. I'll meet with you on Monday to review the results, but I can tell you you've done a great service to your child by bringing him here. We'll have to wait until I'm done reviewing your answers and scoring his tests, but I'm confident that Jacob is going to have a bright future." Dr.

Parker's words were like a Band-Aid of promise to her soul, assuring her that her son would be okay.

With a little more energy than she'd felt in a long time, she thanked Dr. Parker then took Jacob out for a promised ice cream cone. Afterward, she picked up her mother-in-law's pills. Today, not even Judith would dampen her mood.

Jacob sat in the car with a smile on his face as if all his worries had faded away. For a moment, she allowed herself to enjoy the gift of knowledge. The assurance that whatever he faced, they would handle it together. Yet pulling into Judith's front drive caused the grim reaper to slice through her happiness and replaced them with doubt. Doubt that her husband would understand and support what Jacob needed.

Judith shuffled onto the front porch and waved. If Emily didn't know better, she'd swear Judith was actually inviting her into her home instead of chasing her away with a pitchfork and a death glare.

Jacob hopped from the car and ran up the front steps. "Hi, Nana. How you feeling?"

"Well, aren't you the polite young man. Do you still give good hugs?"

Jacob flung his arms around the old woman and Emily worried he'd break her. She'd definitely lost weight since the last time Emily had seen her. "Not so hard, Jacob."

"I ain't that fragile. I might be riddled with arthritis, but I'm tough."

Emily wrapped her purse strap around her hand and held tight as if it would keep her from being thrown off the porch. "I didn't mean—"

"Relax and get your skinny tush inside. Jacob, I need your help. Do you mind going upstairs and retrieving a box for me? I can't climb the attic steps no more."

"I can get it for you." Emily followed them inside the old Victorian home. It was just as she remembered it. The decorative beauty of the stained glass and wood paneling always took her breath away.

"I asked the boy to go. He can handle it. Besides, I thought we could sit and chat."

"I can do it, Mom. If I can sit for hours for that test, I can climb some stairs." Jacob winked and raced up the wide staircase.

"Test?"

Emily tightened her grip on her purse strap, wishing it was a teleportation device. Oh, how she wanted to hop in and disappear before her mother-in-law dug her heels in and gave Emily a good tongue thrashing. She bit her lip and tried to think of a way out of the conversation, but nothing came to mind.

"I won't tell my son if that's what you're worried about. Go sit in that chair and tell me what's got you so troubled."

Emily's head whipped around and she eyed the old woman. This was the same woman who had chased her off the front porch with her gardening hoe and told the town she was a hussy, right? The same one who called her a hideous creature who'd bewitched her son?

"I know I haven't given you any reason to confide in me, but I can see what's been going on between you two. And I'd like to make amends while I still can."

Emily stood frozen in place, racking her brain for a possible motivation. Something to explain this new found understanding and motherly tone.

"I ain't been invaded by body snatchers. It's just that I'm gettin' older and a little more decrepit. Someday you'll be all my son and grandson will have in this world. Now, sit down and start talking. I won't share nothin' with my son you don't want me to, if that's your worry."

Even if that was true, how could she tell his mother about what she'd done? Judith would've never betrayed her husband that way. She was perfect, the original Mrs. Cleaver. Heck, Judith had picked up after her boys even when they were in college.

Judith gave her a shove toward the chair. "Start talkin' or I'm gonna be askin' my son what's goin' on."

Emily sat down, the pharmacy bag crinkling inside her purse. "Oh, here, before I forget. Carter called and wanted me to bring over your medicine."

"Yep, I counted on that getting you here."

Emily pulled the small, white paper bag from her purse and set it on the side table between them. Judith slowly lowered into a recliner with a smile, an actual smile. A devious one that looked like she'd just swallowed the president and became ruler of the free world, but a smile none the less. "So you wanted to get me here? Why didn't you call me?"

"Would you have come if I had?"

Emily eyed her toes peeking through the straps of her sandals. She'd painted them that morning to match her dress.

"No," Judith answered for her, "so let's not pretend you would. I haven't given you cause to come see me."

Emily opened her mouth to give a string of excuses about why she hadn't come by since they moved to Creekside, but she knew they would all be just that—excuses. She took a moment to compose herself, letting her gaze travel around the room. The grandfather clock in the hall chimed, and the smell of old house permeated the air. The sparkle of Judith's grandmother's ring on the side table caught her attention. Why was that sitting out? That was the ring Judith refused to give Carter when he wanted to propose. Emily looked down at her ring finger, bare for over a year. "I should've come sooner. I'm sorry."

"No, you're not, but that's okay. As I said, I didn't give you much reason to visit. You think I didn't want you to marry my son because he was too good for you, but you're wrong. It's the other way around. You're too good for him."

Emily shook her head, trying to make sense of the words. "I don't understand."

Judith huffed and angled to face her. "You see, you're so book smart, life smart, world smart. You'd traveled and graduated top of your class. I worried all that would be wasted on my son."

Emily searched Judith's face for any indication of what she was really getting at. "Carter is smart. And determined and amazing."

Her mother-in-law rocked in her chair, the squeak matching the speed of the grandfather clock in the hall. Slow, steady, methodical. "Yes, he's all those things, but he's a different kind of smart. I'm actually surprised he managed to fool you for so long. What I'm about to tell you could ruin my relationship with my son, but you have a right to know. And knowing may help you do more for your son than I did for mine."

"You're a great mother. All Carter ever talks about is how perfect you were. Honestly, I don't think I'll ever live up to his expectations."

"Hogwash, you're a great mother yourself. I know you've been through a lot, but that's another conversation. Right now, I want to tell you about Carter. He's spent his life trying to overcome a label and now I fear it's costing him his son and his marriage. It's time he faces his past so he can finally let it go and heal. So he can be a better father and husband. When Carter was in third grade, his teachers had deemed him mentally retarded."

Chapter Fourteen

The tall ceilings, white paint, and bright décor did nothing to stop the walls from feeling like they were closing in around him. Carter had long since lost his tie, and his head pounded with stress and aggravation.

The door creaked and he turned to see David standing in the doorway of his office with a smug smile. "The board will be meeting in two hours to vote on whether you should keep your position as CEO. We'll contact you with our decision once the meeting adjourns."

Carter ignored the taunts and glanced at his watch. Three hours until the last flight of the day departed for Tennessee. He longed to make that flight. Funny how he cared more about getting home than keeping his job, but what choice did he have? He had a family to support and as the bread winner, it was his duty to provide for them.

He removed his phone from his pocket and found he'd missed several texts, two phone calls, and had several unread emails as well as a new voicemail. After a quick glance at the door to find it empty, he played the voicemail from Martark.

"I haven't had any dealing with David Aguero personally, but I did find a connection. He's invested in a company that stands to gain a great deal if mine's sold off for parts. If BSMA is unable to secure the proper relationship and documentation to ship to and from China, then Aguero'll recommend that my company be taken apart and the ships sold to Maverick Shipping, which he owns considerable stock in. They'd be able to snatch up the ships, as you'll want to offload them as quickly as possible. He stands to make millions off this other company since they have a connection with China already established. They're small, private, and not something that would be on anyone's radar. I would've never found the connection, but luckily my nephew is smarter than I am. I'm sure glad you recommended he take over my company. I'm not going to let Aguero have his way. My nephew can take this company to the next level and save a ton of jobs."

Carter sat there staring at the phone, unable to comprehend David's treachery. This deceit from a man who constantly spouted company loyalty, who claimed how he dedicated his life to BSMA.

Jim knocked then entered Carter's office and sat in a chair on the other side of his desk, folding his hands on the wooden surface. "If you grip that phone any tighter, you'll crack the screen."

"I can't believe this. I mean, it's unimaginable in my book."

Jim drummed his fingers on the desk. "You gonna tell me, or am I going to have to guess?"

Carter shook off the haze of disbelief and played the message again, this time for Jim. His friend's face twisted from a wide-eyed surprise to furrowed disbelief and finally into a narrowed murderous glare. "This information true?"

"I trust him. He has nothing to gain by lying to me. But I'll need proof to convince the board." The pit of Carter's stomach dropped out, the empty feeling of regret and loss consuming him. "You know, all this time I've been fighting to keep my job, fighting to make everyone see that I had a plan and love for this company. And now, I'm not sure I want to fight anymore. I'd rather be home with my family, working some mundane nine-to-five that guaranteed free evenings and weekends. Not being forced to keep abandoning them to hold onto a job where the board would sooner turn their back on me than listen to reason. I feel like I'm in constant battle mode within these walls, instead of battling against the competition."

"Don't give up on me yet. Not after this. Let's go." Jim stood and opened Carter's office door, the force whooshing air at his face as if to tell him to wake up and see what was going on around him.

"I'll go inform the board, but not to save my job. They can do whatever they want with my position for all I care. But I have to try to save the company."

Jim marched down the hall and into the conference room where some of the members lingered, gossiping about their golf game or the size of the fish they'd caught last weekend. "I need to get the board together now."

"We have another hour before we vote," David said, the edge of his nose lifting in snarling disgust.

Carter snagged Phillip's arm to get his attention. "I think you all will want to hear this," he said in a forced, defeated tone.

"Well, I guess the sooner we cast our votes, the sooner we can get out of here." David twirled one of the tall leather chairs around then plopped down with an air of victory.

"I'll get the others," Chuck announced before leaving the room. Carter didn't know him as well as some of the other nine board members. He'd played a round of golf with the man once, but other than seeing him at meetings or on occasion at corporate functions, they didn't speak much. The man tended to keep to himself.

The rest of the board members filed into the conference room, and Carter glanced at his watch. It'd be a fight to make that last flight home tonight, especially with it being Friday night. There were still two flights left, though. He had a shot.

"We keeping you from something?" David asked. "You can wait outside while we cast our vote. Someone will come and notify you of our decision."

"I'll leave in just a moment," Carter announced, catching the members' attention with his authoritative tone.

"There's no reason to make this uncomfortable for anyone," Charles said.

Phillip sat forward and tilted his head to one side. "Let him speak. He'll only help us come to a quicker decision."

David nodded his agreement.

Tom joined the others at the table. "Go ahead, Carter."

"I'm not here to beg for my job or to offer reasons why I feel I'm a valued member of this team. I believe my record and numbers speak for themselves. I've taken this organization from a blip on the map to a multimillion-dollar company featured in *Forbes* magazine, with targeted projections to hit in the billions if this China deal goes through."

"Or to become a blip again if it fails," David added.

Carter ignored him and pressed on. "I thought this company was important to me, as if it represented who I am as a person. A strong individual. My legacy, if you will. Now, I realize my family is all of those things and more. You're welcome to replace me the minute I walk out that door, but what I won't do is walk out without this board having all the facts. I may no longer be able to identify myself with this company, but I certainly want to see it thrive long after I'm gone, for the sake of our investors and employees."

David opened his mouth, but Carter held up a hand to silence him. He hit the button for the speakerphone then played his voicemail. Martark's voice echoed through the suddenly quiet boardroom.

At the mention of his name, David bolted up from his chair. "Lies!" he shrieked. "This is all a trick."

"Shut up, so we can listen. You can debate its validity later," Charles ordered.

David had no choice but to sit back down and listen to the accusations being made against him. When the message ended, David's eyes pinballed around the room, and he nervously tugged at his collar. "It's a lie. Where's your proof?" he demanded, pointing a finger at Carter.

"It's easy enough to prove with a few phone calls," Carter said. A sense of calm settled over him, soothing his emotions that had felt raw and exposed the past few days.

David shoved his chair back, hitting the wall with a resounding thud. "You'll only distort the truth, the way you're doing now."

Carter slid his phone into his pocket. "Oh, I'm not going to prove anything. I'm done fighting to keep my job. I've been wasting too much time as it is flying back and forth to prove myself."

"If you would've stayed in D.C. instead of gallivanting off to some Podunk town with your family, none of these issues would've happened," David said, his voice rising several octaves. "You wouldn't have lost that contract and the company wouldn't be in trouble."

"Apparently, you missed the point of Martark's message. If that deal had gone through, this company would've been bankrupt, but now it stands to gain billions if this China deal works out. It's you, David, who's in trouble from the Martark deal not going through. But I'll leave that for the board to deal with. Now if you'll excuse me, I have a family to get home to. I'll admit they are a distraction to my job at times, but despite that this company has thrived, thanks to the numerous deals I've closed. While I truly appreciate all this company has given me, it's time I became as good of a father and husband as I am a CEO." He picked up his briefcase. "Good night, gentlemen. I have a plane to catch."

Chapter Fifteen

Emily sat on a stool facing the wall, not allowed to look at her own reflection. Aunt Sue sat nearby, admiring the handiwork of Cathy West, her daughter, Jenna, and her stepdaughter, Rebecca. They'd been working on Emily for over an hour. Between hair curlers, eyebrow plucking, lipstick, and nail polish, she had been primped to perfection. She enjoyed watching Jacob playing in the corner with Jenna's daughter, Sadie. An enthusiastic little girl, full of life and giggles, but didn't like the hairdryer at all. She'd covered her ears and backed into the corner. Jenna explained she had sensory issues. Jacob was good with her. He had a gift with people.

"You think the county will increase the budget for a bus next year?" Aunt Sue asked Jenna.

Cathy waved her spiral brush in the air. "You best believe they will. I'll make sure of it."

Jenna sighed. "Mom, you can't fight every battle for the center."

"I can and I will, for the sake of that incredible granddaughter of mine. I can't wait to see her as the flower girl at your wedding next month. She's going to be the star of the show, next to her mama that is."

Jenna's face blushed, filling with rosy happiness. "You finish the design for the bridesmaid dresses yet?"

Rebecca swept a small brush over Emily's cheek. She wasn't sure how comfortable she'd feel with all this makeup on. Normally, she didn't wear any. "Of course, but you're not going to see it yet. It's a surprise," Rebecca said with a smile. "Trust me, you'll love it. We need to get to beading your gown, though. You picked out the stones yet?"

Jenna bit her bottom lip. "It's so tough to choose."

Emily's mind faded away from their girl talk as her thoughts returned to what Judith had said. Was it true? Could Carter have struggled with the same issues Jacob now faced? Had Carter really suffered such public humiliation in his adolescence that he couldn't face his own son's issues? Certainly, he'd proven his intelligence over the years. He was a CEO. The man had nearly built BSMA from the ground up on his own. How could he ever doubt his own intelligence? Still, to be told you were mentally retarded at such a young age. To suffer a speech impediment, and have issues with reading, writing, and spelling had certainly left permanent marks on his soul.

"Whatcha so deep in thought about?" Cathy asked.

"Oh, nothing. Sorry. I faded away. I'm not used to so much attention." Emily tried to laugh it off. No way she'd share her husband's biggest, darkest secret. One he never even felt he could tell her. By the time he'd moved to Creekside in the fifth grade he was in all regular classes. Sure, he wasn't a top student, but that was because he didn't try. He was too busy being the star of the basketball, football, baseball, and wrestling teams. He was funny, handsome, and everyone loved him. He never had to try in academics. He was able to ride on his talent and charisma. Had it all been a farce? A way to hide his inadequacies from the world?

"Well, get used to it. You live in Creekside now." Jenna beamed. "Hey, I have a question for you. Would you be okay with me asking Jacob to be the ring bearer at our wedding? He's such an adorable young man, and he's so good with my Sadie."

Unaware, Jacob continued to hand the small girl things as she pointed to them. She'd laugh at his funny faces and wacky movements. "I'm sure he'd love that. He's trying to get to know people here."

"Okay, you're done. You ready to see yourself in the mirror?" Jenna asked.

"No, not yet. She has to put on her dress." Rebecca ran to the door and unzipped the garment bag, pulling out the black dress with the burgundy bodice and sash that tied in the back. "I'm so proud of you, Cathy. You really came through on the design."

"I learned from the best." Cathy's hip-bumped her stepdaughter. She was so not the woman Emily remembered. It amazed her how people really could change.

"Carefully. Don't mess up your hair," Rebecca said.

Emily stood and took the dress behind the curtain. She unbuttoned her shirt, thankful they warned her not to wear anything that had to slip over her head. She slid a perfectly shaved leg into the silky material then the other. The dress glided over her hips and fit to perfection. "I'll need help with the zipper." She shuffled out then turned for Aunt Sue to zip her up.

"Wow, you're one beautiful lady. Carter's going to faint when he sees you. Here. Put on the shoes." Aunt Sue reached down and set the pair of slinky sandals in front of Emily. "Okay, now go look in the mirror."

All the women stood around with lips pressed together, hands at their chests or on their faces, waiting for her response.

"Wow, Mom. You look like you belong on one of those magazines in the grocery store." Jacob hopped up and whistled.

She turned to face the mirror and saw a different image of herself. She'd shed the mom jeans and T-shirt, lost the hair tie, and emerged from the Cathy cocoon a beautiful woman. "Is that really me?" She smoothed her hands down her hourglass shape, and for the first time in over a year, she felt beautiful, attractive. Although her hips were a little wider than in high school, the rest of her was proportionate.

"He's gonna go nuts. Do you know what time he'll be home to pick you up?" Aunt Sue asked.

"No." She retrieved her cell from her purse and saw a text with four simple words. She read them aloud. *"On my way home.* It must mean he's on a flight home, so he can't be in Creekside yet. He texted only an hour ago that he was hoping to finish up his meetings soon and get home. I almost feel bad that I'm ruining his surprise. He's going to know when he sees me all dressed up that I found out about our date."

Rebecca let out a cat call whistle. "Trust me, when that man sees you, he's not going to care."

Cathy swatted her with a makeup towel. "You behave."

"Okay, little man," Aunt Sue said to Jacob. "You want to head back to Café Bliss with me? I need to let my help off the hook for the night, but we close up in a couple hours. Then we'll have our own date. Sound good?" Aunt Sue kissed Emily on her cheek. "You don't worry about Jacob. I've got him. You go have a fantastic time with that husband of yours."

"You sure it won't be too much—"

Aunt Sue held up a hand in front of her face. "Don't you dare finish that statement. This is my special night. I've been looking forward to it for days. Trust me. I'm getting more out of this than you are." The new glow she could see in her aunt's eyes told Emily that Aunt Sue had longed for a family in her life. For the first time, Emily was truly thankful to have returned to Creekside. Carter had been right. This move was good for their family.

Cathy, Rebecca, and Jenna all glam-hugged her, careful not to mess up her hair, makeup, or dress. Emily fought the tears welling up in her eyes. "I don't know how I'll ever thank you for this. It means a lot to me."

"Don't you start getting all girly on me. You'll mess up our hard work. Now, get." Cathy snapped the makeup towel at Emily, shooing her from the room.

The short distance home allowed just enough time for her nerves to kick into high gear. A first date kind of excitement fluttered like a new baby in her belly. She shoved the thought from her mind and entered the house. Careful not to wrinkle her dress, she sat on the couch and waited. Within minutes, her nerves drove her from the couch and she paced the floor, straightening a vase on the bookcase, a coaster on the side table, a rug on the kitchen floor. For another hour, she busied herself with small tasks around the house, ones that didn't require any cleaning supplies or much effort until her feet started to ache and she kicked off her shoes.

Another hour passed and she checked her cell phone. Nothing. She sat on the couch, clutching her cell phone as another hour passed then another. She set the phone by her side and leaned against the arm of the couch. When another hour passed, she knew she'd been stood up. Had she gotten it all wrong? Did he make plans with someone else and she'd intercepted a message she only assumed was meant for her? Her stomach rumbled, but she couldn't eat, couldn't move.

No, it wasn't possible. Regardless of their issues, he'd never cheat on her. Carter wasn't that kind of man. Was he? With everything he'd hidden from her about his past, she was starting to wonder if she really knew her husband at all.

Chapter Sixteen

Carter climbed the front steps. The red-eye funk settled over him like a big game tranquilizer. After hours of fighting airlines and rental car companies to get home, he'd never been so happy to see the small rental house.

The early morning hour brought with it pastel hues that washed over the living room and settled on Emily. Beautiful, breathtaking Emily. Asleep on the couch, her hair and face were highlighted by the sun's rays. The dress she wore hugged her body and her hair framed her face. She stirred and her eyes fluttered open.

"Hey, you. I'm so sorry. I was on a plane to get home when there were mechanical issues. We sat on the tarmac for hours only to unload and wait for another plane. I would've called but I thought you'd be asleep." He knelt down and stroked her soft cheek.

"I tried to wait up," she mumbled through a sleepy haze.

"You look amazing. Did you go out with the ladies last night?"

She quirked her head, raising a confused brow. "It was Friday night."

Friday night. "Oh, my goodness. I can't believe I forgot." He pushed from the couch and paced the floor. "I'm such an idiot."

"It's okay," she mumbled.

"No, it's not." He headed toward the master bedroom. "I stood my mother up. I'm gonna shower then head over there to grovel. Man, she's gonna be steamed." He raced to the shower then hopped under the spray. His moment of relief at finally reaching his destination was short-lived, knowing he had to get to his mother's and fast. "I'd love to take you out tonight," he called. "I have some things to talk to you about." He only hoped she understood that he'd made the decision to leave his job so that he could be a better husband and father. Most women would hate their husbands for giving up a big paycheck to stay home more, but Emily wasn't like that. He was sure she'd be thrilled. "How about you see if your aunt can watch Jacob tonight, and we can stay out late and spend some time alone together."

No answer. He stuck his head out of the bathroom and spotted that heart-stopping dress tossed carelessly on top of the bed. "Emily?"

Silence. He toweled off and dressed, then searched the small house for her. She must've taken Jacob somewhere. Disappointed, but determined to make amends as soon as he dealt with his mother, he rushed toward downtown Creekside. He couldn't show up to his mother's house empty-handed.

Carter pulled into a parking space on Main Street. Exhaustion threatened to take him down for the rest of the day, but he didn't have time for sleep. He scrubbed his face with his hands and shook his head in an attempt to get the blood flowing again. With shoulders hunched and eyes fighting to close, he pushed from his seat and stood on the front walk outside of a floral shop. The small letters painted on the window read, *Opening Hours: 10:00 a.m.* With a few minutes to kill, he walked along the sidewalk and peered into the various shop windows, trying to clear his head. The fresh air filled his lungs, reinvigorating him.

The bell above a door chimed two shops up, drawing his attention. Eric Gaylord stood next to an attractive young woman holding a little girl. It had to be Lisa, his wife. "Hi, there. You look beat."

Carter forced a smile. "I am. I thought you were supposed to still be in D.C."

Eric shook his hand. "I was, but everything worked out quickly so I grabbed a flight back yesterday morning." He ran a hand over his daughter's thin, shiny hair. "I wanted to be home with my girls. This is my wife, Lisa."

She nodded, swapping the baby onto her other hip so she could offer her hand. "It's nice to meet you. I hear we'll be getting our families together soon."

"Yes, I hope so." The little girl's hand reached out for him so he offered his finger to her. "It's nice to meet you, too, Amelia."

Eric tickled her feet and she giggled. "You just get into town?"

"Yes, my meetings ran late into last night."

An older lady with reddish hair exited the shop and clapped her hands together at Amelia until the little one launched from her mother's arms. He assumed this woman must be her grandmother. If he remembered correctly, she was Eric's mother, Judy Gaylord, but he couldn't recall her new last name.

"Hi, Mom. This is Carter, the one I told you about."

"Yes, yes. I know your mom. It's so nice to have you back in town. And of course that beautiful wife of yours, Emily." Judy raised and lowered the little girl in the air, causing her to squeal. "I can't wait to see her again, and meet that little man of yours. Will you be at Mr. Burton's surprise birthday party Monday night?"

"I'm afraid not. I need to spend some much needed time with my own family."

"Good man." Eric pulled Lisa into his side and kissed her forehead.

"Mr. Burton's the one who owns the factory and half the town, right?" Carter asked.

Lisa rested her head on Eric's shoulder. "That's the one. He's calmed down a little in the last few years, but he used to be a real bear."

"I was sorry to hear one of his daughters had passed."

"We all were." Judy cuddled her grandchild close to her chest as if providing a protective hug around her. "It's sure a nice surprise meeting you here. Lisa and I own J and L Antiques." She gestured to the shop behind her. "You stop in anytime to say hi."

"I will. Thanks," Carter said.

The sound of the florist shop's lock clicking open drew his attention and he turned to see the florist rolled a display with pretty flowers outside her door. "I'm going to go pick up a few flowers and then head to my mother's. Eric, Lisa, I look forward to getting our families together soon."

"Me, too." Eric took Amelia from her grandmother and they all headed up the street. "Gotta get our morning coffee before work. Stop in after if you can. It looks like you could use a hit of caffeine yourself."

"Thanks." Carter entered the florist shop and found a beautiful bouquet of Emily's favorite flower, lilies. Then he picked up another one of yellow roses for his mom. He took the bouquets from their containers of water in the refrigerator and turned toward the cash register at the front.

"Am I dreaming or is that Carter Davidson?" A sensual voice, one he vaguely recognized from his past, filtered through the shop and settled on the back of his neck causing his hair to rise. Tina Townsend stood in a fitted dress that accentuated her large chest and thin waist. He swallowed so loud he thought the flowers heard him. "Tina? Wow, I thought you'd be off seeing the world."

"I did for a while." She sashayed from around the counter, oozing sexuality. The girl always knew how to lure men. She was a nice girl, but so dangerously attractive. He gripped the flowers tight and held them in front of him like a metal shield to block her advance. And based on her posture, she was ready to charge.

Roses, lilies, tulips, and the seductive scent of perfume flooded his nose, tickling the inside. He sneezed. Twice. When he looked up, she stood at his side, holding a tissue. She leaned into him with her breast smashing against his arm. "Here. Are you allergic to flowers?"

No, just to women who could mean trouble for his undernourished libido. He eyed the exit, but she slid her hand into the crook of his arm and escorted him to the register. "Well, we'll have a quickie and get you out of here."

Carter took a step away from her, his pulse tip-tapping faster than Tina's heels. "Excuse me?"

"We'll get you rung up quick so you can get away from all the flowers. What did you think I meant, silly?" She pushed against him harder and smacked his shoulder before slipping away from him. "Are these for someone special?" she asked. "Your mother, perhaps?" She punched the register a few times until the cash drawer popped open.

"Yes, one of them is. I missed a mother-son date," he mumbled.

"That's so sweet. You're such a good man. Kind, considerate, obviously attentive, and really smart. Last I heard you owned a company or something."

"No. I'm the CEO of one, though. A large mergers and acquisitions company." Well, he was. But why did he even bother to explain that to her? *Tell her the flowers are for your wife.*

Ah-choo. Ah-choo.

"You're obviously allergic to something in here. Go wait out front and I'll bring your receipt to you." She took his credit card out of his hand, and he bolted outside, sucking in a lung full of fresh air. Although the tickle in his nose and libido remained, he felt more in control. Outside, he was safe from too many flowers and attention.

"Here you go." She handed him the receipt and his card then leaned against the brick façade of the building. "Tell me what you've been up to. You were always the most popular guy in school. Tough, handsome, and smart. I heard you just moved back, but I bet you've conquered the world before returning to Creekside." She reached out and stroked his arm. "It's really good to see you."

Her touch seared his skin with the promise of attention and affection, two things he longed for in his marriage. But that was his fault more than Emily's lately. "Wife. I got these for my wife. We moved here together with our son."

Undeterred, she stepped closer instead of away from him. "I knew you married Emily right out of high school. We all thought it wouldn't last a week because you were so young, but look at you. Obviously successful, you took care of yourself, and you're still married. You're doing better than I am. My divorce will be final next week." Before he could stop her, she closed the gap between them and wrapped her arms around him, crushing the flowers to his chest as she kissed him flat on the lips.

For a minuscule moment, he thought about embracing her, to feel the passion of a woman against him, but she wasn't Emily. He wanted Emily's love and embrace, not another woman's. She backed away with a coy smile.

He stood on the sidewalk, unable to move. No other woman had touched him since he'd said his wedding vows, and he knew at that moment he didn't want it any other way. He only wanted Emily.

"Oh, no. Sorry, love. I think you're in trouble," Tina said as she turned to the side, giving him a perfect view of Café Bliss. Jacob was inside, wiping down tables. Emily, Cathy, and a young woman he didn't recognize stood outside the coffee shop, only a few feet away, facing him.

Chapter Seventeen

Emily stumbled back into Rose. Air trapped in her lungs and the world tilted around her. Images rolled through her mind again and again, but each time the same scene played out. Tina Townsend kissing her husband. Her husband holding flowers for that woman. Flowers he hadn't given her in over a year.

The word affair pumped through her faster than the blood surging to her brain, dizzying her with the knowledge she didn't want to face. She whirled around, and with her head held high, she marched toward the café. She heard Cathy and Rose both say something, but nothing registered. Emily only heard noise, buzzing sounds that added to the chaos in her head.

"Tell Aunt Sue I'll pick up Jacob later." Emily bolted around the corner then took off at a sprint for her car. No tears, no hysterics, just a chest that wouldn't expand, as if a large oak branch had fallen on top of her, pinning her to the ground.

She started the car and drove off, not bothering to look back, not able to speak or think until she reached the edge of town and parked beneath the welcome sign at the border of Sweetwater County. Intense pain fisted in her abdomen and drove sound to her throat, a choking cry of loss. She screamed and pounded her fist against the steering wheel. "My fault. I drove him away."

Tears streaked down her cheeks, and she hammered the steering wheel again and again until her arms tired and she hunched over, clutching it as if it were a lifeline. She slumped into her seat and watched a piece of trash roll across the road and tumble over the hill into an open field. "It isn't all my fault," she mumbled. He'd chosen to work harder after Grace passed. He'd buried himself in his precious CEO job and chose to leave her alone with her grief and a son who was struggling in school. Marriage was all about compromise. It takes two to make it work and two for it to fall apart.

It wasn't all her fault. It was both of their responsibility. She was tired of blaming herself. If he chose to see someone else, if that was why he brought them here, that was on him.

She straightened and wiped the tears from her eyes. The scent of leather upholstery mixed with the scent of rain from her vents. A storm brewed along the horizon, echoing the one raging through her marriage. She knew it was time to start making tough decisions. Decisions that would change their lives forever.

She put her car in gear and turned around to head to the rental house. She didn't want to take the chance of running into Carter, but she needed to pack some things so she and Jacob could stay at Aunt Sue's for the night. She'd make it seem like another sleepover, or a celebration for the end of his first week of school. No matter what, she was going to make things better for her son.

With new direction and purpose, she drove around the back side of town in the hopes of avoiding Carter and that woman. The woman he'd kissed back in high school while they were dating. The signs were there. Why hadn't she realized he was a cheater then?

Carter's car sat in the driveway. She thought about leaving and returning later when he wasn't home, but it was time to stop running. It was time to face life and deal with it, even if that meant the end of her marriage.

With shaking hands, she took her purse and slung it over her shoulder then climbed out of the car. On the dining room table sat the bouquet of lilies in a crystal vase. Carter stood behind them with tears in his eyes. "They were for you. I only went to the florist to get you flowers. I didn't know she worked there. I promise you, there's nothing going on between us. She kissed me before I knew what she was going to do." Carter stepped around the table, but she backed away. "Emily, I'm so sorry. I hate myself for hurting you. You're the only woman I've ever loved. The only woman I will ever love."

"Stop. I'm done. I can't do this anymore." Emily headed for Jacob's bedroom to pack some of his things, but Carter blocked her path.

"Listen to me. I can't lose you. We belong together. I don't want our family to break up. What can I do? I'll do anything."

"You can start by not cheating on me." She shoved past him and grabbed a suitcase, but he sat on top of it.

"No. I didn't. That kiss was all her."

"Fine. Then what about your night out at Francisco's?"

He shook his head. "What are you talking about?"

The room closed in around her and sweat broke out on the back of her neck. Her mind searched for an escape as her body went into autopilot, yanking open drawers and tossing clothes onto the bed. "You didn't cover your deception very well. The restaurant called here to confirm. Like an idiot, I thought you were trying, seriously trying to put our marriage back together. Cathy even made me a dress, and the girls did my hair and makeup. I'm such a fool." Her voice cracked, but she continued to yank clothes and throw them at him.

"You looked beautiful." His words only tossed more fuel on the cheating-husband fire. She slammed the drawer, catching her finger inside. With a yelp, she kicked the dresser and whirled around to head to the master bedroom to get some of her own things.

"Are you okay?" He jumped to her side and grabbed her hand, but she snatched it away and made for the door. "Emily, please wait. You've got it all wrong. I didn't take another girl to dinner. I'd never do that to you. I was in D.C. You can call anyone. I swear. David Aguero, one of the board members, demanded a special meeting, trying to have me voted out. I only stayed to save my job. And that reservation was the one I told you about this morning. I'd planned to take my mother out, not Tina."

She turned on him, rage filling every pore of her body. In all the years they'd been married, she'd never once been this angry. She wanted to hit him. "So, you have the time to take your mother out, but not me? You haven't so much as kissed me in the last year, but you're fine making time to take your mother out for a fancy dinner? Fine. But what about Jacob? When are you going to make time for him?" she screamed, her voice cracking under the pressure of her emotions.

"You're right." Carter beat his head against the wall. "I'm so stupid."

She fled to the bedroom and pulled her suitcase from the floor of the closet. Slinging a bunch of clothes off their hangers, she dropped them inside.

Carter removed them and tossed them back in the closet. "The date wasn't meant for you, but it should've been."

All the sorrow, guilt, and hatred toward Carter, toward their marriage, toward the world and God wrapped into a fireball in the pit of her stomach. She balled up her fist and swung, connecting with Carter's cheek. He stumbled back, landing on the bed, his hand over his jaw. She sucked in a quick breath and fell back against her dresser. Anger had never taken hold of her before.

"Do you feel better? I know I deserved that." Carter moved his lower jaw back and forth in an effort to ease the pain. "I've been an idiot."

Thunder clapped in the distance, rolling toward them as if in warning. "Just let me go," she murmured. "We've only been torturing each other this last year. I can blame you for a lot, but not everything. I'm to blame, too. Even if you're not having an affair with—" Words failed her as sobs racked her body.

Carter hopped up and clothes tumbled to the floor. He knelt by her side. "I swear to you I'm not. Please, Emily. Don't give up on us. Don't ever give up on us. I love you."

Emily searched for answers, but found none. "I don't want to be hurt anymore," she said, fighting the emotion welling inside her. "But I know I've hurt you, too. I shouldn't have fallen apart after Grace passed."

"You had a right to grieve."

Emily nodded. "You did, too." She closed her eyes then opened them, looking toward the door. "Jacob knows her name, too. He said that was her name because she was a gift from God."

Carter shook his head. "He's so smart. I tried to tell him the baby didn't come and that you were sick, but he's too smart. I should've known he'd figure it out."

"We've done so much wrong," Emily rasped, fighting to get the words out. To actually have a full conversation with her husband instead of just passing comments and broken promises. "Should we even try anymore? Maybe it's time to separate, to get a divorce."

Carter grabbed her hands and held them tight, not allowing her to pull away. "Don't say that, Emily. I promise there's nothing going on with that woman. There's nothing going on with any woman. I admit I've been lonely and feeling neglected, and the thought did cross my head, but I realized something."

Emily held her breath, looking into his gaze to see if he spoke the truth.

"There could never be another woman for me. There's no other woman like you." He leaned forward, his lips parting, but she leaned away. This time, he let her go, so she stood and walked to the kitchen. With her emotions on hyper speed, she paced between the refrigerator and stove, her mind spinning with crushing guilt, pureed love, blended into a perfect goo of failing marriage. "I don't know what we are to each other anymore. I know I let my family down after Grace. I should have been stronger."

Carter rounded the counter but stayed two feet from her, his hand shaking at his side. "You need to forgive yourself."

"Even if I could, I feel like I'm being forced to choose between you and Jacob. You're so adamant about not getting him any help."

"We'll figure it out together. It's my fault Jacob's struggled so much."

"I had him tested." There. She said it. The wife betrayal. She waited for his reaction, for the yelling, the admonishment, but he only bowed his head.

"When?"

"Yesterday. I'll get the results back on Monday. I did research and based on the patterns that came up when I filled out the paperwork, I think he might have dyslexia."

He rubbed the back of his neck then collapsed onto a bar stool. His eyes turned from pleading to shock with a hint of anger. "This is about us right now, not—"

"If you want us to start working things out, then you need to get over yourself and let me get Jacob some help."

Carter ran a hand through his thick hair. "I just don't want him tortured anymore. This is it. After this, no more testing. No more special classes he doesn't need. I'll pay for a private tutor… I'll figure out how to pay for it."

"If they decide he doesn't have a specific learning challenge they can write an IEP for, then fine. But if they do then we deal with it as a family, together. No running out of town so you don't have to face things."

"I won't. I don't want anything more than to be here with you." He took a long breath. "Emily, I won't be traveling anymore. I quit my job."

Emily sucked in a quick breath and covered her mouth with her hand.

"I couldn't stand being away from you and Jacob any longer. I'll find something soon, I promise." Carter reached out to touch her, but she backed away. "I won't hurt you."

"You already have." Emily fought the tears and managed to keep them from trickling down her face.

"I'm sorry. I promise I-I'll g-get work. I-I won't l-let you down," Carter stumbled over his words. It was something Emily had never witnessed before.

"I don't care about the job."

Carter dared to shuffle a hint closer to her. "Then what is it?"

"I know you've been lying to me all these years, Carter. I know about your own learning issues. All this time, and you didn't trust me. How do we stay married if we don't even trust each other?"

Chapter Eighteen

The café smelled of rich, invigorating aroma of coffee. The couch had been uncomfortable, but Carter considered it a blessing Emily hadn't kicked him out of the house. He had to do something to prove to her how much he loved her, to prove to her that they belonged together.

Sue stood behind the counter, vigorously wiping down the surfaces. "Can I help you, sir?"

Cathy scooted her chair back and joined him at the counter. "I hear there's a great new drink called the Cheating Husband."

"I didn't cheat on Emily," he said, the words leaving acid behind in his throat. "It was all a misunderstanding. I'd planned to take my mother to dinner. The poor woman hasn't been out of her house in months. Only I couldn't make it back in time because I was in the middle of trying to save my job. When I got home, I went straight to the flower shop to get a peace offering for my mother, and a bouquet of Emily's favorite flowers to show her how much I love her. That's when Tina cornered me. Before I could even react, she planted her lips on mine."

"That hussy. I knew she'd be trouble when she came back to town and started working there," Cathy said, a hissing sound in her voice.

Sue paused her scrubbing for a moment. "That's not all you've done."

Carter hunched over, resting his elbows on the counter. "I know. I kept a secret from my wife all these years, lied to her, quit my job without discussing it with her first, and abandoned her when she needed me most. I couldn't handle losing my daughter and ended up shutting my wife out."

"You kept a secret from her?" Sue gripped the rag tight.

He really didn't want to dig up the past again, but as Emily's only family, Sue had a right to know. "Yes, I didn't tell her about being labeled mentally retarded as a child, how I suffered from bullying before I moved to Creekside."

"That's why you didn't want Jacob in special classes. You didn't want him to face the same pain and humiliation." Cathy lowered her hackles.

"You hurt my niece something awful," Sue said, returning to her scrubbing. "She's asked if she could move her and Jacob in with me until she can figure something else out."

"No. She can't do that. I can't lose her. I love her with all my heart. We've been through so much, and all it's done is show me how much my family means to me. I'll find a job, I'll prove my worth to her again."

"She doesn't care about money. She never did. The only thing you need to prove is how you're gonna be a better husband and father. Stop making her feel like you hate her because she lost your child."

Searing panic covered his body with remorse. "Is that what she thinks? That I hate her because she lost our child? Never…I hated seeing her so torn up like that. She wasn't herself. I tried to make her see that life would go on, but she just stayed in a strange, zombie-like state. After six months, I'd had enough and started trying to figure out a way to bring us closer, to get us to start healing. I thought leaving D.C. and returning to her hometown would bring her comfort. I only did it to save our marriage, to bring my Emily back to me."

Cathy tsked. "Well, you sure made a mess of things."

Carter sighed. "I know I have. I'm unemployed, my wife resents me for not telling her about my past, and I wasn't there when she needed me most. I want to show her how much she means to me."

"How are you going to do that?" Cathy asked.

"I have an idea, but I need to ask for your help with part of it." Carter gave the two women his best pleading eyes and tilted his head to Sue. "Do you think you can put together a nighttime picnic at Creekside park near the gazebo, and get Emily to wear that amazing dress?"

"I can probably do that. Why?" Sue tossed the rag to the side and rubbed her hands down her apron.

"You'll see. Cathy, can you bring my mother? Sue, you bring Emily, and Jacob." Carter shoved away from the counter. "We'll meet at the gazebo at six o'clock Monday night. Okay?"

"Whatcha up to?" Cathy asked.

Sue smiled. "I have an idea about what you're planning and I approve, but will it be enough?"

"I don't know. If it's not, I'll just have to keep trying. I'm not giving up that easily." Carter headed for the door. "Oh, and Sue? I need one more thing. Can you handle the flowers? I don't plan on going anywhere near that shop ever again."

"Don't worry. I've got a girl I know in Riverbend. She'll handle it."

"Great. Just have her bill me. I have some shopping to do, so if you'll excuse me." As he walked out the door his phone rang for the fourth time that morning. This time, he decided to answer it. "Hey, Jim," he said as he headed down Main. "I'm fine. No need to worry about me."

"Me worried about you? Heck no, man. I'm worried about our company. You need to agree to take your job back."

"What are you talking about? The board was going to vote me out anyway. I'm not a masochist. I know when it's time to give up."

"Yeah, well, kind of a lot's happened since you walked out. They fired David. That voicemail you played spurred a huge investigation. David's been using his position on the board to try and steer business from the last three deals for his own personal gain. Now, he's facing a criminal investigation for embezzlement. It's a big mess. We need you back, man."

"Forget it. I've had to drop everything and run back to the office too many times already. I'm not doing it anymore. I've got enough savings to live off of for a while. I'll find another job that's less demanding and damaging to my family life."

"You don't understand. The board doesn't care about how often you're at the office anymore. You've won their complete trust. They're working it so you can work from there. Just get deals done and travel when needed. No more running up here for meetings. We'll conference you in, and only have you come up for the critical ones."

Carter continued down the street, determined to concentrate more on his marriage and less on his job. "Give me a couple days to think about it and discuss it with Emily. I've got something to take care of right now, and I can't afford to mess this up. I'll get back to you on Wednesday."

"I understand. I hope whatever needs your attention works out for you. Good luck. We'll be waiting for your call on Wednesday." Jim cleared his throat. "And Carter, I'll always have your back."

"I know you will. Thanks, man." Carter hung up the phone, feeling a little more invigorated. Funny how all he wanted a week ago was to take David down and keep his job. Now that it was a reality, he realized how little it mattered in the grand scheme of things.

He hopped in his car then drove to his mother's house and marched inside. "Mother?"

"I'm in here." She pushed from her recliner.

"Look, I know how you feel about Emily. I know she's more than I deserve, but right now, I might lose her. I'm hoping you'll agree—"

"If you stop waggin' your tongue…" She pulled her hand from her pocket and handed him his grandmother's ring, the same family heirloom he'd wanted to give Emily the day he proposed. "I had it ready Friday night, but you didn't show for me to give it to you. I'd be honored if she'd accept it."

Chapter Nineteen

Emily flipped through a magazine in the waiting room at Riverbend Therapy Center. The decorative clock on the wall ticked away the seconds until she'd find out the truth about Jacob and what he would face in life. She wanted to meet with Dr. Parker alone, to have some time to process what their options were before she talked it over with her son, so she was thankful Aunt Sue had offered to pick him up from school and take him to dinner.

The door opened and she dropped the magazine onto the side table. "Come in, Mrs. Davidson." She stood and followed Dr. Parker to her office. Inside, she found Carter sitting with his hands clasped in his lap. "Your husband's been extremely helpful. He wanted to come in ahead of our meeting to discuss some of his own learning difficulties in the hope it would help us understand Jacob's challenges."

"He did?" She turned to Carter. A strange lightness filled her, making her feel as if she was levitating. "You did?"

He nodded and stood, but didn't touch her. Instead, he just moved to the seat against the wall and waited for her to sit. A hint of disappointment that he hadn't taken her hand inched to the surface. He'd slept on the couch for the last two nights and hadn't spoken a word to her in days. Of course, that was what she said she wanted. They'd agreed that if she was to remain in the rental house until she had time to think things through then he'd keep his distance.

"Please have a seat, and I'll go over the results with you both." Dr. Parker opened a folder on her desk and pulled out a stapled stack of papers. "First, let me start by telling you that your son is an incredibly sweet, smart, and studious young man. He's going to do extremely well in life. That being said, he will need a little extra help."

A nervous queasiness settled in her stomach. She tensed and glanced at Carter, but his face revealed nothing. "How much extra help?" she asked.

"Jacob is struggling with dyslexia and dysgraphia, which is what causes him to be slow at learning to read and write. I'm sure you've noticed that Jacob doesn't like handwriting anything, and many of his letters are backwards when he does write by hand. His grip strength is also weak. These are all things we can work on. As you may also have guessed, Jacob has an extremely high processing speed. He's at genius level."

"Really? I always knew he was bright." Carter beamed from the chair at her side. "But isn't dyslexia where you see things backward?"

"Yes, but it's more complicated than that. While his IQ is well above average for his age, he does have a language disorder." Dr. Parker turned the page around and went line by line over all the strength and weaknesses

Jacob showed during testing, and the results based on teacher feedback and Emily's information.

Emily's head spun. At some point, Carter's hand found hers as they reviewed all the information about their son.

Carter squeezed Emily's hand. "What do we do to give him all that he needs?"

Dr. Parker took out another packet. "Here are some resources. There's an excellent occupational therapist in our building who works on hand strength and a program called No More Tears Handwriting. Also, there are a few online tutors as well who teach Orton-Gilliam, which is explained in this brochure." Dr. Parker held out a tri-folded piece of white glossy paper. "Of course, the best option is a school we have here in Riverbend. It's for children aged kindergarten to eighth grade who are challenged by dyslexia, dysgraphia, or dyscalculia. It's called the Gracepoint School."

"Grace?" Carter whispered.

Emily felt tears roll down her cheeks. There was no disregarding that sign. Perhaps Jacob was right, and Grace really was meant for God.

Carter swiped tears from his own eyes. "That's what we'll do, then. If the Gracepoint School is the best option, we'll enroll him there. We can move to Riverbend, or take turns driving him over every day," Carter stated plainly.

"I'll handle it. You can't miss that much work. Plus, I'm going to apply for classes at Riverbend University to get my degree in Early Childhood Education focusing on special needs."

"I'm unemployed, remember?" He winked at her as if having no money was something to joke about. Carter had never joked about money. "But it sounds like you'll be going to school with Jacob. He'll think that's cool."

"Is it expensive?" Emily asked. Hopefully there was some sort of scholarship.

"Most private schools cost between twenty and forty-thousand for a single year of tuition. The class sizes are around four or five to one, so he'll get the attention and instruction he needs." Dr. Parker placed all the literature and test scores back into the folder then handed it to Emily. "Whatever you decide, I know you'll do what's best for Jacob. If you have any further questions, please don't hesitate to call."

"Thank you." Emily stood and shook her hand then walked out, clutching the folder to her chest.

Carter joined her at the front walk and rubbed her shoulder. "Don't worry. It's going to be fine. We have a direction now. A way to help. I wish I would've had that growing up. This is a gift. He won't have to think he's stupid. He'll understand he has this language challenge, but it doesn't mean he's dumb. And he'll be with kids he can relate to."

"I know. It's just a lot to take in. Do you want me to talk to him tonight, or should I wait so we can talk to him together?" Emily asked. "I have to go to Mr. Burton's birthday party with everyone, so it'll be too late when I get back to the house. Aunt Sue has been so kind, I couldn't say no."

"We can talk to him together tomorrow. I think it's time I tell him about my past, and how proud I am of him."

Emily wanted to throw her arms around him. Those words were everything she'd ever wanted to hear from Carter. Could he really be totally committed to being a part of the family again? To being supportive of Jacob attending a special school. Of her going to college? "You'll let him go to that school then?"

"Let him? I'll drive him there myself. I wasn't joking. Heck, I'll drive you both to school. I'm unemployed for now, but maybe I could set up a little office in Riverbend."

She nodded, wanting to believe, longing to believe, everything would be fine again. But doubt still crept in and shook her resolve to make their marriage work.

"Listen, it'll take time, but don't worry. I'm not going anywhere. Now, go have fun at the party." He took hold of both her upper arms and planted a soft kiss on her forehead. The jolt went all the way to her toes.

She wanted to skip the party. To go home and talk about what could be between them, but she needed more time. There had been too much between them lately. What if tomorrow he changed his mind and hopped a plane back to D.C. and out of their lives for good? "We'll talk to him tomorrow then."

Without another word, she got in her car and drove back to Creekside, hoping and praying they really could find their way back to each other. Love was easy, but trust would be an entirely different issue.

Chapter Twenty

The sun drifted toward the tops of the trees and Carter eyed the street, waiting for Sue to pull up with Emily. This moment took more courage than any multimillion-dollar business deal. He had been young and stupid the first time. Now he understood what he'd lose if she said no.

He clutched the ring box in his hand. Instead of a diamond chip ring like he'd given her when he first proposed, this one was a princess cut solitaire. This ring was special. His mama hadn't parted with it for any of her boys, those who married anyway. It was breathtakingly beautiful, a family heirloom, and Emily deserved it.

Eric clapped him on the back and moved to his side on the steps of the gazebo. "You going to pass out?"

"Maybe." Carter laughed. "Thanks for the help with the lights and the guests."

Lisa took Eric's hand. "She's going to be blown away by this. Any woman would feel special. You did well."

Headlights shone from around the corner, but too large to be Sue's car. By the long front end, he guessed it was Cathy. At least, this time, his mother would be around to show her support. Even after he'd stood her up the other night.

Carter stepped down and straightened a napkin on the edge of the white table on top of a white-and-red checkered oversized blanket. The candles, dangling lights from the gazebo, and fireflies dancing in the park made it romantic.

"I'm here, so let's get this done." His mother shuffled up the sidewalk, her tongue flapping faster than her pace. She hobbled up two steps then stood next to the gazebo in the grass. "You look like a deer caught in semi headlights. You gonna vomit on her shoes?"

"Mother." Carter kissed her cheek. "You behave or I'll send you home. I'm not kidding either. You tell her she isn't good enough and I won't visit you for a month."

"Like you visit me now. More like making an old lady promises and then breaking her heart." She lowered into one of the chairs, holding her low back. "I gave you the ring to give to her, didn't I? I think that says it all." Only the sound of crickets and a distant hum of an engine filled the night air. "Think she's gonna be a no show to the altar?" his mother asked in a teasing tone.

"It's not an altar. It's a gazebo. And as for being a no show, it's possible. I wouldn't blame her."

More headlights slashed through the darkening sky. This time, he recognized the car. "Okay, everyone. She's here." He straightened some flowers decorating the side of the gazebo and picked up the bouquet of white lilies to hand to her.

"Calm down. You look like a pig on Christmas morning."

"I thought the saying was *a turkey on Thanksgiving*."

"Too cliché. I'm not that predictable." His mother stuck her nose in the air.

Jacob ran from the parking lot, down the sidewalk and over to the gazebo. "Hi, Dad. Wow, wait till you see Mom. She's beautiful."

Carter took his son into his arms and lifted him against his chest, hugging him tight. Jacob's little hands clasped together behind his neck and squeezed tight. "I missed you, Daddy."

"I'm here now, little man. I'll be around a lot more, too. I promise." Carter lowered him to the ground in time to catch a first glimpse of Emily. She walked in a pair of stiletto heels like a professional runway model, her long legs going all the way to her thin waist. The dress accentuated each and every curve of her body. Could he skip the ceremony and go straight to the honeymoon? "You're more beautiful than any man deserves."

Her eyes scanned the long table with white chairs, the lights glistening on the gazebo and his tuxedo. "What's all this? I thought we were going to Mr. Burton's party."

"Not exactly. We decided to go a little later," Sue said, joining them.

Eric bent over to shake Jacob's hand. "Nice to meet you, little man. I've heard a lot about you. Your dad won't quit talking about how really proud he is of you."

"He is?" Jacob asked, bouncing on his toes.

Carter couldn't take his eyes off Emily, but he reached over squeezed Jacob's shoulder. "Of course, I am. You're the best son a man could ever have."

Eric guided Jacob by his side. "Stand here. Your daddy has something he wants to ask your mommy."

Carter swallowed hard. Sweat trickled down the back of his neck and his hands shook. "Yes. Yes, I do."

"You haven't gotten to that part yet," his mother teased.

He ignored her and offered his hand to Emily, guiding her up the steps of the gazebo. "Many years ago, we stood in this park and I asked you to marry me. I'd promised to love you always, protect you, honor you, and never disappoint you. I realize now I was young and foolish to promise those things."

Emily glanced at the ground, her lip quivering.

He squeezed her hands and stepped closer to her. "What I should have told you was the truth. That I don't deserve you. That I'm flawed and broken and only with you do I feel whole. I've made so many mistakes.

I've let you down more times than there are stars in the sky. But there's still one promise I made that night that I haven't broken."

Emily inhaled a long, slow breath. Her chest rose and fell as she looked up at him through thick, black lashes. "What's that?"

"That I'll never stop loving you. You're the only love of my life, yesterday, today, and tomorrow. You're my everything. You challenge me. You make me better. You connect with my soul, and my soul would die without you." He pulled the ring box from his pocket and got down on one knee. "Emily Sue Davidson, will you do me the honor of agreeing to stay married to a man who doesn't deserve you? To a man who will fail time and again, who will disappoint and frustrate you, but who will always and forever love you? For you are all a man could ever want. You are my love and my grace. My everything." He opened the ring box and she gasped, cupping her mouth with her hands. "I know you lost a lot a year ago. Your ring is something I can replace, but your love is priceless."

Emily gaped. "It's your grandmother's ring." She stood with her hands over her mouth for a second too long and Carter felt his entire life start to crumble along with his heart.

"I think she should say no," his mother crooned.

"Mother, I told you I'd make you leave if you said anything negative to Emily. She has the right to say no."

"Oh, of course she does. I agree. She deserves better. You've been a terrible husband."

Jacob stomped his foot. "Nana, that's not nice."

Emily cleared her throat. "No, it's not. Everyone makes mistakes. I think it's time we all learn from them and move on."

Move on? Did that mean she was planning to leave him? He lowered his head and stood, fighting to support his weight on the crippling pain of loss buckling his knees.

Emily scooted closer, pressing against him, and ran her nails along the side of his head, brushing the hair back. Her palm cupped his face and he leaned into it, enjoying the warm, the hypnotic touch of Emily. "I won't lie. I've had a bag packed for two days, and one foot out the door for months, but it's time for me to let it all go. To work toward the future and let go of the past. Today, you showed me how much you've changed. That's the man I want to get to know better. I'd love to stay married to you, Carter William Davidson." Emily held up her trembling left hand, and he slid the ring onto her ring finger then kissed her knuckles one by one.

Jacob clapped, but the cheers of their friends and family faded into the distance as Carter swept Emily into his arms and kissed her, passionately, deeply, and with all the love in his heart.

Epilogue

The ferris wheel rotated up and around and down, up and around and down, until Emily's stomach couldn't handle it any longer. By the time it finally stopped and let them off, she'd never been so thankful to see the ground and swore she'd never step foot on another ride. Carter agreed to take Jacob on the rest of them.

"I'm so glad Carter invited all of us to the Sweetwater County Fair. It's like stepping back in time. I see now why he'd rather be here than in D.C." Jim, the man who'd helped save Carter's job, took his wife's hand and kissed it. "There's definitely something special about this place."

Emily nodded. "We're lucky. It's one of the last few towns left where people can leave their doors unlocked."

Jacob ran up to her, carrying an oversized bear in his arms. "Mom! Look what Dad won for me." He beamed, giving her a tooth-bearing smile. He turned the bear's tag over and read the inscription aloud. *"This bear will bring you good luck. Sneeze it tight at night and you'll sleep safely."*

She patted Jacob on the head. "You're doing so well with your reading now. Look at that word again." She pointed to the tag.

"Oh, *squeeze*. Not *sneeze*." He hugged the bear against his small chest and shrugged. "I guess I still have trouble with big words and stuff."

Carter caught up to him and, in a winded tone, said, "So do I, buddy."

"I still can't believe all those years you had dyslexia and you never knew." Jim tore off a piece of cotton candy and popped it in his mouth, swirling it around with his tongue like a little boy. "Yet, you became this successful businessman who's taken our little company to the billion-dollar mark."

Now that Carter had gotten his job back, Emily could relax about the financial strain of sending Jacob to such a specialized school. She only hoped the scholarship fund Carter and she had created would help other families afford the tuition.

"Yes, well, I'm learning alongside Jacob about how to deal with my challenges. Gracepoint, the school I told you about, offers so many resources I never knew existed. It's been great sharing the process with him." Carter messed squeezed his son's shoulder.

"Do you like your school, buddy?" Jim asked.

"Yeah, it's so awesome. Everyone there is blessed with dyslexia." At Jim's puzzled look, her son clarified. "I've learned it's not a curse, but a gift."

"Speaking of gifts, we have one for your new school. The board met and decided to donate all the proceeds of the golf tournament to Gracepoint

School." Jim pulled a folded check from his pocket. "Actually, the entire board also put money into this donation."

Emily gasped at the substantial gift. "You have no idea how much these kids will benefit, not to mention the teachers. They work so hard."

Jim's wife, Gail, gave her a smile. "I hear you'll be working there soon."

"Only as an assistant, but I hope to be a teacher once I finish school in two years."

Carter stroked her hair, sending warmth down the back of her neck. "My Emily's already skipped several courses, and will be ready to take her certification exam soon."

Emily smiled at his words. Carter had never given praise easily, but they'd both changed so much. They'd healed together, and were finally ready to welcome the next big adventure that would come their way. Perhaps another child someday, but for now, she was happy. Really happy.

"Mom is a genius." Jacob leaned into her, his eyes wide with obvious pride.

She stroked his cheek. "You inspire me."

Carter folded the check and slid it into his pocket then offered his hand to Jim. "Please extend my thanks to the other members of the board. I don't know how I can ever express what this means to me, to us."

Jim took Gail's hand and tugged her to his side. "Actually, we were hoping you two could help us. We've decided to copy you. You know, leave the big city and move down here. Gail will love all the antiquing."

Gail nodded and squeezed Jim tight to her side. "It's more than that. It's the people. The community. This doesn't exist anywhere else that I've found."

Emily laced her fingers with Carter's and a rush of Happily-Ever-After adrenaline shot up her arm and injected into her heart. "You'll love it here. We moved to this town to find a new life, and we did. It's not just because our family is here, although that's a big part of it. It also wasn't because we found a school that Jacob loves, even though that's important, or that we found a community that welcomed us. We found a new life here because we were able to find each other again."

Gail scanned the fair, eyeing all the people. "I don't know. I think miracles happen in this place. I've talked to three people today that swear the town's motto is true. And I must say, if you two are any example of what this town has to offer, then maybe Sweetwater County *is* where our hearts and home belong."

The End

Character List

David Aguero
Chairman of the Board, BSMA

Andre
Francisco's (best restaurant in Creekside) employee
Judy Gaylord Benjamin
Mother of Eric Gaylord
Married to James Benjamin
Co-owns J & L Antiques with Lisa Mortan Gaylord

BSMA Board members
Scott Waterman, Shawn Palmer, Nicholas Smith, Daniel Reed, Aidan
Stevenson, Tom Cliver, David Aguero, Jim Stallman, Chuck Morgan

Mr. Burton
Man who owns factory and most of Creekside.
Rose Burton's father

Tom Cliver
Board Member for BSMA
An ex-vet from Vietnam with quiet commanding power

Emily Sue Davidson
Heroine
Recently returned to Creekside after being away for years

Carter William Davidson
Hero who is moving his family back to Creekside
BSMA, Business Solutions Mergers and Acquisitions, CEO

Jacob Davidson
Nine-year-old son
Third grade
Struggles with reading issues

Judith Davidson
Carter's mother

Donald
Carter's brother

Aunt Sue Fletcher
Emily's aunt who owns Cafe Bliss

Amelia Gaylord
Eric and Lisa Gaylord's infant daughter

Eric Gaylord
Judy Gaylord Benjamin's son
Lawyer
Married to Lisa Mortan Gaylord

Lisa Mortan Gaylord
Eric's wife

Girl (unnamed)
Works at Cafe Bliss

Phillip Grant
|Board member; shiny forehead

Dr. Kelner
Creekside Elementary principal; older woman, glasses, hair pulled back in
bun

Mark
Carter's oldest brother; wasn't a preemie; born on time

Matt
|Meredith's son, plays guitar

Meredith
School secretary at Creekside Elementary

Jenna Mitchell Grayson
Cathy West's daughter; in Carter's HS class (& Emily's presumably)
Deputy Walker's Girlfriend

Chuck Morgan
Board member
Well-traveled
Uncle lives in Riverbend

Gail Morgan
Chuck Morgan's wife

Mr. Martark
Owner of Martark

Dr. Parker
Tests Jacob for learning disabilities
Rebecca West   Cathy's stepdaughter
Devon West's daughter

Rose Burton
Cathy's friend
Studying special ed
Volunteers at Center for Autism
Marcus Vega's girlfriend

Sadie Grayson
Jenna's daughter
Autistic

Tina Townsend
Made a play for Carter in HS; head cheerleader

Trianna Mason
Cafe Bliss customer
Married to Sheriff Jimmy Mason

Marcus Vega
Rose's boyfriend

Cathy Mitchell West
Reformed town gossip and expert seamstress who is married to Devon
West

Devon West
Cathy West's husband and (name) father

Dear Reader

Thank you so much for supporting the *Love & Grace* anthology. This project is near and dear to my heart. It began when my son's school, Gracepoint – A School for dyslexia, out grew their temporary home in a local church. They desperately wanted to have their own school home, but as you can imagine that would be costly. Although, this box set will not provide enough money for the school, I do hope that it will give them enough funding to assist with some of their needs. Perhaps it'll help fund a much needed bus to transport children, or some new computers, or classroom supplies.

I hope this story helped shed light on dyslexia, and the struggles families, students, schools, and communities face. Thank you again for supporting Gracepoint.

If you enjoyed this story, please take a moment and start at the beginning of the Sweetwater County stories, with Winter in Sweetwater County. You'll have the opportunity to read Eric and Lisa's story.

For a complete list of my books, please visit my website at www.ciaraknight.com. A great way to keep up to date on all releases, sales and prizes subscribe to my Newsletter here http://www.ciaraknight.com/newsletter. I'm extremely sociable, so feel free to chat with me on Facebook (http://www.facebook.com/ciaraknightwrites), Twitter (http://www.twitter.com/ciaratknight), or Goodreads (http://www.goodreads.com/ciaraknight).

For your convenience please see my complete title list below, in reading order:

Sweetwater County Series
Winter in Sweetwater County
Spring in Sweetwater County
Fall in Sweetwater County
Christmas in Sweetwater County
Valentines in Sweetwater County
Fourth of July in Sweetwater County
Thanksgiving in Sweetwater County

Battle for Souls Series
Rise From Darkness
Fall From Grace
Ascension of Evil

The Neumarian Chronicles
Weighted
Escapement
Pendulum
Balance

The Shrouded Kingdoms
The Curse of Gremdon
The Secrets of Dargon (Coming September 2015)
The Runes of Bramon (Coming March 2016)

A Prospectors Novel
Fools Rush

ONE AUTUMN LOVE

Lindi Peterson

After her mother passed away, Joelle Madison recently moved into her mother's house to find William Scott moving in next door. The handsome neighbor has good looks and brawn. He also has a daughter, Caroline. Joelle already tried dating one man with children and swore she would never invest herself into a family situation again. But William's secrets and past quickly involve Joelle into his life. A life she finds she might fit into if she dares to risk her heart once again.

Chapter One

Joelle Madison never loved planting. Or weeding. But her mother did. So now, on a bright yet windy October afternoon, Joelle found herself, knees in the dirt, pulling the unwanted objects out of the flower beds. There weren't many but Ohio's recent Indian summer caused the pesky green shoots to sprout up here and there in the midst of the beautiful plants and flowers.

The plants and flowers Joelle knew nothing about.

A parallel to her relationship with her mother.

Her mother's passing was so unexpected and sad. Joelle always thought they still had time to become close.

It never happened.

Some months had gone by and now the sadness was becoming distant. Joelle dug into the dirt. Her mother's will included banking information, passwords and the answers to security questions.

It said nothing about hydrangeas and trumpet plants. Or rock gardens. Or weeds.

But Joelle had inherited them all among other beautiful living things she needed to take care of. Like Misty, her mother's Himalayan cat.

Joelle wasn't very good at taking care of living things as Misty would probably testify to if she could talk. Joelle also boasted a black thumb, not a green one. Thoughts of hiring someone to tend to the abundance of plants and gardens her mother built over the years since she retired drifted through her mind the last few weeks. Charlie Lawson had a great lawn service. She was sure they did landscaping as well. Plenty of ladies at the church, who would be a wealth of information if she would ask them, could point her in the right direction.

For hiring someone.

She wasn't interested in tending to this herself.

Her finger closed over the weed. It came out of the ground easily and she dropped it in a cardboard box. At least the ground was soft as it had rained yesterday.

All day.

She had spent her rainy Saturday indoors cleaning and unpacking more boxes. She had also watched the neighbors move in.

Neighbor is more appropriate.

Only one man.

He'd worked all day, rushing boxes and furniture in between downpours. A sweatshirt and ball cap kept Joelle from getting a good look at him. But she knew he was strong by the furniture he carried in by himself.

It wasn't very much furniture though. A couple of beds and dressers. A small dining table with mismatched chairs. She saw no living room furniture. The rental truck left last night and a big pickup truck returned.

Joelle imagined he would be having more furniture delivered soon.

Nostalgia shot through Joelle at the thought of anyone living in Mrs. Bellows house. Mrs. B, as Joelle called her, had lived in that house as long as Joelle had been alive. When Mrs. B died a few months ago, right before Joelle's mother, Mrs. B's son, Ben, who lives in Pittsburgh, took his time cleaning out his mother's things, but after he was through he promptly sold the family home.

Looking to her left, Joelle took in the brick house. Bushes hid the front of the porch, their tops cut evenly with the porch rail. Two colorful yet barren pots hung symmetrically at the front of the porch. They swayed in the breeze along with the porch swing. She wondered if the new neighbor would leave the swing. The last time she was there, when Mrs. B died, the chains anchoring the swing were no longer silver, but a dirty, weathered color. The slats were rotted and needed replacing indicating no one had used the swing in a long time.

That was a shame.

Joelle had always envied the cozy porch next door. Her front stoop with the white awning never seemed as inviting as Mrs. B's porch. You could gather on a porch. The stoop? It protected you from the weather before begging you to go inside.

Focusing back on her weeding Joelle had no idea why a single guy would want to move to Devon Park, Ohio. To be honest she was only guessing that he was single. A wife and kids might show up anytime for all she knew.

But nothing had been happening since she'd come outside.

She pulled three more weeds and dropped them into the box. Moving a little to the left, she dragged the box with her. As she settled into her new spot, her knees aching, her jeans wet, the wind started blowing harder. She grabbed the box, holding it steady. While the box stayed in place, her scarf didn't.

The thin peach-colored scarf started tumbling across the grass. Joelle stuck the box between two bushes then peeled off her gloves. Brown dirt on peach material equaled a dirty scarf. She stood, dropping the gloves into the box. The pink-flowered gloves landed next to the weeds and she was tempted to toss the whole box, gloves and all, into the trash and be done with this task.

Instead she gave the box a little kick to make sure it wasn't going anywhere and turned to find her scarf.

A girl with blonde pigtails, a freckled face and one missing front tooth smiled at her.

Joelle gasped, her hand flying to her heart. "Oh. I'm sorry. You scared me."

The little girl giggled. "I'm sorry. Am I scary looking?"

"No. Not at all. I just wasn't expecting anyone to be standing behind me. I'm Joelle. What's your name?"

"Caroline. It's nice to meet you, Miss Joelle. I caught your scarf." Caroline held the scarf almost like a baby.

Joelle wondered at Caroline's accent. It was southern for sure. "I thank you very much. The wind caught me unawares."

"I thought I told you not to bother our neighbors, Kiddo."

The very male voice caused Joelle to shift her concentration away from Caroline. She almost gasped again, but this time wouldn't have had a good excuse. She kept her hand steady by her side while her heart did a double beat.

Yesterday's baseball cap and sweatshirt had hidden quite a handsome man. Dark hair, darker eyes, five o'clock shadow mid-afternoon. The muscles she saw in action yesterday were very real close up. He placed a hand on Caroline's head. A gentle touch.

"I know, Daddy. But her scarf blew into our yard. I caught it for her. Her name is Miss Joelle."

He held out his hand and Joelle hesitated briefly, her brain moving in a slower motion than the rest of her. "William Scott. Nice to meet you Joelle. And I see you've met my girl, Caro, or Kiddo as I like to call her."

"Cause I'm always kidding around." Caroline looked up at her father and smiled.

"William. It's nice to meet you." She held his hand, but for only a moment.

His gaze lingered longer than the handshake. Joelle wanted to keep staring at him, but that would be rude. And staring too long might give the wrong impression. The impression that she was interested.

And she wasn't.

Good looking or not, relationships were off limits. Especially relationships with children involved.

"I hope Caro wasn't bothering you."

Joelle shook her head. "No. Not at all. I appreciate her rescuing my scarf." The scarf Caroline still held onto.

Tightly.

William looked down. "Why don't you go on in the house? I think Mr. PJ and the rest of your animals are tired of being in boxes. I'll be right behind you."

"Mr. PJ! I forgot! Okay. See you later, Miss Joelle."

With those words Caroline ran across the yard, Joelle's scarf floating like a butterfly in Caroline's arms as she ran up the stairs to the porch. The screen door shut with a slam and the peach material disappeared along with the little girl. Joelle wondered if she would ever see her scarf again.

*****

As the screen door shut, William let out a breath. Safe. Caroline was safely in the house. Rational thoughts said his neighbor posed no threat, but William couldn't take any chances. He would have a talk with Caro later this evening. Again.

No talking to strangers.

Ever.

Although William appreciated his daughter's rescue effort of the pretty neighbor's scarf, he wished Caro would have come to him first. He would have walked over here with her to do her good deed.

The good deed she didn't do. "I'm sorry. I just realized Caro didn't give you back your scarf."

Joelle crossed her arms. "It's okay. I know where to find it."

Her body language didn't match her words, but maybe she was trying to keep warm. Although the sun brought warmth to the day, the wind had a chill to it when it blew.

He tried not to stare as he studied her. Left hand bore no rings, but that didn't mean anything. After all she was playing in the dirt until her scarf got away from her. Golden brown eyes seemed to be taking him in. Soft pink lips and a careful smile appeared genuine.

Her light brown hair was cut evenly just below her pretty chin. She wore jeans and a long-sleeved fitted T. "Devon Park Raiders. Local team?" he asked.

"Yes. The high school. I'm an alum."

He nodded toward the house. "You've lived here a while then I take it."

"I grew up in this house. I recently moved back in after my mother's passing in July." Her voice softened at the end of her words, indicating it was hard to talk about.

"I'm sorry. My condolences."

"Thank you. Where are you moving from?"

The conversation was becoming more personal than he thought it would when he looked out the window and saw Caro conversing with a neighbor they hadn't met. But it was his fault. When you ask questions, questions are sure to be asked of you. "The Deep South."

"Welcome to Devon Park. In the far north."

He liked the fact that she didn't pry. Didn't press him for more details than he was willing to give. He also liked her smile, her attempt at making a small joke.

Although he had no desire to reveal his plans, it might be best considering there would be work trucks and noise starting soon. "I'm renovating this house, so I apologize in advance for any noise or construction mess. I promise not to run my table saw after dark."

Her eyebrows rose while her eyes darkened slightly, something he was sure he wouldn't have noticed if the sun hadn't been so bright.

"What kind of renovation? I thought the house was in good shape."

"The house has great bones, which is why I decided to flip it. Once this old girl is transformed I'll be able to make a nice profit."

Her gaze narrowed. Guess she didn't agree with his plan, but that was all right. He didn't need her to agree. He just hoped she wouldn't make any trouble for him.

Or Caro.

Joelle hoped her smile didn't appear as fake as it felt. Turning Mrs. B's house for a profit? It sounded sinful.

But Joelle knew it only sounded that way because she was so invested in the house. Even though Ben was older than her, she was a regular at the house during her childhood. Mrs. B made the best cookies in the world, and Joelle was often found hanging out with Mrs. B after school since Joelle's mom was at work. Cookies, milk and conversation on the front porch happened more often than not.

Joelle swallowed hard, trying to find her voice. "I'm sorry. That house has almost as many memories as my own. It's hard to hear it's going to be demolished."

His eyes narrowed, and he shoved a hand in his jeans pocket. "Not demolished. Renovated."

"You can't renovate memories. I guess with Ben living in Pennsylvania, this house doesn't have a hold on him."

"I'm sure he's stored up in his mind what he wants to remember."

"And when you say flip, you'll be selling it when you finish? Then what? You'll find another house in town to make a profit off of?" Curiosity drove her question. She hoped her tone didn't evoke sarcasm.

"Selling it is the plan. And yes, I'll have to find another house. But not in Devon Park. I've already got feelers out with friends. I'll travel all over the Eastern states."

"What about Caroline and school?"

"I homeschool her. My projects take a little longer than normal because of it, but I don't mind."

Joelle tried to process the homeschooling aspect. Renovator homeschooler? She'd never heard of such. "That's a big task you've taken on. I'm a tutor. Most of my clients are from the college. A few from the high school."

"So you work from home?"

"Yes. The beauty of the job. I'm almost done renovating my office. . ." The use of the word renovating took on new meaning after meeting William. "Not renovating like you think. Painting, picture hanging. Small things."

"Sounds like redecorating. Which is cool. Totally cool."

Her face heated at the conversation which was becoming more awkward with each word spoken. "I better get back to my weeding. The daylight will be gone soon. It was nice meeting you. And Caroline."

He nodded. "Again, sorry for the interruption. And we'll return that scarf."

Blue jeans never looked as good as they did on William as he walked across the small yard. He seemed too current and hip to be living in the old brick house next door.

Urban.

That was a good word to describe him. He probably had an earring and a tattoo. Not that there was anything wrong with those things. There wasn't.

But unless you were part of the college scene, urban didn't run rampant in Devon Park.

The door slammed once again catching Joelle's attention. A cloud passed over the same time another wind picked up. The breeze blew by her as she stood rock still. Her hair whipped into her eyes, but in moments she was left pushing her straight hair behind her ears. She walked over and knelt down before the bushes taking one more look at Mrs. B's, no, William's house.

Change. Everything was changing.

She didn't realize her hands were chilled until she shoved them into the gloves. The warmth surrounded her fingers and she flexed her hands. As she pulled the weeds she let her tears fall hoping for as good as a cleaning as the flower beds were receiving.

*****

William glanced out of the living room window. No Joelle.

He stared at the scarf that hung on a set of hooks by the front door. Caroline had insisted on prettying up one of her dolls with the scarf. After William took the picture he told her they were going to take the scarf back.

But Joelle had gone back inside.

Darkness had almost completely fallen now, so he decided the scarf could go back tomorrow. He'd place it in her mailbox if he had to.

"What's for dinner, Daddy?"

Dinner? Caro's voice carried well in the small space. Soon the barrier walls would be torn down for the open concept look most buyers wanted now. He walked to her bedroom where she had almost all of her boxes unpacked.

"You've done a great job, Kiddo."

Caro carefully placed Mr. PJ, her stuffed bunny rabbit, on the bed. She pushed its long ear from laying across his eye. "There. Now you can see better."

Her tender voice almost made him believe the bunny could actually see. Such innocence. He didn't ever want her to lose it, but he knew that was impossible. He just needed to prepare himself for all those conversations girls should have with their mothers.

Because her mother wouldn't be having them with her.

Ever.

Not if he had anything to say about it.

"I'm hungry, Daddy."

Oh, yeah. Dinner. He'd already forgotten what question had brought him to her room. Making something to eat was the last thing he felt like doing after unpacking all day, but he didn't feel like driving to town.

He could probably rustle up a box of macaroni and cheese. And he did have the basics—milk, eggs, and butter.

Before he could voice his dinner choice, the doorbell rang.

Caro jumped at the sound. "Daddy. That's loud."

"It is. We'll have to fix that for sure."

He made his way to the front door, Caro close behind, holding Mr. PJ. When he opened the door a young man wearing a delivery uniform stood there holding a box encased to keep it warm.

"Hi." He looked at a ticket he was holding. "One large with everything. Eighteen ninety five."

"We didn't order pizza." William spoke then inhaled the scent of the pizza. He now wished he'd ordered pizza.

"Oh, I'm supposed to be at sixteen eleven—"

"We're sixteen thirteen. Sixteen eleven must be next door. . ."

"Miss Joelle's house?" Caro's voice piped up. "Let's take her the pizza. We can take her scarf back."

The delivery boy shoved the ticket in his pocket. "I'm sorry to bother you." He turned to leave.

"Here." William dug in his pocket then held out a twenty and two ones. "We'll deliver it."

The boy hesitated. "I'm not sure. I might get fired. I better deliver it myself."

William added another one dollar bill. "Trust me on this. She'll get the pizza."

Shrugging, the boy took the bills then slid the pizza out of the protective sleeve. "Thanks, man."

As he ran down the stairs William turned to Caro. "Ready to deliver a pizza, Kiddo?"

"Sure am. Miss Joelle can meet Mr. PJ, too."

"Come on, then."

"Come on, Mr. PJ. You get to meet Miss Joelle. She's super nice. She likes flowers just like me and you."

Tapping his pocket to make sure he had his keys, William turned the lock then pulled the door behind him. "Stay close."

Headlights shone as the delivery boy pulling out of their drive lighted their path for a moment. Enough to guide them toward Joelle's front door.

"She's going to be surprised, isn't she?"

Joelle wasn't the only one who was surprised. He couldn't explain what possessed him to do this, except Caro's excitement. "I think she'll be surprised."

Her blinds were pulled down, but light shone from behind them. He reached for the doorbell.

"Mr. PJ wants to ring the doorbell. Please?"

How could he refuse Mr. PJ? "Sure. Go ahead. But only once."

Almost as soon as Caro rang the doorbell the front door opened. Joelle's look was more confusion than shock.

"Pizza delivery is in your repertoire as well?"

He nodded toward his house. "The pizza guy delivered to the wrong house. We thought this would be a good time to bring back your scarf...which we completely forgot to grab."

"Daddy, I'll go home and get it." Caro looked up at him, an excited expression on her face.

"No. Not in the dark."

Joelle waved them in. "I'll get the scarf later. Come on in."

He followed Caro into the living room. Hardwood floors and a neutral wall color proved to be a nice backdrop for her bluish-gray couch. White pillows with blue stripes accented nicely along with a matching rug. It was obvious no children lived here. "Nice place."

"It's staying just like this. No renovation ideas need to form in your head. Got it?"

Her tone said she was kidding, but he believed her words as truth. "Understood."

"Let me take that." She nodded toward the pizza box.

"The least I can do is carry it to your kitchen. You've been working hard today." He wasn't sure she was receptive to his teasing words.

"Follow me."

Moments later he set the box down on the kitchen counter. He couldn't help but notice how dated this part of her home was. But it had been kept up well. Everything sparkled or shined. A faint scent of cinnamon hung in the air.

"How much do I owe you?"

"My, our treat." He looked down and placed his hand on Caro's shoulder. "Especially since we're still holding your scarf hostage."

"Nonsense." Joelle tried to hand him a twenty dollar bill. When he refused to take it she set it on the counter. "Please take the money?"

He shook his head. "No. Besides you ordered a pizza with everything. Most girls shy away from the deluxe pizza."

"You're speaking from experience. So you take a lot of girls for pizza?"

William realized he needed to watch his words. The less Joelle knew about him the better. "Not too many. Just this one here." He tapped Caro's head. "But she does like the works."

"Well in that case why don't you join me? This is way too much."

"Eyes bigger than the stomach?"

"Partly. Also, I thought I'd have it for lunch for a couple of days. But I always think that, then never eat it. I end up throwing it away. So you can help save the pizza from the trash can."

"When you put it like that, how can we refuse?"

Joelle set out paper plates, poured three glasses of iced tea, and before William could think about saying no for real, they were all seated at the table in the breakfast nook.

"Can Mr. PJ have his own chair?" Caro asked.

"Of course." Joelle smiled.

Caro got out of her chair then settled Mr. PJ in the empty chair. She pushed it up to the table. "He's short. But he's okay."

She then slid back into her chair before taking a bite of her pizza. "This is good."

Joelle nodded. "I do love Taylor's pizza. They've been making pizza ever since I can remember. We'd go hang out there after football and basketball games. Nice place."

William wondered what it would be like to have memories like Joelle. All the constants. She probably sat in these exact chairs as a child. Maybe she had a Mr. PJ that sat in a chair like Caro's stuffed bunny.

The tug to give Caro that kind of life lodged in his heart. But fate, or God, declared it would never be. Not until he knew Caro would be safe staying in one town.

And that was knowledge he didn't have.

* * * * *

Joelle wasn't sure what possessed her to ask William and Caro to stay for dinner. She tried to think maybe she felt bad because he paid for it. But her nagging curiosity about the man next door who homeschooled his daughter had overtaken her thoughts, so when he stood at her front door, she saw a chance to learn real facts about William.

Not the made-up ones she imagined.

Now with the pizza box and glasses empty, she realized she'd gained no information on the man and his daughter. Superficial conversation between bites of pizza happened, but that was all. No deep dark secrets were revealed as they sat in her breakfast nook.

Caro kept giving Mr. PJ imaginary bites of pizza and sips of "the best iced tea she ever had." Which struck Joelle as weird considering the girl was from the South. Joelle learned her love of sweet tea at college but didn't think hers was nearly as good as what she'd had there.

Kids. Who knew what they were going to like.

"Again, Kiddo and I appreciate you asking us to share your pizza." William tossed his napkin on top of his plate then started to stack the other plates on top of his.

"You're welcome. Now I don't have to feel guilty throwing leftovers in the trash."

He stood, his gaze searching the room as he reached for the plates. "Speaking of trash, where is your trash can?"

"Just leave that. I'll get it."

"No, ma'am. We'll do our part, right, Kiddo? Why don't you and Mr. PJ take the glasses to the sink?"

"If you insist." Joelle walked to a small door and opened it. "Here's the trash can."

William dropped the plates in while Caro carefully took the glasses to the sink. What a nice family scene.

But they weren't a family.

Joelle shoved down memories that she thought she had buried. Daniel and his boys, Logan and Sean. They were all supposed to be a family. She still had the dress to prove it.

Pretty.

White.

Hanging in her closet never worn.

A mother to someone else's children she could never be. Daniel and his boys made that clear.

She shut the pantry door harder than she intended.

Caro was oblivious, but William's gaze startled before sharply moving toward his daughter. He blinked and hooded protectiveness took over. Even though she'd never experienced it, Joelle recognized the bond between parent and child.

That unbreakable bond no outsider could intrude upon.

She wouldn't put herself in that position again.

Relief that their conversation never passed the superficial stage flooded her. William's good looks and homeschooling heart could label him a "good catch." Caro changed the game. Never mind the fact that he was already looking for a place to move on to.

"Mr. PJ says thank you for the pizza and tea, Miss Joelle. He loved it."

Caro stood in front of the sink, clutching Mr. PJ.

Her smile caused Joelle to smile. "You tell Mr. PJ you're welcome."

"So you live here all by yourself?" Caro's sweet voice made living alone sound like a bad thing.

"I do. Except for Misty. She's my mom's cat, and she kind of came with the house."

"Oh, I love kitties. Can I see her?"

Joelle shook her head. "She's a scaredy cat, literally. She hides whenever anyone comes over. I'm sorry."

"Me, too. I bet she would love Mr. PJ. I know he would love her."

Joelle wasn't too sure Misty wouldn't drag Mr. PJ all over the house and hide him as well. But Joelle knew enough not to voice those thoughts for Caro to hear. "I think you're right. They would be great friends."

William made his way over to Caro, the kitchen suddenly filled with the man. "We better get home. School in the morning."

A frown that took over Caro's expression. "Yuk."

Spoken like a true kid.

"Yuk or not, it's happening. So let's go. Bath and bed are in your immediate future."

Mr. PJ was the recipient of a tight hug. "Will you read me a story tonight?"

William nodded. "Sure. We can read together."

Caro's gaze dropped and Mr. PJ almost disappeared in her arms. "Mr. PJ says we don't like to read. You read so good, Daddy."

Joelle's tutoring brain worked overtime breaking down the conversation. Caro wasn't a reader. But she liked stories. And she loved Mr. PJ. And she thought William read well. Maybe he just told a great story. Some people had that knack.

Daniel used to tell his sons great stories.

Thoughts of Daniel twice in one night? William and Caro needed to leave. They were bringing up too many memories that she had long ago forgotten.

Or tried not to remember.

"Reading is important. Mr. PJ knows you are a good reader." William placed his hand on Caro's shoulder. "Let's go."

Joelle followed them to the front door. "Thank you again for paying for the pizza. That was nice. Unnecessary but nice."

"It was nothing. Thanks again for sharing with us."

William opened the door. Caro stepped out, but then darted back in. Her arms wrapped around Joelle's legs. "Bye, Miss Joelle."

As Joelle almost lost her balance, William caught her, his hands holding onto her shoulders.

Strong hands.

Gentle hands.

Hands that carried headboards by day and held storybooks by night. Hands that tore cabinets off walls, yet softly brushed his daughter's shoulders.

"Whoa, Kiddo. You almost knocked Joelle over." His firm grasp steadied her as Caro unlatched herself.

"I'm sorry. It was Mr. PJ's fault. He's too strong."

Joelle couldn't help but laugh. "It's all right. Your dad saved me."

Caro shoved Mr. PJ under her arm then clapped her hands. "You're like a princess! And Daddy, I mean the prince, saved you. Just like in the stories Daddy reads to me."

Joelle straightened, wanting to undo any image of her needing to be saved while William quickly loosened his hold on her. Moments later, as he ushered Caro out the door, Joelle still felt the touch points of his fingers on her shoulders. "Bye."

She sounded breathy like he'd just kissed her.

Joelle hadn't turned on the porch light, but light from the living room spilled out over William making him look soft, romantic.

"Bye." He looked at her as he spoke, his gaze locking onto hers. His gaze was dangerous and made her lightheaded, like she wanted to talk breathy again.

So she didn't speak.

She didn't breathe.

Even when he broke his gaze, grabbed Caro's hand, and walked with his daughter hand in hand across her yard, Joelle kept staring.

And then it hit her.

Trouble had just moved in next door.

Chapter Three

Joelle puttered around her office. Her two o'clock appointment canceled.

Again.

Joelle looked at the text, but instead of responding via text, she called.

"Hello?" The male voice sounded irritated.

"Stan, this is Joelle Madison. Are you sure you can't make your session? Even thirty minutes would be helpful."

"No. I can't. And I'm pretty busy. That's why I texted."

Oh, his attitude said it all. But Joelle wouldn't let that sway her. "You've been canceling quite a bit, and it's throwing my days off when you do this. Can I have a commitment that you'll be here on Wednesday? A firm commitment?"

"Look. I'm not sure why you're bothered about it. I still pay even when I don't show. It's not like it's hitting your wallet or anything. I'll try to be there on Wednesday. But things come up. You know how it is. Gotta go."

Her phone went silent. True to his word, Stan paid the full fee every month. Or rather, Stan's family paid the fee. Stan just attended the college. And took classes although Joelle wasn't sure how many times he actually made it to class. He barely made it through high school. Joelle had tutored him his whole senior year. He had aptitude; he simply didn't care.

His parents, who were a big force in this town, hired Joelle again the first day he went to college. But if he attended college like he attended her tutoring sessions, he was playing more than working. And it's not like Joelle didn't let his parents know. She turned in a report to them every month when she sent the bill. A N/S for no-show was plugged in for every session he missed.

She placed his file back in the cabinet. Everything was ready for her three o'clock, so she had forty-five minutes to kill.

Forty-five minutes to think about William. William who doesn't wear a wedding ring. William who never mentioned a wife, girlfriend, or any women's name other than Caro.

So what's their story?

Tragic.

Their story could be tragic. Tragic was different than sad. Sad was different than bad.

She pressed her hands against her head. Her head which she needed to clear of thoughts of her new neighbor.

She wished she could say it was Caro. That her thoughts were consumed by the cute little girl next door. But every time she thought of Caro, the word complication came up. That was thanks to Daniel and that whole situation.

Shoving her phone in her pocket, she left her office. While taking a walk around the block sounded like a great idea, that would entail changing her clothes and shoes then changing back into her dress clothes when her three o'clock showed up.

That wasn't happening.

But she could check the mail.

When Joelle entered the living room, Misty darted out from under the couch. She ran down the hall, ducking into the spare bedroom. Little puffs of fur hung in the air. Great, now she would have to sweep before her three o'clock.

Stepping outside, the wind and clouds from yesterday had disappeared leaving the sun sitting in the midst of clear blue skies. The air had a slight chill to it, and brown leaves fell from the trees that lined the street as Joelle walked to the mailbox.

She would be raking the leaves this weekend. But Joelle didn't mind. She found that task to be peaceful and fulfilling. Maybe because she could do it standing up as opposed to moving around on her knees like yesterday.

Joelle couldn't help but take a sideways look next door. Everything was as it was yesterday. Truck in the driveway. Empty pots still hanging on the porch.

Front door shut tightly.

She wondered what was going on inside? What part of the house would he be demolishing first?

"Excuse me?"

Joelle turned at the sound of a voice. A woman stood next to a car parked across the street. The car had seen better days. The woman seemed hesitant. Her long blonde hair was pulled into a ponytail. She wore jeans, a tight-fitting T-shirt, and flip flops.

Flip flops in October? It wasn't that warm outside.

"Yes?" Joelle stood next to her mailbox. "Can I help you?"

As the woman walked toward Joelle, her gaze darted between Joelle and the house next door. William's house. Little prickly chills covered Joelle's arms despite the sun.

"Maybe you can." She pulled a folded piece of paper out of her purse. "I'm looking for this house. It's for sale. I've looked at so many houses. When I saw this online I knew this would be the one. I thought it was on this street, but I don't see any For Sale signs."

Joelle took the paper. It was a computer printout of the sales listing of William's house. Joelle looked at the top of the page. The date the paper was printed was well over a week ago. "This house has sold."

The woman had a confused look on her face. "Sold? No. It can't be. It is that house?" She pointed to William's house.

"Yes. That's the house. Someone bought it. They moved in yesterday." Joelle handed the paper back to the woman who still had an unbelieving look on her face.

"Are you serious? Who bought it? Wait, I bet an elderly lady with a cat, right?"

Joelle immediately thought of herself, single, living with her mother's cat. But she refused to call herself elderly. "You have something against cats?"

She laughed. "Not really. It's hard to explain. All I know is I had a really good feeling about this house when I saw this picture. I'm sure you've heard the phrase, 'It feels like home.' Well, that's what screamed at me when I saw this listing. Ugh. I can't imagine starting over. All because of an old lady and a cat."

At this point Joelle wasn't sure what to do. Just as she wouldn't want William telling a perfect stranger, "Hey, my neighbor lives alone," she didn't feel comfortable telling this perfect stranger that a child lived in the house. "I'm sorry the house isn't on the market anymore. There are plenty of older houses in Devon Park like the ones on this street. I'm sure you'll find something soon."

The woman shoved the paper into her purse. "Are you sure it's sold? Maybe someone is renting it out. Who knows what can happen when a house is for sale. Have you met or talked to whoever moved in?"

"Even if I had, I wouldn't ask that kind of information. I'm sorry I couldn't be of more help. I need to get back to work." That was more information than she wanted to relay, but it seemed like the only logical way to bow out of the conversation without appearing rude. And she certainly wasn't going to reveal William's renovation plans to a total stranger.

"Just a minute." The woman tore off a corner of the listing paper that was sticking out of her purse. She dug momentarily in her purse and produced a pen. After scribbling on the paper, she folded it and handed it to Joelle. "Please call me if the house becomes available. Or if you find out the people are renting. Please?"

Joelle's fist closed over the paper. "You can always call the agent. I'm sure they'll be more helpful than I can be."

"I've left two messages with no return call. That's why I decided to drive over. Thanks so much."

She ran back to her car, suddenly seeming to be in a hurry, then sped off before putting on her seat belt.

A weird feeling settled over Joelle as she checked her mailbox. Empty. She shut the box wondering if she should have tried to get the woman's license plate.

"Miss Joelle! Hi!"

Joelle spotted Caro standing on the porch waving. Joelle waved back, shoving the folded paper in her pants pocket. "Hello."

"I have to stay on the porch, but Daddy said I could play out here for a while. Do you want to come over?"

Dangerous ground. The little girl was dangerous ground. Joelle could not lose her heart to a child again. A child that wasn't her own. "I'm sorry. I have to work. I have an appointment in a few minutes. You have fun, though."

A slight look of disappointment passed over Caro's face. But it didn't last long. "Okay. Have a fun appointment."

Caro busied herself, Joelle losing sight of her as she was swallowed by the brick railing. As Joelle put a hand on her front door, she glanced one more time at William's house. Maybe expecting to see him?

The sound of a car pulling in her driveway stopped her fantasy thoughts.

Her three o'clock was early. Good. No time to sweep, but at least now she knew she wouldn't spend her afternoon thinking of her new neighbor and his daughter.

Well, at least the next hour would be William and Caro free.

*****

It was guilt.

William ripped a piece of wallpaper off the wall, surprised this section came off so easily. The paper thudded to the floor. He moved the ladder, climbed up then looked for a sweet spot to remove the next piece. Not finding one, he dug the scraper out of his work belt and started shoving the blade under the hideous wall paper.

Guilt was the only explanation William could come up with regarding Caro's reaction to their neighbor. And no, it wasn't Caro feeling guilty.

He was.

Guilty that Caro didn't have a steady female influence in her life. Guilty that he had taken Caro from the small family she did have. But he had no other choice.

The weekly phone calls with Grandma Sue didn't make up for the lack of a woman in the house. So when Caro asked if they could buy a special plant for "Miss Joelle," he found he couldn't say no. The few dollars he spent on the plant wasn't an issue.

Seeing Joelle to give her the plant would be the issue.

He wouldn't trust Caro to go alone to Joelle's house which meant he would go with her. And having already spent one short evening with Joelle, he wasn't anxious to spend more time with her.

Time spent with Joelle was time he could become used to. Easy mannered, nice on the eyes, good to his daughter. What was there not to like about his pretty neighbor?

But liking the pretty neighbor was not on his radar. Too many questions would need to be answered, and he had to protect Caro. For the first time in a long time, he wished his life was different.

A section of paper pulled away from the wall, but sticky glue prevented the whole piece from easing off. Stepping down a couple of rungs, he looked out the window to the front porch where Caro was playing with her dolls. He refused to keep her inside all the time, but he couldn't let her go far.

The front porch was perfect. It was one thing that drew him to this house.

Now he found he was drawn to something else.

Or someone else.

Short brown shiny hair and a sweet smile invaded his mind, settling there and refusing to leave. But it couldn't be.

Certain Caro was all right, he returned to his wallpaper removal task. He was glad he had a job where he used physical energy. He couldn't imagine his mind without this escape.

He heard the sound of the screen door opening then felt the chill of the afternoon sweep into the room. "Hi, Kiddo. How's it going out there? Everybody having a great time?"

"Yes. I saw Miss Joelle. I didn't tell her about the plant. I wanted to but didn't. Does this mean I know how to keep a secret?"

Secrets. "It sounds like it to me." He refused to acknowledge the ping of disappointment that he hadn't see Joelle.

"I told Mr. PJ, though. Is that okay? He promised he wouldn't tell."

William chuckled to himself. He loved the innocence. "I think it's fine to tell Mr. PJ. We all need a friend we can count on and share our secrets with."

"Who is your friend? Who do you share secrets with?"Caro sat on the windowsill. Her coat was too big, her socks too small. Her cheeks were flushed and her hair needed a good brushing. It was hard to ignore the fact that she could use a good female influence in her life.

He kept scraping. "Daddy is fine."

"I think you could share secrets with Miss Joelle. I bet she's a good secret keeper."

Secrets weren't exactly what he was thinking he'd like to share with Joelle. But his thoughts were only thoughts, and they could never come to fruition. "Joelle probably has girlfriends she talks to. She doesn't need an old guy like me."

Caro laughed. "You're not old. You're funny, Daddy. You need somebody to play with."

Play with? He'd played all right. The only good thing to come out of his playing was Caro.

Sweet, innocent Caro.

If she only knew.

But she wouldn't.

Ever.

Not as long as he was around.

Chapter Four

This was risky.

Joelle knew it, yet slid the baking sheet in the oven anyway. In eleven minutes or so she would have a batch of the best chocolate chip cookies in the world. At least that was how she thought of them when her grandmother made them. Whenever her mother made them, they were good, but they never tasted quite like Grandmother Madison's. Her mother was better at balancing accounting sheets than she was at using baking sheets.

Telling herself she was going to all this trouble to make cookies on a Monday night because she wanted something for her clients to snack on this week was one of the better lies she told herself.

She hadn't made cookies in a long time. That was a good reason too, right? How long had it been?

Months.

When she lived across town, she used to make cookies and drive them over to Mrs. B.

"I can cook anything you want for dinner, but don't ask me to bake. I burn everything." Mrs. B's words came over Joelle. In looking back, Joelle wondered at the truth of the words. How can someone know how to cook but not bake?

But Joelle's cookies and Mrs. B's lemonade made for many great afternoons as a child, then as an adult.

Joelle dropped spoonfuls of dough onto another cookie sheet. A scene played out in her mind, one where she would take a plate of cookies next door when Caro was playing on the porch. She envisioned Caro's smile, that missing tooth. Her heart warmed.

Erase.

She had to erase that image.

Just because she could make a decent cookie didn't mean she was ready to throw her heart to people who would crush it to the ground. Fear nudged at her as she realized handsome William and his daughter potentially had that power.

Joelle honestly didn't know what was wrong with her. She knew many good looking guys. She went to church with several of them. She had male friends that were nice looking. And that's all William was, a nice looking man.

His love and gentleness for his daughter lingered in Joelle's mind, anchoring the notion that he was more than handsome.

Thankfully the buzzer sounded and Joelle removed the baking sheet, then shoved in the next one. Setting the timer again, she reasoned with herself.

It was the house.

Relief ran through her.

That was it.

She was having a hard time letting the house go. William and Caro just happened to be a part of this life change. Not only was the house not Mrs. B's anymore, William was about to change everything about the inside of the house.

But the porch.

The porch would remain the same.

A sense of peace that she hadn't felt since she met Caro and William settled on her. Joelle actually felt silly.

The house. She smiled at the cookies as she scooted the spatula underneath them and transferred them to the wax paper lining the counter.

She remembered the woman from earlier today. She was interested in the house as well. How could one simple house speak to so many people? It spoke to William as a profit maker. The woman who gave Joelle her number said it felt like home.

And she determined that from a picture.

Washing her hands quickly, Joelle dried them and pulled the piece of paper from her pocket.

No name.

Just a ten digit phone number.

Joelle turned the paper over. It was blank.

Instinct told her to toss the paper in the trash. Memories of the prickles that Joelle felt at the woman's presence changed her mind. She'd keep the number just in case. . . Keeping the number gave Joelle a sense of being a protector.

Like William needed protecting.

She shook her head as she grabbed one of her mother's cat magnets that was shoved in a drawer and stuck the paper on the front of the refrigerator.

You never know.

The smell of the cookies called to her, and just as she took a bite, her doorbell rang.

Hope then trepidation filled her, pushing aside the sweet taste of the cookie.

She knew who it was.

Her doorbell never rang until William and Caro moved in.

*****

And here he was.

Again on the stoop of Joelle's house.

But he and Caro wouldn't go in tonight. "Remember, we're just giving her the plant then we are leaving. I'm sure Joelle has plenty of things to do this evening. K, Kiddo?"

"Sure. You have Mr. PJ don't you?"

William wiggled the bunny in front of her. "I do."

Caro laughed. "Thanks, Daddy. This plant is heavy."

Before he could respond, the front door opened. He wasn't prepared for the business-looking Joelle, nor the smell of baking cookies.

His mouth watered.

All the cookie's fault, he assured himself.

It had nothing to do with the brown hair tucked behind her ears or her pretty face not looking surprised that he and Caro were outside her door.

"Hi."

Such a simple word could punch him in the gut? But only when spoken by Joelle. "Hi. Caro has something she wants to give you."

"Here, Miss Joelle. We were at the store, and Daddy said I could buy this for you. He didn't even make me use my allowance. He paid his own money for it." Caro held out the plant.

Joelle took it from her. "This is beautiful. Let's see, an African violet. I love it, thank you."

William couldn't help but notice her words sounded forced. Foolishness came over him as he stood behind his hopeful daughter. His daughter whose hands were now empty. He handed her the bunny. "Here's Mr. PJ."

Caro instantly hugged her bunny.

Joelle motioned for them to come in. "Would Mr. PJ like a cookie? I just pulled some out of the oven so they're still warm. I even have milk." Joelle stepped aside, and he didn't have time to refuse before Caro made her way into the living room.

Time to run interference. "We can't stay." Did he notice a flicker of disappointment in Joelle's gaze?

She nodded. "That's okay. Come on back while I grab a container to put some cookies in."

"Yay, cookies! They smell good. Don't they smell good, Mr. PJ?" Caro looked at her bunny as she talked.

William smiled as he followed his daughter and Joelle. Dress pants and slippers. Nice combo.

His heart tugged at the genuineness of Joelle. No faking with her. He felt like she was who she portrayed herself to be.

Unlike Cassidy. Caro's mom was everything she said she wasn't.

Cassidy. He hadn't thought too much about her lately. Except for when he was thinking of Caro and keeping her safe. Cassidy could have nothing to do with Caro.

"Certainly you have time for one cookie." Joelle didn't wait for him to answer as she grabbed a couple of napkins. She placed a cookie on one of them and handed it to Caro. "Here's one for you, and one more," she added another cookie on top of the first one, "for Mr. PJ, of course."

Caro took her cookies and Mr. PJ to the table. Joelle poured milk into a juice glass. She looked at William. "There's a card with instructions stuck in the planter. Can you read me those while I get you a cookie? That's a good trade, right? You tell me how to take care of the plant, and I feed you?"

Words stuck in his throat. Joelle placed the glass of milk in front of Caro then placed two more napkins on the counter.

A buzzer gave him a brief reprieve. Joelle seemed to forget about her request as she pulled a baking sheet out of the oven. She was an expert at spooning more dough onto the now-cooled baking sheet before shoving it into the oven.

Caro was busy feeding Mr. PJ and sipping her milk.

"No instructions, no cookie." Joelle looked his way then laughed. She took a couple of steps, moving closer to him. Her fresh scent replaced any cookie scent and for the first time in a long time he prayed.

"I'm no good with plants," she whispered. "I'm afraid I'll kill it before the week is out."

Her sweet breath and closeness fell over him, through him, causing him to hope for the first time in a long time.

Hope that he could love again.

As she returned to her task he returned to reality. Loving Joelle could never happen. But the fact that the thought even entered his mind left him baffled and afraid.

Baffled at the effect she was having on him.

And afraid that if he were to read the instructions, she might learn one of his many secrets.

*****

He looked stunned.

She felt stunned.

What was she thinking moving so close to him? Did she really think she would stay neutral to him? She was inviting danger and acting like she didn't care.

Busying herself with placing cookies on the napkins, she saw him move toward the counter where she had set the plant. He plucked the instruction card out of the planter. Flecks of dirt fell on the counter.

Looking at the words, he squinted.

"You're not old enough for reading glasses, are you?" She laughed after she spoke, but he didn't join in.

"Making fun of an old man, huh? I'll have none of that. Kiddo," he walked to Caro. "School's in session. Show Joelle what a good reader you are."

He handed her the card which she promptly dropped on the table. "Daddy. It's dirty. I don't want dirt in my cookies."

"What happened to my little girl? You used to eat mud pies." He picked up the instruction card and walked to the sink. "Do you mind?" He looked at Joelle but nodded toward the faucet.

"No."

As he ran the card under the water for a few seconds she pulled a paper towel off the roll, handing it to him when he shut off the water. "When I was checking the mail today a woman asked me about your house."

William shifted his attention from the card to her. "What about our house?"

She shrugged. "She had a copy of the listing when it was for sale. I informed her that the house had been sold. She seemed disappointed. Really disappointed. I guess you bought it just in time."

His gaze narrowed, his mouth a firm, tight line.

He was obviously thinking, but she wasn't sure what was running through his mind. For some reason, she felt like she needed to put him at ease. "I didn't tell her anything about you. Or Caro. Or the renovation."

Walking slowly to the pantry where the trash can was he kept his gaze on her. "That's nice of you. I don't need strangers knowing information about me." After opening the door he dropped the paper towel, which he had crushed in his fist, into the trash. "Or Caro. Especially Caro."

"I know. Trust me, Caro was my first thought."

Ignoring the fact that he hadn't read her the instructions on how to take care of the plant, she handed him the napkin with the cookie setting on it. "Here. You win."

A slow smile spread across his face. "I didn't realize I could lose."

Ignoring her heart which was telling her she could lose her heart to that smile, she watched him take a bite of the cookie, then close his eyes. When he opened them he smiled. "This," he held up the portion he hadn't eaten, "is amazing."

"There are things I do well. And others," she nodded toward the plant, "not so well. I may need some help." She quickly scanned the counter for the instruction card, which she didn't find. Could William have accidentally thrown it out?

"Caro loves plants. She seems to have a green thumb." He wiped his mouth with the napkin. "Thank you for the cookie. Caro. Grab Mr. PJ. We need to go."

The sound of the chair scooting indicated Caro was listening to her dad. She brought her trash with her. Joelle reached in front of William grabbing Caro's napkin. "I'll take this."

Opening the door to the pantry Joelle started looking through the wadded up paper towels in the trash can.

"Lose something?" William asked.

"Did you toss the instructions for that plant? Accidentally, of course? I didn't see them on the counter."

She looked away from her task long enough to see him glancing around the kitchen.

"I may have. Sorry about that."

As she unwadded another napkin, the card fell out. "Ah. Here it is. Now the plant has a chance to live. Maybe." She dropped what trash she had in her hands into the can. She closed the lid, carefully holding onto the card.

She shut the pantry door. Caro was playing with Mr. PJ in the doorway while William stared at her refrigerator.

The cat magnet in particular.

Joelle set the instruction card next to the plant and joined William. "That's a Himalayan cat, like Misty. My mom was such a softie for—"

William grabbed the paper with the phone number. "Where did you get this?"

"That woman I told you about. She wanted me to call her if the house came back on the market again. Or if I found out you were renting. Which I knew you weren't, but like I said, I didn't want to tell her things that weren't my place to tell."

If Joelle thought his eyes were dark the first day she met him, she didn't know what she would call them now. His blacker than black gaze almost made her step back.

"Tell me every word you told this woman." He crushed the small paper in his hand. "Every. Word."

Chapter Five

Pain seared through his gut as he fisted the crumpled paper. Cassidy had asked about his house. His mind scrambled that she might have seen Caro.

His anger flared.

Cassidy had been just steps away from what was most precious to him. His daughter.

He set the number on the counter then reached out to Caro who was still playing with Mr. PJ, oblivious to the danger that had just entered her life. He grabbed her hand.

She looked at him and smiled. The connection calmed him, helped his brain return to somewhat reasonable mode rather than wanting to kick in the door of Joelle's refrigerator.

Calm.

Shutting his eyes he breathed deep.

"I. . ." Joelle started.

Opening his eyes he looked at his neighbor. The unknowing accomplice. "Joelle." He shifted his gaze to Caro. "I know I just asked you a question, but I wasn't thinking clearly at the moment. Would you like to come over for coffee around nine tonight?"

"Nine? That's kind of—"

"I know it's a late, but it will give me time to feed Caro dinner and put her to bed." He refused to talk about Cassidy in front of Caro, but he had to know what went down between Cassidy and Joelle.

Her expression said she'd caught on to his plan. "Sure. I'll see you at nine."

"Come on, Kiddo, Mr. PJ. Let's go."

As Caro gave Joelle a hug, William kept his hand on Caro's shoulder. He wasn't letting go of his girl.

It about took everything out of him to walk out of Joelle's house without knowing what words Cassidy spoke to Joelle, but he always guarded Caro.

Always.

And he'd find his answers in a couple of hours.

"Daddy, you're holding my hand too tight."

He lessened his grip as they walked across the front yard, realizing he wasn't doing a very good job regarding the calm aspect. "I'm sorry. Better?"

"Yes."

He kept mindful of his grip as his gaze darted over the street, sidewalk. He knew he was walking faster than normal but Caro was keeping up. He needed Caro in the house.

Now.

As they walked up the steps of the porch, headlights illuminated the porch. Instinctively, he blocked any view of his daughter. The car drove by at normal speed. No slowing, no stopping. The darkness once again surrounded them.

He was paranoid.

He had every right to be.

Cassidy was in town.

*****

Could time move any slower?

Certainly she could head over five minutes early.

Sitting in the breakfast area, she rolled the bottoms of her jeans up before slipping her feet into her black boots. Her black sweater would keep her warm as she walked to his house so she didn't need a coat. Something she might forget and leave at their house.

Like her scarf was still at their house.

Making a note to remember to ask about her scarf, she stood and picked up the container of cookies she packed. William's intense reaction to the phone number on her refrigerator caused both of them to forget about her offer to send cookies home with them.

The number still hung on her refrigerator, its blue numbers on the crinkled white paper looking harmless.

William's eyes had looked the exact opposite of harmless.

Staring close at the number she saw the area code, four-o-four. Tucking the container of cookies under her arm, she pulled her phone out of her pocket and searched the Internet. Georgia.

The Deep South.

So he was from Georgia.

And someone followed him here.

As she shoved her phone back into her pocket, a sense of foreboding ran through her.

William was super protective regarding Caro. His hair and eyes were dark like the night.

The woman who gave her the number had blonde hair. Caro had blonde hair.

Joelle locked her door before making her way across the front yards. She guessed the good news was that she didn't reveal any information to the woman about William or Caro. The bad news was that she had more than likely been talking to William's ex, Caro's mother.

*****

William opened the door before Joelle could knock or ring the doorbell. Caro had just fallen asleep, and he was sure the doorbell would jar her awake.

The porch light cast a sexy shadow on Joelle, but his brain didn't process fully what that meant as he was focused on one thing only.

Cassidy.

"Hi. Thanks for coming over so late. Come on in." Joelle stepped into his house. "Excuse the mess. We'll go back to the kitchen where everything isn't in such disarray."

He refused to think about how she simply looked like she belonged here. That was a weird thought, especially since the living room was in such shambles.

"So it's begun." Her eyes scanned the room slowly. "I will say that wallpaper had to go."

He smiled, wanting to forget the reason she was here. "No doubt."

Leading the way to the kitchen, he knew by the sound of her boots on the hardwoods she was following him. Her gait was slow, though, like she knew the subject they were going to discuss was unpleasant.

Or maybe she was checking out the house wall by wall seeing if he had made any changes yet.

"I brought the cookies I promised you guys earlier."

He turned as they entered the small space that was the kitchen. "Thanks. You can set them on the counter."

He watched her while her gaze once again perused his house.

A house he knew she knew well.

"Since I asked you over for coffee, would you like a cup?"

She waved her hand. "I'm good, thank you. Coffee would have me awake for a long time, and I have an eight o'clock appointment tomorrow morning."

Coffee and work weren't what they needed to discuss. "Tell me about the woman. What did she look like?" His heart hammered at the response he knew he was going to receive. He wondered if she'd changed much.

"Long, blonde hair. Thin. Pretty. She's your ex, isn't she? Caro's mother."

He guessed it wasn't that hard to figure out. "I felt like I was sucker punched when I saw her number on your refrigerator. She's dangerous, Joelle. She can't get near Caro. Did you say anything about my daughter to her?"

She shook her head. "No. Like I said before, I didn't reveal any information. Not who bought the house, not that it was a man with a daughter. But thinking back on the conversation she was trying to draw it out of me. She said more than once, 'I bet an old lady with a cat bought the house.' That was probably her way of trying to get me to say who really bought the house."

Relief and anger harbored in him. "Thank you for not saying anything. But it doesn't change the fact that she knows we're here. She knows where Caro is."

Joelle leaned against the counter, comfortable like. "You don't have to tell me anything, but she didn't look dangerous at all. She was pretty and bubbly."

"Because she was probably high." Memories of finding the pill bottles set him on even a darker edge. Bubbly wasn't coming anywhere near his daughter.

"Oh." Joelle paused. "You're from Georgia? She came from Georgia to find you? That's a long way."

Had there been more conversation? "She told you that?"

"No. I looked up the area code. It's a Georgia number. That's what you meant when you said the Deep South?"

"Yes. I haven't lived there in a few years. And I'm not sure where Cassidy has been living." He hated being on the defense. His family in Georgia were supposed to be keeping tabs on her. Letting him know if they ever saw or heard from her.

"Cassidy. So that's her name."

"Cassidy Caroline Cambridge. We dated all through high school. She was the prom queen, head cheerleader. I couldn't figure out why she wanted to date a punk like me. I worked with my dad while she went off to UGA. Cassidy was like a whirlwind, you just got caught up in her. I figured while she was at college she'd find another guy."

"Did she?" Could it be Caro wasn't William's daughter?

"No. Between her junior and senior year of college, I got her pregnant. I wanted to get married. I mean she talked a lot about us getting married for years. But she said no." He'd been so naïve back then. A mistake he wouldn't repeat.

"So, you stayed in the picture though, obviously."

"Nothing will keep me from my daughter. Turns out Cassidy was strung out on pills. I found out when I needed to take care of Caro one night because Cassidy was sick. Found the hidden pills. Her addiction. When I confronted Cassidy about it, she freaked. The next couple of years consisted of legal battles, rehab facilities for Cassidy. After four failed attempts at getting clean, the judge awarded me custody. Cassidy vowed to get Caro back. But then Cassidy left town and we didn't hear from her. That's when I started flipping houses. Moving around. Until Cassidy is clean and straight for a long time, I don't need her around Caro. Even then, I may not let her."

"What kind of visitation does she have? Legally."

"None. Well, I take that back. Supervised visits only until she was clean for a full year. Then we were to go back to court for a hearing. But she never got clean, and she left town. That was five years ago."

"Yet she's here. In Devon Park. Asking about your house."

His brain scrambled with the unknown. "I can't take a chance with Caro. If Cassidy is up to no good, I have to find out. I guess I'll have to call her. Confront her. Remind her of the judge's orders."

"So legally, she could see Caro. With you around, of course."

Darkness invaded his brain. "Not happening. It would only confuse Caro."

"Agreed. Is that why you homeschool her? So she's not out of your sight for long?"

Was he that transparent? He thought he was clever at his methods of madness. "I like to know she's safe. It's as simple as that."

"I get it. Totally. I wish there was something I could do."

William soaked in her words. Words that were probably hollow. In his experience people said those words all the time out of concern and habit. Yet, when you tell them there was something they could do, a look of fear came into their eyes.

Was Joelle different?

Only one way to find out. "There is something you could do. If you don't mind."

Chapter Six

Joelle's heart jumped. "You think I can help?"

"You can do me a favor. And yes, it would help a lot."

A sense of belonging ran through her. She tried not to make more of it than she needed to. Of course she would have that feeling standing in Mrs. B's kitchen. She'd always belonged at Mrs. B's house.

Joelle was just as sure she wouldn't have that feeling regarding William. He was so private and guarded. Even though she now knew why, she didn't feel like he was going to open the floodgates of his life to her. If he asked her for anything it would be so he could protect Caro. "What's the favor?"

He hesitated. Either he was trying to word his favor right, or he was rethinking it. His gaze locked with hers. She trembled at the intensity. William Scott was a passionate man. She imagined he didn't do anything halfway.

"Call Cassidy."

Her eyebrows raised and she knew her eyes widened. She purposefully widened them more as she stared. "Why?"

"First, ask to meet with her. Tell her you have some information on the home. But offer to have coffee with her in town. Don't have her come to your house."

"Okay. . ."

"When you meet with her tell her you found out the house is being renovated and might be on the market at the first of the year. Then see what she says. How she reacts."

Realization dawned on Joelle. "I get it. I'll see where her interest is focused. The house itself, which we know it won't be, or how I found out the information. Did I meet my neighbor, who is my neighbor, right?"

"You've got it. And see how she's acting. Can you tell if somebody is high?"

"I can't say I've been around it a lot."

"Me either. She got away with it in front of me for years. Just look for anything unusual. But tell her nothing about me or Caro."

"Of course not."

He ran his hand through his hair. As his black hair fell past his fingers, Joelle connected to his helplessness. Was William ever vulnerable? If so, he wasn't likely to admit it. He seemed like a proud man. But not proud in a bad way. Just in a way that said he could take care of his own by himself.

And he would.

She firmly believed that about him.

It was sad in a way. Joelle guessed that no one would be able to break past the heart that guarded his little girl. He'd been betrayed by Cassidy, and William didn't seem like a second chance kind of guy.

"It means a lot to me that you would help."

His voice broke a little as he spoke.

Witnessing the small crack in William, Joelle's heart raced. "It means a lot to me that you would ask."

He half-smiled as he uncrossed his arms and pushed away from the counter.

She straightened taking a step forward, her gaze never leaving his. Would she ever slip into that tiny crack she witnessed moments ago?

Would she want to?

His arms slipped around her waist.

She placed her arms around him, resting her chin on his shoulder. She never imagined this as she walked across the front yard earlier.

"Thanks for helping. Protecting Caro is my life."

William's words whispered their way into her heart.

*****

Hugging pretty Joelle was unexpected.

And nice.

She smelled nice, felt silky-soft, and could snag his heart in a minute if he wasn't careful.

And he had to be careful.

He had no idea why he trusted her, except that he didn't have a choice. That phone number on her refrigerator could be his downfall.

Ending their embrace, he swore it wouldn't be. Cassidy would leave here never seeing him or Caro if he had his way.

"I haven't hugged anyone but Caro in a long time. Thank you." Why he felt the need to explain his actions, he had no idea. Except that he didn't want her expecting hugs from him on a regular basis.

"Hugs are good for the soul. Mrs. B used to tell me that. My family wasn't into hugging, so I was always overwhelmed by Mrs. B's affections. And her cooking. We spent a lot of time in her kitchen."

William wished he could see spending time with Joelle. But he never became involved. He hadn't lied to her when he said he hadn't hugged anyone in a long time. He hadn't even thought of dating since he and Caro started moving around.

Their adventure, Caro called it.

But Joelle had a way of bringing different kind of thoughts into his mind. Thoughts of sticking around. Thoughts of hugging.

Joelle was as dangerous as Cassidy.

But Joelle was a good kind of dangerous.

And that was bad. He needed to get back on track. Focus on the real reason Joelle was here. "Are you going to call her tomorrow?"

Her. He didn't even like saying her name.

"Yes. I have appointments all morning but I'll call her around lunch. Do you mind giving me your number? I can keep you posted." She pulled her phone out of her jeans pocket.

Her request startled him. No one but his family and business acquaintances had his number. Giving Joelle his number would indicate she had a place in his life. It would mean more than he could commit to right now. "I'm always here. If I'm gone, it's not for long. I'll catch you in person, if that's okay. For now." Why did he add that last bit? Like his stance might change?

Joelle stared at him for a moment, smiling. After a few moments, her smile turned into a straight line. "You're not kidding. You aren't giving me your number."

"It's not a long walk." Now he smiled, trying to make light of his decision. Which was not a light decision at all.

She shrugged, shoving her phone back in her pocket. "Your call. No pun intended."

He laughed. A real laugh. Another aspect of Joelle that he found he liked. She could momentarily make him forget his troubles. Which was another reason he couldn't become close to her.

He might lose focus. "You're funny. That's cool."

"It's a coping mechanism. It's not every day I ask a guy for his number and get turned down. To be honest, I don't usually ask."

Her eyes had a twinkle to them, her tone was playful. He needed to be careful. "You kind of go with the flow, don't you?"

"I'm flexible. Hey, I better be getting home. It's late. I'll let you know tomorrow if I reach Cassidy. I guess I'll come over? Knock on your door?"

And I'll see your beautiful face. Shift thoughts. "Ring the bell. It's really loud, and I'll hear you no matter what I'm doing."

They walked through the house to the front door. This time he followed her. He liked the view.

He liked Joelle.

The thought slammed him. Threatened to take his breath at the absurdity of it. He simply needed her to find out what Cassidy was doing. Misplaced feelings? Something like that. He refused to acknowledge anything else. Needs were different than wants.

Very different.

He opened the front door for her, trying to ignore her scent, her hair, her everything. Thinking the cool air might help, he stepped onto the porch.

Reaching back into the house, he flipped off the porch light then pulled the door shut. "Sorry about the light. I feel safer with it off. You understand."

"I do. But I can't ever imagine you feeling unsafe. Cassidy must really threaten you."

"Caro. She threatens Caro. I couldn't care less about me."

Joelle turned toward him. They already stood close together.

"Maybe I should care about you."

Joelle's words caught him off guard. "Don't do that. Don't."

She took a step back. "Don't forget about you, William. You need caring for just like Caro."

The cool night surrounded him as he watched her walk away, her voice lingering in his mind. Caring for? He needed caring for?

Caro was all he needed for now.

Although, he must say, Joelle was someone he could care about.

He wasn't sure if his heart could handle that.

Chapter Seven

The dreaded number went to voice mail as Joelle put the finishing touches on her ham and cheese sandwich. Shoving the mustard back into the refrigerator, she left a short message asking Cassidy to call her.

Of course Joelle didn't use Cassidy's name.

Joelle's first mission would be to get Cassidy to reveal her name. That way there was less chance of Joelle slipping up causing Cassidy to wonder how Joelle knew her name.

Even through her morning tutoring appointments Joelle found herself thinking of William and his dilemma. She couldn't imagine what he'd been going through the last few years. He and Caro had such a great relationship, a special bond between father and daughter.

He felt threatened by Cassidy. It was natural. And he had every reason not to want Cassidy near Caro if she was abusing pills.

Just as Joelle finished her bite, her cell phone buzzed indicating she had a call.

Cassidy.

Joelle's fingers shook slightly as she pushed the button. "Hello?"

"Hi. I missed a call from you and you left a message wanting me to call you? This is the woman who was interested in the house next door to you."

No name. "Yes. My name is Joelle."

"Did you have some information?"

So Cassidy wanted to play a game. "Possibly. Can you meet me in town around three? There's a coffee shop called DP Perks."

"You can't tell me on the phone?"

Honestly, Joelle hadn't thought this far out. Hadn't thought Cassidy would object. "I have something I wanted to show you. If that's okay."

Hesitation. Then a "Sure. I guess. I'll see you there. Bye."

"Bye." But the call had dropped.

Or Joelle had been hung up on.

After glancing at the clock she grabbed her sandwich and headed outside. She had half an hour before her next client would arrive. Since William wouldn't give out his super secret phone number, she'd go and tell him in person what her plans were for meeting Cassidy.

And ask him what she should take.

After all, she promised Cassidy she wanted to show her something.

It took him a minute to come to the door. She was thankful she had finished her sandwich while walking over, otherwise she probably would have dropped it.

A skin-tight T-shirt, low hung jeans, boots, and a brown belt succeeded in accentuating all of William's finest features. In fact, she didn't think he had a feature that wasn't fine.

"Hi." His voice another fine feature.

"Hello. I wanted. . . Is Caro around?" She lowered her voice.

He shook his head. "She's actually napping. Come on in."

"I can't stay long. I have a client coming shortly. I wanted to let you know that I'm meeting Cassidy at DP Perks at three o'clock."

He nodded. "Okay. Cool."

"Maybe not so cool. She asked me why I couldn't tell her what I needed to tell her on the phone. So, I said I had something I needed to show her."

"Okay. Good thinking."

"Except I have nothing to show her."

He bit his lip. "I see."

Joelle saw his lips. Her thoughts drifted far away from Cassidy and lingered on what it would be like to kiss those lips.

The lips she'd never kiss.

"What about some other home listings."

William was a quick thinker. "That might work. I'll tell her about the renovation, but tell her I printed these listings in case she can't wait."

"That's mighty friendly of you." He winked.

"It is considering she won't give me her name."

"No?"

"Not on the phone. I said 'my name is Joelle' as a lead in, and she just asked me a question like I hadn't said anything."

"She's up to something. I'm sure of it."

"She's being careful."

"She needs to careful herself right out of this town. I do appreciate this, Joelle. I really do."

The way he spoke her name reminded her of melting chocolate. So yummy. "I haven't really done anything. Except back myself into a corner. Thanks for helping me out of that. I'm going to run home and start printing those listings."

"Why don't you come over for dinner? Caro always plays afterwards and we can talk."

She knew William was issuing the invitation so he could find out what happened with Cassidy. He didn't have to include dinner. But the way she saw it, that was who William was. Nice, considerate, friendly. No ulterior motives with him. "I'd love to. Can I bring anything?"

"Just don't bring Cassidy."

Hurt jolted Joelle. "You don't—"

"I'm sorry. I don't think you would do that. I know you wouldn't."

Joelle backed away.

He took a step, too.

And then another.

Before she could speak he wrapped her in his arms. "I'm sorry."

She longed to relax into his hug. Her body eased close to his, his scent washing over her. She gripped his waist. Breathing in William meant rattled nerves and flourishing hopes. Neither of which she could afford. "It's okay. But I need to run. I'll see you later."

She slipped out of his arms, but his pinky found hers. "Six is good."

Unlatching her pinky, Joelle pretended she didn't hear his words as she ran down the stairs. That way if she decided she didn't want to come for dinner she would have an excuse.

Hinting that Joelle would bring Cassidy to them indicated he wouldn't ever let anyone into his family, his heart.

Which was good, Joelle thought as she brushed a tear from the corner of her eye. Ready-made families weren't her thing.

And William was a good reminder of that fact.

*****

At three-thirty Joelle sipped the last of her coffee and stood.

Cassidy wasn't going to show.

As Joelle took a step away from the table though, Cassidy walked in. Breezed in really. She didn't smile when she saw Joelle, simply floated her way over to the table.

Something was different about Cassidy and Joelle's radar went on full alert.

"I'm sorry I'm so late. I had an appointment to get my hair done and the gal was running late. But she's such a sweetheart, you know? I couldn't even pretend to be mad at her. But here I am. I guess you were about to leave."

Cassidy's southern flow of words threatened to overwhelm Joelle. Cassidy spoke fast and sincere all while smiling. This was a different Cassidy than the gal who approached her at her home. And not just because her hair was a little shorter and blonder.

"I figured you were delayed. But I'm glad you made it." Joelle sat, hoping Cassidy would do the same. Joelle held out her hand. "Hi, I'm Joelle."

Cassidy shook Joelle's hand for about one second. "Do you mind if I order a coffee? I'll be happy to buy you another one." Cassidy nodded toward Joelle's cup.

"I'm good. Thank you for asking."

Still, no name.

Joelle kept a wary eye on Cassidy while trying not to be obvious about it. Tapping the manila folder, Joelle waited while Cassidy appeared to charm the young man behind the counter. Although unable to hear the conversation, Joelle couldn't miss the huge smile the young man boasted or the fact that he kept moving his gaze downward, like he was embarrassed.

Physically, even with the new hairstyle, this looked like the same woman who asked Joelle about William's house, but the personality seemed to have taken a happy pill.

Which was what William suspected.

Disappointment filled Joelle. She'd like to think Cassidy had it all together. That's why she would chance coming a long way to see her daughter.

And William.

William talked about Cassidy and Caro, but not too much about him and Cassidy. Sure he revealed their history, but he never indicated his feelings for her now. If he had any.

The fact that she had been strung out on pills upset him. But Joelle knew couples who had gone through similar issues. It didn't mean you stopped loving the person.

You simply stopped trusting them.

Joelle wished there weren't as many people in the coffee shop talking. The barista would call Cassidy's name shortly.

But he didn't.

Before he could, Cassidy raised her hand like she was in school. "I believe that's mine. Mocha latte. Thank you."

The barista nodded then handed Cassidy her cup.

Cassidy slid into the chair across from Joelle. "Thanks again for waiting. So you have news about the house for me?"

Direct. That was the word Joelle would use to describe Cassidy. "Um, some. But I wanted to bring you these listings." Joelle shoved the folder toward Cassidy. "Here are some houses that I thought you might like."

Cassidy sipped her drink while not even glancing at the folder. She kept her hands around the cup, so there was no way Joelle could read her name. "What about the house next door to you?"

Talk about conversation take over. Joelle needed to reign in Cassidy. "It's actually being flipped. So it will be on the market again in a few months. For a higher price, I'm sure."

A thoughtful expression came over Cassidy. "So you've met the person who's flipping the house?"

Nervousness caused Joelle to hesitate. She did not want to reveal too much information. "I've heard some talk. And there's been construction-type things going on at the house."

"Have you been inside?"

Joelle relaxed somewhat. This question would be easy to answer. "Sure. I spent a lot of time in the house while I was growing up. . ." Her eagerness at answering the question caused her to overlook the amount of information she was giving Cassidy regarding her own life.

"So you've lived in your house a long time?"

"Yes." No need to reveal her recent move back. Let Cassidy come to her own conclusions.

"You probably know your neighbors then."

"Some." Joelle had to be careful here. Cassidy had yet to even acknowledge the manila folder Joelle had given her.

"You know William then."

Joelle tried not to let the surge that went through her at the mention of William's name show. "William?" She repeated his name as a technique to stall Cassidy until Joelle could decide if she wanted to own up to knowing him or not.

She and William hadn't talked about this.

Why didn't he warn her that Cassidy was so forward?

"Yes, William Scott. I looked up the records, and it shows that he bought the house."

Now thoroughly confused, Joelle batted her empty coffee cup between her two index fingers. At least if Cassidy owned up to knowing William, Joelle knew what battle to fight. "I believe a man did buy the house."

"So, he's flipping it. You said it would be for sale again in a few months?"

"Just an assumption. But I did bring you some more listings. Or maybe you've already found something?"

Cassidy pushed the folder back to Joelle. "I've decided to rent. Just for six months. I hated the thought of being rushed. And now, it looks like everything might work out perfectly."

Perfectly for whom?

William wouldn't like the news that Cassidy would be in Devon Park for at least six months.

Joelle took a chance and really stared at Cassidy. She was beautiful. Joelle could see that Caro took after Cassidy in more ways than one. Her eyes, her smile.

Cassidy's eyes were clear and normal. Deep brown and curious like Caro's.

"He still wears the same cologne."

"What?" Uneasiness crept through Joelle.

"William. He still wears the same cologne. I can smell it on you."

Chapter Eight

Joelle resisted the urge to smell her sleeve. "I don't know what you are talking about."

"You know exactly what I'm talking about."

Joelle stood. "You won't even tell me your name, so I think this conversation is over."

"Cassidy. And I didn't give you my name because I knew you already knew it. You have to help me."

Picking up the manila folder, Joelle realized she had wasted her time printing those listings. Cassidy had set her up all along. "I can't help you."

After she dropped her cup into the trash, Joelle walked outside, the cool air taking her breath. That Indian summer had spoiled them all. Now, the real Ohio weather was showing up.

"Wait. Please?"

Cassidy's voice tugged at Joelle's heart. This was Caro's mother. Joelle stopped walking.

"Thank you." Cassidy stood next to her. "Can you help me?"

"No. I can't. It's not my place."

"I want to see Caroline. She's my daughter." Either the cold wind had done a number on Cassidy or those were real tears at the corner of her eyes.

Joelle shook her head. "Again, it's not my place."

"Talk to William for me, please? I would never hurt Caroline. I've been clean for almost two years now. Will you tell him that?"

"I don't know. I just don't know." Joelle started walking, half expecting Cassidy to follow her. But she didn't. Joelle quickly jumped in her car and started driving.

How had she become so involved so fast? This situation was really none of her business, yet here she was in the middle of all the business.

It was almost five by the time Joelle walked into the house. She purposefully avoided looking at William's place. Joelle took her jacket off and hung it up. As she went to take her sweater off, the scent hit her.

William's scent.

The giveaway scent.

Memories of their hug, their arms wrapped around each other, lingered in her mind.

Joelle grabbed her jacket back out of the closet. No use waiting until six. Joelle would explode if she didn't tell William right away what had happened.

Spying Misty sleeping on the back of the couch stopped Joelle at the front door. The cat was always sleeping. Of course she had some age to her, but Joelle wasn't sure what normal sleep times for cats looked like. She'd never had a cat before, didn't realize the laziness of their lifestyle.

Joelle wondered what it would be like to lounge around all day and night.

It didn't sound like much of a life to her.

Joelle made double sure the door was locked as she left for William's house. After all, Cassidy knew where she lived.

That thought unsettled her a bit as she walked across the front yards.

William met her on the porch. "How did it go?"

Joelle shoved her hands in her jacket pocket. "Badly. She knows you live here. She knows I know you."

William's eyes darkened. "Tell me the conversation."

Joelle relayed what she remembered. "Then she told me that you still wear the same cologne and she smelled it on me."

Shifting his gaze right, he bit his lower lip and shook his head. "She's right. I have worn the same cologne for a long time. And we, you and I. . ."

"We hugged. Closely. For a decent amount of time." Thoughts of being in his arms warmed Joelle. She knew the hug wasn't something that would happen again, but she could cherish her memories if she wanted.

"Then what? Did she start questioning you?"

"Not really. She wanted me to tell you she's been clean for two years. And she wants to see Caro. I did not promise I would relay these things to you. I never acknowledged that I even knew you or that you lived here. But of course she knows."

William kept glancing back, probably making sure Caro wasn't lingering around the front door.

What it would feel like to love like that. To care that much about someone. Joelle was ready to find out. But not with a ready-made family. "My honest opinion is that she isn't a danger. I mean she asked me to talk to you. She wouldn't have done that if she was up to something terrible. Agreed?"

He shook his head. "Not agreed. Cassidy is capable of anything. In fact, I have another favor to ask of you. It's a really big favor. One I can't believe I'm about to ask you."

Joelle took a breath, thankful for the chill in the air. Otherwise, the flush of her face would be more heated. "Go ahead."

"I would like Caro to spend the night with you."

*****

William couldn't believe those words came out of his mouth. But he didn't trust Cassidy at all. The thought of Cassidy and Caro in the same room gutted him.

He couldn't chance it.

"Just for tonight. I wouldn't put it past Cassidy to show up here. She's like that."

His heart ached at the thought of not having Caro in the house. It ached even more thinking about Cassidy conversing with Caro. Spending the night at Joelle's was the lesser of two evils. Not that there was anything evil about Joelle.

Not at all.

Joelle was kind-hearted, nice, and everything cool that a woman could be. Nothing like strung-out, pushy Cassidy. He couldn't trust her word about being clean.

He could trust Joelle with his daughter.

"Sure. That will be fine. I'll hype it up, talk about a slumber party. She can bring Mr. PJ, of course."

He ignored the nudging of his heart. Joelle cared.

She paid attention and she cared.

That was a first to him regarding women. Women other than his family.

"Let's go in. Give Caro the good news. But we'll wait until after we eat. Otherwise she'll be too excited to eat."

He held the door for Joelle. His half-demoed living room seemed to mock him. An indication of the unfinished business in his life. Pushing that thought down, he indicated to Joelle to head for the kitchen. "Kiddo! We have company."

"Coming!"

Standing close to Joelle, probably too close, he whispered in her ear. "Thanks, again, Joelle."

"Miss Joelle!"

Caro came running into the kitchen full force.

William quickly stepped away from Joelle, not wanting to give Caro any false ideas. He hadn't dated at all and wasn't sure how Caro would react if he started. He had talked to her about Cassidy a long time ago, told her that her mother was very sick and had to stay at a place that could make her better.

But that was years ago, and Caro had never mentioned her mother again.

William liked it that way.

"Hi, Caro. It's good to see you." Joelle gave Caro a hug.

"Are you eating dinner with us? Please?"

Joelle nodded. "I am. Thank you for the invitation."

Caro's smile could light up the world. "You're welcome. Daddy promised to cook hot dogs on the grill."

William leaned against the counter, taking in his girl and her interaction with Joelle. Caro took to Joelle fast. That was unusual for her usually reserved nature. But something about Joelle brought out the best in Caro.

It was nice to see.

Even though he homeschooled Caro, he always found a church to go to once they moved into a town. He wanted Caro to have friends, and he had found church people to be friendly. And most of them didn't ask questions.

Too many, anyway.

He wasn't very good with questions.

Or maybe he simply wasn't good with answers.

"Grilling in October? That's different."

Joelle's tone was easy, fun. He liked that simple things surprised her. "We grill a lot. Our kitchens are in demo mode so often grilling is our way of life, isn't it, Kiddo?"

Caro nodded. "I love Daddy's hot dogs. And we get to have potato chips when we have hot dogs. That's the only time. Except when we have guests."

"Caro, you're giving away all our secrets." He found he liked having Joelle in on a few things that he and Caro shared. But she couldn't be in on everything. "French fries don't do so well on the grill."

"I can see that. But I do love potato chips."

She pushed her hair behind her ears, looking natural in this environment. Way too many thoughts of Joelle could occupy his mind. And he couldn't lose focus on Cassidy and the harm she could cause. *Focus, William.* "I'll get dinner started then."

"I can help set the table or something."

William grabbed a package of hot dogs from the refrigerator. "Do you want to tell Joelle another one of our secrets?"

Caro cocked her head, like she was thinking. "Which one?"

William's heart beat fast as he realized he left Caro wide open to tell Joelle anything. Caro's thought process didn't work like an adults. "About setting the table. What kind of plates do we use?"

"Paper."

"You got it. Why don't you show Joelle where they are and you two can start that while I fire up the grill."

Grabbing a plate and a set of tongs, he shoved the hot dogs under his arm and stepped outside. The night was clear, yet no stars were visible as they were too far into the city. Taking the cover off the new grill, he turned the knob on the propane tank, then started the grill.

While he was thankful for this opportunity to take a breather, he could only relax momentarily. Cassidy was too loose of a cannon to let him truly relax. She could show up here at any time.

He actually bet money that she would.

That's why he needed to have Caro gone. But he didn't want to confuse her. Although she'd asked many times, she'd never spent the night away. He still wasn't sure how he was going to tell her she was staying at Joelle's, but he was sure he'd figure it out.

A twig snapped, and the hairs on his neck began to rise.

He pulled out his phone, turned it to flashlight mode, and scanned the backyard. "Hello?"

To the right he caught a fleeting glimpse of a tabby cat escaping into bushes at the edge of his property. He breathed a sigh, moving his phone light toward the grill.

He could not let Cassidy turn him into a paranoid freak. Getting to the task at hand, he focused on the sizzle of the hot dogs as they hit the heated grid. He thought of Joelle.

Joelle, who probably had no idea she sizzled.

Or made him sizzle.

Chapter Nine

As Caro shoved the last potato chip in her mouth, William started second-guessing his decision to let her stay at Joelle's. According to Joelle, Cassidy had a six-month lease. What was he going to do? Caro couldn't stay at Joelle's every night for six months.

But for tonight?

With all that today had brought, tonight would be perfect timing for Cassidy to try to wreck his life. Plus it would give him time to think. Time to plan how he would handle this Cassidy situation.

After all, it would have to be handled. Especially if she really had been clean for two years.

But Cassidy knew everything about him. His faults. His struggles. If she knew or found out he was homeschooling Caro, he had no idea what she would do.

Would she have a claim in court? How many judges would let a man with dyslexia homeschool a child?

Caro was smart. She read at a grade level higher than hers. Surely that would count for something. And Joelle. What would she do if she knew about his disability? She was a tutor after all. How would she view his homeschooling venture?

Why did he care what her views were?

He pushed away from the table as he realized he did care. And that wasn't in any plan he'd ever had. "I'll take the plates, ladies."

"Easiest clean up ever," Joelle said, pushing her and Caro's empty plates toward him.

"When you reno you learn to live a different lifestyle. No time for washing dishes."

"I love my life." Caro held Mr. PJ tight. Such a grown up thing for such a small girl to say. But she'd been around adults most of her life. These types of statements quit surprising him a while ago.

William shoved the plates into the trash can. "Well, I have something else you may love."

"Ice cream?" Caro asked.

"No. Better. How would you like to spend the night with Joelle? Miss Joelle."

His heart thudded at the widening of Caro's eyes. "Daddy, really? Spend the night with Miss Joelle?"

"Mr. PJ can come, too," Joelle added.

Caro pushed her arms in the air. "Yes! My first overnight! I'm going to pack my suitcase, okay?"

"Not too much," William said. "You're only staying for one night. A pair of pajamas and clean clothes for tomorrow."

"And Mr. PJ's things, too." Caro ran out of the kitchen, singing.

"Wow. You made her day." Joelle stood and pushed the chairs to the table.

"No, you made her day. Thanks so much. I'll come over in the morning to bring her home. I don't trust her outside alone for even a minute right now." William ran his hand through his hair. So much to think about in such a short time.

"Cassidy is making her life here for the next six months, so it looks like you'll have to confront this situation sooner rather than later."

Wishing life were simpler, yet knowing if it was he wouldn't have met Joelle, he nodded. "I know. If she doesn't show tonight, I will be phoning her tomorrow. I can't live like a powder keg's about to explode. Especially in front of Caro. She'll know something is up. She's a smart girl."

"She has a smart father. Of course she's smart."

"I'm not sure I'd put me on the smart train." For the first time in his life he wished he could tell someone about his dyslexia. Cassidy had helped him hide his troubles all through school. He was a great student, a lover of history, science, and math. He soaked information in like a sponge. Cassidy helped him by showing him the best way to learn, and he did very well in school. But only because of Cassidy's continued help.

He found he continued learning by homeschooling Caro. It actually helped him as they advanced each year. But Cassidy didn't know that.

"You ooze smartness." Joelle cocked her head. "Look at how you've adapted to your reno life. I know people who would have bucked the system trying to figure out how to do everything the same way they had always done things. You, you revamped life. I like that. That's using your brains."

"It doesn't take a—"

"Rocket scientist. And hey, I know a couple of rocket scientists, so no judging."

He took in her easy manner, her way of simply fitting into his life.

Joelle made him wish for all the things he didn't have. Comfy couch. Overstuffed chair. End table with a remote. Fire burning in the fireplace. All he had was a couple of camp chairs and a milk crate. He wasn't a bachelor. He was a father.

And now he wanted to be more.

He could envision a life with someone he cared about.

Someone like Joelle.

*****

Joelle shut the bathroom door giving Caro her privacy.

William had walked them over looking left and right as he did. Joelle was sure it was only Caro's excitement that kept her oblivious to William's paranoia. Joelle assured him she would make sure every door was kept locked while Caro was here.

Glancing in the guest room, Joelle smiled as she saw the pile of stuffed animals Caro had shoved into the suitcase. A pair of jeans and a long-sleeved shirt spilled out as well.

She hadn't brought a book as far as Joelle could tell.

Flipping the light on in her office, Joelle scanned her bookshelf. The bottom shelf held books for children.

She grabbed a favorite of hers. It had been a long time since she'd read to a child. She walked out of her office and into the guest room. She set the book on the bed then pulled the covers down. It only took a couple of minutes to arrange the stuffed animals on the bed. Then she folded Caro's jeans and shirt and set the small, pink suitcase against the wall, out of the way.

Joelle heard the bathroom door open, then little footsteps coming down the hall. But instead of stopping at the bedroom, they continued on. Joelle followed Caro, who was almost running, into the living room.

"What's the rush?" Joelle asked.

Caro fell to the floor and laid on her stomach, her head turned so she could see under the couch. "I saw the kitty. He's so pretty. I really want to pet him."

"He's a she, remember? Misty? And she's really not very friendly."

Caro stood, frowning. "He should be friendly."

"She."

Caro rubbed her nose. "She. Miss Misty should be friendly."

Joelle held her hand out. "Come on. She might warm up to you one day, but I can't make any promises. She hasn't warmed up to me yet." Joelle cherished the feeling of Caro's soft fingers wrapped in hers.

"That's probably because you don't like her."

Joelle steered Caro into the guest room. "Why do you say that? How do you know I don't like her?"

"Your voice. It's never friendly sounding when you are talking about Miss Misty." Caro jumped into the bed, pulling her stuffed animals toward her. She singled out Mr. PJ and hugged him tightly.

Joelle smiled at Caro's insight. "Miss Misty and I are still getting to know each other. How about we read a story before you go to sleep."

Caro scooted up the pillow a ways. "I would like that. Sit here." She patted the space next to her on the bed.

Joelle squeezed about half her body onto the bed as best as she could. "This is one of my favorites from when I was little, like you. Do you want to read it?"

Caro shook her head. "No. Please read it to me. I just don't like reading. But I do like hearing stories. Daddy reads me some of the best ones."

A slip of uneasiness rippled through Joelle. It was true not every child liked to read, but Caro seemed downright opposed to it. It wasn't Joelle's place to size up Caro's school work. There were tests children had to pass when they were homeschooled. Joelle was sure William kept up with those things.

Still, as she started reading, that uneasiness refused to leave her. Her tutoring instincts were kicking in and Joelle knew something wasn't right.

She also knew that it wasn't her place to question anything concerning William and Caro.

*****

The French toast wasn't too badly burnt. Gobs of syrup would cover up a rough spot here and there. Joelle had gone in and woken Caro about ten minutes ago. She should be coming in the kitchen for breakfast any time now.

But instead of hearing footsteps coming into the kitchen, Joelle heard the front door screen slap shut. She turned off the stove and ran toward the front door. Sure enough the big wooden door was pushed against the wall, the door wide open.

Surely she would have heard William knock on the door. And surely he wouldn't have taken Caro without talking to Joelle. Heart beating wildly, she stepped onto the front porch. She almost tripped over the paper laying on the stoop.

Funny thing was, she didn't get the paper delivered.

"Here, Miss Misty. Here kitty, kitty."

Relief swarmed over Joelle as she heard Caro's voice. But how did the cat get outside?

"Caroline."

Joelle grabbed onto the wrought iron post holding the awning in place. The black metal was cold, but not as cold as the fear that ran through Joelle as she saw Cassidy at the edge of her yard calling for Caro.

Fortunately, Caro was almost all the way under a bush and apparently didn't hear Cassidy calling her name. Joelle started toward Cassidy, but veered toward Caro as she saw William run down his porch steps.

"Caro, come on. I'll get Misty later." Joelle scooped Caro up. Mr. PJ tumbled out of her arms.

Joelle bent down, grabbed Mr. PJ, and quickly ran into the house.

"Am I in trouble, Miss Joelle? I didn't mean to let Miss Misty out. I just saw the paper lady, and wanted to surprise you by bringing you the paper. Miss Misty ran outside and I just went to get her. That's all."

Tears brimmed in Caro's eyes and her throat was choked with tears. Joelle's heart broke into pieces. Pieces she'd hoped not to have to put back together again. She hugged Caro, while wondering what was taking place outside.

Considering Caro said she saw the paper lady, Joelle's guess was that Cassidy had put the newspaper on her porch. But why? She couldn't know Caro was here. And what did the paper have to do with anything?

"It's okay. I thank you for being considerate and wanting to surprise me. Miss Misty will be fine. I bet she'll come running in shortly." Joelle wasn't sure at all what Misty would do, but it seemed okay to reassure Caro that all would be well.

"I'm sorry." Caro hugged Joelle tightly.

"Why don't we eat some breakfast? I made French toast. How does that sound?"

Caro sniffled. "Good. I like French toast."

Holding hands, Joelle walked while Caro shuffled into the kitchen. Joelle set Caro at the table with two pieces of toast and a lot of syrup. "Would you like some milk?"

"Yes."

Joelle poured a glass of milk and set it in front of Caro. "You sit tight. I'm going to check on Misty."

Caro tried to scoot off her chair, but Joelle stopped her. "No. You eat your breakfast. If she doesn't come back by the time you finish, we'll look for her together. I promise."

"Okay." Caro steadied herself in her seat and picked up her fork.

Joelle walked calmly out of the kitchen then ran to the front door.

William stood there, his hand ready to knock.

"Hello," Joelle said, trying to look behind him for signs of Cassidy.

"She's gone," William said. "Where's Caro?"

"Eating breakfast. Come on in." His dark as night eyes and clenched fists almost deterred her from asking him in. She didn't think he'd be in the best mood, but she also knew he was determined to keep Cassidy from Caro.

"Where's her things. We need to leave."

Joelle's heart dropped. "Leave? As in leave town?"

William shook his head. "No. Here. Caro needs to be home. Where I know she's safe."

"Look, the cat got outside—"

"Joelle." His voice cut off her words, his finger touched her lips. "I was wrong to ask you to keep Caro overnight." His words were whispered, but rung loudly in her ears. "Caro is my responsibility. We should never have involved you. I'm sorry that we did. We won't be troubling you anymore."

She wrapped her hand around his finger, gently drawing it away from her lips. "There is no trouble. I would always keep Caro safe. Always."

He leaned in and she held her breath. Cupping her face with his hands, he kissed her forehead, the feel of his lips on her skin threatening to undo her. She lifted her face, knowing full well what might happen, the thought of his lips on hers almost making her feel faint.

Gently rubbing her cheeks with his thumbs, he stepped away from her. Her face felt naked without his hands. "I know you would. My heart is full with caring for Caro. Then you slipped in. You're in here, Joelle." He tapped his chest with his fist. "And it's too much. I don't ever want to hurt you."

"You won't." The words came out naturally, like she really did mean them. And she did. But the girl. Caro. William was a package deal.

Pretty paper and bows didn't mean the package was always the best for you.

But she was willing to try again.

With a man that had a family.

Joelle had no idea what he had said to Cassidy. But whatever it was, it set him on a mission. A mission to stay away from her.

A mission she had to stall.

"Don't walk away from this, William. From us."

His dark eyes turned soft, his expression one of regret. "I don't have a choice," he whispered.

"You do have a choice." She took a deep breath. "I have a wedding dress hanging in my closet. A dress I bought because a man proposed to me. A man with two sons. I loved them. All of them. But the man, Daniel, decided that his secretary was who he really loved after all. He broke off our engagement to marry her. That was his choice."

For a brief moment she saw compassion in his eyes. "I'm sorry that happened to you."

"I didn't tell you the story so you would be sorry. Sometimes making the right choice is hard. Daniel did make the right choice by breaking if off with me. If he hadn't, I would never have met you."

William closed his eyes, shook his head. He opened his eyes. "Joelle, I can't. Kiddo!"

Her throat clogged with unshed tears, Joelle stepped back as she heard the chair scrape away from the table.

"Daddy!" Caro ran to him, and he whisked her into his arms.

"Did you have fun?" He ruffled her hair and kissed her on the cheek.

"I did. Except, I let Miss Misty outside. Joelle said I could help her look for her after I ate breakfast."

Joelle prayed that William would back off. That he would let Caro stay. He could stay, too.

"Honey, we need to get home. Show me where your things are and we'll head home."

"But Daddy—"

"No buts." He set her down. "Where is your suitcase?"

Joelle watched them walk down the hall. Moments later they reappeared, Caro pulling her pink suitcase, its wheels groaning down the hardwood-floored hallway.

"Bye, Miss Joelle. I had fun. I'm sorry about Misty."

"It's okay. I told you she'll be back." She gave Caro a hug.

She didn't look at William.

They walked out the front door, leaving Joelle standing alone in the living room. Giving them plenty of time to walk across the yard, she made her way over to the door. Opening the screen, she stepped onto the porch and picked up the paper.

The paper that Cassidy had left on her porch.

As she did, she heard a rustle in the bushes. Misty came running out, wrapping herself around Joelle's legs.

Tucking the paper under one arm, Joelle bent over and picked up Misty. She carried the cat into the house, shutting the wooden door behind them.

She tossed the paper on the couch and set the cat down.

Only then did she remember that William and Caro still had her scarf.

Her scarf that she knew she'd never see again.

Chapter Ten

William checked the door for the tenth time.

Locked.

Just like his heart when it came to Joelle. Locked.

Leaning against the door, he let his body take a break from the work he'd been doing all day. Every swing of the sledge hammer into the drywall was him convincing himself he had no choice but to say goodbye to his pretty neighbor today.

Life was becoming complicated.

Cassidy was back and real, and he had to deal with her. If her claims at being clean were true, he had no right to keep her from Caro. But he needed time. He told Cassidy he'd be in touch with her.

His anger had been so strong as he barreled down his porch steps that morning. That Cassidy would attempt to see Caro without him knowing was the final straw.

Cassidy admitted that trying something behind his back wasn't the right way to go. She seemed agreeable to having a conversation regarding Caro. He promised to call in her a couple of days. Cassidy gave him the address of the home she was renting and swore she would stay away until he called.

"I've changed, William. I need to prove it to you. I have a job, and they let me transfer here. You and Caro would both be proud of me."

Her words drove through his mind. Could he trust them?

She seemed perfectly sober when he confronted her. Her skin looked smooth and healthy. She looked healthy. She wasn't shaky, her gaze didn't flit around. She'd held her own.

But one thing was for certain.

He wasn't in love with her anymore.

Caring and concern could be feelings he'd admit to when it came to Cassidy. But love?

No.

Visions of Joelle loomed in his mind. He wasn't in love with Joelle either, but being in love with Joelle was something he could see happening. Light-hearted, fun, loving. Girl-next-door beautiful.

The look on her face when he told her he and Caro wouldn't be troubling her anymore cut through him. He didn't want to hurt anyone. Ever.

A part of him told him he'd already hurt Joelle.

It was for the best. He had too much to concentrate on without having his heart wrapped up in a woman he could fall for.

Pushing away from the door, he grabbed a screwdriver. He walked over to the last wall standing. Joelle's scarf hung from a peg that was mounted on a board that hung on the wall. He removed the scarf from the peg, letting the soft fabric run through his hands. Her scent lingered in the peach material, it's power threatening to change his mind about his decision.

But he couldn't.

He shoved the scarf in his pocket, then grabbed his sledge hammer.

Time to demo another wall.

*****

After seeing her last client, Joelle changed into jeans and a sweater. She decided to go and grab some take out for dinner. She'd been cooped up inside all day after this morning's drama. Her clients kept her mind occupied, but moments of darkness and sadness snuck up on her at odd times.

No more William and Caro.

She thought about walking over and asking for her scarf, but knew she would look desperate. William might think she was just using her scarf as an excuse to come over, which would be entirely true.

But she respected him.

Respected his decision.

Didn't like his decision.

But she liked him.

A lot.

Still.

As she was putting her boots on there was a knock at her front door.

Not a William knock.

No, more of a soft knock. Like a woman's knock.

One boot on, one boot off, Joelle opened the door knowing who she would find standing there.

Cassidy.

"Hello," Cassidy said. "I don't want to bother you, but can I talk with you? Please?"

It was full on dark outside. Joelle didn't see Cassidy's car parked on the street. "Does William know you are here?"

Cassidy shook her head. "No. But we talked today. He's calling me in a couple of days. Please?"

Joelle stepped back and opened her home to Cassidy.

"Thank you," Cassidy said.

"We can sit if you'd like." Joelle moved to the couch. She sat at one end, Cassidy sat at the other end.

"I think William is going to let me see Caroline. Not right away, but soon."

Joelle nodded. "That will be nice."

Cassidy set her purse on the floor. "Yes. I'm sure William told you all about my struggles. My addiction. But I'm clean. Like I said, over two years now. It feels good."

"I'm glad. I'm sure you feel much better." Joelle guarded her words. She didn't want to reveal anything to Cassidy. Joelle didn't trust her. Although Cassidy seemed genuine. Real. If she was lying about being clean, William would figure that out.

"I parked down the street because I didn't want William to know I was here. I wanted to apologize for this morning." Cassidy pushed her hair behind her ears.

"I'm sure you've told William all that needs to be told."

Cassidy smiled and laughed a short laugh. "It was stupid, really. I bought a few papers, thinking I could act as a paper boy, you know, tossing papers on porches. I thought maybe Caro would be outside playing since it was a nice morning. Stupid, stupid idea. I should have been upfront with William from the beginning."

Joelle nodded toward the chair. "The paper's still there if you want it back."

Cassidy shook her head. "No. But I was surprised to see Caro coming out of your door."

"I was surprised, too." *Keep that guard up, Joelle.*

"William cares for you."

Cassidy's words caused Joelle to feel. "He's a friend."

"If he let Caro stay with you, he cares. My family has been keeping me posted on William and Caro. I know he's led a pretty solitary life. He even homeschools Caro. He really doesn't need to be afraid of me. I wouldn't do anything to him or Caro."

Her gaze locked with Joelle's, and she believed her.

"I know he's worried about me spilling the beans regarding his dyslexia. But as long as Caro is learning and advancing, again, he has nothing to worry about from me."

Joelle knew her eyes widened. She tried to stop the action, but she was too late.

"You didn't know, did you?" Cassidy asked.

William is dyslexic. Memories of him not wanting to read the instructions for the plant rushed into her mind. Caro's words about William's great stories. If he was having trouble reading, Caro wouldn't know necessarily. He could probably tell a story well.

It was all Joelle could do to sit on the couch. She wanted to fly off it and over to his house. She wanted to wrap her arms around him and let him know what an amazing dad he was. But she stayed put. She didn't answer Cassidy.

But she didn't have to.

Cassidy knew Joelle didn't know.

"Don't tell him I told you, okay? I'm just now gaining ground."

Joelle grabbed her remaining boot and put it on. "No worries. William and I won't be talking too much, so I don't think it will be a problem."

"I'm sorry to hear that. Caro would do well having you in her life." Cassidy stood. "Thank you for opening your home to me. And one day, I'd like to have coffee with you. As friends."

Joelle stood. "Maybe one day. Welcome to Devon Park, though. I'm sure you'll love it here."

"I already do."

Cassidy picked up her purse and left.

Joelle stood alone in her living room.

Well, not really alone. Misty walked in and rubbed against her ankles. Great. Cat hair on her suede boots.

At least the cat was showing signs of liking her.

*****

William and Caro walked into the Burger Barn. It was crowded. He glanced around and after seeing no signs of Cassidy, he gave the hostess his name.

"Table for two will be about five minutes, sir. Is that okay?"

"It's fine."

An old George Strait tune played overhead. Caro sat on a bench, Mr. PJ in her lap. She was making him dance to the beat of the music.

"To go, please. Madison. Joelle Madison."

William looked up to see Joelle standing at the hostess station.

"I'll be right back." The young hostess disappeared, leaving Joelle standing alone.

Looking up, like he could see past the ceiling, he wondered at the coincidence of him and Joelle being here at the same time. She was staring toward the back of the restaurant and hadn't seen him yet. Caro hadn't spotted her either.

When she did it would be all over.

He looked down, and he saw it.

Her scarf. Still in his pocket.

Okay, God. I get it.

Caro had half-turned and was playing with Mr. PJ on the bench.

William pulled the scarf out of his pocket and walked toward Joelle. "Excuse me, are you missing a scarf?"

Joelle turned, surprise written all over her face.

She glanced at her scarf before focusing on him. Then she smiled. "Why, yes. I am."

She reached for the peach material, but William pulled it back. "Whoa. Are you in a hurry to retrieve it?"

Joelle shrugged. "Well, it has been missing a few days, now."

William pushed the scarf back into his pocket. "It's been quite happy in its new home."

Shifting her weight, she said, "Oh, it has? Please tell me I've been missed at least."

William's heart thudded with her double meaning. It had only been a few hours, but he felt the absence of Joelle like he never imagined he would. "You've been missed."

"That's nice."

William knew he needed to talk to Cassidy and put things right with her regarding Caro. William also knew he needed to trust Joelle. And that meant with everything. "While you have been missed there are some things I need to talk to you about."

"I'd like that."

"Here you are, Ms. Madison. That will be twelve forty-five." The hostess had returned. She set down a bag containing a Styrofoam container.

William grabbed the bag. "Put it on my tab. And, I've made a choice. We are no longer a table for two. We are a table for three."

Joelle's expression eased his mind at this admission. "For three," he reiterated. "Forever," he whispered.

The hostess looked down and did some scribbling. "That will make your wait a little longer. Is that okay?"

William looked at Joelle. "I've been waiting my whole life. A few more minutes won't hurt."

"William—"

"Will you have dinner with us? Caro and me?"

She smiled. "Yes."

His heart was happy. Caro to his right, Joelle to his left. "Like I said though, I have some things I need to talk to you about. Some things you might want to know."

She glanced at Caro. "I know everything I need to know about you, William."

He cocked his head. "I may have some hidden secrets."

"I've loved every secret I've learned about you so far. You aren't scaring me off."

The hostess came from around her podium holding three menus. "Your table is ready, Mr. Scott. Follow me."

"Kiddo. Our table is ready."

Caro stood, holding Mr. PJ. "Miss Joelle! Are you eating with us again?"

"She is. Let's follow the lady."

Caro hugged Joelle quickly then fell in step behind the hostess.

William grabbed Joelle's hand as they started walking. "This is the beginning of something special, Joelle. I just need to take things slowly." He squeezed her hand before letting go.

Joelle looked at him. "To quote the words of a smart man, 'I've been waiting my whole life.' I can do slow. As long as it's with you."

"It will always be with me."

They reached the booth. Caro slid in one side, Joelle slid in the other.

"Kiddo. Do you mind if I sit with Joelle?"

Caro smiled. "No. That way Mr. PJ can sit with me."

William set the bag with Joelle's food on the table, then slid in next to her.

Life in Devon Park was looking up.

He was sitting across from his beautiful daughter and sitting next to his beautiful neighbor.

William held Joelle's hand in his, knowing she was his future.

*****

Joelle reeled at the feel of his hand on hers. *Table for three, forever.* She knew she found forever in William. Sure, this was only their first date. He hadn't even kissed her yet, except on her forehead.

But there would be time for that later.

For now, she wanted to take in all she could of William and Caro. She already felt so comfortable around them. And yes, she and William had things to discuss, but nothing that would hinder moving forward.

"Caro, Misty came back. She's home safe and sound."

Caro smiled. "That's good, Miss Joelle. I'm glad she came back. She's not lost."

"No, she's not lost. I think she's starting to like me, actually."

"Have you talked nice to her?" Caro asked.

"I think so. Thank you for that advice."

"You're welcome."

Caro busied herself with Mr. PJ.

"She loves you, you know," William whispered in Joelle's ear.

Instead of panic, hope filled Joelle. "I love her, too. And I think I'm kind of falling for her dad." She kept her voice quiet so Caro wouldn't hear, not that she was paying attention.

"Keep falling. I'm good at restoration."

Joelle looked into his deep brown eyes. "I'm counting on it."

The End

Dear Reader

I hope you enjoyed reading One Autumn Love as much as I loved writing it. William quickly captured my heart in a way I didn't think possible. Caro was fun to write and well, Joelle deserves her happy ending. Don't you think?
There will be four Devon Park 'Single Dad Next Door' Novellas. I love the thought of men raising kids. So many storylines there.

I want to thank my critique partner, Missy Tippens, my beta reader, Jill Vaughan. You two are always there for me, even in the last minute rush. I'm so appreciative of you. Also my editor Emily Sewell. This gal is the rock behind my stories. She's amazing.

Ciara Knight who put this project together and sparked ideas for not only me, but for so many other authors. Thanks for making us dig deep for stories. (Actually there isn't a whole lot I could do without Ciara Knight!)

My husband and children are always supportive and I love them from the bottom of my heart. And Jesus, yes, Jesus. The why behind everything I do.

Again, thank you for reading One Autumn Love.

Lindi P.

Follow Me
Facebook: https://www.facebook.com/Lindi-Peterson-103631776422502/
Twitter: https://twitter.com/LindiPeterson
Website: http://belindasblogging.blogspot.com/

If you enjoyed One Autumn Love here are links to other books I've written.
Uptown Heiress
Uptown Flirt
The Little Black Wedding Dress

MONTANA BORN

Hildie McQueen

Love of land brings Sully Cole back to Alder Gulch, Montana. A multi-million offer although tempting is hard to accept, even if it includes dealing with the beautiful designer Elle Tyler.

Elle figures the best way to get the arrogant landowner to understand she doesn't sleep with clients for a land deal is to bring out a secret weapon... the crazy women in her family.

Dedication

This story is dedicated to a wonderful bunch of crazy friends, who are there for each other through thick and thin.

Janet, Elle, Stacia, Jennifer, Sharon, Margie, Deanna, Lori and Sandy.
I Love you gals!!!

Chapter One

Sullivan Cole leaned back on the hood of his truck allowing the serenity of the surrounding landscape to engulf him. Too many years had passed since he'd been to Alder Gulch, Montana and nothing had changed. The century-old cabins remained. The remnants of stables and fencing were reminders of generations of Coles who'd always lived on the property and a testament to good workmanship.

In the distance just past a large pond, there was a newer structure. It was his uncle's log cabin, a stark contrast to the older dwellings and it stood proud.

His uncle, a wealthy rancher had ensured the property remained maintained while at the same time the beauty of it untouched. Many a summer as a child he and his family had returned here for reunions and festivities.

As they'd grown into adulthood, and their uncle too old to keep abreast, the property had remained taken care of by his brother Bennett, cousin Regina and himself. Therefore, it was not a surprise to anyone when at his uncle's death, he bequeathed the land to the trio.

With a deep breath, he looked up to the clear blue sky in hopes of an answer to his current predicament.

The sound of the wind rustling leaves in the nearby trees was the only reply. Sullivan kicked at a rock. "Yeah, I don't blame you for not helping me out right now," he muttered figuring God had better things to do at the moment.

He was conflicted at the sudden changes in his life. The turn of events forcing him to make decisions that would affect the surrounding land and future generations of Coles. Sullivan wished to go back two days when his main preoccupation had been the sale of a motorcycle.

He rode bikes, horses and loved Jeeps. Besides his work in Helena at Cole Ranching Supply with his older sister, he dated sporadically and rarely the same woman twice.

After all, he planned to remain single for a few more years. If and when he settled, it would be with a woman chosen carefully. He'd ensure she would sign a prenuptial agreement, which would spell out that she'd not have any rights to any of his properties or business ventures.

At thirty-five Sully had time to work his personal life out while carving a successful career in the United States ranching industry.

A vehicle neared. The silver Ford truck easily traversed the bumps of the unpaved road to where he waited. The truck rolled easily over the uneven terrain of the hill where he'd chosen to meet. Sullivan was prepared to meet with whomever the development company had sent to represent them.

A few feet away, the truck stopped and two people emerged. Both of them wore designer sunglasses and dressed in business attire.

Sullivan huffed and shook his head at the showmanship. In worn jeans and a plaid shirt, he could easily buy their company out from under the suits now walking toward him. They'd probably rented the truck, as their Prius would not make it over the bumps in the landscape.

The pair, a man and a woman exited the vehicle. The man was of average build with the clean-cut look of an office jockey. The woman, however, caught his attention. She wore a navy blue pantsuit and low heels. Her long, blonde hair was pulled back into a high ponytail and she carried a pair of binoculars in one hand and a binder of sorts in the other. With the composure of someone who rarely loses at anything, her head moved side to side as she took in the landscape.

"Mr. Cole," said the approaching man, holding out his hand. "Gary Burch of Burch and Tyler."

The woman came to a stop beside her partner. "Good morning, Mr. Cole, I'm Elle Tyler." He took her hand in his, noting the sparkle of a pink rhinestone bracelet peeking from her long sleeve. *Interesting.*

"Call me Sully." He lifted his sunglasses to meet the reflection in theirs. "Should we get down to business?"

*****

Elle was taken aback first by the breathtaking beauty of the Cole lands as the sun burned the early morning mist off them and secondly by Sullivan Cole's unusual eye color. She'd never seen a blue shade like his. They had to be contacts. No one had turquoise eyes. Not that she knew of anyway.

"Miss Tyler?"

Crap, he had been talking and here she was drooling over the color of the man's eyes. "Yes," she replied, hoping it was the correct answer.

When he made his way to the passenger side of the Jeep, she realized he planned to drive her and Gary.

She followed and climbed into the front passenger seat. Leaving Gary to take the back seat, which she knew he hated.

To be fair, Gary was a good business partner, although at times a bit over the top. Nevertheless, the man was persistent. He rarely gave up on business deals, which made him the perfect balance to her "stand back and allow potential customers time to think things through" approach.

Sully drove slowly for a few minutes, purposely allowing them to look around at their leisure. They'd been there several times already to scope it out. He had to know that. However, whatever the purpose of this tour was, she'd wait and see what he'd say.

Gary, of course, could not remain silent. "Mr. Cole...err, Sully, my partner and I have been out here several times with your cousin Regina's permission, of course. Have to say, I'm impressed by it. Although there is plenty of land out here in these parts, none compare to yours."

The silence of the man in the seat next to her was intriguing. Relaxing back into the seat, she lowered her sunglasses to get a better look at a field of blue flowers.

Sully stopped and looked through the windshield. "My relatives, dating back to 1820s are buried there." He paused before continuing. "Not sure why the flowers always bloom here, but they have for over a hundred years."

He removed his sunglasses and slid them into his front chest pocket. His gaze was fixed on the tombstones. "Looking at it now I'm realizing I can't sell this land to you. I'll buy my brother and my cousin out before I allow it to be destroyed."

"With all due respect," Gary blurted, "we're talking about a lot of money. Millions. A development of the size we're talking about is monumental. It has never been done." Unfortunately, Gary's voice had reached the high pitch of desperation, so Elle cut in.

"Mr. Cole, I understand your attachment to your land. I don't foresee a problem working around this portion. I can assure you that your ancestor's remains won't be disturbed."

His astonishing eyes met hers. "No you can't. Once the deal is signed, there is little you can assure me of, Miss Tyler."

Unable to keep eye contact, she looked to the field. There had to be a way around it. Unfortunately, the property deal had to include this portion, as it was located almost in the center of the planned project.

"You're right, I can't. But I can assure you, I will work hard to find a solution."

One brow lifted. "Do you always make so many assurances?"

Unable to keep from it, she smiled. "Only when I mean it."

Feeling left out, Gary scooted forward. "Of course we can find a way around it. Elle and I are good together. Once we get our minds set on something, we find a way to work it out."

"Good to hear," Sully replied. "But I'm not going to change my mind. Sorry to waste your time."

The engine came back to life and he drove back toward where they'd parked. Gary talked the entire time, making promises, throwing out numbers and plans so fast Elle wanted to slap him silent. However, she could see Sullivan Cole was listening, his dark head moving up and down every so often.

He was a smart businessman. Sullivan was a wealthy entrepreneur who worked hard to maintain his family business prominent in Montana and all over the country.

Although she hoped he would accept their offer, somehow she got the feeling that once he made up his mind, it would take a great deal to change it. The brother and cousin would no doubt follow his lead since they'd sent him to represent the trio of owners.

"So, dinner then?"

Elle blinked and looked from one man to the other. "Excuse me?"

Gary's eyes rounded at her lack of focus during this crucial time. "Mr. Cole has requested to discuss my proposition over dinner with you."

"Yes, of course. I'm sorry. I was admiring the view and became lost in thought."

Since Sully turned to look to where she'd directed her gaze, Gary rolled his eyes and gave her a pointed "don't screw this up" look.

With mountains in the background, the expanse of land and aged buildings resembled a beautiful painting. The bright blue sky was almost as breathtaking as the man's eyes. She let out a long sigh. "I could stare at that scenery all day."

"Let's give Mr. Cole time to think." Gary had appeared at the passenger door and opened it. He took her elbow to assist her from the vehicle.

Seeming deep in thought, Sully walked to stand at the front of his vehicle and leaned on it, his arms crossed over his chest while waiting for them to near. He was the perfect picture of an all American cowboy with his brown Stetson, faded jeans and dusty boots.

"See you this evening, Miss Tyler." He shook both their hands and met her gaze. "I'll pick you up at your office at five."

"Why don't you meet me? I'll text the info."

"Sure."

Once they were settled into the truck that Gary had insisted on renting, she jabbed at him with her index finger. "What the hell did you set me up to do?"

"I told him you would gladly meet with him over dinner to discuss any further details. Hey, it's a Hail Mary. The man is not budging unless we do something drastic."

Elle narrowed her eyes. "So you think pimping me out to a client will work, huh?"

"What? No! Of course not. Its just dinner."

"You're darn right. That's all he'll get, too."

She huffed with irritation. Men were so dense. Did Gary think Sullivan Cole didn't see through the ploy? Did Sully think she met potential clients for intimate dinners on a regular basis and hoped for a "good time"?

Realizing she already had dinner plans with some very interesting people who would definitely teach the rancher a lesson, her lips curved into a smile.

"I'm looking forward to this evening. It will definitely be unforgettable."

"Don't do anything stupid," Gary said.

Chapter Two

"I really need to get one of those Spanx girdles," Elle's Aunt Janet exclaimed inspecting herself in a full-length mirror. "What are you thinking having a mirror in the entryway where people can scare themselves to death?" She frowned at Elle and waddled to the kitchen. "Have any of those cookies Margie made left?"

"No Aunt Janet, I don't. Scott came over yesterday and ate them all," she said, referring to her brother.

Wednesdays were Tyler women, girl's night out. Along with her Aunt Janet, who lived next door, her mother, Margie, and Aunt Janet's daughters, Deanna and Jennifer, they went to a nearby Mexican restaurant for food and margaritas.

More times than not, her other cousins, twins Lori and Sandy, would join them. Her uncle's daughters were an odd couple of twins. They were always together but argued constantly.

Lori was more restrained, while Sandy cussed like a sailor and changed the color of her hair depending on her moods. Sandy's moods seemed to change rather frequently.

Today, all seven were meeting at a Mexican restaurant. It was truly cruel that she'd asked Sully to meet her there. It was obvious he would not change his mind about the land and if Elle were to be honest, she didn't blame him one bit. Although she'd hate typing the email to the conglomerate planning to purchase the land, it was not the end of the road on the project.

Always ready for a Plan B, she'd already scoped out another property, which, although not as nice as the Cole land, would suit the purpose for the venture.

The commission would have been nice. She'd already earned very well on the architectural plans for the combination dude ranch, condo and adult resort. If she and Gary bartered a land deal for it to come to fruition, Elle could relax and only take jobs she was passionate about.

"Aunt Jane, I asked a client to stop by La Veranda tonight. I don't suspect he'll be there long."

Her aunt stopped with a chocolate halfway to her mouth. "Is he single and good looking?"

Elle eyed the chocolate. "How did you find my stash?"

Her aunt shrugged and popped the expensive truffle into her mouth. "It was right there in the open for anyone to take."

"In the third drawer down, under a kitchen towel you mean?

Aunt Jane waved her remarks away. "Back to the subject at hand. Who is this client of yours?"

Her lips quivered in anticipation of her aunt's reaction. "Sullivan Cole."

"Oklahoma!" Her aunt exclaimed. "Dallas and Toledo," her voice lowered to a reverent level. "Isn't he the most eligible bachelor in the entire state of Montana?"

"He's also a male chauvinist pig, who thinks I do 'dinner' with clients," Elle replied making air quotes. "So anyway, you don't have to be nice to him."

"Honey I'm not just going to be nice to him, I'm going to buy him dinner. " She picked up the nearest cell phone, which happened to be Elle's and stared at it for a moment then poked at it. "Listen up, buttercup, tell your sister to fix up nice for dinner. Tell her to put on some makeup and wear that green dress you wore to Jenny's wedding. Tell Jennifer tonight is not the night to be wearing those tacky romance reader t-shirts. And tell her for God's sake slap some lotion on those feet!"

Her aunt listened for a few seconds. "Sullivan Cole is joining us for dinner. That's what's going on."

Elle's mouth fell open. "No he's not. I was going to sit him at a table next to ours for the few minutes he'll stay."

"Hello is this Lori? Come to dinner tonight. You may want to leave Sandy behind..."

Elle shook her head and dug in the drawer for a chocolate. Maybe she'd just made the biggest mistake of her life.

*****

The ambience at La Veranda could only be described as tacky with a twist of Mexican flair. Armando, their usual server, rushed to Elle and Aunt Janet and ushered them to a table on the far side of the restaurant.

Elle couldn't figure out if it was to give them privacy, or because he feared them running off other patrons. She ducked a beer bottle piñata and hurried to hug her mother who'd arrived along with Deanna and Jennifer.

Her eyes rounded at her cousins' appearance. Both looked like a trailer park version of the Kardashians. "Hey, Cuz," Deanna said looking past her toward the entrance. "How are ya?"

Jennifer didn't bother to greet her. Instead, she clapped her hands up over her right shoulder like a Flamenco dancer. "Armando, I need a strong margarita. Throw a shot of vodka in it."

The server's eyes rounded. "You want a margarita with vodka? That's just wrong."

"The tequila don't care. Tequila is very friendly to other liquors. Oh, and bring everyone a shot of your best tequila while you're at it. Elle is paying for those."

Armando hurried away after counting heads and promising shots and margaritas for everyone except her mother.

Margie Tyler was a proper lady. How she'd ended up with a circus for a family was a mystery. She didn't cuss, drink or ever raise her voice. She dressed tastefully and was so sweet sometimes it made Elle's teeth hurt.

"Why in the world would you bring an important client to dinner on a Wednesday night?" Her mother grabbed her arm and steered Elle away from the others. "They won't give the poor man a chance to get a word in edgewise."

Just then Lori and Sandy walked in. Sandy clung to her twin's arm to keep from falling off her four-inch heels. Both wore what looked like belly dancing costumes, except, thankfully, their midsections were covered.

It was a stupid mistake. She'd call Sullivan Cole right away and make excuses. "I'm going to call him and reschedule." Elle held up her phone and hurried to the doors. When she attempted to round her cousins, Sandy latched on to her arm. "What are Deanna and Jennifer doing here? Who invited them?"

"Since when does anyone need an invitation for Wednesday night?" Elle yanked her arm away.

Sandy screamed and flapped her arms twice before falling backward into Armando's tray full of margaritas. Unfortunately, Elle tried to save a pitcher only for it to flip forward and splash all over her feet.

"Dang it!" She leaned forward just as Armando straightened the tray slamming her in the face.

Elle wobbled backward and would have landed on her butt if not for someone catching her around the waist.

Huffing, she pushed her rescuer's hands away. "Lori, get your sister to the table. I have to go outside and cancel with my client. Although I don't like the man, even he doesn't deserve to be around my crazy ass family."

"Should I leave then?"

The deep voice crashing over her was colder than the frozen margarita mush between her toes.

Sullivan Cole had arrived early it seemed.

Chapter Three

Apparently, the one thing Elle Tyler had not found out about him was how much he enjoyed a challenge. He'd not only stay, but also make her regret whatever she'd planned.

Sully took her elbow and peered down at her shoes. She wore tight faded jeans and what used to be off white sandals. They were more of a green shade now.

"Miss Tyler, you may want to rinse your shoes off. They'll be sticky."

Her wide eyes went from him down to her shoes and then over her shoulder towards where the woman who'd fallen was now being helped to sit. "Ah...yes, well there apparently has been a mix-up. I forgot my family would be here tonight. We should reschedule. Or better yet, how about we meet at your office.... or...or mine?"

Totally different from the woman in the business suit. This Elle was dressed casually, with gleaming blonde hair flowing past her shoulders. Her makeup was precise without being overly done and the off the shoulder t-shirt made him wonder what it would feel like to touch the smooth olive skin.

The waiter came to them and gave him an apologetic look. "Do you need a table?"

"No," Elle answered for him. "Sorry to trouble you, Mr. Cole. I'll call you to arrange another meeting."

From the table, six sets of expectant faces watched them with interest. "No need for all that extra work. How about I go and sit with your family while you wash up."

He directed her towards the neon bathroom sign and then walked toward the table.

*****

Elle ran into the bathroom and kicked off her shoes. She did the best she could with wet paper towels on her feet before running her sandals under tap water. She danced in place with nerves. He'd gone to the table. He was there right now with her relatives who'd waste no time in spilling every ugly detail of her life. That, combined with her cousins fighting for his attention, could potentially ruin any future business.

She had no doubt he'd overheard her comment about not liking him. To be fair to the man, didn't know him well enough not to like him. It could have been Gary who orchestrated the entire dinner thing. Although she doubted it.

"Miss?"

"Huh?" She jumped as a woman tried to get to the paper towels. "Sorry," Elle muttered and walked out holding the drenched shoes.

At the table, Sullivan Cole had been seated in the center, her cousins, Deanna and Lori, at his elbows. The other two, who'd obviously lost the battle, sat across from him.

Letting out a breath, she neared only to freeze when all the women laughed. Her mother clapped at whatever he'd said and shook with mirth. Her. Mother.

"What's going on?" Elle narrowed her eyes at Sully. "Why is my mother laughing?"

"Sit down," Aunt Janet tugged her to the only empty chair, which was in between her mother and aunt. The Untouchables section.

Great.

"Sully was just telling us one of his childhood antics." Jennifer all but fell across the table toward the man, who seemed to be enjoying the attention tremendously. "You missed it."

"So Sully," Lori said leaning against his arm. "What is your drink of choice? Elle's buying drinks tonight."

"He can't stay for drinks," Elle said, meeting his gaze. "Didn't you tell me you had a meeting with another client Mr. Cole?"

There was a gleam of challenge when he looked to her and lifted that damn brow. "They cancelled. I'll have a beer since you're buying. Can't turn down a free drink. Momma didn't raise no fool."

The women all laughed as if he'd invented the saying. She turned to her mother and whispered, "They are acting like sex starved maniacs. Deanna's married for lord's sake."

"Oh, it's all in good fun. He is very charming after all."

Charming? He certainly had the entire table eating out of his hand. And if she was to be honest, she did envy Lori and Deanna just a little. When Aunt Janet announced she had to pee, Sully stood. "Please allow me."

"Aunt Janet doesn't need help, she's in very good shape," Elle told Sully.

"My knee has been acting up lately," Aunt Janet interjected and waited for him to take her elbow and assist her to stand.

"Thank you dear," she actually blushed and smiled up at him. "You're a good boy."

"Can it get any deeper in here," Elle muttered only to be shushed by her mother.

*****

They finally called it a night after Lori's false eyelash plopped into her margarita and everyone shuffled to the door. It was like a dysfunctional parade with Aunt Janet leading a crew that included a limping Sandy clinging to Sully's arm while her mother, of all people, clutched the other. Elle shuffled behind everyone hoping zombies waited outside and she wouldn't have to deal with whatever her client would do next.

After overly exaggerated goodbyes and too-long hugs, finally, everyone left. Her aunt scurried to wait for her in the car after Elle announced to the group that she and Sully hadn't had time to talk business.

Once again, the challenge twinkled in his eyes as he lifted a brow. "This was one of the most enjoyable evenings I've had in a long time. Thank you so much for arranging it."

"I'd honestly forgotten about it being family girl's night," she replied looking him square in the eye. She attempted to lift a brow but, unfortunately, she had never been able to accomplish the task no matter how much she practiced in the mirror.

"I've learned that when someone reinforces a statement with 'honestly', 'truly' or 'I swear', they are usually stretching the truth."

Elle gasped. "Are you calling me a liar?"

"No, truly I'm not."

She took a long breath. If the man were to change his mind about the land deal, which she doubted, it was not in her best interest to insult him. "I believe our business is pretty much over, Mr. Cole. I will contact you in three business days to confirm you will not sign the deal. That should give you time to discuss the matter with your family."

The jingle of his keys was followed by the curve of his lips, which of course, made Elle wonder how it would feel to be kissed by him.

"Goodnight, Miss Tyler. I will see you tomorrow at nine o'clock sharp. My office." He strolled off, leaving her without a choice but to study his well-formed back end.

The roar of a motorcycle shook Elle out of her trance as Sullivan Cole rode off. Could the man get any sexier? He was the devil and she did not trust him one bit.

If she was to be truthful, it was herself she didn't trust around him. Silly, of course, since it was doubtful the most eligible man in the state would lower himself to be interested in her.

After letting out a long sigh, she trudged to her car. Aunt Janet laughed. "He's somethin' else, huh? Hard to look away from those firm buns."

"I didn't notice," Elle quipped refusing to look her aunt in the eye.

Chapter Four

Sully hated to admit the woman had somehow gotten under his skin. He'd meant to tell her at the end of the night the deal was over and, after shaking hands, going on his way. Instead, he'd arranged for a meeting first thing this morning.

It was eight o'clock and while reviewing his emails for the day, he kept thinking back to the night before.

She'd been on edge the entire time acting as a referee with her unruly, but nice family. The women had kept him laughing all night. After the initial shock of what Elle had planned, he'd actually relaxed and enjoyed dinner.

When he'd told Elle he'd had an enjoyable evening, it was the truth. He couldn't remember the last time he'd spent time with women that although at first flirted had resumed their true personalities and began a constant banter of jokes and competitive digs at one another.

His own family was close, with three sisters and a brother. They often enjoyed evenings with their cousins and parents where laughter filled the room. The dynamic of the night before which Elle had set out to trip him had been more familiar than his usual stoic business meals.

"Sully, what time do you want the nine o'clock conference rescheduled to?" his assistant, Stacia, asked.

He smiled at the pretty woman, who'd become his close friend over the years. "Nine-thirty. I doubt this visitor will stay long. She doesn't like me." He smiled at Stacia and shrugged.

"Oh boy."

"What does that mean?" He attempted an innocent look. "There are women on the planet who don't like me. It's a strange phenomenon, yet it happens."

Stacia gave him a droll look. "I can think of about twenty people who don't like you right off the bat. Give me a minute and I'll come up with another batch."

"Women don't count."

With a shake of her head, she went back to her desk.

"So I don't like to date someone more than once. It's not a crime," he called after her.

At nine o'clock sharp his intercom dinged. "Miss Tyler is here."

It troubled Sully when his stomach tumbled. He stood to meet Elle at the door. Once again, she wore business attire. This time she had on a red dress with a navy blue jacket. She carried a slim handbag and he spotted the bright pink sparkling bracelet on her wrist again. The only hint she was not all business all the time to a potential client.

By her austere expression, she was not happy to be there. When he held out his hand, she hesitated before shaking it. "Good morning, Miss Tyler."

"Mr. Cole."

"I thought we'd agreed to you calling me Sully?"

After a barely noticeable nod, she went to the chair in front of the desk he motioned to. While making his way to the chair opposite her, he raked his brain to come up with a reason for their meeting.

"Tell me, what plan were you considering that would ensure my family cemetery would not be disturbed?"

"There are conditions that could be written into the sales agreement. I can include it into the plans and make the cemetery a type of remembrance to the history of the area. Your family has been central to Alder Gulch for a couple centuries."

It was a good reply, which Sully presumed had been practiced. "What is your plan B?"

She blinked, indicating to him the question was unexpected. "I have scouted out some land east of yours near where the mines are."

It was impressive. Although her partnership banked on his land, she'd gone out of her way to ensure there was a backup plan. It was interesting that Elle said "I" and not "we", which meant her partner was not as motivated to pursue another area. The man had already called him twice leaving invitations for lunch.

"Your partner seems to think I could be persuaded to change my mind."

"Is that why you agreed to dinner last night? Did you think I was part of said tactic?"

"If you'll remember, it was me who suggested dinner. It was not because I'll change my mind, but because I am curious to know more about you."

Bristling, her eyes widened and she swallowed visibly. "Exactly why am I here this morning?"

"I wanted to explain why I am not selling..."

"No need. I understand. It's your family. No matter what happens in life, to have a good family is priceless. Even mine, as crazy as they may seem, they are my glue, the ones who will be there for me through thick and thin."

Sully nodded. "True."

"So other than that I don't think there is anything to discuss. You need to explain your reasons to me."

"I want to know what your plan B is. If I can be of assistance, it will make me feel better about not selling."

She seemed to soften. "Thank you, but I will handle it. I have done it a time or two."

"I don't mean to offend you, Miss Tyler. My business in ranching allows me to get to know many of the landowners in the area. The land you are speaking of belongs to my friend Jared Redstone. How about a ride on Saturday?"

"What?"

"Horseback riding. My horses are boarded at Jared's while I build my own house and stables."

She pondered his question for a moment. Her pearly top teeth bit down on her bottom lip and her brow creased. Obviously, she didn't realize how sensual the expression was.

Sully cleared his throat. Not because he wished to hurry her in making a decision, it was to clear his mind and stop from drooling.

"Very well." Her reply was reluctant. "On one condition."

"I'm listening."

"Let me do the talking if and when the appropriate time comes up to discuss his land."

"Deal."

Her cell phone buzzed and she glanced down at the display. A warm smile brightened her face as she read the text. When she looked back up at him, the smile lingered, making him wish it were he who'd caused the reaction.

Without anything more to say, he stood and waited for her to do the same.

"I will see you on Saturday then."

"Please text me directions to the stables if you don't mind." She handed him her business card.

*****

Elle waited until she reached her car and replied to the text. Her nephew, Billy, always brightened her day. Deanna's son rarely smiled or spoke. The seven year old melted her heart with his messy mop of blond hair and askew glasses. He would only hug her, which peeved her other cousins to no end.

The shy boy was homeschooled by Deanna since he was severely dyslexic. However Billy was gifted in creativity and kept her jeweled by making her pink sparkling bracelets. Elle wore one every single day.

After a hug, he would inevitably check her wrists. Sometimes he'd be displeased with a design and take it back and replace it with another. It was their private affair and she loved it.

With his mother's assistance, he often texted pictures of his latest creation. The picture of a soft pink bracelet along with three words, "See you Saturday." Made her heart squeeze.

She replied with a smile.
Super Pretty!
I will stop by this evening at five o'clock.
I love you Billy.
Aunt Elle

*****

Elle pushed send and looked back toward the four-story building she'd just left. Sullivan Cole confused her. When he'd commented that the dinner was his idea, for a second, she thought he would confess to being attracted to her.

When he'd clarified his wish to assist in the business venture, she was both disappointed and relieved.

The man was dangerous. With the appeal of a seven-layer chocolate cake and a dose of designer clothes and rugged good looks, it was easy to understand why he was constantly featured with a different woman in the society pages.

Underneath it all, Sully was a good man. She'd been surprised to find out how nice he actually was. He'd not been faking interest in her family. He had laughed until wiping tears a couple times. Confusing and alluring, a very dangerous combination.

Chapter Five

Saturday morning was perfect; sunny with briskness in the air. After discarding several wardrobe choices, Elle finally settled on a pink plaid shirt, jeans and a denim jacket.

After parking near Redstone's stables she walked closer as the two men turned toward her. They exchanged a couple words and Redstone chuckled. It was in that moment she realized perhaps Sully had planned something in retaliation for her setting him up at the Mexican restaurant.

"Oh man," she mumbled. "What to do?"

The men neared, both tall and handsome, but she could barely pull her gaze from Sully. With an easy saunter, every step toward her made her breathing more labored. In a dark blue shirt, which brought out the brightness of his eyes, he could only be described as breathtaking.

Jared Redstone was also a good-looking man. With an easygoing vibe and a messy mop of brown curls, he instantly made her more comfortable. He smiled and held out his hand. "Jared Redstone. Welcome."

"Elle Tyler. Nice set up you got here." She glanced over to the stables.

"It's home," Jared replied raking his fingers through his hair. "I hear you are interested in the land over by the mines."

Although he maintained the relaxed stance, it was easy to see his mind was all business by the directness of his hazel gaze.

"That's correct. I represent Miller Associates, who are looking to build a one of a kind resort complex." She gave Sully a pointed look. He'd spoken to Redstone after she'd asked him to allow her to do the talking.

"Don't care much for the idea of a resort in our mix to be honest, Miss Tyler. I had discussed it with Sully when your partnership first approached him," he clarified.

"I share the same reservations he does. This is our home." Redstone motioned toward the open land. "Although many families have long since sold to allow for subdivisions and such, the Coles and I have not, as of yet."

If she didn't produce a suitable place for Miller Associates, it could prove disastrous. "Is there a compromise we can come to? Perhaps if we could meet and I show you my plans? I am ensuring the beauty of the land remains forefront."

Months of work were about to sink into a deep, black hole. Elle battled with what to say next.

Sully moved to stand beside her. The solidness of his body helped her regain balance. "I believe Jared and I may have come up with a workable solution."

They shouldn't have, but his words angered her. Why was Sullivan Cole getting so involved in the project? Was there an underlying reason she'd yet to discover?

"I'm listening." She looked to Jared for an explanation.

"I have land near Missoula. I believe it will be a good location for your resort." Jared gave her a bright smile and held out his hand once again. "I will have my office call and set up a time for you and your partner to see it."

He sauntered away not giving her a chance to say anything further. Finally she turned to Sully. "Why are you doing this?"

"Helping?"

"Yes. I get it, you felt bad about backing out of the deal, but there is no need for all of this. I appreciate it, however, I feel indebted and I..."

"You don't like owing anyone anything," he finished for her. "Is that it, Miss Tyler? If something is to be done, you'll work it out alone. Is that why you are working on this deal without your partner? You feel as if you let him down since you were the one to insist on my property."

She was taken aback. "Not that it's any of your business, but my partner is fully informed of each step I take on this project."

"He's called me four times."

"You're infuriating." She blew out a breath. "I've changed my mind. Enjoy your ride."

Just as she turned away, he moved to block her path. "I'm screwing this all up, aren't I?"

"No...I mean, you're being nice. I'm just overwhelmed. I have a lot of work to do."

He looked down at her, making every nerve in her brain go haywire. "Relax, Miss Tyler. Things will work out. Although I may just frazzle you a bit more."

"How?"

His fingers cupped her chin and he bent down and pressed a soft kiss to her lips. "Like this. Have a good day, Miss Tyler. I will call and ask you to dinner."

This time when he walked away she didn't watch. Her mouth fell open and her feet were rooted to the spot.

*****

The entire drive back to her house, Elle couldn't stop going over what happened at the stables. Had he really kissed her? What about dinner? Was it going to be an actual date?

"No." The word rang out against the silence in her vehicle. "I'm not going to join the endless string of women he dates and dumps."

She turned left instead of right and headed to her mother's.

"I think he is interested in you. Kept looking at you at dinner the other night." Her mother sipped her Diet Coke and placed items into a gift basket she was making for a local charity auction for an activity center for dyslexic children.

Every year the center where Billy went for tutoring counted on her mother's baskets to make enough money to sustain their programs.

"I went shopping and bought these," Elle said and lifted two bags, placing them on the dining table. "Got some really cute stuff."

Elle was quiet for a moment. "I'm not going to dinner with him," Elle announced while pulling price tags from a picture frame. "It's not a good idea."

"What harm can come of it?" Her mother took the frame and nestled it into the basket. "I think you like him."

"He's nice, but...he's also way out of my league."

"Nonsense. If anything, you're both in the same league. You do very well and are independent. It's refreshing. I'm so proud of you and your cousins. Every single one of you taking care of business, not depending on any man to make it."

She met her mother's warm smile and instantly felt better. "You are my world. Always set me straight. You're right. That man is not out of my league."

"Then you're going to dinner with him?"

"No. It's a very bad idea. He's too...I don't know...."

"You like him."

Her mother's quiet response seemed to echo in the room.

"Yeah, maybe I do. Therefore, I don't need to tempt myself by going out with him. That man is no closer to settling down than I am flying to the moon."

*****

The candlelight on the table made the booth where they sat seem even more intimate. While Sully ordered wine for them, Elle wondered for the millionth time why she'd said yes to dinner.

The server, a smartly dressed young man, smiled just a bit too warmly at Sully and Elle realized the guy was flirting. It was refreshing when Sully returned the smile and slid a look toward her effectively sending the signal he was interested in women. The guy gave a light shrug. "I'll be right back with your wine."

The server moved closer to her. "More water ma'am?" He poured and left.

"He likes you," she said, smiling in spite of the nerves tumbling in her stomach. She reached for the water, hoping he didn't notice the slight shaking. "Your charm disarms both men and women."

"It's a curse." He chuckled and took a healthy draw of his water. "Thank you for agreeing to dinner. You surprised me."

You and me both, she wanted to say. Instead, she looked around the restaurant. Just west of Helena, the Italian bistro's interior décor was a thing of magazines. With marble statues at the entrance and murals depicting archways with different Italian city themes, it was the perfect place for a date.

"I've never been here before. It's beautiful."

"I like it. Come here at least once a month." He leaned back and looked to the wall across from where they sat. "That one is my favorite. I love Florence. Have you been?"

"No. I went to Rome with my mother and father. We visited Venice, too, but didn't make it to Florence."

"You should go."

"Perhaps I will one day."

"Never say that." His words were clipped and she jerked back to meet his gaze.

"What?"

"Make plans if you wish to see something. Assure it with 'I will'. Don't say 'one day', that usually means the day will not come."

So the man had interesting quirks. She smiled at him. "I will go to Florence. I will look at The David's junk up close and personal."

Sully relaxed and smiled. "I believe you will."

While they ate dinner, conversation became more focused on work and the resort project. Although Sully seemed interested in talking business, Elle couldn't help but notice he kept guiding the conversation away to more personal matters. No matter if she did find the man attractive, the last thing she needed was to turn their professional relationship to more than that.

As for the kiss, she preferred to act as if it never happened. Surely it was a ploy to get her off balance and turn her into his latest conquest.

"So tell me, Sully," Elle began, "what do you plan to do with your land? I was led to believe you'd not been to Alder Gulch in years."

There was slight movement at the corners of his mouth. He knew she was avoiding any personal discussion. "Do I make you nervous?"

Yes, of course he did. The man was too attractive for his own good and to make things worse, Elle couldn't keep from staring at him.

When he reached for her hand, she didn't pull away. His blue gaze met hers as Sully lifted it and pressed a kiss to her knuckles. "I'd like to get to know you better, Elle."

Despite the warning bells of knowing he was a serial dater, her lips curved. "I'm sure we can work something out."

Elle's heartbeat picked up and she excused herself to go to the restroom, mostly to avoid pulling Sully across the table and kissing him until they were breathless. Walking on clouds, she waltzed into the bathroom.

Chapter Six

This could be it. The woman he'd been waiting for. Sully let out a breath and contemplated where to go from there. When Elle returned from the bathroom, he'd escort her to the car and kiss her goodnight.

He'd ask her out for a casual follow up date, perhaps a picnic. Hell, when was the last time he'd been on a picnic. Okay, so he'd never done that. That was what made Elle so attractive. He wanted to try new things, have different experiences with her.

A buzzing got his attention and he realized that she'd left her cellphone on the table.

Sully didn't mean to, but his eyes locked to the screen at seeing her partner's name pop up. He leaned forward and the text message became clear.

"Nice to hear you're not giving up on the land deal with Cole. Doing what you have to do to get the job done. Let me know..."

Sully's blood ran cold. A lump lodged in his throat almost gagging him. The land deal was the only reason she'd accepted his invitation. Had he become so arrogant he'd read her signals all wrong? Before Elle had gone to the restroom, there was definitely a connection between them. Or so he'd thought.

Anger simmered to the point that when she returned he could not look her straight in the eye.

She didn't look at the phone. Instead, she seemed nervous about having left it on the table and dropped it into her purse. "So tell me what do you like to do in your spare time?" Her genuine, warm smile almost made him falter. He wouldn't be surprised to see her win an Oscar for the performance.

"I enjoy night activities."

"Such as?" Her gaze didn't lower from his.

It was time to find out how far she'd go for the land deal. Sully reached for her hand again, the softness of it made him wonder about the rest of her body. This time he nibbled at her knuckles. "Come back to my place and find out. We can talk about my land in between the sheets."

For a second she didn't respond. Her eyes slowly rounded and her mouth fell open.

Elle let out a soft breath and as if repelled, she snatched her hand away. When she bent to retrieve her purse Sully sat back. He wouldn't go through with it, of course. Once she agreed to come with him, he'd call the deal off.

Producing her wallet, she pulled out five twenties and threw them on the table. "That should cover dinner." Her voice was shaky and the gaze that met his was so full of pain, he could not respond. "Don't contact me ever again."

Elle stalked off while Sully could only watch as she weaved around tables, her head down.

*****

Thankfully, she'd met him at the restaurant. Elle was shaking from head to toe by the time she sat in her vehicle. The few seconds it took to jam the key into the ignition and throw the vehicle in drive seemed to stretch. More than anything, she needed get away and put distance between herself and the pompous Sullivan Cole.

When she'd returned from the restroom, she'd noticed a change in his expression. It was as if she'd returned to a totally different man than when she'd gone. Had he actually thought she'd sleep with him to get a contract?

As soon as she arrived home, Elle rushed to the bathroom and threw up. What had been a delicious meal had turned into a revolting ball of grease in her stomach.

In the mirror, her reflection mocked. So different than when she'd gotten made up for an evening full of promise. Now her eyes were hollow, hurt radiating from them. She moved back and studied her outfit. She wore a simple loose-fitting tan dress with matching strappy sandals. Around her neck, two thin gold chains and simple hoops at her ears. Did she somehow give the vibe of being a woman who slept around?

What a fool. She'd actually felt as if they had something going. How could she have read him so wrong? It was probably how he seduced so many women and dated so often. It was easy to fall for him, but what she didn't understand was how blunt he'd been. Was it that women were so blinded by the fact he was rich and attractive they'd allow for disrespect?

More than anything, it was what bothered her the most. He'd insulted her without batting an eye. Expected she'd go to bed with him over a contract. It was clear he'd not sell his family lands. He'd taken her for not only being greedy enough to try, but for a bimbo in believing there was a possibility to change his mind.

Elle trudged to her kitchen and poured a glass of wine. Hopefully, after a good night's rest, she would move forward to forgetting the evening ever happened. She would do everything in her power to avoid the man from that day on.

"What an idiot!" her aunt Janet, exclaimed between sips of coffee. "If I ever see him, I'll cut him."

Elle couldn't help but chuckle. "You will, huh?"

"Heck yeah, he insulted my favorite niece. I should call him and tell him what to do with his land."

Needing company, Elle had walked next door to her aunt's house. There was always something going on there and she'd made a habit of stopping by on Saturday mornings. "I should check with Gary and make sure he doesn't call the man again."

She'd left her cell phone at her house, so she let out a sigh and drank from her cup. "I need retail therapy. A day of shopping always makes me feel a hundred percent better."

"Good idea," her aunt said. "I'd go with you, but your mother's coming over. We're planning our road trip to six romance reader conventions."

Later that day Elle sat in her living room with a wide grin, surrounded by shopping bags. Her cell phone dinged and she ignored it. Other than a quick chat with her mother, she'd ignored her calls and texts. If there was one from Sullivan Cole, it would ruin her day and she refused to let him ruin another one.

On Monday, she would deal with the situation and start contacts for the resort deal with the landowner of the land near the mines.

Sullivan Cole was not going to be a factor in her life and that was final.

Chapter Seven

Four horses fed while their tails swished from side to side. In the distance, goats wandered, the younger ones jumping and prancing happy for the warmth of the sun. Sully leaned on a fence while his cousin, Regina, and his brother continued arguing over which of them would get the portion of land closer to the creek. Sully spoke to them about the land deal and offered to either buy them out or split it three ways with the agreement they'd not sell the land.

The only balk Regina had was a college fund for her daughter, but after Sully disclosed he'd set up a college fund, she agreed to split the land.

"I want to build a house with a view of the water," Regina said, her arms crossed. "You don't even plan to move here," she said to Bennett.

Bennett, a well-known country singer cocked his head to the side. "I might. You can see the water from the other side. I need to be close to the water for my cattle."

"You don't own any damn cows!" Regina stomped her foot. "Sully help me out here. Bennett is being unreasonable."

"All three plots have a portion of the water. The eastern portion is secluded and surrounded by trees. It has the privacy you're always whining about Bennett. Besides, if you get cows, you can let them graze on my portion. Although I think there's plenty of space on that portion."

His younger brother gave Sully a grin he suspected usually got him whatever he wanted. "Yep, I'm going to buy cattle and settle down to become a rancher."

"What exactly are you planning to do with the cows?" Regina asked giving him a pointed look. "Your whole life, you've had a fit over killing animals. Never even liked fishing."

Bennett gave her a droll look. "I'll milk them."

"Right," Regina replied with a roll of her eyes.

Sully had corrals built and moved his horses closer to newly built stables. Next to the structure, a new RV had been set up along with his favorite grill and a sturdy shade tent with outdoor furniture and table underneath. He planned to live there one the weekends while what was to be his new home was constructed. Although he agreed with Regina, he pretended not to, otherwise his stubborn brother would never relent.

Finally, the two walked off while discussing which one would get what and Sully leaned on the corral in thought. He'd been surprised by Elle's reaction to his statement. The pain he'd seen in her eyes tortured him all night. She'd been genuinely hurt and if he'd misunderstood the text, Elle had every right to be. As much as he wanted to move on and let the entire experience go, his thoughts kept going back to her reaction.

There had been no calls from either her or Gary, and he figured they were moving on to another project. No skin off his back, although a part of him wanted to apologize to Elle. Whether she'd meant to seduce him or not, nothing ever warranted a man disrespecting a woman like he'd done. It went against his every fiber. He'd been hurt in the past and, in that moment, retaliated without thought.

The society pages made it seem as if he dated scores of women. Gossip pages rarely checked sources to discover it was mostly friends or cousins who accompanied him. On occasion it was a woman he'd not date afterwards.

Since his fiancée, Diana, died, three years earlier, he'd rarely dated. He smiled thinking of her ongoing bucket list obsession, often making him write lists and then completing each one.

After being diagnosed with a rare cancer, Diana was unable to do much, so instead, she'd accompany him when she was able and cheered Sully on.

Warmth filled him as usual when thinking of her. On her deathbed, she'd balked at him planning their wedding, while insisting she'd never get better. "I'm not going to get better, Babe. Accept it. Go do something useful like eating ice cream."

He'd planned the wedding instead, clinging to hope. On the day she'd died, he promised himself never to let time steal any chance to do something.

"Hey Uncle Sully, dinner's ready." Regina's daughter waved at him from the RV.

The lanky teen chased after his dog and he thought back again to Elle. Did she own a dog?

Not caring for the constant guilt, he attempted the coward's way out and typed a text of apology to Elle. He reworded it and then once again tried to convey he'd not thought clearly and didn't mean to offend her. The words didn't quite seem adequate enough, so he tried again, then erased the message, tucked the phone in his pocket and walked to meet his dog that bounded toward him, tongue lolling out the side of his mouth.

*****

Monday came too soon. Elle reviewed an architectural drawing and bit her bottom lip. Something about the setup of the pool and open beach area didn't sit right. She cocked her head to the side and once again visualized walking through the space.

"Hey, you busy?" Gary walked in and plopped down on a chair. Obviously, her reply didn't matter. "How did it go?"

She frowned up at him. "How did what go?"

"I ran into your aunt Friday down at town center square. She said you were going out with Sullivan Cole. I assumed it was to discuss the land deal."

It took a lot of willpower not to snap at Gary. He'd been her friend since freshman year at college and, although annoying at times, was smart and funny. "It didn't go well. I don't know why I even went."

"You two seemed..."

"Come look at this," Elle purposely interrupted. "Something is missing. What is it?"

Gary moved to stand beside her. He drew an imaginary line with his finger. "The bar should be over here so it won't obstruct any views of the ocean."

"Oh my goodness. You're right." Elle smiled broadly at him. "Sometimes you can be useful."

"Jeez thanks a lot," Gary chuckled and then looked to the doorway. "Good morning."

She knew who stood at the doorway without looking. Somehow Sully's presence seemed to fill the room and immediately she fought not to look at him.

"Miss Tyler, may I speak to you in private?"

Before she could reply and make Gary stay, the idiot scrambled to leave the room. "See ya around," he said to Sully and hit his shoulder, as if they were buddies, on the way out.

Elle moved to stand behind her desk needing the barrier and reminder it wouldn't be professional to throw a potted plant at his head.

"I thought I made it abundantly clear any business between us is over." She finally met his gaze directly almost flinching at his pinched brow and obvious consternation. "There is nothing further to discuss."

"I came to apologize. My behavior and what I intimated to you is unforgiveable. I am sorry for what I said. Please accept my sincerest apology."

She wasn't sure what to say. The embarrassment and hurt camped out in her chest with popcorn and an extra-large Coke. With what she hoped was a careless one shoulder shrug, she directed her gaze to the door. "Understood, and I agree you acted like a chauvinist pig. I will strive to forget the entire night. Now, if you don't mind, I have a lot of work to catch up on." She looked down to her messy paper-strewn desk.

When she looked back up, Sully was gone and she let out a long breath. Why didn't she feel better?

Not even a minute later Gary was back. "What was that about?"

The man was nosy as all get out. "He's not selling the land. I prefer if we keep from doing any business with Cole Corporation in the future."

Her phone dinged. "Dang it, I wish texting didn't exist. I have like twenty I haven't read."

"I know. You never replied Friday night." Gary lingered but when she didn't return to the subject of her visitor, he finally gave up and left.

"Let's see what the family is up to now." She sat and began scrolling through her messages, replying when needed.

At seeing Gary's message from Friday night, she jumped to her feet and stormed into his office.

Gary's eyes rounded. "What's wrong?"

She jammed her display to within inches of his face. "What did you mean by this?"

"Noth...nothing, it was a joke. I mean, I figured you were out on a date. Now that I read it again, I guess it was rude."

"You think?"

"Crud, you think he saw it?" Gary, the idiot, gave her a silly grin. "Hope not."

"Ugh!" Elle turned on her heel and stormed. "Men are so stupid."

Their admin assistant, gave her a knowing nod. "They are."

Elle sat at her desk unable to focus on work. Was it possible Sully had seen the text and assumed the reason for the dinner was to go to any lengths to get the contract? She looked at the time of the text and it didn't really tell her much.

She had no idea at what point in the evening it could have arrived. The only time she left the table was to use the restroom and... "Oh my God." She lowered her head to her hands.

He'd seen the message. She'd left the cellphone on the table.

If he read it, then it explained his change in demeanor when she'd returned to the table.

For a scant second, she considered texting him and telling him she accepted his apology. Unfortunately, it wouldn't do anything to repair what was done. He'd insulted her, period. And no matter what he read into the message, it had been wrong.

Her phone rang and Elle relaxed. Work was the best way to put the entire debacle behind.

*****

The land was perfect for the resort. The seller and their clients hosted an outdoor cocktail party, which included champagne and an elaborate display of Elle's architectural plans for Big Sky Resort Ranch. It was a beautiful, sunny day and unlike the few days prior, Mother Nature cooperated with a light breeze and no rain.

Elle held a glass of champagne and discussed the possibility of a future project with a guest. While scanning the crowd for Gary, she caught sight of him standing a bit too close to a woman, his free hand moving along with whatever he said. Full flirt mode.

It had taken two months, but finally a contract was signed and she could put the project behind. From here, the lead in the project would take over, only contacting her if minor changes were needed, which she doubted.

"I hear Cancun is in the near future," her friend, Cindy, quipped as she approached with a glass of champagne. She smiled at the man Elle had been talking to. "Maybe we should plan a trip to Mexico. It's been a while."

The man was handsome with streaks of grey on his temples, which accentuated his dark eyes. He smiled easily at Cindy. "I'll call you and we can discuss it." He nodded at both and sauntered away.

"Well, well," Elle said, lifting a brow. "You know Edgar Hughes?"

"Dated a few times," Cindy replied, taking Elle's arm. "How about you? Dating anyone?"

"No. I am looking, but they all run scared." Elle laughed, ignoring the pang in her chest and the immediate picture of Sully forming in her mind.

*****

Brow furrowed, Billy slid beads onto a wire while Elle watched from across the kitchen table. As was their custom, she visited during the weekend, usually hoping to be fed. Her cousin, Deanna, was a fabulous cook who was used to the rest of her unmarried relatives popping in with growling stomachs and feeble excuses.

When a lock of blond hair fell across Billy's face, Elle itched to sweep it back. Instead, she smiled at him. "I love the colors you're using this time."

"They are shades of pink," her sullen nephew replied. She never tired of his creations, often hating to return one in exchange for another. He rarely allowed her to keep one longer than a couple weeks.

"Can I keep this one?" She pointed at the one she wore.

"No." He looked to the kitchen where Deanna cleared her throat.

"It would be nice to let your aunt keep some Billy. The bracelet box is full."

For a long moment, his gaze locked to the sparkling bracelet on her wrist. "I suppose you can keep it. Let me check my box first." He ran toward his bedroom.

Deanna let out a sigh. "We're going to be on *Hoarders* if he doesn't stop making bracelets. It will be a very sparkly episode." Her eyes widened and she pointed at the patio doors to her back yard. "Queue the freak parade."

Twins Lori and Sandy appeared followed by Aunt Janet. They carried floats, beach bags and what looked to be an oversized floating bed.

"I don't think your pool is big enough for all of that." Elle studied the above ground pool. "What are they up to?" Unable to resist, she got up and went out.

"Hey!" Her aunt narrowed her eyes. "You didn't tell me you were coming over here. I could have used a ride."

"You have a car."

"I hate driving the damn thing."

"What are you doing with all that stuff?"

Lori turned to her, revealing a fully made up face. "We're taking pictures for online dating sites. Doing something different. Also for our social media profile pictures."

Her face red from blowing up a beach ball, Sandy nodded and grinned. "We've decided to advertise for twins and get married at the same time."

There was a beat of silence as Elle couldn't think of a thing to say.

"Nobody is going to marry you freaks!" Deanna called out from the kitchen window. "Pictures by an above ground pool with all that crap, scream white trash."

"Takes one to know one," Sandy screamed back.

"Make me a sandwich," Aunt Janet said settling into a foldout chair and lifting up a camera that would make professional photographers drool. "Model photography makes me hungry."

Deanna's sister, Jennifer, traipsed to stand by the pool and posed like a pin-up girl. She wore a string bikini, a huge multicolored hat on her head and bright yellow sunglasses. "I go first. This extreme wedgie is giving me a rash."

*****

Elle chuckled at the scene she'd left at her cousin's house. An argument over who'd pose with what prop culminated in a tug of war with a blow up flamingo, which ended when Lori fell on top of Aunt Janet. The chair collapsed and when Jennifer hurried to help, Deanna's Great Dane stuck his nose in her butt.

Before long, everyone laid around talking and laughing; the flamingo the only thing in the pool.

*****

The quiet of the coffee shop beckoned and she adjusted her laptop strap. The weather was perfect to sit outside and work. She loved Sunday afternoons, especially when she could review her emails and read over local articles on upcoming projects. After Sundays like today, she could go to work on Monday without having the extra pressure of email and such.

She spotted an empty table next to a man with a Labrador. The dog sat on the ground watching him read. The scene was cute.

The closer she walked, the tighter her stomach. Was it Sullivan Cole? The man wore sunglasses and his dark hair gleamed in the sun. Not wanting to go any closer than necessary, she couldn't get a good look without being obvious.

He'd not lifted his head. Instead, he read the book and every once in a while petted his dog.

If it was Sully, she'd prefer not to deal with whatever awkwardness it would bring. Although after he'd apologized for his reaction after reading her text, she'd hoped not to see him so soon after. The annoying butterflies fluttered and her breath caught when the man smiled at the dog and broke off a piece of bagel for it.

It was Sully.

"Crud," Elle mumbled, lowering her head and walking past. She'd order a latte and find a place inside. If she left, it meant walking past him again.

"Elle?" His deep voice washed over her and, in that instant, she knew for sure. Sullivan Cole mattered to her.

Swallowing, she stopped.

*****

Sully wasn't sure how to proceed. When she turned to him and their eyes met, it was all he could do not to reach for her. "Are you working today?"

Before replying her hand went across her body to her laptop bag strap. "Yes. You?"

"Nope. I don't work on Sundays." He motioned to the table. "Would you like to join Buddy and me?"

It was an awkward moment of silence as Elle looked toward the dog who watched them. "He's cute."

"I think so."

"I don't know. I'll be reading and working on email and won't be much company. Maybe some other time."

"Sit down, relax. Tell me what you want and I'll get it. My treat." He took her elbow and guided her to the table. "We don't have to talk."

There was no way in God's creation he'd allow this opportunity to pass. For weeks, he'd been racking his brain to come up with a way to see her. No matter how hard he tried to not think about Elle, she constantly popped up in his thoughts.

Although seeming unsure, she lowered to the chair. Immediately, Buddy leaned over and proceeded to lick her face, his large body shaking and tail wagging furiously.

Elle's laugh made Sully smile. He'd have to reward Buddy later for breaking the ice.

"Be still, Buddy," he commanded. With obvious reluctance, his dog obediently relaxed onto the ground, seeming happy when Elle continued to scratch behind his ears.

"He's so well trained. I could use you with my cousins," she said. Then seeming to realize her implication of them becoming friends, she swallowed visibly.

"What can I order for you?" Sully asked with a nonchalance he didn't feel.

"Latte, with two honeys please."

*****

Elle looked down to Buddy who'd lowered his large head to between his paws. If only she could be as relaxed. Here she was, waiting on Sullivan Cole to bring her coffee and all she could think of was how to run to her car and leave. Now that she accepted feeling more than attraction for the man, it would be hard to not be nervous around him. His actions were disconcerting. If anything, she expected resentment.

After all, she'd not accepted his apology and, for all intents and purposes, their last parting had been less than amicable. Way less then friendly.

When he reappeared and held open the door for two women who giggled with overly bright enthusiasm, Elle let out a long sigh.

He placed the latte on the table and looked to her bag, which she'd placed in the empty chair. "You're not working."

"I need to tell you something." She waited for him to sit and leaned forward, placing her elbows on the table. "When you came to my office to apologize. I should have accepted it."

His gaze moved to the side as he considered her words. "Do you?"

"Yes. At that time I was angry and hurt. But I understand what happened."

"My actions were not to be understood or accepted. I disrespected you and deserved what I got."

*****

Taking a break from replying to emails, Elle opened a request for a quote and realized she'd received a great deal more work lately. Thankfully, due to the ranch and resort deal, she was able to be choosier about which jobs she accepted.

Over the laptop, she caught a glimpse of Sully. The corner of his mouth lifted at whatever he read and she had to admit that spending the afternoon at a café with a handsome man across the table would be hard to beat.

"What are you reading?" His hand covered the cover of the book so she couldn't make the title out.

"Espionage Thriller." He showed her the cover of a well-known author. "Helps me prepare for the week ahead." With a boyish grin, he looked to her laptop. "I should probably do what you're doing."

"Everyone has their own way of relaxing. I don't do anything most Saturdays and Sunday mornings. On Sunday afternoons, I do this and am ready for Monday."

Sully remained quiet as she clicked her document closed and shut the laptop. When she slid it into the bag, he stretched. "Time to go?"

"I have to get something to eat and get home." As soon as she said it, hope sprung he'd want to join her. Truthfully, she'd been done with work over an hour earlier, but prolonged it to stay with Sully.

Oblivious, Sully picked up their empty cups and took them inside the shop. He returned and poured what was left of his water into a dog bowl and waited for Buddy to drink. "What are you planning to eat?"

There it was. The possibility of more. "Probably a wrap from over there." She pointed to a small restaurant with outdoor tables. "I love their chicken salad." Elle hesitated. "Would you and Buddy like to join me?"

He looked to the restaurant and then to Buddy. "Sure. I'll meet you there, let me walk him around and see if he needs to visit a bush or something."

Moments later, they were seated outside. Without the distraction of the book and laptop, Elle wondered a how conversation would go.

Almost two hours later of interesting discussion, jokes and even more butterflies, Sully walked Elle to her car. She placed her purse on the seat and turned to say goodbye.

Sully stood close, his eyes looking from her eyes to her lips. "I'd like to see you again, Elle. Spend time with you."

"I'd like that, too." Just before his lips covered hers, Elle closed her eyes and gripped his shoulders. This time the kiss was not as chaste as the time before. Perhaps a bit too intense for being out in public, but the thought would not occur to her until later.

His arms circled Elle's waist and Sully pulled her against him. Not wanting him to move away, she leaned against him and nibbled at his bottom lip. His body was hard and felt right against her. Sullivan Cole was in very good shape.

He was...

Perfect.

Chapter Eight

"I'm glad you cleared things up with the young man." Her mother poured soda into a cup and lowered to sit next to Elle on the wicker loveseat at her mother's screened in porch. "I wondered how long before you both bumped into each other."

Elle let out a breath. "I am looking forward to our date. We seem to get along very well, but I still worry about all the women. He seems like a serial-dating-gigolo."

Margie laughed. "I doubt he's a gigolo. He's very wealthy, so Sully doesn't have to sell the goods."

"Oh my God, Mom!" Elle laughed. "The goods?" She chuckled and her mother nodded.

Her mother patted her hand. "It's all about grace dear. You shouldn't judge based on perception. Let his actions and words speak to you, not what you hear or read about him. That's where people go wrong all the time, allowing others to influence how they feel or see things."

"You're so right Mom."

They were going to see an action movie and then have a drink at a small pub Elle loved. Much to her amusement, he'd suggested the latest chick flick, which she wanted to see, but feared sobbing in front of him.

"Hopefully I won't show up on the society pages as his latest conquest." Elle flicked at a fly. "Shoo."

"Did you hear your cousins are all on dating sites. It's going to be a hoot hearing what they've gotten into. I can't wait for tonight." It was family night at the Mexican restaurant and, of course, her aunt had already called to remind them.

"I have to agree with you on that one, Mom. It's definitely going to be interesting."

*****

Sully stood just a short distance from the grave. He'd not brought flowers that day. Her family kept the vases filled and he rarely caught them empty. He neared and lowered to the ground on one knee. "Hey, Diana. I need to talk about something..."

An hour later, the office loomed and he hurried into the building. There would be a roomful of people waiting for him, partners surrounding the large conference table and secretaries fretting over whatever was demanded of them that morning.

Sully exited the elevator unable to keep from smiling at the rush he always felt when facing the prospect of a day filled with work and problems to deal with.

"Mr. Cole," a young man neared. "I am Phillip, Sharon Logan's assistant. She is here and requests a word with you in private before the meeting."

Sully glanced at his watch. "I don't have time. Will barely make it in time..." In his office, the woman awaited him. As usual, everything about Sharon was attractive. Her long hair fell in waves past her shoulders. In a power red dress and black heels, her slim figure was accentuated.

"Good morning, Sullivan. I just need a minute of your time."

"Sharon. As you know, we have several execs waiting in the other room. I don't want to waste their time. Perhaps after."

"No now."

"What is so important that it cannot wait?"

"I'm pregnant."

"That's not possible. We used precaution. And it was that one time about a month ago. Are you sure?"

She lifted a shoulder. "I'm going to keep the child."

Immediately, his thoughts went to Elle and how he'd not have a chance to get to know her now. There was no way he'd allow a child of his to grow up without him in his or her daily life.

"We'll get married."

"Of course."

She waltzed out of the office, not waiting to discuss anything further, leaving Sully reeling. His life had just taken a turn he'd not expected. No matter how shrewd or aloof Sharon was, he knew she'd not lie about something that could be easily tested.

The woman was as rich as he, if not wealthier and owned one of the biggest horse breeding programs in Montana.

"Sully, the meeting is about to start." His assistant, Stacia, gave him a curious look. "Are you all right? You are pale."

"I'm fine. Just great."

*****

Elle could only stare at her cell phone display dumbfounded. The text was short and to the point. Sully cancelled their date and added he'd not be able to see her again.

When the first tear slipped down her cheek, she rushed to the door, closed and locked it. Leaning on it, she allowed more tears to fall. It was silly, of course, to cry over someone she'd not gotten to know well.

At the same time, something about him had felt so right. It was as if she'd been waiting her entire life for him. The peace in her soul, the lightness in her chest that came when spending time with Sully was like nothing before.

Finally behind her desk again, Elle wiped away tears and blew her nose. It was time to finally put Sullivan Cole in the past. He was not the man for her no matter what her heart demanded.

The phone rang and it was her cousin, Jennifer. "Hey you're not going to believe what I just heard at work?"

Jennifer, who worked for the state protocol office, always had the best gossip. Most business executives came to her office on a regular basis with their assistants in tow. The bored underlings made for easy prey and if anyone could wheedle information from them it was Jennifer.

Elle smiled, glad for the distraction. "Tell me, what did you hear?"

"Phillip, Sharon Logan's assistant told me his boss is preggers." Jennifer waited for effect. "Guess who she says the baby's daddy is?"

"Brad Pitt?"

"Close. Sullivan Cole."

Elle's jaw dropped. "Are you serious?" Her voice elevated two octaves at the thought Sullivan was sleeping with someone while pursuing her. "That low down..."

"Wait," Jennifer interrupted. "Phillip knows for a fact, Cole is not the father."

Sometimes Jennifer's flair for drama was a bit much. "How would Phillip know?"

"Oh honey, assistants know everything. The last time Sully slept with Sharon, she was already pregnant." Jennifer laughed. "I bet the girl outside your office can probably tell me how many times a day you fart."

"Jenn...who's the baby's father?" Elle snapped, which made Jennifer excited at knowing she'd hooked her.

"It's Randall Newman. The owner of the Double Wabble." Double Wabble was a new franchise that sold hot dogs and steak strips encased in batter that was popular with teens. No one else seemed to like the food. Elle suspected the teens gathered because the Double Wabble logo looked suspiciously like twin phalluses.

"Seriously?"

"His assistant, Nancy, is a total bitch. I don't like her. All about getting all the attention. But all I have to do is start acting like I'm jealous of her and she spills faster than an oil tanker in the Gulf of Mexico."

It almost worked, Elle was curious to know more about Nancy. Instead, she focused on Sullivan's issue. "Why would Sharon not want the guy, Randall, know he's the baby's father?"

"He's greasy and slimy. I'm sure she was drunk when she had the relationship. From what Phillip said, it lasted about a month. You think someone can stay drunk that long?"

"Eww. He is not very attractive if I remember the commercials. Is it the guy in the bright orange jumpsuit that parachutes into a huge bowl of batter?"

"That's him. Isn't the thought of Sharon with him totally wacky?"

Elle sighed. "How does she plan to sell the baby off as Sully's? He can get a DNA test. I'm sure she wouldn't lie about something like that."

"Phillip says Sharon is counting on Sully believing her because she never lies. Actually she lies a lot, but never gets caught. Also, she told Phillip that he would have to seduce Sully's secretary, Stacia to make sure she has the inside scoop on whatever Sully is doing."

"Oh my goodness. Is he going to do it?"

"Oh crap. Gotta go!" Jennifer hung up.

What to do about the situation? There was no way to warn Sully without throwing Phillip under the bus. She leaned forward, not exactly feeling better. So he'd had relations since they'd met. Yes, the woman had purposefully seduced him, but nonetheless, it still hurt her.

There had to be a way to let Sully know. Perhaps if she put her mind to it, she could be as creative as Sharon Logan.

*****

It turned out that evening the choice became clearer. Elle sat back with a glass of water. She'd done her yoga routine and was ready for a lazy evening of television and the couch. Although her mind kept returning to Sully's predicament, she decided to relax that evening and not worry too much over something she had little control.

At the sound of the doorbell, she groaned. Hopefully, it was a package being delivered. The delivery guy would usually ring once and leave, so at the second ding, she reluctantly got up.

Sully, framed by the doorway, gave her half a smile. "Need to talk. Got a minute or two?"

"Of course." She moved back to allow him in only to be engulfed in a tight hug. It was not for her that he held on so tight. Sully needed reassurance so she rubbed his back and allowed the hug to linger.

When he finally released her, she took his hand and led him to sit. "How about a glass of water, straight up?" It was hard to keep her voice neutral when she wanted to scream at the top of her lungs and let him know the truth about Sharon.

The dejected man did not deserve to be lied to. It was obvious he was torn between the right thing to do and what he truly wanted.

After handing him the glass, which he emptied and placed on the coffee table, he remained still, not looking at her. "I want to apologize for cancelling. I told myself I would step away from you because of a sudden change in my life. But I can't stop thinking about you."

"I feel the same about you, Sully." She nudged his shoulder with hers. "I need to tell you something. However, I can't explain anything and I just need you to trust me on this."

His blue gaze met hers, moving from her eyes to lips. He leaned forward and she allowed the kiss. Her heart melted when his lips pressed against hers. Eyes fluttering shut, Elle cupped his jaw with her hand loving the feel of his unshaved skin.

When he moved back he smiled and nodded. "Okay, hit me."

"Ask for a DNA test."

He blinked and frowned. "How did you know?"

"I'll allow you this one question. Let's just say one of my cousins has a lot of contacts. She calls me with gossip and inside info."

"Who did she..."

She pressed her finger to his lips. "No more questions." She reached for the remote. "Let's watch people make stupid choices." The latest episode of house hunting came on the screen and she settled back against him. "Relax, Sully, things will work out."

When he let out a sigh and rested back putting his arm around her, Elle prayed Jennifer was right. Otherwise, this would be their last time together.

Chapter Nine

His horse nickered. It grazed on the young grasses while Sully looked across the expanse of his land. How many of his ancestors had sat on this very same hill and did the same? It was Cole land and, as such, he could not imagine anything but the lushness of trees and flowers there.

Although his cabin's construction was well underway, he'd become quite accustomed to staying at the old house where his great-grandfather, Grayson Cole, had lived. It was rustic living, but after spending the week in his modern condo, sometimes the basic life there would bring him to realize what was important in life.

Sully expected to hear back from Sharon since leaving her a voice mail. However, he'd purposefully left his cell phone behind at the cabin. This was time to think things through and clear his mind of clutter.

At the moment, he wasn't sure how he felt about Elle knowing he'd slept with Sharon. A moment of weakness had proved horrible results. He could have fathered a child, but that he'd be tied to a woman he had no deep feelings for.

Now all that was left was to ensure who the child's father was. If the child were his, he would provide him or her with the best life possible. Divorce was not in the Cole vocabulary. Once he gave his word to marry someone, it was for life. He tried to imagine a life with Sharon and had to urge the horse forward until galloping across the field back to the cabin.

She'd called.

Her voice was hesitant, as if unsure, which was nothing like Sharon.

"I'm sorry you feel the need to question me. As you know, I never speak untruths. I will do no such thing as a test to prove I'm being truthful and I am fine with raising your child alone."

She'd hung up without a goodbye.

"Hey Sully," greeted his cousin, Regina, as she strolled in with Buddy. "Saw you riding back and had to come and make sure you didn't fall and break your neck."

"I'm a better rider than that."

"Um hmm," she leaned closer and peered at the phone in his hand. "Something wrong?"

"You can say that. A woman saying she's pregnant by me."

"No way. Who's the father?"

"Good question."

He pressed the replay button and let Regina listen to the message. She snatched the phone and pressed a couple buttons.

Before he could react, Regina was speaking. "Sharon, this is Regina, Sully's cousin. I need to clarify something to you. If he's asking for a DNA test, it's not to insult you. You know how men are, he should have explained more. It's just that every Cole has two things. A recessive gene for Doracks disease, and a crazy birthmark on our butt. I'm sure if you slept with Sully, you've seen it."

There was a beat of silence as Regina listened.

"Oh yes, well I have it, too. Every single one of us has it. So you see there is no need for any kind of test to make sure the child is a Cole. We come marked. Kind of like an omen or something." Regina laughed and ducked away when he reached for the phone.

After a few uh-huhs and okays, Regina ended the call.

"The baby is not yours. Said she just found out this morning, but was hurt by your request. Probably feels slutty or something."

"What is Doracks disease?" He followed her out when she walked after Buddy.

"I made it up."

"Do you really have the same birthmark as mine?"

"Nope. Only you and my brother have it. Remember I made fun of you guys and pulled your swim trunks down every summer?"

"You were annoying as all get out."

"My being annoying just saved you from having to marry a lying....you know what."

"True. Thank you, Regina." He did a side hug and she punched his shoulder.

Family could be great. Although Regina was demanding and strong willed, she was a great person to have in his corner.

Six months later

"I love it!" Elle turned in a full circle, her arms extended outward. "It's a perfect place to get away and enjoy nature."

Sully's weekend cabin was finally complete. He'd surprised Elle after asking her to a picnic. Yes, he'd finally had a picnic date and everything had gone off without a hitch thanks to Regina's help.

They'd gone for a short horseback ride and now he ended the evening by bringing her to the cabin.

Her eyes sparkled. "Sully, you'll spend many happy days here. How could you not?" She went to the large picture window overlooking a shaded area he'd specifically built for entertaining.

Although summers were short in Montana, there was always time to squeeze in a couple family barbeques.

Sully neared and wrapped his arms around her. "Do you think your family would like to come out here sometime?"

Wide eyes met his. "Are you kidding me? They would probably scar the horses and any other critters for life."

"I'm hoping they come out. I think it will be nice to have them here."

She placed her arms around his neck and brought him down for a kiss. "You are the sweetest man. I would have never guessed."

"If inviting your family brings me kisses like these, I'll invite them every week." He laughed when Elle pushed him away and shook her head.

"Could you see yourself living here?" The question left his lips and Sully held his breath to see what she'd say.

Elle's gaze slid to him and then his girlfriend looked around the living space. "I could, it would be very relaxing."

"Good," he replied.

*****

Sully had been acting strange all day. He'd ask a question and then wait for her reply. It was as if he tested her.

In her opinion, she'd garnered a big fat "F". Whatever he was thinking, she was ahead of him.

If he worried she'd pull a Sharon and force him to marriage, it would not be happening. If and when they did sleep together, which she figured would be soon, she would insure full protection for both of them.

"Sully, don't worry about what will happen between us. I'm telling you upfront now. If you have something on your mind, just say it. Right now I'm thinking you are still reeling over the Sharon thing. I care for you, heck I may as well admit it, I'm head over heels crazy for you."

He moved closer, but did not speak, so she continued.

"I want us to spend time together and, hopefully, find out we have a future. But if and when we decide that, it will be because we both want it. I demand a prenup and let me add, I don't want to have any kids for a few years yet, so when we are intimate, which I hope is soon, we are using triple protection."

His lips quivered. "What is triple protection? It doesn't sound romantic."

"You know what I mean, pills, condoms.... Okay, you got me there." She laughed when he pulled her in for a hug and nuzzled her neck.

Serious eyes met hers. "I won't sleep with you until you agree to something."

"Are you playing hard to get?" Elle pretended offense, but couldn't help but giggle when he placed his hands over his private parts. "Sully, I'm being serious."

"So am I."

He dug in his pocket and lowered to one knee lifting a sparkling diamond ring. "I will only sleep with my fiancée. So, Elle Tyler, will you sleep with me from now til my parts don't work?"

In spite of herself, Elle laughed. "Yes, Sullivan, I will marry you and sleep with you even after your parts don't work."

Moments later she snuggled against her fiancé cocooned with him beneath a blanket as they watched the sun set from the front porch. They'd had a glass of wine to celebrate and then settled onto a double rocker to talk about their future.

With a content sigh, she lifted her head from his shoulder and looked at the handsome face. "Can we go to Florence for our honeymoon?"

"I've already bought tickets."

The End

Dear Reader

Writing is my dream come true. There is nothing I love more than bringing my characters and stories to life and sharing them with you.

I live in a small town in Georgia with my husband and two unruly Chihuahuas.

I had fun writing Sully and Elle's story. If you enjoyed *Montana Born,* please recommend it to your friends and family. There are more short western contemporaries, so be sure to read *Montana Bachelor, Montana Boss and Montana Beau* next!

I would sincerely appreciate a review.

I love hearing from my readers and am always excited when you join my newsletter to keep abreast of new releases and other things happening in my world.

Website: http://www.HildieMcQueen.com
Facebook: http://www.facebook.com/HildieMcQueen
Email: Hildie@HildieMcQueen.com
Newsletter sign up: http://goo.gl/PH6D00

Keep Calm and Read On!

Hildie McQueen

STANDING ON THE PROMISES

Sally Kilpatrick

It's funny what a pinky promise--or two--can do.

Katrina ridiculed Seth mercilessly in elementary school, and now she and the town of Kingdom Come need to ask of him a big favor. A tornado has destroyed their community center, and the city council is hoping their native son, now a Christian music star, will do a benefit concert to help fund repairs. Katrina's job is on the line, but she's even more concerned about how she can ask Seth's forgiveness. For Seth, forgiveness for the past is easy, but fighting his present feelings is a lot harder.

Chapter 1

Today was shaping up to be the Mondayest of all Mondays to ever Monday.

First, she forgot her purse and had to go back home for it even though she was already running late. Then she got a flat tire and got a grease stain on her favorite capris while changing it. Her reward upon walking through the door? Her boss wanted her in a meeting. Right then.

It was bad enough that her Aunt Faith was her boss, but now Katrina also had to live with her. She'd always had the feeling her aunt didn't like her, but now that her aunt had moved in with Katrina and her mother, the constant carping carried over from home to work and back to home again. Sometimes Katrina thought she was catching all of the vinegar that should've been spewed on her spoiled brat cousins. They'd taken their father's side in the divorce that had sent Aunt Faith packing.

Katrina took a deep breath and mentally prepared herself as she took the seat across from her aunt. "I'm sorry, but I couldn't make it to the town council meeting last night. Makayla had one of those twenty-four hour bugs and—"

"You could've left her with Hope."

Katrina bit her tongue to keep from pointing out that maybe her mother didn't want to catch the twenty-four hour stomach virus of death, and, besides, she'd already raised a daughter and shouldn't have to raise her granddaughter, too. "Just tell me what I missed, please."

Aunt Faith droned on about several happenings in the little town of Kingdom Come, Texas. Descended from one of the founders of the town, she would tell you all about its history as a sanctuary for evangelicals of the hottest fire and brimstone. Her favorite pastime was reminding her niece in every way, subtle and not, that she had not saved herself for marriage and was reaping what she had sown. Katrina dozed with her eyes open, her aunt's voice now that of a 'Charlie Brown' grownup, when she heard a name that made her sit up straight, awake and in a cold sweat. "Did you say Seth Bridges?"

"Yes, of course I did. I told the council last night that you would be his handler since you don't have as much on your plate while we're waiting for the funds to fix the old auditorium."

"Not as much on my plate?" Either Katrina's hearing was faulty, or her aunt had lost her ever-loving mind. The softball season was underway, and soccer registration had begun. There were three continuing education classes going on, and she had to find new places for them to meet now that a tornado had damaged the old school that served as Kingdom Come's Community Center. There were contractors to meet and mailings to send out and the website to update and—Seth Bridges to chauffeur around?

"I don't think it's a good idea. Surely there's someone else around here, someone more educated maybe, who could take care of Seth." The words hardly came out over the lump in her throat. She hadn't spoken to Seth since he left during the fifth grade. She'd tried to talk to him when he came back to town to attend high school, but she'd been too embarrassed.

Yeah, that and you were a good seven months pregnant.

Okay, sure, part of her didn't want to talk to him while she felt like a blimp. He had turned out to be so handsome, while she had turned out to be just the kind of girl who was stuck working for her aunt because she'd dropped out of high school.

"I don't really care if you think it's a good idea," Her aunt was saying. "I told him earlier that you would meet him at the Doomsday Diner this afternoon and that you would be his point person for anything he needed while he was in town."

"This afternoon?"

"Yep, and I told Hope on my way out the door so you wouldn't wiggle out of it. She said she'd be happy to watch Makayla for you."

Katrina's mouth opened and closed as she searched for the words. After discarding several of the four-letter variety, she said, "You had no right to do that."

"Look, you need to make something of yourself, and I'm going to help you whether you like it or not."

Katrina sighed. Part of Aunt Faith's make-something-of-yourself program included her taking the GED in two weeks. Truth be told, she should be studying for the math and science portion of the test rather than running errands, but her aunt was the boss and Katrina worked three times as hard to avoid cries of nepotism.

Nepotism: noun, a practice of favoritism based on kinship.

Her vocabulary skills were just fine, but math and science? Not so good.

"Katrina, did you hear me?"

"What? No. I'm sorry."

"Seth's due to arrive in an hour and a half." Aunt Faith looked over the rims of her glasses

"Oh! I gotta go." Katrina's hand flew to her hair before she remembered there was no need for her to primp. She lowered her hand slowly then stood with deliberation.

"Oh, and Katrina?"

She turned to face her aunt.

"Make sure you aren't *overly* nice with Mr. Bridges, please."

Katrina's face burned scarlet. There was the dig. She'd known it was coming, but it had managed to catch her off guard again nonetheless. "Yes, ma'am."

"You might want to change pants before you go, too."

"Of course," Katrina murmured.

She walked out of her aunt's office quickly and made a beeline to the closet of an office she called her own. She considered marching back into Aunt Faith's office and telling her that she wasn't careless. She considered marching back in there and telling her secret, but she didn't. She hung on to it as she always did.

She had other problems to worry about, bigger fish to fry, as her mother always said.

Fish like Seth Bridges.

She wondered if tartar sauce improved the taste of apologies. Either way, she would have to ask his forgiveness.

Chapter 2

Katrina parallel parked about a block from the Doomsday Diner. She would've dearly loved to have parked right in front of the cafe, but an old fashioned hitching post sat out front. Sometimes residents of Kingdom Come still rode their horses into town and made use of that post, but today was too hot to be one of those days.

She paused at the door. She'd arrived early in the hopes that she would be able to get her bearings, but what if Seth were ridiculously punctual, too? What would she say to him? What *could* she say to him?

I have all of your records.

She wouldn't be lying. She did have all three of his contemporary Christian albums. Still, it felt like an inane thing to say.

Inane: adjective, silly; stupid.

She recited the definition as she entered the dive and quickly scanned the patrons for Seth. When she didn't see him, she took a seat facing the door. Maybe she should just play it cool and pretend like nothing had ever happened between them.

No, she needed to swallow her pride and apologize to Seth first thing, just get it out into the open. Either he would take her seriously and accept her apology or he would look at her as if she were crazy and tell her she had nothing to apologize for. She was hoping for the latter since she would be at his beck and call for the next few days.

She checked her watch to see it was one minute until their appointed meeting time of three. When she looked up, he stood in the door scanning the room for her. She sucked in a breath, taken off guard by how handsome he'd become. If anything, he was even better looking than in high school. Tall with wavy black hair, his face had taken on more angles and more scruff, but his brown eyes still twinkled. Now those eyes locked with hers.

She stood as he walked toward the booth, feeling silly for doing so. Even though she was a good five foot ten, she still had to look up to him when he stopped in front of her. "Hi."

Smooth, Katrina.

"Hi." He pulled her into a quick awkward hug, unfairly smelling of nothing more than woodsy cologne and man in spite of the brutal Texas heat. She backed away as soon as she respectably could because a) she could only hope her deodorant and perfume were holding up, b) she didn't deserve a hug from him, and c) his strong embrace felt entirely too good.

Great. She'd been studying for so long, she was even thinking in multiple choice.

"So," she said as she slid into one side of the booth and he took the other.

"So," he echoed.

"I have something I need to say before we go any farther—"

"Y'all ready to order?"

Katrina closed her eyes for the merest of seconds before looking to Seth to see if he wanted to eat. She only had fifty dollars in her checking account, but she could afford one meal. Maybe.

"I believe I would like some of Juanita's world-famous chocolate pecan pie."

"A la mode?" The waitress asked.

"Is there any other way?"

She grinned at him. "Coffee?"

"Of course!"

Thoroughly charmed, she looked to Katrina. "What about you?"

"Oh, nothing for me—"

"C'mon. My treat," he said.

She couldn't guarantee he'd keep smiling at her, and she really liked his lopsided grin. "I suppose I could have some coconut cream pie and a coffee."

"Coming right up."

Katrina didn't even look after the waitress because she was too busy looking into Seth's eyes and trying to see in his soul. Maybe she hadn't hurt him as much as she thought she had.

"Now what were you about to say earlier?"

"I, ah, I was going to say," she began. She almost chickened out and told him about those records she had, but she forced herself to soldier on. "I owe you an apology that's been a long time coming."

"For what?" Either he was an excellent actor as well as singer, or he really had forgotten all about fifth grade.

"The things I said back in fifth grade. My parents were getting a divorce, and it was a hard time. Not that that's any excuse, but I'm sorry. I'm really, really sorry."

They waited for their pie in silence. Of course, she hadn't picked the best place or time. She felt as though everyone in the diner were watching and waiting to see what he would say to her apology even though she knew the few patrons there were wrapped up in their own conversations.

"What are you talking about?"

Her face burned red hot. "I said you read baby books back in elementary school because—"

"Trina Rawls," he murmured. "I could've sworn my publicist had said Christina Rowland would be meeting me, but, no. It *is* you."

The lopsided grin disappeared. So did the twinkle in his eye.

He had thought she was one of their other classmates. He had only been friendly when he thought she was someone else.

She cleared her throat, telling the tears that threatened to fall that they would just have to wait until later. "Christina moved to Corpus, and I go by Katrina now."

"Katrina it is."

She didn't want to be Trina. The summer after her fifth grade year, she had demanded that everyone call her by her full first name, Katrina. She told them she wanted a more grown up name, but the reality was that she wanted to be a different person than the one who'd tormented Seth and hung out with a bunch of girls who dropped her the minute her parents got a divorce and she had to move away from the house with the swimming pool. By some miracle, Katrina had stuck.

She shook her head. "For what it's worth I'm sorry."

"Long time ago," he said as their slices of pie arrived. "Water under the bridge."

She opened her mouth to try again, but he looked away and attacked his slice of pie with such force that she knew he wanted to get out of the diner as soon as he could. Her body ran hot and then cold, and she almost choked on her first bite.

Water under the bridge.

That wasn't quite the same as "you're forgiven."

Chapter 3

Suddenly that chocolate pecan pie Seth had been looking forward to since Dallas tasted like sawdust, but he forced himself to take the requisite bites so he could leave the aptly named Doomsday Diner.

As if he could *ever* forget or forgive Katrina Rawls. That girl had hated him back in elementary school, and he'd never been able to figure out why. Yeah, she'd accused him of reading the baby books and had made fun of him when Mrs. Winterbourne made him read out loud, something he'd detested because he lived in fear that he would mess something up. And mess up he almost always did, causing Katrina and her girlfriends to titter at him.

Every day, Katrina'd put a different book on his desk, usually a bulky one she knew he couldn't read like Tolstoy's *War and Peace*. Sometimes she'd mix it up and bring an old board book from the Kindergarten rooms instead, though. She'd stand in the corner with three other mean girls, and they would laugh and point. He wasn't their only target, but he was their favorite.

At least until the day they made him cry.

They had picked on him and picked on him. When they were tired of calling him stupid, they made fun of his pants with the patches or how he didn't get his hair cut as often. One day, Katrina had said, "I bet you get your stupid from your daddy."

That day he snapped. He turned over his desk with a growl. He broke his ruler on the side of his desk, and one piece went flying. It sliced Katrina's cheek just under her right eye. He swiped books from all of the desks near him, but, as he stood there in the silent aftermath watching a line of blood trickle down her cheek, his anger dissipated. The tears came to his eyes, hot and fat, and then the class began to laugh.

Mrs. Winterbourne, who was ready to retire and oblivious to the constant teasing of Katrina and her crew, had grabbed him by his ear and dragged him to the library where Ms. Riley had offered him hot cocoa and let him tell his side of the story between hiccupping sobs. She even coaxed him to read to her—just a little bit. Once the principal came for him, he'd been suspended for two days, but he'd never gone back. Instead, after a call from Ms. Riley, his mother had swallowed her pride and called his grandparents in Plano. He'd never met his grandparents, but they'd been ready to take him in and send him to a special school where, lo and behold, he'd learned to read. As it turned out, there was nothing *wrong* with him; he had dyslexia, which only meant he looked at the world different way. He'd found Jesus at that school, and he'd learned how to play the guitar, too.

That summer he shot up in height, and he'd never had anyone else make fun of him ever again.

Well, at least not until he became a performer and opened himself up to the critics. They weren't always complimentary, but they didn't make things personal. Katrina Rawls and her posse of mean girls had made things very personal. His faith told him that he should forgive and forget. He was having a little trouble with the former and a lot of trouble with the latter.

"Well, that was tasty," he finally said. "But I think I'd like to take a look around the auditorium, if that's okay."

She put her fork down, and he noticed she hadn't taken more than two bites of her pie. Maybe she really had felt guilty all those years.

Good.

"Sure. I'm at your disposal for the next few days," she said with a small smile. When she smiled, her eyes crinkled causing the little white scar from his ruler to pucker.

The waitress put the bill on the table as she walked past, and Katrina swiped the bill.

"I told you I'd get it," he said.

"No, really. You're my guest," she said, her smile tighter and her scar even more noticeable.

He should insist. She probably didn't make anywhere near the kind of money that he had in the bank. Living in Kingdom Come, there was no way she could. He let her take the check anyway.

Some petty part of him still wanted her to pay for insulting his Daddy. He thought, too, of the morning before he returned to Kingdom Come High School after having been in Plano for five years. He didn't want to go back to high school there, but his grandfather had passed. His grandmother was headed to assisted living, and there was no more money for a special school. Everyone told him he had the skills he needed and that he would be just fine, but all he could think of that morning was the day in fifth grade when he'd busted up Mrs. Winterbourne's classroom and injured Katrina. He'd spent thirty minutes that morning breathing into a paper bag and then putting his head between his knees. His mother had slipped him a Xanax to get him to school, and somehow he'd made it through that day and then another. And then another.

Yeah, Katrina Rawls owed him something for that, too.

She held out a bill to the cashier behind the counter, and he told himself not to notice that she filled out her jeans well. Instead, he slid a folded up twenty under the two dollars she'd left on the table as if over-tipping the waitress might ease his guilt for making Katrina pay for his dessert.

"Ready?" she asked when she stopped by the table.

He nodded and followed her outside. Even though he knew how to get to the high school, he let her lead. She drove a little banged up Toyota, and he felt even more remorse for sticking her with the bill. She *had* apologized after all.

Seth, that was petty. You should've paid the bill.

He ran a hand through his hair as they paused at the one traffic light in town. He knew she wouldn't take the money if he tried to give it to her now.

The light changed, and they turned left to get to the old high school. Both of his parents and at least one grandfather had gone to this high school before him. Now, plywood covered the windows of the old two-story brick building, and blue tarps splayed across the roof. The auditorium, added to the side of the building in the fifties, looked better, but not by much.

Seth parked his truck alongside Katrina's car, noticing the weeds creeping up between cracks in the pavement.

"They stopped using it as a school a few years back," Katrina said. "We had just started using the building for community classes when the tornado came through. Now that so many businesses in town have dried up, we don't have the money to repair it."

"And what is it you do?" he asked in spite of himself.

"I work for my Aunt Faith, arranging classes and keeping up with all of the rec league schedules. I recruit teachers and coaches, advertise what's going on, and make sure that everyone gets paid."

He nodded.

She led the way to the auditorium, wrestling with the key to get the old door to open. He stepped inside and it felt as though he'd walked into a musty, humid wall.

"Air conditioner's broken," she said with an apologetic smile.

"We'll pass out paper fans," he said.

He walked down the aisle to the old, scarred stage. This was the room where he'd first played his guitar for an audience. He'd thrown up before his number because he'd been nervous, but he'd made his way on stage and discovered that the footlights blinded him to the people of the audience. He could pretend that he didn't know a soul out there, and so he did. He brought the house down with his rendition of "Friends in Low Places," and he'd never looked back.

He climbed the steps to the side of the stage and walked to the middle, noting that one of the curtains was frayed and had fallen. Three talent show wins in a row on that stage, the last one with a song he'd written himself. He owed it to the town of Kingdom Come to do this concert and to hopefully get the building back up to snuff. Heck, he had more money than he'd ever need so he'd chip in some of his own money on the sly.

He bristled at the thought of doing anything to help Katrina Rawls, but he was an adult. He wasn't doing any of this for her. He was here as a favor to his mother. He was here for any other students who might need this stage the way he once had. He was here for Kingdom Come.

Seth, you need to let your anger with Trina go.

He could hear that still voice that didn't quite seem to be his own, and, as it so often did, it was saying things he didn't want to hear.

After all, you were about to ask her on a date when you thought she was Christina.

True, but his grandmother had always said, "Pretty is as pretty does, and he'd already seen the ugly side of Trina. Or Katrina. He'd have to get used to that.

"Mommy!"

A young girl squealed and ran down the aisle to Katrina, slamming into the woman almost hard enough to knock her over.

Seth swallowed hard. He hadn't seen a wedding band, and he'd looked when he'd thought she was Christina. He looked at the child who was almost as tall as her mother. He was no expert on children, but this one had to be old enough that. . .

Well, old enough that Katrina Rawls had been pregnant back in high school. How had he missed that?

Chapter 4

Per usual Makayla almost knocked the wind out of her, but Katrina wasn't about to complain that her daughter was being affectionate. For one thing, it was good to see her girl child back in good spirits after her stomach bug. For another, Makayla's preteen moods sometimes swung so fiercely that Katrina got whiplash. She'd take happy over pouty or whiny or any other emotion that sounded like one of Snow White's rejected dwarfs.

She reminded herself not to worry for one minute what Seth Bridges thought about her, either. It was none of his business.

"Mommy, who's that?"

"That's Mr. Seth. He's going to give a concert in a week or so to help us raise money for the old building."

"Oh, yeah. So you can keep your job."

Katrina blushed beet red. She didn't want Seth to have any idea how little she had in her checking account, and she sure as heck didn't want him to know that she was in danger of losing her job if Kingdom Come couldn't find a place to hold the community classes, a program she had just started a couple of years before.

"Oh! Oh! That's the guy who keeps popping up on your iPod!"

A hole couldn't open up in the floor and swallow her fast enough. If she'd thought talk of her employment embarrassing, she'd obviously forgotten the first rule of living with Makayla: Never say or do anything you don't want repeated to the world at large. In her defense, she hadn't known her daughter would run into Seth.

"Baby, what are you doing down here?"

"Nana saw your car and pulled over. She took me for ice cream!" As she said the words, Makayla jumped up and down and even started shouting "boing boing boing" in time with the jumps.

"I see your nana has sugared you up," Katrina said as she ruffled her daughter's hair.

Her mother appeared in the doorway, walking briskly. "I hope you don't mind our stopping. I wanted to make sure our future dance studio hadn't sprung another leak."

"Stopping's not a problem, Mom. The sugar? We may have to talk. You remember Seth Bridges, don't you?"

"How could I forget?" her mother asked. Katrina bit back a stab of envy as her mother passed. Trim and neatly dressed in a billowy blouse and capris, her mother exuded more sophistication than Katrina would ever manage.

Seth hopped down from the stage and shook hands with her mom. "Nice to see you again, Mrs. Rawls."

"She goes by Stevens now," Makayla helpfully supplied.

"Honey, we don't correct people on my last name. It's not that important," Katrina's mom said.

"I do apologize. I sometimes forget that things in this town do actually change," Seth said.

"It's nothing." Katrina's mom waved away Seth's concerns, and Katrina wondered if there was a woman alive he couldn't charm.

Her daughter stepped forward and stuck out her hand, too. "My name is Makayla, and I think you should sing some old hymns."

"Makayla Colleen!"

Seth only chuckled, though. "You think so?"

"I like the hymns they sing in Nana's church, but you sing the new ones where they just keep saying the same thing over and over and over—"

"That's enough," Katrina said through clenched teeth. She didn't need her daughter to be criticizing Seth's music.

Seth crouched to look Makayla in the eye. "Tell you what, I'll sing an old hymn or two along with my new songs. How about that?"

"You should sing one of the songs from the little brown book," Makayla added. "Nana says those songs are the best songs."

Seth held both palms out. "I do *not* want to argue with Mrs. Ra-Stevens, so I'll see what I can do."

Makayla held out her hand, littlest finger extended. "Pinky promise?"

Seth hooked her pink with his. "Pinky promise."

He started to take his hand away, but Makayla held it fiercely and trained her hazel eyes on his. "You can't break a pinky promise ever. No matter what."

He nodded solemnly, and something about the scene made Katrina tear up. If life had gone the way if was supposed to go, then Makayla would have a father who loved her very much and who made pinky promises with her.

Instead, she had a coward for a father.

Blessedly, nurture could overcome nature. Katrina was making sure of that.

"Makayla, baby. I think we've bothered Mr. Seth long enough. Why don't you run on with your Nana, and I won't be far behind you." She turned to Seth. "I'll lock the door on my way out. Just make sure it closes all the way behind you."

He got to his feet, his eyes shuttered again. "I thought I might play a bit and get a feel for the old place," he said. "But I'll make sure the door closes behind me."

Chapter 5

Seth's acoustic guitar echoed over the empty seats.

All that time he'd spent hating Katrina, and he'd forgotten another memory, a happier memory. They'd been in kindergarten—maybe first grade—playing at the edge of the playground where the honeysuckle grew. She'd worn her blond hair in two ponytails, looking almost exactly like her daughter had looked tonight. They'd been taking honeysuckle blossoms apart to get that single drop of nectar from each one.

"Seth, will you always be my friend?"

He hadn't thought much of it other than how Katrina never drank her chocolate milk at snack time. Maybe if he agreed to be her friend, then he could be the one to always get her chocolate milk. "Yeah, I'll always be your friend, but only if you'll let me have your chocolate milk when you don't want it."

"Pinky promise?" She'd held out her pinky, and he'd hooked his with hers, wondering what the heck the strange girly ritual was all about. When he went to take his pinky from hers, she'd latched on with a surprisingly strong grip. "You can't break a pinky promise ever. No matter what."

He'd broken his pinky promise.

Of course, so had she, but the whole thing had reminded him of something his pastor was fond of saying: the Bible is full of the promises that men break and the ones that God keeps.

He sighed deeply. He was too old to hold on to the things that happened to him when he was just a kid. But keeping Makayla's promises? Now that was something he could do.

He riffed on several of the old camp meeting hymns just to see how they'd bounce around the empty auditorium. "The Battle Hymn of the Republic" was too much pressure; it reminded him of his Vacation Bible School days. He loved "Amazing Grace," but it didn't quite feel right, or maybe he didn't feel quite ready to sing it. Then he tried "Love Lifted Me," which was one of his mother's favorites. None of those felt quite right, but he was enough of an artist not to push it—especially since he was going to be playing solo and didn't have to worry about a set list or getting the guys up to speed.

He'd decided against bringing the rest of his band, Fishers of Men, for a few reasons. One, they deserved a break after the tour they'd just finished. Two, no one had seemed that enthused about driving into the West Texas countryside, and, finally, his town was trying to raise money. Bringing his whole band would've added to the cost. Since there was only one hotel in Kingdom Come, he didn't even know where he would've put everyone. If he'd brought them home to his parents, they would've eaten well, but they would've been up at a ridiculous hour gathering eggs and doing who knew what chores. His mother believed that all guests were family and, as such, they should have the "privilege" of participating in the chores.

Funny how things had a way of working out.

When he'd made his decision to go solo, he hadn't thought about the state of the auditorium, but he should have. At some point during the last round of storms, the building had sprung a leak, and the entire back part of the stage had suffered water damage before someone could put up a tarp. If Seth performed by himself, he could pull the curtains and block that from view—assuming he could get the curtains fixed.

His melancholy led him to play his saddest songs. He'd mainly agreed to do this because his mother asked him, and she didn't ask for much. He did have a sense of nostalgia for the old building that had shown him he had something to offer the world. Back then he'd thought he would go on to play country songs, but Christian music had captured his imagination.

He chuckled as he thought about Katrina's little girl with her earnest eyes and solemn pinky swear. He liked to think he didn't sing the kind of songs that she described. He liked to think he used his interest in country and rock to create a different kind of song. Even so, he wondered if she was right.

Something about the girl had touched him. Maybe it was how she wasn't that impressed with him. Maybe it was that she spoke her mind freely, a trait he found to be quite refreshing. Maybe it was that she had reminded him of a different side of her mother. Either way, he would sing her one of the old songs, and he was beginning to think he knew just the one

When he was a little boy, about Makayla's age, his mother used to sing a version of one of the old hymns as a way to get his attention when he was being careless around the farm. She would start by telling him to open his eyes, but she was particularly fond of altering one of the verses and singing, *"open your ears that you may hear voices of truth from your Mother Dear."* Yes, he'd sing that old song. He'd sing it for his mother and also for little Makayla.

After all, he had made a pinky promise.

*****

Katrina couldn't help but wonder how Seth's session was going, and she worried that he might prop the door open with a rock and forget to close it when he left. If someone found their way in and trashed the place, then it would all be on her, of course.

She forced herself to work on Makayla's hair, a tangled mess that had recently held the remains of her ice cream. As usual, her daughter shouted at every knot she attempted to untangle. To make matters worse, she insisted on sitting on the ottoman in the living room which meant Katrina had to bend over to get to her hair and sometimes tripped on the corner of the ottoman as she worked her way around. Goodness knew, Makayla wasn't going to turn her head and miss whatever cartoon was on the television. Katrina would turn the television off altogether, but, at least occasionally, Makayla would get absorbed enough in the program to forget to be indignant about every little tangle.

"Ow!"

Then she would remember.

"Child of mine, please hush. I know it's tangled."

"Mom. It *hurts*."

"Then let me take you to Miss Fiona, and she will give you a sassy cut."

Makayla stuck out her bottom lip and crossed her arms. "I don't want a sassy cut."

Katrina shrugged. "Nana has a very sassy cut."

Makayla uncrossed her arms. In her world, Nana could do no wrong. "Maybe. But I don't want my hair to be as sassy as Nana's."

Katrina chuckled. Her mother's hair was quite short, but Makayla definitely had the edge on being sassy. She finished combing out the tangles, still worrying about the auditorium. "Go brush your teeth so I can put you to bed."

Her daughter bounced into the bathroom, and Katrina turned to her mother who'd been watching the exchange instead of whatever cartoon was on.

"A *very* sassy cut, huh?"

Katrina shrugged. "A mom's gotta do what a mom's gotta do."

"She does have your hair. We went round and round like this, too."

Katrina lowered her eyes. She and her mom had gone round and round about a lot of things, especially during the time her parents were getting divorced. Now she knew her parents had split because her father had been having an affair, but back then her mother hadn't told her because she didn't want to poison the man in his daughter's eyes. He had taken advantage of his wife's good faith for a while. That good faith had been vitiated by the evening Katrina caught her father with his secretary in a state of undress.

Vitiate: verb, to make something less effective; to ruin (or spoil something).

As mother and daughter had battled their way through Katrina's preteen years, her father had let her believe that she could come live with him. Of course, she'd wanted to live with her father! Her mother was the one who enforced all of the rules. Finally, one day in the midst of a particularly heated argument, her mother had said, "Look, Katrina, your father doesn't want you. He doesn't even want to pay child support, but he's going to whether he likes it or not."

That day was the turning point in Katrina's relationship with her mother. Oh, she hadn't changed overnight. No, she'd had to make at least one more big mistake before she'd come to terms with how much her mother loved her and just how right her mother was. She looked over to her mother now and felt the weight of her disappointment that Katrina hadn't even finished high school much less gone to college.

"Mom, do you mind keeping an eye on Makayla? I want to make sure Seth closed the auditorium door all the way."

"Paranoid, are we?" Her mother said with a chuckle.

Katrina got up and kissed her mother on the check. "I come by it very honestly."

"Go ahead before it finishes getting dark. I'll get the kid in bed."

Katrina drove over to the old school as the sun set behind her. Seeing a rock propping open one of the doors, she felt vindicated in her paranoia and burst through the door. She would make sure the premises were empty and give him a piece of her mind the next day. Then she heard Seth's mellow voice echoing through the auditorium. She froze. Should she go? If she left, she would worry about whether or not he remembered to remove the rock. Besides, he had to have heard the loud crash of the door behind her.

"Well, you might as well come in and sit down."

She walked down the aisle. "I'm sorry. I didn't realize you were still here. I'll go."

"Don't leave on account of me."

She took a seat, bewildered by his tone. Was this the same man who'd been angry with her earlier? Now, he seemed. . . indifferent?

He started playing what was going to be "Open My Eyes That I May See," and she sucked in a deep breath. The hymn had always been one of her favorites. As a really little girl, she'd always liked the line, *"place in my hands the wonderful key"* because it was something she could picture in her mind. She'd daydreamed about getting a mystery key that would take her beyond closed doors to a magical world. Her mother was fond of the second line, though. She liked to say that she could see God in those little moments when people were at their best. Those were the *"glimpses of truth."*

Katrina felt she had seen one of those glimpses of truth when Seth made a pinky promise with her daughter. She caught a chill. How could he have known that hymn meant so much to both her and her mother?

Seth finished the song and put his guitar back in the case.

"Don't stop on my account," she said. "That one's my favorite."

"That's all I have in me for now, but I would like to come back tomorrow and set up the equipment for the concert on Saturday," he said.

"Just tell me when, and I'll open up for you." She said the words lightly, but didn't like how he'd clipped his words.

So much for the indifference.

He came down the stairs and stopped in the aisle where she sat. "How about ten?"

"I can do that." She sucked in a deep breath. "And Seth?"

He took his case and walked a little way up the aisle but stopped and turned back to her. "Yeah?"

"I really am sorry. I was a stupid, snot-nosed kid who said mean things to you to feel better about myself."

"I'm not mad, okay?"

He hadn't turned around to face her, and he still hadn't said that he'd forgiven her. It shouldn't bother her so much, but it did. She would tan Makayla's hide if she found out her daughter was being as mean to her classmates as she had been to Seth. "Is there anything I can do to make it up to you?"

At that, he placed his guitar case carefully on a row of chairs and came back to where she sat. She stood to keep him from towering over her.

"Woman, you had me breathing in a paper bag before my first day back at high school here. That's how much trauma you caused." His eyes bugged out as though he couldn't believe he'd just admitted such a thing.

She swallowed hard over a lump in her throat. "I had no idea."

"I got my butt whooped for the two-day suspension and for that scar under your eye. Yes, *I* got a spanking for hurting *you*."

She winced. That was hardly fair, all things considered.

"I had to go to a new school in Dallas where they made fun of me for being from the country. Then, once I finally made friends, the money ran out, and I ended up here again."

"At least you got to leave."

"What does that have to do with anything?"

"Nothing. Forget I said anything. I can see that you'll never forgive me, and I understand," she said, her voice wavering in spite of herself. "I won't mention it again."

She brushed past him but only got halfway to the door before she thought of one more thing she wanted to say to him. "Look, I messed up, and I get that, but. . . trust me. I got what was coming to me, and I'm so tired of paying for past mistakes."

She walked quickly back to the entrance, careful not to brush her tears away until he couldn't see the motion. The door slammed behind her with a satisfying clang. So what if he didn't lock up? If someone snuck in and burned the place down then she wouldn't have to deal with him anymore.

Chapter 6

Trust me. I got what was coming to me, and I'm so tired of paying for past mistakes.

Either the acoustics in the auditorium where the best he'd ever heard, or Katrina's words were still echoing in his imagination. Why hadn't he just forgiven her? He knew he should, but he couldn't make the words "I forgive you" leave his lips. He couldn't forgive her, but he also had an irrational urge to hunt down whoever had hurt her and punch him on her behalf.

Of course, he might as well punch himself since he'd made her cry.

Not one of your prouder moments, Seth.

No, but in elementary school, he'd wondered if she even had the ability to cry.

Something about the way she'd said those words, her voice wavering over an obvious lump in her throat, cut him to the bone. He'd spent many a lonely night in Plano wishing horrible things on her. That was before he started going to church again. He hadn't actively tried to forgive her, but he had stopped wishing those horrible things on her at least.

At the time, he'd thought that was enough. Now he couldn't help but thing of something his mother was fond of saying: *You don't have to like someone to love them.* Anytime he'd point out how hard it was to love his neighbor as himself, she'd broken out that little gem. He sighed. He didn't have to *like* Katrina to want what was best for her, and wanting what was best for her would mean forgiving her. And somehow slipping her the money for his pie the other day because that had been petty, too.

Three more days. He had three more days before be could leave Kingdom Come and never have to speak to her again. He would perform his concert and take care of the old school. Then he would spend some time with his parents before he left for Plano. He could stand anything for three more days.

*****

The next morning he was still thinking about Katrina Rawls, and it was eating him alive along with that nagging voice saying, *Forgive her.* He almost got kicked by one of the sassier Holsteins and then almost snagged himself in the electric fence while checking on the Longhorns because he was so distracted. He sat down to a breakfast table full of all sorts of things that would hide the abs he'd worked so hard to find: biscuits, country ham, grits, scrambled eggs that he had gathered, and homemade strawberry jam. "Mom, what happened to Katrina Rawls after I went away?"

"Why are we talking about *her*?"

His mother had no love lost for the girl who'd caused her son to create such a commotion. He was also pretty sure his mother had had something to do with the firing of the elementary school principal who'd suspended him without doing a thing to the girls who'd tormented him. She might look like a sweet farmer's wife, but his mother had a spine of steel. No one crossed her babies.

"I just want to know. She has the girl and doesn't appear to be married."

Her mother clucked her tongue. "Came up pregnant in high school and didn't even graduate," she said. "She got pretty wild there after her parents divorced."

Seth's father grunted. "Is this really good breakfast table talk?"

"No, sir," Seth said. He knew how his father felt about gossip. Fortunately for him, his mother liked to collect it. Gossip, she liked to say, was her only vice.

He turned his attention to savoring his breakfast and thinking on Katrina. Now that his mother mentioned it, he didn't remember seeing her in high school after their junior year. Of course, he'd been busy ignoring her and considered it a happy circumstance. He'd never thought much about what not being in high school might've meant to her.

He'd heard rumors even back then, of course, but he didn't have that many friends, and they knew he didn't want to even hear her name. But what about the others? He could only imagine the taunting, not to mention how hard it had to be to find a good job without a diploma. And why hadn't she graduated? Other girls in their class had had babies but still finished high school.

He didn't need to be thinking about Katrina Rawls or whether or not she'd received some kind of cosmic punishment. He sure as heck didn't need to be feeling sorry for her or worrying about her. She'd made her bed, and she could just lie in it. He had one more day to get ready before the big concert, and he couldn't very well go back to the auditorium smelling of cow.

"Thanks for breakfast, Mom," he said, leaning over to kiss his mother's cheek before taking his plate to the sink.

"You're welcome. You got too skinny, off gallivanting around the country."

He chuckled. His personal trainer had a whole other way of looking at the matter. The man would probably lose his mind if he knew Seth had been eating biscuits made with lard. "I'm fine. Really."

His mother grabbed his hand as he made to leave the kitchen. "I don't know why you're asking about her, boy, but you steer clear of that Rawls girl. She's nothing but trouble."

He squeezed his mother's hand, but he didn't make any promises.

Chapter 7

By the time Katrina got to the auditorium, Seth was already there. He sat on the tailgate of his truck playing his guitar, looking nothing like the rising star he actually was.

"You're here early," she said, trying not to notice just now handsome he looked. At first glance he looked like any number of guys around town—faded jeans, cowboy boots, and a hint of scruff—but his shirt gave him away. He wore a pale yellow shirt with the Reading Rainbow logo.

"I'll just let you in and go back to the office," she said as she headed for the auditorium door.

"Wait!" he said as he put his guitar in the cab of the truck. "I was hoping you might show me some of the projects the foundation has in mind. You know, so I can talk about them during the concert tomorrow."

"All right." She didn't believe that for an instant, but she was supposed to be at his beck and call. She waited for him to catch up and started walking toward the old high school's front entrance.

As usual she paused just inside the front door, thinking of the last time she'd been in the lobby as a student. That day, she'd been eight months pregnant. She didn't have friends, but she could always feel the stares. They gravitated to her belly, to her waddle as she struggled to get to class. She'd been running late that morning, and she huffed as she entered the school. A group of guys to her left burst into laughter at the sight of her.

She didn't even know what they were laughing about, but suddenly her chemistry test didn't seem all that important. She was going to be a mother. The guys laughing to her left, the girls gossiping to her right? They were only concerned with what to wear to the prom next month or who was taking whom out on a date that Friday night. She didn't have time for dating, and no one made maternity dresses for prom.

So she turned around and walked out, and she didn't come back.

"Katrina, you okay?"

"Yeah." She rolled her shoulders back and forced herself to take a deep breath. The good thing about the school these days was that it was empty. Mind you, if the concert went well, they would start making strides to fill it, but most of the students would be adults looking to learn a new skill or seniors taking classes to keep their minds sharp or even immigrants coming to learn English. For now, it was just her and Seth.

She showed him the old physics classroom. "Most of the damage looks about like this," she said as she gestured to the room. The contractor told her it wasn't as bad as it looked. Sure, each room had some water damage, but she and several volunteers had caught most of the leaks and placed five-gallon buckets strategically around each room to catch the worst of it.

Every now and again, some of the boys from the Beta Club at the new school would come to empty the buckets for her.

"We're lucky that the auditorium isn't attached to the main building," she said a few minutes later as they walked through the gym, her voice echoing through the musty air. "It and the gym sustained the least amount of damage. I mean, the windows all have to be replaced, but the gym roof had been repaired a few years back and held up well."

Seth nodded, and she wondered why he wanted to go on this tour since he'd said absolutely nothing for the past fifteen minutes as she'd yammered on.

"They stopped in the hallway on the other side of the gym, and she pointed one way. "The cafeteria is a lost cause, but we're hoping to save the library and the front offices."

"Where's the dance studio?"

She jerked her head around, surprised that he remembered what her mother had said the night before. "Actually, Mom's hoping to make the old library into a dance studio. She can teach tap and clogging, and she's looking for a ballet teacher. I keep telling her not to get her hopes up considering all of the damage, but Makayla likes to dance and is getting beyond Mom's capabilities, so there you go."

"What about the front office?"

"I'm hoping to make that the office for all of the community center events," she said. All of the sports fields are behind the school, so it'd be a nice central location for everything."

"And this is what you've always wanted to do?"

She felt his eyes on her before she turned around. "What do you mean by that?"

"I mean, you've told me what your mom and Makayla want to do. You've told me about the woman who wants to teach pottery and the guy who's going to teach French. You told me about the woman who's all about scrapbooking and is putting together a scrapbook for the high school as well as teaching a class. There will be basketball leagues and cloggers and writers and a brand new computer lab, but all you want to do is watch a bunch of other people take classes?"

"Sure. I guess."

He shook his head.

What was this all about? Why did he even care? "Look, Seth, we can't all go off chasing that neon rainbow. It's good work. It puts food on the table."

"Last night you said something about how at least I got to leave town. What did you mean by that?"

She sucked in a deep breath. "I got pregnant with Makayla, and that was the end for me. I wish I'd never been so mean to you, but at least you got to go to another school. Look at you now, you're a star. I'm just. . . stuck here."

His eyes bored through her, and she would've cleared out the last of her checking account to know what he was thinking. Finally, he spoke, "So leave."

She laughed. "I can't get a good enough job to support Makayla and myself. I have nowhere to go."

"Make Makayla's father pay his way."

"Great idea. I'll get on that as soon as I figure out who he is."

She had been so angry the words had come out before she could stop them. Now she blanched then her face burned beet red with shame. Why had she said that? No one knew her secret but her mother. And now Seth.

"What do you mean by that?"

She took a deep breath. "Look, no one knows this so you can't go telling people. I was a little wild after my parents divorced, but I wasn't sleeping around—not to the point I wouldn't know who'd fathered my baby—and I was careful. But I went to this party one night and—"

Tell him. You can trust him.

Why? Why should she tell him this?

"Someone put something in my drink. I woke up the next morning in a strange bed, and someone had raped me. I had Makayla nine months later."

She didn't know why exactly it was so important for him to know that she wasn't careless, that she hadn't made the mistake others supposed, but she would rather him know the truth. It wasn't anybody's business, but still.

"And Makayla's father has never stepped forward?" His eyes flashed, and she had a vision of him going from door to door looking for Makayla's father to make him do right.

"Nope, and I'm not sure that I want him to. Did you know that here in Texas he technically has parental rights? I'd rather her have no father at all than to have the sort of coward who drugs a girl to have sex with her."

"Trina, I don't even know what to say."

She shrugged. "There's nothing to say. It is what it is, and I've worked hard to come to that conclusion."

"Understood. If I could help. . . ." He let his voice trail off, and she respected his desire to help even as he realized there was absolutely nothing that could be done.

She laughed, the hysterical sound of it bouncing off the lockers. "Why would you want to help me? And what exactly do you think you could do?"

"I don't know. I could help you go to school," he said. "Interest-free."

His brown eyes shone earnest.

"I don't get you at all," she said. "But I couldn't accept a gift like that from you. Next week I take the GED and then I'll start college applications. Maybe Makayla and I will graduate together."

"Well, I'm sorry I've been a jerk to you."

You should be. "Does that mean you've finally decided to forgive me?"

He ran a hand through his hair and gave her that lopsided grin she'd enjoyed the day before. "Yeah. I think I forgave you a long time ago, but I had to think on some things.

"Such as?"

"Well, when you mentioned that I got to leave, I realized that I might never have learned to read if you hadn't pushed my buttons until I had that fit. Ms. Riley was the one who figured out why I had trouble reading, and the suspension was enough to have Mom make up with her grandparents so I could go to a different school. In a perverse sort of way, I should be thanking you."

She swallowed hard. "The Lord works in mysterious ways."

"That He does. Because that's one heckuva kid you've got."

Her heart swelled. She had often thought that Makayla was quite the consolation prize for such an awful night, but Seth was the first person to really say it—other than her mother. "That I do."

She leaned back against the bank of lockers, and it was almost as though she and Seth had gone back in time to be two teenagers who didn't have such baggage between them. The slate had been wiped clean. They were a boy and a girl in a deserted high school hallway, and she could think of a time before she looked over her shoulder constantly and questioned the intentions of every man she met.

He leaned one arm against the locker, completing the illusion of two teenagers dancing around attraction or maybe even love. Her breath hitched, and she wondered if he felt it, too.

"If you could do anything in the world, what would you do?" he asked.

"That's easy. I—" Only she couldn't finish the thought. When was the last time she'd thought about something she wanted to do rather than something she *should* do? She had to look like a fish as many times as her mouth had opened and then closed. "Okay. It's not easy. I have no idea."

"Come on. There has to be something."

She searched her memory banks. Her most current fervent wish was to work for someone other than her Aunt Faith. Before that, she'd wanted to sleep for Makayla's first four years since the child wouldn't sleep through the night until she started kindergarten. And before that? Was there a time she didn't have Makayla?

"What about when you were a kid?"

Well, if she thought all the way back to her sophomore year in high school, she remembered thinking that she would love to teach American history. She especially loved all of the nooks and crannies of time that the textbook forgot or ignored. She still liked to read books about what her history teachers hadn't told her or about the "forgotten" history of the

United States, in general, and Texas, in particular. Once upon a time she had imagined herself in front of a group of students teaching them to think for themselves so they could dig for all the things others didn't want them to know.

"There! Something sparked your interest."

She'd forgotten Seth was even there, until she came out of her reverie to look up into his eyes. "I used to want to be a history teacher."

"Then do it!"

She blushed and looked away. "By the time I finish the GED and take all of the classes I need to be a teacher, I'll be old enough that everyone my age will be retiring."

"So?"

"So? I'm so far behind now, that I'll never catch up."

"It's not a race," he said, his hand cupping her cheek. She drew in a sharp breath. No one, other than family members, had touched her in so long. She couldn't even remember the last time she'd been on a date. She couldn't remember the last time she'd wanted to go on a date. Or to be kissed.

Then he was leaned closer, his eyes locked on hers.

I should stop him.

Even as she thought the words, she felt her body lean toward him. Her hands traveled to his chest, but she couldn't make them push him away. Her fingers wanted to curl into his tee shirt, and she considered it a moral victory she kept them from doing so. His thumb trembled ever so slightly on her cheek, and she realized he was touching the scar from his broken ruler.

"I really want to kiss you right now." His low voice reverberated through her since his lips were only half an inch away from hers.

"I wish you would."

His lips met hers, and she wanted to melt into the lockers from the sensation. Her traitorous fingers curled into his tee shirt, and he drew back only to kiss her again, this time drawing her closer and burying his hand in the hair at the nape of her neck.

"Oh, Katrina!"

At the sound of her Aunt Faith's voice, they broke apart.

Katrina cleared her throat, willing her heart to slow down. "And this is the front office. We'll take payment here and oversee all of the classes and sporting events from here."

"That's, ha, interesting," Seth said. He was having a hard time taking his eyes off her, and she couldn't help but smile at that.

"What are you doing in here? I have been looking for you all over," her aunt scolded. "Monsieur Guillaume needs that sample syllabus to create one for his French class, and three of the softball coaches need to check out new equipment. Oh, and Silas Britton is looking for his check."

Those were all things her aunt could've done, but Katrina had a feeling Aunt Faith mainly wanted to make sure she wasn't being "overly nice." To be fair, she was being quite nice to Mr. Bridges and might be amenable to being a little nicer, should the opportunity arise.

"I'll go take care of it," she said. "But could you let Seth into the auditorium. We were so caught up in the tour that I didn't have the chance to do that for him."

"Of course," her aunt said.

Seth put a light hand on her arm as she turned to go. "Hey, I was wondering if you might want to have dinner with me tonight."

Even her aunt's icy glare couldn't stop her from saying, "I'd love to."

Aunt Faith cleared her throat. "You go on back to the office, and I'll take care of everything here."

Katrina walked down the hall, suppressing the urge to whistle. She was having dinner with Seth Bridges, and he just might kiss her again.

Chapter 8

"So, Seth, how's Kingdom Come been treating you?"

"It's been great to be back home, Ms. Stevens," he said as they left the old school and walked across the parking lot to he auditorium.

"Please, you can call me Faith."

"Well, I can try," he said.

"I've heard that some reporters may be here for the concert tomorrow," Faith said as she opened the auditorium door.

"That so?" He only half-listened to her because he was thinking about Katrina, about how much he'd like to kiss her again.

"Be a shame if they were to catch wind of you kissing a woman who had a baby out of wedlock."

"Mmmhmm."

"Might put a damper on your career in Christian music."

"Yeah. Wait. What?" Her words had finally caught up with his brain, and his body chilled despite the heat that hung in the auditorium.

"Look, Seth, she's my niece, but I don't think she's right for you. I saw the two of you kissing and went back around the corner to yell because I didn't want to embarrass her. Tell me, though, do you think scrutiny from journalists would be good for you? Or her?"

He hadn't thought that far ahead. Truth be told, he hadn't been thinking at all.

"I'm not having this conversation with you," he said. "Thanks for opening the auditorium door. I'm going to set things up and play the concert tomorrow then we'll see what happens. Katrina and I are both adults, and we don't need supervision."

Her lips pressed together to form a thin line. "All right, but you can't say I didn't warn you."

Seth shook his head as he watched the older lady leave. He wasn't a big enough star to merit paparazzi. He made good money and enjoyed a healthy following, but he wasn't going to see his mug on the tabloids any time soon. Truth be told, that was just fine with him.

But what would people say? What would his record label say? His fans?

He shoved the thought aside. One kiss did not a relationship make.

With some difficulty, he threw himself into finalizing his set list and making sure that he had the equipment he would need. First, the concert. Then, he would figure out what to do about Katrina.

*****

Katrina's makeshift office in the basement of town hall was in a state of pandemonium.

Pandemonium: noun, uproar: wild and noisy disorder or confusion.

She found the softball equipment that had come in the mail and gave it to her anxious coaches. She distributed checks to both Silas Britton and Violet Dandridge. She even managed to find the sample syllabus for Monsieur Guillaume. Just as she was about to go for a break, someone from the ball fields called to say that a sewer main had broken and flooded the soccer field and one of the softball fields so she would have to send out notifications canceling that evening's games.

By the time five o'clock rolled around, her stomach could no longer be ignored—especially since she'd forgotten to eat lunch. She had her purse on her shoulder ready to go when she heard the knock on the door. Her shoulders wanted to slump at the thought that another person needed yet another thing, but she forced herself to turn around with a smile.

Her reward for doing so was her Aunt Faith.

Katrina's shoulders slumped in spite of themselves. "Please tell me you don't have anything else for me to do because I was so swamped today that I didn't get lunch. I'm thinking about gnawing off my own arm."

"No, I was just thinking you might want to have supper at your place instead of with Seth Bridges."

"Do you have to rain on every one of my parades? I don't get that many, you know."

"Yes. Listen, what do you think is going to happen to Seth if his fans or the media find out he's going out with a teen mom who never married the mother of her child?"

Katrina thought about pulling out her hair in frustration. She reconsidered because it was one of her better features. "I'm not a teen mom. I'm a quarter of a century old. Also, last I checked it's not the nineteenth century, although if you would all like for me to wear around a big T for 'Teen Mom,' I guess we could try to revive the good old days of Hawthorne."

"You know that and I know that," her aunt continued with a condescendingly patient tone of voice, "But the fans of Christian music hold their artists up to a higher standard."

Am I just kidding myself?

Katrina didn't want to believe her aunt. She wanted to believe in grace. She wanted to believe she wouldn't be punished for the rest of her life for something she did as a teenager, especially since someone out there had meant her harm. That was the person everyone needed to be saving their lectures for—not her.

"Look, I need you to stay out of my business. I know you mean well, but I've about had it with your little comments about me. You don't know me as well as you think you do, and I'm going to be finding a new job. Soon."

"But you've always worked here. Where are you going to go since you don't have a diploma?"

Katrina shrugged. "You've been after me to get my GED, and I'm going to do it. Then I'll go back to school."

He aunt shook her head. "There you go just like your mother: going off half-cocked without having a real plan. You think Seth Bridges is after a real relationship with you? Maybe he's just after a little fling while he's here in Kingdom Come. You know he's going to leave and go back to touring and writing music. He's certainly not going to stick around here."

Katrina couldn't take any more of her aunt's negativity. Deep down, Aunt Faith meant well, but she hadn't had a positive thought since her own divorce. Usually, Katrina could avoid her worst-case scenarios, but even her mother had given up on dating since Aunt Faith had moved in with them.

Katrina was beginning to see why.

"Ready to go?"

She looked up into Seth's chocolate brown eyes and recanted.

Recant: verb, to withdraw or repudiate a statement or belief, publicly and formally

There was no law that said she couldn't have dinner with a handsome man and maybe, if she were lucky, even kiss him.

Chapter 9

Seth reached for Katrina's hand and laced his fingers with hers then looked down at his hand in surprised. Why had he done that? He wasn't really a handholding kind of guy. But Katrina's hands? They seemed to fit his, and she didn't seem to mind.

"So, where are we going?" she asked.

"Well, after an extensive study of restaurants that are open right now, we can have fast food or—"

"We can go to the Doomsday Diner?"

Her stomach growled, and he smiled. "Based on what your stomach is telling me, you'll never make the thirty-minute drive into Logansville."

"You're probably right. I was so busy I forgot to have lunch."

"That's no good," he said, but his own stomach growled.

"Ha! You worked through lunch, too!"

As they walked the two blocks to the diner, he told her about his attempts to rehang the fallen curtain and how he'd almost fallen from the ladder.

"Don't do that! You should've called me, and I would've sent someone to help you."

He shrugged. "Maybe I like living on the edge."

They entered the diner and sat down. Their waitress from the day before jumped at the chance to wait on them, probably anticipating another huge tip. Seth didn't plan to disappoint her.

Conversation flowed easily, and dinner was tasty. Seth could only think how comfortable it was and how completely different from the day before. Never in his wildest dreams had he thought it possible that he would voluntarily sit down to dinner with Katrina Rawls in what some might classify as a "date."

"Excuse me, are you Seth Bridges?"

Occasionally, he did get autograph requests—especially in this area of Texas—so he turned around with a smile until he noticed the petite brunette wore a pantsuit that screamed journalist. "I am," he said cautiously.

She started with a spiel that he didn't quite catch because the thought of someone following him to middle-of-nowhere West Texas was too much to process. She mentioned something about his new album and one of his bandmates being arrested for driving under the influence. As she spoke, he took his phone from his back pocket and realized that it was dead.

"Georgia Steele of the *Dallas Morning News*. I was hoping you'd be willing to make a statement about Fishers of Men drummer Leif Gibbons."

She had her pen poised over a notebook, and Seth didn't need his publicist to tell him what to say, "No comment."

"Is this your new girlfriend?"

"Also no comment."

"Are you seeing anyone?"

"No comment."

"Is the band breaking up? Is that why you're here doing a concert by yourself?"

That he could comment on.

"No, the band isn't breaking up. I'm here to help my community raise funds to repair the old high school. That's a good story. Why don't you tell that one?"

She scribbled in her notebook, but he didn't have high hopes. The news always seemed to prefer the bad to the good.

"Could I get your name?" Georgia Steele had turned to Katrina, whose expression resembled that of a deer in headlights.

"Don't answer that," he said as he fished through his wallet. He motioned for the waitress to come over and handed her more than enough money to cover the bill. "Come on, Katrina."

The reporter scribbled down the name, and Seth inwardly kicked himself.

Katrina took his hand and followed him from the restaurant. Their nemesis tried to follow them, but Seth held out a hand. "No more questions."

They made it about a block before Katrina asked, "Does that happen often?"

"Nope. First time actually," he said. "My phone died, so I must've missed whatever is going on right now."

"Listen, Seth. Maybe this isn't a good idea."

"Wait. Whoa. We don't even know what's going on yet."

By this time, they'd reached her car. "Yeah, but I know you don't need to have that reporter asking too many questions about me. What are your fans going to say?"

"Who cares?" He got the words out, but not as quickly as he should have.

"That pause," she said, and his heart sank as he realized she'd caught him. "You do care, and you're right to care. Besides, you're going to leave in a couple of days. Then what would we do? You're one heckuva kisser, but I think I'll have to be happy you've finally forgiven me and let you move on with life."

"One last kiss?" he asked, still dizzy from everything that had happened and how a day so filled with promise had suddenly gone so very wrong.

She extended her hand instead. "One last handshake, and then you need to charge that phone and find out what happened today."

Chapter 10

Katrina got into her car before she could take Seth up on his offer of a last kiss.

She wanted to just sit there and catch her breath after her roller coaster of a day, but she had to leave. He was still looking at her, shell-shocked by the sudden appearance of the reporter. As she backed away, he looked down at his phone as if it were a traitor to lose its battery and thus not share its secrets with him.

Katrina Rawls, you have a very vivid imagination.

Yes, yes she did. She also had a broken heart. No, not broken because she hadn't allowed herself to fully fall in love. It did, however, have a fissure of deep regret that she'd never find out what could've been.

Fissure: noun, oh who the heck cared what the word meant.

She might be sad, but she would never regret this weekend because she'd finally earned his forgiveness and finally stood up to her Aunt Faith. She had a plan now, and having a plan would mean a much better future for Makayla.

She pulled into the driveway at the same time as her mother did. Makayla bounded out of the car and tackle-hugged her mother. "Mommy, mommy! We went to see a movie and Nana let me get a frozen drink, and do I have to go to bed right now?"

Katrina looked over to her mother. "You let her get cola, didn't you?"

Her mother shrugged and left Katrina to listen to Makayla's summary of the movie she'd seen in excruciating detail. The child talked through her shower and then through their evening ritual of combing out her tangles. She tried to talk while brushing her teeth and even managed to get a few salient plot points into her evening prayers.

Salient: adjective, most noticeable or important.

Finally, Katrina kissed her baby girl on the forehead and turned off the light before retreating to the sofa and collapsing.

"How did your date go?" Aunt Faith asked from the recliner.

"It wasn't a date."

"You had a date? Was it with Seth?" her mother asked.

"It wasn't a date," Katrina repeated.

"I saw you kissing him in the hall. It was a date."

Katrina turned to chew out her aunt, but Makayla's bedroom room creaked and she appeared in the middle of the living room, effectively blocking her grandmother and great aunt's view of some show where celebrities danced with professionals. "You kissed Mr. Seth? Is he going to be my daddy?"

Now what? She had a strict policy of not lying to her child after everything that had happened with her own father, but she certainly didn't want to tell her daughter that she'd kissed Seth because Makayla would only hear the word "kiss" and anything that might've happened between her and Seth wasn't going to happen so there was no need in stirring things up.

But, still. . . no lying.

Katrina gestured for Makayla to come to her, as much to get her out from in front of the television as to make sure the child was listening to her. "Yes, I kissed Mr. Seth, but we decided that we wouldn't make a good couple because he has to go back to making music after he plays his concert tomorrow."

"So? We can go with him. I saw this show where kids of actors and singers get their own tutors. Nana won't miss us that much."

Nana, who had just taken a sip of water, spewed the beverage.

"It was one kiss. People need to share more than one kiss to get married, and they also need to date for a lot longer than one day. Now, you go to bed and mind your own beeswax." She gave her daughter a kiss on the forehead and a pat on the rump. "Now, git."

Makayla blessed them all with her patented pouty face but eventually trudged in the direction of her bedroom. "Can you tuck me in again? Please?"

"What are the rules?" asked Katrina.

"If I pop out of bed then I can just pop myself back in?"

"You got it, sugar plum. Now, scoot."

The three women lounged on sofa and recliner as dancers whirled about and a studio audience clapped.

"You're a good little mama, Katrina Faith."

Katrina looked to her namesake. "Thank you, but I'm still going to quit working for you at the end of the year."

Aunt Faith snorted. "Good. It's about time."

"Have you two been at it again?" Katrina's mother asked.

"Yes, Aunt Faith was in my business about Seth," Katrina said. Then she sighed. "Unfortunately, this time I think she's right."

*****

Seth disconnected his phone and left it charging on his bedside table before flopping down under the covers. Apparently, a lot had happened while he was touring schools, kissing Katrina, and fixing up the auditorium. The drummer for his band, Fishers of Men, had been arrested for drunk driving. Since he was headed to rehab, all tour plans had been suspended indefinitely. Seth wanted to call Leif and make sure that he was okay, but he wouldn't be able to speak to his bandmate until he'd reached certain benchmarks in his recovery.

Some talk show bigwig had seized upon the story as a platform for the hypocrisy of Christian music stars and all of his social media blasts had gone viral. Now Seth's agent was telling him to expect more reporters than usual at his concert the next day.

As an upshot, sales of Fishers of Men albums were skyrocketing, which proved the old adage that all publicity is good publicity. After five years of working their way up, Fishers of Men were finally getting exposure beyond the sphere of Christian music. The bass player, John Dixon, had made a statement based around "Judge not lest ye be judged," and that was generating good press. Even so, Seth couldn't get excited about the attention or the sales. Instead, he felt as though he'd lost something.

He knew it was stupid. They'd shared precisely one kiss, but he felt as though he'd walk out of town in a couple of days and always wonder *What if?* He also didn't like the idea of not pursuing her because of her past. After all, he wasn't a candidate for sainthood. He'd had some honky-tonk moments he wasn't too proud of back when he was trying so hard to be a country star. He'd lost his way, but he'd found it again. And wasn't that the human condition? To make mistakes but to learn from them and to hopefully get better each and every time?

If no one sin was any worse than any other, then he didn't understand why he couldn't be allowed to decide for himself whether or not Katrina Rawls was a good person. Heck, people didn't even know the whole story, and he could only hope and pray that Makayla's "father" was in a place where he couldn't hurt anyone else.

The whole thing made no sense to Seth. Shouldn't his label trust him? Shouldn't his fans trust him? Shouldn't he be able to make decisions for himself?

Shouldn't you *respect Katrina's decision?*

Yeah, he should, but he had to know if she felt the same way he did. He thought of the look on her face when he paused just a second too long. He had been thinking about what might happen to him and his band if the press eviscerated him for being someone not already "perfect," and she could see it.

He couldn't go back in time to change his last conversation with Katrina, but he did have the stage to himself tomorrow night, and he was going to use that to his advantage.

Chapter 11

"Mommy! Mommy! You're in the paper!" Makayla shook her mother mercilessly, and Katrina longed for the days when she could pull the child into bed and snuggle with her until she fell back asleep.

"I thought I told you not to get up so early," she said with a yawn.

"I was so excited about the concert today and how Mr. Seth is going to sing an old song just for me and Nana that I had a hard time sleeping. And then I heard the paper hit the driveway, and I thought it would be nice if I went to get it for you. Oh, and I'm also making pancakes."

That got Katrina out of bed in a hurry. The child knew not to mess with the stove in a theoretical sense. Unfortunately, Makayla could rationalize a lot of things in the name of "being helpful." By the time she got to the kitchen, egg yolk was running down the counter from a breaking that had been too forceful.

Katrina had almost forgotten about the paper altogether in her quest to finish the pancakes and brew some coffee, but then Aunt Faith said, "What is this?"

"Pancakes?" Katrina asked with a smile.

"No, thank you. I'm thinking about going paleo."

"Coffee?"

"Sure. If cavemen didn't drink that, then they should have."

Katrina passed her aunt a cup of coffee and attempted to read over her shoulder. Makayla danced in her chair while she ate her pancakes, having forgotten about seeing her mother in the paper. Underneath a mug shot of Leif Gibbons was a tiny picture of "Katrina Rawls." She caught "single mother" and "possible love interest" and wondered when the newspaper had devolved into a gossip rag.

"Well, you made the Religion section," her aunt said with a tight smile that had entirely too much of a smug I-told-you-so tone. She passed the paper to Katrina.

"I'm guessing they're not nominating me for sainthood," Katrina said.

"Nope. It wasn't as bad as I'd thought it would be. Just a line and your picture."

Katrina scanned the article and saw that most of it pertained to the sins of Christian bands both past and present. She was but a footnote. This time. She put down the paper and concentrated on her coffee.

"Is it time to go to the concert yet?" Makayla asked.

"Honey, the concert isn't until tonight," Katrina said. "Why don't you go play in your room for a while?"

"But it's Saturday! Time for cartoons."

Katrina did her best not to roll her eyes. Now cartoons played every day and weren't relegated to Saturdays only. This idea was something the child had picked up from her very tired grandmother. "Fine. But you're not drooling in front of the television all day."

Makayla kissed her cheek and bounded off in the direction of the living room.

Katrina waited until her daughter was out of earshot. "I need both you and mom to take Makayla to the concert tonight."

"Excuse me?"

"I don't think it's a good idea for me to go. There are bound to be more reporters and more questions for Seth. It has to be better for him if I keep a low profile."

Aunt Faith leaned back in her chair. "Well, it's going to be really difficult for you to introduce Seth from the living room here."

Katrina waved away her concerns. "You can do that."

"Oh, but I can't. I don't speak in public. That was part of our arrangement when I hired you."

"Mom can do it."

"She doesn't officially work for the City of Kingdom Come."

Trina's knuckles went white as she grasped the corner of the table. "What are you playing at? I thought you would be happy if I stayed home and away from Seth where I couldn't be 'overly nice' to him."

"The minute you said I might be right? That was the moment I knew I was wrong."

*****

Seth couldn't believe the number of people who'd gathered outside the old auditorium.

Faith had come by to tell him they had officially sold out and that everyone was scrambling to find a way to show the concert in the gym for any overflow attendees. He nodded. He was too nervous to eat anything until the whole mess was over, and he tried to tell himself that his nerves had more to do with not wanting to let his hometown down than Katrina, but his self knew better.

Finally the time for the show came, and there Katrina stood looking like the All-American girl she was in a floral sundress and cowboy boots. She gave him a smile as she stepped out on stage to introduce him. "Folks, I'd just like to thank you for coming tonight to support our endeavors to get the old school up and running. We have a lot of great plans for community classes and other recreational activities, but all of that can wait. Tonight we're here to celebrate our local boy who's done good, Seth Bridges!"

Seth came out on stage to applause and he wowed the crowd for over two hours with his songs, country covers, and a few from the fifties. That same crowd wowed him, too, because they seemed to know the words to all of his songs. Even though the auditorium was sweltering, they waved their fans and sung on. Finally, he'd come to the part of the evening that he'd been both dreading and eagerly anticipating. "I got an education on pinky promises day before yesterday," he started. "Miss Makayla down there told me I needed to sing some of the old hymns to go along with my new songs, and I have to do it because we made a pinky promise."

The crowd whooped at the idea.

"Before I sing her song, though, she made me think of another pinky promise I made when I was just a little boy. Katrina Rawls, you haven't been sharing your chocolate milk with me as of late, but I would still like to be your friend."

She looked as though she wanted to become one with the hard wooden auditorium chair where she sat, but Seth continued. "It just so happens that Katrina's favorite hymn is one my mother used to sing to me. So, ladies, this one's for you."

Chapter 12

Katrina had completely forgotten about that day at the edge of the playground when she made Seth pinky promise to be her friend forever. Now the day came back to her, complete with the memory of honeysuckle's intoxicating scent.

Then he started strumming the intro to "Open My Eyes That I May See," and she sucked in a breath. He had remembered. He sang her favorite song even though she'd been mean to him so long ago and even though she'd sent him packing the night before. She would miss him when he was gone.

He finished the song and tipped his hat to Katrina before turning to Makayla, "Think you might come up here, Miss Makayla?"

Trina's child jumped from her seat on the front row and ran up the stairs to where Seth stood. He swung his guitar behind him and crouched down to be at her level. "How was that for an old hymn that doesn't say the same thing over and over and over and over?"

She put one hand on her hip and cocked it to one side. "It was good, but it wasn't a fast song."

The crowd tittered, and Seth, a natural showman, let them react.

"I thought you might say that," he said before grinning at Katrina. Her heart squeezed with something that felt suspiciously like the infant stages of love. He turned back to Makayla, "So, you want an old hymn that's a fast one?"

The little girl nodded, her blond ponytails bobbing.

"Ever hear of 'Standing on the Promises'?"

"Yeah," she said as she clapped and jumped up and down. "I like that one!"

"I'll sing it, but only under one condition."

"What's that?"

"You have to sing it with me, of course." He motioned to someone offstage, and one of the drama club kids brought one for Makayla to sit on. Seth lifted her easily and placed her on the stool. He looked offstage, "Think y'all can project the words behind me so we can all sing?"

The old screen once used for movies slowly descended, and someone managed to get the hymn's words to show behind Seth and Makayla, although they had to shift to the side to keep their shadows from blurring the middle of each verse.

"Well, Makayla," he said as he extended his pinky. "Let's take care of this promise with a song about promises."

And so they sang every verse of "Standing on the Promises." The crowd sang along, clapping and stomping their feet. At the end, Seth had

Makayla take a bow and then sent her back to sit with her mother while the auditorium gave him a standing ovation.

He thanked them all for coming and waved once more before he disappeared from the stage. Katrina was still trying to etch every moment of the last two songs into her mind as Makayla pulled on her hand. "Did you see that, Mommy? I sang on a stage! I think that's what I want to do when I grow up."

Katrina clasped Makayla's hand as they weaved through the crowd. She listened to her daughter's chatter as best she could, but she was preoccupied. A part of her hoped that Seth would part the crowd to find her, but, of course, he didn't. She had to remind herself that he needed to do what was best for him.

As they finally pushed through the doors and into the night, a reporter sidled up beside her. "Miss Rawls, what is the status of your relationship with Seth Bridges?"

She froze for a moment but then thought of what Seth had said, "No comment."

"So you *do* have a relationship with Seth Bridges."

"No comment, I mean no." She wasn't good at this sort of thing, and she shouldn't have to answer such questions.

"What she means is that she doesn't have a relationship with Seth Bridges *yet*."

Katrina turned, and Seth had, indeed, parted the crowd. "What are you doing?"

"Well, at the very least I owe you friendship. A pinky promise is a pinky promise."

"Seth," she began, ready to release him from the childhood agreement until she decided that might be letting him off way too easy. "Maybe I would've shared my chocolate milk with you if I'd known where to find you," she said.

"From now on that won't be a problem," he said, his eyes serious even if his lips were still turned up in a smile. "After all, you can't break a pinky promise ever. No matter what. A couple of wise ladies once told me that."

"So you do have a relationship with Miss Rawls?" asked the reporter they had both forgotten.

"If she will have me, then I would like to have a romantic relationship with her," he said, his eyes on hers.

"But—" Katrina began.

"No buts. I don't care what this lady or anyone else thinks. You're kind enough to care about something you did a million years ago and you're raising a really great kid. That's more than enough for me."

"Then, yes. I would like to have a 'relationship' with you," Katrina said with a big smile.

"And how would you describe your relationship?" the reporter asked.

Seth decided to answer her by drawing Katrina into kiss. She wound her arms around his neck and kissed him back until Makayla pulled on her elbow, a gentle reminder to keep everything PG.

"Are you sure you want to be a part of this craziness?" Seth asked.

"Oh, they'll get bored with us soon enough," she said.

His thumb touched her scar, and she closed her eyes to lean her face into his hand.

"Maybe, but I don't think I'll ever get bored of you."

"You say that now," she said.

"I think you underestimate yourself. Besides, I *know* I could never be bored by Makayla."

Her daughter took Seth's hand and swung it, and Katrina's heart wanted to burst from the honest affection he showed her daughter.

"You promise?" she asked as she extended her pinky.

"Promise," he said, as he linked his pinky with hers.

Promise: noun, a statement telling someone that you will definitely do something or that something will definitely happen in the future; an indication of future success or improvement; an arrangement between two people made all the sweeter by honeysuckle, chocolate milk, or pinky fingers.

Dear Reader of Mine

I hope you enjoy "Standing on the Promises" because I've wanted to write a series of stories based on the hymns in the *Cokesbury Hymnal* for quite some time. I don't always write sweet, but I do always write about how hope wins in the end.

I'm originally from West Tennessee, but you'll see that I put the town of Kingdom Come in Texas because, well, it sounds like a Texas kind of town doesn't it? I've traveled in Texas and have a lot of love for the state, but I usually write about a small town in Tennessee called Ellery. If you would like to read more of my stories, I'd greatly appreciate it. You can find out more about me and about my stories at sallykipatrick.com.

I do love to interact with my readers, and one of the best places to do so in on Twitter. My handle is @Superwritermom. I'm also on Facebook at https://www.facebook.com/Superwritermom/.

Thanks again for reading! Remember: leaving an honest review on Goodreads or at any retail site will always earn you a star for your celestial crown.

With love,
Sally

Other books by Sally Kilpatrick
The Happy Hour Choir
Bittersweet Creek
Better Get to Livin'

Sally Kilpatrick is the author of three published novels. Her first, The Happy Hour Choir, won the "Duel on the Delta" and was a finalist for the Maggie Awards and 2012 Golden Heart® Awards. Sally's third novel, Better Get to Living, was a 2013 Maggie finalist. Both *The Happy Hour Choir* and *Bittersweet* Creek are finalists in the 2016 National Readers' Choice Awards. Sally lives with her husband and two children in Marietta, Ga., a suburb of Atlanta.

CHRISTMAS BELLS

Linda Joyce

After grieving the loss of her husband and son, TV host Morgan Marshall is ready to embrace life again. But she won't risk a relationship with the father of her favorite cooking student, Avery, since the girl's happiness is more important than her own.

Advertising executive Alex Blake never thought another woman could pique his interest after losing his wife to cancer. Yet every time he's in Morgan's presence, she brings sunlight into the room. Plus, she's a role model for his daughter, always assuring Avery that dyslexia can't hold her back. But if he asks Morgan for a date and then she refuses a second one, the person he loves the most, Avery, could get hurt the worst because she adores Morgan.

When Alex is injured in a fall, Morgan insists on caring for him and Avery. As they share holiday fun, Avery topples Morgan's beloved crystal bell collection, shattering it to pieces. Through it all, they discover love of one another is more priceless than any object money can buy. Love rings in the air at Christmastime.

Chapter One

Tapping two fingers to her bottom lip, Morgan scanned the studio kitchen at the television station. Bright spotlights brought every item on the cooking island into sharp focus. Her set needed a few personal touches before today's shoot of *Cooking with Kids*. Had she healed enough to bring the item out of storage? Maybe.

Her crew had decorated the set professionally with a winter theme, but it still needed something special. A featured item. The perfect statement piece waited tucked in the back of the prop room. It was handmade locally. The kids on her show would love it, not to mention it would be new to most of her viewers, since the last time it graced a set was three years ago.

Bryce had presented it to her when he crashed the taping of the show dressed in a Santa suit complete with bulky belly padding. She wanted to be mad at him for ruining her timing on the show, but his infectious, "Ho. Ho. Ho," put everyone in stitches. Now it was one of her favorite memories of him.

She remembered the day like it happened only a week ago...and how she wished she hadn't wasted even a single minute being irritated. Regret, she'd learned the hard way, was like an anchor weighing her down. After years of grieving and finally moving out of depression, she promised herself she would truly embrace living. So it was now or never. At least for the decoration.

"I'll be back in a second, Corinna," she told her assistant. Her heels clicked on the polished concrete floor. The *tap-tap* sounded upbeat to her ears, more evidence of her returning happiness. She made her way to the closet beyond the brightness of the set in search of the oyster-shell, conical shaped tree. It would add a southern touch to the table and bring in a visual element of height. Mentioning the artist on her show would hopefully be a boon for his holiday sales.

She slid a box across the floor to keep the door ajar. Confined spaces still made her a bit anxious, something that started three years ago. Everything changed her back then. Trying to shake off panicky sensations of walls closing in, she reminded herself, "Breathe."

Calmness settled over her nerves a few breaths later, enough for her to continue the hunt.

Ambient light from the set lit the long narrow room enough to allow her to spot the item she sought covered in plastic. It was perched high on a shelf and would require a ladder and some assistance to get it down.

As she was about to call out for her assistant, she heard a voice from within the studio say, "Hey, Corinna."

Morgan waited for the newcomer to finish her business with Corinna, her younger assistant.

"Tina, I'm working." Corinna sounded annoyed.

Morgan didn't recognize the woman's voice, but Corinna had proven herself to be capable over the last year and could handle anything, so Morgan redirected her attention to various items in storage. A six-foot wooden heart she'd used at Valentine's Day leaned against the back wall. With a bit of work, lights could be added to it to give it a refreshed look. Red, white, and blue banners for the 4th of July needed replacing. A beach ball-sized pumpkin for Halloween was a new acquisition a couple of months back. Stroking the orange velvety surface, she stopped when she heard the tinkling of a little boy's laughter. She glanced from side to side and waited, but the sound didn't return. It came from nowhere. Lasted long enough for to capture her attention, but never as long as she wanted to hear it. While it used to make her sad, now it wrapped her in a deep feeling of motherly love.

"I just wanted to tell you. I have a date," the woman said to Corrina.

"Date?"

"Alexander Blake. Score the big time for me."

Hearing Alex's name, Morgan eavesdropped on the conversation.

"Tina," Corinna snapped. "This is a place of business, not a dating service. I got you the job as an intern to help you out. Do not embarrass me. Besides, he's too old for you." Corinna's harsh admonishment surprised Morgan.

"It is business." The words dripped sweetly. "His company does the station's advertising, and I just happen to work in the marketing department. We're going to discuss a new campaign for next year. Over lunch."

"That's not a date. I'll tell you now. He's not interested in you."

Satisfied that Corinna had the conversation well in hand, Morgan reached for a green, felt-covered box. She hadn't looked inside it for three years. Maybe this year the pain had finally lessened enough for her to find joy in opening the box again. She'd brought it to work to hide it. The pain of having it at home was just too much.

"How can you be so sure?" The woman's voice took on an accusatory tone.

"Because the only time his eyes light up, since his wife died, is when Morgan walks into the room."

Morgan's heart quickened. They were friends. He was Avery's father. No, Corinna couldn't be right about Alex.

"But she's *old*," Tina whined. "She's like thirty-two or something."

That's old?

"Ms. Marshall isn't old. And Mr. Blake is thirty-five," Corinna shot back.

"So what's a dozen years between soulmates?"

Corinna snorted. "Soulmates? No darlin', you're mistaken. We both know you're looking for a sugar daddy. Besides, the man has a daughter he adores, and *you* are not stepmother material."

Morgan straightened and pushed her dark brown hair behind her ears. Clearly, Corinna paid attention to those around her if she noticed all the things she told the other woman.

"Want to bet how long it takes *me* to get him into bed?"

Morgan had heard enough. "Corinna? Would you mind helping me in here?"

Surprised at her reaction to the dialogue taking place out of sight, Morgan pursed her lips. It was none of her business what this Tina person did or with whom. Nor was Alex's private life any of her concern. Except she liked him as a friend. Admired him as a gentleman. After all, he had been devoted to his wife who passed more than a year ago, and his daughter Avery held a special place in her heart.

The sweet girl was a regular on her show and came to her house weekly for cooking lessons as part of an afterschool group. The eight-year-old girl with the dimples, smiling brown eyes, and fawn-colored hair captured her heart the first time they'd met. She was the same age as her son…or the age her son would've been if he had survived.

Chapter Two

Phone to his ear listening to his mother's voice message, Alex stood at the window of his fourth-floor office and gazed at the people enjoying Johnson Square, one of the twenty-two historic squares in Savannah, Georgia. The city of his family for generations. Except that at that moment, his parents weren't in residence, in fact, not even stateside. It was his own fault they were vacationing in Europe for three weeks. Waiting for them to return was like waiting to spot Rudolph and his fellow reindeer in the sky on Christmas Eve.

"Alexander, honey, we're going to Austria today." His mother's voice sounded breathlessly excited. "We're having such a good time. Although, this time zone difference has turned me around. Hope I didn't wake you."

He saved the message before ending the call as a reminder he'd made the right decision to give them their Christmas present early. Europe lit up for Christmas was the top of their bucket list. They needed to enjoy it while they could. No one knew what tomorrow would hold…the adage of not putting off important things hit home when his wife died suddenly from pneumonia eighteen months ago.

This year, for the first time in his life, he would undertake December traditions without his mom or his wife overseeing everything. He was a topnotch elf, and would do as instructed, but he didn't have the eye for all the extra details. Like coming up with an original theme for decorating the Christmas tree. Or picking a different wrapping paper for each person in the family—something his mother insisted and his wife had considered a brilliant idea.

The holiday to-do list was daunting enough, but managing life *and* the holidays… He could barely wait for his parents' return. After five days of juggling his schedule, plus melding his daughter's school and social calendar, he wondered how his mother managed it—more importantly, would he survive fatherhood?

Never before had a Friday held as much appeal as it did today. He couldn't wait for the day to be over. A pizza and a cold beer tonight would remind of his less complicated years.

"Knock, knock." Emma entered his office. "Boss, you need to leave for that lunch meeting with the TV station staff. As in, leave now. Also, don't forget Avery's choir program tonight. Do you need me to have a car pick her up from school today? You wanted me to remind you to buy a Christmas tree tomorrow."

"You still think I need a fresh tree this year? It's not like my mother can object. It will be a done deal by the time she gets back on the 23rd." Alex sighed. Emma, his secretary, was efficient and helpful. She and her husband had provided a great deal of support since his wife, Casey, had died, which made last Christmas a somber affair. This year, he wanted to restore joy to the holiday, most importantly for Avery's sake.

"Don't even go there again. A fake tree? No." She handed him a slip of paper with an address. "That's the place to get the tree. Your mother will kill me if she finds an artificial tree in her house."

"We're decorating my house this year, not hers. She agreed."

Emma grabbed his suit coat from the hook behind the door and motioned him out of his office. "Go. Now. To make life easier, I'll have Avery delivered here when school gets out. Then you can have a nice father-daughter dinner before her program tonight. We'll see you there."

How had he ended up with so many bossy women in his life? At least, Casey, crafty woman that she'd been, had a way of finessing him in to doing things.

"I'm going." He snatched his coat and scooped up the folder on his desk. As he crossed the threshold, he turned back to Emma who was straightening up his desk. "I do appreciate you, just in case you were wondering."

"I know you do. When I think you don't, I remind you what a fabulous secretary you have." Her impish grin let him know he was back in her good graces.

Driving to Harbor Grill for lunch, he wondered when Peter, the head of the public relations department, would approve the new campaign his firm proposed. It was more contemporary than in the past. Over the last five years, he and Peter had been on the same page. They both wanted tasteful quality advertising when presenting the station to the public. However, this time, the commercials projected a hip and edgier vibe to capture a younger audience. Did Peter like the latest ideas, or was the reason for the lunch away from the office a pretext for delivering bad news in private?

He arrived at the restaurant exactly on time. The hostess led him to table covered with a crisp white linen tablecloth.

"Hello, Mr. Blake." Ms. Ward, the intern from the marketing department, was seated alone at a table set for two by the window.

"Hello." He glanced at the table and then back at her.

"Hey there." She tilted her head slightly to one side and smiled, holding out her hand, wrist bent and palm down. He wondered if she expected him to kiss it rather than shake it. After setting a folder on the table, he reached for her hand, clasped it in both of his, and then gave it a couple of pumps before releasing it.

"It's nice to see you again, Ms. Ward."

Where the heck was Peter?

"Why, Alex, I thought we'd moved past formalities. Call me Tina, please."

He was pretty rusty, but if he didn't know better, he'd think Ms. Tina Ward was flirting with him. She was certainly attractive, the kind of woman who stood out in a crowd, and everything about her said expensive and demanding. He appreciated her appeal the way he appreciated a fine piece of art—nice to look at, but he couldn't afford it, and even if he could, he wouldn't want it hanging in his home.

When she dipped her chin and looked up at him, his discernment went on high alert. If he wasn't careful, things might take a wrong turn. He remembered Morse Code from his Boy Scout days, but female code…not his forte. "Are we waiting for Peter?"

She shook her head. "No, today it's just me."

Taking a seat across the table from her, he motioned the waiter over.

"What would you like to drink?" Alex asked her as the waiter stood eagerly ready to grant her any request. He wanted the young man to put his eyes back in his head.

"I'll have sparkling water with a twist of lime." She reached across the table and placed her hand on his side of the table. "But once I get your new advertising plan approved, I'll let you buy me champagne."

"I'll have glass of water and a cup of decaf with my lunch," he told the waiter as her words settled. "When the plan is approved, I'll throw a party for the department at the station. Cater the food."

"Well…" She batted her lashes and smiled coyly. "I had a more intimate affair in mind." She drummed her fingers languidly as though an invitation to him.

"Ah…that would…be…interesting. Would you excuse me, please?" He sounded like an awkward college boy. It hadn't been since those days that a woman had flirted so outrageously with him. Heading for the men's room, he pulled out his phone and voice-texted Emma.

Call Peter. Tactfully ask about changes in his department's procedures. As in—is there anything new I need to know before pitching our new campaign to him? Check my schedule. Invite him for drinks at the marina where he docks his boat. Then call me in ten minutes with an emergency. I've got to get out of here.

"Shall we order?" he asked Tina when he returned to the table. A second later, the waiter appeared with their beverages and rattled off the lunch specials. She ordered crab salad. He ordered a sandwich with fries he had no intention of eating.

"I'm a little surprised," she said.

He raised an eyebrow and waited for her to explain.

"You're clearly someone who works out regularly. And you eat French fries. I like a man who knows what he wants and goes for it."

He forced a smile. She was being about as subtle as sunshine on a sunny day. But he didn't want to insult her or embarrass her in any way.

Ring. Ring.

He pulled his phone from his jacket pocket. "I'm sorry," he told her. "I have to take this."

She nodded in understanding.

"Hello, Emma?"

"Avery called. She doesn't feel well. I spoke to the school nurse, and she wants to send Avery home."

"Yes, I understand. I'll leave here immediately."

"Alex, this is not the emergency you asked me for. This is the *real* thing."

"Okay," he said slowly, his mind latching on to the news with alarm. His pulse raced. Avery hadn't been sick a day since her mother had passed away. "I'll leave now." Looking across the table at Tina, he patted her hand. "I'm very sorry to do this, but I have to cut our lunch short. My daughter is sick at school—"

"I would love to meet Avery. Shall I come with you?"

She knew his daughter's name? He paused. Her persistence was more than a little bold. "I think it would better for you to meet her another time." He turned to get their waiter's attention.

"I love children," Tina gushed.

"Sir, how may I help you?" the waiter asked.

"I need to pay the check. I have an emergency and must leave."

"Right away, sir."

Alex stood. "I'll have my secretary contact you to set up another time for a meeting. My firm is ready to *wow* the station. Please give Peter my best regards."

"Of course," she said brightly. "I hope we can wrap up this deal before the end of the year. What better way to ring in the New Year than with a new campaign in place?"

Alex nodded and smiled. How could he respond to the question when he wasn't quite sure what kind of deal she had in mind?

As he stepped from the restaurant to the sidewalk, he called the school nurse, who surely would call an ambulance if Avery was in any serious distress. The woman gave him vague answers, and then he asked to speak to his daughter.

"Daddy, you're coming to get me now, right?" she wailed.

The pained whine in her voice caused his pulse to skyrocket. "Yes, Sugar. I'll be there in a few minutes. What's wrong?"

"Stomach ache. Bad. I want to go home. Please hurry, Daddy."

"Hold tight. Daddy's coming." God help him if she was sick because of the breakfast he'd made for her. A bacon and peanut butter sandwich. She'd insisted, and he complied. He wanted to prevent any morning drama that might carry over and hinder her evening performance. He'd even let her walk halfway to school when she insisted rather than dropping her at the front as he or his mother did most mornings.

Stalking toward the parking garage, he couldn't remember any illnesses Avery had suffered. No chicken pox or measles. No mumps or even whooping cough. This was a time when she needed a mother…and when he wished for a caring woman in their lives to help guide him. His mother doted on Avery, but nearly to the point of smothering. But she didn't like craft projects—she hated to mess up her nails—nor did she know about contemporary music or kayaking, two of Avery's favorite things.

Ring. Ring.

"Yes, Emma." Alex started his car. "I'm headed to pick up Avery."

"I think it's a case of the nerves," his secretary said. "I think Avery is scared to sing her solo tonight."

"What? I don't understand. She's been singing on stages since she was four."

"Just talk to her. You'll figure it out. Just don't go rushing over there, blowing stop lights, and causing any accidents. I think she'll be fine."

He sighed. "Her voice sounded scared. It shook me. Thanks for letting me know. Now my heart won't pump out of my chest."

After making it safely through several intersections on green lights, he caught a red one a block from the school. Waiting for the light to change, he drummed his fingers on the steering wheel.

He wanted his daughter to grow up with a mother, but life took an unexpected turn and robbed them all. But he also wanted a wife. A woman who would bring love and laughter to him *and* Avery. His mother had been encouraging him to consider dating. She'd be shocked to learn he had given it some thought. But when he tried to make a list of women he would consider, only one name had come to mind. She had beauty and brains. Beauty in that wholesome woman-next-door kind of way, not the drenched-in-makeup-and-jewelry kind of woman several of his friends had married. High maintenance wasn't his thing. Her inward beauty shone, too. It was revealed in her kindness and patience with kids. Her laughter was lilting and infectious. Her smile heartwarming. Her conversation was informed and stimulating. She could tell a good story.

He'd met Morgan Marshall during a fundraising event for the television station about three years ago. Unlike most other hosts, she drew people in, more interested in finding out about them than boasting about herself. She exuded a quiet grace and radiated an inner strength. He'd offer his condolences back when he heard about the tragedy. She thanked him, and they'd never spoken of it again.

Yet, she always talked eagerly about Avery since his daughter started taking her afternoon cooking class. Most recently, her eyes danced with delight when she told him about his daughter's accomplishments with food.

Yeah, he'd made a list of women he was interested in. A list of one. And then he had completely dismissed it.

When the light finally changed, Alex spotted a red SUV. He waved. Morgan waved back. Would she be surprised to learn he had just been thinking of her? Her friendship was important, not only to him, but Avery, too. Morgan had shown his daughter great compassion since Casey died. She even helped Avery with her schoolwork whenever he arrived late to collect his child. She inspired his little girl to keep trying. He couldn't think of a better woman to be in Avery's life.

"Dyslexia isn't a prison sentence," she'd told Avery, "but a challenge to overcome for the world to see how special you are. Whatever else may happen, you can never give up."

After that, Avery sang Morgan's praises every week after cooking class. Not only was his child gaining an understanding about cooking, but also about where food came from and how to tackle recipes.

He wanted to know Morgan better, but he feared the problems it would create if she didn't like him well enough after the first date to join him on a second one. Her relationship with his daughter ranked higher than his needs. Avery had to come first.

But a daydream about Morgan now and then couldn't hurt anything, he hoped.

Chapter Three

Morgan arrived home, excited anticipation tingling through her. She carried a box with a treasure from her car inside to the kitchen. Her heart beat with lightness, a new experience since Bryce and Justin died. This year, she looked forward to actually finishing her holiday decorating, unlike the past two years. Memories lifted her up in joy, rather than plummeting her into sadness.

Gingerly taking a crystal bell from a red velvet-lined box, she placed it on the top shelf of the special wooden stand for her bell collection that Bryce had purchased the first year they were married. Round ball feet supported a wide round base and hosted three, round tiered shelves. The top one could hold a single bell. From the base upward, each shelf grew smaller. The entire stand resembled the conical shape of a Christmas tree, and it greeted everyone who entered her front door from its perch on the mahogany antique table in the foyer.

She gazed at the bell and the display from different angles. This new bell was different from all the others. Larger, with a faceted crystal clapper. Hundreds of sparkling tiny crystals covered the upper portion of the bell. It was a special edition by a famous crystal company. She'd spied it in the window of a jewelry store after lunching with one of her cousins. Somehow, it triggered her desire to decorate again. Her cousin had staunchly reminded her that decorations were just things. Developing an attachment to them or assigning them any emotional value was just not appropriate.

But she couldn't help it. The bell was beautifully made, ornate, and unique. Her hands went to her chest as she stared at it. She breathed in joy and serenity.

"I hope you love it as much as I do," she whispered. "It's in honor of you."

The tinkling laughter of a boy floated for a brief moment in the room. Morgan smiled, comforted by the sound. "Thank you."

Walking to the living room to turn on Christmas music, she noticed the flashing light on her home phone. Only work and her cooking students called that number. Everyone else used her cell phone. Morgan reached for the phone, punched in the code, and waited for a message.

"Miss Morgan, this is Avery Blake. Could I talk to you? Please call me back." That was twenty minutes ago. A long time to an eight year old. The urgency in the girl's whispered message alarmed her.

Hitting redial, she called the Blake home.

"Hello?"

"This is Morgan Marshall. May I speak with Avery, please?"

"Oh, thank God," Alex said. "I don't know what to do. Avery's crying. My mother usually handles her tears, but she's away on a trip in Europe. Besides, my daughter says she only wants to talk to you. That you'll understand."

"Is she sick? Running a fever?"

"Honestly, her vital signs are normal. But the tears... You have to help me."

Alex's anxiety surprised her. He always projected a calm and relaxed demeanor. "Could I speak with her?"

"Avery, Sugar, Daddy has Miss Morgan on the phone."

A heart-wrenching sob came through the phone's speaker followed by, "Daddy, I...*hiccup*...want to *see* her."

"If you can't come here," Alex said in a rush, "then I'll bring her to you. *Anything* to calm my child. Her tears make my heart hurt. Her sobs are stabbing me like swords. She's been this way since I picked her up from school."

"I'll be over as fast as it takes for me to drive there." Morgan grabbed for her purse. "Tell Avery I'm on my way."

"Thank you." Never before had she heard a man sound so relieved.

Morgan drove five blocks to the Blake residence, worry pushing her along. She hadn't met Avery until after five-year-old Justin died. Soon after, she discovered that she and the girl shared something significant in common. While she couldn't protect Avery from the downfalls of her condition, she could help her cope with the misunderstanding arising from the ignorance of others.

She gripped the steering wheel tighter and focused on the road. Treelined streets. Manicured landscapes. The angle of the afternoon sun cast long shadows. The neighborhood changed as she traveled the short distance. Single-story cottages dotted her neighborhood, but the style of the houses changed the closer she got to the Blake's home. They lived in a large, brick two-story colonial. Pulling onto the driveway, she parked.

Alex opened the door before she pressed the doorbell. "Up there. Door on the right." He pointed.

She shoved her purse at him when a sob tore through the silence of the house. As she bounded up the wooden stairs, her steps were muffled by a wool runner.

"Avery, I'm here." Morgan thrust open the door. A girl's room covered in pink. On the floor, her back to her bed, knees and head bent, hands covering her head, the girl's body shook as she cried harder.

Rushing to her side, Morgan sat down beside Avery, pulling her over onto her side, resting Avery's head in her lap. "Oh, Avery." She whispered her name over and over as she stroked her hair. "Tell me what's wrong."

Avery sniffed and fought to catch her breath. "She—she—she said, I was…stupid."

Morgan's heart seized. "Who said that?" She had been on the receiving end of that kind of bullying when she was a kid. "You and I know that's not true." Children with dyslexia were often singled out and cruelly labeled.

"But—but—I have to *work* so hard…to—to learn new words…when I read."

"That makes you brave and smart. You're strong. You don't give up." Morgan stroked the girl's hair. "Who said this about you?"

"Penelope Hiller."

Morgan was well acquainted with the Hiller family. The girl's mother, a socialite with more money than all the Christmas lights in Savannah, bragged on her daughter, but rarely spent time with her. Nannies and drivers cared for the girl. Penelope's father ran a shipping company. He also ran around, not so discreetly, on his wife. He'd even tried to seduce Morgan after her husband died. The scumbag. Sadly, Penelope paid the price for neglect from her parents.

"That little miss is not an expert on anything. She's jealous because you have a solo tonight, and she doesn't."

"But," Avery wailed, sitting up to face her. "She said I sing like a bellowing cow."

Morgan laughed. "Oh baby, I doubt Penelope's ever even heard a bellowing cow. You're a sweet, angelic soprano. A bellow is a deep masculine sound. They're nothing alike. She's just trying to throw you off your game."

Avery sniffed and raised her eyebrows as though she wanted to believe, but couldn't quite get there.

"Trust me on this." Morgan began planning the conversation she would have with Mrs. Hiller, one the socialite wasn't likely to forget. How would Mrs. Hiller feel if her darling Penelope never got another slot on the *Cooking with Kids* show?

Avery held on to her. The sniffles lessened. Patiently, Morgan waited for the girl to sort out her feelings.

When Alex appeared in the doorway, Morgan shooed him away with a flick of her hand. She continued to stroke Avery's hair. "How about a cup of warm tea? Do you want something to eat before your performance?"

Avery's breathing soon returned to normal. She looked up. "I think Daddy wants to go out to eat. Mimi isn't here to cook, and Daddy isn't so hot in the kitchen."

Sitting up, Avery faced Morgan and cocked her head. "Hey, I'm pretty funny. It's hot in the kitchen when Daddy's trying to cook. He's good at burning things."

Morgan rose and stretched out her arm to Avery. "How about you show your daddy some of your cooking skills? Let him know he's getting something with the hard-earned money he's paying me to teach you every week. I'll be your sous chef. Let's go raid the fridge."

The smile spreading across Avery's sweet face was worth more to her than all the diamonds Mrs. Hiller owned. Morgan pulled the girl tightly into a big hug. If she had a daughter, she'd want her to be just as sweet, bright, and smart as Avery.

Holding hands, they descended the stairs. Alex rose from the bottom step and looked up at them. The furrowed brow disappeared. He leaned against the newel post. "Ladies, may I take you to dinner?"

"No, Daddy. I'm going to cook for you."

Alex's gaze connected with Morgan's. His warm brown eyes twinkled. A little flutter started deep in her chest.

"What doesn't kill you makes you stronger." She smiled at him instead of telling him to trust Avery.

When the girl reached the bottom of the stairs, she ran for the kitchen. "Come watch me, Daddy."

Morgan started to follow, but stopped when Alex touched her arm. "You're sure about this." He tilted his head toward the kitchen.

"Oh ye of little faith," Morgan admonished, teasingly. "Your daughter can cook a 4-star meal. Just you wait and see."

"Well, Miss Morgan, if my child gives me food poisoning, I'm going to hold you responsible. I'll insist you nurse me back to health." He winked and then bowed, waving his hand in a flourish, suggesting he would follow her lead to the kitchen.

Morgan took a step, stopped, and glanced over her shoulder. Alex was grinning wider than she'd ever seen. A tingle shivered along her spine. Was the man flirting with her?

"Tell me what you need me to do," Alex said once they were all in the kitchen.

"Set the table, of course," Avery piped up. "You do what I do, and I'll do what Miss Morgan does—cook."

Morgan put together a bowl of salad from the items Avery pulled from the refrigerator—cucumber, apple slices, and dried cranberries. She helped sliced sweet potatoes into chips for baking after they were peeled. Without a word of instruction, she kept an eye on the girl as she melted butter to sauté shrimp. Avery's mother had a dream kitchen. Everything exactly in a perfect place, but sadly, the room would fit better in a showroom than in a house. She'd heard that Casey rarely cooked. Why would someone want a dream kitchen and then not cook?

When they sat down to eat, Avery asked, "For dessert, how about ice cream with sprinkles?"

"You're going to make ice cream, too?" Alex asked his daughter. "Wow, I'm feeling extra pampered tonight. Two beautiful ladies and ice cream after dinner. But first, we say grace."

"No, Daddy," Avery laughed. "You're going to buy us ice cream on our way to my recital."

Alex bowed his head. Morgan and Avery followed. He offered thanks for the meal and threw in a word of gratitude for friends willing to help at the drop of a hat. Morgan smiled at his not-so-subtle hint.

After the last "Amen," Morgan said, "We could wait and have hot chocolate and a brownie at my house after your performance. The kind with cream cheese you like so much, Avery."

The girl's eyes grew wide. "Daddy, can we?"

Alex paused, appearing reluctant. Morgan wondered what his objection might be.

"It will be late, Sugar, when the program ends. We don't want to impose on Miss Morgan."

Morgan hid a grin at Avery's wounded expression. "*Are* we an imposition, Miss Morgan?"

"No, never you. Your father on the other hand," she teased, "he might be."

Confusion swept across Avery's face. "Daddy, whatever you're doing to impose, stop it. I love Miss Morgan's brownies, and I think I deserve a reward after the day I've had."

Morgan stifled a giggle at the very adult-sounding girl.

Alex let out burst of laughter. "Sugar pie, it's seems like it's been a long day for all of us. Miss Morgan, we'd be honored to take dessert with you in your home after the recital."

While they finished dinner, Morgan soaked up the feeling of comfort Alex and Avery brought to her. For a moment, they were like a family. Morgan's heart settled into a warm comfortable rhythm, something she could grow to enjoy. When the tinkling sound of a little boy's laughter drew her attention, she glanced around the room fully expecting to see her son. Instead, her gaze landed on the glowing angelic face of an eight-year-old girl.

"I really like this." Avery spooned up a large shrimp and slipped it into her mouth.

"Shrimp?" her father asked.

"Well, that, too. I like the three of us. Dinner at the table."

Morgan's heart melted at the expression of satisfaction on the girl's face. Turning in Alex's direction, she caught him nodding. His brown eyes lit with delight and locked on hers. He winked. "I agree."

Morgan felt heat rising into her cheeks. Alexander Blake was definitely flirting with her. Flustered, she didn't know how to respond.

Chapter Four

"Bye, Sugar." Alex waved to Avery before leaving her in the care of her choirmaster back stage.

He wound his way to the auditorium to find Emma. She waved, and he headed to where she and her husband sat.

"Hi. Thanks for the seat, but if you don't mind, I'm going to sit with Morgan Marshall."

Emma smiled so wide, he thought it had to hurt her face. He'd bet big money she'd be texting to his mother about this development before he could take a seat.

Leaving his friends, he sought out Morgan. Dinner had proven a very enlightening affair. The cooking teacher, cookbook author, and television host most definitely captivated his attention. He didn't know what she said to his only child to quiet her and put a smile on her face, but she'd worked magic. She represented what he considered wholesome and genuine in a woman. He couldn't call her the girl-next-door type because she clearly wasn't a girl, yet she held the same appeal. Morgan Marshall was a woman to be trusted. Someone he was very interested in spending time with alone. But for an unknown reason, he sensed her unease whenever he directed his attention at her. He'd been disappointed when she refused to ride with him and Avery, instead choosing to take her own car and meet them at the recital.

"Hello, Tom. Susan." He spoke to the parents of Avery's schoolmates, nodded to several more. He stopped and scanned the large room decorated in swags of red and green velvet hanging from the rafters, searching her out—her dark brown hair that hung in soft curls at her shoulders. She had gone off to secure seats while he escorted his daughter to the appointed spot backstage as instructed.

"Morgan, where are you?" He didn't expect her to have ESP or to even hear him, but saying her name helped him focus in the sea of people.

When Morgan stood and waved, he spotted her and waved back. Making his way through the crowd, he couldn't imagine better company for the evening. He wasn't even sorry his parents were out of town. And, he realized, he was smiling. Genuinely smiling.

"Excuse me." He bumped the knee of an older woman as he made his way down the aisle to his seat. He repeated his plea to each person he passed. Morgan had picked prime seats. They lined up with the center of the stage, ten rows back in row J. Was that coincidence? J stood for joy. Something that vibrated in him for the first time since… he and Avery had buried Casey.

"Thanks," he said, sliding into the seat next to Morgan.

"She's calm now, right?"

"Smiling like there had never been a meltdown."

"Good." The smile that played on her lips made him smile again, too.

After a deep sigh, his tensions of the day melted away, and he relaxed. He started to stretch out his arms, but then stopped. He wouldn't want her to think he was making a play for her with some sort of high school move—the awkward arm stretch around the girl. He turned slightly in his seat and tilted his head closer to hers. "Are you going to share with me what caused Avery's tears today?"

Looking straight head, she smiled, and he watched it form easily on her lips.

She shook her head. "No. Not now. It was special girl talk. We can discuss it parent-to-parent later."

Alex turned when someone from behind tapped his shoulder. "Yes?"

"You two are the cutest couple. So you have a daughter in the program tonight?" A silver-haired lady draped in strands of pearls asked. "I'll bet she's beautiful, looking at the two of you."

"We—" Morgan began.

"Thank you." Alex interrupted, cutting her off. "Avery Blake is her name. She has a solo. It's listed in the program." He smiled brightly at the lady and then turned his gaze back to Morgan. She appeared surprised but didn't contradict him.

He figured the lady didn't need to know the intimate details of their life. It was enough that she considered them a couple. If others could see it, would it be possible for Morgan to see it, too? It wasn't until that moment, he understood how much he truly missed being a family of three and having a wife after being forced to let go of the woman he loved. It proved tougher than he imagined. Eighteen months later, he looked forward to a new chapter of his life. Maybe one with Morgan Marshall playing a major role.

The houselights dimmed. A hush fell over the audience. The school's choirmaster appeared under a spotlight. "Good evening, ladies and gentlemen. Friends and family. Tonight, Savannah's all-girl Preparatory Academy presents its annual holiday show. Each year, we feature a solo artist from each grade level. It could be a singer or a musician. These students, singled out for this honor, have shown marked improvement over the course of a year and exemplify the kind of tenacity we seek to nurture at the academy. Without further ado, I give you the Preparatory Academy choir and band."

The applause was deafening as the curtain rose to reveal the stage. All the kids he'd seen running around backstage were now garbed in white robes. All that was missing was their halos. Alex settled in his seat and rested one hand on his leg. His hand brushed Morgan's. Instantly, they looked at each other. He patted her hand before she folded hers together in her lap. If the lights hadn't been so dim, he'd swear he saw her blush. Yes, indeed, Miss Morgan charmed him more and more.

With rapt attention, he took in each performance. It was too hard to choose which age group he enjoyed more. The sweetness of the voices of the younger children or the delicate harmony of the other students. The musical solos—one on the piano, another on a violin, and the last one a flute—convinced him the decision he and Casey had made to send Avery to the Academy had been the right one for her. She thrived with the smaller class size, and she received special attention for her dyslexia.

Three quarters into the program, Avery moved from her lineup in the choir on the risers to take center stage. The choirmaster lowered the microphone to suit Avery's height. His adorable daughter began her first note a cappella. She projected her voice and hit a high note, a note he hadn't known she could sing. The auditorium filled with applause as his daughter continued her solo, the choir backing her up.

When Avery finished her selection and began to take her place with the others, the lady in pearls behind Alex, tapped him on the shoulder again. "You and your wife must be so proud," she whispered. "What an angelic voice."

Alex watched as Morgan smiled and nodded, her face damp with tears. With all the restraint he could muster, he kept his hands to himself, though he wanted to gently wipe away her tears and fold her into his arms for a comforting hug.

The program ended about fifteen minutes later with the performers receiving a standing ovation. As the house lights rose, so did Morgan. "I'm going to scoot out. I'll get dessert ready. Avery did a fantastic job. I know you must be so proud of her."

"She really moved you with her singing, didn't she?"

Morgan nodded again and then moved through the exiting crowd. There was something sweetly vulnerable about her. A slight tremble of her bottom lip. The way she cast her glance away. He wanted to hug her and reassure her that everything would be okay. But given her stance, he couldn't bring himself to cross the short distance. Something told him to be patient, to wait for her to say something more. He offered a silent prayer, "Lord, if she's the one, and I think she is, you have to give me a clear sign, even if it takes a bump on the head."

He stared at the stage, curtain closed, while people around him swarmed for the exit doors. Watching for a sign, he half expected the curtains to part and an angel to sing out *Hallelujah*, which in his mind would be the perfect notes. But he was far from perfect. If he received a perfect sign from Heaven above, it just might bowl him over dead.

That wouldn't do at all. Because then he would miss the pleasure of getting to know the lovely Morgan Marshall better.

He paused to focus on her in his mind's eye. "I wonder what her favorite flavor of ice cream might be." He truly wanted to know everything about her. But would she want the same?

Chapter Five

Morgan's hand trembled. She squeezed the steering wheel tighter to stop the tremors.

"Get a grip." Then she laughed at her own pun.

Traveling the most direct route home, she hurried, running a yellow light. A turning car honked and startled her back to a clear reality. Nervousness had taken hold mixed with sweetness—she adored Avery and she really liked Alex. However, apprehension bubbled inside her. She recalled her darling in-laws encouragement about dating again, but until the last six months, the thought was out of question. Their accusation about her staring at a closed door way too long made her ponder their observations of her.

They insisted when one door closed, another opened—at the right time—but if she wasn't looking, she'd miss it. Though she appreciated their loving concern, she thought they had been too cavalier in putting the past behind them. Her time of grieving had taken much longer than theirs, maybe because they had each other. When Bryce and Justin died in the car accident, she had no one of her own. A few cousins scattered here and there, but no immediate family. Her therapist assured her she was doing just fine. To take her time.

But when last summer turned to fall, she had a new spring in her step. The color of light made things around her glow in a new way. The sense of life surrounding her brought a renewal to her aching soul. At Labor Day, for the first time in a couple of years, she had an inkling from a vivid dream that Christmas would deliver a miracle to her. To her. Of all the people on the planet, she would be blessed with a miracle. Yet, that knowing deep in her soul made her flinch and look away. Why would she be more deserving than someone else? Her needs were small compared to so many others. Could she trust the feeling? Or was she no better than a doubting Thomas?

Maybe having an interest in a man is a miracle.

She liked Alexander Blake. He was kind. Something about him gave her confidence that in a crisis, he would seek to do the right thing and at the same time, he would be strong, a strong arm of support. And she would be remiss in admitting she like the way his eyes twinkled when he teased and the curl of his mouth when he smiled. Yes, the man was quite good-looking.

Was the tingling vibrating deep in her gut a sign that a doorbell was ringing, and she needed to answer it?

Was Alex interested in her as a woman?

Or mostly for Avery's sake?

Could she hope to fall in love with the same depth and commitment she'd experienced with Bryce?

"Angels in Heaven, I need a sign. If I'm supposed to open my heart and give a relationship a try, is it supposed to be with Alex? I like him. I'm interested." If only the curtain covering the auditorium's stage had opened before she left and a winged angel had sung out *Hallelujah*, then she could trust her instincts. But that hadn't happened. She intended to keep her eyes peeled for a signal. Hope was growing in her heart.

Pressing the button to turn on the car's stereo, she turned up the volume on the classical station. A baritone sang deeply and broadly. Shivers raced through Morgan when the choir sang the chorus to *Halleluiah*. Her body relaxed fully for the first time in years. The music hypnotized. A deep contentment filled her. Gratitude swept through her. But the comfort she experienced—scary. She couldn't stay in that space for long.

"Okay, so it's Christmas time," she argued. "This song is to be expected. I need a real sign. A true sign," she pleaded as she pulled into her garage. After closing the door behind the car, she exited and started into the house. The tinkle of a little boy's laughter tickled her ear. She paused to hear more, but it had drifted away as though the trade winds had swept it along. Instead, silence loomed loudly.

After washing her hands, she went to the pantry and pulled the ingredients for the brownies, setting them on the kitchen island. She turned on the oven to preheat, and then she gathered eggs and cream cheese from the fridge.

The brownies were in the oven when Morgan pulled plates from a cabinet and spoons from the drawer. She wished she'd already unpacked the rest of the Christmas boxes. The pretty red cloth napkins would go nicely with the cream-colored china plates trimmed with green holly, red berries, and rimmed with gold. They had been a gift handed down from her grandmother, to her mother, to her when she married Bryce. It would be comforting to use them again.

"Hot cocoa. I promised Avery." She crossed the kitchen to the fridge when the doorbell rang. It had to be them. She smiled. For a second, the image of them as a family sitting around the kitchen at night, all cozy and close, gave her heart a shot of joy.

She turned on Christmas music and then opened the door. "Hello. Welcome."

Alex and Avery stepped inside.

"Your light is out." Avery pointed to the darkened porch.

"Thank you for letting me know." She hugged the girl. "You were beyond wonderful tonight. I enjoyed the program very much."

Avery blushed and cast her eyes down. "Thank you," she whispered.

"Let's celebrate," Morgan told her, lifting her little chin. "You know where the kitchen is. Brownies are in the oven. Why don't you wash your hands? I still have to make the cocoa. Would you get the milk out?"

"Sure!" Avery scampered off.

"You probably don't come in and out this way much." Alex pointed back to the porch before closing the door. "If you have a bulb and a stepstool, I'll be happy to change the light for you."

"I appreciate your offer." It was nice to have him ask. A very gentlemanly thing. However, she didn't need a protector or a handyman. She was quite capable of changing a light bulb. "Thank you, however, I'll take care of it tomorrow when it's light outside."

His forehead crinkled. "You would deny me the privilege of doing something nice for you…while you treat Avery and me?" He leaned in close. She stood very still, half wanting him and half-afraid he would kiss her cheek. "I'm not that good in the kitchen. You and Avery could have some girl time. Her grandmother's been gone all week, and I think she really misses talking with her about girl stuff. It's only a light bulb, but my thank you for rushing over to handle the meltdown earlier. I don't know what I'll do when she reaches those teenage years."

Morgan laughed. "Okay. I'll get the stool and light bulb, but let me put the milk on the stove first." She crooked her finger. "Follow me. I even have a tool belt, if it will make you feel more official."

"You have a tool belt?" He was only a step behind her. She chuckled at the curiousness in his voice. She enjoyed surprising him.

"It is the twenty-first century. Do *I* need to teach Avery how to use a hammer and a screwdriver?" She entered the kitchen where Avery sat on a stool at the island. The carton of milk in front of her.

"Daddy has prepared me," Avery said.

"Alex, I don't know what you're worried about. You're raising a daughter to cook and wield tools. That's quite an accomplishment."

"Yeah, but he's really glad you're teaching me about cooking." Avery nodded. "I think he's waiting for me to get older and learn more so I can cook for us more often."

"Then you've come to the right place. I promise you'll be on your way to being a chef if you stick with me."

Walking into a small closet off the kitchen, Morgan reached for a bulb in the box where she stored extras. On her way out, she hoisted the two-step stool. "Here." She held the items up for Alex. "Make sure the switch by the door is off. Safety first."

When Alex headed out of the kitchen, Morgan turned to Avery. "Why don't you get the large measuring cup? Pour four cups of milk into that pan." She pointed to the one already on the stove. "I'll get the cocoa."

Morgan glanced at Avery to keep an eye on her, but she allowed her to handle the task without helicoptering. The worst that could happen would be spilled milk, which in the scope of life was nothing more than a ten-minute clean up.

She secured the cocoa and held up the package for Avery to see. "Would you get a scoop from the drawer?"

Turning on the gas, Morgan began whisking the milk in a circle, making it swirl. "Now add the cocoa," she instructed Avery just as the timer for the oven dinged, a reminder to remove the brownies.

"YOW!"

The holler came from Alex. A clatter followed. A thud hit against the front door.

Morgan turned off the stove and pressed the timer button to make it stop. She and Avery raced to the front door. When she opened it, the step stool toppled over inside, clattering against the wooden floor.

"Owww," Alex moaned.

"Goodness. What happened?" Morgan searched in the dark to locate Alex. A moan came from below the porch. He lay on the ground, three feet below, beside the brick porch. He was almost sitting, his head against the house, and holding his shin. In five steps, she reached him, searching for signs of blood.

"Did you hit your head?" Did he have a concussion? "I think I need to call an ambulance."

"Daddy?" Avery wailed. "Daddy, please be okay." She began to cry. "Please don't let them take him away in ambulance."

"Shhh, Sugar," Alex said hoarsely. He tried to push himself up but melted back against the house. "Avery, Daddy is okay."

"Alex, I really think I should call an ambulance," Morgan insisted. In the dim light, he shook his head.

"The worst of this is a sprained ankle. Could you help me up?"

Squatting beside him, Morgan reached an arm around his back. As she stood, Alex grabbed the porch for stability. She leaned him in that direction, fearing his injured ankle wouldn't be able to support his weight.

Avery, tears trickling down her face, hugged him from behind. "Daddy, you're okay?"

"Yes, Sugar, I am."

Morgan worried he might pass out given the pain flashing on his face. "Avery, go get my purse in the living room. In the kitchen closet, grab the broom." Like it or not, Alex Blake was going to see a doctor.

Avery returned with the requested items in tow. "Here."

"Alex, use the broom for stability. I'll get my car."

A minute later, she drove her SUV across her manicured lawn. The closer she could get the vehicle to Alex, the easier it would be to get him inside with the least amount of pain. Or so she hoped.

"Avery, please grab the throw from my couch." Avery raced away.

"Alex, let's get you to the ER."

With Avery buckled in the back and Alex in the front passenger seat, reclined as far as it would go, Morgan backed out of her yard and into the street. The nearest hospital was only a handful of minutes away. But going there was a path she dreaded. It dredged up memories of the evening she raced there hoping to hold her child before he took his last breath. Over time, the sharp pain of the memory turned to a dull ache, but the same urgency she felt then pushed her to get to the ER now as fast as possible.

In the backseat, Avery whimpered, "Momma. Momma. Momma."

Morgan's heart broke. She couldn't be sure, but she guessed somehow Avery connected the hospital with her mother's passing. If there were any other way, Morgan would've spared Avery the pain of this experience, but with Alex's parents out of town, she had no one to call upon to care for Avery this late at night.

After pulling up to the emergency room entrance, she got out and opened the door for Avery. "Honey Bear, I want you to walk in there very calmly and tell someone at the desk that your daddy hurt his leg and needs a wheelchair. Can you do that? Very calm and very grown up."

Avery's bottom lip quivered. She nodded. With her fists by her side, she marched rigidly to the sliding doors that *whooshed* open for her. Morgan closed the car door and went around to the passenger's side. "Alex," she whispered. "We're at the ER. Going to get you help."

He nodded, though his eyes remained closed.

"What's going on?" A man in scrubs jogged out the door. Avery, Morgan noticed, wasn't with him.

"Where's Avery?"

"Little girl is being taken care of inside. What happened?"

"He fell off a step stool. Hit his head, maybe his back. He can't put weight on his foot, or maybe it's his ankle."

Alex nodded slightly. "She's right."

"Be right back." The man jogged back inside. A second later, he rolled out a wheelchair and assisted Alex into it.

"I'll move my car and be right inside," Morgan called to Alex. Gripping the steering wheel, she tried to stop her hands from trembling, this time for a completely different reason than she had only hours ago.

"What if his injuries are worse than I think?"

Chapter Six

Wearing a gown in place of his shirt, Alex sat in the bed in the ER examining room and waited for his turn for X-rays. The nurse had checked him for a brain injury, palpated his back to get a sense of the injury there, and then cleaned up the scrapes. Luckily, he hadn't sustained a concussion, but his head sported a goose egg of a bump, and a headache throbbed like a flashing red light in Savannah's harbor, reminding him there was something inside his skull.

"Does this hurt?" The nurse manhandled his leg.

"No. Of course not." He winced, refusing to cry out in pain, but if he had superpowers, she would've been vaporized.

"X-rays in just a minute." She turned and left the room.

He stared a hole in her back when no one was looking. The intensity of the pain had subsided a bit once the torture the nurse inflicted had stopped.

The doctor arrived a few minutes later and checked him over. The diagnosis so far: blow to the head without loss of consciousness, sprained back, and severe sprained ankle with possible fracture.

Alex added sprained manly-pride to the accounting of injuries.

He hated hospitals. The sound of activity outside the door. The clock on the wall ticking loudly. The odor of cleaning supplies. Each minute had to be five in a hospital bed. He drummed his fingers and then stretched his hands. These folks could hurry the process along. Cast the foot. Send him on his way.

But...the injury was to his right foot. How would he drive? Rubbing his fingers through his hair to his scalp, he didn't know how he would handle things until his parents returned. Telling them was out of the question. They'd cut their trip short. He'd call Emma in the morning and have her help him make arrangements. Like a driver to take Avery to and from school. Someone to cook meals. Then there was the laundry to do.

Of all the times he could've picked to have an accident, this was the worst.

And his poor baby—although Avery would object to that moniker since she was eight, sometimes going on sixteen—she'd suffered tonight. At one point, he considered asking the doctor to prescribe a med for her anxiety, but thankfully Morgan stepped in, took control, and distracted Avery in a unique way—teaching her about the machines and medical terminology. She showed her how to check a heartbeat rate and explained about blood pressure. The nurse was kind enough to allow Avery to listen to his heart with a stethoscope, which calmed her down significantly. Afterward, Morgan carted her off for hot cocoa.

When they had returned, his heart surged with a rush of happiness.

He wasn't falling for Morgan in a big way because she brought joy to his child—she would do that for any child in need. Her ability to bring out the best in others, to nurture when she'd suffered so much. The generosity of her spirit. These characteristics made her truly beautiful to him. He was more than a bit infatuated, giving him a natural high that painkillers couldn't touch.

Since September, he'd noticed a change in her whenever he visited the station. When he asked Peter about her, his friend shrugged and explained how she rarely spoke of her private life. He couldn't say whether or not she'd dated since her husband's passing. But Peter had thrown out a challenge—invite her to the New Year's Eve bash, the fundraising benefit for the station. The worst that could happen—she would say, "No."

He hadn't found the nerve yet to ask her.

In the chair beside the bed, Morgan held his sleeping daughter and dozed. What a disaster. He made a fool of himself and imposed on Morgan. She had better things to do than play nursemaid to him and his daughter. Friday night in the ER. Not the best impression. His chances for a real date in the future were probably pretty slim.

Gazing at Morgan, her mouth slightly parted and expression relaxed, she dozed peacefully. To him, she was lovely. Her manicured hands appeared delicate as they held his daughter. And yet, those hands had great strength and gripped him tightly when she helped him to the SUV. Earlier in the day, he'd looked on as her hands tenderly cupped the face of his daughter. She worked feminine magic, soothing Avery's fears and tears. Now sparkling sensations pinged in his chest, coming at a moment when he was able to gaze unabashedly at her, and she was unaware of her effect on him.

She was an angel.

"Mr. Blake," the nurse said, barging into the room, interrupting his thoughts, and turning on the bright lights. "I'm taking you for x-rays now."

Avery rubbed her eyes, groaned, and squirmed in Morgan's arms. Rising and slipping his daughter into the chair, Morgan draped her jacket over the recliner like a tent and blocked the light from his daughter's face, and then she stood next to the bed.

"May we wait here?" Morgan whispered and pointed to Avery.

"That would be fine."

"I'll take good care of her," Morgan told him when he slipped from the bed into the wheelchair the nurse provided. She squeezed his shoulder.

The quiet of the ER struck him as the nurse wheeled him down the hall. He needed to get out more. Live again. What did he have to lose? Yes, he would invite Morgan to the party.

No patients waited ahead of him when he reached the designated room. The whole x-ray process took only a few minutes.

"Officially, I have to wait for the doctor's approval to release you." The nurse delivered him back to the examining room. Morgan put her finger to her lips and pointed to sleeping Avery. "But, I have it on good authority, no fracture," the nurse continued in a whisper.

Morgan nodded as she listened as though committing all details to memory.

"You have a severe sprain," the doctor said, walking into the room. "Crutches. No weight bearing for a couple of weeks, could be up to a month or more, depending on how quickly it heals. Keep icing it to reduce the swelling for several days. Follow up with your primary doctor for further care in a week. I expect you'll need PT." The doctor nodded as though everything was settled. He left as quickly as he came.

"PT? Why would I want to do that? It'll heal. I'll be fine." Alex shook his head. The idea of spending any more time than necessary dealing with the foot seemed unwarranted. He had a busy life, especially with the holidays only two weeks away. Of course, he'd be up and walking in a few days. Okay, a week at most. A bum ankle would hinder dancing with Morgan on New Year's Eve.

"You're released to go, Mr. Blake. Remember about the follow-up care."

"Thank you, nurse," Morgan inserted. "I'll make sure he follows up as needed."

"There's a bright side to this, you know," the nurse said.

"What's that?" he grumbled.

"You're going home to spend the holidays with your family. Not everyone who came through those doors tonight is so lucky."

Morgan paled. Was this the hospital where her son and husband were brought after their accident? If so, he could only imagine what she must be thinking. The nurse sure put him in his place. He had a lot to be grateful for, including the woman who'd given up her evening to help him and care for his daughter.

"He will do everything to the letter that he's supposed to." Morgan's clipped tone shone with insistence. "I shall make sure of it."

"Someone will be by with crutches and a wheelchair to roll you out of here," the nurse said as she left the room.

"Really, Morgan, you've done enough. Just get me home," Alex told her.

"Home? Really, Alex? How are you going to navigate stairs? Get sheets and bedding? Let alone make up the couch to sleep on? Who will cook for you and Avery? Who will take care of her? Help her get ready for school? Cook dinner? And according to Avery, you have only a half-bath downstairs. No, sir. I've made other arrangements for you."

"You what?" He was taken aback by the general standing at his bedside. Where had the mild-mannered Morgan gone?

"You can be stubborn all you want. If so, I'll leave you to fend for yourself, but at the very least, Avery stays with me. My house is a single story. I have two spare bedrooms. I'm on hiatus from work until mid-January."

"I can't impo—"

"Hush. This is not open for debate. You need help, and I'm available to give it."

Begrudgingly, Alex grinned. "Whether I like it or not, eh?"

"Yes." Her fists went to her hips. He never should have doubted her ability to persuade. After all, she dealt with some pretty tough customers regularly—a group of eight year olds.

"All I'll commit to is 'a try.' There's lots to do before Christmas. My mother is expecting a fully decorated house."

"You can negotiate later, Alex. Right now, let's get you out of here." She gently woke Avery. "Honey Bear, come with me. We'll get the car and pick up your daddy. Let's go home."

As Avery followed along in tow, her hand fitting together with Morgan's, he couldn't help but wonder if Morgan's words, 'Let's go home' were a turn of phrase or a prophecy of better things to come.

"God bless us one and all," he said under his breath and meant it.

Chapter Seven

Morgan's mind swirled. She hadn't had overnight guests in nearly a year. Beds had to be made. Pillows retrieved from plastic bags high on a shelf in the hall closet. Did she have enough eggs for breakfast in the morning? There was probably a package of bacon in the freezer. She had to remember to take it out before she went to bed. Eggs, grits, biscuits, toast, and fruit. Or maybe Avery would prefer pancakes?

She would set a table for three.

The memory of another time when her table was set for three popped into her mind. She smiled feeling the presence of Bryce and Justin gazing down on her, giving her a big thumbs-up for helping Alex and Avery.

"Morgan?"

"Huh?"

Alex pointed to the right. "I think that was your street."

"Oh?" Flustered, she blinked to focus her tired eyes on the street sign. Sure enough, she'd missed the turn. Alex must think her an idiot…a woman who can't find her way home.

Pulling into a driveway to turn around, in the illumination of the headlights, she glimpsed a couple standing at the back of a car kissing.

"Oh my. Sorry for the intrusion," she called to the couple whom she was certain heard none of her apology through her closed car windows. Her cheeks heated. Thankfully, Alex wouldn't be able to see her embarrassment in the dim light. "That happened to me once. Only it was my grandmother's porch light. I was seventeen." She'd never told anyone that. The only people who knew were her grandmother and the boy she'd been kissing. Both now passed. She married the boy a few years later. It had remained a sweet memory for her and Bryce. But now she was babbling about it to Alex.

"Lucky guy," Alex teased.

"Yes," she mused, happily. "He was." A lightness filled her. The ability to talk about memories of Bryce with Alex seemed natural. Comfortable. "And I was a lucky girl."

"I'll just repeat myself. Lucky guy."

"Here we are." She pulled onto her own driveway. "I'll unlock the door, and then I'll carry Avery inside. I'll come back and help you, so please sit tight."

"Take care of my baby, please. I can manage on my own with the crutches." Something about the tone of his voice made her believe he wasn't a man used to being unable to help.

After Morgan opened the rear passenger door, she unbuckled the seatbelt for a sleeping Avery. Scooping up an eight-year-old girl proved to be more of a weightlifting challenge than she anticipated, but she accomplished it without fully waking the sleeping child, and even better still, not injuring either of them as she ran the obstacle course inside her home. Avery had to weigh three times her regular weight. Morgan vowed to add weightlifting to her weekly workouts.

Once inside the bedroom that had been her son's, she gingerly placed the girl on the bed. Six months ago, the bedroom looked like a toy museum and the bed resembled a car. A thrift store bedroom-set find and then some elbow grease transformed the room into a gender-neutral space, comfortable for nearly anyone. The color scheme was taupe and turquoise. She'd been proud of handling it all by herself.

She removed Avery's shoes, pulled up her sox, and then covered her before turning on the night light. The door remained ajar as she backed out. Hopefully, Avery would sleep peacefully through the night.

Returning to assist Alex, she found him out of the car and navigating one slow step at a time with crutches.

"Tomorrow, we'll make a few adjustments to make things easier for you. I have a rolling desk chair you can use as sort of a wheelchair."

Still in the hospital gown, he sat on the couch in the living room while she made up the second guest room. Moving quickly, she wished for eight arms to make the task go quicker. The image of an octopus in a maid's uniform made her giggle.

She finished the task and then rolled her office chair to Alex. "Rather than risk you falling over tonight because of those metal legs"—she pointed to the crutches—"sit here. I'll roll you into the bedroom. You can hop over to the bed."

"Thank you." Exhaustion etched his face. His brown eyes had lost their earlier sheen. Her heart ached to see him so tired. It had to be tough, especially with his support team away. But she was committed to helping him. No matter how much he tried to refuse. There wasn't a man alive who handled being a patient well, let alone dealing with a daughter only weeks from Christmas.

She rolled Alex into the bedroom and parked the chair next to the bed. He insisted on climbing into bed on his own.

"I put out three pillows. You might want one to prop your foot on and another beneath your knee, and of course, the last for sleeping." She sounded more like a mother hen than a friend. That wouldn't do at all.

"You're a godsend. I appreciate your help. Tomorrow, I'll get things situated so Avery and I won't impose on you more."

"In the morning, we'll have a new day and a new perspective. Once again, you're not an imposition. It would be fun to have you and Avery help with the decorating while you recover. You point, and I'll hang ornaments, something I haven't done in few years."

"You don't decorate every year?" Alex laid back on the pillow and closed his eyes.

She paused and wondered how to explain without sounding maudlin. "I haven't celebrated the holidays in a while. This year, I'm excited to renew the tradition, and I can't think of two people I want to share it with more."

"I'm too tired to launch a campaign against Saint Morgan." He yawned. "Good night, Alex."

When Morgan laid her head on her pillow in the darkness of her room, she remained still and listened to the sounds of her house. The tinkling of a little boy's laughter caused her to strain to hear, hoping for more. She waited expectantly. Silence filled the room. Sighing, she drifted off to sleep, the image of dancing gingerbread men in a chorus line made her smile.

The next morning a knock at her door woke her. She blinked several times. Was she dreaming? Someone called her name. Bolting upright, she recalled her houseguests.

"Miss Morgan?" Avery's sweet voice penetrated Morgan's still sleepy brain.

"Come in." She yawned. For some reason, she'd slept better than she had in a long while.

The girl slowly opened the door. Her sweet face appeared around it. "Daddy's still asleep. I'm hungry."

"Of course you are. I'll get dressed, and we can make breakfast together. How's that?"

"Miss Morgan," Aver said, inching closer to the bed. Her small hands began to knead the holly and ivy quilted cover on the bed. "Do you like me?"

Surprised, Morgan nodded. "Yes. In fact I adore you." She patted the spot beside her and motioned for Avery to climb up. Fluffing a pillow, she placed it behind the girl's back for support.

"Can I talk to you about something?" Avery's downcast eyes were worrisome. Morgan ran her fingers along Avery's forehead, pushing the girl's hair aside from her face. "Anything. I promise whatever we talk about will be just between you and me."

"What about Daddy?"

"What about him?"

"You won't tell him what I tell you, will you?"

Concern sliced through Morgan. She would do anything for Avery, but if his child was in danger of any kind or something had happened, she couldn't keep serious information from Alex. Having been a parent, she would want to know, and she suspected Alex shared that expectation as a devoted father.

"Well…How about if you tell me what's on your mind? If I think your daddy needs to know, I'll tell you. Together, we'll find a way to tell him. I won't go behind your back. Is that fair?"

Avery crinkled her nose and after a moment nodded. "So…people think because kids are small we don't hear some things." Avery rolled her eyes as though some adults were too stupid to live. "I've heard a few women talk to Daddy, give him their phone numbers or email addresses, but later I've seen them helping at school or at church, and they stop me and ask me things about Daddy."

"Such as?" She couldn't fathom where the girl was going, but she intended to stick with the logic of an eight year old.

"Silly things. Does he drink coffee with cream or sugar? Does he like steak or seafood? Does he date?"

"What do you tell them?" Morgan held her breath. She was afraid to hear the answer. As cute as the girl was, every child had a moment when just about anything could come blurting out. She steeled herself not to laugh.

"Usually, I shrug. Act like I don't know anything. But *I* know what's going on. Momma talked to me, before she died. She told me one day Daddy would hopefully bring a new woman into our lives. Momma said I had to be patient and caring. To try to love that woman, too, especially if we became a family."

Sadness flooded Morgan's heart. Avery's mother had tried to prepare her child for a stepmother coming into her life. What a brave thing to do. And yet so heartbreaking to endure.

"I think…" Avery looked up at Morgan with hopefulness shining on her face. "I should get a vote about making a family again."

"Oh, Avery. I can't imagine your daddy trying to add a woman to your family without talking with you about it." The Alex she'd gotten to know over the last few years was patient, thorough in his work, also considerate. And most caring to his only child.

"I asked Daddy about it. He said to find someone to bring into our family to love us like Momma did, he would have to date."

Morgan smile and adjusted her pillow. Talking with Avery was like a rollercoaster ride. The girl had adults pegged. They didn't give children enough credit for knowing what was going on. The girl beside her was wiser than her years. Any woman would love to have Avery for a daughter.

Avery reached over and patted her hand. "Miss Morgan, would you date my daddy?"

Surprise ricocheted through Morgan. She tried to keep a neutral expression. Of all the things she anticipated, those words coming from Avery's mouth were unexpected. "Date? Ahhh…"

"That's what daddy says he has to do to find a new person." Avery's words rushed out. "If we're going to add to our family."

"I see." How in the world did she explain adult relationships to a child? What words could she use to explain chemistry, attraction, compatibility, and, most of all, committed love?

"If you date him, then those other women can't, right?"

Stunned, Morgan stared straight ahead. Little Avery had given this topic some consideration.

"I think it will solve all our problems," Avery insisted.

Morgan swallowed. The eight year old beside her sounded more like a thirty year old with an uncanny grasp of her father's situation. This was most definitely a discussion Alex needed to have with Avery. Just the two of them.

When Avery waved her hand in front of Morgan's face, she flinched and tried to think of a way to skirt the topic of Alex dating.

"Miss Morgan, I have only one question about this dating thing."

"Okay, Avery." Morgan's voice wavered. "I'll try to answer it."

Outside the door, a rumbling noise sounded, drawing closer to Morgan's open bedroom door.

Morgan leaned down when Avery quickly motioned to her.

"Miss Morgan, would you please tell me what happens on a date?" Avery whispered.

Before Morgan could formulate an answer, Alex rolled into the opening of the doorway and smiled. "There you are. Good morning, ladies."

Morgan pulled up the covers around her shoulders and chuckled. In a very short time, the father/daughter duo had captured her heart. They brought happiness to her life she hadn't expected. Joy was truly one of the miracles of the Christmas season. But how in the world did she explain dating to Avery and tell Alex his daughter was setting him up?

Chapter Eight

"I came to see who wants breakfast," Alex said, sitting in the doorway to Morgan's bedroom, aware of the fact that the hospital gown hung down over his pants and he looked more pathetic than manly. Not the image he wanted to impart to the lovely Morgan Marshall. "I think I can manage a frying pan, a spatula, and flipping eggs. I'll cook."

"No." Avery and Morgan said in unison. The two faced each other and shook their heads, and then giggled.

The intimacy of the scene before him was a bit unsettling. He hadn't seen a woman in bed since before his wife died, but he'd been married to her. However, Morgan's sunny smile allowed his momentary discomfort to slip away. It filled his heart with a warming joy to see his daughter smile.

"How are you feeling this morning?" Morgan asked.

Avery hopped down from the bed and hugged her daddy.

"I'm happy it wasn't worse. I rewrapped my ankle. I gotta say, it ain't lookin' pretty."

"No significant pain?"

"The pillows kept it propped up. I don't think I moved all night."

"Good to hear. Now, why don't you and Avery roll into the kitchen?" Morgan asked. "I'll change and meet you in there. Avery, you know where the things are to set the table. Please wash your hands and start with that."

"Okay, but Miss Morgan," Avery wailed. "I *still* need an answer to my question." Avery's eyebrows wiggled. Her head bobbed to the side, and her shoulder twitched. Alex rolled closer. Was she having some weird spasm attack? A second later it stopped.

"Girlfriend, we'll talk later. I promise." Morgan held up her hand, pinky lifted. His daughter hooked her pinky through Morgan's, and they shook.

He shook his head. This was one of those times when he needed his wife to interpret life for him. Maybe later, he could pull Morgan aside and ask her to explain what that was all about.

"Marching orders, young lady," Alex said. "Let's go." He used his good foot to push off against the floor and send the chair in reverse. Morgan needed some privacy before breakfast.

Rolling through Morgan's house, he decided she was right. Trying to survive a two-story house on crutches would be a nightmare. Maybe Morgan would make help him by making up the sofa bed in his downstairs office, but that left Avery upstairs at night all alone. If she needed him for any reason, climbing the stairs with crutches could result in a tragedy of errors.

When Morgan arrived in the kitchen, Alex rolled over to her. "I found everything to make coffee. I hope you don't mind that I rummaged through your fridge and pantry. What I don't know is—how do you take your coffee?" On the kitchen island sat a small pottery bowl with green packets of natural sweetener and a tiny pitcher filled with cream.

"I took a guess," Alex said. "Cream and sugar."

He was glad to see delight spread across her face rather than a frown. His wife had mostly banned him from the kitchen. She claimed when he even walked through, it usually resulted in a mess, so the only meaningful time he spent in the kitchen was when he helped clean up. Since her passing, his mother did most of the cooking—coming to his house a couple times a week to prepare and store meals. In return, he had earned a Ph.D. in microwaving.

"I got the bacon and eggs." Avery beamed. "I put the bacon on the sheet, just like you showed in cooking class. Daddy insisted on putting it in the oven. Please tell him I won't burn myself."

"She's quite good in the kitchen," Morgan said. "We do a fair amount of baking, so she knows her way around the stove. And safety first."

Alex rolled to the table. He bumped his foot on one of the table's legs. Turning away, he didn't want Avery and Morgan to witness his grimace. The ankle hurt more than he imagined. To distract himself from the throb, he drank coffee while Morgan and Avery finished making breakfast. They decided on pancakes. Alex mused—if he ever wanted Avery to get a job, she'd do well in a diner, given all she'd learned from Morgan.

"Avery," Morgan said, "Please find the pancake recipe in that cookbook." She pointed to one on a stand at the end of the counter.

"If you read me the ingredients, I'll gather them." Avery stood at attention and saluted.

"Well, now…how about you take control? You did the bacon, right?"

"Yes, ma'am."

"You read the ingredients and the directions to me. We can conquer dyslexia with continued practice."

Alex held his breath, expecting his daughter to balk. Usually, she avoided reading with a thousand different reasons. He fully expected her to grow up to be an attorney. No one launched a better argument than his child. Once, she'd refused to eat if she had to read the instructions for boiling spaghetti.

Avery scrunched her face and pursed her lips. He expected to hear an excuse.

"Okay. But you have to help me so it doesn't take forever. I'm hungry. I want to eat—this morning, not this afternoon."

Avery made it through the ingredient list as the timer for the oven went off. Morgan retrieved the bacon and set it aside. Returning to the kitchen island, Morgan helped Avery read the directions and to Avery's delight, Morgan played sous chef. Alex learned just how bossy and demanding his little angel could be.

"Miss Morgan, will you please put the bacon on the table?" Avery asked.

Morgan nodded, "Yes, Chef. Good idea."

Yet, as Morgan played the helper role, she asked questions, and it was obvious to him, Morgan was boosting Avery's confidence.

His heart wanted to hug her as much or more than his arms.

"Shall we eat?" Avery flicked the corner of the napkin and placed it into her lap as though ready to dine at a five-star restaurant. "Daddy, please pass the syrup."

They chatted through breakfast with Avery recounting the behind the scenes details of last night's choir recital. Had it been only last night? How interesting that an emergency could bond two, well in this case, three people together so quickly. Quietly, he observed Morgan. By all accounts, she appeared genuinely happy to have them as company. But staying beyond breakfast could wear out their welcome.

"What were your plans for today?" Morgan turned and asked Alex.

"We were going to buy a live tree and set it up at home."

"A real tree? Really, Daddy? I love the smell."

Alex chuckled. "Well, your grandmother wasn't happy with the short artificial one I purchased last year."

"I have a suggestion," Morgan said. "I think you each could use a change of clothes. Why don't I drive you to your house where you can pack a few things? I'd like you to stay with me, until you"—she pointed to Alex—"are able to get around better. Or until the cavalry returns to rescue you. Whichever comes first."

"I don't know…"

"We could pick up a tree for you. Take it to your house and put it in water. It would be ready for you when you're able to decorate it," Morgan suggested. "In the meantime, we could come back here. I had planned to decorate today, too. You could help me."

"Please, Daddy. How will we eat if we don't stay here? Momma would be mad if you ordered pizza every night until Mimi and Pops came home."

Alex hated whenever Avery invoked something about her mother. It made him feel less than a good father.

Morgan looked down and sucked on her bottom lip. Her shoulders shook a bit. She considered the not-so-subtle guilt Avery applied humorous?

Avery had kicked a field goal through the center of the uprights. Food was an important element in their life. At breakfast, he and Avery talked about what they looked forward to that day. Over dinner, they discussed all that had happened, along with some current events. He wanted his child well versed in the world around her.

Besides, his mother had always teased his wife with the old saying about the way to a man's heart was through his stomach. If he allowed Avery to cook, he'd have a nervous breakdown. If he tried to cook for them both, they could end up in the hospital with food poisoning. He'd eaten Morgan's food a time or two—and the woman could cook.

For a little while, it made sense to accept her generous hospitality. Staying with her would provide more insights into the woman whose smile and glow attracted him, especially first thing in the morning.

Somehow he would find a way to show his appreciation. But what would she think of his growing affection?

Chapter Nine

"Avery, will you wait on the bench in the foyer? I'll be ready in a minute. I need to get your dad a new toothbrush. After we get you both a change of clothes, we'll be ready to pick out a Christmas tree. I think people might worry if he shows up in a hospital gown."

"Men," Avery huffed and rolled her eyes. "Sometimes they take the longest time in the bathroom. When Daddy shaves, it takes him longer than me to get ready. At least, he's got pants on."

Morgan chuckled. "I see." She retrieved the item for Alex from a stash in the hall closet and offered it to him along with a small tube of fresh toothpaste.

"Do you think of everything? Are you related to that Martha woman? You're organized. You have a television show. And a string of cookbooks. Wow, when I say it aloud, I realize what a celebrity you are."

"Just brush your teeth, Mr. Blake."

Smiling, Morgan pointed Alex to the bathroom sink. The tasks of life were no longer ordinary when shared with people she cared about. A sweet affection settled in her heart. She enjoyed Alex's teasing.

"I'll be finished in a minute. Would you mind getting those crutches? I can't exactly roll your chair out of the house."

"Meet you in the foyer with them."

Crossing the living room, Morgan sucked in a quick breath when Avery picked up the crystal bell from the display in the foyer. "Honey bear, I would prefer you not handle the bells."

"Oh. Okay. This one is *so* pretty." Avery stood on her tiptoes to try to replace the bell. It struck the side of the shelf. The *clank* sent fear up Morgan's spine. Had it cracked? It was the last one the store had, and she couldn't replace it with a new one before Christmas.

"Wait. Please let me," she said when Avery started to try again.

"It was easier to take down." Avery examined the bell, turning it around in her hands and then placed the crystal ornament gently in Morgan's outstretched one. "I don't think I broke it." Her tone was fearful.

"It's okay. Let me take a look." After a quick examination, Morgan set the bell back on its perch. "All good. No worries." She let go a sigh of relief. "I'll be happy to show you each of the bells. They're a very special collection."

Avery counted. "One. Two. Three…Nine bells."

"Each one has meaning."

"What's that one mean?" She pointed to the one Morgan had replaced on the top shelf of the display.

Morgan paused. What words did she use to explain that the bell represented her turn to the living. "That bell is new. I picked it up yesterday. It represents good friends in my life, like you and your dad."

"And this one?" Avery pointed to one on the bottom shelf etched with baby booties.

"My husband gave me that one the year our son was born."

"You had a son? Where is he?" The surprise in Avery's voice took her aback. "Did his daddy take him away? That happened with a girl at school."

"Avery," Alex said gently, as he rolled into the foyer. "We don't pry into other people's lives."

The girl cast her eyes downward. "I'm sorry, Miss Morgan. I didn't mean to be impolite."

Morgan squatted beside the girl and lifted her chin. She wanted complete eye contact before explaining. There was no need to overwhelm the child with more information than necessary, yet at the same time, she wanted to be sure Avery understood what she was explaining.

"I like to talk about him. His name was Justin. In a way, his daddy did take him. It was three years ago." Morgan swallowed before continuing. "They were in a car accident. Another driver ran a red light and hit their car. They didn't survive the crash."

Avery's eyes grew large and round. "You mean the way my momma didn't survive at the hospital when she was sick? They're in heaven?"

As Avery's eyes filled with tears, Alex reached over and put a hand on her shoulder and gave a little squeeze.

"Yes, Honey Bear, my guys are in heaven." Morgan tried to smile.

"Oh. I'm very sorry for your loss." Avery sounded so grown up. She wiped her eyes before any tears fell.

Morgan shifted her gaze to Alex and gave him a quizzical look.

He shrugged. "She heard it over and over when her mother died."

"Miss Morgan?" Avery took a step closer. Morgan opened her arms, and Avery fell into them. "Do you think my momma is sharing time with your husband and Justin like we're spending time with you?"

Morgan drew in a breath as the girl's words washed over her. "I don't know, darlin'." She pulled Avery tighter to her. "But it would make me so happy if they were."

For a minute more, Avery clung to her. Morgan soaked up the love that only a child's arms can offer. She stroked Avery's hair. It had been so long since she hugged a child so thoroughly. Usually, she offered her students a quick embrace; it pained her too much to hug in earnest since Justin had died. Until now.

Drawing back, Avery said, "That would make me happy, too. I wonder what Christmas is like in Heaven."

"I'm sure it's grand," Alex said. He stood from the chair and grabbed for the crutches. "They're surely outdoing us. Let's go get a tree."

*****

"Hopalong Cassidy couldn't do it faster." Alex hobbled on crutches up the front steps to his house. With a quick glance over his shoulder, he sighted Morgan. She followed closely, ready to catch him if he fell. It was a comforting thought. Morgan as his spotter. Though if he fell forward, he'd end up tackling his daughter and hurting her.

"Who?" Avery asked. She pulled the house key from her pocket and inserted it into the lock.

"A cowboy. My grandfather used to tell me stories about him."

"Who names their kid Hopalong?" Avery scrunched her nose and then pushed open the door. She disappeared from sight.

"Mrs. Cassidy?" Morgan suggested barely loud enough for him to hear. So she had a dry sense of humor. He liked that. Just wanted to see a bit more of it. For some reason, she seemed shyer around him than when they met for functions at the television station.

"Watch your step," Morgan warned as he crossed the threshold.

Did she intend her words to have a double meaning? Was his conscience throwing up a warning to him regarding his physical movement or was the warning intended to caution him about rushing her into…romance?

Romance? Wow. Romance.

Well, there it was. The true intention of his heart. He wanted to win over Miss Morgan Marshall. But he wasn't a fool. He would tread carefully.

Then maybe he'd have a chance.

Chapter Ten

The piney scent of Christmas surrounded Morgan like a familiar dream. Christmas carols played through speakers placed on poles throughout the tree lot, and she bobbed her head as she walked in tempo with the beat. Ahead, a fence displayed different types of tree lights. Children raced round and shouted, "I found one!" referring of course to the perfect specimen Christmas tree. The cool December afternoon was creating the perfect heartwarming memory.

Avery ran on ahead to scope out trees. So far, each one she had picked, Alex had nixed. Too tall. Not properly shaped. Too round. Not round enough. He insisted on at least an eight-foot tree, no more than ten feet round at the base. She never imagined the man could be so picky about a pine for his living room. Ornaments and lights often covered imperfections, and actually she preferred a less-than-perfect tree, one that had character. But she had to admit, she appreciated his dedication to his ideal. He had tenacity and patience for the hunt

"When we get back home, I mean to my house," Morgan said, following behind Alex down a row created by Christmas trees already set up on stands, "I'll get a foot tub and you'll soak that foot. The doctor didn't intend for you to be on crutches for half the day."

"Yes, nurse. After we find the perfect tree, I promise to be a good patient."

"But you're going to try *my* patience," she teased. This was the third tree lot they'd visited. Soon it would be time for lunch. At this rate, they wouldn't make back to her house until dinner time. She unbuttoned her jacket. In one day in Savannah, she could experience the temperatures of spring, summer, and fall on a winter's day. This had a way of making her tired. But she looked forward to another meal with three plates on the table.

"What to make for dinner?" she pondered.

"Food?" Alex called out. How was it he heard her muttering over all the activity going on around them? She'd have to remember he had eagle ears. But could he hear the quickening beat of her heart whenever he looked at her with smiling intensity in his eyes? It was as though he was trying to memorize every detail about her.

"Daddy, halt! I've looked at everything. I want *this* one." Avery pointed to a tree next to her.

"I love that one." Morgan stepped up for a closer look. A Frasier fur. Perfectly shaped. With enough branches for her to thin some out and use them for a wreath. She and Avery would create something special for the door. After rubbing needles between her fingers, she sniffed. The needles had released a fragrant pine scent. Freshness of the tree proved evident by the sap on her fingers.

"Looks like it's unanimous. Three votes." Alex raised a crutch high in the air. "Over here, my good man." His voice deepened as though he played a theatrical role in a play. "We shall take *this* one. Wrap it up."

"Daddy, you're silly sometimes," Avery giggled. She began to do some hip-hop moves and sing, "Wrap it up. Wrap it up. We. Be. Treed."

"Why don't you two start the trek back to the car? You can direct the guy to the correct vehicle while I pay." She handed her keys to Avery.

Alex steadied himself and reached into his pants pocket and pulled out a handful of bills. "This should cover it." He handed her the money.

"I would like to treat you and Avery to the tree."

Alex shook his head. "Nope. Absolutely not. I'm paying for my tree."

"But you paid for mine. Let me do this."

Nodding, Alex said, "Your tree is a gift from me and Avery for all your kindness. Trust me, what you're doing for us is worth the price of all the trees in this lot."

"Fine. You win this round. But you're still soaking that foot tonight."

With Avery in tow, Alex headed back toward the parking. Morgan looked on fondly at the father and daughter. A day on crutches helped him get his hop-a-long walk down. Morgan didn't worry about him falling backward, or worse, doing a parking lot nose-plant.

Morgan waved over one of the attendants.

"You've found what you were searching for?"

She paused before answering. The guy had no clue how his words carried a double meaning. Later that evening, when she discussed dating with Avery as promised, she would share how much she looked forward to a date with her dad. She hoped it might lead to something more. "Yes, I think I have," she said softly, a smile playing on her lips.

"Ma'am?"

"Sorry. This tree, please. Wrap it and tie it to the top of the red SUV parked on the left in the parking lot. You'll find a guy on crutches if you need more direction."

"Will do. You pay over there."

With her wallet out, she stepped up next in line to check out.

"You've got a sweet family," a woman's voice said from behind.

"Pardon?" Morgan asked, turning half way to see who spoke to her. A short, gray-haired lady with a round face, round glasses, and apple cheeks when she smiled, nodded.

"I watched you with your husband and daughter. What a lovely family."

Morgan remembered hearing similar words last night. She followed Alex's example. "Thank you." She didn't feel the need to explain the extent of her relationship with the father and daughter duo. "They're pretty special people to me."

"That's so nice to hear. You have a Merry Christmas, dear." The lady left the line and wandered away.

"You, too," Morgan called out, but a choir signing *Halleluiah* drowned out her words.

When she finally reached her car, Alex was dozing in the passenger's seat while Avery, in the driver's seat, pretended to drive. Morgan chuckled. When she was growing up, her father taught her to drive their ski boat. Later, when she learned to drive a car, it was much harder and scarier. But she wouldn't tell Avery that. For now, the girl needed her own daydreams.

"Hi," she whispered. "The patient is napping?"

Avery nodded and hopped out of the car. Morgan opened the back door for her.

"Don't forget, Miss Morgan." Avery's brow furrowed.

"About?"

"You said you would talk to me about dating."

"I haven't forgotten. Once we're back at my house and we've had some lunch, we'll talk before decorating my tree. Deal?"

"Yup."

As Morgan started the SUV and put it in reverse, she wondered how she would've handled this same question with her son. As though on cue, the tinkling laughter of a little boy rang out.

"Avery, do you hear that?"

"That what?"

"Little boy laughter."

"Oh, sure. I hear it a lot. I didn't know he was your son. I thought a nice ghost came with your old house."

"Out of the mouth of babes," Morgan said. Avery's surprising response made her smile. Justin was with her everywhere. A happy, laughing little boy. Now that Avery knew about Justin, it would be easier to talk about him with her.

Traffic was snarled at nearly every intersection. Had all of Savannah left home to shop? "Patience," she muttered. Everything will get done with perfect timing. All she needed was trust.

Two hours later with chores completed—the tree on a stand in water at Alex's house waiting to be decorated at another time, Alex's ankle iced, her tree up at her house, and lunch finished—Morgan filled a foot tub with warm water and Epson salts and set it before him on the kitchen floor. Alex rolled a little closer to it.

"Sit here and soak, Alex. I promised Avery private girl talk. I'm going to turn music on low. Is there something in particular you'd like to listen to?"

"What's your favorite musical genre?"

Morgan thought for a moment. "I love Christmas carols."

He shook his head. "What would you normally listen to?"

"Classical. Jazz. Blues."

Alex brightened. "Jazz. That we have in common. How about some smooth jazz? It will help me relax whilst you heap your foot torture upon me."

The soft strains of Chris Botti and his trumpet floated on the air as Morgan went to the living room and dropped onto the couch next to Avery. It was her favorite spot in the house with a view through the front window of her manicured lawn and a view of the fireplace. A great spot to curl up and read. Meanwhile, the Christmas tree, set in the corner, waited to be decorated.

"Why do you call me Honey Bear?" Avery asked.

"Why?"

"Yeah. I mean yes."

"I don't know…you're a sweet cuddly girl?"

"My momma used to call me that." That was not the response Morgan expected to hear. What were the odds that they both used the same nickname? Was it creepy or sweet?

To Morgan's delight, Avery leaned and rested against her shoulder.

"I talked to Daddy about dating. He said I couldn't date until I was thirty—but I know he was just kidding. When I told him I was talking about him dating you, he said—"

"Wait." Morgan put her arm around Avery and cuddled her close. "I thought you wanted to know what dating was all about. I don't think I'm comfortable talking with you about me dating your dad."

"But it's only dinner. Movies. And a good-night kiss."

"Is that what your daddy told you?"

"No. I called Bethany and asked her while I was upstairs packing my clothes this morning. She has an older sister, ten years older, who dates. So I asked her. You mean you won't go out on a date with Daddy?"

If ever she used the word flummoxed, which she didn't, this would be the time for it. "Maybe. I'm not saying yes. I'm not saying no." Dating Alex…the idea shot a pin of excitement through her, spreading a warmth of anticipation. He was fun. There could be enjoyable times. Picnics. Art exhibits. School events for Avery. And Christmas every year.

But as the kaleidoscope of images turned in her mind, a panicky sensation bloomed in her chest. It might be too big a risk. If she and Avery grew more attached and things didn't work out between her and Alex, Avery might suffer—she'd already lost her mother. Add that to losing Justin—even if Avery were resilient, she couldn't withstand the loss of another child she cared for deeply.

No. Dating Alex Blake was not a good idea at all. Better not to play with caution. Keep his friendship and keep Avery safely in her life.

"Daddy *said* sometimes dating was harder when one person had a child. Is it harder because of me? I thought you liked me. Or is it because I remind you that your little boy is gone?"

The depth of the conversation and the turn it had taken slapped Morgan dead center into reality. Avery was her Honey Bear. She would protect her like a mother bear. She would never hurt Avery.

The idea of dating Alex could only be a sweet daydream.

"Will you *please* tell me what dating means? It's not what Bethany's sister said?"

"Well… A date is when two people share a common interest and they spend time together to learn more about each other. Dating is when the two people like each other enough to have several dates."

"Then you get married?"

Morgan sat up straight forcing Avery to straighten, too. "What? No… not necessarily. Sometimes when people date, they discover, they don't like each other as much as they thought they might."

"That sounds like a guessing game or like a scavenger hunt."

Morgan chuckled. "Actually, I think you discovered the secret to dating—for most people, it's some kind of game. Or maybe a test of sorts."

"Well, that's okay. Daddy is good at tests. I think you need to give him a chance. He said he only needed two dates to know it all."

Stunned, Morgan looked down at the girl. She pushed Avery's hair from her forehead and planted a kiss there. "Your daddy is a smart man. I don't know if I'm smart enough for him. No games. No tests. Not with me."

Two dates? Two dates? That's all he needed with her? To then do what? Break things off before they got serious?

It was time to plant her feet in reality. She and Alex Blake would not be a couple, no matter how cute others thought they looked together. It pained to her to be excluded from the gift of raising Avery, beyond teaching her cooking and maybe attending future recitals.

Trying to maintain composure, Morgan crossed one leg over the opposite knee. No need for a couple of pity dates with Alex. If he asked her out on an official date now, she would turn him down.

Friends. That had to be enough of relationship. Now and forever.

She just hoped she didn't dream about him when she closed her eyes at night.

Chapter Eleven

Alex rolled to the kitchen door. "Morgan, I insist on paying for groceries." Her mood had changed, and he couldn't discern why. When she left, he'd talk with Avery to see if his daughter's chat with their hostess revealed any insights. If luck smiled on him, after dinner, he would have a chance to make a romantic stand and invite Morgan to the New Year's bash. But would she want to be seen with a guy in a wheelchair? Dancing with a chair couldn't possibly be as endearing as it was made out to be on television and in movies.

"Alex, when I want your money, I'll ask for it. I'm trying to do a nice thing here. Please just accept my friendship." Morgan bolted out the door.

"Wait," Avery called. "I want to go with you."

Alex grabbed his daughter's arm as she raced through the kitchen. "Sugar, let her go alone. I fear we're overwhelming Miss Morgan."

Tears welled in Avery's eyes. "But Daddy, I wanted to go. Momma used to take me."

Was his child trying to replace Morgan for her mother? Trying to find a place of comfort? It broke his heart to watch tears slide down her face.

"Sometimes, the holidays can be…difficult for people. Like it was for us last year, after Momma went away."

Avery stomped her foot. "Stop it, Daddy! Momma died. D. I. E. D. I know about dying. People go to heaven and never come back. At least, Miss Morgan has Justin. He comes and laughs with her. Momma has never come back for me!" Sobbing, Avery ran from the room.

"Oh, crap." Alex shoved his fingers through his hair. Grief was such a tricky bugger. Maybe staying with Morgan was a bad idea. For her *and* for Avery. His sweet girl needed to fill the hole in her heart left raw by her mother's death…and it looked like she wanted Morgan for that. Morgan had her own grief to deal with, and holidays, he'd read, were often most difficult.

What did Morgan want?

Alex rolled to the guest room where Avery lay face down on the bed and sobbed into a pillow. Had he pushed Avery and Morgan too far? The fall was an accident, but he'd used it to get to know Morgan better. Too much, too soon?

Stroking his child's hair, he said, "Sugar, are you okay? You need to catch a breath."

"Go. A…a…way!"

"I can't do that. I'm here for you."

Avery's sobs slowed. He continued to stroke her hair. Patience, he'd learned was as much an art as a virtue. After a few minutes when Avery turned on her side and moved out of his reach, he offered a few tissues. She snatched them from him.

Alex sighed. "Did I do something wrong? Did I upset you or Morgan?"

"You."

He'd gotten good a twenty questions with his daughter since Casey died. "I'm sorry. I apologize. I would never purposely hurt you or do something wrong. Could you please share with me what I did? Then, I'll try not to do it again." The family therapist he saw to help with Avery's grief and frustrations explained that he needed to always remain calm. Never raise his voice. And try to get Avery to verbalize her feelings.

She sniffed and blew her nose, then tossed the tissues at him, landing on the floor. He didn't move to retrieve them. Instead, he handed her a few more.

He waited for her breathing to even. When no more tears fell, he tried again. "I love you. I want to help you. Please tell me what I did so I can fix it."

"You can't."

"Well...sometimes I have talents beyond the obvious." Was he no longer her hero? The thought was crushing, but he was unwilling to give up. "Okay, maybe I can't. However, you might feel better if you talk about it."

Avery pointed at him. "It's *your* fault."

"Okay. It's my fault."

His daughter rolled close to him and stared him down. "You made Miss Morgan feel stupid."

Shaking his head, Alex stared at his crazed child. "Ah, how did I do that?"

"I don't know. I told her what Bethany's sister said about dating— dinner, movie, and a goodnight kiss. Then I told her what you said. She told me that you were smarter than she was. You must have done something to make her feel that way."

"Sugar, I swear, I don't know what I did. But what if we talk with Miss Morgan when she returns?"

Avery sat up, scooted until her back rested against the headboard, and then she crossed her arms. Her bottom lip trembled. "Do you think Miss Morgan won't go out on a date with you because she doesn't want me around?"

"Oh, Avery." Alex hoisted himself on the bed and pulled his child into his arms. She let loose another flood of tears. He rocked her while she cried. "I don't think it has anything to do with you." He certainly hoped it didn't. Couldn't imagine a child being a barrier to any sort of relationship with Morgan. From all he had witnessed, she loved kids, and she was especially fond of his.

Stretching out on the bed, he lay beside his whimpering child, his heart breaking, and tried to offer comfort. He always tried to be careful with his words and explanations about life, but sometimes he was just a guy, never able to offer the tender nurturing support a mother could give.

A few minutes later, Avery's breath evened again. She had fallen asleep. Closing his eyes, he wished for time when grief and heartache were no longer landmines to navigate, that memories were sweet and cherished.

A bit later, he woke with a start. He must have fallen asleep, too. A sound startled him. Disoriented, he sat up carefully, not wanting to wake Avery. A second later, he recognized the room. Morgan's house.

As though poked with a grappling hook, Avery suddenly sat up and charged from the bed. "Morgan!" The scream was one of desperation.

Alex followed, hobbling with his injured foot.

Morgan was at the front door and turning around when Avery raced toward her, launching herself at Morgan. Horror seized Alex. He ran. His daughter's foot kicked the foyer table. Bells began to *clink* and topple.

Morgan caught Avery in her arms.

The bell stand rocked off the table onto the floor. Glass and crystal shattered everywhere.

"Ohhh!" Avery wailed.

Morgan stood statute still.

As Alex knelt to search for any unbroken bell, Avery broke from Morgan's embrace and raced out the front door. "Wait!" he called after Avery. A piece of glass sliced his hand. Before he could do or say anything more, Morgan turned and followed after her.

"What a mess I've made of things." Making it to the kitchen, his foot throbbing, he grabbed a piece of paper towel and found his crutches. He offered a silent prayer that Morgan had found his child. And offered another prayer for the misery they'd caused Morgan.

Her bell collection was irreplaceable.

There was no way to make that up to her.

That knowledge could crush his sensitive child.

"Avery?" he called as he walked through the front door. Heart-pounding fear slammed in his chest. A list of disasters rolled at warp speed through his mind—What if she ran out in front of a car? What if she tripped and was knocked unconscious? What if someone lured her away? "Avery," he shouted at the top of his lungs. "It's okay, Sugar. Come here!"

"Avery!" Morgan shouted a block down the street.

Morgan looked through bushes in her neighbors' yards. A woman came out to ask what she was doing. "I'm looking for a girl. She's very upset. She's only eight. Light brown hair and cute dimples. She was wearing jeans and a t-shirt, but no shoes or jacket."

"It will be dark soon," Alex called out. "Avery is my daughter. Would you help us search?"

Hobbling on the sidewalk, Alex continued to shout out messages, encouraging his daughter to appear. He wanted to scream and demand she show herself, but not because he was mad, but because terror wracked his entire body. He couldn't lose his precious child.

Within twenty minutes, a half dozen of Morgan's neighbors joined the search.

Morgan raced up to him. "She couldn't have gone far. I'm going back to the house to check. If we don't find her in fifteen minutes, I think we need to call the police. I am sooo sorry about this, Alex."

Shouts for Avery popped off every other second like an off-key calliope. Fear scratched its way up to Alex's throat. He swallowed against it and continued to search. "Where are you?" he begged.

Minutes ticked by. No Avery. His foot throbbed. His hip hurt. His back ached. But none of it compared to the raging fear in his chest. Where was his daughter?

Five minute later, Morgan stood on the front porch of her house. "Alex! Found her!"

The neighbors applauded.

As fast has his crutches allowed, Alex moved at a quick hop-a-long pace. Reaching the steps, he dropped the crutches and ran up to Morgan's door. The pain in his ankle tame compared to the pain in his heart.

Morgan greeted him, her expression troubled. "Go easy, Mister. She's quite upset still."

Inside, he spotted Avery on the couch. Hands folded. Head hung so low, he couldn't see her eyes. Between where he stood and where she sat, the foyer table had been removed. No trace of the bell stand. No broken glass.

With a hitch in his step, Alex crossed the room to his child. He knelt down on the floor in front of her and pulled her into his arms.

"I'm so sorry," Avery wailed between small gasps of air.

"You're all right?" Alex cupped her face, kissed her nose, and ran his hand along her arms. "Lord, child, you scared me senseless."

"Daddy, I'm so sorry."

"Shhh." He hugged her, memorizing every ounce of her. "Just don't ever do that again."

"I can't." Avery hiccupped.

"Okay… good to know."

Avery whimpered. "Can't replace the bells I broke."

Morgan appeared by their side. "Avery, you're what's important to me." Morgan threw her arms around Avery and him. "Group hug."

They clung to each other. One of the neighbors came up on the porch and closed the front door. Alex wondered if Morgan was being nice so as not to make a bad situation worse. Was she placating them until they were gone from her sight?

"I'm sorry for being so…stupid, Miss Morgan. I didn't mean to break your things. And Daddy, I'm sorry I ran away. Please don't hate me."

"Shhh. No Sugar, I could never hate you."

"Avery, you're safe. Unharmed. That's all that matters to me," Morgan insisted. "And I never ever want to hear you call yourself—or anyone else—stupid."

In his arms, Avery finally relaxed a little bit. Alex noticed her feet, scratched and dirty. "It's been a long day. Avery and I should go. If it wouldn't be too much trouble, after all the damage we've done, would you take us home?"

Morgan shook her head. "You have to stay. I get my turn to tell the two of you how I'm feeling."

She folded her arms over her chest and eyed him like a determined general.

Confused, his thought swirled like eddy in the Savannah River.

This was a side to Morgan he'd never seen.

Chapter Twelve

Morgan set the table for three. Paper napkins with poinsettias on them. Spoons. Forks. And knives. She hummed *Hark the Herald Angels Sing* as she placed a mixed green salad on a small plate beside each large bowl and then slid a pot of grits into the center of the table. Hoisting a sauté pan, she placed it next to the pot. Shrimp and grits. A low country favorite. Pouring sweet tea in each of three glasses, she stood back and surveyed the table. The meal might be their last together. If so, it had to be as positive a memory as possible. The events of the last twenty-four hours could crush a weaker person. Not Alex. And certainly not Avery. She hoped she could be as brave as them.

"Smells great." Alex rolled into the kitchen with Avery behind him dressed in reindeer pajamas.

"Hungry, Honey Bear?"

Avery nodded her head shyly. Morgan ruffled her hair. "Let's sit down."

Once everyone was at the table, Avery said, "Could we hold hands and tell what we're grateful for?"

Alex raised a quizzical eyebrow at Morgan. She smiled. "I think that's a wonderful idea."

Avery stretched her arm across the table. Morgan reached for it. In her hands, she held the hearts of two special people. She squeezed both Avery and Alex's hands.

"I'll start," Avery said. "I'm very sorry for ruining your bell collection. Thank you for being kind to me."

"I'm thankful you're safe." Alex nodded at this daughter. "I'm very grateful we have a wonderful friend in Miss Morgan."

"I am very grateful we're together. I find family-style dinners very comforting."

"Amen," Avery said, smiling.

After each had finished their salad, Morgan pulled warm garlic bread from the oven. She served up grits in each bowl, and then ladled the shrimp and broth over it.

"This is so good." Avery rubbed her tummy. "Will you teach us how to cook this in class someday."

"I'd be happy to have you help me make it next time." Morgan took a bit and savored the flavors. She would forever remember this meal whenever she ate shrimp and grits in the future.

"I want to keep things on a lighter note. I planned to slide this under the Christmas tree so it would be your first present." Alex nodded to Avery. She pushed her chair back and walked to her father's seat. From behind him, she lifted out a gold foiled rectangular box.

"This is from us." Avery presented the gift.

Morgan's hand went to her chest. "For me? Really? Oh my. I don't have presents for the two of you yet."

She stared at the box and chewed her bottom lip. "I have something I would like to say before I open this, if I may."

Her dinner guests nodded.

"I've been told by two other people whom I know love me well, that I have stared too long at a closed door. In doing so, they feared, I wouldn't see when a new one opened. So while the events of the twenty-four hours have been strange and sometimes painful, I believe I've stumbled through a new door without even know it. Until now. Alex, I'm sorry you were hurt, but my front porch never attacked anyone before, so I didn't know to warn you. Avery, if I put a table in the foyer again, I'll be sure to either nail it down or glue it. What I'm trying to say is that while I shopped alone and talked to the onions and celery who have given their life for this dinner, I found it's more meaningful to talk with people. Not just any people, but the two of you."

Avery's mouth formed a small 'o'.

Alex grinned. He reached for her hand. With her hand in his, he rubbed his fingers over the top of her hand. The slight friction warming her hand and her heart. He winked. "Why don't you open your present now?"

Carefully lifting the lid so as not to damage the gold foil, she set it aside. In a bed of red velvet lay a silver bell with a polished wooden handle.

"It's lovely." Morgan lifted it from the box. A little shake and a beautiful tone emanated from the bell.

"I've had it for a long time. Actually, since birth. My grandmother collected all sorts of bells. This was a gift to my mother when I was born."

"Oh, Alex, I can't accept this." It would be a family heirloom. Something he'd want to pass to Avery someday.

"Oh, Morgan, yes, you can. I'm hoping you'll use it to summons us to dinner many times in the future."

The tinkling of little boy laughter caught her attention. Clearly, Justin approved.

Morgan shook the bell again. "Yes, I'm sure I can do that."

*****

After dinner was cleared from the table, Morgan popped corn and set a big bowl on the coffee table in front of them. She joined Alex and Avery on the couch to watch a Christmas movie. "This is so relaxing." She sighed and dimmed the lights. From her spot, the dim light glinted off the silver bell she'd placed on the mantle.

Avery popped up and grabbed the bowl of popcorn and then nestled herself between Morgan and Alex.

"Now, here are the rules for this evening," Alex said to Avery. "After the movie, no excuses, you're off to bed. Just one movie. Agreed?"

Avery smiled wide. She shook her head three times.

Alex felt her forehead. "Are you okay? Where's my daughter?" He tickled her.

Avery giggled. "It's a date."

"What?" Alex and Morgan said in unison.

"It's just like Bethany's sister said. 'A dinner. A movie. And a kiss good night.' That's what we're doing. It's date night."

Morgan tried to hide a grin but gave up.

"See, Daddy," Aver said with glee in her voice. "We're going to date Morgan."

"Well…" Whatever Alex intended to say, he never finished.

When the movie began to play, Morgan reached her hand into the bowl of popcorn and felt a warm palm as Alex grasped hers for a brief moment. On the television, a choir sang *Hallelujah*.

Thank you, she mouthed, looking heaven bound. *Got the sign loud and clear*.

Looking over Avery's head at Alex, Morgan whispered. "This is the best date I've had in years. And it's good to know in advance that it will end with a kiss."

Alex nodded in agreement.

Morgan leaned down and kissed Avery's cheek. "Honey Bear, you need to learn to share the popcorn."

"God bless us one and all," Avery said and reached for another handful of popcorn.

The End

Dear Reader

Thank you so much for supporting the *Love & Grace* anthology. It's a labor of love by this wonderful group of authors. My story, *Christmas Bells*, is the story of Morgan Marshall, Alex Blake, and a very special girl, Avery. Here's a sneak-peak:

After grieving the loss of her husband and son, TV host Morgan Marshall is ready to embrace life again. But she won't risk a relationship with the father of her favorite cooking student, Avery, since the girl's happiness is more important than her own.

Advertising executive Alex Blake never thought another woman could pique his interest after losing his wife to cancer. Yet every time he's in Morgan's presence, she brings sunlight into the room. Plus, she's a role model for his daughter, always assuring Avery that dyslexia can't hold her back. But if he asks Morgan for a date and then she refuses a second one, the person he loves the most, Avery, could get hurt the worst because she adores Morgan.

When Alex is injured in a fall, Morgan insists on caring for him and Avery. As they share holiday fun, Avery topples Morgan's beloved crystal bell collection, shattering it to pieces. Through it all, they discover love of one another is more priceless than any object money can buy. Love rings in the air at Christmastime.

I hope you will enjoy their journey, and I hope you'll share mine. Let's connect!

Website: http://www.linda-joyce.com
Facebook: https://www.facebook.com/LindaJoyceAuthor
Twitter: @LJWriter https://twitter.com/LJWriter

LETTERS TO RACHEL

Airicka Phoenix

Dear Rachel,

Accepting failure has become the backbone of my existence. Without you, I am no longer a daughter, no longer a sister, no longer a friend, or even a person. I have been resorted to that girl. The one no one quite understands what to do with, but can't really write off.

Then I met a boy with a guitar.

Chapter One

Their story started with a letter.

Dear Rachel,

I want to start this off by stating very clearly that it was a bad idea from the start. Knowing that and still going through with it made me a special kind of stupid, but I walked through those glass doors with its smudged fingerprints and gold lettering like I owned them. I crossed the sticky linoleum. I weaved around the tables. I locked eyes with the sweaty, hairy man behind the counter, who paused in his scrubbing to stare back.

Then, in a lot less steps than I'd counted in my head, I was there ... and every word in the English dictionary made a mad dash from my brain.

"Kaylee?"

If you ask me now what it was I said back, I couldn't tell you, except that it was a series of Orc grunts followed by an assault of my papers being thrown into his face; you know I don't do well under pressure. You always teased me about becoming a doctor, what with my nerves of steel.

"Girl, what's the matter with you?"

Rachel, I was sweating like I'd just been caught lying to Father John during confessional by God himself. It was everywhere. I was damp in places I didn't even know I had places. You would have laughed—and I would have kicked you, and then slipped on a massive sweat puddle and died.

Bailey glowered at me in that way he used to when you and me would sneak into his yard and pick all the strawberries off his side of the bush. You always justified that it was partially ours since that one branch always crept through the fence into our yard, but I don't think he ever saw it that way. He certainly yelled enough about it.

Oh, speaking of strawberry bushes, he moved it. Can you believe it? He literally pulled that bush out by its roots and replanted it on the other side of his yard. The man's a monster, I'm telling you.

"Girl!"

I don't know why he was yelling at me. I'd given him the papers stating very clearly why I was there. I didn't feel like I needed to clarify, but he was squeezing my head like a grape with the powers of his mind.

Rachel, I'm afraid to inform you that I think he might actually be developing those powers, or at least perfecting them. I could have sworn I felt my skull beginning to cave in at the sides the longer I stood there. We might need to inform someone. Professor Xavier, maybe?

"Job," I blurted with all the dignity in me. "I'd like one ... here." I motioned at a bit of crack splitting open the red leather on a stool "Not at this chair, but the diner," I clarified. "Not that this isn't a very nice chair. It's done many great things for mankind."

So, I was rambling. You're rolling your eyes. I know you are. I can feel it.

Bailey looked no less impressed. To think, I actually got dressed up for this man. I didn't even do that for my dates. I had to borrow one of your blouses, the white, silk one with the pearl buttons. I might also have borrowed your black, pencil skirt ... and black, suede pumps. You may only want the latter back. I'm not sure how to get yellow pit stains out of silk and the skirt might be staying up by the sheer grace of a safety pin. You need to take better care of your things. That button was hanging on by a thread long before I arrived.

"You? A job? Here?"

It was insulting how he broke every word up with a laugh, like the very idea of me with a job at his stupid pub and grill was ridiculous. I'm not lazy. At least, no more than anyone else. I'm reasonably quiet. I am very consciousness of my hygiene. People occasionally like me. And to be fair, that whole strawberry business was your idea. I only went along because I didn't want you to get them all.

"Yes. Me. Job. Here," I said back, my Irish temper getting the better of me (yes, I'm very well aware that I'm not Irish). "Why not me job here? I know the menu better than anyone."

Well, that certainly wiped the grin off his face. I thought for sure he was about to tell me to get lost, but he surprised me by snorting. Actually snorting, like a hog. It was the strangest thing.

"Today's your lucky day." He tossed my poor, defenseless—now grease stained—resume into the trash bin. "You're hired."

I was still mourning the loss of my twenty-five cents at the library making copies that I almost didn't hear him. My head snapped up so fast, I felt it in my neck for the remainder of the day.

"You're hiring me?"

Not my best moment, I'll grant you that, but you know you're just as surprised as I am.

"You want the job, don't you?" he said, looking a bit smugger than I like.

I said yes, because I did want the job, but I had a little voice in my head sounding off the alarm bells, Abort! Abort! Normally, I would have listened. It had never steered me wrong. But my pride was on the line now. He was expecting me to back down. I could see it in his pudgy face, quietly mocking me. Well, Kaylee Elizabeth Cooper backs down to no man.

I told him I'd see him bright and early tomorrow for the opening shift.

"Oh, no, no, no, no."

Do you remember when we were kids and we'd sneak into the basement to watch movies off the top shelf? The adult *shelf? And there would always be that one scene where the monster would cackle just before lowering the chainsaw? I expected a chainsaw.*

"Be back here at five tonight," Bailey said in a low, menacing drawl that made me wet myself a little. "You're working the night shift."

Not going to lie, I'm scared.

I got home and Mom was in one of her moods. You know what I'm talking about. No matter what you do, or how quiet you tiptoe up the stairs, she'll still yell at you for breathing. I swear it's gotten worse since it all happened. It feels like she just finds reasons to scream at everyone. Dad won't even come home anymore. It's just me and her, and I don't know how much more I can take. Every day, I go home to that house, the one we filled with all our memories and it's just darkness. I never knew a house could hold so many shadows. I keep waiting for you to walk in, ~~to stop goofing around and put everything back together again~~ and laugh at how stupid we're all being.

I'm sorry.

I don't blame you. I could never blame you. It would be a lot like blaming myself, because you deserved to go. It was the right thing for you. You wouldn't have stood in my way if I was the one with the fully paid scholarship to some fancy pants art school in New York. You would have made me go.

I just ~~hate it~~ miss you.

Chapter Two

Dear Rachel,

Mom's telling me to stop writing. She says I'm wasting my time. You'll never write back. I don't believe her. I have this image in my head of you opening them one day and us sitting on the porch, like we used to, discussing all the things I've written to you about in the last two years.

Mom says I'm embarrassing myself, that every time I write your name on an envelope—my E's backwards like I'm back in the first grade, learning to write—I'm further proving just how incredibly pathetic I am.

"Just because you're sick in the head, doesn't mean you need to prove it to the world," she says.

Dyslexia isn't sickness. Words may not like me very much, but at least I'm not her.

I called her miserable and bitter. I hated myself afterwards, but you know what they say about angry words—it's always how you truly feel, and I felt them, Rach. I feel them and so much more, and I keep bottling them all up inside. I think it might kill me one day, all these unsaid things. Sometimes, at night, I lie in bed and I feel them pushing inside me, a heavy pressure, kind of like when you blow a balloon too far and you know ... you know it's about to burst, but you keep blowing. I'm always waiting for someone to find me in the morning, chest cavity cracked open, lungs in tatters. But I wake every morning like the morning before and nothing's changed.

I can't breathe sometimes. I wake up gasping over the side of the bed, my fingers twisted into the sheets. Other times, I want to scream. Not just scream, I want to rip my throat raw. I want to howl until I no longer have a voice. It's all there, Rach. All packed up inside me and I just want to ~~hate~~ see you.

I know I can. I know you're only eighteen blocks away, a fifteen-minute walk, but it's not the same. It will never be the same. The hour I visit every day to leave you these letters is testament to that. I've tried staying longer, thinking it would make a difference. I try talking to you. I try shaking you. I try and I try and I will never stop trying. I will never stop writing or talking or seeing you, but it's not enough and it kills me. It's chipping away at me like it did with her. It's slower, but each blow is a new cobweb in the strength I'm trying to keep and it scares me that one day I will shatter like she did. You are the only thing keeping me together, knowing you're there, seeing your face, it's a fine thread of hope that I am clutching on to with everything in me and it's been so long that I don't know how I can ever let go.

I can't. Not like she did. She gave up. She stopped believing and I won't do that. You will come back. I know you will. You're strong. You always have been. She's an idiot for not realizing that and I hate her for it. I hate her for her uselessness, for her brokenness. I hate her so much I am shaking as I write this. And I'm scared, scared of the creature crawling around inside me when Mom's in the room. I'm scared of how my insides writhe and grow hot with an unimaginable fury that just surges up my body at the sight of her.

She's not the woman you left behind, Rach. She's not the woman who would bake us cookies and laugh because, just because. I haven't seen her smile in years, not since you ~~packed your things~~ left. She's miserable and cold and I'm becoming like her a little more every day I stay here. I wish I could leave. I wish I could be brave like you. But you were the one with the courage, the one who always made her own path. Besides, even if I found the nerve, I can't leave, not now. Who would take care of her? Who would make sure the bottles were picked up before they filled the house? Who would drag her dead weight inside when she'd passed out on the lawn? Dad won't. He said as much.

"Call someone else, Kaylee. I can't do this anymore."

That was two months ago. I haven't seen him since.

I'm in the parlor as I write this. I'm sitting on your favorite window seat, watching the rain cut tracks into the glass. Sometimes, when I huff, I can almost see the lines your fingers have made.

It's crazy of course. Mom scrubs everything with a single minded purpose of erasing you forever in between binges. Then she looks at me and I can see it in her eyes—if only she could erase me with a squirt of Windex.

I don't think she's ever going to forgive me.

*****

I started my first shift tonight. I like to think I survived it. I'm pretending I'm a better person for the opportunity and that I have somehow grown to becoming a wiser, sophisticated soul who has the proper grasp at coffee pouring, but who am I kidding? It was horrible.

I arrived fifteen minutes before my shift was supposed to start like a responsible nineteen-year-old. I walked in there confident and ready to kick butt and take orders. It was just beginning to fill up with the evening rush so my strides were more dodge and weave, but it was purposeful. I reached the counter and declared myself to Darlene—you remember Darlene. She used to sneak us extra helpings of ice cream when Bailey wasn't looking— but this wasn't the Darlene we knew and loved. This Darlene was rushed and red faced, and meaner than Mom when we used to run through the house with her lipstick trailing after us along the walls and her expensive French perfume soaking our clothes. This was scary Darlene.

"You're late!" she barked even before I opened my mouth. "I don't have time to be running after you. Get back here."

She threw open the hatch and stormed off. I took that as my cue to hurry my butt, so I ran after her.

"Don't follow me!" she said, whirling around so suddenly, I teetered on my toes when I skidded to a stop. "Get over there and get your uniform on."

I won't lie, I had no idea where over there was. She had both hands balled up on her hips and she only nodded in some random direction behind me with her chin. But I turned and went back, slowly, searching for a sign that said, you are over there.

Rach, there was no sign.

"Lord help me."

Darlene physically grabbed my elbow and hauled me through the swinging doors we were never allowed to pass as kids. That's right, I entered the Do Not Enter zone. It was exhilarating ... and hot. I swear, the temperature jumped six hundred degrees, and it was loud.

Pots and pans clanged. Meat hissed and sizzled on the grill. Water boiled. People were shouting. It was chaos and I was shoved forward like a sacrificial lamb by Darlene and abandoned before a man wielding a bloody butcher knife.

"Best hurry," Mr. Wallaby mumbled, never looking up from the rack of ribs he was cutting into quarters. "Darlene doesn't like waiting."

"I'm new..." I began to explain, hoping someone would take an ounce of pity on me.

Mr. Wallaby looked up and I was struck by this memory of you and me going up to his door on Halloween and him smiling all grandfatherly and letting us pick our own chocolate from the plastic bowl. Was that something my crazy mind made up, because this man was not that man? This man was sweaty and tired, and speckled with drying blood.

"Uniforms are on the rack." He pointed with the end of his knife in the direction of the back.

Most of the space was lone sheets of metallic countertop with towering shelves bolted into the walls all around. There seemed to be some kind of system. The hot stuff was on one side of the counters and the cold stuff on the other. At the end was a narrow corridor that held three doors. One was a bathroom. The second one was a cramped staffroom. On the third was a sign taped to the door: Bailey's Office. I took that at face value and didn't go in. Plus, I could hear voices inside and I'd been yelled at enough for one day.

The staffroom was what you'd expect, small, a table at one end, a row of lockers in the other with a bunch of shelves next to it, and that weird, gym room smell, like if sweaty feet and week old meat got into a brawl and somehow, cheap perfume won. It's the worst smell. I can't even begin to tell you. I came home with it still clinging to me and nearly took off five layers of skin trying to scrub it off.

But, I'm happy to report that I found the uniforms on my own. They were in a box, on the shelf, wrapped in plastic. Not so happy to report that it looks ridiculous on me. The only sizes they had was a small and six extra larges, and since I didn't relish the idea of walking around in a potato sack, I squeezed all that God has given me into a small.

Don't laugh. I know you are.

It was awful. The light pink material was stiff and clung to all the place I was pretty sure I wasn't allowed to show at a family friendly establishment. I couldn't even close the top two buttons without the fear of it popping off and blinding someone.

"Girl, what in blazes is the hold up?"

Darlene found me in the staffroom, trying to stretch another inch in the skirt. The thing was short enough to show London, France, and Australia.

In short, Rach, I looked like I deserved my own wall in the men's bathroom.

"Good Lord, child." Darlene looked me up and down, head rocking slowly from side to side in a mixture of distaste, sympathy, and pure annoyance. "What are you wearing?"

There was a moment where I actually prayed I'd put on the wrong uniform. That somehow, these were the old ones and she'd point me to the right ones. But I knew that wouldn't happen. The thing matched the one she was wearing, except hers didn't give off the vibe that she belonged on a stage, wrapped around a gleaming rod.

"Bailey's going to have himself a heart attack," she mused, still shaking her head. "But at least the tips'll be good."

The tips were good, once you overlooked that pesky modesty business. The pub was brimming with lonely, half-drunk men just dying for a chance to watch me bend over and show 'em a bit of heaven. You would have loved it. All that attention. You were always better at accepting it with grace and that flick of your blonde hair and a bat of your blue eyes.

"She has all the charm in the family," wasn't that what Grandma used to say? Then she'd look at me, click her tongue and say, "What happened to you?"

It never seemed to matter that we were identical, that I was born only three minutes after you were, you were the one all the boys wanted and all the girls wanted to be. Strange how that works, huh? But I never minded. I honestly always preferred you taking center stage. You seemed to always need it more than I did. I liked being Rachel Cooper's younger twin, the one just slightly less pretty than her sister.

Anyway, I made it through the first portion of the evening with only six broken dishes, twenty wrong orders, and only one instance when I bent down too far and gave a little too much friendly service to a freckle faced ten-year-old who blushed so hard, I thought his head would explode. I was a bit more careful after that. Besides, that was the least bad thing to happen. It was about midway through when things got really bad.

Do you remember that piece of garbage jukebox Bailey kept in the corner of the diner? The one that only worked when you kicked it in just the right spot? I don't know why I didn't spot it right away, but it was gone. I only noticed when mic feedback cut through the usual chatter. We all turned to watch as a man took the spot, a stool behind him and a guitar strapped across his back. He fiddled and tweaked with the mic stand, lowering and lifting until it was level with the most incredible pair of lips.

Rach, there are no words to properly describe them, except truly edible. They were perfect, thick and full on the bottom, thinner on top and tipped just enough in the corners to make a girl swoon.

I swooned, Rach. Me. The girl who rolls her eyes at romantic movies and Hallmark cards. I looked at that man's mouth and my heart dipped. My stomach tightened and every nerve ending in my body prickled to life. It's only while I'm writing this that I realize it's the exact same sensation as falling, like that brief moment when you miss a step going down and your stomach lurches. My breath actually caught. I think the last time that happened, The Backstreet Boys *were going on tour. It was an incredible, surreal, so unbelievably remarkable moment. The kind* Jane Austin *would have been proud of. The sort I wanted to write poetry over—if I was any good at it. How did something so utterly perfect exist in a world where I was dressed like a bit of sushi swaddled in tight, pink saranwrap?*

They curled, a bit sheepish, and oh my God, my knees quivered.

"Sorry," he said in a thick, guttural drawl of man. I don't know how else to describe it, except that I felt it glide across my skin, teasing and hypnotic. "How's everyone's evening?"

He had stubble. The right kind, you know? The one worn by poets and heartbreakers. It darkened a jaw chiseled to the deepest kind of perfection. Not too rugged, but firm and strong. His chin had a dent, a tiny little cleft that made my hands tremor with this crazy urge to stroke. I could almost feel the prickle of his five o'clock shadow tickling my skin as I took his face between my palms, pulled him close, and...

That's when it all went south.

The plate tipped in my hand and the clump of spaghetti slipped off the surface and straight into Mr. Hagerman's lap. Poor man leaped out of his seat so fast that he upended the entire table on Mrs. Hagerman, who squealed and toppled, chair and all, into the couple at the next table. *All over the place, people were jumping out of their seats. Glasses were being knocked over. Drinks were pouring in fountains to the floor, mixing with shattered dishes and wasted food. People were just tripping all over themselves trying to get out of the chaos. And there I was, smack in the middle of it all like the true idiot that I was.*

All because of a pair of lips.

Rach, I ran.

He looked up and I looked up and our eyes met across the expanse of that battlefield and I ... I dropped the plate, shattered it with all the others and I left that place at a run that would have made a marathon man proud. I didn't even bother to get my clothes from the locker. I ran until my feet were thundering on the front steps and I was locked in the safety of my bedroom.

I have never been so mortified. I can't believe what an absolute loon I was. What sort of person falls apart over a ~~boy~~ man? A crazy person, clearly. It's not even like I've never dated. Our town might not be overflowing with Calvin Klein *modals, but we have our share of a few decent blokes, right? I've dated. I've had a boyfriend. So, what on earth happened back there?*

More importantly, who was that and ... would I ever see him again?

Chapter Three

Dear Rachel,

His name is Austin and I'm going to marry him.

It's not official and he doesn't know it yet, but I've got it all figured out. We'll date for a year before I suggest we move in together, but he'd be old fashioned and insist we get married first, which I'll agree to, because we'll be madly in love. We'll wait two years before having children. Two years seem like a good number don't you think? We'll have gotten used to each other's weird habits and everyone says the first year's just the honeymoon phase. We'll have two children. I haven't decided what they'll be, but they'll be beautiful because he's beautiful. So beautiful. So painfully, violently, passionately beautiful.

All right, I'm getting a bit carried away. Let's back up a bit.

I went to the diner today to get my clothes and apologize for the night before. Bailey looked like he wanted to smack me on the head with a frying pan when I pushed through the doors. He set down the clipboard and pen he'd been holding, and only then did I dare approach him.

"Hey," I said, hoping to soften the blow with my winning smile, which I might have left at home, because it didn't work.

Bailey's face only deepened in color. "Three hundred dollars," he said. "That's what you cost me last night."

In a perfect world, I would have ripped out my checkbook and offered to cover the cost, but I didn't have three hundred dollars. I didn't even have a checkbook.

"I'm really sorry," I started, feeling genuinely horrible for the way it all went down.

"You owe me three hundred dollars," Bailey said, folding his arms.

He wasn't joking. His eyes had gone very little and his nostrils kept flaring. Mine only did that when I was forced to run.

"I haven't got three hundred dollars," I told him. "But if you keep me on, I will and I'll pay you back."

Clever, right? I was pretty impressed with my fast thinking as well.

Bailey just stared at me like that was the stupidest thing he'd ever heard.

"Are you serious?" he blurted at last. "Why on earth would I keep you after that?"

"Because I owe you three hundred dollars and if I don't have a job, then I can't pay you back."

I may not be able to read words properly on paper, but sometimes, my brilliance stuns even me.

"Just give me another chance," I went on quickly before he could really make up his mind. "If I mess up again, then I'll never darken your doorstep ... except on Wednesdays," I added. "That's when you get your baked goods delivered fresh."

I like to think that, by knowing that, it meant I did my research and I was truly dedicated to being part of the food industry and his business. But we both know it's because I'm an absolute pig.

"I know when my deliveries come in." He grumbled. Then he exhaled. His arms lowered to his sides. "All right. One more chance, but you drop so much as a spoon and I will use it to scoop out your brain."

Horribly graphic, but understandable.

So, I returned that evening in my tight, pink saranwrap uniform, my blonde hair scraped back in a decent and tidy ponytail, and I applied just enough make up not to make people think my outfit was an invitation—which is to say light. I grabbed my purse, your sneakers—sorry! Seriously, I'll try not to wreck these ones—and stalked from the house like a woman on a mission.

The entire way, my stomach whimpered like that time you and I ate too many fiber bars and paid for it dearly the rest of the week. Halfway through town, I was walking with my knees pressed together. Really, it was that bad. My pits were drenched. I could feel the stiff fabric rubbing my skin raw and I wanted to rip it off and pitch it into the street.

I arrived exactly fifteen minutes early again, but this time, I was smarter about it. I immediately went to work. I checked all the salt and pepper shakers on all the tables. I refilled the ketchup bottles, the vinegar bottles, and even helped Mr. Wallaby stack frozen patties in a metal container for easier grabbing through the rush.

That's right, your little sister was on her game. I had it all under control. I only dropped two spoons, which, thankfully, Bailey wasn't around to see. I was so proud of myself. I truly believed that my first day of bad luck was really at its end.

Then he *arrived.*

I wasn't holding anything—thank God. But I was arranging a table after having cleared it when the door opened and there ... he was, just standing there, all of him, the parts of him I hadn't really paid much attention to the night before and it was all equally breathtaking. I wish I could say the only thing he had going for him was his mouth, but, oh, he was wrong. The kind of wrong women fall for, the kind that can change your life in a single night and never look back. He was the perfect kind of wrong and I wanted all of it. Maybe that made me the biggest crazy person in the world, wanting something, knowing it would break my heart, but, oh, Rach, I physically ached with the sheer force of that want. Maybe I was crazy, because I didn't even know what color his eyes were until they locked onto mine.

Do you remember that china doll Grandma brought back with her from that trip she took to England to see that Tea Club lady? What did you name that thing? Lacy? Carrie? Anyway, do you remember how incredibly blue her eyes were? Like cornflowers sitting on a field of snow. You could see them clear across a room, no matter how bright or dark it was.

His eyes were that blue. They were the endless blue of an open, summer sky on the highest point in the world. They were vast and bottomless. I could have fallen into them, an abandoned leaf just drifting head over heels, forever. But I'd already held his gaze longer than I'd held anyone's and my nerves wavered.

I looked away.

You must think I'm such an idiot, going on like this about some guy I haven't said two words to. Honestly, I wasn't entirely sure I hadn't lost my mind. The whole thing was some fantastic story I'm really sure I'm not doing justice.

God, I'm a mess. So pathetic. This is why you need to come back. I need someone to slap me upside the head and snap me out of it. I could ask Bailey. I'm sure he'd love to clap me one.

"Hi."

In the process of staring absently into space, I nearly jumped out of my skin when the voice cut into my thoughts. I turned, expecting a customer, someone who'd been waiting ages to get my attention and now stood behind me with his family, anxious to be seated.

It wasn't.

It was so much worse.

He stood there with his messy mop of unruly brown hair and scatter of boyish freckles. His guitar was strapped to his back, the arm part jutting up over his left shoulder. I remember vaguely thinking the country style instrument clashed so hopelessly with the dark jeans, skulls and bones t-shirt and leather armbands. Didn't he need one of those heavy metal guitars? You would know the name of it. The one rockstars always shattered in a fit of glorious inspiration on stage while shrieking wildly.

I know. Focus, Kaylee!

Well, there he was, inches from me—two feet, to be exact. And he smelled phenomenal. Like spices, musk, and wood polish. It was a manly sort of smell. The kind that made me want to nuzzle into the side of his neck and kiss his Adam's apple and move up his chin and...

God, Rach, I'm losing it. I'm actually losing it.

Okay, anyway, I just stood there, as dumb as a bag of bricks. I might have been staring. No, I was definitely staring. I couldn't talk. I had no spit.

I forgot the English language. No joke. Everything I'd ever learned in the last nineteen years ... gone. Evaporated from my head like vapors.

"Hello?"

He was watching me with concern now. It was in the tilt of his head, the neat little furrow between those gorgeous eyebrows. In the mortifying shift of his gaze flicking away from me, around me the way people did when things were getting awkward and they were looking for a way out.

"Hi!" I blurted ... loudly. Really, really loudly, Rach. I mean, I practically screamed it at the guy.

Then, I just wanted to die. I wanted to crawl under the table, pull my knees to my chest and wait for the world to end ... or until Bailey stormed out and tossed my butt out.

He chuckled. "I didn't mean to bother you," he said. "I'm looking for my stool."

His stool? I thought my brain was malfunctioning again. I wouldn't have doubted it.

"I'm sorry?"

He cleared his throat, and I wondered ... was he ... nervous? Then, of course, my brain ran with it: what kind of nervous? Like, dear Lord, get me away from this girl, *nervous, or* I can't live without her, she needs to be mine, *nervous? Bit melodramatic, I know, but we weren't all blessed with the ability to understand men like you.*

"I had a stool," he said, gesturing towards the square patch of rust that stained the linoleum where the jukebox used to be and where a mic stand now stood. "I thought I left it there last night, but someone might have moved it." He looked at me. "I was just wondering if you'd see it."

I shook my head. "I haven't, but I can look."

He smiled and I forgot how to breathe. I forgot to think. All I could do was stand there and stare at that cleft in his chin and the sensual tilt of his lips. They were even more delicious up close.

"Thank you."

He walked away and I found myself stumbling almost drunkenly to the kitchen. I asked Mr. Wallaby, who shook his head and told me to go ask Darlene. But Darlene had her, talk to me and I'll cut you, *face and I was in that happy, floaty place.*

I went searching for the stool myself. Shouldn't have been too hard, right? It was one stool and the diner wasn't that big.

Rach, it took me twenty freaking minutes. Twenty. I don't know how that's even possible, but ~~some poophead~~ someone had left it in the stock room, tucked behind an entire wall of freshly delivered boxes.

I hauled it out and took it to him, feeling a bit proud of myself. He was adjusting the mic and glanced up when I approached, treasure in hand. He beamed like I'd just saved the world.

"You found it!" He took the seat from me and set it aside. "Thank you..."

"Kaylee."

"Austin." He thrust out a hand, a large hand with long fingers decorated in an assortment of colorful Band-Aids. "Hazards of being a musician," he explained when he caught me looking. "I accidentally picked up a box of children's colored ones at the pharmacy. I don't mind it, honestly. It's a great conversation starter."

Was he talking about this? Us talking? This conversation? I had no idea, not even when he peered up at me through some of the darkest, thickest lashes I'd ever seen and I became painfully conscious of my sweaty palms and the palm he was still holding out for me.

I swore a little in my head. Okay, a lot. I had an angry, drunken sailor in my head. But what was I supposed to do? I couldn't shake his hand, not when mine felt like a clammy fish. I couldn't not shake his hand either. Why couldn't life just be fair for once?

I bolted down my nerves and I put my hand in his. Then I held my breath, waiting for him to yank away in utter disgust.

He didn't.

Those long, musician fingers curled around mine and my lungs stuttered. My knees trembled. I was so excruciatingly aware of that simple gesture that I nearly gasped.

"It's nice to meet you, Kaylee," he said and the gruffness in his voice coursed through me.

It, combined with the feel of his callused fingers, the rubbery grip of the Band-Aids, sent my system into an odd sort of shock. I don't honestly know how to explain it, except that it was a little like getting my nerves electrified. Each nerve ending sizzled with an awareness that was impossible to ignore. The contact of his warm skin, the subtle, but firm grip of his fingers, I have never been so enraptured by anything.

I don't know how long we stood there, our palms mashed together, our skin and sweat exchanging DNA, but it felt like hours. Days maybe even. The entire world had ceased to exist. There was nothing but me and him and that single contact.

Have you ever felt that? Am I even making sense? I feel like I'm just rambling, trying to sort through the chaos he keeps causing in my life. I don't know if what I'm feeling is normal or if I've finally become those women who go so long without contact that they can't help but crave it all the time. I don't want to be that person. I don't want to be so desperate and hungry for love that I find it in all the wrong places. We all know what happens to women like that.

God, Rach, I need you. ~~Why can't you be here?~~ I know why you can't be here, but I'm so lost. Not just over the whole Austin business. Life in general is slipping completely out of my grasp. Everything is falling apart. It was gradual at first, little things, but sitting here now, writing this in the room we used to share, there is a void in the middle of everything. It's like my life is a long stretch of highway and everything before the incident is fields of flowers, sunshine, and laughter. Then, suddenly, out of nowhere, there's a hole. This enormous, looming, bottomless abyss in the middle of that road that spans the entire world and somehow, we—me, Mom, Dad— we survived it. We got on the other side and you didn't. You're still somewhere back there and I keep looking through the back window, searching for you and there's nothing. The road has become dark, desolate, and barren. The sky is dark. The fields are dead. There is nothing ahead, but an endless span of my existence yawning forever without you. I don't ~~want to face~~ know how to face that.

On nights like tonight when the sky is calm and the wind holds the faint remains of summer, I think about all the things we were supposed to do together. The promises we made. The dreams we spilled into the room. There had been so many and we were supposed to make so many more.

I'm so alone, Rach. So incredibly empty. How is that possible when somewhere beneath this flesh is a network of bones, veins, muscles, and origins, and whatever else? Is it my soul? Is my soul screaming for something I ~~can't~~ don't know how to give it? I don't even know if I believe in souls. I just know that I am here and you are not and I'm supposed to be okay.

Chapter Four

Dear Rachel,

Today marks three years since you left. Three years since you ~~*abandoned me*~~ *followed your dreams* ~~*and never came back*~~*. I woke up this morning feeling like someone had pumped me full of lead overnight. My limbs ached. My head throbbed. I wanted to stay curled up under the sheets until it all went away. Until life ended.*

But I wasn't the only one remembering what day it was. I could hear Mom downstairs. The bang of cupboards closing, the shatter of glass as things were pulled from their shelves reverberated through the house the way I always imagine an earthquake would start, slow and then all at once.

She was the earthquake, the natural disaster I dreaded facing. I knew, even before I pushed back the blankets and stepped out of that room that one of us would not survive the day.

I just prayed it would be me.

Mom threw a cookie jar at me. The cat, not the rooster. Thank God. I don't think I could have ducked that one. She was already three sheets to the wind and it wasn't even eight in the morning. The stale stench of whiskey ... I swear, it's coming out of her skin now. I don't know where she's been hiding the bottles. I've looked. I'm sure they'll turn up.

"You miserable, stupid, useless brat!" she slurred at me, wobbling with every violent wave of her skeletal arm. "This is your fault!"

I know she doesn't mean the carpet of broken pottery strewn across the kitchen, the cupboard doors ripped off their hinges and pitched far into the dining room, or the water cascading over the countertop and soaking the ground from the overflowing tap. No. She means you. Your absence. I'm not entirely sure she's even really talking to me. Might be.

"Mama, let me help you to bed."

I try to edge around the glass and smudged food, but it's everywhere. It's a carpet of devastation and she's ankle deep in it. Closer, I could see she'd already cut herself. Streaks of blood stain the floor, but I can't tell how bad it is.

That's when she threw the cookie jar. I barely dodged it in time. It sailed over my head and shattered into a million pieces over my shoulder.

I got her to bed. I got her cleaned up and tucked away. I ignored her profanities, her deep wishes for me to join you so she could live in peace. All the usual things. Some days, I can't help but wonder if she wouldn't be better off somewhere they can monitor her. Somewhere she can get help and counseling. Maybe that makes me a bad daughter, but I can't trust that she won't hurt herself one day when I'm not home. I have Tally from next door come in during the evenings while I'm at work, but it's only a matter of time.

I'm done living, Rach. You're probably rolling your eyes and calling me ridiculous. You'd no doubt tell me I have so much to live for, but I don't. I am trapped in this house, in this town until the day I die. That is my life. I will be Darlene. I will work at Moosehead Bar and Pub until my fingers are too stiff to undo the salt shaker caps. I will be buried in a hole next to Grandma and all the others just six miles before the town line ends, so, even in death, I will be here. This is my prison. I don't know what I'm being punished for, but I don't know if I don't deserve it.

I went to work today under a bright, beautiful sky. People waved and I waved back, because to them, it's just another day. No one asks about you. No one has in years. I hate them for that. I'm so grateful. I don't want to talk about you. I don't know what I'm supposed to say.

Darlene was already at the counter, polishing the surface for all it was worth. It was fifteen minutes before my shift, but I headed into the back, left my things and started anyway, needing the distraction.

Austin arrived at six, guitar in tow.

He met my gaze and he smiled.

I looked away.

I had no smile to give back. Not even for him.

I got through the night. I don't know how. I don't remember any of it. The seven hours between me walking in and me getting ready to leave were just another black hole. I was relieved, truthfully. I wanted today to end the moment I woke up.

"Hey." Austin caught up to me while I was walking down the street, arms folded, head bowed as the entire world weighed down my shoulders. "Where are you headed?"

I don't want to talk. My lips feel glued together and I have no will for anything.

Then I looked at him. I took in the way the light from the lamppost turned the ends of his hair silver and how it reflected in his eyes, making them glow in the darkness. His freckles were barely visible and I wondered just how old he really was.

He's twenty-five.

I asked afterwards, after I'd made the boldest move of my life. You would have been proud. You would have laughed and clapped your hands while jumping up and down on the bed until Mom screamed at us to knock it off. I did something I had never done before—I grabbed him. I bunched my fingers into the soft, worn material of his top and I shoved him.

It caught us both by surprise. His guitar case hit the pavement with a final whine of disturbed strings that vanished beneath the scuffle of our feet.

I didn't stop until I'd properly slammed him into the wall of Bow and Bits Hardware store.

Then, my darling sister, I kissed him.

I kissed him like I had five minutes to live. I kissed him like everything was ending and I needed to feel something, anything, just one last time. I was crying. I realize now how pathetic that sounds, but the taste of him, the lingering sweetness of cherry pie and coffee mixed with the saltiness of my despair and I couldn't stop.

I expected him to shove me away. I was violating him and drowning him in my tears. What sort of girl did that? I almost shoved myself away. Disgusted.

His arms slipped around me. They enclosed me to him, a firm, but gentle cradling that honest to God destroyed me.

I broke.

No. I shattered.

I fell so far apart that I was literally on the ground ... sobbing hysterically as everything ... the last three years came crashing down around me. And he was there ... on the ground with me, holding me, pressing me into him, crushing me so close I couldn't breathe. This person that I'd met only the day before. This man whose last name I didn't even know. He gave me something no one, not one person in that entire town, that town I grew up in had ever given me.

And I hated myself.

I hated you.

I hated the world.

But I loved him.

"It's all right," he whispered when I finished wrecking his shirt with tears, snot, and saliva. His hands were running down my back, stroking my hair and soothing the tremors. "Let it out."

"I'm sorry..."

"Shhh." He shook his head and tightened his hold on me. "Nothing to be sorry for."

"I shouldn't have—"

"I didn't mind." There was a smile in his voice that made my cheeks warm.

I peeled my face off his shoulder. It was too dark to see, but I knew I would need to buy him a new shirt. I had no doubt most of my makeup was now smudged all across the fabric. I didn't even want to imagine what my face looked like and prayed to God it was too dark for him to see.

"All right?"

I nodded, careful to keep my head down. "Thank you and—"

His fingers, warm and gentle, slipped beneath my chin and tipped it to his. It was so unexpected, I could do nothing but sit there and fall into his eyes while he smoothed my tears away with the pad of his thumb.

"Want to talk about it?"

I wish I could say that I'd gotten a hold of myself. I wish I could tell you that I got up and walked away, feeling better. But the moment he asked, I was crying again. Not sobbing, thankfully. But the tears welled and spilled in hot, wet rivulets down my face and dropped off my chin. I could feel them hitting my bare chest where the buttons didn't close and rolling until the fabric soaked them up.

"Go on," he urged. "Tell me."

I did.

I spilled nineteen years into the twilight between us. I purged my burden onto him, uncaring that he would have to carry them. I never liked those people, the ones who forced others to share their pain. But he let me. I bled all over that sidewalk, Rach. I cut open every vein I'd spent the last three years sewing up and I drowned him in the aftermath. And he just sat there, long legs sprawled around me, arms keeping me grounded against the soft patter of his heart. His warm breath ruffled the hairs at the top of my head and, once or twice, I could have sworn I felt his lips skimming there lightly.

When I finished, when there was nothing more to tell him, no more wounds left to open, we just sat there, his guitar case a few feet away, bathed in the pale halo of light. The night swayed around us, shifting from one day into the next in a seamless tick of a single clock hand. I closed my eyes. I probably would have slept, but he couldn't have been comfortable.

"You must think I'm just..." I didn't even have a word for what I thought I was.

"Human?" he prompted.

I said nothing.

"I lost my brother last year." His confession took me completely by surprise. "He was older by eight years. Shot during a domestic disturbance call. He was a cop."

"Rachel's not dead," I told him.

He considered that a moment. "No, but is there much difference?"

I wanted to scream at him that there was a world of difference. That you—Rachel—could wake up at any moment and things could go back to normal. That his brother would never come back. How was that not different?

"What was his name?" I asked instead, too exhausted to fight.

"Jackson."

A smile turned up my lips. "Austin and Jackson."

He chuckled. "My dad's a cowboy."

"Didn't know Canada had cowboys."

"I'm not from here." His fingers slipped bits of hair behind my ear. "Montana—born and raised."

Would you believe me if I told you that we stayed there, wrapped in each other, against that wall for three hours before I realized what time it was? The only other person I'd stayed up that late talking to was you. But there I was, telling this stranger all my secrets and listening while he told me his. I learned that he was the youngest of three. That his parents own a cattle ranch. I learned that he left home after the accident and backpacked across the US and most of Canada and that he played his guitar for extra traveling money. I learned that his favorite color was blue.

"The pretty blue," he explained. "Like the blue on a peacock's feathers."

I learned that he can't dance, he puts ketchup on his eggs, and he has a deep love for gummy worms.

"Anything gummy, really," he said. "I like how they squish between my teeth."

Disgusting, but I ~~think I~~ want to keep him. Can I? Can I have him for myself? Can I have this one thing? I have no idea what any of it all meant or what will happen when I see him again, but I do know one thing—I am falling for a cowboy from Montana.

Chapter Five

Dear Rachel,

I am in so much trouble, and I can't stop smiling.

I woke up this morning to Tally knocking on the back screen. I knew it was her because she's the only person who knocks and then sings, yooohooo loudly. I went out and was told Mom had wandered her way into Tally's begonias. Most of the flowers were crushed, but there was Mom, sprawled face down in the dirt, in her bathroom robe, one foot missing a slipper.

She was a sad mess. I was almost tempted to leave her there, but Tally kept pattering on about her precious begonias and how she'd planted them so she could see them grow from her back porch.

God.

I took Mom home after promising to replace the flowers. I cleaned her off and stuffed her into bed. Then I got dressed, grabbed my purse, and I marched to Aunt Judy's house. She was already on her porch, dressed in the ridiculous floral moomoo. She smiled and waved when I stalked up her garden path.

"Hello sweetheart," she said as I stomped up the steps. "Here to see your dad?"

"Where is he?"

Because enough was enough, wasn't it? I didn't marry the woman, he did. Wasn't it in the vows, something about sickness or health? I wasn't doing it anymore. I was tired of being made to feel like my pain and my problems somehow meant less than everyone else's. I lost you too. I've had to live with that just like they were. But they're my parents too and I'm still here. I'm still their daughter and I needed them to get their crap together.

Dad was in the kitchen nook, sipping coffee and reading the paper like nothing in the world was wrong. He looked up, his face clean shaven, his hair combed and not a single dark circle under his eyes.

"Hello—"

"Don't you hello me," I roared, my hurt and fury boiling over. "What are you doing?"

He looked down at his coffee mug, bemused.

"No," I shouted. "What are you doing? Why are you here? You have a wife who needs you at home."

He set the mug down with a resigned sigh. "Kaylee—"

"She's your wife!" I interrupted. "You married her. You had a family with her ... I'm in that family, Dad. I'm part of this. Part of all of it. I am your daughter and I need you. I need my parents." I was gasping and

yelling and crying, because Lord knows I didn't cry enough the night before. "I lost her too. She was a part of me, literally a part of me. She was my sister. My best friend. And I lost her just like you did. But I'm here. I'm right here and I need you. I need Mom. I need not to be made to feel like I no longer matter. I matter, damn it!" I stomped a foot and felt the vibration of pain ripple up my body. "And I'm done. I'm finished. I can't do this anymore. I can't ... I'm dying. You don't even notice. None of you. You're sitting there, happy as a ... as a clam and everything is falling apart and you don't care."

"Of course I care!" He lunged to his feet, a bear of a man with a bright, furious face. "I told you to come with me."

I laughed. "Come with you? That was your solution? Let's just abandon your mother, the woman who bore my children, and live happily away from her while she drinks herself to death. Is that it?"

He said nothing. What could he say?

"You and Mom are two of the most selfish people on the planet," I told him, my voice eerily calm in my ears. "You pushed Rachel away because she wanted better than this pathetic town and now, you couldn't care less what happens to me. I don't know why I bother with either of you. You both deserve each other."

I left. I walked past a stunned Aunt Judy and out of the house.

It was beginning to rain. I hadn't brought an umbrella. Didn't really need one. The warm wetness actually felt nice soaking into my clothes and dampening my skin. I could feel my anger lifting, rising off me like steam and evaporating into the nothing.

Have you ever noticed how the world seems to breathe a little easier after a storm? Even people seem calmer. It's like the rain has the power to soothe the soul, tame the beast, calm the fires. It can swoop in on a whim and, with its wet and cold, bring peace. My favorite memories seem to always happen when it's raining, like sneaking out to run in the puddles, like building a fort in the living room and making shadow puppets against the blankets, like telling each other secrets late into the night while the heavens cried. All beautiful things I long to revisit with you when you wake up.

It was raining that night, wasn't it? The police hadn't been clear, or maybe they'd said and I hadn't heard over the roar of blood in my ears. All I remember is them standing there, two of them in uniform, looking somber and weary.

"There's been an accident."

But it wasn't an accident, was it? You don't accidentally get drunk and then climb behind the wheel of a semi. That isn't an accident. That's murder, or at least, it would have been if you'd been killed. I sometimes wonder if this isn't worse. I imagine you in that hospital bed, strapped to tubes and wires, breathing because a machine allows it, and I wonder—is this what you want? Is this how you would want to live the rest of your life, brain dead and empty? Are you even in there anymore? Can you hear me when I beg you to wake up? Do you try? Are you awake in there, screaming to be heard, a prisoner in that body, that body that looks so much like mine? The doctors swear you will never get better. Some have even insisted we should ... no. I won't even think about it. They're wrong. They don't know you. They don't know how stubborn you are, how much you love living. You will come back. I know you will.

I didn't go home. I walked around town, not really going anywhere. I considered going to see Austin at the motel. But I was utterly mortified by my behavior the previous night. Mostly the crying. Only the crying, really. The rest had been wonderful. I do wish I'd focused a little more on the kiss. I don't remember much of it, except an angry mashing of our lips, well, my lips and the tang of salt. I can't imagine what he must have been thinking after he left me on the doorstep with a loving squeeze of my fingers.

"Good night," he'd said. "I'll see you tomorrow."

Obviously he meant later that evening at work, but what if he was only being nice? Country boys were like that, weren't they? Polite and attentive to weeping, dramatic women who assault them in the middle of the night. Yet, a part of me was actually excited. I hadn't anticipated much of anything for years so I was a bit rusty, but I couldn't wait to see him. I couldn't wait to get to work so I could hear the low croon of his voice as he sang about love and loss, and the joys of youth. Most of his songs were country, music beyond my realm of expertise, but a few I recognized from the radio. The customers liked it. It always brought with it a sort of calm serenity to the place. Even the rowdy drinkers seemed to do their medicating in a contemplative manner.

Maybe that was his talent. Austin's, I mean. That was his superpower. He calmed demons. He made them feel better. Maybe I was just feeling a bit indebted, a little uncharacteristically loyal to a stranger, but I honestly believe he can fix me.

I was in the market when I heard my name. In a town the size of ours, you know that's not entirely unusual. I immediately expected any number of people and instinctively slapped on my smile. Only, the moment I turned, it slipped straight off my face. I blinked, but the image remained until he was standing directly in front of me.

"Austin." His name rushed out of me in a breathy whisper.

He smiled, looking every bit as beautiful as he did cloaked in shadows. He held an umbrella over his head, a navy blue one that was not at all the kind of blue he preferred. His sneakers were soaked and the hem of his jeans was darker than the rest. He had on a light coat with the front open, revealing some band t-shirt I'd never heard of.

"I've been looking for you," he said.

I would have believed him if he'd said he'd been in the area and spotted me. Him actually setting out to find me had my mind twisting for a loop.

"Me?" I blurted. "Why were you looking for me?"

Now, he looked uncomfortable. "I was worried, partially. After ... well, I just wanted to make sure you were all right. I went by your house—"

"You went by my house?" A cold sort of panic seized me. "Who did you talk to?"

I couldn't blame him when his eyes went wide. I was acting like a nutter.

"Uh ... no one?" he hedged cautiously. "I rang the bell, but no one answered. I assumed you'd gone out."

Of course no one answered. Mom was out cold and Dad was a coward.

"Sorry." I couldn't even look at him. I traced the cuff of his damp pant legs instead.

He shook his head. "It's all right."

He took a step forward. I know, because I'd been staring at his feet. His umbrella extended over me, shielding me from the downpour. I lifted my chin, partially surprised by the gesture, partially curious. He was already watching me, so attentive, like he was actually trying to read the state of my emotional and mental health in my eyes.

"I'm all right," I assured him. "I shouldn't have fallen apart the way I did. I'm so embarrassed."

He was quiet for a long time, long enough for me to start counting the rapid taps of raindrops on the fabric above our heads.

"You know when people say strong as a rock, *or* endure life the way a rock endures the river?*"*

I hadn't, so I shook my head.

He shrugged. "Well, I seen them on these inspirational posters at some music shop in San Francisco I think, I can't be sure. Anyway, and it's absolute rubbish. Even a rock will eventually crack beneath a constant stream of water. So, if you want to be strong and enduring, you need to be the water. It might take longer to get what you want, but persistence and perseverance always win out, right?"

"So, you're telling me I should ... what?"

"Well..." He rubbed the back of his head and squinted off into the distance over my head. "I suppose that you can only be strong for so long and it's okay not to be sometimes."

I laughed, not because of his brilliant wisdom, but because he seemed to have absolutely no idea what he was talking about, yet he was trying so hard to make me feel better.

He grinned at me, a little sheepish, a little amused, but a whole lot distracting. The man had one dazzling mouth when he smiled.

"Can I join you?" he asked once I'd sobered.

"Join me?" I lifted an eyebrow. "You mean just randomly walk about?"

He considered that a moment, then nodded. "I can wander. I'm almost a professional at it."

I already knew he'd traveled for almost a year before finding his way to my little town, but he hadn't gone into details and I had an inexplicable need to know everything. Not entirely about him, but where he'd been, what he'd seen, who he'd met. I wanted to know where he was going next and ... and when he'd be leaving.

He would be leaving. I mean, I knew that. He'd told me as much. But I hadn't really fixated on it until that moment.

"What?" He must have seen the realization on my face, because his grin was gone as well and he looked almost concerned.

"How long were you planning to stay here?"

I probably should have softened the question with a few pre questions. I probably shouldn't have sounded so anxious about it. After nearly destroying the diner the first time we'd met, attacking him the second night, and now this, I really didn't want him to think I was a loony stalker.

If he was thinking it, he'd been very careful not to show it. His expression remained thoughtful as he contemplated my question carefully.

"Don't know," he said at last. "I don't really have a schedule."

I didn't like the non-answer. I didn't like not knowing just how long I had him for.

God, maybe I am loony.

"How long did you stay in the other places?" I ventured, thinking I could calculate a pattern.

"A few days, a week or two."

My spit tasted gritty going down with my swallow. "You've been here nearly a week."

He scratched his head. "Yeah, but..." He bit his lip and I had to work hard not to stare. "I never had a reason to stay in any of those places."

The kick of my heart could have been heard for miles. I was sure of it. The knock of it was violent and fierce and filled with a hot, expanding joy that overruled all my other senses. I started to ask him if he'd found that here ... now, but I didn't. I caught myself. The last thing I wanted to do was presume I knew something when there was a good chance I was completely wrong.

"You can join me," I told him, already digging my heel into the damp earth and starting to turn away, a mischievous grin on my face. "But only if you answer a few questions."

His brows lifted in immediate interest. "I'm intrigued. Lead the way."

I asked him a million questions. I wanted to know everything. I made him tell me in detail every scene, every smell. I even shut my eyes and pretended I was there, in a tiny café in New Orleans, listening to the sultry purr of jazz and smelling the sweet, sugary scent of coffee and beignets. I was so happy and so miserable all at the same time. I longed to be there in person, to see it all myself, to experience the hills of Montana, the dirt trails of British Columbia, the warm sands of Miami. I wanted it all so much I wanted to cry.

"Have you gone anywhere?"

I couldn't look at him. Shame was a powerful force burning into my cheeks. I managed a shake of my head.

"There's still time, you know," he said. "I ... I could show you."

I stopped walking and stared at him, not expecting that at all.

"I don't mean..." He grimaced. "I'm not a pervert. I don't go around offering to take off with girls I just met. I just..." he broke off, blew out a breath and shoved five fingers back through his hair. "I feel like I know you, like we've met before, a long time ago, does that make sense? It's not a line or anything. I'm not trying to pull one over on you. It was just an offer." He glanced down at our feet, soaked to the ankles in a puddle. "I'd like the company." He peered up at me through those lashes. "I'd like your company. As friends even, if that's what you want."

I had no idea what I was supposed to say. I know you would have told me to do it, to take the chance and explore the world. But I couldn't. The words were trapped in my chest even while my blood hummed.

"You don't need to answer this second," he went on quickly. "I can wait, Kaylee. I will wait if you want."

It was that moment that I knew I would leave with him. Not today or tomorrow. Maybe not even next month. But one day. If he really waited, I would see the world with him. I would sit in that café with him. I would take air balloons and trolleys and maybe even a moped through the narrow roads of Rome. I would do it all. Just not yet.

Chapter Six

Dear Rachel,

I'm sorry I didn't come see you this weekend to finish the next chapter of Wuthering Heights. *It's been a miserable few days what with the rain keeping most people locked inside and it being my first weekend free since starting at the diner. I spent most of Saturday at home anyway just cleaning up and resting. Austin dropped by later in the evening and we shared leftover pasta and talked about our favorite movies. He suggested we should see one together. I loved the idea, except...*

"We don't have a very big selection at the theater in town," I told him. "It's been showing the same four movies since I was a girl."

Sunday, he took me to see Practical Magic, *but only because he didn't believe me when I told him the movie theater in town was still playing it.*

"That movie's a hundred years old," he argued.

"Eighteen," I corrected. "And I'm serious."

Well, we went and took a seat at the very back. We shared a bucket of buttery popcorn and talked through most of the show. No one else was bothered by it. We were the only ones there.

When it was over, he took my hand and I showed him around town. We walked aimlessly for hours, just talking and walking, and laughing. So much laughing. My stomach ached all day Monday from having used muscles I no longer thought I had.

"I like your laugh," he said once I'd unfolded myself and wiped the tears from my eyes. "You don't do it often enough."

I snorted. "That's a line if I've ever heard one."

We were standing on the sidewalk outside Kelly's shoe repair shop. The air smelled of leather and him. Mostly him. Even in the theater where the scent of popcorn and sweat was dominant, I only smelled him and that warm, spicy fragrance I couldn't get enough of.

"Not a line." His eyes shone in the dwindling light, reflecting a darkness that had my heart skipping a beat and my lips tingling with anticipation. "It's not just the sound. It's the way you do it."

I blinked. "Do it?"

Warm fingertips swept back a lock of hair the breeze had knocked loose from my French braid. They whispered just lightly along the curve of my face and I was swarmed in tingles. My skin erupted in pimples. A heat surged up from the base of my stomach and I shivered almost violently.

"Your eyes light up first." The strand was tucked behind my ear. "Then your lips curve, just slightly, not too much. You roll your eyes and shake your head like whatever I just said is absolutely ridiculous, and then, just

then, your nose crinkles, just ... there." He skimmed a finger over the bridge of my nose. His eyes never left mine. "It happens right before you laugh."

One of us moved. I think it was him. It might have been me. It's a bit hazy, but that doesn't matter. What matters is the disappearance of space. What matters is that split second our gazes met, that silent spark that passed just before we sealed it with our lips.

It wasn't violent and aggressive like the first time. It wasn't a collision of bodies, a mindless heat of mouths taking and demanding. No. That had been about control, about pain and soothing that pain. This kiss was a delicate exploration of two people relinquishing control and submitting to a power stronger than love, or lust, or hate. It was shallow, delicious sips, light, feathery nips. It was unspoken poetry whispered between tangled wisps of breath. It was pure.

I never wanted it to end.

But it did.

My perfect night came to a close beneath the halo of our porch lights. It concluded with a final brush of his lips over mine and a promise to see me tomorrow. It ended with me crawling into bed, a smile on my tingling lips, and a release of the sash around my lungs.

I slept that night with a smile and my very first breath in forever.

Chapter Seven

Dear Rachel,

How are you? I know I haven't written in a while. I promise that wasn't intentional. Life has become unexpectedly complicated. But it's the good sort of complication. The kind that drives me out of bed in the morning, eager to see where the day will end and wishing it wouldn't. I love every waking moment, even those spent cleaning up after Mom. It's becoming more and more impossible to will myself to sleep at night, terrified that I'll wake up and the world will be that dark, miserable nothing that seems like something from a nightmare. But every time I open my eyes, he's there—my Montana cowboy with his blue eyes and dangerous smile and the world is bearable again.

I came to see you a couple of times. I don't know if you heard me that last time. The nurse had moved my box of letters off the shelf where I always place them and I might have lost my temper a bit with her. She found them and put them back and apologized, but I was too angry to care.

"Those are private," I shouted at her. "No one is allowed to touch them."

She claims she'd been dusting and just forgot to put them back. I don't know if I believe her. I counted them, all one thousand and ninety-five envelopes neatly labeled with your name. I made her stand there while I did it. They were all there, untouched, waiting to be read by you. I don't think I've ever felt such crippling relief.

Austin was with me. He asked if I was all right after the nurse had fled. I couldn't answer him. I was livid. I couldn't stop shaking. It was insane and I knew I was being ridiculous, but I wanted to find her and hit her.

It scared me. I think it might have scared Austin a bit as well. He didn't say as much, but he was a little more watchful of me the rest of the day, like he was waiting to catch me when I fell apart. I almost did a time or two. I could feel that familiar coiling of hysteria tightening in my chest, that gnawing, violated sensation you get when something personal has been touched by strangers.

I knew the nurses cleaned your room. I just never expected they would move the box when they did. Clearly they would have to, but it was never a worry. Now, all I can think about is someone reading what I've written and knowing just how unhinged I really am. Austin knows. Lord knows why he stays. Maybe he's unhinged too, or maybe he'd been right that day we sat huddled outside the hardware store. Maybe our situations are similar. You might not be gone physically, but you are gone in a sense.

I don't mind saying it here. I could never speak those words out loud. Not even to myself. I wouldn't dare, not while the doctors are making little comments about doing the unthinkable. I think I'll slap the next one who even opens his mouth. What do they know, right? It's only been three years. I read about a man who woke up from a coma nearly seven years later. I see you doing that. I see you just opening your eyes one day and that'll be that. It would certainly show them, wouldn't it?

Anyway, I need to run. Austin's coming over in a bit and I need to make sure Mom won't unexpectedly get out of bed and wander downstairs. She hasn't met him yet, and if I have any say, she never will. That's a poison I don't want anywhere near him. Us. Her and her toxic ways can just stay locked up in her room, lost in her booze induced haze.

But I will write more again. I promise I will. I have so much to tell you. I could write whole novels with how things have been the last little while. They're not perfect, but they are when I'm with Austin. I can't explain it. He just makes me feel ... everything.

Some nights, when we're in bed and the house is quiet, we'll whisper our secrets into the room. We'll share our dreams with the stars. And sometimes, his dreams intertwine with mine in the darkness and become our dreams, a unit, a promise. I love those nights, because they always end with his soul capturing kiss and a vow that we'll do them all.

Chapter Eight

Dear Rachel,

I'm going to do it. I'm going to leave with Austin. It's been six months since he asked me, six months where he waited and I waited, and I don't want to wait anymore. I realized several mornings earlier, while watching coffee drip with agonizing slowness that my whole life has been a series of lost minutes, seconds just gone and me still standing there ... waiting. Waiting for you. Waiting for Mom to get her act together. Waiting for Dad to realize he's still part of this pathetic family. Waiting for the doctors to give up. Waiting for my life to begin. Waiting for it to end. Waiting. Waiting. Waiting.

I don't know where we'll go or how long we'll be gone, but we'll be back. This is my promise, in writing. I also promise that I will write every day, no matter where we are or what I'm doing so that when I return, I will have thousands of memories to share with you. The very idea has me delirious. I haven't slept a wink since I blurted it out over dinner two nights before.

I'd only had half a mind on the pork chop I was moving around on my plate. I kept shifting restlessly in my seat, anxious and antsy. I honestly have no idea what was wrong with me. Maybe it was the heavy slush of snow outside or the impenetrable gloom that always followed the holidays, once the lights and pretty decorations were gone and there was nothing, but dirty roads and angry winds. I missed summer. I missed walking through town with Austin. We still do that occasionally, but you know how I feel about winter. I'd die happily in my own bed before willingly going anywhere in snow.

Poor Austin, he had no idea how I was during the winter seasons. He kept darting me concerned glances from across the table.

"You all right, love?" he asked.

I opened my mouth to tell him I was fine. Instead, what came out was, "Okay, let's do it."

He set his utensils down on his plate with careful slowness and studied them for several long heartbeats.

"Do what, exactly?" he ventured at last.

"Go." I shot out of my chair, amped and ready to hit the road. "Let's go. I don't care where."

His lips had parted, the only outward show of his surprise. "You mean it?"

I nodded and reached for the hand curled loosely next to his plate. I tugged him up after me.

"I'm ready. I want to do this."

He studied my face, eyes narrowed warily. "You're not just saying that, are you? Because I can wait, Kaylee. I'd wait forever for you."

I put my arms around him. "I want to."

There was a smile tilting the edges of his mouth, but it stopped before it could fully bloom. "What about your job?"

My eyebrow lifted. "You're right. How will I ever find another waitressing job?"

He poked me teasingly in the side. "All right, what about your mom?"

That stopped me. I hadn't thought of her. She hadn't been more than a passing thought in my exasperation, a flicker of inconvenience before my decision had solidified. But she hadn't been an importance. Dear God, I would have left her. I would have packed my things, climbed into Austin's car, and driven away without so much as a ... what was wrong with me? What had I become? I was horrified by my own pettiness, my own blinding, crippling selfishness. You would have been disgusted, Rach.

"Hey, it's all right." Austin tried to pacify me. He pulled me into his arms, comforting a person who didn't deserve it. "We'll figure it out, yeah?"

Figure it out how? Dump her in some home? She wasn't old enough even if that were a possibility. And could I? Could I really put my own mother in some shoe box just so I can jet off and have adventures? That somehow made me seem even worse than when I'd forgotten her. Dad clearly didn't care. He hadn't said two words to me since I stormed out of Aunt Judy's house. I couldn't leave her. She'd drink herself to death or stumble off and get hit by a car.

That was it. I wasn't going anywhere. I never would.

"It's not going to work, Austin." I pulled away from him. I couldn't stand to feel him around me when I knew what I had to do. "You should go." I tried to smile, tried to act like I wasn't dying all over again. "Take lots of pictures and email them to me—"

"That's not going to happen," he cut me off. "You're coming with me."

"I can't!" I moved away from him before he could think to reach for me. "I will never leave and I'm not going to keep you here."

"It's a bit too late for that, isn't it?" He grinned when I dared a peek at him through the heavy curtain of tears threatening to abolish my bravado. "You probably should have thought of that before you made me fall in love with you. Now, you're kind of stuck with me."

I just stood there, torn between thinking, oh my god, he loves me *and* I'm imagining things. *The latter was persistent and unavoidable. I couldn't stop wanting to ask him to repeat it, to say it again, if he meant it. Of course he meant it. Austin meant everything he said. It was an annoying and endearing quality. He has many of those—qualities. He's a good person, a warm, loving, generous person. He's the kind of person who deserves a good girl, someone fun and friendly, and beautiful. Not someone who forgot their own mother in some stupid, desperate grasp at their own freedom. I'm a horrible person. I don't deserve him.*

"I'm not saying it back," I partially shouted back at him, my voice choked and thick with tears. "If I say them back then you'll stay and you can't stay."

He took this in as he took everything in, with a quiet, contemplative manner that drove me insane.

"All right, I'll go back to the hotel and—"

"No!" God, how was I screwing this up? "You can't stay here ... in this town. You need to leave. You need to continue your adventure and finish seeing the world and doing amazing things. If I say I love you back, then you won't go. You'll give it up for me and I..."

"And that would be just awful," he finished dryly, clearly not taking me very seriously. "Did it ever occur to me that my adventures were what led me here to you? You're the pot of gold at the end of the rainbow, Kaylee. This is where I was supposed to end up, here ... with you. You don't have to say it back, but either way, I'm not leaving without you."

I wanted to hit him. Why couldn't I just be strong and push him out and tell him never to come back? Instead, my traitorous arms were throwing themselves around his neck and I was holding him so tight he actually squeaked.

"I do love you," I breathed into that warm stretch of skin connecting his neck and shoulder. "I shouldn't and it's selfish, but ... I love you."

I do love him. I've never loved anyone the way I love him. Even just thinking about him, I can feel myself growing warm inside. It brings a smile to my lips and an odd little skip to my heart. He was the embodiment of the word. Cliché and corny as it sounds.

But I accepted my predicament. Whatever he said, I already knew it wouldn't happen. I couldn't leave Mom. That was the short and long of it.

At least, so I thought.

Austin proved to be far more resourceful than I'd expected. I've always known he was clever, but he certainly proved it earlier today.

I'd changed shift hours at the diner—I'm not sure I mentioned that before—but I asked Bailey for day shifts. That left my nights free to spend time with Austin and be home in time to keep Mom tucked away. Some days, I swear that seems to be my main job—keeping her out of sight. Austin once asked me about it, even insisted he didn't mind meeting her, but I minded. Add it to my accumulating mountain of sin, but I am ashamed of her. Mortified. I live in fear that she'll find her way out and he'll be there. I don't know what she'd do or what she'd say. I don't want her spiraling into one of her rages and throwing something at him. He might think he was okay with the idea, but he wasn't. I wasn't.

Anyway, I came home to find Austin already on the porch, waiting for me. It was strange because he usually picked me up and we walked together. Then he'd leave me on the porch and make a run out for dinner or whatever and I'd take the time to send Tally home and sort Mom out. But today, there he was.

He got up when I drew closer and kissed me softly. Even then, I felt that simple brush all the way down to my toes.

"I've got a surprise for you," he said, pulling back.

He motioned me to follow him inside, which I did, wary and a bit afraid. He walked in and all I could think was, please, Lord, please let her not be passed out on the kitchen floor again.

She wasn't.

She was on the sofa, swaddled in a blanket, awake, slightly alert. She looked up when I walked in. I waited for the assault, verbal and physical, but she turned her head away, as disgusted by me as I was by her.

That was when I noticed the woman. She was tall and slender and had the darkest eyes to match her slicked back hair. She wore a nurse's uniform with colorful giraffes all over it. But it was the smile that sparked the vague memory.

"Heather?"

You remember Heather, don't you? She was a few years ahead of us in school, really quiet, really nice. I only remember her because I occasionally see her at the hospital when I come see you. We say hello on occasion, but we haven't talked since she graduated.

She smiled at me. "Hey!"

"Heather's a nurse," Austin said, like I didn't already know.

"Was," Heather corrected. "I mean, I still am, of course. I have my certificates and license, but I'm not working at the hospital anymore. I was let go due to cutbacks."

I understood that. It's been happening everywhere lately, people getting fired because there just wasn't enough money being made. The whole thing makes my stomach hurt.

"What are you doing...?" Then it hit me. "Is my mom okay?" I start moving towards the sofa. "Did Tally call you?"

Mom flinches away from me even before I'm three feet from her. She balls the blanket closer beneath her chin and curls in on herself. I stop, but I keep watching her, looking for blood or bruises, which are hard to see with the wrapping.

"No!" Heather says quickly. "She's fine."

Austin takes a step deeper into the room. "I ran into Heather when I was leaving the hotel. She was leaving one of the rooms..." he paused and grinned sheepishly at Heather. "Maybe you should tell it?"

Heather smiled and I wished everyone would stop grinning and smiling and tell me what the heck was going on.

"A friend of mine called me this morning. Her boyfriend is staying at the hotel while he's in between places and he was having chest pains. She said she'd pay, so..." She gave me a pointed, what was I supposed to do, *look and I nodded, understanding perfectly. "I went and I looked him over. Anyway, long story short, I was leaving when I ran into Austin."*

"Tommy's in the room next to mine," Austin explained. "I've been hearing him hacking and coughing for days, so I asked if everything was all right."

Heather nodded. "And we started talking about me losing my job and all that money I wasted going through training..."

"And I got the idea that maybe..."

"I could help with your mom."

I'm not going to lie, them finishing each other's sentences really pissed me off, but I understood enough of it to grasp that there was a bigger picture that I needed to focus on.

"Help her how?"

Heather hesitated. Her mouth opened and closed a couple of times and she glanced at Austin, but I guess the telepathic link must have worn out, because he just shrugged remorsefully and left her to explain.

"Well, your mom—"

"Is sitting right here and ain't deaf!" Mom snarled. "I don't need no thumb sucker doing anything for me."

Do you remember that? I had completely forgotten that Mom used to babysit Heather back when you and me were still in diapers. Mom, apparently, had not.

"Yes, I understand, but—"

"Get out of my house." Mom was struggling to untangle herself from blankets and cushions and was having zero luck on both accounts. "Get..."

She tumbled sideways and hit the ground between the sofa and coffee table. The crash made my bones hurt.

"Mama!"

I ran to her, hands reaching even before I rounded the sofa. She was a tangle of blankets and flailing limbs. I tried grabbing something, anything and earned a kick in the thigh that nearly sent me backwards on my butt.

"Don't touch me!" she shrieked, still thrashing like a cat stuck in a bag. "You lying, deceitful..." The rest of her rant cut off when she finally popped free.

Her head swung around, her short, cropped hair sticking up wild like a startled octopus. She saw me and her flushed face turned crimson. I had just enough sense to leap out of the way when the fake plant on the coffee table was hurled at me. It struck the floor where I was standing and shattered.

"Hey!" Austin charged forward, but I stopped him.

"Get out!" Mom screamed. "All of you. Get out of my house."

No one moved. I don't think any of us could. We all just stood there, rooted to the hardwood as she staggered and pushed her way up to her feet.

Without a word, she weaved her way in a zigzag formation towards the kitchen. Cupboards opened and closed, each crack resonating through my bones. Each shrieking curse when she couldn't find what she was looking for making me flinch.

"Where is it?"

Something shattered. More followed. Forks and spoons clattered to the floor. Pots and pans crashed across the room.

"Go," I said quietly to the pair standing frozen as the war raged. "I'll take care of this."

I didn't wait to see who would follow my orders. I took a deep breath and went to face our mother.

She was pulling rags from the drawer by the sink and pitching them like confetti. Glass littered the ground, a carpet of jagged diamonds. I was relieved I had my shoes on when each one crunched beneath my feet.

"Mama, let's get you upstairs."

I never saw the backhand coming until the world erupted into a shower of sparkling stars. The clap of it rang in my ears, harsh and violent, contradicting the utter numbness I actually felt. But the skin was hot beneath my palms. Gradually, the heat began to throb and a stickiness coated my fingers.

Her ring had cut me. It stung, but I couldn't tell how bad it was.

"Kaylee!" Austin was in the doorway, eyes wide in horror, then narrowed in rage as I felt the trickle of blood making its way down my cheek.

"Austin, no!" I planted myself between them, not because I believed for a minute that Austin would ever lay his hands on a woman, but because I didn't want her hurting him. "I'm fine."

Mom laughed. She said things I won't put in the letter, things that had my face burning hotter than any slap. I wanted to leave. I started to. I was at that point where I wanted to march out of the house and never look back. But Heather hurried in, holding a syringe and a determined expression.

It took all three of us to hold Mom down just long enough for Heather to sedate her. Austin took her upstairs and I helped tuck her in. Then I stood there, cheek blazing like an angry burn, wondering what in the world I was going to do now.

"She needs a facility," Heather said when we were all downstairs again, standing in a freshly swept kitchen. "She needs help, not just for the drinking, but what's happening with your ... family."

"I'm not putting her in a home," I said. "That wouldn't be right."

"It's not a home. It's a resting facility where they will help her regain control of her life. She needs this or you may walk in one day and find her dead."

I wasn't sure why I was hesitating. I knew she needed help. I knew I couldn't give it to her, not when she couldn't even stand the sight of me. I knew if I didn't, she could die and no matter what, I didn't want that. But every time I even considered the possibility, I was consumed by guilt.

I started to shake my head, when it finally hit me; it was too convenient. There I was, dying to leave, to just dump her off and live my life and here was the perfect excuse. She's a drunk, let's toss her into a facility while I jet around the world with my boyfriend. It was low, a horrible copout. I felt sick just thinking about it.

But could I keep her? I clearly wasn't doing a very good job of taking care of her. I couldn't even tell you how she got the drinks half the time. I don't drink, neither does Austin, yet there are bottles everywhere and the house perpetually smells like a brewery, vomit, and sweat. What good was I doing her? I clean up after her. I drag her to bed from wherever she may have passed out, I mop up her vomit and whatever else, and then what? I lock her up in her room. Was it even helping her? No. It was tucking away my shames so others wouldn't see it. So I wouldn't see it. If it was out of sight, it was out of mind, right?

"This is the only way you can help her," Heather prompted quietly, misunderstanding my silence. "She will die, Kaylee. If not from alcohol poisoning, then from choking on her own vomit or liver failure. I know you're all going through a tough time, but this is the only way. I promise you."

What would you do, Rach? If you were in my place? She was our mother at one point. She was the woman who raised us, who laughed and played with us, who sat up night after night when we were sick. She may no longer be that woman, but she was still Mom, wasn't she? She wouldn't have given up on ~~you~~ us.

I turned to Austin, my decision a stone wall of determination. "We can't leave. I won't leave, not while she's locked away somewhere."

Austin nodded. I expected nothing else.

"I'm okay with that."

So, my loving sister, you're probably reading this and thinking, but you said! You said at the beginning that you were leaving. What are you doing, Kaylee?

I am leaving. Not to Morocco or Kenya, but Austin is taking me out of town, one city over, for a weekend. It's not much, but for someone who's never been outside the town perimeters, it's practically another planet.

Chapter Nine

Dear Rachel,

Mom is doing better. At least, that's what the doctors keep telling me. That's all they can tell me. She refuses to see me and Doctor/patient confidentiality restrains them from telling me anything else. I have tried. I went every day for two weeks and got turned away each time with the same instructions: she's not accepting visitors right now. *It's been four months. One would think she's angry with me for putting her in there, for wanting to help her, but she never liked me before that anyway. You were always her favorite, strange considering we're identical.* ~~It never bothered me before~~ *It doesn't bother me. Things just are the way they are, right?*

So much has happened since my last letter. I still haven't gone anywhere outside the province, or the country, but Austin has been planning little trips, little getaways close enough around town so we can return if Mom needs anything. It wasn't even my idea. He's wonderful like that.

We've come to see you a few times since. I never had a letter, but things have been so busy and we've been doing so much. I did leave photos. Each one has a description, location, and date on the back. They're better than letters, aren't they?

It's raining today, which made me think of you and I thought I would write something for my next visit. Austin's in the next room. I can hear him talking to his mom. She sounds nice. I've talked to her a few times, and his dad. They want to meet me and I'm scared silly, which Austin tells me is ridiculous.

"They love you," he keeps telling me. "My mom is already making plans to adopt you into the family."

I tell him he's crazy, but I'm secretly thrilled. I like being accepted into his family. I like that his mom and dad like me. I want them to like me. I want them to accept me. Pathetic, right?

They would have loved you. I sometimes wonder if things had been different, if you never had that accident and if you had met Austin, would he have chosen you? Would he have even seen me past you? None of the boys in school ever noticed me when you were in the room. It never bothered me. You were my sister. We were twins. Hating you would be like hating myself.

I honestly don't even know why I'm bringing this up. It's stupid, really. Austin loves me. I am confident in this. I am secure in our relationship. I don't tell him, obviously. But I still wonder.

Austin's off the phone. He asked if I was writing to you and I told him I was. He's asked me to say hi.

Chapter Ten

Dear Rachel,

I tried to see Mom again this morning. The nurses are beginning to get upset by my attempts. I honestly can't say I blame them. A normal person would have gotten the hint by now, right? But she refused my visit. Again. So, I came to sit with you a while. I'm with you now as I write this. You look better, by the way. Someone's combed your hair. It's extra shiny. I know you'll appreciate that. The machines have an irregular beep today. I keep talking to you about random things and I like to think you're agreeing with me every time it beeps a little higher. The nurse says it sounds the same, but she doesn't seem very bright.

I poked you with my finger. I don't know if you felt it, but you didn't move.

Oh, I nearly forgot, I told you this already, but I'll write it here in case you're actually sleeping.

Austin and I booked our first international flight last night. We're going to go visit his family in Montana. It was why I went to see Mom. I wanted to let her know Heather has my itinerary in case of an emergency. I gave one to the facility as well, in case. The woman said she'd put it on file, but since I'm not even listed as her emergency contact, or any contact, odds aren't very high they'll call me. They wouldn't tell me who is listed. Maybe Dad. Or Tally. Heck, it could very well be you. I don't know.

You know what bothers me most about the way she's behaving? The fact that I wasn't the one driving that semi. I wasn't the one who pushed that twentieth beer in the driver's hand. I wasn't the road. I wasn't even there, but she blames me for you being here. She blames me because I didn't stop you when you got your acceptance letter and wanted to leave. She knew that you would never have listened to her or to Dad, but you would have listened to me. I could have stopped you. I should have stopped you. I should have made you stay. She thinks I encouraged you out of spite. That I wanted you gone. That I made this happen with the power of my mind.

It's disgusting. How could she think that? I would never hurt you. I've never even been mad at you. I love you more than I life itself. I would give anything for you to wake up.

The nurse was just here. The doctor's on his way to run some tests. I'm being asked to leave.

I love you, Rach. I hope you know that.

Chapter Eleven

Dear Rachel,

Guess where I am! Browning, part of Glacier County, Montana. We arrived early this morning and drove through the tiniest town, tinier than even ours. But they have mountains, Rach. Mountains! I have never seen mountains before. Beautiful, snow capped slopes that set the most incredible backdrop. Austin's dad laughed when I practically tripped over my own feet to get a better look.

"We'll get you closer before you leave," he promised.

Tim Paige is an enormous man. I think he might even be bigger than Dad. At least six foot seven with a laugh that you can feel vibrating through your bones. Austin looks like him. They have the same eyes and jaw, but Austin is slighter, a few inches shorter.

His mom, Ellen, is dainty. I mean tiny, tiny. She's shorter than even me with these delicate little bones that could snap with the flick of a finger. Standing next to Tim ... I honestly feared for her life. But they had three kids so I guess they figured out a system. She smiled so big when she saw me, I was sure her face would rip apart.

"Kaylee!" She darted off the porch and embraced me. I don't think I've ever been embraced by a stranger before. "I'm so happy to finally meet you."

She smelled amazing. I don't know if that's something normal to mention, but she was warm and soft, and she smelled like a mom, if that makes sense. She smelled comfortable, like cookies and sunlight. She smelled a little like Mom used to, before the drinking. I'm embarrassed to admit that I didn't want to let her go.

"Austin's told us so much about you," she said, leading me to a gorgeous log cabin nestled on a bed of endless green. "I feel like you're already part of the family."

I wanted to tell her I hadn't had one of those in years. I might not be very good at it anymore. But she takes me inside, into the warm, sugary scent of freshly baked chocolate chip cookies, wood polish, and something hearty and meaty—stew maybe.

Their home is simple, worn, relaxed. A lot like how our house used to be before. Lumpy furniture you know will cradle and comfort, soft lighting, mostly natural through the wide windows—there's even a seat on one—the wood is dark, not mahogany. Rosewood, maybe. And there are photos everywhere. Literally a collage of new and old, past and present, all clustered together in a tangle of memories. I was enthralled by them as I followed the progression of Austin as a baby, brand new born, bundled in a blue blanket, clasped to his mother's chest, all the way to Austin graduating university, grinning into the camera, draped in a navy blue gown, and waving a rolled up bit of paper.

His brother was there—Jackson. With Austin. With Tex, the other brother. I didn't meet him until supper. But they'd been close. You can see it in each picture. There were thousands of the three of them, huddled close, grinning and holding something up—fish, game controllers, kites, ice cream, or just waving. They looked alike. All three brothers seemed to have the same blue eyes, the same unkempt hair, the same mischievous grin. But Jackson had been taller. Maybe it seemed that way, because the other two were younger, but he was always in the middle and always taller.

"Austin says you have a sister."

Ellen had come up alongside me, her eyes fixed on a photo of the boys at a campout, wielding squares of marshmallow speared on sticks. A fire blazed behind them, painting shadows across their faces, but you could see just how much fun they were having.

"Yes," I said. "Rachel. She was in a car accident. Drunk driver hit her on her way to university three years earlier." I don't know why I was telling her. She hadn't asked. But the words just kept pouring out. "It would have been her first year. She got in on a full scholarship at only sixteen. She was brilliant, Rachel was. Incredible at charcoal drawing. Very artistic. I can't draw a line." I laughed shakily. "The accident caused swelling in her brain. She went into a coma and hasn't woke up ... yet. But she will, because she's incredibly stubborn."

Ellen smiled at me, not condescending or pitying. You know how much I hate those. I think I might have left if she had. But it was an understanding smile, the kind you give when you believe what you're being told.

"Of course she will," she said, and I immediately liked her. "I read about a man who woke up after seven years."

I burst out laughing. "Me too!"

Do you remember when the Anderson's split up when we were in the fifth grade and Mom said, you can tell what type of people a family holds by the tragedies they're able to withstand? *Or something like that. I hadn't been listening. But I would think about it every time Mom would have one of her episodes. I'd look at her and think,* what type of family were we? *Clearly not withstanding or durable. One horrible tragedy and we toppled like a house of cards. At least the Anderson kids still had their parents and two Christmases.*

The Paige family had withstood a death. They had lost a part of them, a piece that made them a whole and the gap was there, you could see it in the shadows of their eyes and even their brightest smiles, but they had remained together. They loved each other. They laughed and joked and talked about Jackson even though it had only been a year. They told stories of when he'd been alive and what he'd been like. No one screamed or threw anything. Ellen had a glass of red wine and I expected her to have another, but she didn't. Tim never left her side. He remained a strong force next to her tiny frame. He seemed to always be touching her, kissing the side of her head, touching her arm, holding her hand. He was always looking at her like she'd hung the moon and painted the stars. And they treated Austin and Tex like their children, not a burden or something they couldn't stand the sight of.

I love them, Rach. I've only been with them a day and I never want to leave. I want to bathe in their happiness and let it wash away the last three years of my life. I want to pretend that this could be my home and my family. But we both know that's not possible. I can't forget you or Mom. I haven't abandoned the idea of seeing her, seeing how much better she's gotten. I'm hoping that once she's no longer prisoner to the bottle, she'll hate me less. That's my wish, anyway. ~~And maybe, once Dad sees her sober, he'll come back.~~

No. I take that back. He doesn't deserve to, not when he left us when we needed him most. Maybe we're better off. I don't know, but it's like that saying by Marilyn Monroe *about accepting a person's worst before deserving their best. I'm probably saying it wrong, but he didn't accept any of us.*

Oh! I never told you about Tex. You would like him, Rach. He would be perfect for you. You need to wake up so I can introduce you.

He's adorable, but not cute. He's sophisticated and quiet, but you can see he could be a devil if he wanted. He's got this glimmer in his eyes that makes me wonder what he's thinking sometimes, because you know whatever it is, it'll be hilarious, and he drives a motorcycle which immediately made me think of you and that phase you went through where you would only date boys with a motorcycle. Tex laughed when I told him. He said no girl's ever been on his bike, but he'd let you—after I'd shown him a picture. A good picture, don't worry. It was the one of you at the fair that summer before you left and you have one hand on the straw hat the wind is trying to snatch off your head. You're laughing at me, your hair a soft gold in the setting sun. I love that picture. It captured so much of you.

"Oh, she is beautiful," Ellen said, looking at my phone over my shoulder. "You didn't mention you were twins."

I'd thought Austin would have told her.

"Yes, but she's older."

She took the phone from me and peered more closely at you, then at me. I felt her comparing us and I shifted in my chair. I wondered if she was thinking how much better suited you were for her son and that Austin had made the wrong choice picking me.

But she grinned and returned the phone, saying, "You're similar, but you're not entirely identical. You're different in the eyes. Yours are softer. Hers are restless."

I looked at the photo afterwards, trying to see what she was talking about, but I couldn't see anything. It was like looking at myself. It's always like I'm looking at myself, except ... she's sort of right, isn't she? You always were restless. You were never happy being like everyone else in town. Traveler's feet, *isn't that what Grandma used to say? You always wanted to leave, to see the world. I did too, but I was never as driven as you. I never applied for a million scholarships or sent thousands of applications to every school in the world, but ours. I never really even thought about what I would do once high school ended. That was where we always differed. You always had a plan. You knew what you wanted. I envied that about you. I felt it most when you got back all those acceptance letters from all those schools desperate to have you. I didn't understand how I could be born with no talent, unless wandering through life is some kind of accomplishment.*

Doesn't matter. That's all in the past now, I suppose. No use drudging it all up and trying to sort it out. Besides, I know what I want now. I've known for a while, and it's not exactly a talent, but I at least have a goal. I want to see the world, or at least as much of it as I can. Then, I want a family, one I can call my own.

Chapter Twelve

Dear Rachel,

I saw Dad today. He was in line at the grocery store, a basket of canned beans hooked on his arm. He saw me and we both stiffened. It would have been hilarious, except it was so uncomfortable. I imagine it's how couples feel after breaking up and seeing each other for the first time since. It's even more awkward since he's my dad.

I tried to count how long it had been since I screamed at him in Aunt Judy's kitchen. I count back almost a year and I'm amazed; in a town as small as ours, how on earth had I not seen him since? That's not the point, I think and try not to turn and leave. It was tempting. My buggy was empty. I could have just abandoned it there in the middle of the aisle and walked out. But I couldn't. My flats had grown hooks into the ground and I was stuck to stand there and watch with growing panic as he left his spot and started towards me.

"Kaylee," he said. "It's good to see you."

Clipped. Polite. I expected a handshake.

"I've been out of town," I tell him. "Went to Montana for a couple of weeks."

It wasn't any of his business where I was or what I was doing, but I was bragging a bit. I wanted to show him that he wasn't the only one who was capable of moving on and living their life.

He blinked. "Montana? USA?"

As far as I know, that is the only Montana I know, but I don't say that. There's a Miami in Manitoba so maybe somewhere in Canada, there's a Montana?

"Yes," I said. "With my boyfriend. We went to see his parents."

His eyes widened. "Boyfriend? Parents?" He rubs lightly at the back of his head as though the concept was completely foreign. "I didn't know you had a boyfriend."

"Well, seeing as how you cut me from your life as a daughter, I didn't think it was any of your business," I told him flatly. "But, yes, I have a boyfriend. It'll be a year at the end of this month."

"A year?" His eyes practically bulge out of their sockets. "I had no idea ... I didn't think..." He puffed up his cheeks and exhaled. "Well, good for you, I guess. Glad you're happy." He shifted, the tins of beans rolling back and forth in his basket. "And your mom? How is she?"

"Doing fantastic," I said without missing a beat. "She's cleaned herself up and couldn't be happier."

"Yeah?" He was no longer looking at me. "That's nice." His answers were vague and distant and I could see the wheels turning in that thick skull of his. "Maybe I'll—"

"Don't you dare," I warned him, my anger clouding my better judgment.

He started and blinked down at me. "What?"

"You leave her alone," I tell him. "She is in a good place. She's working hard to better herself, no thanks to you. You have no right to return to her life now when you weren't there when she needed you most."

I knew I'd hit the nail on the head when his shoulders sag a bit. It only makes me want to pitch the cans at his head.

"I wasn't..." he trailed off. We both knew he was lying. "It's good she's better. I hated seeing her like that."

I don't say anything.

Finally, when the silence becomes an over strained elastic about to snap, he drew back.

"I should..." He jerked a thumb back over his shoulder.

"You should," I said and promptly maneuvered my cart around him and stalked off.

It felt good. Seeing his face, seeing the realization as it became clear that he'd royally messed up, priceless. I couldn't have asked for a better resolution. I just hope he takes my warning seriously and stays away from Mom. She really is on the mend, at least, as far as I've been told by the doctors. Her recovery is coming along. Lots of ups and downs, but she hasn't had a drink since her admittance and that's the important thing. I asked them to call me, but they won't. Instead, the doctor will bring me up in her next therapy session and see if he can't get her to see me. I'm not entirely sure that will ever happen, but I'll go if she wants me there.

We're back from Montana, in case that wasn't made clear. We returned to a flood of rain and a miserable sky. Didn't matter though, being home had been worth it. While I loved being with his family, it was comforting being back with my own things.

I got tearful leaving. Ellen crying didn't help matters. She held me so tight, I almost couldn't breathe, and she kept telling me, over and over again, come back, okay? You better come back. Anytime. Promise me. *I promised.*

"Let her go, Mom," Austin teased. "You'll see her again."

Ellen nodded, rubbing tears off her cheeks and sniffling. "Thanksgiving, right? Both of them. American and Canadian, and Christmas."

"You missed New Year's," Tex had said, standing a bit away next to his dad, hands in his pocket, grinning at the exchange.

"Yes!" Ellen said, eyes going wide. "You need to stay for New Year's."

"And Valentines," Tex added.

"Why don't we just move in?" Austin said, laughing.

Hope sparked in the brilliant smile that spread across Ellen's face. "You could. You really could. We have the space and Kaylee's welcome, of course."

"I'm joking, Mom." Austin leaned in and kissed her cheek. "But we will see you again soon."

I managed to contain myself until we were in the car. Then the tears came and Austin laughed at me.

"Will you two stop it?" he said, reaching across and taking my hand. "You're both acting like you'll never see each other again."

It didn't feel like that at all. I couldn't wait to see Ellen again. And Tim and Tex. I've just never been any good at goodbyes, but this felt worse.

Chapter Thirteen

Dear Rachel,

It's happened. Austin asked me to marry him today. I wasn't expecting it. I guess no one ever really does. We'd gone for a walk and we passed our favorite spot outside the hardware store as we always did, and he stopped. I'd been holding his hand so I jerked to a stop, not anticipating it, and there he was, just standing there, in the same spot I'd kissed him that first night.

He did that sometimes. He'd pull me to him when we reached that exact patch of concrete and he'd kiss me. I waited for it, for the tug, for his lips. Instead, he'd gone down on his knees, right in the middle of the town, in the middle of the afternoon and he'd looked up at me with those clear, crystalline eyes and I knew. God, I knew what was coming. I knew it and I was already gasping. My heart was racing. I was crying and he hadn't even asked me.

"Kaylee?"

My palm was clammy in his grasp. I knew he could feel it, but he didn't let go. People were beginning to gather. A low murmuring was taking over the whispers of the wind. But I could only focus on him, on his mouth, that beautiful and distracting mouth.

"I had this all written out," he said, chuckling sheepishly, a bit nervously. "I don't really remember much of it now."

"Yes!" I blurted.

I don't know why. Maybe he was taking too long. Maybe I needed to just get it over with so I could have his lips on mine.

He laughed. "I haven't asked."

I licked my lips. "Right. Sorry."

He squeezed my fingers. "But I like your answer."

It was my turn to giggle tensely.

He cleared his throat. "Do you remember that night we first met?"

I thought about the kiss and had a clear image of his guitar case lying in a puddle of light as he held me.

"No, when we first met," he said, inexplicably reading my mind. "The first time, when you destroyed half the diner."

My face blazed hot at the vivid memory. "Vaguely," I lied.

"I remember it like it was yesterday. I can't see spaghetti without remembering—" I laughed. He grinned and continued. "I remember looking up and ... there you were, just standing there, eyes such an amazing blue. I didn't even notice the chaos until it was already over and you were gone. I came back the next night only because I wanted to see you again. I didn't leave because every time I was with you, I was already exactly where

I wanted to be. You're my home, the place I belong. You're the best adventure I've ever had and I don't want it to end. I need you, Kaylee. I need your light and your laughter, and your chaos, in my life. I need to see us on a porch one day, watching the sunset with our hands, old and wrinkly, clasped together. I need to be the man you wake up with every morning, the man you turn to when you need a friend. I need to be the reason you never feel lonely again. Maybe I'm being selfish, but in return, I swear I will never leave you. I will never hurt you. I will love you until there is nothing left of me but ashes. I will give you everything you need and work to give you everything you want. Just..." He fished out a small, velvet box from his pocket and pulled back the lid. "Please say yes."

I might have said yes ... again. I just remember throwing myself into his arms and sobbing into his shoulder. I remember him putting a ring on my finger—a delicate band of silver with a square diamond on top—and kissing me, the kiss as salty as it had been that first time.

It was perfect, Rach. So perfect. How could anything put a damper on that moment? Except something did, a realization that this wasn't so perfect. How could it be when the most important part of my life wouldn't be there—you? The one person I want to rush home to tell, the one person I always imagined sharing this moment with me, and you're not here. You won't be my maid of honor. You won't help me find my dress. No one will. I'll have no one in the change room with me, fixing my veil and promising me that everything would be all right. No one will be there to walk me down the aisle. No one will be sitting on my side of the church, wiping away tears, and watching me start a new chapter in my life.

You would think that by now, I would be used to it. It really shouldn't have bothered me nearly as much as it did, yet I couldn't escape the sickening realization that I truly was completely alone.

"You're not alone," Austin told me when I expressed my fears to him earlier. "You have me, and my family."

I did have his family. I really shouldn't have asked for more. The moment we called up his parents on Skype *and he told her he'd proposed, Ellen had promptly burst into tears. Tim had to press a Kleenex into her hand and calm her down before she pulled herself together to ask to see the ring.*

"It's a beautiful pick, Austin," she told him once I'd lowered my hand away from the camera. "Have you picked a date? Will it be here or there? Was your mother excited, Kaylee?"

"We haven't picked a date yet," Austin said for me, my throat too stuffed with emotions to speak. "We'll sort all that out later. Where's Tex?"

The conversation was momentarily derailed as Tim talked about the hundred new heads they'd bought the day before. I would have been terrified if I didn't know what they were talking about. Cattle, in case you're curious.

"Putting them down for the evening," Tim said.

But that conversation only lasted as long as it took for Tim finish his explanation. Ellen jumped right back to weddings, asking about dresses and cakes and if I'll be wearing gloves and if I had a theme yet.

It was all too much. I couldn't answer any of those things. I didn't know any of those things. I never had anyone to talk to about them. I never looked at those glossy magazines at the store for ideas. That was always you, Rach. You were the dreamer, the one with fantasies about your special day. I had nothing.

"I don't know!" The moment the words burst out of me, I was mortified. I couldn't believe what I'd done. My hands flew to my mouth. "I'm sorry. I'm so sorry!"

Ellen said nothing, but the look ... oh, Rach, the look. I'd hurt her. I'd taken her excitement and happiness and thrown them back in her face. She hated me. I knew it. I couldn't blame her. What sort of person shouts at someone just for being nice to them? It wasn't her fault my family was screwed up. It wasn't her fault I wasn't you.

I shot off the sofa and ran, unable to sit there and feel her staring at me. I could hear Austin talking in the next room, low murmurs. No doubt he was explaining that I was an orphan and, despite having a perfectly healthy mother and father, I had no one. Now, she was probably pitying me.

"Kaylee?" Austin found me in the kitchen, slumped over the sink.

"I can't do it," I panted. "I can't have a big wedding. I can't have cake and themes or ... dresses." I turned when he pulled me up and around. "I don't know anything about getting married and this is supposed to be special—"

"For us," he said quietly. "It's supposed to be special for us, and if you want the wedding here, at home, with just two people, then that's what we'll do. If you want to go to my parent's ranch and have it in the yard or in the ocean, or on the moon, we'll do that. It doesn't matter what you're wearing or if the cake's bought from the shop down the street, I just want to be with you."

"But we're supposed to have memories of this day," I told him. "It's the start of our lives together. We need to make it amazing."

He shrugged. "All right, so we will. Come on."

He took my hand and led me back to the living room. His parent's faces were still wedged in the tiny screen of his laptop. They both smiled when Austin nudged me down on the cushions opposite the coffee table.

"I'm sorry," Ellen said. "I shouldn't have been so ... pushy."

Now, I felt like an absolute jerk.

"No, it's not you. I promise it wasn't. I'm just..." I licked my lips. "I don't know what I'm doing," I confessed and felt my eyes burn and my throat tighten. "Rachel was supposed to be here with me. She was supposed to do all the things sisters are supposed to do, you know? She was always the one with the best advice and she's not and I don't..."

Austin put his arms around me when my voice broke. I tried not to cry, but tears still escaped and dampened his shoulder.

"Sweetheart." Ellen's soft voice pulled my face back to the screen. "You're not alone, love. You've got us and there are many, many of us." She laughed a little at her own joke. "And you, my lovely girl, are one of us now. You just tell us what you want and we'll make it happen."

Tim nodded. "Austin's got about five hundred cousins, aunts, uncles, and grandparents on all sides. Plus, friends that are like family and an entire town that'll move oceans to make sure you two are all right. You don't worry about a thing, and uh..." He cleared his throat and shifted a notch closer. "I'd be right honored if you'd let me walk you down the aisle. That is if you don't already have someone."

It really didn't seem possible. How on earth did I get so lucky?

Chapter Fourteen

Dear Rachel,

It's nine am on a beautiful Sunday afternoon and I'm wearing the most stunning dress anyone has ever seen and I'm sitting alone in the bathroom of my changing room in the church I booked almost eight months earlier and it's all wrong. Not the dress or the church, but the day itself.

Outside these doors are people who have spent the better part of half a year helping prepare for one of the biggest days of my life, people who I have laughed with, cried with, celebrated with, called family, people who have accepted me for everything I am ... and I would give them all up right now for just one day with you. This day. This moment. I need you here. I need you by my side. I need to look over and see you in the crowd, smiling and happy for me. Every day until this moment, I kept telling myself that I got this, that I could go out there and marry the man of my dreams and be okay with you not being here. But I can't lie to myself anymore.

I'm not okay.

I'm not okay.

I'm not.

I don't want to do this alone. It's not right that it's my big day and no one I care about is here. Not you. Not Mom. Not Dad. To be fair, I didn't invite him. But I did send a card to Mom six months ago, and then again four months. I even went to the facility and tried to ask her in person, and was informed that she'd been released nearly two months before. They wouldn't tell me where she'd gone and no one in town had seen her so I'm thinking she wants to be alone. I don't know. Doesn't matter I guess. I really don't care about them. It's you I want.

Austin's at the door. I guess I've been in here too long. They're worried about me. God, he must think I've got cold feet.

"I'm all right," I tell him. "I just need a minute."

"Baby, let me in," is his response and there's fear in his voice that cuts deep into my very heart.

I'm going to let him in. Of course I am. I'm going to walk down that aisle, because everything I want is at the end of that carpet. I will do it and I will smile and I will be happy, but inside, I will hurt. I will bleed for all the lost opportunities, all the things I may never do with you.

I miss you, Rach. I miss you so much.

Chapter Fifteen

Dear Rachel,

I hope you're getting my letters and postcards. The nurses at the hospital swear they've been leaving them for you, but I won't know until we get back next month.

It's been amazing. I've been seeing so much. I never knew all of this was out there, just there, waiting to be seen and admired. Austin and I spend most of our days wandering through museums, following winding paths deep into various parks and trails, and taking pictures at every statue we come across. Austin is in deep love with the new camera his parents gave us as a wedding present. He insists he's not, but he practically leaps out of his skin if anyone so much as touches it. It's adorable. I love watching him when he's lost in his element. He has an amazing eye for capturing the most beautiful things. He says his favorite thing to photograph is me, but I like his landscape photos. Each one takes my breath away. I want to frame them. I think I will when we get home. I want to put them everywhere for people to see.

He's telling me I'm being silly, but I know I'm not. You'll see. I've sent you a few for your letter box.

We're currently in a tiny French village on the south of Quebec. The people are gracious and welcoming and everything smells like freshly baked bread and summer. It's our last night here before we drive out to New Brunswick. From there, we're going to go to Nova Scotia to explore their many cemeteries. Austin's excited about that. I worry about him sometimes.

Anyway, I'm having such an amazing time. I wish you were here.

Chapter Sixteen

Dear Rachel,

You're going to be an auntie. We found out this morning and I have never been so terrified. I keep wondering if we're ready. What if it's too soon? We've only been married a year. What if we make a mistake? What if I do something wrong? There are so many questions, so many concerns, so many ways I could drop it. It's a very serious possibility. My clumsiness hasn't magically vanished. I still drop things all the time. A baby squirms and fusses and cries ... oh God...

"You're not going to drop him," Austin keeps repeating, grinning like the biggest fool. It's been the same one since we found out. This huge curve in his lips and an almost dazed look in his eyes. It's incredibly endearing if I could just focus past my own churning terror. "You're going to be an amazing mother."

A mother. I'm going to be a mother, Rach. I can't even wrap my head around it.

Chapter Seventeen

Dear Rachel,

It's a girl!

Chapter Eighteen

Dear Rachel,

June 16, 2016 at three-twelve am, weighting six pounds, three ounces, Richelle Jacklynn Paige came screaming into the world. She has ten fingers and ten toes and a head full of soft, dark curls. Her eyes are blue, and she is the most perfect little soul I have ever looked upon. I even forgive her for the twelve hours of labor and the realignment of my sanity. The moment they put her in my arms, it hit me that this was the thing I'd been missing in my life, that piece I couldn't find. This tiny bundle of pink with just a blink of her eyes has filled the void inside me.

"She's perfect, Kaylee." Austin stroked the top of our daughter's head, his hand enormous compared to her tiny head.

"Yeah, she is." I nuzzled her against my cheek, loving her soft scent of baby and the downy tickle of her hair against my skin.

"Thank you," he said and I looked up at him, bemused. "She's the greatest gift anyone's ever given me."

I felt myself smile. "That makes two of us then I guess." I peered down at Richelle's small, slumbering face. "You've given me everything."

Ellen and Tim arrived later that evening. Ellen, actually, arrived a full second before Tim, bursting into the room, hair in disarray, eyes wide and shiny with excitement. They swung over the room and latched on to me and Richelle and widened. She made a loud oh sound and hurried over to the bed.

She bent over my arm and studied Richelle, what little was visible beneath the swaddling blankets. Tears welled and spilled down her cheeks, making my own eyes burn.

"Oh, sweetheart," she breathed, half choked. "Look at her. She's perfect."

"We thought so," Austin said, clapping hands with his father. "It was touch and go, but ultimately, we decided to keep her."

His mother wasn't listening. She was tracing the soft lines of Richelle's cheek with one bent knuckle.

"May I?"

I passed Richelle to her and watched, feeling the loss of her weight, as she was cuddled against a chest that wasn't mine. I didn't like it, but I let Ellen sway with her, kiss her pert little nose, her cheeks, her brow.

"My perfect girl," she was saying, nuzzling Richelle's cheek with her lips. "What a beautiful girl you are." She sniffled and raised her head just a notch to ask, "What's her name?"

I looked to Austin who shrugged and motioned for me to tell them.

"Richelle Jacklynn Paige."

Ellen stopped rocking. For a moment, she didn't move at all. She simply stood there, staring at Richelle like someone had just stabbed her through the heart. I began to wonder if I'd said something wrong, I was about to apologize when she made a sound between a moan and a whimper and curled the bundle higher against her chest, high enough to press her face into the crock of my daughter's shoulder and cry.

"Mom?"

Austin took a step forward, as stunned and concerned as I was as the subtle tremors in her shoulders quickened, becoming gut wrenching sobs that shook her entire body.

Tim got to her first. He guided her over to a chair, where she dropped with Richelle and just wept, dampening the blanket.

"Darling," Tim was saying softly, giant hand stroking his wife's heaving back. "You're going to scare the baby."

The crying didn't stop, but she raised her head, her face shiny and contorted with unimaginable pain. She kissed Richelle's cheek, streaking it with tears.

"Your Uncle Jack would have loved you," she croaked. "He would have loved you so much."

Now I was crying. I hadn't thought when going through names with Austin just how much they would affect me and Ellen. Both were picked to honor the people we loved, people who couldn't be with us, couldn't see our daughter grow up. We wanted her to know them, to carry on their memories.

No matter what, Rach, you and Jackson, you will never be forgotten.

Chapter Nineteen

Dearest Rachel,

Mom's made the decision. I don't know how. Maybe over the phone. Maybe in person. Maybe through fax. However it was done, however she came to this ground breaking decision, she never came to me. I wasn't even aware she was back in town. She would have to be, wouldn't she? There's papers to sign and an order to things, isn't there? But she couldn't take two minutes to call me and inform me of this life altering decision.

I want to hurt her. It's powerful and maddening, this feeling writhing inside me. I want to find her and shake her and demand to know what she's thinking. How could she do this? I could she not tell me?

I'm sitting outside the doctor's office now, Richelle is sleeping in her stroller. I'm waiting for someone to tell me how to stop this. There has to be a way. There has to be someone in this building with the power to overrule the deranged decisions of a mad woman. I've called Austin as well. I need him here with me. I need him to help me stay calm. I need him to take Richelle if I can't.

But don't worry. Whatever happens, I won't let them take you, Rach.

*****

Dear Rachel,

This is Austin. I'm sorry. I don't normally read Kaylee's letters, but it fell out when I was going through Richelle's snack bag and ... I'm not entirely sure Kaylee will be finishing it. The letter, I mean. But I know she'd want to. She'd want you to know she tried, Rachel. She fought hard. I was there. I watched her. She's always been incredible, but she was a warrior standing in that doctor's office. But she wasn't able to change their mind and I'm so sorry. Your mom is legal guardian over you and her decision is final. Kaylee threatened to sue. She told them she'd get a lawyer. She'd fight this—and we would have. I promise you that. But it was already done. It was too late. I'm so sorry.

She's resting right now. She's in pieces and I don't know what to do for her. I don't know how to help. But I'm going to do my best, I swear it. I hope you know that. I hope you'll pass on knowing that I'll be here, keeping her safe and happy, and loving her with every bit of me.

Your loving brother in law,
Austin

Chapter Twenty

Dearest Rachel,

Your room is empty. I went there today. I don't know why. You'd been buried almost two years now. Maybe I wanted to see if I could feel you again, if the sound of your heart beeping through machines still echoed along the walls.

It doesn't.

I waited and listened for hours. The nurses must have thought I was mad, just standing there, in the doorway of an empty hospital room.

But it's gone.

You're gone.

I'm waiting for the peace part to kick in. Everyone keeps telling me it'll happen. But how do you feel peace when a literal part of you is gone?

I'm holding this letter, standing here in the room that was once yours and I have no idea where to put it. The box is gone. I don't know what Mom did with it. I haven't seen her. She wasn't at the funeral. Maybe she kept them. Maybe she had them buried with you. I hope she did. I think I'd sleep a little better knowing a part of me is with you, too.

I love you, Rachel. I don't know if I ever told you enough. But I will, over and over again, when we meet again.

Love always, your clumsy, sarcastic, annoying sister,
Kaylee

P/S Richelle has gotten to stealing Bailey's strawberries. I don't know how she found the notch in the fence, she's only two, after all, but I heard her giggling and I have a feeling you had a hand in it.

Have You Tried…

The End

To my darling readers

I think this is my favorite part of releasing a book, the part where I get to thank you for taking time to read my work and hope you've enjoyed it. It's been such an honor working with the authors of this boxset on such a worthy cause. Those of the school, Ms. Sherrilyn Kenyon's moving and heartfelt foreword have all served as a great reminder of just how much we don't know about dyslexia. I've heard people use it in passing as a joke and it never really dawned on me just how it affects people until having worked so closely with so many wonderful people. It's truly been inspiring.

So, I thank you again, my lovely reader, for giving Letters to Rachel a chance, and thank you Ciara Knight for allowing me the honor of participating, the authors who have been so welcoming and gracious, Ms. Kenyon for opening my eyes to the cause, and finally, the men, women, and children of GRACEPOINT. I would also like to give a huge shout out to my beta readers, Sam, Jaime, Nanette, Diana, Ashley, Amber, and Kim. I love you ladies so much. And my editor, Katherine, who is my unwavering strength and voice of reason. Never lastly, my family for never failing to love me, flaws and all. Thank you all for always being my sunshine. You are all blessings I am forever thankful for.

With all the love in the world,
Airicka Phoenix

About Airicka Phoenix

Airicka Phoenix lives in a world where unicorns, fairies and mermaids run amok through her home on a daily basis. When she's not chasing after pixies and rounding up imps, also known as her four children, she can be found conjuring imaginary friends to play with. Airicka is the prolific author of over eighteen novels for those who crave strong, female leads, sexy alpha heroes and out of control desires. She's a multi genre author who writes young adult, new adult and adult contemporary and paranormal romance.

For more about Airicka and the realm she rules with an iron fist—and tons of chocolate—visit her at: www.AirickaPhoenix.com

TRANSCENDING DARKNESS
Crime Lord Interconnected Standalone
Book 1

One: Sign the contract.

Juliette Romero had a debt to pay, a debt that wasn't even hers. But it was the only way to keep her family safe and all she had to do was sell her body and soul to the devil.

Killian McClary wasn't called the Scarlet Wolf for nothing. He'd been the head of the McClary Organization since he was fifteen and had built a reputation for being a ruthless son of a bitch when it came to running the city's underbelly, not to mention merciless when it came to punishing those who betray him. He didn't believe in weaknesses. Only results. Juliette, with her shy smiles and hot little body was a weakness unlike any other and yet he was powerless to resist one more taste of her sweet flesh.

Two: Become his for a year.

When given the choice between her life or her body, what could Juliette possibly do, but submit to a man whose very name invoked fear in the hearts of others? She just never anticipated falling for his dark, hungry eyes and clever hands, or the way the beast in him made her feel oddly safe and cherished.

But what will happen when Killian's dark past finally catches up to him and threatens the woman he can no longer imagine himself without? What will happen when both sides find themselves caught in a web of passion, lies and broken promises? Can Juliette tame the wolf or will her love for him devour them both?

Three: Don't fall in love.

Boundaries will be crossed, loyalties will be tested and lives will be changed forever.

AVAILABLE in Paperback & eBook

Also by Airicka Phoenix

TOUCH SAGA
Touching Smoke
Touching Fire
Touching Eternity

THE LOST GIRL SERIES
Finding Kia
Revealing Kia

REGENERATION SERIES
When Night Falls

THE BABY SAGA
Forever His Baby
Bye-Bye Baby
Be My Baby
Always Yours, Baby

SONS OF JUDGMENT SAGA
Octavian's Undoing
Gideon's Promise

CRIME LORD INTERCONNECTED SERIES
Transcending Darkness
The Devil's Beauty

STANDALONE
Games of Fire
Betraying Innocence
The Voyeur Next Door
My Soul For You
Kissing Trouble

ANTHOLOGY
Whispered Beginnings: A Clever Fiction Anthology
Midnight Surrender Anthology

WHERE YOU BELONG
A Runaway Series Novella

MK Smith & Lori Freeland

A girl can run from her roots, but she can't escape her heart.

Six years ago, after a practical joke gone wrong, Hendrix Marshall blew the single stoplight in the town of Runaway, Wisconsin, and never looked back. But when Grandpa Joe—retired hippie, Jimmy Hendrix devotee, and the man who raised her—ends up in the hospital, she reluctantly agrees to take a cab home. As long as she can keep the meter running. But then she comes heel-to-boot with Alexander Ryland—former best friend, sometimes nemesis, always secret crush. And his ocean-blue eyes still have the power to launch cartwheels in her belly. Too bad his freestyle attitude makes her certifiable. He's the reason she left. He won't be the reason she stays. Even if he's determined to collect interest on the kiss she's owed him for the last ten years.

Chapter 1

As far as small towns went—
Runaway, Wisconsin was pretty much the perfect cliché.

John Mellencamp once said you could breathe in a small town. Maybe so. As long as you didn't mind everyone knowing what your breath smelled like.

The local cab that had picked me up from the county airport pulled into Papa Joe's driveway at the end of the cul-de-sac. The house hadn't changed in the six years I'd been gone. The L-shaped, brick ranch with narrow rectangular windows still had the same 1960s doctor's office vibe.

According to Papa Joe, his house on a hill was the trifecta of prime real estate—surrounded by the highway for a quick escape, a corn field for Norman Rockwell photo ops, and a golf course for culture and class. He dismissed the bull-breeding farm at the other end of the street. No use for bull semen, I guess.

I shoved a twenty over the seat to the cabbie, who also happened to be Mr. Jensen, my former fourth grade teacher. Filling me in on his life story, he'd explained he was too old to teach and not hip enough for Uber, so he'd invested in an old cab.

Not sure how he paid the bills, since in the tiny town of Runaway, Wisconsin, you could pretty much hoof it anywhere you needed to go.

"Not taking your money, Hendrix." My ex-teacher slung an arm over the seat and twisted toward me.

Yep. Hendrix. That's what happens when you let a hippie with an obsession for 70s guitarists name a kid. I'd be living Papa Joe's legacy forever.

Mr. J. cocked an eyebrow the way he did when I'd turned in my homework late. "Papa Joe's gonna be real glad you're back."

My grandpa had been everyone's grandpa ever since I could remember—his kitchen table more popular than Runaway's one and only bar.

"I'm just here for a quick visit." I thought about asking Mr. J. to keep the meter running, but that might get expensive. With Papa Joe in the hospital, I figured I needed to be here at least through the weekend. Wednesday tops. Then I'd hightail it back to Orange County. Even if I no longer had a job to hightail it back to. But that wasn't something Papa Joe needed to know.

"Thanks for the ride, Mr. J." I slung my purse over my shoulder and pulled my carry-on with me out of the cab.

As soon as I shut the door, the cab engine sputtered, wheezed, and died. A small black cloud drifted from under the hood. And something inside me sighed.

Not a good omen for my homecoming. I'd stayed away for a reason. A number of them actually. But they all rolled into two words—small town. The big-city girl inside me had been trying to claw her way free since the day she realized there was a bigger world out there than cow-tipping, cornfields, and cheese curds.

Mr. Jensen stepped out of the cab and pulled up the hood.

"Need any help?" Not that there was anything I could do. Machines weren't my thing. Marketing was. Or it used to be. Unless one of the thousand resumes I'd scattered over Southern California suddenly revived my shorted-out career.

"Happens all the time." He waved me off and bent into the smoke for a closer look.

Missing half a wheel, my rolling bag swayed and limped behind me like a drunken tractor. Couldn't make myself replace the plastered carry-on with a sober suitcase. It was part of the set Papa Joe got me for high school graduation.

As I passed, I saluted the statue of Mary bumped up against the bronze bust of Martin Luther on the front walk. Even though Papa Joe was full-on Lutheran, when it came to the ever-after, he believed in hedging his bets.

A sudden prickle of dread rooted me to the concrete and in the reality of why I came—assess the situation, get him out of the backwards county hospital, and set up some kind of home care. Or better yet, get him to come back to Orange County with me where I could keep an eye on him.

Couldn't lose the only family I had. Couldn't leave him alone and weak and vulnerable. Not the grandpa who stepped in as dad when my mom didn't want me. The man who bedazzled my bike, took an online course in the *Art of the French Braid*, never once booked me on a guilt trip for hightailing the heck out of this going-nowhere town, and traveled to see me on every major holiday.

This whole situation could turn out for the best. He could move to an apartment near me, live near a real hospital, and we'd see each other more often. Win, win, and triple win.

I waited outside a moment in no hurry to enter a silent, empty house void of Papa Joe's laughter and Old Spice. My hand shook when I stuck my key in the door.

But the house wasn't silent. Or empty.

Shouts and laughs and an occasional groan drifted from the lower level.

Letting my purse and carry-on fall to the worn yellow linoleum, I beelined for the wide staircase at the end of the living room and tore down the carpeted steps.

Not a stellar idea.

Where the wall opened up to reveal the giant walk-out family room, my heel slipped. I stopped, dropped, and skidded down the next three steps on my butt, my skirt shimmied up my thighs, and a mess of hair escaped from my blonde-business bun.

Using the iron railing like a guard rail, I grabbed on tight, using my wrists as bungee cords to slow my fall. Only they didn't stretch—they jerked me to a hard stop that came with an embarrassing grunt and a sharp pain shooting up both arms.

"Bug! You're here." Papa Joe stood in the middle of the room shaking what I hoped was a drained bottle of Budweiser at a field full of life-size football players on a TV screen that covered the entire wall.

And he wasn't alone or weak or vulnerable.

Tall and reedy, his trimmed mustache matched his gray ponytail. Wearing a threadbare Jimi Hendrix T-shirt and a pair of wide-bottomed dark jeans, he looked like a first-generation hippie who found his way home from Woodstock after a forty-year detour.

His three VA buddies—my self-appointed uncles—sprawled on the couch and recliners, decked out in leather and jeans and square-toed boots, resembling retirees from Grizzly Adam's biker gang.

What. The. Heck.

"Bug's back." Coop jumped up, twisting his Yosemite Sam mustache. "Grab some pizza, girl."

"It's Chicken Supreme, your favorite." Papa Joe gave me a sideways grin, before going back to yelling at the Packers' offense.

Bo and Duke tipped their beers at me.

That prickle of dread grew into pissed-off porcupine needles. I pulled myself up, yanked down my skirt, and marched in front of the screen to a multitude of boos and a pelting of popcorn. "You're supposed to be in the hospital. Sick."

"I am sick." Papa Joe pointed to the screen. "Did you see that turnover? The Packers are 27-26, two minutes left at the fifty-yard line, and that wuss just took a knee." He motioned for me to move.

I locked my knees and stared him down. "You called me from the hospital." I'd read the caller ID.

Taking my shoulders, he guided me out of the way of the end zone. "Big playoff game. Hospital screen's too small, and they nixed the beer when the guys showed up. So I checked myself out."

"You checked yourself..." I surveyed the empty pizza boxes piled on the coffee table and the beer bottles scattered around the room. "You had a heart attack, and you're throwing a frat party?"

"More like a kegger." Duke chuckled, patting a belly that hadn't missed a meal since '75.

Grandpa shot him a look obviously meant to shut him up. Or shut him down. "Not a heart attack, Bug. Just a little angina."

Those pissed-off porcupine needles bristled up and down my back. "You sounded like you were dying." John Mellencamp lied. I'd been back a total of twenty minutes, and the last thing I could do was breathe.

"Are you really mad I'm not?" He popped the top of another beer on the edge of the scratched coffee table and offered it to me. "Kick off those fancy L.A. heels and take a load off."

"I live in Orange County." Believe me, it mattered. I crossed my arms. "Stop acting like you're nineteen. When you're sixty-five."

"Only on the outside." Bo swiped the beer I didn't take from Papa Joe and downed it in one chug.

"Hey, Bug." Papa Joe balanced on the arm of the couch. "If you don't want to watch the game, can you run down to City Hall and collect something for me?"

"An arrest warrant for an illegal frat?" A lie detector for whatever else he was about to tell me?

"No. The mayor." He punched up the volume on the game.

Had he lost his mind? "You want me to bring you old man Miller?"

"He retired. I need the new guy." He checked his watch. "The annual scavenger hunt started ten minutes ago. Playing for HECC this year, and I'm in for a Benjamin."

In a town of a few thousand, the only two churches—Hope Eternal Catholic Church (HECC) and Last Chance Lutheran—were constantly in competition. And since it wasn't the Middle Ages, they vied for God's ear via the annual scavenger hunt. Weirdly, whichever church won had the most attendance, the highest baptism rate, and the most tithes that year.

I wanted answers, not a job. "I'm not bringing you the mayor."

Papa Joe reached into his pocket and tossed me the keys to his old VW Bug. Didn't know if he got me or the car first. "I don't actually need the mayor. Rules changed. The scavenger hunt's gone digital. I just need a pic of the mayor in his office."

Digital? A pic? Did I miss the invasion of the pod people? "Who are you, and what have you done with Papa Joe?"

"Future don't slow for no one, girl," Coop said.

"Got to jump into all that cloud nonsense." Papa Joe waved his hand heavenward.

And officially lost his mind. Or I did. Because I headed to the garage, got into his car, and took the three-mile trek to City Hall.

Chapter 2

*Runaway's jail had a ticket machine installed in 1974
with a thousand-ticket roll. Now serving 376.*

Runaway hit its peak in the late 60's with a storefront combination City Hall, Sheriff's office, pizza place, post office, and library—if *library* meant a couple hundred donated paperback romance novels.

I parked out front and tried the double doors into City Hall first. Locked. Since I wasn't hungry, had nothing to mail, and I'd lost my library card six years ago, I went in through the Sheriff's Office—which was open, but empty.

"Hello?" I called down the hall, my voice bouncing off the recently repainted block-cement walls and carrying back in a creepy echo. "Anyone here?"

If I didn't know better, it was like I'd stepped into a reboot of *Scream*. But in Runaway, the lunch hour tended to runaway—for at least two hours every day.

The building's usual ode to mildew mixed with the oil paint, and gave me an instant headache. But I moved farther inside, careful to make noise.

Didn't want to risk getting shot by Sheriff Dixon. Thanks to Vietnam and a purple heart, he had one working eye, one good ear, three-quarters of a trigger finger, and a platoon's worth of PTSD.

Just as I turned to retrace my steps, a deep voice yelled, "In the back."

And not just any voice. A voice that twist-tied my chest. A deep, throaty, guitar-thrum of a voice I hadn't heard since I'd bailed on this town after graduation. Actually, Alexander Ryland *was* the reason I'd bailed after graduation. I'd always planned on leaving, but he triggered a much earlier departure.

The pressure in my chest didn't stop my feet from making their way down the hall to the jail—where he was cuffed to the far end of the only cell, bent over, picking the lock of his metal bracelet with…wait…was that a *Hello Kitty* hairpin?

Even if the voice hadn't given him away, he didn't have to turn for me to recognize him. Not with the way his upper body owned his T-shirt, that boy-band hair, or those skinny jeans.

Zander Ryland might be the only guy in history to actually rock a pair of skinny jeans. Voted Most Likely to Die in a Dare, the source of my kill-me-now moment, and in a strange way my best friend, he was also the one guy I'd played Spin the Bottle with and not followed through.

Of all things, why had I thought of that?

Lifting his head, he turned—as much as he could with his wrist attached to the bars—and locked me into place with his intense gaze. My breath caught in a short gasp, and his hairpin skidded across the floor, out of the cell, and landed by my toe.

Making no qualms about totally checking me out, he cracked an award-winning grin, his appreciative whistle trailing out as long as his head-to-heel survey.

Six years, and he still had the ability to throw me into a steep spin. *Pull it together. You're mad at him. And you're not some high school wallflower.*

"Wallflower!" Zander belted out the nickname he gave me in eighth grade—the night I refused his spin-the-bottle advances.

The nickname, the tone, the town, the skinny jeans triggered my go-to defense—steaming sarcasm. "Zander the Great." I pointed to the cell. "Guess Runaway finally had the sense to recognize a miscreant." It's not like I was surprised. Well, the hairpin did throw me a little. But the bars? Right on target.

Smoothing my skirt, I went for calm, cool, and collected. Took a step forward, slipped on the hairpin, barely caught my balance, and ended up with frazzled, freaked, and frenzied.

Zander's grin deepened. "Help me out?" He nodded to the fugitive hairpin that almost took me out. "I'm kind of on a time crunch here." He shot a look over my shoulder like he expected to get caught any second.

I stepped on the pin. "I think the idea is for the cuff to stay on your wrist."

"Maybe you could give that hairpin a small kick." He winked at me. "It'll be our secret."

And that deep spin dropped into my stomach and turned sour. "Like how you kept my underwear a secret during the last performance of *The King and I?*" And sent me bolting out of town covered in humiliation because of a stupid dare?

"Aww, come on, Hendrix." Those blue eyes burned into me. "It was supposed to be a tiny little slit down the back of the dress." He held his thumb and index finger apart. "Not an entire costume malfunction."

"You can't cut tulle." And my sarcasm came screeching back.

"Clearly." His grin didn't even toe the line of repentant.

"It wasn't just a costume malfunction it was…" Sweat pooled under my hair on the back of my neck. An anxious rhythm rippled through my heart. My fingers shook, and I steepled them behind my back.

His grin fell. "It was what?"

The launching pad for my escape. The end of my career in theater. The reason I had to pick a new major.

Every time I got on stage my freshman year, I flashed back to that night.

Standing under the hot lights, facing away from the audience, my knees bent in a deep curtsy. And the dress made the most hideous ripping sound, tearing from the neck down, leaving a hundred pairs of eyes privy to my Barbie boy shorts.

I kicked the hairpin under the filing cabinet and pivoted toward the hall where I came in.

"Look," he called after me. "Nobody even remembers."

Whipping around, I nailed him with a glare that screamed—*right!*

He ran his free hand through his hair, fine-tuning the messy style. "A month after you left, Ms. Blaska's dementia went full-throttle, and she took a Sunday stroll around the park *without* her Barbie boy shorts. Or any other clothes." His pointed look digs into me. "Now that, people remember."

"Time's up." A little girl—maybe six or seven—came barreling down the hall, zipped past me, and pressed her face to the bars. "Did you pick the lock?" Brown curls fell from two Princess-Leia buns on each side of her head.

"Got distracted." He tipped his head toward me.

She turned, gave me a once-over like she was deciding if I was worthy of the interruption, then broke into a crooked smile. "You're pretty."

"Uh...thanks?" Kids weren't really my thing. Too sticky. Too unpredictable.

And to prove my point, she rushed me, throwing her arms around my waist, squeezing hard. She sniffed my blouse. "You smell good too."

I lifted my hands, not sure where to put them, and silently pleaded help from Zander. "What happened to that stranger danger video we had to watch in kindergarten?"

Zander laughed. "The school board yanked it for not being culturally diverse."

The girl loosened her grip and backed up. "I'm Abby."

"That's my friend, Hendrix," he said.

"Good try." I walked closer, turned so Abby couldn't see me, and whispered, "Friends don't let friends flash their underwear."

"Papa Joe's favorite guitarist is Jimi Hendrix," Abby said.

"Hendrix is Papa Joe's granddaughter," Zander told her. Then he looked at me. "He's giving her guitar lessons."

"So, Abby." I grip one of the bars. "You spend a lot of time visiting Zander in jail?"

"It's Take Your Kid to Work day." She skipped back to the cell.

Zander had a kid? Sliding from shock into some kind of hollow feeling I didn't quite understand, I stumbled into the file cabinet, then shoved my hip against the side and rested my elbow on top, like I meant to make that move. "You got busy fast after graduation." I tried to check out his ring finger without him noticing.

"Flying solo." Laughing, he wiggled his left hand—definitely noticing—and clanked the metal cuff against the cell. "There's only one girl I'm marrying. I'm holding out till she says yes."

I remembered the posters taped to his locker. "Don't think Angelina Jolie is available."

He shrugged. "I moved on."

In my head, I flipped through the girls he'd gone out with in high school and came up empty. He'd been sweet to all the girls, but he'd put more effort into planning and pulling off dares than setting up dates.

I resisted the urge to ask him any questions, not happy about my sudden clawing need to know who Zander Ryland was dating.

Just stop. Remember, you're mad at him. Furious. He didn't even apologize about your underwear.

I cleared my throat and tipped my chin toward Abby, who had bent over to tie her *Hello Kitty* shoes. "So what's that—forty-four out of fifty of Reverend Lovejoy's Banned Behaviors broken?"

The pastor of Last Chance Lutheran had a print-out taped to his office door—his personal addendum to the Ten Commandments—because apparently, God wasn't quite strict enough.

"No comment." He looked at Abby. "Be a good girl and find me that hairpin. I think it slid under the file cabinet."

She got on her knees, felt around the file cabinet, and pulled out the dusty pin.

"He's handcuffed for a reason," I told her. Although Zander as a dangerous criminal I couldn't quite buy. Zander as a screw-up—now that was probably most of his rap sheet.

Before I could pluck the hairpin from her hand, Zander's older sister walked down the hall dressed in Runaway's Sheriff's uniform, her dishwater-blonde hair pulled back in a low knot, showing a few inches of brown roots near her scalp.

"Brynn?" Zander's sister was the sheriff? What was she now? Like thirty? She'd been older than us, gone off to college, and apparently gotten sucked back into the vortex of small-town hell.

"Hendrix." Her gaze ping-ponged between me and Zander.

"What happened to Sheriff Dixon?" I asked her.

"Retired last year. That crop circle scandal triggered his PTSD." She blasted an accusatory glare toward her brother.

Abby got off her knees and ran to Brynn. "Mommy, Uncle Zander lost the bet." She held up the hairpin.

Uncle Zander. *Uncle* Zander. That hollow feeling I'd had when I thought Abby belonged to him started to fill in around the edges. "So why are you locked up?" Probably should've asked first. Judged later. But this was Zander.

Brynn rubbed her daughter's head. "It's Take Your Kid to Work Day and we were fresh out of bad guys, so Zander volunteered."

He jiggled his cuff. "Anytime now, Brynn."

She waved the key in the air. "It'll cost you a park day."

"You know I'd spend the day at the park with Abby for free. Should've asked for an overnight weekend."

"Okay, Deputy Abigail." Brynn unlocked the cell. "The criminal's done his time. Let him free." She handed her daughter the handcuff key and headed back down the hall. "Meet you in the car, Abs. You can play with the lights. We got a call."

Abby struggled for a few seconds before she opened the cuff holding Zander's wrist to the bar.

With the cuff still attached to his wrist, he walked right into my personal space.

A good head taller, his shoulders a lot wider, he wasn't quite the boy I remembered. He'd filled out. Matured. He did however smell exactly the same—like electricity in the air just before lightning hit. And that's how he made me feel. Tingly and anxious and on the brink of an oncoming storm.

His eyes went hooded, and then he shook his head and jangled the cuff. "I know why I'm hanging around the jail. How about you?"

"I'm looking for the mayor."

"You found him."

Chapter 3

Zander Ryland was Runaway's new mayor?

In spite of the fact that half a handcuff dangled from his wrist, and that he was back-dropped by a jail cell, something inside me grew in respect.

Until my memories of the last time I saw him shriveled that something into nothing. I glanced around for plastered-over bullet holes in the concrete wall. "Did you stage a coup?"

"Elected fair and square." His easy grin bantered with my sarcasm. "That and no one else wanted it. Although Papa Joe had a few write-ins."

Not a surprise. Everyone loved my grandpa. But imagining *Zander Ryland* printed on the nameplate on the mayor's desk? That took me for a ride.

Which was probably why I missed Abby sneaking up behind us—until after I heard the *click* of the cuff securing my wrist to Zander's.

In the middle of my outraged gasp, she giggled and raced down the hall after her mom, whisking the key away with her.

"That's one way to do a reunion." Zander broke into a soft laugh and tugged my cuffed wrist with his.

The sound I made was at least five emotions from laughter. I tugged back harder. "What if I don't want a reunion?"

Something I couldn't read filled his eyes and cut off his chuckle. But he recovered fast and found a new smile. "In that case, I have bolt cutters in my office."

Trying to pull off stern, I shoved my hands on my hips. Bad idea. Zander came along with the cuffs. I cleared my throat like I hadn't just yanked him kissing-close. "You have bolt cutters in your office?" A subtle side-step gave me room to breathe.

"And a flatiron and three pairs of toe shoes." He reclaimed the step I took. "Abby's into *Dance Moms*."

"Why don't we just find another key?" I forced him to come with me to the metal desk on the other side of the file cabinet.

He let me rifle through all six drawers—and Abby's art supply bin—before he said, "There's one key. Abby took it."

I kicked the bottom drawer shut and faced him. "There's only one handcuff key in the Sheriff's Office?"

He lifted his eyes, like my question put him in a mental spin. "Last few times I was locked up, yeah."

"Last few times..." I sat on the edge of the desk. "How many times have you been locked up?"

"Twice on Take Your Kid to Work Day." Two fingers popped up on his free hand. "Two times on Tour Your Town Day." Two more fingers. "Once on Meet the Mayor Day." He stuck up his thumb. "Again when Runaway auditioned for *Undercover Boss*. Oh, and that time I got arrested during the great crop circle scandal." He added two fingers from his imprisoned hand.

"Let me guess," I said dryly. "The crop circles were a dare."

"No. Well, yes." He dropped his fingers. "Derek and Chase were bored, and you weren't here to be the voice of reason."

Derek and Chase. Twins. Zander's sidekicks. Egging him on since '98. And the other two members of The Double Dare Club. "So it's my fault you and the Double Dare Brothers did time?"

"It was only a night. What can I say? You left our collective conscience high and dry. But the case of beer, the four-by-fours, and the railroad spikes didn't help." He shrugged exactly the way he used to when he teased me—with one shoulder and a flirty quarter-grin.

It affected more than I wanted to admit. "They still elected you Mayor?"

"Got a lot of tourism traffic that summer." His eyes held mine. "And this town needs more cash inflow."

I shook off his ocean-blue stare, desperate to put more space between us. A lot more space. Before I forgot why I left. Before I forgot what he did. Before I forgot everything I hated about Runaway. I rattled our cuffs. "So...how about those bolt cutters?"

"Coming right up." He took me down another hall that led to the mayor's office. His office. Unlocking the door, he attempted to wave me through first, but the chain between the cuffs was too short. We did an awkward two-step into the room, his arm brushing mine.

Goosebumps rallied on my skin everywhere we'd touched.

I rubbed my arms and took in the view—of the claustrophobic room, not him. His office was a quilt-work of old and new. The scarred desk was Runaway original and had probably served a line of mayors stretching back to the twenties. But the leather office chair had just rolled out of an Office Depot. Same contrast with the threadbare orange carpet and the shiny white blinds covering the only window.

The walls were plastered in a decorator's nightmare of unevenly spaced frames—black-and-white pictures of former mayors, town events, framed newspaper articles, and Zander's Small Town Mayor of the Year award for...I looked closer...three years running.

I managed to keep my mouth from falling open and contain my caustic comments. Stupid little ball of pride forming in my chest.

"How long have you been in town?" Zander moved behind me and put a gentle hand on my elbow to turn me to face him.

A small touch, but everything about his fingers on my skin felt familiar. Achingly familiar. I pulled my gaze from his and checked the clock hanging on his wall. 4:40. "An hour."

His expression seemed to say—*huh*. That flirty quarter-grin returned. "And you came looking for me right away?"

No. No. No. "I most certainly did not." I jerked from his touch and got yanked back by the matching metal bracelets. Handcuffs really messed with my ability to pull off incensed. I settled for a glare.

Which only spurred on his grin. "You said you were looking for the Mayor."

"Papa Joe was looking for the Mayor. He put a hundred bucks on this year's scavenger hunt."

Leaning forward, startling me, Zander whispered, "I missed you," out of nowhere. Then squeezed me into a catch-and-release hug so fast I couldn't move.

"Zander—"

"On to the bolt cutters." He pulled me to a locker in the corner—like he hadn't just rattled everything I thought I knew about me and him and us.

"Is that your high school locker?" I ran a shaky finger over the small black letters where I'd signed my name on the bottom right corner—in one of the few dares I'd accepted.

Getting into trouble wasn't something I'd been into. Still wasn't. Which is why even standing here was worse than going cow-tipping and finding a bull. Trouble wasn't just Zander's middle name, trouble was his motto.

He leaned a broad shoulder against the metal door. "The school remodeled after graduation and sold off the lockers as a fundraiser." He brushed across the letters in my name where the tip of my finger had just been. "Remember how nervous you were that they'd make you pay for defacing school property by taking your scholarship away?"

In hindsight, stupid. But back then, that scholarship had been my one-way, don't-pass-go ticket out of Runaway. Papa Joe didn't have the money to pay for college. Neither had I.

His hand left the locker to toy with the ends of my hair, his pinky accidently skimming my cheek.

And I felt the touch all the way to my perfectly-pedicured toes. "So?" I shook it off and held up my cuffed wrist. "Are we going to do this?"

"What'll you give me?" His voice dropped.

So did my stomach. I could listen to his smooth baritone all day. When we were in high school, I used to make him read to me. Our history textbook of all things. But it was the only way I passed the exams.

And…I needed one of those wristbands you could snap anytime you went off-course and were tempted by a bad habit. "What do you mean what'll I give you?" I gestured to our close proximity like we'd just run a 10K and were covered in sweat. "Your freedom. Your personal space. Some mouthwash." I went for his Achilles. One girl, one time, told him he tasted like jalapeños when he kissed her after lunch, and he never got over it.

But he didn't freak out like he used to. He didn't blow in his hand and smell his breath. He moved in closer. Confidently closer. "Already hit the mouthwash after a late lunch."

Not a lie. I could smell the cool mint on his breath.

I backed up and dug my heels in—as much as they'd go on the industrial carpet. "Can we get this over with?" Before I did something stupid—like thought about thinking about considering kissing him. "I'm supposed to collect you…I mean your picture for Papa Joe. Then I'm gone."

"You want bolt cutters and a picture?" His eyes sparkled. "What are you going to do for me?" He tilted his head and his hair flopped over one eye, begging me to sweep it back.

There was a time when it would've been second nature. Even though all those years ago we'd never kissed, in some ways we'd been closer. Comfortable. Friends with the sweet kind of benefits that let me hold his hand, fix the collar of his shirt, brush his hair with my fingers when it fell his forehead. Bump his shoulder when we sat side-by-side.

"Wallflower?" He waved his hand in front of my face. "What are you gonna do for me if I let you take my picture?"

"Let you get back to your *busy* day." And your life.

He glanced around the empty office. "It's Runaway. I can find five minutes, or a few hours, for you."

"Well, I'm busy." If you counted agonizing over filling the hours of my future now that I no longer had a job. Marketing was my thing. I just hated marketing myself.

With an overly-done sigh, he opened the locker. Right next to a flatiron and some ballet shoes leaned a pair of small bolt cutters. He grabbed them and shut the door.

I dug for my phone in my pockets. But my pockets—like my cell— were conspicuously absent. Great idea to wear a skirt. "How about you snap a selfie and send it to Papa John?"

"Now you want me to *take* the picture?" His eyebrows lifted. "You're just racking up favors."

"I left my phone in the car."

"Sorry." He shook his head, not looking the least bit sorry. "No selfies. The picture has to be full-size of me behind my desk."

"Okay. Whatever. Cut the cuffs. I'll stand on the other side of your desk with your phone and you can text me the picture."

"You can't just take it. You have to post it on the Scavenger Hunt Pinterest Board for it to count. There's rules to this year's scavenger hunt."

"Rules? Pinterest Board?" I shot him a glare that said—*you've got to be kidding.*

"We're law-abiding people in this town." His tone took on mock authority, and he set down the bolt cutters and squeezed us sideways back out his door to the posting board in the hall.

A printout titled, *Official Scavenger Hunt Rules,* hung next to children's drawings from the elementary school, a blown-up photo of a squirrel, a property-tax increase notice, and the city's most wanted—two men I didn't recognize who'd gotten a little too zealous with the cow-tipping.

The hundred reasons I left this town, besides Zander, bullet-pointed themselves in my brain.

"This is a serious contest this year," he said in that same mock sober tone. "Church attendance has dipped to an all-time low. Everyone's fighting for tithes." He steered us back into his office and through the doorway. "Papa Joe set up the Pinterest board."

Had everyone in this town lost their minds? "Did my grandpa happen to get an accidental lobotomy during his stay in the hospital?"

Zander grabbed the bolt cutters. "You came back to see *him.*"

I swear I heard a tinge of disappointment in his tone. I let it go. "He called me from the hospital." He hadn't actually asked me to come back. But he'd painted a grim-reaper picture of his health and silently manipulated me into a trip he knew I otherwise wouldn't make. "I rushed back to find he'd checked himself out and invited the guys over for a kegger."

Zander winced. "Probably not a great idea after the heart attack."

My heart stuttered. Kicked once against my chest. "Heart attack. He said it was angina." I grabbed Zander's arm.

"Angina that led to a heart attack. Guess he didn't tell you they're sending him to the University Hospital for more tests this week."

"He didn't tell me anything." I sagged against him.

With a strong arm around my waist, he led us both to his desk to sit on the edge. "He'll be okay."

"He has to be okay." Didn't care that I was hitting the quarter-century mark this year—I still didn't want to be an orphan.

Zander lifted the chain between our cuffs. "Grab the other handle?"

With him holding one side and me the other, we pushed and snapped the chain connecting us with the bolt cutters. Taking my wrist, he set my hand palm up on his thigh and carefully broke my metal bracelet. Then he replaced my wrist with his and offered the cutters.

I tried. And tried. And tried. And the darn thing would not break.

His grin turned solid. "Let me brace this…" Setting one handle against the wall and using his hand on the other he shoved till the veins in his neck swelled. Nothing.

Shrugging, he shook his wrist. "Souvenir." He put the bolt cutters back in the locker and dug around the bottom. When he came back, he set an empty crème soda bottle on the desk.

The bottle. From the Spin the Bottle game we'd played with our friends after the last eighth-grade dance. The bottle we'd initialed. The bottle that pointed to me on Zander's last spin and rattled the friendship line.

My lungs hollowed. "What are you doing with that?"

"You want my picture for Papa Joe?" He spun the bottle. "I'm collecting on that kiss you owe me."

Chapter 4

Only in Runaway could a simple visit home
turn into a game of handcuffs and hacksaws.

The crème soda spinning on Zander's desk wound down, rolled to a stop, and pointed at me. What was he? A bottle-whisperer? "Why do you have that again?"

"Proof." His earlier you-owe-me attitude dimmed in favor of something that seemed almost unsure. "Been waiting a long time. Wanted to make sure you didn't forget."

"I didn't forget." I remembered everything about the bewildered boy I almost kissed. Before he got a little crazy. Before the dares. Before the girls who giggled in his wake. Before he ever would've thought to cut the back of my costume.

He touched the bottle, then stepped out from behind the desk to stand in front of me.

My heartbeats went shallow like my breath. I could still see him that night, sitting by the bonfire out at The Resort—the old lodge his grandparents used to run, but let waste away. He'd smelled like lake and smoke and s'mores. And when Eric had thrown another log on the fire, Zander leaned into me, the awe in his eyes mixed with the reflection of showering sparks.

Until Papa Joe drove up and found us unsupervised playing with fire and saved our friendship. If Zander and I had crossed the kissing line, we couldn't have gone back.

"It would've been our first kiss." He said it like he was watching the same visual. "Yours and mine. Together." He leaned closer, exactly the way he did that night. Only this time, the sparks were coming from me, he just smelled like *him*, and there was no Papa Joe to interrupt us.

Forcing a swallow, I tried to ignore the warmth simmering in my stomach.

His fingers came up to brush my cheek. "Do you ever regret giving that kiss away to someone else?"

I nodded before I could censor. At least I didn't admit that I'd waited until college, and that the poetry-reciting TA from the English department had turned out to be a major dud in the mouth-to-mouth department.

Zander touched the corner of my lips with his thumb, raising that simmer in my stomach to a warning boil.

Zander would not be a dud. I already knew that, and his mouth hadn't even touched mine. I wanted to move. But the ocean churning in his eyes held me in place, asking every question I'd ever had about us dancing over the fine line of our former friendship. Questions that made me want to put a thousand miles between us.

Or lean in and see what happened.

"I regret giving that kiss to someone else too." His head tilted—on a crash course for my mouth.

Just in time, I took a self-preserving step back.

He followed. "Hendrix?" The heavy confusion in his voice backed me up one more step.

He followed again, this time tangling his fingers in my hair.

I shook my head no. I couldn't kiss him then. I couldn't kiss him now. It would be the end of me.

He let go of my hair, but those eyes, they didn't let me off so easy. "Maybe you could make an installment."

"Installment?" I blinked. "How can you make an installment on a kiss? You either kiss or you don't."

He slid closer. "Do you trust me?" His tone turned into a coaxing tease that kept me from wanting to bolt.

"No." Not quite a lie. I didn't know what I felt when it came to him. I knew what I wanted to feel—nothing. But that wasn't working out very well.

"Fair enough." His face softened in agreement, like maybe he thought he deserved my answer. "Let me just…" He held up his hands, not touching me, not blocking me, but definitely invading my space.

I let him *just*. I let him tip his head back down. Breathe across my jaw. "Back then, I would've settled for this." He brushed warm perfect lips across my cheek.

And left me trembling. Everywhere. My legs were having serious issues holding me up. It was all I could do to stay standing. All from a two-second kiss on the cheek.

When he pulled back, I looked at him, studied his face. He let me see the kiss had rocked him too. And knowing I wasn't alone somehow made it better. "And now?" My voice strained over the words.

"Now I'm a little more grown-up." His hand wound around my neck slowly pulling, pulling, pulling me toward him until his mouth hovered inches from mine, and I could almost taste that minty mouthwash.

The shrill ring of the phone on his desk jarred me back to reality. My reality—where Zander and I weren't even friends anymore.

Removing his fingers from my skin one at a time, I made my unstable legs work long enough to put some desperately needed space between us. Reality check. Mad at him or not, I wasn't immune. I needed to leave before we had anymore near misses.

The phone stopped ringing and started again.

"You should get your phone."

He picked up the receiver and set it right back down. "What just happened?" His voice dipped low and husky, like we'd been having a moment.

A moment I couldn't afford. "What happened is that I'm not *making good* on some stupid game from eighth grade." I inched backward until my back hit the doorframe.

He rested his hip on the desk and crossed his arms, the sleeves of his shirt stretching against some not too shabby biceps. "You leaving without your picture?"

"Unless you're going to stop acting twelve and quit trying to claim some stupid kiss that's never going to happen." I wrapped my hand around the doorknob as an anchor.

"Maybe I'm reliving my youth." He pushed his hand through his hair. "Working on a do-over."

"I don't want a do-over." I smoothed a damp palm down my skirt.

"Liar." His eyes sparked the way they did when he accepted a dare.

And something beyond attraction for him sparked inside me. Something that scared me almost as much as Papa Joe's hospital phone call.

"You still want your picture for Papa Joe?" He leaned his hip against the desk.

I nodded. A hundred bucks was a hundred bucks.

"I have a compromise to the kiss."

The sly glint in his smile made me afraid to ask, so I didn't.

"Come with me to The Resort," he said.

Our old high school hangout? I glanced at the bottle. I'd never seen a rattlesnake in Runaway. But that crème soda grew fangs. "Why would I do that?"

"Nostalgia. Old time's sake. One last hurrah. A walk down memory lane. Pick a cliché. Any cliché. As long as you say yes." On the surface, his shrug appeared casual.

But I knew better. And I didn't want to pick a cliché. I wanted to run far, far away. Because being back here with him confused the heck out of me.

"Wallflower?" He even made that horrid nickname sound enticing. "Will you come?"

I opened my mouth, formed the sound *no*—only that wasn't what came out. "Yes." What? Wait. Seriously. Something had to be majorly wrong with me. I gripped the doorknob tighter, officially a mess. "I meant no. No. No. No."

He moved off the desk, dropped another kiss on my cheek, and walked past me. "Tomorrow's my day off. See you out there at nine a.m."

Chapter 5

You can get your body out of a town—
But you can't get a town out of your head.

Instead of clearing the Zander-haze from my head, the drive from the Mayor's Office whipped it into a dense fog of memories.

Barfing bad cheese curds at Miller's bowling alley. Lying on our backs at midnight under the single stoplight in Runaway. Falling through the not-quite-frozen ice of the pond by the bull-breeding farm. Illegally diving for golf balls in the stream that ran through the golf course. Getting kicked out when we tried to make a profit on them later. And setting off fireworks from the roof of the Old Palace Theater. Well, that one was all Zander. Instigated by the Double Dare Brothers.

Then there were the past-curfew bonfires and friends and fun at The Resort. Where I was going tomorrow. Even though it was the worst idea since I'd agreed to that stupid game of Spin the Bottle.

When I got to Papa Joe's, the driveway sat empty. Either the Packers lost, or his *frat brothers* went on a beer run.

My stomach tightened as I parked the VW in the garage. Papa Joe and I had to talk about the heart attack he hadn't owned up to. If his health was failing, I couldn't leave him here alone.

And I couldn't come back.

Even if I got over my small-town phobia—which would take a bottomless bottle of Xanax and a thousand hours of therapy—I'd never find a marketing job. And I wasn't donning a triangular cheesehead at The Mouse House to serve the Chicago tourists who exited the highway for the perfect squeaky cheese curd. Or putting my life in the toes of a pair of rollerblades to carhop the A&W that shared the parking lot.

I powered myself inside the house on a long sigh and found Papa Joe alone in the kitchen, shaking his butt to "Night Fever." He was cleaning the stove in a pair of yellow gloves, Grandma's old Kiss-the-Cook apron, and a man bun.

Couldn't go there with the man bun, so I focused on the apron. Grandma had died when I was four. Papa told me so many stories over the years, I felt like I knew her. But all I remembered for myself was her smell. Lilacs and roses and that hairspray in the big pink can. Could you have separation anxiety from someone you'd never met?

I cleared my throat.

Turning down the Bee Gees on the old radio on the counter, he faced me. "Did you get the picture?" He tossed his sponge and gloves into the chipped avocado sink.

"Not quite." I looped the VW keychain by the door on the painted hook of a cow udder.

He washed and dried his hands, then pulled off the apron. "Why not?"

"Because it's going to cost me a trip out to The Resort." I slumped into the closest kitchen chair and put my elbows on the scarred table.

Aside from the odd knife rut and fork divot, every gouge had its own story. This table had logged more conversational miles than NASCAR. Papa Joe and me. Neighbors. Friends.

And underneath the left corner, Zander had carved our initials along with several curse words with his *Power Rangers* pocketknife when we were twelve. On a dare. As far as I knew, Papa Joe had never found them. "Why didn't you tell me Zander Ryland was the mayor?"

"What would be the fun in that?" Not bothering to hide the amusement in his eyes, he ignored my flash-glare and sat across from me at the table.

"I found him in jail." I kicked off my heels and flexed my toes. "Locked up."

"Yup." He flattened his hand on the table and rubbed his scratched wedding ring. "Take Your Kid to Work Day. Man, your boy sure stepped up for his sister when Barry Appleton knocked her up and left. He's practically been a father to Abby."

"Zander as a father. Maybe in some alternate universe." So why did a tiny part of me soften? "And he's not my boy." All the reasons why waited to jump off my tongue.

"Whatever you say, Bug." Papa Joe's eyes sparkled. "Anyway, I'm teaching his niece to play guitar. Sweet kid."

"For a girl who knows her way around a pair of handcuffs." At his quizzical look, I refocused the conversation. "We have to talk." I squared my shoulders and my spine.

"That sounds serious. Stay right there." Going to the fridge, he pulled out a plate of cling-wrapped meatloaf and cut us each a piece.

Thirty seconds into the heating process, I recognized the smell of Harriet Dixon's cooking coming from the microwave. Not only was she the old sheriff's widowed and much younger sister, but she headed up Last Chance Lutheran's Home Brigade, and made the best meatloaf in the county. Had the big, poofy, blue fair ribbons to prove it. If she'd been by with food, the church had been notified and people were worried.

Or bored.

Or nosey.

All three weren't out of the realm of Runaway possibility.

I poured us some water, and we met back at the table. Before he could dig in, I grabbed his hand.

He dropped his fork. "We didn't say grace."

Papa Joe's idea of grace was humming "Stairway to Heaven." A dinner tradition we didn't share with Reverend Lovejoy. Pretty sure if we had, he would've added it to his Banned Behaviors as an addendum of what not to do. What happened at this table...stayed at this table. And out of church. Sort of like Papa Joe's collection of blown-glass bongs and his Sunday-afternoon beer fest.

I touched the top of his hand to get his attention. "I call Huddle."

Huddle was the code word he'd used when he shook off Hippie-Mode long enough to lecture me like a normal parent. Although those conversations were too much of a back-and-forth to be considered actual lectures. Hippies have a thing about freedom of choice.

I'd only called Huddle once before—when I told him I was leaving for college at the beginning of summer, rather than at the end.

He blew out a breath. "I should've served a side dish."

"Alright. Huddle up then." He gestured to me with his fork, indicating I had the table since I called the meeting.

"We live too far apart." I started with a solid opener.

"You're not wrong."

"And I miss you." I offered my big-eyed, need-you stare.

"I miss you too, Bug." His welcome-home smile said he liked where this was going.

"Orange County has fabulous weather, great golf courses, and cutting-edge cardiologists." Perks a man his age would find relevant.

And all the welcome-home disappeared from his smile. "Zander told you." He leaned away.

"That you had a heart attack for real? Yes, he did." No matter what I thought about Zander, he did care about Papa Joe. Always had. "I shouldn't have had to hear it from him."

"I'm gonna be just fine." He patted his chest. "County General just got a new MRI machine."

"Why do you need an MRI?" I pointed my fork at him. And a hunk of meatloaf fell off. "You never know." He shrugged like he wished he could take back the words.

I cleaned up my mess with a holiday-printed napkin—even though Christmas happened five months back. Papa Joe had a thing for buying in bulk at Sam's in the city.

Enough of this Sunday-drive conversation. I cut right to the you-need-to-move chase. "I think you should come to California with me. Live in my building."

"Building?" He didn't cross his arms. But I could feel it coming, and when it did, him agreeing to move would be a hard sell.

"Papa Joe—"

"You think I can live in a high rise? I need space. And grass." He took a deep sniff toward the farm behind our house. "And manure." He shoved back his chair and grabbed his plate. "I got my fishing spot all set up by the bull-breeder's pond. And what about skinny dipping off Bo's dock?"

"You and Bo skinny dip off his dock?" My skin shriveled a little.

"Only in the dark." He set his plate on the counter. And crossed his arms.

There it was. His version of putting his foot down. But this conversation was nowhere near over. I took my plate to the counter and stood beside him. Touched his arm over his flannel shirt. "Why are you wearing flannel in June?"

"I'm cold. Old people get cold."

"You're not that old." People with poor circulation—and bad hearts—got cold. I needed to up my Orange County pitch. "They have great A/C in my building. A park close by with acres of *grass*. And I'll map you out some fishing spots." Couldn't help him out with the manure though. And I wasn't going near the skinny dipping.

His arms stayed crossed.

"Remember McLoud's?" My tone was overly coaxing as I gently tugged on his forearms.

"The sports bar with the swords on the wall?" He let his arms drop to his sides.

"And chicken wings, and barbecue meatballs, and micro-brews." And I was back in business. Time to reel him in and wrap this up. "All on the ground floor of my building." I pitched my closer. "Sports seven days a week on the big screen."

He leaned forward. "My screen's bigger."

"True." Forgot about his new man cave addition. "But…" Can you pitch a closer on a closer? "When you have parties there, there'll be no cooking. No cleaning. No running twenty minutes up the road if you run out of beer."

"And who am I going to party with, little girl?" And the arms folded back over his chest.

"You're like a people magnet. You'll have more friends than I do the first day."

"Bo and Coop and Duke—they're not just friends, Bug." The lines by his eyes deepened, and he gripped the counter. "They're family. Our family."

And this was why I lost my job. I could make something look good, but I just couldn't sell it. Right now, I had nothing. Not against a fifty-year friendship that turned people into family. I ran a hand through my hair. "Would you just think about it?"

His eyebrows knit together in a way that said he was trying to find a way to say no and let me down easy.

"Please."

"Two conditions." He held up a pair of fingers.

Any chance of Papa Joe living near me had my full attention.

"One, I need a couple days to think about it, and I want you to stay with me."

"I don't need to stay—"

"I've got some medical tests scheduled, and it would be nice to have you with me."

All my objections died. "What else?"

A sly smile slowly spread across his face, past his eyes, high enough to lift his eyebrows. "I want my picture of the mayor."

Chapter 6

There's something about a small-town guy
and his big-attitude truck.

Out at The Resort, I parked behind a Ford 4x4 I assumed belonged to Zander.

The black metal tubes on the extra bumpers were thicker than the cell bars I'd originally found him behind. The monster-truck tires could've swallowed Papa Joe's VW. And the black body was so spattered with mud, he had to have spent the morning off-roading. The whole package was a beast compared to the butterfly-decaled Pinto he drove in high school.

When his mom passed the car down to him on his sixteenth birthday, we'd spent an entire weekend trying to scrape those suckers off. A waste of a pack of razor blades, it was a total no-go. But like the skinny jeans, he'd rocked his emasculating ride.

Speaking of skinny jeans, Zander walked up the dock, one hand in his pocket, the other over his eyes to block the morning sun, even though he was wearing a cap.

Water glittered off the lake. But the flashes of light weren't enough to detract from *him*—all six-feet, tanned, he'd-clearly-been-working-out *him*.

A tingle of nostalgia sparked in my heart. Needing a change of focus, I got out of the car, leaving my purse and keys on the seat, and took in the Resort.

The property sat on the outskirts of town, located on a hill overlooking a meadow and bordering an old apple orchard. The trees had grown together, forming a woody canopy, and the apples had gone wild, breeding like bunnies. The blackberry patch still grew next to the storage shed. But the two-lane road out here had been freshly paved, and the lawn in front of the lodge had been mowed and manicured.

In the six years I'd been gone, the lodge had done a *Benjamin Button* and aged backward. The broken-out windows, rotting logs, and sagging roof had been redone in a style that gave the place a French Colonial feel. I especially loved the copper lights and window treatments.

The nostalgia tingling in my heart turned into a sharp stab. When we were kids having parties out here, we used to graffiti our names on the inside walls, and no one cared. But now someone had cared enough to bring this place back to life. I'd put my MasterCard on Zander being that someone.

"You made it." His boots hit the dirt next to the truck, and he paused for a quick look in the panoramic side mirror, then swaggered over.

Yes. That hip-rolling walk was truly a swagger. And had he just done a mirror check?

"You like?" he asked.

"You or the truck?" Stupid flirty gene. It flipped on at the most inopportune times. Schooling my features, I switched it out for something lightly sarcastic with a side of innuendo. "It's almost like you're compensating for something." I tipped my head toward his decked-out ride.

He rolled a measured gaze up my heels, pantyhose, pencil skirt, and silk blouse as if to say—*County kettle, meet big-city pot.* "Yeah, I'm compensating. For you leaving. The truck doesn't quite fit the hole in my heart, but what are you gonna do?" His casual shrug accentuated the width of his shoulders. "At least I can take her off-road." His mocking glance toward my wardrobe implied I wouldn't last a second out on the back country trails.

I cleared my throat. "This beast is a she?"

"I'm exploring my feminist roots."

"Feminist? Your mom is a collage of Betty Crocker, June Cleaver, and Martha Stewart."

"Not anymore." A wistful look crossed his face. "Now she's a snowbird in Florida. Hasn't cooked a meal since she and my dad moved two years ago. Seems Whole Foods has an endless selection of dinners for two."

"You miss your mom's pot roast," I teased him.

"I miss my mom." He got quiet for a minute and kicked the dirt with his boot. "Silly for a grown man, right?"

"Actually, it's kind of sweet." Whoa. I put a hand on my stomach. Were those warm, fuzzy feelings floating in there? Fluttering around for Zander? I needed to stop that right now.

And on that note, I picked my way across the dirt to stacks of building lumber and shingles past his truck—in heels I shouldn't have worn because they planted themselves in the dirt like stakes.

Following me, he aimed a pointed gaze down at my three-inch slingbacks.

"What?" I looked down at me, then up at him. "This is what I wear now."

"I liked the tight jeans and 70s band tees better." The sound he made wasn't complimentary.

Irritation slid along my skin. "I don't." That was a lie. But I had an image to fake. Well, I used to have an image to fake. "My jeans weren't that tight."

"Your jeans were a second skin." The new sound he made turned that irritation to a shiver. "Don't mess with my memories, Wallflower." He yanked on the brim of his cap. *HECC* was stitched in big swirling letters above the words *Hope Eternal Catholic Church* across the top.

As if anyone in this two-church town needed the acronym spelled out. "They're giving out hats at Mass now? Thought you were supposed to take your hat off when you hit the pew."

"Won it at bingo Friday night." He grinned. "Don't you kind of miss Father Morris?"

Even though I'd risked my Lutheran roots by sneaking into HECC's bingo nights with Zander, I did miss flicking the dried corn kernels we used for markers at him. And the native Wisconsin animals printed on the cards in place of numbers—*B Badger. G Gopher.* Too bad BINGO didn't have an M so we could represent the state bird—*Mosquito.* "Does it still take Father Morris seven tries to call out the squares?"

"He's down to three. The stutter's really improved since he started speech therapy." Zander grinned.

I grinned back. His smile was like a cold. Easy to catch. But filled with unpleasant and lingering consequences. I needed to think about something else. "About the picture Papa Joe needs for the scavenger hunt…"

"Already posted on Pinterest."

I gave him a questioning glance. "What if I wouldn't have—?"

"I knew you'd come." His answer was as rock solid as his truck.

Something in his voice, in his eyes, just sort of grabbed onto me like they didn't want to let go. I turned toward the lodge.

The changes were impressive. The pillared porch he'd added to the front of the restaurant reminded me of a lakeside Cracker Barrel. All he needed were white, slatted rocking chairs. Yep. Those would be perfect. Along with a few of those barrel tables that doubled as checkers-slash-chess boards.

I couldn't believe I was marketing this place in my mind. I shook off the selling points and looked at Zander. "Did you do all this?"

"I did." He tugged on his cap again, wearing his thinking face. There was something unsure in his eyes, then he straightened, coming to some sort of silent decision. "I want to talk to you about something." He took my hand and started walking.

And those fuzzy feelings I had for him grew wings. Great. If I pulled my hand away, he'd know something was up. So I didn't. Because in the whole time we'd been friends, I'd never pulled my hand away. Holding hands was something we just did. Something that meant absolutely nothing.

Those fuzzy wings beat on my stomach in a loud protest to my lie.

To shut them up, I concentrated on making sure my heels didn't quicksand into the wet grass every time I took a step, and let him lead me toward the lake.

"Do you remember our last high school party here?" He squeezed my hand.

I pretended not to notice. "The day before I left. The Double Dare Brothers used gasoline to light the campfire."

Zander stopped by the old fire pit. "Never had marshmallows quite that toasted before. Haven't since." The longing on his face suggested he might not be talking about the marshmallows anymore.

I took back my hand and sat on a log we'd carved our initials into. There was evidence of a recent meal of catfish next to the fire pit. "You still butcher those poor fish?"

"Filleting, Wallflower." He sat next to me, and the log felt much smaller than it ever had. "And they don't feel it. They're dead."

All I remembered were their big giant eyes. I stared over the lake at the peaceful ripples playing across the water. The scent of flowers bloomed in the breeze, and the cool wind off the lake played with my hair. Hadn't felt this…free in years. Tension I didn't realize I had drained out of me.

"There's still something about this place, huh?" He bumped my shoulder with his.

Yes, but I wasn't about to agree. "Why are you renovating now? What do you want to do with this place?"

"My parents left it to me when they fled south. At first, I thought I'd fix it up and sell it." He stretched out his long legs. "Before the tornado hit, it used to be quite the getaway. At least according to my grandparents. They ran it for years. But for whatever reason, they never rebuilt and just gave it to my mom."

"What happened to college in—"

"Georgia." He finished my sentence just like he used to. "Abby happened." He pulled off his cap and set it on his knee. "Her dad left before Abby was a month old."

"You gave up college for her?" Wow. That didn't sound like the Zander I knew. Not that he'd been so gung-ho on college, but he'd wanted to get out of this town too. Just not as much as I had.

"I moved in with my sister. Took online classes so Brynn could work." He said it so matter-of-fact, so responsibly, so seriously. When he'd never been that much of a serious guy.

That was part of the reason I never thought too much about us being more than friends. How could you date a guy that would do anything on a dare?

I glanced at him. Even sitting, he was taller than I let myself remember. Still had that goofy half-smile. But his eyes were sincere. Caring. Grown-up. Those warm fuzzies came back with a vengeance, determined to make me see him in a new way.

That couldn't happen. Standing, I walked toward the old willow near the lake.

Zander gave me less than five seconds of space before he was at my side. "Family is important to me. So is home." He set a warm hand on my shoulder. "That's what I wanted to talk to you about."

I ducked from under his hand before that warm could settle into me. Before I settled into him. There was a much bigger world than Runaway out there. And I needed to get back to it.

"I want to reopen The Resort. See if I can get tourism back on the menu for Runaway. Most of the city council is onboard."

"All two of them?"

"Four actually. Wilbur Morris is a holdout, but he'll come around when I agree to mow his lawn until the first snow."

"So September then?" Remembering the arctic Wisconsin winters made me shudder.

He laughed. "Or maybe October if he's lucky." His hand found my arm again and slid down till he intertwined our fingers, tugging me to face him.

The move so familiar, so much like home, I was trapped in the depths of his eyes and their solid determination.

"The lodge is almost done." Pride flooded his voice. "Now I need a plan to get the word out."

"What's your plan?"

"You're my plan."

"Me." Something strange gripped my heart. Something that made me pull my hand away, his familiar touch suddenly constricting. "What do you mean me?"

"Papa Joe's been updating me on your life for years. You're in marketing. You could launch our website. Make brochures. The City of Runaway would like to hire you as a contract consultant to get everything up and running on the advertising side."

I didn't know what was more disturbing—that thanks to my gossiping grandpa, Zander knew way more about my life than I did his, or that he was actually asking me to stay in this godforsaken town past Wednesday. "I'm a pharmaceutical sales rep. Not a small town tourism advisor. And I already have a job."

"I thought you got laid off."

"How do you know that?" Anger tightened my chest. "I didn't share that news with Papa Joe."

Guilt flashed through Zander's eyes. "I might've Googled you. And then there was that whole... scandal."

Panic replaced some of my anger. Not because of the scandal. Because of what Zander might've told Papa Joe. "Did you tell him I lost my job?"

The guilt in his eyes deepened.

My stomach hollowed. "Thanks for that." I stalked back toward my car. Didn't get far before my left heel dug into a muddy patch and stuck. My upper body kept going, my foot did not. I went down hard. And my skirt ripped up the side in an ironic replay of the day Zander cut my costume during *The King and I.*

Zander was kneeling in front of me before I could scrape together even one part of my dignity, his hands running over my ankle.

"I'm fine," I snapped, slapping his fingers away. The helpless-girl humiliation burned worse than my ankle or my bleeding knee. I'd worked hard to put small-town me in the past.

"Wallflower—"

"No." I sat on my butt. Yanked off both my heels. "I won't work for the city. I won't stay."

"Papa Joe and I talked—"

"So you planned this together." I hooked my shoes by the slingbacks and pushed off the ground. "Get Hendrix out here. Poor girl lost her job. Well, I did my job. Pelvavox passed under the FDA bar. It worked. Relieved constipation. So what if it caused uncontrollable flatulence." I slung my shoes around wildly, almost clipping Zander in the chin.

"Whoa." He did a duck-and-dodge.

I kept going. With my rant, and my high-heeled swing. "We were upfront in the microscopic print. But noooo…people had to be haters. So what did they do? Went on the warpath for a scapegoat. Blamed marketing. Fired Hendrix. And now you're offering me a last-pick pity job in a town I can't stand."

"Step back from edge." He managed to grab my flailing arms before I scarred his pretty face with the sharp tip of one of my heels. "You're not a last pick. And it wasn't a setup."

"Sure, it wasn't." Barefoot, I trudged back to the car.

"The town needs you." Zander was fast to follow.

I threw my shoes on the passenger seat, slid in, slammed my door, and hit the lock, almost missing his quiet voice when he touched the window and said, "I need you."

My fingers shook as I turned the engine over, those three words threatening to bring down the wall between who I'd been and who I wanted to be. A wall I'd spent the last six years building.

Putting the car in reverse, I backed up, turned around, and pulled away from him. From The Resort. From the memories begging me to stay. Done with Runaway. Done with Zander. Done with the volatile emotions he stirred inside me.

Chapter 7

Coffee. Bacon. Biscuits. And sausage gravy.

The smell of my breakfast favorites pulled me out of bed and into a pair of old pink gopher slippers I'd left buried in the back of my closet.

Lurching down the hall in early-morning Zombie mode, I finger-combed my bedhead and wiped yesterday's mascara from under my eyes.

Not exactly fashion-diva fare, but Papa Joe had seen me looking worse.

I rounded the corner and froze. Because Zander had not. My suddenly sweaty feet stuck to the faded yellow linoleum along with any dignity I hadn't already left at the lake.

"…sounds like an amazing trip." Zander leaned back in his chair across from Papa Joe.

"We brought in a dozen catfish." Papa Joe wiped his mustache with a napkin, then glanced over to me. "Morning, Bug."

Just as I peeled my left foot from the floor to backtrack, Zander zeroed in on me.

"Nice." His quick grin turned into a wolf whistle.

I yanked down the white-and-purple striped tail printed near the bottom of my PJ top to meet the matching shorts and covered the slice of skin I'd accidently put on parade.

"*My Little Pony's* a good look for you." He twisted sideways in his chair and slung an arm over the back. "But Diamond Tiara? An unusual choice."

Since I lost the option of sneaking away, I left my pride on the linoleum and owned my outfit—and my favorite pony—and stalked over to the old Corning Ware coffee pot. It looked as 1960 as the rest of the avocado-and-lime-colored kitchen. "Diamond Tiara was redeemed at the end of season five."

"That's a matter of opinion." Zander's friendly banter dissolved a layer of yesterday's anger.

"As if you're into *My Little Pony.*" I swiped the last clean mug off the row of hooks next to the coffee pot. The mug that read—*Caffeine rules. Decaf drools.*

"I'm all the way in. I DVR it for Abby. Highlight of Runaway's rocking Saturday nights."

"OMG." I pitched my voice cheerleader high. "Zander's a Brony."

"Darn right. Abby and I have collected every Happy Meal pony. I'm partial to Fluttershy. She's Team Rainbow Dash."

And didn't that just shoot a rainbow flutter through my stomach.

I mixed one third half-and-half with two-thirds brew and brought my coffee to the table, wishing I'd spent time with my toothbrush. I took the chair farthest from him and tried not to breathe.

"Got a little morning breath going on there, Wallflower?" Turning back to sit straight in his seat, he took a sip of coffee from a mug that read— *World Peace. Free Love. Good Coffee.*

Papa Joe pointed at Zander with its mate. "Be nice to our Bug."

"I was very nice to *Bug*." His tone teased across the nickname. "And she cut our date short anyway."

My mug clattered to the table. Hot droplets splashed my wrist. I slid my hand across my shorts and blew on the burning skin. "It wasn't a date. It was a set-up." An equal opportunist, I turned my you're-so-busted glare on both of them.

"I just wanted you to hear Zander out." Papa Joe tried to soothe me with a glass of my favorite organic, no-pulp orange juice. "You used to be so close. And you didn't have anything left in California to keep you there. So I thought you might be able to help him—"

"So you wanting me to market The Resort *was* a pity offer," I asked Zander. Instead of the fire of self-righteous anger, everything inside me fizzled out.

"Wanting to hire you was a business call," he said. "That's all it was about."

"No, it wasn't." Papa Joe rounded his gaze on Zander. "There's nothing business about the way you look at Bug." Then he swung his attention to me and leaned on the table. "I guess I was holding out that somewhere deep down you'd find your way back to each other and admit you've always been in love. I do want great grandchildren before I'm dead, you know."

Zander snapped instantly and awkwardly to attention, like he hadn't been expecting that.

I choked on my coffee, and it flowed scalding hot down my throat.

Frantically sucking in air, I dived for my glass of orange juice and downed it in one swallow.

"Are you alright?" Papa Joe rushed around the table and thumped my back, like he could dislodge the fire burning me from the inside out.

Zander flanked my other side.

Not even close to alright, I choked on the burn and chugged Papa Joe's orange juice too.

When I stopped dying, I pushed my chair back and stepped away from him. "So that's why you really wanted me to come home. To play matchmaker." My voice sounded as raw as the inside of my mouth felt.

"Well now, Bug." Papa Joe tugged the collar of yet another flannel shirt in June.

Zander moved to lean against the counter, his expression no longer awkward, but suspiciously thoughtful. Like he might actually be onboard with Grandpa's great-grandchildren campaign.

I couldn't go there. Not now. I focused on Papa Joe. "You called me from the hospital. Made it sound like you were dying." My gut clenched all over again. I'd been so wound up that night, I'd thrown up twice.

"I didn't actually *ask* you to come—"

"No, you made me think you were in the homestretch to the afterlife. And when I threw together a suitcase and took the next flight out, I found you at home, drinking with your buddies clearly not anywhere close to waiting in line at the pearly gates."

"How about some biscuits and gravy?" Moving toward the stove, he grabbed a plate and started piling on food from the covered pans. "Made them just for you."

"Why did you do that?" I crossed my arms.

"You love biscuits and gravy." He pivoted with the plate in his hand.

"Not that." I gestured to the food. "You scared me half to death the day you called. All you had to do was tell me you needed me and I'd have come."

"Would you have come?" Zander's quiet question came with a deafening cry of doubt—that almost doubled me over.

"Maybe not that day." I kept my gaze on Papa Joe. "But I would've come." I crossed my arms over my waist. Less as an I'm-closed-off statement, more as a countermeasure against the churning in my stomach. "What really happened with your heart?"

Papa Joe shared a secret-club glance with Zander.

"Just tell me." I couldn't hide the desperation in my voice.

"It was just a small…" Papa Joe pinched his fingers together and held them up. "Miniscule little angina episode that—"

"Led to a heart attack," Zander finished for him.

"A teeny, tiny, microscopic attack." Papa Joe gave him a sharp look.

Tears burned in my eyes, but I pushed them back. Leaving both of them in the kitchen, I ran down the hall to my room and shut the door a little too hard. On cue, the graduation picture of Zander and I throwing our hats up together went crooked and fell off the wall.

I slumped to the floor and clutched the picture, drew up my knees, and bent my head. Zander hadn't been lying about the heart attack. I saw it in Papa Joe's eyes. Heard it in his silence more than his words. The reality of my grandpa being sick pulled me under a rushing river. And refused to let me breathe.

The door quietly opened, and Zander padded in and sat beside me, barely making a sound. We sat there for a while, then he touched my knee. "Wallflower."

I lifted my head. "Is he going to die?"

"Not if he takes care of himself. He needs to slow down. See a specialist. Stop eating biscuits and gravy."

I squeezed the picture frame. "Maybe he'll be fine. Maybe—"

"I was the EMT on duty when Papa Joe's 911 call came in." His piercing eyes grabbed me and held on. "It wasn't a small attack."

EMT.

Ambulance.

911.

Specialist.

My brain fizzled and instead of asking everything I should, I said, "You volunteer at the fire department?"

"Hendrix." Zander said my name as if were trying to ground me.

But it wasn't enough. And I burst into tears.

Chapter 8

High school was the epicenter of small town religion—
a full-contact revival on the football field every Friday night.

I drove forty minutes of back-country roads, processing the cardiology appointment I'd gone with Papa Joe to this morning, before I ended up in the gravel lot behind Runaway High School.

The school was first on the list of Zander's summer hangouts that Papa Joe felt the need to share. A list I'd memorized, then filed under—*no-fly zones*. My feelings for him were already dangerously close to veering off course.

But I couldn't turn the car around anymore than I could stop myself from getting out to go in search of him. Braving the hot sun and thick humidity, I walked toward the track, where he was rumored to be coaching cross country.

Uncle. Mayor. Renovator. Brony. EMT. Still my sort-of best friend. Otherwise I wouldn't have come here—even subconsciously.

A glance at the high school's theater entrance brought back an unwanted flash of my last night on stage. They'd probably enshrined a picture of my *King and I* fiasco in the blooper case next to the charred branch from *Seven Brides and Seven Brothers* when the stage lights accidently caught Zander's live tree on fire.

And for the first time, when I thought about the night he'd cut my costume, I didn't automatically sizzle. What he'd done was stupid. But maybe I wasn't any less stupid, using an accident to push him away because being angry made it easier to leave him—when I'd been having doubts on whether to stay.

The mixed feelings I had for Zander churned me up inside. I'd wanted to run from him. And I'd ended up running to him.

Sounds from the sports field drew me under the faded billboard advertising the Runaway High mascot. He was supposed to have been a giant, axe-wielding Viking. But a printing mishap or budget cuts or plain old artist error gave the town a design more like a massive, potbellied dwarf decked out in a perpetual scowl. The Double Dare Brothers had a yearly competition to see which of them could paint a beer mug in the dwarf's free hand first in honor of the homecoming game.

Our hulking dwarf proudly overlooked the triple-threat football-baseball-track that was a liability waiting to happen. Despite being in the country with acres to spare, the sports fields were crammed together into one entity. The orange track circled the football field and acted as the far edge of the baseball diamonds' outfield. Signs warned runners to *Watch*

For Flying Footballs, and football players were reminded to wear their helmets at all times to avoid a fastball-induced concussion.

This afternoon, teens in gym shorts and tees circled the field, the steady pounding of their feet on the orange gravel track a relaxing rhythm against the cloudless blue sky. In the visitor's end zone, a dozen baseball players stood in two rows passing balls back and forth. And the football players huddled up in the middle of the field shouting plays.

Nothing like getting an edge on all the sports. What happened to summer vacation?

I walked to the bleachers and stretched, letting my hair down from its tight twist. Didn't see Zander. But the nostalgia of the hours I spent here in high school watching him lap the track coaxed my butt onto the first row of hard metal benches.

A paper blew by and caught on the railing.

"Dang it." A peeved voice came from behind me.

Shading my eyes, I looked up.

Abby sat on the top row wrestling with a stack of papers trying to take flight, her brown curls blowing into her eyes.

Kids were so needy. And so not cute.

A tiny string tugged on my chest. Nope. Nothing even remotely cute about the way Abby scrunched her forehead and bit her lip in concentration.

Her not-cuteness had me climbing the bleachers in a skirt not fashioned for leg range-of-motion and three-inch heels.

Abby's head lifted. "Hendrix." An insta-grin killed every trace of her frustration.

Must be nice to be optimistic on command. I snatched up several wandering pages of what looked like first-grade homework and handed them to her.

"Thanks." She shoved the papers under a thick *My Little Pony* binder covered with pictures of Rainbow Dash.

"Are you here alone?" I sat next to her, smoothing my skirt. She had to be like six. Didn't six-year-olds need supervision?

"Mom's at work. I'm waiting for Uncle Zander to take me for pizza." Abby gestured toward the field.

I shielded my eyes and followed her finger. Dressed in shorts and a tee, he set down a clipboard and joined the group of well-paced kids jogging around the top curve of the track.

Not only keeping up, he stayed ahead on the outside lane, and by the way he held himself back, I knew he could've lapped them if he wanted. Even at this range the definition in his calves was obvious. He'd loved to be a show-off with his double calf-muscles.

I forced my gaze off his legs and studied Abby. "What are you working on?"

She flicked her eyes at the sky as if she was calling on divine aid and let loose a long sigh. "Summer school."

"How old are you?"

"Seven."

"Seven-year-olds go to summer school?"

"I don't read good." Her gaze dropped, like she was embarrassed.

I resisted the urge to correct her *good* to *well*. She probably didn't need another bash to her self-esteem. When I struggled with something—like losing my job, being back in this town, seeing Zander, Papa Joe's illness—I didn't need someone pointing out what was already biting me in the butt.

"Let me see what you're working on." I held out my hand.

"We have to write a report." She gave me a book about a dinosaur named Fred. "On all fiiiive chapters." The amount of frustration in her eyes made it seem as if her teacher had asked her to dissect five hundred pages. "But the words don't work right."

"What do you mean?" I rubbed my fingers over the triceratops tail on the cover. "On the report?"

She opened the book on my lap. "On the page. The words don't work." The frustration in her eyes spread to her voice. "The letters don't go together. They're all mixed up and…" Her exhale shook, and for a second I thought she might cry, but then she rubbed her hands over her legs and caught her breath.

"Abby." I looked into her pinched face. "Are you dyslexic?"

She scrunched up her nose. "Dis-what-ic?"

I didn't know one darn thing about kids—other than I'd been one—but I knew my way around dyslexia. I'd spent my last two years of college tutoring dyslexic students in the writing lab.

First grade was prime time to notice the condition, if the teachers were trained. But I doubted Runaway had the budget.

Scooting closer, I put us hip-to-hip and placed the open book on her knees, then took her finger and traced a random word in the middle of the page—*hi*.

"*Hi*." She stabbed the page. "That's an easy one."

"Why?"

"'Cause I mesmerized it." Her curls shook along with her head. "I mesmerize lots of baby words in reading group. I'm in the baby reading group." Her voice slid past embarrassment into shame. "I learn them. I do. But the next day they look different." She shut the book and threw it on the bleachers next to her.

"That's because you need a secret code to figure out the words." It wasn't her fault. Runaway Elementary was still clearly teaching whole language. Even though a good chunk of kids couldn't learn that way.

Abby touched my skirt with her hand. My heart with her eyes. "Do you know the secret code?"

Ugh. I was helpless against her big brown eyes and trembling lips and the direct line she'd attached to my heart—then tugged.

My sigh came on the tail end of a deep exhale. "Yes, I know the secret code." I took her finger again and this time we traced the *h* and *i* on her leg by her knee. "There's too many words to memor...*mesmerize*...so you learn the sounds instead."

"*H* is easy. *H, h, h.*" She puffed out the sound.

"Exactly. But *i* can have two sounds. In *it* it says *i*." I highlighted the short staccato of the sound. "In *hi* it says *i*." This time I drew out the letter's name, all the while moving her finger to draw the letters on her skin.

Then I accidently glanced down at the track at the same moment Zander passed by. And got lost in his stride. He still packed a lot of power when he ran. It showed not only in his legs, but in the way he carried his upper body.

"That's the secret code? The sounds?" The confusion in Abby's demanded my attention, and I reluctantly gave up my view.

I twisted my knees toward her so I'd be less tempted to be distracted. "The secret code is figuring out the different sounds a letter makes, depending on whether it's at the beginning, middle, or end of a word."

"Umm..."

I drummed my nails on my knee. Adults caught on much faster. And I wasn't used to teaching kids. "Okay. It's like this. Do you ever have to stand in line?"

"At school for recess." She nods quickly. "And lunch."

"Okay. A word is a line of letters." I waited for her nod. "The letters change their voice depending on where they stand in line."

"Huh?"

Tugging her hand, I pulled her with me to stand on the bleachers— stepping a centimeter from losing the point of my heel off the edge. Saying a Hail Mary prayer that I hadn't just broken my ankle, I shifted to the middle and faced her.

She looked at my feet. "You should take off your shoes."

Who made Zander's niece the voice of reason? Stealing one more peek at the track, I stepped out of the heels and set them where I'd been sitting. "Let's start with the short sound of *i*. I'm going to be the *t* and you're going to be the *i* in *it*. After I say my sound, you say yours. But I want you to draw the letter's name out."

As soon as she started to drag out her *i*, I leaned into her and cut it off with a sharp *t*. We went back and forth like this until we could've been doing a clip from the old *Electric Company* on PBS. "Your sound is at the beginning of the line, but I'm next, so I get to cut you off. Stop you from saying your whole name. Because it's my turn to talk."

This time a mini light-bulb moment went off in her eyes.

Switching gears, I became the *h*, and we did the same thing with *hi*. Only this time, I let her string out the long *i* sound until she ran out of breath. "See how there's no letters after you in line to stop you from screaming out your name?"

"I get to be free." She giggled. "Because I'm *i*." She shouted out the letter's name again. Loud enough that Zander looked up. When he saw us together, a sunrise-smile lit his face, and he waved.

My traitorous little fingers lifted and wiggled right back. Wiggled. Like I was some awestruck track bunny. I slid my shoes out of the way, sat hard on the bleachers, and shoved my disloyal hands under my legs. "Stay." I hissed at them.

"Zander thinks you're pretty." Abby sat too.

Why did that melt something inside me? "Zander thinks a lot of girls are pretty." I dug out my sarcasm, but with a small shovel. Abby was only a kid after all. And she didn't understand—

"No, he doesn't." She slid closer. "But the other teachers think he's pretty. Especially Ms. Eberhart." She pointed to a tall woman with a dark ponytail and a come-get-me chest, who'd taken over Zander's clipboard to time the kids as they lapped the track. Her fingers might be on the stopwatch, but her eyes were trained on Zander.

And I instantly unmelted—if that was a thing.

The meaning of the rest of Abby's words came rolling on in on a five-second delay. "Zander's a teacher?"

Abby nodded. "He teaches shop. And track. 'Cause he's always out working on The Resort."

I watched the teacher watching him.

And something tightened under my ribs.

I twisted my head toward Abby. "Does Zander think Ms. Eberhart's pretty?" Did I really just pump a kid for information…on a guy I had no business asking about?

She shrugged and puckered her lips like a fish. "They kissed."

Something inside me went green-eyed at the thought that Ms. Eberhart knew what Zander's lips felt like and I didn't. I slumped on the bench. Sunk on the inside. "So he likes her."

"Nope." Abby's wide grin showed two missing teeth. "Zander loooves you."

Chapter 9

Living with dyslexia is like sailing under a starless sky.
A good teacher can be a lighthouse.

Zander loves you. Abby's words skipped through my chest—without the sing-songy twang.

I twisted toward her so quickly both my heels took a nosedive off the bleachers and *thump, thumped* to the dirt below.

Abby got on her knees and peered between the metal steps. "Wowwww. They bounced far. And there's kind of a lot of mud." She pulled her face from between the bleachers. "Want me to get 'em?"

No, I wanted her to backtrack.

I tugged on her elbow until she sat next to me. "Why do you think Zander loves me?" My overzealous, middle-school pitch came with a nails-on-the-chalkboard cringe. This was ridiculous. I was ridiculous. Gossiping with a first grader about boys. "Never mind. It'd be great if you could find my shoes."

I needed to leave before I got stuck inside middle-school me and was forced to relive eighth grade *Groundhog-Day* style.

Eighth grade. The bottle. That kiss-that-didn't-happen.

Instead of running down the bleachers to retrieve my shoes, Abby burst into song. "Zander and Hendrix sitting in a tree." A loud song. "K! I! S! S! I! N! G!" A song that carried across the entire field, gathering up glances and stares along the way.

"Hey." I clamped my hand over her mouth. "Can you not sing so loud?" I whispered like I could cancel out her musical shout-out. "Or maybe change it out for some Rihanna."

I waited for Abby to nod before I ungagged her.

But it was too late. *Boom. Boom. Boom.* The bleachers rumbled under me as Zander jogged up the seats toward us.

My brain yelled—*bolt!* But my butt missed the message and merged with the bench.

He plopped down next to me, leaned back, slung his elbows on the step behind him, and stretched his legs. "Nice song, Abs." His nuclear grin threatened to swallow me whole.

If humiliation didn't devour me first.

Deflecting with the first thing that popped into my head, I gestured to his outfit. "Blast to the past. You wearing the school colors again." The anti-dwarf, he did the Viking T-shirt proud. Exceptionally, muscularly, double-calved proud.

"Stalker," he teased, bumping his knee against my leg. "Didn't expect to see you here."

I caught myself twirling the ends of my hair. I really had reverted to thirteen. Shoving my hands behind my back, I forced a smile to stop an oncoming groan.

"Hendrix was helping me with my homework." Abby's eyes danced, as if I'd come specifically to see her.

Why she liked me so much, I had no idea. I didn't even like me lately.

"Are you finished?" Zander's tone was one-hundred-percent parental.

"No." She huffed an overdramatic breath and pulled her book back on her lap.

While she worked, I studied Zander. "I can't seem to escape you. You're everywhere. City Hall. My breakfast table. The school." I swallowed hard. "The ambulance." And that's why I was here. To talk about Papa Joe with someone who understood what was going on.

Zander straightened on the bench, suddenly serious. "How did it go with Papa Joe this morning?"

"Not great." I picked at the hem on my skirt. "According to the doctor at University Hospital, he's basically another heart attack waiting to happen. All those little chest pains he's had over the years? Congenital angina. That he never did anything about." The frustration I'd wrestled with all morning swept through my voice. "If he pushes himself too hard, eats the wrong things, stresses out, and a thousand other things, he'll end up in the ambulance again." I flattened my hands on the bench to keep from shaking. "Or worse."

"Sounds like he needs a major lifestyle change." Zander slid his hand over until his pinky bumped mine.

Just that tiny touch soothed me enough to take a deep breath. "Sounds like..." My gaze lingered on our touching fingers. "I need to make some decisions."

"*He* needs to make some decisions, Wallflower. You can't hand him a project plan and expect him to check off your boxes. He's a grown man."

"He's a stubborn man." My shoulders shook a little.

Zander brushed his pinky across mine. "He has to want to change."

"Like that's going to happen. Based on the casual way he drifted through the appointment, he wasn't too hip on listening to anything the doctor said. With the exception of yoga. Which he told me he'd do, but only in his *natural state*." If the skinny-dipping had been TMI, the birthday-suit yoga made me gag.

Zander he covered my hand with his palm and squeezed. "I'll talk to him."

"And say what?"

"I'll remind him that he wants to stick around for those great grandbabies." His grin ran so wide, it crinkled his eyes and sent me scrambling into a blush.

"Can we forget about that?"

"Not a chance." He met my eyes, his grin settling into an encouraging smile. "He'll come around, and when he does, he'll be okay. Angina is something he can live with."

Abby slammed her book closed and touched my knee. "What's a gina?"

"Ummm...."

"Hey, Abs." Zander leaned over me. "Why don't you run down to the coolers on the field and grab us some Gatorades? Hendrix likes orange." His yeah-I-still-remember shrug curled my toes.

"Sure." Abby took off. The enthusiasm of her *boom, boom, boom* as she hopped down the steps was louder than Zander's when he'd run up, even though she weighed far less.

"You're good with her." The way he talked to her, the way he handled her made him a great dad. Even if he was only the uncle.

"I love her." It wasn't the words that wrapped around my heart and squeezed. It was the *way* he said them—with layers of emotion that were so profound, they were simple. Like he couldn't possibly feel any other way.

"I can see that," I said softly, watching him watch her.

"Can you?" He turned his gaze on me. And the look settling onto his face wasn't one you'd wear for a daughter or a niece. It was entirely something else, something just for me, that took that pressure he put on my heart from powerful to...something more.

I couldn't look away.

Not when he twisted on the bench. Not when he leaned toward me. Not when he tilted his head and the space between our lips vanished inch by inch.

Chapter 10

*The Double Dare is one of the few sacred rites of childhood—
it teaches responsibility, consequences, and stupidity.*

I shut my eyes, anticipating Zander's kiss.

Leaning closer on the bleachers, he skimmed a finger down my cheek and across my jaw, his mouth descending in slow motion until his breath feathered across my lips, and—

A blast like a cargo freighter's foghorn sent us flying apart.

My butt slid off the bench, and I plopped to the bleacher below—arms, legs, and indecent skirt flailing in the middle of our crumbled moment.

Scrambling to tug down my hem, I conducted a frantic search for my poise. But it dropped off the bleachers somewhere next to my heels. Not gonna be a fun search and rescue.

"Are you okay?" Standing, Zander lifted my arms and helped me up.

The horn honked again, drawing us up two more steps to the railing to peer over the bleachers.

Down below, in the back section of the parking lot, a man pulled in on a four-wheeler with a hulking chrome engine.

Massive wasn't enough adjective to describe the ATV. Or the guy. I brainstormed a few more—tall, wide, thick, tree stump. Nope. Every adjective fell short. Literally.

In a white cotton shirt, dark blue jeans, and brown leather boots, the guy was a Mack truck souped-up with the swagger of a country boy.

"Is that the Derek half of the Double Dare Brothers?" I turned to Zander.

"Yeah." He nodded. "Both of them hit a growth spurt around twenty-two."

"Or ate a bear."

Zander laughed. "Or that."

A redhead in gigantic sunglasses with hair blowing in the breeze rode behind Derek, a hand attached to each of his Paul-Bunyan biceps.

The woman pushed up her sunglasses, and recognition sent a happy tingle racing through me. Emma Austin had been the closest thing to a girlfriend I'd had. Although she wasn't supposed to be here any more than I was. She'd hopped a plane to Europe the summer I left.

Derek parked the ATV and swung off, carefully helping her down.

I watched them together. The way he took his time setting her on the pavement. How she held his hand a little too long after. "Derek's with Emma?"

"Derek doesn't know who he's with." At my curious look, Zander added, "It's complicated. You should probably ask her."

Abby pounded up the bleachers and squished between us to yell over the railing. "Are you taking me for a ride, Uncle D?"

"Later, Firefly. Emma needs to grab something from the library, then I need to run her home." He lifted his head, and did a double-take that sent him a step back. "Hendrix Marshall—is that you?" His voice rumbled all the way up to the bleachers like he was standing next to me.

"Hendrix?" Emma squinted at me, pulled her sunglasses back down, and waved. "I'm coming up."

"I'll come to you." I darted barefoot down the bleachers and onto the orange track.

Emma sprinted around the fence, almost getting plowed down by a mass exodus of football players rushing off the field toward the locker room.

Zander's runners, and the baseball players, had already cleared the track so once the stampede passed, we were the only people left on the field.

Emma wrapped me in an it's-been-forever hug.

"Looking good, Hendrix." Derek joined her. Not in the hug. On the track.

Didn't feel like being suffocated in his chest. And he wasn't my favorite person.

"Doesn't she?" Emma stepped back and held out my arms. The compliment rang genuine. Something I wasn't used to. The compliments my coworkers gave me tended to come with an ironic bite. "And you're so tan."

"California will do that to you." California will do a lot of things to you. Like take away your job and eat your self-esteem. And…did I just dis Orange County? Was Zander pumping something into Runaway's air to make it seem more appealing?

"I'm still pale." Emma held out a white arm next to mine.

"Yep. Still an albino. With freckles." Derek's backhanded comment made her frown.

I frowned at him too when I really wanted to stick out my tongue.

"Hey." He crossed his beefy arms. "I didn't say she didn't look—"

"Shut up, Derek." I turned my brightest smile on Emma. "You look amazing, Em. Totally amazing." And she did.

The scoop neckline on her white-and-navy striped shirt and her white shorts set off her slender figure. A figure a few sizes smaller than she'd worn in high school. Her sleek red hair had been cut six inches and layered to brush the tops of her shoulders. But the Julia-Roberts smile—that hadn't changed one bit. Sadly, neither had the barely-hidden longing in her eyes every time she glanced at Derek.

Did she come back for him? And oh-my-living-gosh why?

"Uncle D! Catch me." Abby bounded down the bleachers like she was getting a running start, then jumped from two steps up straight for Derek.

I had a mini-heart attack the millisecond before he caught her and hugged her close.

She wiggled in his arms. "Can't breathe." But she was laughing. "Take me for a ride."

"I don't know, Firefly." He pretended to think about it. "You're getting awfully big."

I snorted. He could carry ten of her. Bare minimum.

He let her slide to the ground, then squatted so she could hop onto his back.

"We're getting pizza." She wrapped her arms around his thick column of a neck. "Want to come?" She glanced at Zander who was taking the bleachers at a much slower pace—because his gaze was glued to me.

A flush spread over my face, and I turned back to Emma. "I thought you were backpacking in Europe never to return. Tell me everything." I pulled her down onto the first bench with me.

"We'll see about pizza, Firefly." Derek took off down the track at a slow trot. Sort of like a pony. God, and everyone else in Runaway, knew he was big enough.

"Let's see. Europe. Running summary." Emma kicked into high-school list mode. "Living out of a few cubic feet was overrated. That backpack was a rock. And the food was crap. So I gave it up for Paris."

"The French Conservatory?" That had been second in her five-year plan.

"*Oui. T'as raison.* You're right." She nodded. "Studied lit. Came back here to be the school librarian."

"Really?" That hadn't been in her any-year plan.

"Really. Mrs. Price retired." Emma twisted her hair into a severe bun and put on a pinch-faced grimace—nailing our former librarian's twenty-four seven sour expression.

"You weren't in love with Paris?" I was guessing no, since she still appeared to be in love with Derek. Who still seemed densely oblivious.

Who would give up the sophistication of any guy in France for a corn-fed lumberjack?

She shrugged. "Paris lost its charm. All those near-misses with bicycles. Second-hand smoke. Dog poop on the sidewalk. Kind of killed the whole romantic fantasy." Her eyes darted to Derek's back. "And I missed the…cheese."

I waved my hand in front of her face to get her attention. "France has cheese. They're sort of known for it."

"It's not the same."

Zander made it down the bleachers, and Derek came around the track.

"What's up with Attila the Hun's ATV?" I asked him.

He helped Abby slide off his back. "Four-time state champion." His already massive chest puffed with pride.

"State champion of what—the monster-truck pull?"

Emma shook her head. "Don't ask."

"Don't ask," Abby repeated, stepping onto the first bleacher. She threw out her arms and walked the length airplane-style.

Zander pounded Derek on the back with a solid *thwack*. "He'd still be using that thing to haul hay if I hadn't dared him to race."

"That ATV's a honey in a race," Derek said. "Best dare I ever got."

"You guys are doing that again?" I looked down my nose at a both of them, like a stern look could force them to grow up.

"They never stopped," Emma said.

"Gotta keep things interesting." Zander's smiled was a little too wide and a little too directed at me.

Curiosity sparked all over Derek's face. He flicked an appraising glance between us. "You collect on that kiss yet?"

And why did we keep coming back to that? I ran my fingers through my hair.

Abby snickered and started singing the kissing song again. Thankfully, softer this time.

Zander grinned. "Not yet."

"Not ever." I couldn't tack that on fast enough. Which made me a complete hypocrite, considering that a centimeter of space had been the defining factor between our almost kiss and an actual kiss at the top of the bleachers. But what I couldn't figure out was if my quick refusal came out of habit or fear.

"Shoot, girl." Derek looked at me, but clapped Zander on the back. "Collecting on that kiss has been Zander's numero-uno topic of conversation since Papa Joe texted him you were on your way back."

Zander's grin floundered.

I said, "Papa Joe texted you..." at the same time he said, "Now wait a minute."

Derek went on. "He wouldn't stop telling me that before you blew out of town again, he was going to make sure he sealed that—"

Zander rammed his shoulder into Derek's chest. And I couldn't tell who *oomphed* the loudest. "Business arrangement. I wanted to make sure you thought seriously about that job offer to do marketing for The Resort. That's all."

"That's all?" Derek lifted a shoulder.

Zander massaged his. "Yup, that's all. Just a two-week job."

"Why don't we let Hendrix decide." The sly look in Derek's eye put me on edge.

"She already decided," Zander said. "It was a no go."

"I don't think you laid it all out for her." Derek spun to me. "You know, in terms of *I'd Rather*."

"I'm not going to play a game of live-action *I'd Rather* with you." I put my foot down with my tone.

"Good choice." Emma patted my leg. "That game never ended well. Remember last time?"

We looked at each other and grimaced.

Couldn't forget the lesser evil of the *I'd Rather* pair I'd been forced to carry out. Who knew that when I agreed to lick a leaf, I'd pick the only patch of poison ivy in the woods?

"Let's play a different game then." Derek's sly look slid into wicked. "Zander's favorite game."

"*I Dare You*." Abby named the game with a high jump off the bleachers.

"Right, Firefly." Derek gave her an air high-five.

They'd dragged a seven-year-old into their madness? "I have a pass from *I Dare You*, Derek." I glanced at my ticket to amnesty—Zander— who'd always pinch hit my dares.

"I think your pass expired six years ago when you left." Zander's easy-going tone said he was kidding. His hard eyes said otherwise. Like this might payback for running out on him.

A sinking sensation tugged my insides into a swirl until they felt like they were about to spin down a bottomless drain.

"Finally! Hendrix is fair game." Derek gave a victory yell, crossed his arms over his chest, and smirked. "I dare you to take Zander's two-week job. Or pay up on that kiss—right now."

Chapter 11

Somewhere deep down,
there's a kid inside us waiting to come out.

Work for Zander. Or kiss Zander—in front of everyone. Two more long weeks in Runaway. Or two quick seconds now. No brainer, right?

The stubborn, indignant girl inside me stomped her feet and demanded I shout—*Neither*. But the other girl, the girl pushing to be heard, the girl who was falling for Zander, she wanted me to say—*Both. I want both.* Maybe not such a no-brainer.

The second Derek had challenged me to the dare, he, Emma and Zander locked their eyes on me, and we waited in front of the bleachers in an uncomfortable, bated-breath moment. Even Abby had gotten quiet and moved to stand behind me on the bench.

A fear-of-falling sensation swept through me. Like I was suspended from a thread-thin tightrope stretched between both choices.

"This is stupid." I pushed on Derek's Mack-truck chest. I couldn't believe I'd let him corner me into a dare. "We're not twelve."

"I want to be twelve." Abby twisted my hair, piled it on my head, and used her fingers to hold it there. "When you're twelve you get to play Spin the Bottle."

Emma hid her laugh with a quick tilt of her chin.

Zander shot her a dad-look, then turned to Abby. "No, Abs, that was supposed to be a life lesson about what not to do. Twelve is way too young to—"

"Kiss?" Abby let my hair fall back to my shoulders.

"Get your heart stomped on." Derek lifted an accusatory eyebrow at me.

His barb stirred up that indignant girl inside me. This time she did stomp her feet. Or rather, she stomped mine. Right off the track and toward the exit to the field. "You I didn't miss, Derek," I called over my shoulder.

"Hendrix." Derek's deep voice boomed after me. "I up my challenge—to a double dare."

Derek's biting taunt turned me around. But it was the tight look on Zander's face—like I'd kicked his ego to the curb enough times for him to take the kiss off the menu—that drove my answer.

"The job," I said. "I'll take the job."

Emma did a girlie fist pump the way she used to when she was excited and spun in a circle that whipped her hair into her face.

Abby hopped off the bleachers and copied her—even though she'd lobbied pretty loud for that kiss.

Derek grunted something that sounded like, "I tried, man." And slapped Zander on the back.

And Zander met my eyes, his refusal to look away a different kind of dare.

I walked away, off the field and through the parking lot, head held high—as smoothly as I could on hot pavement with no shoes. With every step, flutters of could-have-been's dive bombed my stomach.

Zander didn't get it. It wasn't that I didn't want to choose the kiss. I was done lying to myself about crossing that line with him. If you counted from the Spin-the-Bottle day in eighth grade, that kiss had been ten years in the making. Ten years overdue.

But I sure as heck wasn't putting on a show for Derek. I wasn't going to put my first kiss with Zander on display. We're weren't teenagers anymore, and I wasn't into PDA. That kiss should be private. Between us. Except I'd pushed Zander away hard enough that I'd lost my chance.

I took a quick shallow breath. That's what sucked about the past, you couldn't change it, even if the past was a minute ago.

I was opening the door to the VW when I looked up to see him jogging toward me, holding my mud-caked shoes. I dropped my keys on the seat and my pride on the pavement, tempted to ask if he'd managed to salvage my poise too, because I didn't have it. "I'm sorry. I made the wrong—"

"Hendrix." He stopped on the passenger side, resting my shoes and his elbows on the roof of the car.

Hendrix. Not Wallflower. An unexpected feeling of loss stole the lift right out of those reckless, aeronautic flutters in my stomach. "Thank you for knighting up and rescuing my shoes."

An awkward span of silence moved into the space between us more solid than the car—something that had never happened, not even when we'd been mad at each other in the past.

I glanced behind him. "Thought you were taking Abby for pizza."

"I pawned her off on Derek and Emma." His tone was so matter-of-fact, so no-big-deal, it was as if the dare had never happened.

"Why?" I hung on to the open car door.

"Come with me a minute." He tilted his head toward the school.

I shut my door and followed him to the theater entrance.

The lock still stuck, and he had to jiggle it left then right, the move as familiar as everything else in this place. He held the door for me. Also familiar. And very Zander.

I walked past him and down the center aisle, running my fingers along the auditorium chairs, until I stood in front of the stage.

Racks of costumes had been lined up for the once-in-a-blue-moon inventory purge. But in my mind, I saw the set for *The King and I* on the last night of our performance. And I saw me in my ball-gown costume twirling across the stage, seconds before the impending disaster.

I heard the door close and Zander's footsteps coming down the aisle. Instead of moving next to me, he lined his body up behind mine. But his chest didn't touch my back. His arms didn't wrap my waist. His chin didn't rest on top of my head.

But I felt him all the same. And he didn't feel matter-of-fact or no-big-deal anymore.

"I'm sorry, Wallflower." His voice was quiet next to my ear. "Sorry for our last night here."

On stage, I watched myself bow. Heard the ripping of the dress. Imagined what I must've looked like to the audience. And instead of all the shame and humiliation churning up inside me, I felt...nothing. All these years, I'd been holding onto something that just wasn't important anymore.

"It was funny, wasn't it?" I took the smallest step back, just enough for my shoulders to barely graze his chest, and his breathing picked up in synch with mine. "Bet Runaway High will never top that theater moment."

"You were right to be mad." His hands found my arms and drifted slowly down to my wrists and back up again, his light touch on my skin throwing my heartrate into the same choppy rhythm as my lungs.

"When I cut your costume, I wasn't thinking about you." His hands stopped roaming. "I was thinking about the look on Derek's face when he realized he owed me a hundred bucks."

"You bet a hundred dollars?" I leaned all the way back against his chest, against the steady thump of his heart.

With a barely muted sigh, he wrapped his arms around me, and rested his cheek against mine. "Yeah. He didn't think I'd do it."

"Why?" His solid body sheltering mine and his lips by my ear made me work harder to have a coherent conversation. Thoughts that Zander was touching me, Zander was holding me, kept getting in the way. "When...have you ever turned down a dare?"

"I turned them down all the time..." He lowered his voice to a sweet rumble. "If they involved you."

I closed my eyes, soaking that in. "So why that night?"

"Because both dares were about you. He dared me to cut your costume..." He tipped his head so his breath fanned across the side of my neck. "Or admit how I really felt about you."

Derek wanted us together? "Why didn't you tell him we were just friends?" I held my next inhale, waiting for his answer.

"Because we weren't." He didn't even hesitate.

Deep down, I'd always known that. On the outside we'd danced on the line of all those friend-zone rules. But on the inside we'd always been more. "Why didn't you ever ask me out?"

He brushed his nose along my ear, sparking tingles that ran all the way down my neck. "You wanted to leave, be someone different, long before the wardrobe incident. You weren't going to be happy as a small-town girl. And I didn't want you to stay for me."

I turned in his arms. Put my hands on his chest. "You wanted to leave for college too."

"Yeah," he held my gaze, "but I was always planning on coming back. I'd been thinking about trying to put The Resort back together before we even graduated."

And I blurted out, "I'm sorry I picked the job." Then flattened myself against him, burying my face in his chest. There. It was out. I'd said it. And if it was too late—

"Why are you sorry?" He ran his hands down my hair.

"I didn't want our first kiss to be in front of Derek and Emma and Abby. I wanted our first kiss—"

"You *wanted* our first kiss?" Stepping back, he cupped my cheeks, raising my face.

I nodded.

Then with no warning, no hesitation, no lead-in, Zander crashed his lips against mine.

Startled, I fell into the kiss. Felt it everywhere. In the warmth of his mouth, in his hands on my face, in the frantic way he worshipped my lips with pressure that alternated between not quite enough and almost overwhelming.

Desperation seemed to direct the way his hands slid into my hair and gripped me. The way his mouth nipped and grazed across mine. The way he pulled me closer and closer and closer until everything faded away and all that was left was him.

Just as desperate, I fisted both my hands into his shirt and hung on. Rode through the butterfly-band beating their wings in victory, spinning me dizzy, shooting tingles from my lips to my pedicured toes.

Finally, breathing heavy, he broke our connection and lifted his head.

"What was that?" I touched my mouth.

"Just making sure I didn't miss my chance. I waited too long that night we played Spin the Bottle. I waited too long on the bleachers."

I smiled. Extremely glad that kiss had been just him and I.

He palmed the back of my neck. "And now that your debt to me is cleared...with interest—" his eyes danced "—I can take the rest of the afternoon to do this." He tilted his head and brushed his lips across my jaw in a slow, sweet move that left me trembling. "And convince you to still take the job."

"I'll take the job." Easiest sell ever. His lips had super-persuasive powers.

"Two weeks." He stroked his fingers across my cheek and down my neck, pausing on my pulse point. "To see where this is going with us."

I nodded.

"Then we can reevaluate." He trailed soft kisses over my face, coming close, but never quite brushing my lips. "Maybe you'll decide to stay longer. A lot longer."

"Maybe." A shiver swirled across my skin. I wrapped my arms around him. If he kept this up, there wouldn't be a lot of maybe about it.

His thumb skimmed the curve of my ear. His finger traced my spine. And he kept teasing me with those almost kisses until I was dying for him to press his lips to mine.

The next time he got near the corner of my mouth, I grabbed his jaw and turned my head, leading him exactly where I wanted him to go.

He grinned against my mouth and took the hint, fusing our lips together, taking the kiss deeper and deeper and deeper, until I couldn't think about anything but his hands sliding across my back and his mouth claiming mine.

Kissing Zander fast, kissing Zander slow—it didn't matter—I was kissing Zander. And it made coming back to Runaway more than worth it. It made staying a possibility I never thought I'd entertain.

And right in the middle of my happy kissing high, just when things went from amazing to rock-my-world, my stomach growled.

Because it wouldn't be a me-moment if something embarrassing didn't happen.

Zander lifted his head, laughing. "Do you want to meet them for pizza?"

"Heck, no." I pulled his head back down. "We have ten years to make up for."

Chapter 12

Family doesn't have to be blood.
Family is the people you love.

Didn't matter if you were five, fifteen, or fifty—if you lived in Runaway, Papa Joe was your grandpa. Not that you'd find him posing for a Norman Rockwell. With his beatnik wisdom and his ability to talk to anybody about anything, he was a combination Hippie-Santa Claus, therapist, and bartender.

If you needed something, it wasn't unusual to find it wrapped in hemp paper on your front porch. His kitchen table never closed for business, his insight didn't come with an hourly rate, and happy hour never had last call. The only downside to drinking with him was that he insisted on serving Duke's moonshine, and that stuff could sprout hair on a bald man.

There were a lot of things about this town I could do without. Like the four-screen theater that showed movies a month late, night life that consisted of stoplight-gazing in the middle of the only four-way intersection, and the pizza place that only served reheated pepperoni. Yum.

But as my first week working for Zander closed out, things I didn't realize I'd wanted lined up to beat down the door of my heart and beg me to stay. Skipping stones at the lake with Zander. Chasing lightning bugs with Abby. DIY mani-pedis with Emma. Gossiping with the blue-haired ladies in the library over lunch.

Not to mention Sunday supper with whoever happened to bring a side dish and show up when church—either church—let out at noon.

Today's whoever turned out to be Zander, his sister, Abby, both Double Dare brothers, Emma, and of course the Grizzly Adam's Biker Gang—Duke and Bo and Coop. We wouldn't be hurting for moonshine.

But Papa Joe would. I leaned against the kitchen counter by the sink and snatched the tipped glass out of his hand before a drop hit his mouth.

"Bug," he whined. "It's the new batch. You can't just go cold turkey."

I rolled my eyes. "It's not LSD." Although it came with its own version of flashbacks. "You don't need a withdrawal plan."

"You know, if I'm supposed to give up Duke's brew for light beer and pizza for salad," he shuddered, "you're going to have to make it worth my while." His mournful eyes would've rivaled the best hound dog in the county, and he looked at my ring finger expectantly. Then at my flat stomach.

"Back off the great grandchildren bandwagon. Zander and I have only been together a week."

"Fine. Be that way." He reached for the moonshine.

I pushed the glass farther across the counter. Then changed my mind and dumped it down the drain.

"Bug!" His tone horrified, he slapped a hand to his chest. "You can't—"

"Are Grandma's deviled eggs done?" I grabbed a towel and wiped a chunk of mayo off his apron.

"Done and on the table." Zander stepped behind us, taking a beat to lean over and kiss my cheek in a move that made Papa Joe sigh.

I swear he was about to wax poetic or burst out into a flurry of beat poetry about *love, man, love*. When he watched us together, he seemed to melt quicker than I did over my guy's sweetness—and my swoon level over Zander this last week was pretty hard to beat.

In a loud crash, the back door swung open, and The Double Dare Brothers came through carrying plates of grilled ribs. Derek set his on the counter where I'd been setting up a buffet and thundered past me before I could nail him with a glare. It wasn't a secret that the friends-not-friends bipolar *thing* he had going with Emma scraped my skin the wrong way.

Chase acknowledged Zander with a fist bump, left his plate next to his brother's, and turned to me. "Welcome back, Hendrix." Although he was as massive as Derek, I didn't fear for my life when he pulled me into a hug, I hugged him back.

Emma and Abby came in next, wearing sundresses and matching smears of barbeque sauce on the corners of their mouths.

"We're the taste testers," Abby said.

I rolled my eyes. "More like you called first dibs."

"First ribs." Abby laughed and ran out of the kitchen yelling, "Uncle D."

"Not quite sure what that girl sees in your brother," I told Chase. But my gaze didn't trail after Abby, it landed on Emma.

Chase held up both hands, shook his head, and backed out of the room.

Busying herself, Emma grabbed the pan of fish I'd made and added it to the buffet behind a sign that had Papa Joe's name and a healthy, happy heart. Or at least as close to one as my limited artistic skill could render. It kind of looked like a dancing squiggle with a smile and stick legs.

A large burst of shouts came from the family room downstairs where Duke, Bo, Coop, and Zander's sister, Brynn, had disappeared the second Papa Joe started delegating kitchen duties.

Ripping off his apron, Papa Joe took off for the family room. "You're recording the game, not watching it. Turn it off..." He groaned. "Oh for the love of world peace." His voice rocketed up the stairs. "Was that a touchdown?"

The back door burst open, and Harriot Dixon's beehive hairdo entered first. She handed off her pans of Last Chance Lutheran's Home Brigade meatloaf to Zander. "There's lemonade in the car." With that announcement, she disappeared toward the chaos coming from downstairs, fussing about Papa Joe getting too worked up.

Interesting. When had Mrs. Dixon gotten so concerned over Papa Joe?

"I'll go grab the lemonade." Emma went outside, leaving Zander and I in the kitchen.

Zander looked around, peeked in the cupboards, lifted a dishtowel, then turned to me with a devilish grin. "Alone at last."

The teasing look in his eyes made me smile all the way to my toes. "I forgot how many people come through this house on a Sunday afternoon."

"Too many." Stalking over, he backed me against the counter, putting one palm on either side of me. "Way too many when all I want is some private time with you."

"Private?" I widened my eyes. "Why do we need to be private?"

"Cause you're not into PDA, Wallflower. And I've been dying to do this since you held my hand in church." He lowered his head and dropped a kiss on the corner of my mouth.

I leaned back like I was shocked. "You were thinking of kissing me during Reverend Lovejoy's sermon? I'm pretty certain thinking about kissing in church is near the top of the list of his Banned Behaviors."

"Well, since I'm Catholic, I think I'm okay. But a Lutheran girl like you might have a problem." His fingers slid up the back of my neck into my hair, and he gripped my waist, quit playing around, and kissed me exactly the way I liked. Like there wasn't anyone else in the world but me.

Chapter 13

If you won't ditch your plans,
you can't choose a new life.

Inside my office at City Hall—behind a door labeled *Janitor's Closet*—I leaned back in a 1920s Runaway-original office chair. In California, the chair would've been labeled retro and sold for the price of a small car. Here, Zander had to raid the stash down the hall that had been marked *dumpster*.

My desk was new. If you counted a folding plastic table as a desk. But at least Zander had used his mayoral superpowers to get me something to write on other than metal shelving or mop buckets.

And then there was the view. If both our doors were propped open, I had a direct shot to his desk across the hall. A direct shot to him. Which negated the recycled furniture, the musty smell pouring from the walls, and the cement with the drain under my feet that kept catching my heel.

Zander had spent most of the morning on the phone negotiating a better deal on catfish to stock Runaway's lake, arguing where the sewer system split off into the next town, and agreeing to cut the ribbon at the seventeenth grand re-opening of The Palace Theater. Small town problems.

Now he was glued to his computer screen, headphones on, nodding his head in time to his Icelandic heavy metal playlist—a habit he firmly denied when I called him out on it.

A video would solve that. I picked up my phone and hit the camera app, then glanced at my laptop. The changes to The Resort's website and the city's tourist page were almost up. If Runaway's network connection wasn't strung between a pair of tin cans, the sync would've been done in seconds.

My phone rang. An international number. London. A weird vibration in my chest pulled me out of my chair, and I stared at the screen. Who did I know in London?

Across the hall, Zander caught my gaze and gave me a question-mark look, tapping his headphones—his way of asking if he should take them off.

I smiled and shook my head. Everything was fine. Probably the wrong number.

So why was my quick, "Hello," so shaky?

"Miss Hendrix Marshall?" a man asked in a very British accent.

"Yes?" That weird vibration amped.

Zander's sudden air drum and chair spin grounded me into a low laugh.

"I have Mrs. Roberta Bristol for you."

I glanced away from Zander and scrambled to clear my head. Roberta Bristol. The VP of marketing for PharmaZen's worldwide operations? One of the most powerful women in the pharmaceutical world, she made drugs into household names on a global scale. And she was on the phone. For me. Right now. I wanted to hyperventilate a little. Okay, a lot.

The line clicked. "Miss Marshall." A professional female, also British, came on the line. "Roberta Bristol with PharmaZen here."

"Ms. Bristol." My pulse thumped.

"One of your former supervisors passed me your resume. I must say I'm impressed. Even with Pelvavox's poor initial positioning, your ad strategy gave the drug a fifteen percent market share."

"Fifteen percent?" Throat tight, I clenched my fingers around the phone. "No one told me that." Not when they gave me my severance package. Not when they showed me the door.

"You didn't know?" She sounded amused. Which for a British person meant she made an attempt at a barely-there chuckle.

In his office, Zander pulled off one side of his headphones, took a call, and resumed air drumming with his free hand—like a little boy playing dress-up in the Mayor's Office.

When I didn't respond, Ms. Bristol said, "Typical for a startup not to recognize their talent when a drug does not make initial target figures."

I cleared my throat over the anger still trying to choke me out over that fifteen percent.

"We have a new product launching in eighteen months. Global release. And we want you to head up that team. Reporting to me."

Global release plus Roberta Bristol? A career game-changer. A squeal of delight rode right past the tightening in my throat and almost bubbled out. "You're offering me a job." I tried to be smooth. And failed when a tiny bit of joy burst out.

"Of course we'll pay for a full relocation to our New York office, and you'll spend a third of your year in London, so I hope you like the rain."

New York. London. Zander. My joy fizzled.

Ms. Bristol continued with some of the job details.

While I listened, I glanced at the office across the hall and watched Zander lean over his file cabinet and shake his butt in those skinny jeans.

He turned and threw me a hundred-and-twenty-watt smile that expressed everything he felt about me without any words.

My face felt like lead, but I smiled back.

"So," Ms. Bristol wrapped up, "shall I send you the formal offer?"

My heart pounded out options to Ms. Bristol's question in a fast beat that bruised my ribs. If I said no, that one word would end my pharmaceutical career. If I said yes, the job would take me from Runaway. And from Zander. I'd be lucky to get a fly-by holiday or two a year. And he wouldn't leave. Not The Resort or his sister…or Abby. I couldn't ask him to.

"Miss Marshall? Would you like to see the formal offer? Yes or no?" Ms. Bristol's cut-to-the-chase tone indicated the offer was a one-time, take-it-now-or-lose-it-forever deal. And that she had better things to do than wait on me.

I breathed over the pressure building in my ribs and looked at Zander again. What if yes meant maybe? If I turned her down, I'd lose the chance. If I didn't, I could buy time to think it through.

"Yes." I forced the words past the giant piece of cotton clogging up my throat. "I'd like to see the offer."

"My assistant will send it. I'll call you Thursday." Ms. Bristol hung up with a *click* as clipped as her accent.

Three days to decide. Not enough time. I glanced at Zander, then at the phone, and sank onto my desk.

And the table gave at the seam, folded in half, and sent me sprawling onto the cement.

Chapter 14

*Small-town relationships don't stay small—
because everyone in town has an opinion.*

Most girls ugly-cried. I Medusa-cried.

But I held back—even though my hip stung and a shockwave pulsed through my elbow and I'd just gotten the take-me-away from Zander offer of a lifetime.

"Wallflower?" Zander came rushing in and dropped to his knees beside me and the tipped-over table. "Are you okay?"

I sat on the cement floor of my pseudo-office, and balanced on the hip that wasn't in need of a bottle of Ibuprofen and an ice-pack. A white hot mess, my hair fell into my face from my shaken-loose French twist, my skirt hiked high on my thighs, and tears burned for release behind my eyes. So not okay. But I nodded anyway.

Slipping into EMT mode, he touched my elbow with gentle fingers. "Am I hurting you?"

"No." But I might hurt him. And the thought of hurting Zander sent my heart careening around a sharp curve so fast my chest caved.

Sliding his fingers across my cheek and into my hair, he kissed my forehead, then carefully lifted me to my feet. "I'm going to buy you some tennis shoes and elbow pads for Christmas."

Christmas. My heart picked up speed. Zander's casual comment implied so much. That I'd still be here. That we'd still be together. And what was I supposed to say to that? Hey, I got this great job offer that's everything I wanted, and by the way, I'm moving to New York and London, so thanks for the last two weeks and maybe we can do this again in another six years.

I massaged my hip and straightened my long, layered skirt, glad I hadn't worn my short black mini. Then tried to fix my wayward hair. "Am I never not a mess around you?" My deadpan laugh was thick with unshed tears.

Grinning, he swooped in to press his mouth against my ear. "Don't tell anyone, but I kind of like you a little…messy."

And my heart drove right off that curve. If he said one more thing like that to me, I wouldn't be able to hold back the truth about the call.

I stepped away and tried for a normal smile, but my lips weighed ten pounds and curved the other way. "Weren't we going to lunch?" I tugged him toward the library entrance where there'd be fewer people to witness my nursing-home gait. I was already feeling the bone-deep bruise forming on my hip.

Thick blue carpet in the small room packed with paperbacks silenced our footsteps. The only sound was the steady drone of the air conditioner. The shades had been pulled over the front windows as a barrier against the hot summer sun. The librarian was missing as usual. Two-hour lunch and all.

"Who was on the phone?" Zander stopped me next to one of three revolving book racks devoted to pirate romance.

The guys on the covers were all the same—glamour-shot hair, chiseled faces, open shirts flapping in the breeze showing off shaded-in abs. The only difference between the cover clones was the color combinations of their shirts, hair, and eyes.

I tipped my head toward a book on the bottom rack. White shirt. Black hair. Green eyes. "Just someone from a pharmaceutical company."

Taking my hands, he played with my fingers, then searched my eyes like he knew something big was up. "You got a job offer, didn't you?" His voice caught.

I didn't want to do this now, but the instant ache in his eyes pushed me to answer. "It was nothing. It's just—"

"Where?" He set a hand on top of the spinning rack like he needed something to hand onto.

I shook my head. I needed time. To think. To breathe. To stop the terrible tugging on my heart between the girl I used to be and the girl who didn't know who she was anymore. Two weeks ago I'd never have imagined being so torn up over the possibility of leaving Runaway. Today—?

"Where?" he asked again, lifting my chin.

"New York. London." I blinked back that earlier burn in my eyes.

"Wow." That one word laid the first brick in the wall going up in his eyes. The wall that covered an ache that spread to me. "The offer would have to be amazing for you to be so upset."

"It was from PharmZen—one of the top pharmaceuticals. My dream job." But Zander was my dream guy. And I wanted both. Why couldn't I have both?

I already knew why. Dream jobs came with price tags. Sacrifices. Obstacles. Mine was geography. I couldn't work remotely from here. Zander wouldn't—couldn't—relocate.

"So these two weeks with me have been what?" Another row of bricks piled on that wall rising in his eyes. "A drive through the past before you move on to your future? A place to park until something better came along?"

"No." I palmed his jaw. "No." Zander was the best thing to happen to me in...forever.

He circled my wrist with his hand. "I thought we were giving us a chance." The wall grew again. "I thought we were figuring things out."

"We were. We are." How was this happening to me? Three weeks ago, I couldn't even get an interview for an interview, and now I was getting an offer from the top in my field? Life, fate, whatever had the world's worst timing.

"Which one is it?" He pulled my fingers from his face. "We *were* figuring things out? Or we *are*?"

"This job offer? It's my career, Zander. I'll never get anything better. I may never get anything at all if I don't take this. And there aren't any opportunities for me around here."

"That's funny. Because I thought there was an opportunity for you right here." He touched his chest with his index finger.

"Zander." I covered his hand with mine over his shirt and pressed against his heart. "I have three days to decide."

The last brick in that wall slid into place. "It sounds like you already made your choice." He stepped back.

My hand fell to my side. "I haven't made any choices. How can I when I've only known about the offer for ten minutes? I need a chance to process. Think things through."

"What's to think through?" Unlike the wall he'd built in his eyes to protect himself from me, he didn't shield me from the betrayal or the sarcasm in his tone. "It's your dream job."

"That's not fair." This time I stepped back. "What if I asked you to come with me to New York right now?"

He raked an aggressive hand through his hair. "I can't leave my job or The Resort or my family—"

"Exactly." I nailed him with a single word. A single word that said everything.

Our eyes met in a silent stand-off over what we wanted, what we needed, and what we couldn't have.

Zander was the first to walk away.

Chapter 15

A good mani-pedi is ointment for the soul.

Roberta Bristol gave me seventy-two hours. Zander walked away in less than one.

The first day without him, I changed into my *Pony* PJ's, wallowed in a pint of moo-ca-licious ice cream, and resurrected my Barbie collection—brushing their hair until it started to fall out in chunks.

The second day without him, I donned a pair of ripped sweat pants and hid in my room in an attempt to shutdown Operation Stay in Runaway. Didn't work. At breakfast, Papa Joe brought me biscuits and gravy and went on and on about how lonely Emma had been without me. At lunch, he served cheese curds from the ten-booth farmer's market in the square and mentioned how beautiful Zander's babies would be. At dinner, he grilled me a beer brat, made himself a salad, and sat next to me on my bed spouting statistics about the dangers of living alone with angina.

On the third day, I slipped into a pair of yoga pants and checked my social media, my job boards, and spammed everyone I knew—and some I didn't—about potential employment in my field. Nothing within driving distance of Runaway compared to PharmaZen's offer. Unless I wanted to commute three hours to Chicago, twice a day, for forty percent less pay.

My future skidded to a screeching halt in front of a two-pronged fork in the road.

Veer left. Cruise the career boost of PharmaZen. And give up Zander.

Choose right. Coast at Runaway's tourism office until their funds ran out, then hawk cow-shaped cheese at the Mouse House. And keep Zander.

My head was spinning *Exorcist*-style over that unfair fork in the road when Emma's text popped onto my screen—*Girls' Night. I'm on Abby duty. Me. You. Her. Nail polish. Now!*

Dizzy and torn up and nine-tenths of the way to heartbroken, I pulled on a pair of holdover jeans from high school and went.

Nothing was far in Runaway, including Emma's place. She'd bought the old 1920s one-room, brick schoolhouse on Main Street when it went up for auction last year. And turned it into an IKEA shrine.

"Wow." I stood in her entryway, attracted to the bright color she'd splashed throughout the large open-floorplan.

"What do you think?" She motioned me all the way inside and shut the heavy double wooden doors.

I grinned. "I think I want to move in."

Three walls of the interior were left in the original brick, but she'd stucco'd the back wall, swirled it with white and yellow paint, then hung frames of all shapes and sizes in a collage of modern art.

A kitchen area took up the back left corner. A circular staircase on the right wound to a small loft I assumed to be her bedroom.

And in the middle, arranged over a woven-fabric rug, sat a couch, a few chairs, and one of those huge bean-bags-for-eight. Brightly-colored throw pillows and blankets accented the look. Such an ultramodern contrast to the sixties chic at Papa Joe's.

"You really like it?" Emma clapped her hands together like she was five, and her eyes danced. I wondered how her bubbly personality worked when she stepped into her role as a librarian. I couldn't reconcile Mary Poppins meets Headmistress McGonagall.

"I love it." I smiled because her excitement was catching. And because I needed this tonight. Needed a friend. Hadn't had a real one in a while.

"Hendrix." Abby flew down the spiral staircase, barely holding onto the railing, and barreled into my arms like I hadn't seen her in a year. "We're having grown-up girls' night. And it's late."

I checked the big world clock Emma hung over her stove. 9:00. Late for a seven-year-old.

Abby squeezed me hard, then skipped away. Someone had flat-ironed her curls.

"I like your hair," I told her.

"Emma did it. And my makeup." She pointed to the soft swipe of cherry lip gloss on her mouth.

"Welcome to spa night." Emma took my keys and my wallet and dropped them on an art-deco table next to a cute, cut-glass lamp.

"Sit down." Abby plopped onto the far edge of the rug near a salon's worth of nail polish and patted the tarp Emma had smartly spread over the floor. "We're gonna paint each other's toes first."

"Kick off your shoes." Emma pulled me toward her makeshift spa, while I was trying to de-shoe. Should've worn sandals instead of tennis shoes. "Pick your color, girls. I'm going with *Scarlet A*. French and mod."

I picked up a few colors. Definitely not drugstore polish. "You didn't get this stash in Runaway." Mod and Runaway were not words that went together.

"Amazon." She laughed. "And the post office. It's not like we're living on the moon."

I picked up a burnt-brown polish. "No, because that would at least be interesting." Weird how my Runaway sarcasm fell flat. It just didn't have the same bite as the first day I'd come into town.

Abby slid the bottle from my hand and gave it to Emma. "I want to do your toes, so I get to pick your colors."

I shrugged. How bad could her pick be? There wasn't a color in Emma's collection I didn't like.

Emma arranged us on the tarp in a weird version of seated *Twister*, so that she could reach Abby's toes, Abby could reach mine, and I could reach Emma's. It took a little maneuvering, but we stretched and adjusted until we made the odd circle work.

Abby's idea of picking my color turned out to be ten colors. She was halfway done painting each of my nails—and the surrounding skin—a different shade, before it clicked that I was letting a seven-year-old give me a pedi. A few weeks ago I'd never have let a little girl come near me with a bottle, or ten, of nail polish.

Emma finished Abby's toes first. "Don't get up until they dry."

"Okay." Abby screwed the top on the Neon Purple she'd used on my big toe and set it next to the Lemon Lime she painted on my pinky toe, then appraised me with a critical gaze—as critical as a first grader can after she's done your nails in tens shades of I-don't-match. "So are you going to take that highfalutin job or what?"

My brush slipped, and I painted a stroke of *Scarlet A* on top of Emma's foot.

Wiping it with her thumb, she offered one word. "Derek."

I turned to Abby, my gaze more critical than hers. "Derek told you I got a job offer?" Had Zander driven his monster truck straight there from the library and told him everything? Our private everything?

"No." Abby shook her head thoughtfully. "But I heard him tell Emma and Chase and Mrs. Dixon—"

Ohmyeverloving gosh. "Why would he tell Mrs. Dixon?"

"I don't know." She shrugged. "She was there, I guess. Dropping off meatloaf."

"At Derek's?"

"At Zander's," Emma said. "She feeds him when he's in crunch-mode working on The Resort. He doesn't have that much time in between all his other jobs."

My chest squeezed hard. I pushed against the Zander ache and caught Abby's gaze. "Back to Derek and his loose lips. Does everyone in this town know about my job offer?"

"Umm…" Abby shifted her mouth to the left and blinked toward the high ceiling. Then looked at me. "Just Miss Eberhart from his school and—"

"His school? Like Zander's school? *Derek's* a teacher too?"

"Yep. He teaches calculated."

"Calculus?" I accidently swiped another coat of paint on Emma's skin. "You've got to be kidding me."

She took the bottle away and put it behind her.

"Oh." Abby tilted her head and flexed her Apple Red toes. "He also told Mr. Henry at the post office. And Reverend Lovejoy."

"Well, great." I leaned back on the tarp. "Now I can't even go to church."

"You're not allowed in church?" Abby's pupils doubled in size.

"Probably not." Because even though Zander spent most Saturday nights at Hope Eternal's mass instead of Sunday mornings at Last Chance Lutheran, Reverend Lovejoy preferred him over me. "Does this spa night come with a wine bar?" I asked Emma.

"There's sparkling apple juice in the fridge." She smiled toward Abby. "It's under-twenty-one night."

"Apple juice it is." I got up, walked toward the kitchen area, and poured myself a glass, careful not to the paint her stained-cement floor with my still-drying feet. There was more polish on skin than there was on nail. And Abby had polka-dotted all my nails with globs of runny white.

"Why don't you just say no?" Abby trailed after me and pulled a plastic cup from a lower cupboard, like she knew her way around this kitchen.

"I don't mind apple juice." I filled her cup.

"No, silly. About the job." She took a sip and set the juice down. "Just say no. Like you're supposed to with drugs."

Were the schools already freaking out about drug awareness in first grade? It was Runaway. I looked at her over my cup. "It's not like drugs."

Emma joined us by the fridge and put the juice away. "It kind of is. You work in pharmaceuticals. And I think you should say no, too. No to drugs."

"Yes. To. Uncle. Zander." Abby punched the air with one of Emma's famous fist pumps.

"Yes to Zander," Emma agreed. "Yes to Zandrix."

"You shipped me and Zander?" You couldn't miss the what-the-heck leaking from my tone. Or my grow-up eye roll.

"Zandrix. Zandrix. Zandrix." Abby and Emma chanted the combined version of our names.

"Saying yes to *Zandrix*…" I set my glass on the counter a little harder than I'd intended. "Isn't that simple."

"Yes it is. Which do you love more?" Abby closed both hands like she was hiding something inside and held them out. "Drugs or Uncle Zander?"

"It's not drugs or Zander. It's my career or Zander. You want me to pick one and set women's lib back seventy years?" Why was I explaining my life choices to a seven-year-old?

"Don't be stupid." Emma laughed. "You're not even into women's lib. And it has nothing to do with choosing a career over a man."

"It doesn't?" I crossed my arms in a pose as sarcastic as my tone.

"It's choosing one career over another. I wanted to be a lit professor. Now I'm a librarian. But I love my job."

No. She loved Derek. In vain. I glanced at Abby. But now wasn't the time to point that out. "I loved my job." My instant statement gave me pause. Had I really? Or had it just been the means to locking down the small-town girl and going big city?

"You can't marry your job," Abby said.

"Trust me. That's not true." I'd seen enough people married to their jobs. Isolated. Lonely. Empty people. Even if they'd taken the time to grab a spouse and a few kids along the way.

Something inside me went hollow as I tried to imagine my life with the PharmaZen choice. Meetings. Travel. Hotels. Shallow relationships. Surface appearances.

My gaze swept over the warmth of Emma's house—the warmth of Emma—and slid toward Abby's lip-glossed smile, and my crazy toes.

"Welllll," Abby drew out the word like she was thinking really hard. "You can't make babies with a job."

Her kiss song from the bleachers rang through my head. "I don't want babies." I hugged my waist.

And Abby hugged me. Right over the barrier I'd made with my arms. "Yes, you do."

That hollow place inside me bottomed out. What if she was right? What if Papa Joe was right? What if wanted babies? Zander's babies. Not now. I wasn't ready. But later. Much later. I wiggled my arms from between Abby and me and rubbed my hands across her back.

"Don't take the job. Don't leave." Abby sighed against my shirt.

"Yeah." Emma joined our hug. "Don't leave."

Their hugs and their words—what Papa Joe would call their free love—combined with every moment I'd spent with Zander since I'd come back and rushed through me in a whirlwind.

I knew what I had to do. Squeezing them tight, I pulled away. "I gotta go."

I scooped up my shoes, my wallet and my keys, pulled up Ms. Bristol's number on my phone, and ran barefoot for my car. And my future.

Chapter 16

As far as small town cliché's went—
Runaway, Wisconsin was pretty much perfect.

I got pulled over on my way out to The Resort. But Officer Little—one of Runaway's four full-time policeman—was more interested in finding out if I'd taken the job with PharmaZen than writing me a ticket.

Apparently, he played right field for the town's summer softball league on Derek's team—*Lithe Lumberjacks*. If the other players were tree trunks like him and Derek, whoever christened them *lithe* was screaming for a gift-subscription to Dictionary.com.

I turned the VW onto Zander's property, and Officer Little gave me a flashing-light salute in my rearview mirror and made a choppy Y-turn on the narrow two-lane road. I'd declined the police escort, but since my late-night visit involved the best interests of the mayor, he'd insisted.

Everyone in this town was Team Zandrix.

I parked in front of the lodge. Tapped my fingers on the steering wheel. Trained my gaze on the glow from the curtain-covered window on the second floor. My brief brush with the law had dragged down some of my win-back-the-boy momentum.

What if *Zander* wasn't Team Zandrix?

What if he wouldn't take another chance on me? What if he didn't want to? Maybe in the three days we'd been apart, the Hendrix section of his heart hadn't grown three sizes larger. Maybe it had shrunk. Maybe he was glad I was leaving.

Only I wasn't—leaving.

I picked up my phone and looked at my call log. Considering it was four in the morning in London, I figured I had a couple hours before Ms. Bristol retrieved her voicemail. Not that she'd be getting back to me. Not after I turned her down.

Darkening the screen, I dropped the phone onto the seat, rallied my resolve, and got out of the car. With or without Zander in my life, I'd walked away from everything PharmaZen represented, waved goodbye to the big city pull, and chosen to embrace the small-town girl inside me.

I touched the hem of my Pink Floyd tee, an across-the-world contrast to my usual uniform of blouses and skirts and heels. Wearing nice clothes had made me feel important and in control. Poised and powerful. Like I'd made something of myself. Or at least I thought so.

Now I saw my uniform for what it really was—an illusion.

My concert tee, comfy jeans, and even my Abby-painted toes, felt real. Felt like home. Being back at The Resort felt the same. And for the first time since I'd gotten out of Mr. Jensen's cab, I was excited to stay.

I looked back up at the lit window, hoping *Zander* would be excited for me to stay.

Something creaked behind me, turning me around.

A lantern snapped on, offering a shadowed view of a shirtless Zander sitting at the edge of the dock drinking a beer.

Choosing to take that as a sign he wanted to be found, I gained back some of the momentum Officer Little stole and walked barefoot through the thick grass. When I got to the rough wooden planks, I stepped carefully across the dock, praying I didn't get a splinter. The last one Zander had tweezered out of my toe—after the graduation bonfire—had been the size of a small tree.

Zander trailed a foot through the water. "Probably would've been better if you hadn't stopped to say goodbye." He took a swig from his long-necked bottle.

Restless flutters filled my heart as I sat next to him under the clear, star-spattered sky. "Better for you or for me?"

He didn't answer. He also didn't ask me to leave.

The smell of the lake was stronger at night, mixing with the smoky scent of a recent bonfire every time a light breeze floated by.

I dipped my feet in the cool water and leaned back on my hands, watching the way his arm flexed every time he lifted the bottle. "You don't look like those book-cover clones."

"What are you talking about?" He cracked his neck, then twisted toward me.

"The pirates. From the library." At his narrowed eyes, I added, "It's a compliment. They're generic and bumpy with all those overdone, airbrushed muscles. But you're…kind of beautiful."

He rotated back toward the water, shooting those restless flutters full of anxiety. "Why are you here?"

To jump into your arms and claim my happily-ever-after. Only it wasn't quite working out like the movie in my mind. Of course, I'd come with zero of the script memorized and no plot—so there was that.

Maybe I needed to open the scene with a hike down memory lane. "How many nights a week do you think I broke curfew sitting right here with you?" I'd always joked there was zero nightlife in Runaway—but that hadn't been accurate. There'd been a lifetime of nightlife right out here at The Resort.

"Enough." He offered me the beer.

Something he'd done a hundred times in high school. Only now we were legal. I took a sip. And choked. "You're still drinking this nasty stuff?" I handed the bottle back.

He was careful not to brush his fingers over mine. "We don't all have a wine collection to go with our kale and sushi."

"What if I gave up wine?"

"Why would you do that." It wasn't a question. Not even in the realm of rhetorical. It was a veiled, stop-dragging-this-out directive.

I pulled my feet from the water and drew up my knees, moving ahead with my win-back-the-boy plan anyway. "Maybe wine isn't as awesome as I thought. Maybe I could relearn to like the beer."

"Maybe you shouldn't."

His words opened spiked wings on those flutters, and they scraped my heart raw. I got up from the dock and walked away, every step pushing them to gouge deeper, until I stopped and turned around. "If me taking this job was your choice, would you tell me to go or ask me to stay?"

His back stayed toward me, but he lifted the beer and toasted me with a resigned gesture. "I'm not gonna get in your way, Hendrix. You've been absolved. I'll go to confession for you Saturday night. You can leave guilt-free."

"I'm not here because I feel guilty." I shifted my feet on the dock and pressed on the burn in my chest. "I'm here because I turned down the job."

Silence hung over the dock for one inflamed heartbeat. Two. Three. Four.

"You still standing there, Wallflower?" Zander set down the bottle.

"I am." I started the heartbeat count again. One. Two…

He pushed off the wood planks, turned, and shoved his hands into the pockets of his jeans, his expression heavy. "Say that again."

"I'm still standing here."

"Not that." He took a few steps forward. "The other part."

"I turned down the job." My feet stuck to the dock. My heart stuck to my chest. And since it wasn't really beating at full capacity anyway, I said the rest. "I've decided to stay—with or without you in my life."

"With or without me?" He stayed where he was as if my inability to move my feet was catching. But there was something hopeful in his voice that kept me talking.

"I'm choosing the future I want for myself. But just so you know, if I do this without you, I'm blaming you for the fallout. It only took three days of wallowing in ice cream for my hips and butt to pile on collateral damage. The months it'll take me to put a Band-Aid on my broken heart will push my dress size into a new zip code."

"I guess we can't have that." The heaviness on his face lifted. And then he moved. Sprinted across the dock. Caught me up in a hug that lifted my feet and soothed the stinging ache inside my chest. "I like your dress size."

"You do?" I wound my hands around his neck.

"I do." He let me slide down his body, then shaped his hands over my waist. "I like your dress size a lot."

"And what about me?"

"I like you a lot too." He ran a hand through my hair, then cupped both my cheeks. "But if you're really staying, then you're *staying*. I'm not letting you drive away from me or Runaway again. If we decide to leave one day, we leave together."

"You promise?"

"I more than promise."

That first conversation we'd had the day I'd gone looking for the mayor and found Zander handcuffed to the jail cell came back. The way he'd watched me, the words he'd said, and the puzzle pieces of Zander clicked into place. "What about the girl you're holding out to marry?" I danced back a few steps.

He held out his hand. "I've been waiting for her to come back to me."

This time I sprinted into him, held his jaw, and pulled his head down.

Meeting my lips, he took his time making up for the last three days. His hands wound in my hair. His mouth moved firmly over mine. His lips strayed to graze softer kisses at the corners, to trail up my cheek, across my forehead, and even over my closed eyes. Then he worked his way back down to a deeper kiss that fused us together and lasted the rest of the night.

Or at least, it felt like it did.

John Mellencamp once said you could breathe in a small town. True or not, I didn't care as long as I could breathe Zander Ryland's kisses.

The End

Dear Reader

Thank you for reading *Where You Belong*. This is the first collaboration between MK Smith and Lori Freeland, longtime friends and editing partners, and the novella that kicks off their upcoming *Runaway* Series. Watch for Emma and Derek's story, *Where Your Heart Is*, next.

MK and Lori love to hear from their readers.

Visit with MK at authormksmith.com on Twitter @AuthorMKSmith and FB authormksmith

Look for Lori at lorifreeland.com on Twitter @LoriAnnFreeland and FB L.A.Freeland

MK Smith, coffee connoisseur, Danish lover, full-time dreamer has a BS in psychology, a Masters in something complicated, and loves to spend java-fueled nights weaving stories filled with quirky imperfect characters trying to survive life, friendship, and each other. Because love really does spin the world. In addition to writing contemporary romance, MK is also the author of *Serena's Fall*—an urban fantasy with attitude.

Lori Freeland loves flavored coffee, the perfect kiss, and a happy ending. She could do without early mornings, parades, and long cold winters. A GoldenHeart® Finalist, author, freelance editor, and writing coach, she holds a BA in psychology from the University of Wisconsin and currently lives in the Dallas area. When she's not snuggled up with her husband and worrying about her kids, she spends her days dreaming up romance and messing with the lives of imaginary people.

THE RIGHT ONE

MK Smith

A girl can't change her past, but she can choose her future.

Eight years ago, Anne Archer stood on her front porch with the two guys who'd shown up to take her to the Valentine's Dance. And made the wrong choice. A choice that left her ringless on the Kent State pitcher's mound. But when Maddie, Anne's high school BFF, talks her into helping make their ten-year reunion a magical night, she's hoping some of that magic will rub off. Especially after she runs into Kevin Tyson—bachelor number two from her front porch mistake. But Kevin hasn't forgotten her choice or his humiliation, and he made a promise to take care of his dead Marine brother's fiancé. Too bad Anne can't get his deep chocolate eyes out of her mind or scrub the memory of his touch from her skin. She was the reason they missed their first dance. She won't be the reason they miss their second.

Chapter 1

Whoever said love could endure anything never met Anne's high-school crush.

Or wasted eight years following, loving, and supporting him all the way through college graduation—the day he left her.

Anne sipped her chardonnay, and ran her ringless finger down the polished bar. The lit cabinets behind rows of polished brass taps glittered with a wide array of local and exotic liqueurs. The bar at the Lake Champlain Lodge was a grownup version of Cheers—minus a handsome Sam Malone—with stools for thirty and tables for forty-five.

But Friday at noon, Anne was the only customer. And she definitely needed another drink. Or seven. Because in a few hours she'd walk on stage in front of everyone who'd voted her *Most likely to Marry*, and kick off Sunset High School's ten-year reunion. Alone.

A bored bartender with more fishing stories than listening skills wiped the counter and kept her glass full.

"Anne Archer." Maddie's lyrical tone announced the arrival of her High-School bff. Maddie's curly dark hair was held back with a glossy red headband. Her blue eyes were bright, and her designer *everything* announced the kind of casual success that didn't have to try to be trendy.

Or announced crushing credit card debt.

But she'd married Bryce Mason. Who, last Anne heard, definitely didn't have crushing debt of any kind, unless you counted the mortgages his firm owned on other people.

They hugged, and Maddie's eye slid over to Anne's newly filled glass. "Chardonnay? Seriously? It's waaaay early for wine."

"What do you suggest?" Anne's eyes filled with mischief.

"Whiskey." Maddie grinned and tossed a flock of folders onto the bar. She hit the stool and a drink was in her hand by the time she reached for one. The dayshift bartender was fast. And he knew how to keep his guests happy. "Ready for tonight?"

"Sure, I just have to get the final music list to the lodge people."

Maddie pushed a folder to Anne labeled *Playlist*. "I hope he's got a good DJ."

"They brought in Katt." Anne smiled at her and raised her glass. "We got it done." With Maddie, she'd always felt unstoppable. Two girls on mission to have the most fun the law would allow, and try out plenty of options it didn't. But now Maddie had Bryce, and hanging out as couples was awkward when two plus two turned out to be three.

"We are the best reunion committee our class has ever had." Maddie tapped her glass with Anne's.

"We're the only committee."

"Even better."

Anne had to admit they were pretty amazing, for a committee of two.

Maddie designed the decorations. Anne coordinated the invitations. Everything else they split. Except location.

Maddie had insisted on the Lake Champlain Lodge, even though it was a three-hour drive from where they grew up, and many hours more from a major airport. But someone on the hotel's staff actually came from their tiny spec of a school, so they couldn't beat free. Well, the space was free. Not the Alcohol. Alcohol was never free.

Without Maddie, Anne would've sat out trips down reunion lane until the twenty-year anniversary, and memories of her and Chad as the Inevitables—the couple that couldn't fail—were long faded.

But Maddie had other plans. She lived their BFF life to the last F. Both in her High school and College days, and especially in her definition of friendship. So she made sure Anne came out to play. In Maddie's world, friendship, like diamonds—*diamond wedding rings that is*—were forever.

Too bad none of the forever stuff had rubbed off on Chad. She'd followed him all the way from upstate New York. Way upstate, all the way down to Kent state, and stood at his side until he left to play baseball in the major leagues.

But the only diamond he'd left behind for Anne were the empty bases of the college baseball field where they'd met for the last time. The time she thought he was going to propose. The time he left her standing in an empty stadium.

At least he'd let her keep a signed ball—present for her dad. He was so absolutely wonderfully incredibly thoughtful she just wanted to scream. Scream until he dropped dead from the guilt he'd never feel.

Anne forced a deep breath. She refused to get angry. Most days. Today she was riding the fence.

"Anne," Maddie's voice pulled her back to the present, and the realization she had no idea what Maddie had said for the past several soon-to-be-embarrassing minutes.

"Yeah?" Anne set her glass on the mahogany bar.

"Were you in your Chad Place?"

"No," she said a little too fast.

"Liar." Maddie swirled her whiskey sour like it was a magic Eight Ball brimming with all the answers. "Don't dwell."

"I know." She blew out a long breath. "No dwelling."

Maddie snorted. "You got Chad out of your head three years ago. You finished working off the chocolate calories from your breakup—"

"He. Walked. Away." Anne grabbed Maddie's drink and finished it in a single swallow. "It wasn't *my* breakup." The whiskey went down smooth and simmered in her belly.

"Fine." Maddie's smile had to be suppressing a sigh. "You burned off the chocolate from the *walkaway* two years ago. Got back into circulation last year. So no backsliding."

Tom hadn't exactly been circulation. Three dates. Or just long enough for her to notice the gap in his tan line for a wedding ring. She went back to her wine and took a long, slow steadying sip.

"I'm just saying, three years and fifty gallons of Rocky Road are plenty of time to heal."

"I get it." Three years was also enough time for Anne to turn her BS in sports management, earned when she thought she would be involved in Chad's career, into something that made her proud.

Running the business side of a ten-store dealership chain that wrapped the major roads from the Manhattan skyline through northern New Jersey might not be glamorous, but it'd taught her how to spot and handle manly men and their Suburban-sized egos.

Most men from the service side—where grease and muscle ruled—saw her medium-build and sandy blonde hair and figured her for a pushover. They figured wrong.

But at today's reunion of her half-way to the end of nowhere high school, she felt like a freshman who'd wandered into the school assembly naked. And the party hadn't even started.

At least Chad wasn't coming.

She'd triple-triple checked the RSVPs to make sure. But with or without a plane ticket, he'd be there in spirit. While Maddie showed off a wedding ring so large it got satellite reception, Anne would have the pleasure of telling all her old friends how her prom king had ridden off into the sunset—without her.

What part of tonight was supposed to be fun?

Okay. Deep breath. How hard could it be to enjoy a weekend with Maddie on the lake.

Anne scooped up the playlist folder. "Who do I talk to? When I had questions, I emailed *staff*."

"Did *staff* email back?"

"Sure." Anne shrugged. "They were helpful."

"They?" Maddie's smile was way too wicked. "You have no idea do you? Only one person answers staff mail around here—Kevin."

Anne shot her best friend her no-clue look.

"Kevin Tyson. Your inseparable from middle school." Maddie paused to see if any recognition sparked in Anne's face. When she got nothing, she rolled her eyes. "The guy you dumped before the Freshman Valentines Dance to go out with Chad."

"No." Anne's next swallow was like shoving down a heavy stone.

Her breakup with Kevin was school legend. Even though the dance was supposed to be their first date.

Chad had glowed. Kevin was a nerd in braces. When Chad showed up at her house the morning of the dance and asked her to go, she said *yes* so fast her brain didn't have a chance to remind her she'd already promised Kevin.

Nothing got through her Chad fog until that night when they both showed up for her—and she did the wrong thing. The very wrong thing. The very very very wrong thing.

She left Kevin standing on her front porch. And walked away with Chad. The rest was in the yearbook. Four years dating the most popular boy in school. While Kevin faded into the background.

And now she had to hope he'd either forgotten or forgiven or didn't recognize her.

With a sigh, Anne snatched up the folder and went looking for the one man in the world who had every right to hate her.

Chapter 2

Anne left the safety of the bar and ventured into the lodge's massive main room. She tugged her blouse, adjusted her skirt, and ran a hand through her hair to add an extra bit of sexy bedhead.

Not that she cared what Kevin thought, she hadn't spoken a word to him since the one-way breakup.

But that was high school history. They were adults, they had a job to do, and she had no doubt they could both be professionals. Hopefully. Since she and Maddie had decided to make a long weekend out of the reunion, she didn't want to stir up any bad memories she'd have to talk to every day.

Her heels echoed on the hardwood, the sound plucking her already taught nerves like an out-of-tune love song.

Everything around her, from the oversized leather couches to the staff's smart uniforms, had a renovation feel, as if the whole lodge had gotten a modernizing facelift after years of neglect.

She passed the reception desk and forced a pleasant smile for the check-in clerks.

"Do you need any help?" A young porter stopped.

"I'm looking for Kevin," she said.

"Kevin?"

"Sorry." She forced herself to stop smoothing her skirt. "Kevin Tyson."

"Oh, you mean the general manager. He's on the front drive with a customer." He pointed toward the main doors.

"Thanks." She pressed a few dollars into his hand and was already headed for the door before he could thank her.

General manager? The title was surprise. He must've gotten a college degree to get to run a place this large.

And him being with a customer was perfect. She could approach him while he was distracted, giving her the perfect opportunity for a quick walk-by. She could check him out, hand him the music list, and get away without awkward questions.

Controlled calm settled her stomach. She went out the main door and took a deep head-clearing breath of the fresh breeze off the lake. The cove was beautiful.

Outside, a sidewalk ran along a half-circle drive in front of the hotel. Twenty feet overhead, a crescent roof shielded the entire drive from sun and rain, anchored at either end by a pair of giant carved wolves. A dozen cars could unload at once, but only a single minivan and a Harley Davidson motorcycle were parked on the drive. No people.

She was drawn to the Davidson. The massive motorcycle still radiated the heat of a recent ride. And from the gleaming chrome to the polished black leather seat and saddlebags, the dragon on wheels was a thing of beauty.

She loved motorcycles. Had her own red Ducati racer back home. But compared to this Harley, hers was sleek—a Greyhound next to a Rottweiler. She ran her fingertips over the smooth leather. The letters *K T* had been embossed into the side of a saddlebag.

KT? Kevin Tyson…could the bike be his?

She held back a laugh. The scrawny boy she'd known wouldn't know how to handle a bike this powerful.

*****

Her bike was a crotch rocket, where she leaned in and glided curves and raced the straightaways. This bike was make for riding, seeing the countryside as much as the road.

Voices came from a side exit.

She snatched her hand off the bike and thought about dashing inside, but her heels were several inches too tall for dashing.

It didn't take more than a glance to take in the three people walking onto the curved drive. But Kevin required a long stare. He walked behind an elderly couple, carrying their bags toward the back of the van.

And he was—amazing.

The skinny boy with the scraggly mustache she'd left on her front porch to follow the High School hero had filled out into a man. Tall, muscular, with shoulders broad enough to balance a boulder, he had long dark brown hair that fell loose down his neck.

A white silk business shirt rolled up to his thick mid-forearms, and his fitted blue jeans tucked into heavy square-toed riding boots. When he bent at the waist to lift a heavy trunk, his shoulders strained the fabric of his shirt.

Anne's eyes strained to stop staring. She wondered if Kevin had to try to be this handsome.

The elderly woman noticed her watching and gave Anne the kind of warm smile a happy older woman gave to someone young and in love.

Startled, Anne stepped back, raised her hands and opened her mouth to say *no, I'm just here to drop off a folder,* but the words never had a chance to come out.

Kevin turned around, meeting Anne's gaze.

His hazel eyes were fifty shades of *wow*.

She stepped back from the intensity of his gaze and tumbled into the Harley. And his perfectly polished bike tipped onto the hard concrete.

In a moment, he was at her side. He could've saved the bike. She would've saved the bike. Instead he grabbed her arm and pulled her into his chest to keep her from falling. "Are you okay?" The deep rumble of his voice passed right into her and made her heart sigh.

"Um…fine…yeah." So articulate. Someday she might be able to form words. *Okay, calm down Anne. He grew up. We all grew up. But ohmyLord, he grew up.*

He slid his eyes over her shoulder, to his knocked-over bike laying at an angle on its long chrome foot guard.

The worst first impression in the history of first impressions. And she owned it.

The older woman watching them covered a laugh with her hand and pushed her staring husband into the van.

Kevin looked into her eyes for moment, like he was searching for something deeper than his reflection. He steadied her and stepped back.

"I'm really sorry." She took a deep breath and tried to not think about the thousand scratches her accident had etched into the bike's perfect chrome. She smoothed her blouse. Tried to find the composure she must have dropped on the ground. "I'm Anne." Not knowing what else to do she stuck out her hand to shake his. And instantly wished for a do-over on her day.

Shake his hand?

She had to fight from rolling her own eyes at herself. Twisting a finger through her hair would've been a cliché, but a million times flirtier than a handshake. How much worse could her first meeting in ten years with the guy she dumped, the guy who turned out to be the Fabio of her generation, the guy who saved her from the pavement over his motorcycle, possibly get?

Just looking at him made her stomach flutter like she'd been drinking butterfly champagne.

Kevin took her hand with surprising gentleness. "I remember you. In fact, I've never forgotten you." His beautiful hazel eyes turned into glaciers.

Chapter 3

Kevin dropped Anne's hand. "Is this for me?" He picked up her folder from the ground.

The icebergs in his eyes made her heart sink faster than the Titanic. "It's the playlist for the DJ in the order we want the songs."

He thumbed the folder open and stared for long seconds at the pages of names and numbers. Concentrating. Or unsure. "I'll handle this."

She nodded.

He flipped the folder shut and walked away.

Words Anne. Words would be nice. "Are you…going to the reunion?" she asked his back.

Shrugging, he turned. "Maybe."

Disappointment pinned itself to her heart. "You should. I'd like to— save you a dance?" She dropped her eyes and flashed him a forgive-me smile that used to melt starry-eyed high school boys.

He moved to the opposite side of his bike. "I've got a lot of chrome to polish and a lot of last minute prep. I'll probably be too busy."

"Oh." Because Kevin wasn't a boy, his eyes didn't have stars, and they weren't in high school anymore, her smile had zero effect.

He rocked the bike on the chrome foot guard. One hard shove and it came up in a single motion, the bike so heavy the strain showed in the chorded muscles of his neck.

She sucked in a breath. Glanced at the mosaic of fresh scratches on the metal guard and exhaust pipes and cringed. "Yeah. Maybe next time." In ten years.

He wheeled the bike off the drive onto a river-stone path running between the outer wall of the main room and the hotel side of the lodge. From the drive, the path between buildings was hidden behind sculpted bushes, so Kevin seemed to disappear down a secret tunnel.

Anne crossed her arms and turned toward the lodge's main entrance. Maddie was inside. And Maddie plus wine always equaled escape. Especially when they were single.

She took a step.

But Maddie wasn't single. She was probably texting Bryce, telling him what a great weekend was he was missing. While the word lonely tattooed itself to Anne's forehead.

Anne swung back where Kevin had disappeared. A knot of worry tightened her gut. She'd walked away from Kevin ten years ago. Correction, she'd walked away from the wrong guy ten years ago. Leaving him every reason to hate her. But that didn't mean she had to walk away from him now.

Worst thing that could happen? He could shoot her down. Hard. But she had Maddie, and the walk-in freezer in this place had to have a half-gallon of Rocky Road hidden inside.

She straightened out her blouse, her skirt, and her confidence. But whoever said it was better to try and fail than not try at all had to be married.

A few fast steps down the sidewalk in stilettos seared the balls of her feet worse than a hundred-meter dash. And the river stones covering the path between buildings were the size of ankle-breaking fists, and with her luck one of her heels would snap and take her ankle along for the ride.

She pulled off her shoes, scooped them up, and made her way down the rocks barefoot.

Overhead the third floor walkway served as the roof of the tunnel. Kevin was almost halfway down the path between the buildings.

"I've got a Ducati." She yelled, picking her way over the rocks as fast as she could. "Let me help you polish the chrome."

"A crotch rocket." He didn't turn around. "Figures."

"Excuse me?" More than a little attitude torched through her tone.

He looked over his shoulder. "Ducati's are crotch rockets. You can't catch the wind."

"On a Ducati, you are the wind." She flipped her hair over her shoulder and walked on the opposite side of the bike from him. "I didn't know Harley riders were such bike snobs."

He laughed, the sound deep and rich. "Yeah. You did." He smiled and glanced at the shoes in her hand. "If you want to help, hop on."

"I'm good walking." She liked his smile, it was natural, and it made her smile back.

"Maybe now," Kevin patted the seat, "but are you sure you want to risk bruising your feet on these rocks before a three-hour dance?"

He had a point.

Anne's polished and pedicured French nails were less riverbed and more fifth avenue. And so was she. What was she doing? Why was she chasing yesterday's guy?

She looked into his steady eyes, ready to make an excuse and leave. But his gaze twisted her up inside. For a moment she was back on her porch. But this time there wasn't a Chad to burn through eight years of her life. This time she only had Kevin. This time felt right.

"Are you alright?" He arched an eyebrow.

"I am." She bit her lip. "Help me up?"

He held the bike while she swung onto the seat, careful to keep her skirt from getting a mind of its own. She planted her feet on the forward foot pegs to keep their legs from touching. But also kept her skirt from covering them.

He walked next to her and pushed the bike. The position had to be awkward, but he didn't complain.

Cool lake air blew steadily down the tunnel. "Where are we going?"

"I've got a small garage where we keep the four-wheelers. I'd ride back there, but the rumble echoes in the tunnel and bothers the guests." He kept the bike steady and ran his eye down her bare leg. "You've got great…balance."

"Thanks." A warm flush fanned through her cheek. "I run a group of ten car dealerships. I ride between locations every day."

"Ten?" He whistled. "You've done a lot for yourself." He pushed them out of the tunnel onto the back lawn. Privacy hedges separated picnic areas, and large trees dotted the shoreline.

"It's beautiful."

He looked a little embarrassed. "You should've seen it last year."

"Good or bad?" She swung off the bike and let her feet sink into the thick grass.

"Bad. Parts of the hotel weren't livable, and the main lodge wasn't much better."

"Well the whole place looks great. I guess you've done a lot too." She tried a dialed down version of her forgive-me smile from earlier.

His smile back was tiny, but it was a start. And it let the dimple come out to play on his cheek. "Are you sure you can polish chrome?" He glanced at her hands. "Your skin looks soft."

"Don't you know how to wear gloves?" She kept her tone even. But the way he looked at her made her chest felt lighter. "I hurt your bike. I'd like to make him whole."

He looked her over from hair to heel with a wry grin. "Ducati huh?"

"Yeah. And she's sweet." Anne glared a challenge.

"Alright." He held up a hand. "No offense meant. Follow me then, Miss Ducati."

He couldn't see her smile or feel the fluttery emptiness in her stomach. But she was pretty sure he could hear her breath get faster.

She followed him into a whitewashed barn that looked too clean for mechanical work.

Inside, opposite a row of polished four-wheelers stalled like horses, racks of tools and a welder set ready for use. His workshop smelled like oil and leather.

Kevin put his bike up on a stand and pulled out a box of fine steel wool. "Gloves are in the top drawer."

Above the workbench drawers were a few faded photos. One showed Kevin in military fatigues next to a blond man of equal height and build. They could've been brothers. Tucked into the glass corner was a creased picture of the blond man again, with his arm around the shoulders of a thin woman with long red hair.

She opened the drawer without looking and pulled out a pair of gloves. Underneath them she found a slim wooden box.

Curiosity did bad things to cats, and Pandora should've known better than to open strange boxes, but Anne ignored the warnings tingling up her spine and took a tiny peek inside.

A purple heart shaped medal on a bright ribbon. Her breath caught. She flipped the medal over. On the back it said—*For Military Merit, Kevin Tyson.*

The purple heart. Given to soldiers wounded in battle. Not her business. She snapped the box shut and pushed it to the back of the drawer.

Kevin cleared his throat right behind her.

Chapter 4

If Anne had been a cat, Kevin would've cost her eight-and-a-half lives.

She spun and planted her palms against his chest. "What are you doing?"

"Isn't that a little cliché?" He looked at the open tool bench drawer and the newly closed box which held his purple heart.

"What?"

"You're searching through my private stuff, and you're wondering what *I'm* doing."

"You scared me." The ca-thump of her heart knocked against her ears. "You need a bell around your neck." He was good at moving into her personal space unnoticed. Not a trait she admired in a man.

"How about," he reached past her and pushed the drawer closed, "you shouldn't be in there."

She rotated to keep their bodies from touching. "You told me to get some gloves. If I wasn't supposed to see…"

"The work gloves are in the *top* drawer."

A sinking feeling dropped through her body and she glanced at the gloves in her hand. Camo. Definitely not work gloves. And the drawer she'd pulled…second row.

She dropped her gaze and sighed. "Sorry, I wasn't paying attention. I was too busy looking at the pictures."

"So you're spying on me?" His dead neutral tone sprang her eyes back up to his.

"I didn't mean…" She swallowed. She would ask herself if her worst-first-impression-day ever could actually hit a new low. But she already knew the answer. "Can we start over?"

"I thought we were."

"I'm not used to—"

"Not being in control?" He couldn't hide the half-smile that landed on his face.

"Exactly."

"Come on." Kevin handed her a pair of work gloves. "Let's get to work. If you want to get done in time to get ready for the dance."

He set a tub of chrome polish next to a box of super fine steel wool pads. He dipped a pad into the polish and started on the peg guard with long smooth strokes.

"Think we can get all these scratches out before the dance?" Anne pulled over a stool.

"No." He glanced at her and laughed.

"Is that a challenge?" Mr. Kevin Tyson was about to learn she wasn't afraid of a little work. Except, she glanced at the web of scratches again, *little* might not be the right word.

Gloved up, Anne started in on her end of the bike, thankful the scratches didn't look deep. She worked in silence, focused on the circular rhythm. When her steel wool pad wore thin she replaced it, and dipped out more polish.

Kevin nudged her arm. "Not bad."

She flicked her gaze and caught him eyeing her legs. "The bike?"

"Yeah." His easy tone and embarrassed expression triggered a churn Anne's gut. "What else?"

She reached down unconsciously and tried to pull her skirt over her knees. But the short A line skirt wasn't designed for fingertip length, and it slid right back.

"Don't worry." He might have rolled his eyes before turning back to the bike. "We don't have a dress code."

She let her gaze wander the hills and valleys of his shoulders. Okay stop. What was she doing? She knew a preening man when she saw one, and he wasn't preening. He was calm. Too calm. Interested? Maybe. But not...

He turned to face her, and she whipped her eyes back to the bike so fast the world spun and took her heart along for the ride. Being with him after so many years was almost too much, like emotional whiplash. She focused on her hands.

"Is Chad coming?" Kevin said.

She dropped her pad. She bent over to pick it up. "I think he's at the Mets training camp in Port St. Lucie." The words came out in a jumble. She didn't have to think. She knew. She'd memorized the Met's whole schedule when it looked like they were going to sign Chad. She wasn't a stalker, the plan was supposed to be her as his manager and his wife.

"Are you okay?" Kevin let his concern about her hang in the air on unsteady strings.

"Let's drop him."

"Drop him?"

Off a building. "It. I mean let's drop it. Let stop talking about Chad. Okay?"

Jerk had to sign with the Mets. Her parents had moved to Florida, and now that he trained there he'd ruined the whole state for her.

"Sorry." Kevin didn't sound sorry.

But was it the not-sorry of hoped for revenge, the not-sorry of polite curiosity, or the not-sorry of boy-meets-girl-again interest. Her pulse quickened. And which did she want?

.

"Who's in the picture with you?" Anne decided a simple probe into Kevin's past would be fair game.

"Let's not talk about him." Kevin's answer was quick and final.

"I talked about Chad."

"You hardly said anything." He shrugged. "Besides, it's old news."

"So were me and Chad."

"You don't give up."

She pointed her Brillo pad at him. "No, I don't."

Kevin stared over her shoulder for a moment, like he was deciding something. "The man with me in the picture was Frank. Frank Jessup. We enlisted the same day."

"You were buddies?" She scooped a heavy dollop of polishing cream.

"Yeah." He took the kind of long breath men take when there's sadness in the story.

She let the silence hang while her heart ached for the loss in his eyes. She just wanted to learn more about him. But her cursed luck had struck again, she almost glanced up to see if she was under a ladder holding up a black cat dancing on a broken mirror.

She'd probably just brought up the saddest moment of his whole life. Maybe she should get him a puppy and run over it in front of him to finish off this perfect afternoon.

"Frank was a top notch soldier." Kevin shut his eyes as if reliving a movie in his mind he didn't want anyone else to see. "He helped me survive the tests. Wouldn't let me fail. When I made officer ahead of him, he was the first to slap my back."

She could sense the *but* flying toward her like a fun seeking missile.

Kevin stared off into nothing. "He died. Ambush."

"Is that…" She really needed to stop now. "Is that where you got your heart?"

He shook his head. "I was recovering in the hospital when he punched out protecting a little girl."

"I'm sorry." Anne put her fingers on his arm.

He didn't answer. And he didn't move away.

Strong men couldn't always handle a woman's comfort. He could. Chad never showed his true feelings—good or bad. Kevin had already shown both at the deepest level. A mix of respect and attraction grew inside her.

"So." He looked into her, his dark eyes pulling her in and sending warm flutters cartwheeling through her belly. "Reunions, huh?"

"Yeah. They're great." His laugh pulled the corners of her mouth into a flirty smile.

"Let's see how it's going." He claimed the space between them and reached around her with a finishing cloth. Wiping the metal polish clean, the fine scratches were gone. Only a few larger ones still needed work.

She turned toward him. Their faces inches apart. "So what do you think?"

He swallowed and looked straight into her eyes. "I think it looks good. Really good."

So close to his body, his heat brushed across her skin and set the hairs on her neck quivering. He smelled like cologne and sweat and motor oil. And Kevin. She wet her lips.

"Kev." A young, perky sounding female voice came from outside the shop.

Kevin stood and took his warmth and cologne and deep dark eyes with him. "Alice."

Anne shut her eyes. Stupid. Stupid. Stupid. As if a man like Kevin was just waiting around.

She stood, prepared to be nice and gracious, and then sprint back to her room.

Alice walked in with the kind of familiarity that said this wasn't her first time in the barn. Her long red hair fell all the way down to the kind of thin waist that made women rush for rice cakes and Pilates.

Dressed in a smart blouse and jeans with designer boots, she looked like a Wall Street accountant gone country. And she was definitely the girl from the photo. The girl Frank had his arm around.

"Welcome to the lodge." Alice gave her a welcome-home smile. But Anne didn't miss her head-to-toe evaluation.

Kevin took the playlist folder from the workbench to Alice. "Alice, this is Anne."

Alice's eyes narrowed. "*This* is Anne?"

Kevin cleared his throat. He stood in the kind of close side-to-side posture with Alice that would've made Anne's HR department say something about not sending *messages*. "Could you help me?"

"Sure." Alice flicked defensive eyes at Anne like Kevin had said something she shouldn't have heard. "How about I take care of it?"

He nodded.

"Staying long?" Alice held out her hand to Anne.

"For the reunion." Going for formal nice play, Anne smiled like they were sisters and took her hand.

"Great." Alice tucked the folder under her arm. "This is going to be so much fun."

Chapter 5

The good tension in the motorcycle barn had evaporated. Anne wiped polish from her hands on a rag and stepped away from Kevin's Harley.

Alice stood next to Kevin by the motorcycle barn door and slid him a coffee mug. "Your favorite morning brew."

He let out a low hum. "Why am I getting it now?"

"I thought you'd need the energy boost. The reunion party won't close out till two AM."

Anne walked over to Kevin, uncertain. Alice was in the picture with Frank—but Frank was dead—so what did that make Kevin and Alice to each other? "I think we've brought your bike back to life. I should probably get going."

"Wait." Kevin's voice wrapped Anne and twisted inside her chest. "Let me show you around."

Alice stepped next to Anne. "I'll take care of her." She put a fingertip against Kevin's chest. "You need to freshen up and get your best suit on. Based on the money they're spending, tonight's going to be a classy affair."

"The kind of affair we need." Kevin gave a half-shrug.

"Usually." Alice tucked the DJ folder under her arm.

Alice didn't say anything remotely rude, but her critical glances, her tight posture, the judgmental subtext in her tone lifted the hairs on Anne's neck.

"Alright." Kevin's gaze paused on Anne's face, fluttering her insides. "Guess I'll go change. Alice will take care of you."

The woman's sly smile did nothing to convince Anne she was in good hands.

Kevin left, and Anne watched him go. He didn't amble, or stroll, or saunter. He walked with purpose, like a man in control of his destiny.

Anne let out a long breath. Why couldn't she have a little more of that and be in control of her own destiny?

"Well, you've probably seen enough of the barn." Alice nodded toward the door. "I could show you the grounds."

Alice wanted out of the barn, but Anne wanted to know something more about her before she lost her chance. She glanced at the picture of Frank and Alice on the wall. "Is that you with Kevin's best friend?"

If Alice was surprised that Anne knew about Frank, she gave no sign. Instead she took a deep breath and let it out slow. "That's me."

Anne glanced at her left hand. No ring. No tan line. Not even a tattoo. "Were you—?"

"Engaged?" Alice crossed her arms.

Anne stopped. What was she doing? Quizzing a woman about a dead man to figure out Kevin's relationship status? Checking social media would be kinder. "Sorry."

Alice walked over to the picture and pressed it flat against the wall with her fingers. "Frank and I weren't married. We planned to after his deployment was over. We didn't even have a ring. But I was with Frank. Till he died."

And now? Anne couldn't stop the question from bubbling up inside her mind, but she kept her lips politely shut.

Alice walked over to a stall where a tarp covered what could have been another, smaller motorcycle. She lifted one end revealing a black on black Harley—smaller and sleeker than Kevin's metal monster. "This is my bike. The day after Kevin and I met Frank's coffin at the Air Force base, he took me out and bought it for me. Taught me to ride. I'd probably have gone insane if he hadn't stepped up and taught me to catch the wind." Alice's expression turned wistful and far away.

Anne guessed if she had a Chad Place, Alice probably had a whole island for Frank. She wiped a stray sympathetic tear from her eye.

Alice lowered the tarp and walked outside into the breezy afternoon air.

Anne followed in silence across the golf course grass that ran like a carpet over the slope between the Lodge and the shoreline. Numbered metal arches were setup across a section of lawn between two wooden poles.

"Croquet." Alice said, following Anne's eyes.

"Never played. I'm not into golf, or anything like it."

"Me either." Alice looked like she might have smiled for a moment, but she forced it away. "Come on, I'll show you the dock."

"The lodge is a long drive from town," Anne said. "Do you commute? Or live local?"

Alice's expression said nothing, but her pause said she knew Anne was fishing for information. "I live down the road. You could say Kevin and I are neighbors." She nodded at the opposite wing of the lodge from the hotel. "He's the only one who lives onsite, aside from the night janitor."

Anne looked over the waters of Lake Champlain. "That's almost *Shining*-creepy in winter. Good thing Kevin's not a writer."

The friendly parts of Alice's expression dropped like cheap mascara in the rain. "Why would you even?"

Anne took a step back. "What's wrong?"

"What's wrong? Kevin has dyslexia. And you're joking about whether he can be a writer?" Alice's territorial tone built a wall between her and Anne. "There are teachers who have dyslexia. Scientists. He can do anything he puts his mind to. He even used his GI benefits to get his MBA."

"I never said he couldn't do anything. I was just joking about the movie. I...I didn't know about his dyslexia." How could I possibly not know?

Kevin had been my friend since the third grade. We weren't super close, but he was always around. Always—

"How couldn't you know? He left Arborhale Academy mid-spring semester of his Sophomore year to go to a special school." Alice stared at her like she was somehow responsible, not for his leaving, but for holding him back from leaving.

Kevin left? Anne sifted memories of her sophomore year, but she couldn't remember seeing him very often after the Freshman Valentines Dance. After Chad. And her memories running from her Sophomore summer till the end of college were a Chad haze of parties and friends and fun. But no more Kevin.

Her stomach twisted. And her throat closed, like it didn't want to say anything incriminating. "I didn't know about any of that. He was a great guy. But he just... he kind of... disappeared."

"I understand." All the anger had drained out of Alice's voice. "I heard the stories, but now I get it."

Anne didn't want to know what was coming next. Knowing wouldn't let her go back in time, and even if she could—unless she knew the future—she'd chose Chad all over again. Because her teen self was a teen. And being with Chad meant prom court, meant going from merely popular to the top clique, meant having every jealous eye in school on her.

All that stupid stuff that meant soooo much in the tiny world of Arborhale.

Anne met Alice's gaze. "I thought Kevin and I were friends. I guess I was wrong. I didn't know he left."

Alice shook her head like Anne was sitting in the corner with the pointed hat on, wasting her time. "You still don't get it. Leaving was the best thing that could have happened to him. His mother moved to Georgia and got him into Gracepoint—a school for dyslexia."

"That's great." So why was Alice so mad, at her?

"The problem wasn't that he left, and you didn't know. You were popular. He wasn't. I get it." Alice paced the grassy shoreline. "The problem is the only reason he stayed, the reason he didn't go to Gracepoint sooner, was because of you. He wanted to be with you since the elementary school. And you... Never. Even. Noticed."

A whirlwind of memories rearranged themselves in Anne's memories of Arborhale. Kevin. The scrawny kid. The guy who ran for his bike whenever Anne rode down the street. Who always left flowers at her house on Valentine's and her birthday. Who helped her with her math homework. Who finally asked her out her Freshman year to one dance.

He stuck around Arborhale for her? But he was friend-zoned. He had to know he was friend-zoned. He had to know...

"We've gotten close since Frank... Really close. And I won't let anyone hurt him."

Anne dropped her gaze to the ground. Numb. "I better get back to my room and change."

Even if Kevin had feelings then, and Anne didn't notice—or want to notice—did that mean they couldn't have feelings now?

Because the carousel of guilt spinning in her chest didn't just want to apologize for being a clueless love struck teen, it wanted to scoop up the new Kevin and take him for a ride.

Chapter 6

Anne's room at the lodge was a grade-F fashion fiasco.

While Anne had been in the garage with Kevin, letting herself get caught in might-have-beens without even considering that might be another woman, Maddie had gone up to the room, detonated an explosion of dresses, tops, and shoes.

And Anne didn't like any of her outfits.

"What about the strapless black?" Maddie's asked from the bathroom over the steam and sizzling smell of her flat iron.

"Maybe in Manhattan. In this town, that hemline's a felony." Anne tossed the body-hugging dress onto the pile.

"A felony you can fill out."

"I'm not a Kardashian."

"The white maxi, then."

"Too sheer. I don't have the right slip." Anne could tick off a hundred reasons each dress was wrong.

"The Valentino."

"Too asymmetrical."

"The Karan. The Chanel. The Furstenburg."

"Too Nice. Too classy. Too out-of-my-league."

If Maddie sighed it was covered up by the roar of a hair dryer. "What about the red pumps?" she yelled over the roar of the hair dryer. "Start with the shoes and work your way up."

Red leather, heart-shaped front, six-inch spike. Anne might have gone for them in a better mood. "They're perfect—for a pole dancer."

The hairdryer turned off. "I shouldn't have come without Chad." Which really meant she shouldn't have come.

"Coming without Chad is the perfect way to show everyone what he lost and how you've totally left him behind."

Anne scanned the room. Seven cast-off dresses scattered across her bed. A half dozen pumps, flats, and even a pair of boots littered the floor. An hour wasted trying on clothes and trying to convince herself the night was going to be wonderful, and no one would think she was *over* anything.

Behind her, the bathroom door swung open and Maddie stepped into the room. "Well?"

Anne swung around. In a tight black dress and savagely high heels, Maddie was put-together perfection. "You look great."

"I know how *I* look. The question is why you're still in your just-arrived outfit."

"Chad—"

"Chad isn't on your mind. This room has windows. And I saw you playing with a Harley on the back lawn. Not to mention the Harley rider."

Anne's attempt at a whatever smile missed the mark as soon as she put it on her face. "He was nice."

"Tall." Maddie crossed her arms.

"Great eyes."

"Great shoulders."

"Alright, I get it." Anne launched a pillow at her friend's face. "But he also has a legs-up-to-her-eyeballs red headed girlfriend."

Maddie picked up a red deep V halter top dress from her own pile. "Is there a ring on her finger?"

"No. But I'm not the kind of girl who goes after taken men."

"Well, did you stick around after she showed up to ask?"

"Ask?"

"If he was taken."

"No." Who asked a man if he was taken?

"Then you don't know whether he's taken. Friend-zoned. Or just not interested in her. And in this dress and heels you're *going* to find out." She tossed the strappy red pumps at Anne.

"Hey, those are dangerous."

"I luuuuve the shoes." Maddie coaxed Anne out of her old attitude and into the new red dress. "And this dress will do them justice."

"Or get me propositioned." One look in the mirror and Anne couldn't stop herself from finding a smile.

"Tonight you're not the tough girl who runs car dealerships. Tonight you're Anne, the woman who's here to get noticed. So tonight, less is not more."

"Then what's more?"

"You are." She looked Anne over from neckline to hem and beamed. "Now sit so I can help you with the shoes."

"Does this make you my fairy Godmother?"

"Why not." She sat on her bed and slid each shoe on Anne, adjusting the thin straps that slung around her heels. "You will own the room tonight. You deserve to own the room tonight."

"What if it's a total disaster?"

"If everything falls apart?" Maddie tapped a finger to her lips. "Well, how many of these people besides me will you see for the next ten years?" At Anne's blank stare she continued. "Exactly."

Maddie moved on to help with the lipstick, the flat-iron, and fussing over dress adjustments until Anne was pulled, tugged, and pushed-up into place.

Anne looked at her Cinderella transformation in the mirror and did a little twirl. "I'd kill for a dose of your confidence."

Maddie turned her around and popped a dose of translucent finishing powder on the tip of Anne nose. "Poof. You have it, and midnight is so old fashioned. My fairy magic doesn't expire till you wash it off. At least that's what the bottle says."

Anne laughed. "Alright, alright, I'm ready."

"Not quite." Maddie scooped up a pair of her diamond studded earrings from the nightstand. "Wear these for luck."

"I couldn't. They're…"

"Too expensive?"

Anne couldn't stop watching the light play in the precious stones. "It's like you caught rainbows."

"Actually, I caught a big chunk of Bryce's bonus. And you deserve a little luxury." Maddie brushed back Anne's hair and helped her put in the diamonds.

Earrings in place, they linked arms and headed to the fifth floor elevator. On the second level they walked around the balcony overlooking the main entrance.

Anne spotted a few dozen high-school memories walking around the lobby. Even from this height it didn't take her diploma to sort out the camera-ready smiles from the real hugs and handshakes.

"Is that Chris Elkins?" Maddie whispered. She pointed to a built, balding man in a designer suit, holding a pretty little girl in his proud arms. Chris used to be in their clique. Football linebacker. Scholarship to Ohio State. Only guy Anne knew who could lift a beer keg over his head and drink.

"I can't believe it. We dated a few times." Anne laughed. "But he was completely in love with—"

"Lisa Mercer." Maddie leaned so far over the railing, Anne put a hand on her back to keep her from falling. "There she is, with her son in tow."

"Son? And she's pregnant..." Anne couldn't merge the sight of a light blonde Lisa against the black haired indie-rock girl who used to dance by herself in the corner.

"They married in college—after a night of partying led to baby number one." Maddie's tone was light, but her gaze probed Anne. Probably to see if she's slipped into her Chad Place.

"Well I guess they enjoyed it. They've got two plus womb now. Isn't he in insurance?"

"Tires." Maddie leaned back. The pity in her tone at Anne's subject change hurt worse than a patronizing arm squeeze. "He sold enough insurance to buy a tire store in Jersey City."

"You're kidding. Tires? But that suit looks expensive."

"It's bespoke expensive. One-of-a-kind tailored. He started with one store, now he owns a chain of five and counting."

Anne whistled. "He was such a muscle head. I wouldn't have imagined he'd end up an entrepreneur." Seeing Lisa—*Most likely to Goth Out*—looking normal and happy and suburban pulled Anne's insides. Maybe if Anne had chosen someone less flashy, less into a baseball career, she'd be the one with four kids, a wedding ring, and a chain of tire stores.

Regret mixed with hindsight into an acid cocktail in her stomach.

Maddie grabbed Anne's arm with gentle fingers. "You never know where you'll end up."

For a moment she almost sounded fatalistic, but Maddie's bounce returned and she tugged Anne away from the edge. "I need to stay away from railings, and you need to check the reunion room before everything kicks off."

"I do?" Anne plastered on her I'm-just-perfectly-fine smile that never fooled Maddie.

"Since you're giving the speech, I thought you'd want to see the room."

Anne's heart stuttered. She'd let herself forget the inconvenient detail that she was kicking off the event. "Can't we let the valedictorian do it?"

"George Yohan McBriar?" Maddie laughed. "No one's seen him since he washed out of grad school. Sorry, but you're taking center stage tonight."

On the way to the north wing of the lodge, they passed an old wrought iron elevator with a *Private Use Only* sign next to broad carpeted stairs that had been roped off.

"I wonder what's up there?" Anne ran a finger over the worked iron calla lilies.

"Movie theater I think, and the lodge manager's apartment. The brochure said that back in the day this place was also a theater for the locals."

"Back in my grandparent's day."

"More like our great grandparents." Maddie pushed her on. "Let's go."

At the end of the freshly-carpeted hall, three sets of double doors barred entry into the Elk Horn Room, largest of the reception halls, where the tenth reunion would start in a few hours.

Staff in tuxedoes pushed drink carts into position, ready to circulate the alcohol that would help reunion goers remember the good times, forget the bad times, and decide ten-year-old grudges and petty feuds could be forgiven and forgotten.

Maddie walked toward the stage, but Anne stopped cold.

Alice stood in the middle of the room directing staff in a body-hugging red flame dress with strappy red pumps. Anne's red pumps. And a dress so close to hers they might as well have been rack neighbors. Or twins.

Anne's insides twisted so tight they knotted. The last thing she wanted to be tonight was a fashion victim on a *Who Wore It Better* blog.

Chapter 7

Alice stood in the center of the Elk Horn Room directing the staff setting up for the reunion with a pen and a pad and an aura of control.

Anne didn't want to be anywhere near her aura, her identical shoes, or her identical dress.

If she left now, she could get to her room and switch into the Kardashian black before the reunion started. If she hurried.

She swung around and found herself face to face with a champagne bar on wheels.

The man pushing the cart didn't look old enough to be out of high school. He had bottle black hair pulled down over one eye, piercing holes on his lips and nose, and a hint of greasy eyeliner he hadn't quite gotten off in time for work.

"You're in a punk band." The words were out before Anne could engage her social filter. The filter that said some people didn't want their personal lives on display for strangers.

"How'd you know?"

"Instinct."

He smiled. "You look like you could use a drink."

Her turn to smile. "How'd you know?"

"Instinct." He pulled a wine glass from under the cart and poured her a deep dark red.

"I need more than a drink, I need a life preserver, this hasn't been my day."

"Then make it your night." He handed her the glass and glanced over her shoulder, his eyes warning of an approach.

The only people close enough were Maddie and Alice. And with her luck it wouldn't be Maddie. "My queue to leave."

"Mine too." He dipped his head and pushed the cart away.

Anne turned around, excuse for leaving on her lips, and stepped for the door. But her heel caught on the carpet, and she fell glass-first into Alice.

For one adrenaline frozen second Anne's horrified eyes met Alice's shocked ones before a wave of red wine splashed across her designer silk.

Panic opened her hand, and Anne dropped the glass. It fell, hit the carpet, and launched the last of its high-stain cargo in a spatter across Alice's legs.

Alice looked down at the modern-art spray of damage. Her fingers passed over the stains. Came away wet with wine.

Cleaning staff passed, their voices dropping to horrified whispers. And a few snickers.

"I am so..." Anne's voice failed when she locked gazes with the nuclear fire burning in Alice's eyes.

Alice stood in smoldering silence. Fists clenched. The flame in her face seared its way down her neck, across her cheeks, over her nose, and all the way up to her eyes. Anne had never seen that kind of body blush. "What's. Your. Problem?" The string of expletives in Alice's tone remained unspoken, but implied.

"I am so sorry." For the first time in her adult life Anne wished she had her favorite childhood blanket, her stuffed rabbit, and a place to hide. "So sorry."

"I heard how self-centered you were in High School, but isn't ruining my dress too far—even for you?"

Self-centered? She had no idea what Alice was talking about, but decided this wasn't the time to press for clarity. Anne snatched a fistful of napkins from a cleaning cart.

"After what you did, you better stay away from him." Alice jerked back from her hand with a laser beam glare that etched her threat into Anne's soul.

"What do you mean—what I did?" A swirl of confusion scattered Anne's thoughts. Did Alice go to their High School? Anne didn't recognize her or remember anything she ever did to anyone that would make them this this angry after ten years. Unless she meant Kevin...

The question seemed to make Alice angrier, and she turned and marched from the hall.

"I guess that's one way to handle a dress twin." Maddie walked up from her discretely positioned-to-eavesdrop distance, her smile wicked.

Anne's chest hollowed out to make room for an extra serving of guilt. "I would never...I didn't mean for that to happen."

"I know," Maddie motioned for a pair of glasses from the champagne cart. "It was obviously an accident."

"What do you think she meant—stay away from him?"

Maddie arched an eyebrow. "I don't think you need a translator for something that crystal clear."

"She thinks I'm after Kevin."

"Is she wrong?"

Anne fought the tight feeling in her chest. He was a handsome man. Nothing more. And after this weekend she'd never see him again. Unless he still ran this place when they came back in another ten years.

Maddie clinked glasses with her. "Cheer up. You still don't know how he feels."

Anne stared into her champagne glass. The tiny amber bubbles bouncing and racing to the top lifted her mood and her smile. She toasted

Maddie and they laughed like the time they'd staged a midnight break-in and TP'd the cafeteria with three hundred rolls of pink toilette paper.

"Here's to finding out." Anne smiled and took a shallow sip. Champagne went straight to her head, and she wanted to keep her focus.

Maddie nudged her and pointed toward the main hall door.

Kevin entered the room. He had changed into a white dress shirt and an understated black tux. His transformation from biker to Bond put a hitch in Anne's breath. He was so easy on her eyes, she had already started toward him before she even knew she was walking.

Kevin watched her approach, his head to heel appraisal robbed her breath and set the beat of her heart from waltz to salsa.

A dozen conversation starters flitted through her head but before she could use her best, or even her second best, he turned away and held up a hand.

"What happened?" His tone was matter of fact, a police detective who already knew the answer.

Her heart took a one-way elevator ride to the floor. He'd seen Alice and probably already heard her version of who was responsible. "I'm not having a good night."

His slow ironic smile plucked smooth notes on her heart strings. "Say that to Alice."

"It was an accident. A stupid accident. I tripped…"

"And ruined her dress."

"And ruined her dress." Anne's stomach folded into origami knots.

"I can't believe you did that to her. This isn't High School. You can't always have what you want."

"Kevin." She put her hand on his arm. She wasn't sure what High School he went to, but she definitely didn't recall getting her every wish fulfilled. "It was an accident."

Touching him sent her insides into a slow warm spin. And for a moment he looked at her with eyes that wanted to believe. But he stepped away, and let her hand fall.

"I better get back to work. It's *my* job to make *your* night special." He walked past her to the stage trailing an arctic front in his wake.

Maddie stepped up cautiously and put a hand on Anne's shoulder. "Are you okay?"

Anne thought about all their friends and classmates gathering in the lodge. All the people who names she remembered. Faces she'd never forget. But when they looked at her, who did they see? "Were we those kinds of girls?"

"What do you mean?" Maddie slipped her arm around Anne's shoulders.

"Were we the kind of girls that would trash a girl for wearing the same dress?"

Maddie shook her head. "We were the kind of girls who walked down the center of the hall. The kinds that made other girls jealous. But we weren't stereotypes."

"But I would never have sabotaged another girl's dress."

Maddie took Anne's free hand in her own. "No you wouldn't have. A really confident girl, or a really confident woman, doesn't have to play that kind of dirty."

"But Kevin thinks—"

"I saw. I heard. And he's wrong about you." Maddie's gaze was fierce, the kind that sent people about to hurt her friends running.

"Well at least I know how he feels about me."

"You have two choices. Set him straight. Or walk away."

"Walk away is a lot easier."

"Definitely." Maddie said the word way too easily. "But here's your problem."

"My problem?" Anne definitely didn't want any more problems.

"You're not the kind of girl who walks away."

Chapter 8

Anne headed for the DJ platform. The crew had worked with machinelike efficiency to speed setup on the last of the decorations. Hardest had been the pink champagne fountain in the center of the room.

She wasn't even sure it was technically legal to serve anything out of a ring of peeing cherubs, much less champagne. But the effect was beautiful.

Maddie had her own problems fixing up the ice sculptures. The hunting Centaur was so large it had to be made in two pieces, and the horse's rump had partially melted leading to a severe case of droopy butt that no amount of freezer aerobics could lift.

Kirk, Arborhale's top jock, slipped in early and was leaning on the brass rail of the long bar telling cocktail waitresses his college glory stories. Okay, so he won the Heisman trophy and started for the Tennessee Titans. He'd done a few football things worth bragging about.

When Anne passed he slipped free and intercepted her. "Anne. Hey." He ran a hand through his buzz-cut blond hair.

She remembered his big hands. Those hands were pretty busy in high school, but she didn't remember him being this all-body-big up close. "Hey Kirk. It's been—"

"Ten years?" His smile brought out the cleft in his chin.

"Ten years." She bit her lower lip.

"I heard about Chad."

A whirlpool started up in her stomach. "Yeah."

"You're better off. He was a jerk." He couldn't stop his eyes from checking out her legs. "If I'd heard sooner…I'd have called."

"I didn't know you wanted *to* call." A little ball of self-confidence bobbed up out of the whirlpool.

"Well, yeah." His aww-shucks-mam smile definitely melted hearts back at Arborhale, and could evaporate them now.

Anne felt the heat blossom in her cheeks. But not the butterflies in her belly that Kevin set off. Kirk's attention was wonderful. His interest, exactly the boost she needed after her worst first impression day ever.

And part of her said—*Whoa. Desirable man right here. Stop and do not pass Go. But do collect his phone number.* But the part of her that had been intrigued by Kevin, by his smile, his touch, his story—that part won.

"Thanks, Kirk. I needed to hear that more than you know. But I might have a date tonight."

"Might?" The part of Kirk that won trophies and started in pro football games stepped up in a voice that said *might* equaled opportunity.

Anne nodded her head and brushed back her hair. "I hope so."

"And I hoped to catch you before everything started. Looks like I was a little too late."

"You're too sweet." Anne put her hand on his arm and gave it a friendly squeeze.

"Just let me know if you need anything, or if he's an idiot." Kirk walked back to the bar, his eyes on her.

Maddie was right. Reunions were magic. And seeing Kirk had done far more than let her know someone was interested. It was just the right confidence boost on an otherwise glass-of-wine-before-bed kind of day.

Anne made her way up to Katt, the DJ, and got her attention. They'd flown her in from The Towers, a posh Manhattan nightclub, for the full weekend. "Change of plans."

"Okay." The short purple-haired girl with more piercings than tattoos pulled up a tablet. "Go ahead."

"After my speech I want you to queue up song 97."

"Lady in Red?" Katt asked.

"Yes, and can you give me a slow remix. Add a few minutes?"

She smiled. "Your remix is my command. Care if I blend in another song?"

"Keep it classy?"

"Some violins. You'll love it." The DJ turned back to her mixing boards. "Now I need time."

"You'll have it." Anne headed back toward the stage for her mic check.

Maddie stepped back from an ice sculpture and waved Anne over. "Check out David."

"David Meyers?" Chess team captain, robotics nerd, and youngest MIT professor in history. Anne hadn't seen him since her senior year in college when a group of Arborhale alums met up at Miami Beach. He did math problems in his head to make sure he hadn't had too much to drink. Problem was, no one else knew enough to check his math.

"No." Maddie pulled Anne next to her. "Michelangelo's David. In Ice."

The monumental ice sculpture was frozen sculpture perfection. From David's lean muscled arms, down past his impossibly good abs, to the runner's legs. Everything was flawless. Except the shorts.

"Why is he wearing shorts?" Anne turned her head sideways to get a different perspective.

"You noticed."

"Everyone will notice."

Maddie sighed. "The ice company didn't tell me I was ordering the PG David."

"What's the G David?" Anne started laughing.

"He's wearing a shirt."

"Wait. Do they have a PG-13? An R?" Anne's laughter threatened to give her the hiccups.

"Yes. Yes. And an NC-17." Maddie looked increasingly embarrassed. "I meant to get the R. That's the original."

"Then what's the NC-17?"

"Don't ask."

Anne shook her head and forced herself to stop laughing. "If you gave him a surfboard, he'd look just right."

"That's it." Maddie spread her arms toward the statue.

"A surfboard?"

Maddie stepped around the statue excitedly. "Yes. It's exactly what he needs."

"But Arborhale Academy was almost as far from real surfing as Maine. And where will you get a board? We're in a lodge off a lake."

"This is art. Don't trouble me with details." Maddie grabbed her phone off a table and sent a flurry of texts. "Now what are you doing? Are you almost ready? You're on in less than thirty minutes. And I saw you…with Kirk."

Maddie's question barrage had Anne spinning to answer, but the Kirk observation made her stop and swallow everything. "I'm not going to the dance with Kirk. I have a plan."

"Plan?" Maddie stopped mid-text.

"Kevin won't talk to me because he thinks I purposely dissed Alice."

"I knew that part." Maddie sat on the statue pedestal. "So how're you gonna fix?"

"I need time with him, so he'll hear me out." Anne leaned against David's frozen thigh.

Maddie tapped a finger to her lips. "You're not giving up on him, are you?" The amused twist to her voice said she'd won a bet with herself. "Even though you got a clear offer from Kirk?"

"I've never been into Kirk. Blame chemistry." Anne took Maddie's hand, sure sign that she was about to do something crazy. "After my speech I'm calling out a Sadie Hawkins dance, and I'm going to ask Kevin—in front of everyone."

Chapter 9

By five-thirty, the Elk Horn Room had been transformed into the reunion's theme—*Changes*. The walls were floor-to-ceiling renditions of the world's most famous skylines, the windows glowed with lights and illuminated sunsets, and the tables had been set to match the nearest wall-mounted city.

Anne stepped next to Maddie and the fourteen life-sized ice sculptures. A pink champagne fountain flowed from three cherubs into a heart-shaped crystal basin five feet across. And at the front of the room a DJ was messing with her soundboard.

Anne felt her smile lift all the way to her eyes. Three years of planning had come into perfect focus.

"Ready?" Maddie took Anne's hand.

"What about your Fairy-Godmother magic?" Anne squeezed Maddie's fingers.

Flashing her billion-dollar smile, she gently touched one of the diamond earrings she'd loaned Anne for luck. "The magic's in place."

"Then let's do this."

Maddie raised her hands and signaled for the doors to open.

Hundreds of former classmates—friends, BFFs, cheerleading sisters, crushes, rivals and even a few special invitation-only teachers—flooded the room.

The Rachel twins, nicknamed Tall and Tan, reached the center first. They weren't related by blood, but shared a resemblance so close it was impossible to tell them apart.

Tall Rachel hugged Anne while Tan Rachel, her skin as dark as a Coppertone commercial, snapped selfies with Maddie.

"Chad's a loser." Tall Rachel didn't waste a second diving straight into Anne's only forbidden topic.

If Chad hadn't gotten a contract with a major team, the words might have had a softer impact. Instead they hit like a fastball. Anne smiled anyway. Tall Rachel's heart was in the right place.

A girl walked in behind both the Rachels.

"Lisa." Anne waved her arm to get Lisa Mercer's attention.

She looked around, confused, then made eye contact. Surprise registered in her face, but she gave Anne a quick finger wave.

"I didn't know you talked to Lisa?" Tall Rachel said.

"I'm past the cliques," Anne said. "And she has the kind of cool you can't buy."

"Plus she married royalty." Maddie laughed. "Chris was homecoming court."

Stefan and Alex, linebackers from Arborhale's glory days, joined their group and they caught up on careers, and in Alex's case, family. Two kids and counting. What was it about football guys and big families?

Anne's smile said she was listening, but her attention was focused searching the room for Kevin. When she saw him near the DJ's stand, her heart did a loop-de-loop.

"Ready for your speech?" Maddie whispered to Anne.

"As long as everyone's had time to get a drink. I'm funnier through wine googles."

Maddie gave her a gentle shove. "Get up there."

Somehow volunteering to give the opening speech made a lot more sense three years ago when the reunion had been a project to plan. Before the speech ended with her asking Kevin to dance and possibly—probably—facing his rejection in front of all her friends, enemies, and otherwise.

When it came to fear, picking between giving her speech and asking Kevin to dance, there was no contest. She'd rather speak for hours than risk a gut-twisting, nausea-inducing public rejection.

So why had she thought this was a good idea? But for better or worse, despite the sick feeling in her stomach, her plan had already been set in motion.

Anne made her way through the crowd toward the stage.

At the bottom of the short flight of stairs a giddy lightheadedness grabbed her, turning her nerves into a tight anchor weighing down her stomach.

Deep breath. You can do this. Put on a little happy. Going for giddy, she skipped up the stairs two at a time. One tap on the mic got everyone's attention. "Hello, Arborhale."

Across the room of applause and cheers, Kevin straightened, a glass of wine in his hand, his eyes on her.

"I had a speech. It was funny and it was pretty and Maddie helped me write it." Anne gestured Maddie's direction and Maddie took a bow. "But that's not the speech I'm going to give."

Her cheer sisters, the Arborhale varsity cheerleaders that formed the ring around the Chad-center of her Arborhale life, began to chant—*Anne. Anne. Anne You go!*

"Ten years is too long. And not long enough. Because we all have dreams, and we're all on a journey. I started my journey over three years ago." Anne gripped the mic, searching for the strength to be real. Vulnerable.

"I've made choices. Good. Bad. Fun." She brought her lips close to the mic and gave her voice a naughty twist. "A lot of fun."

The class, friends and barely remembered acquaintances, reacted with yells and laughs and even a few whistles.

She waited till the noise died down and continued. "And along the way I figured out how to stop pretending and be myself."

"A gorgeous girl in an on-fire red dress?" Kirk spoke at exactly the right time for everyone to hear.

"That's woman to you. Jerk." Anne pointed at him and glared him down with a smile. "If you track the TMZ moments of each other's lives, you know Chad dumped me on our college graduation day."

A hush swept the crowd.

"And I've been worried this whole time how I was going to handle the questions, the looks, the whispers. Because I thought after five and a half years of following him and waiting for that magic ring I would look like a failure."

Maddie took a step toward the stage like she wanted to rush Anne with one of her over-the-top, tele-novella drama hugs. But Anne held out a hand to stop her.

"But you know what? If Chad had stayed with me, I might never have found out what I could do, who I could be, on my own. Or found the determination to succeed in a job where I truly belong." As the words came out, they came out easier, and Anne breathed deeper and smiled more.

"I may have lost Chad. But I didn't lose much. Chad was a grade-A…jerk. But he did do one thing for me. He set me free. Free to be myself. To find my own success. To live my real life. And that's what I want for you, Arborhale. All of you. Even those of you who left school early." She spoke directly to Kevin. "I want you to find your real life and—catch the wind."

From across the room it was impossible to tell for sure, but when she said *catch the wind* he seemed to smile, and he definitely took a step toward her.

The room erupted in cheers and laughter and a chorus of flashes as hundreds of pictures hit social media.

Kevin's eyes never left hers. And he walked across the room. Set his glass on a passing table. And moved to the front of the crowd.

"And now Arborhale I'm officially opening the reunion with something a little different." Anne let out her playful smile that boys used to find oh-so-charming. "A Sadie Hawkins opening dance. And I get first pick."

"Not my guy," Tan Rachel yelled.

The varsity girls laughed and pretended to shield their dates.

But Anne's pulse quickened for only one man in the room. She walked down from the stage, crossed the floor, and stopped in front of Kevin.

He said nothing, but if a silent gaze could say anything, she hoped the warm chocolate darkness in his eyes meant desire.

The sound of her own heart pounding in her ears almost drowned out the opening chords of *Lady in Red*.

Anne reached up and smoothed the lapel of Kevin's tux with one hand, and his breath stopped. "Kevin Tyson. Will you dance with me?"

Chapter 10

Anne wasn't on stage anymore. She was standing in an ocean of stretched-out silence in front of Kevin and his dark chocolate eyes, waiting for him to say yes to her Sadie Hawkins proposal. She might as well have lost her bikini in the undertow, because that's the way she felt—naked and bare and vulnerable.

The longer the silence went on, the more her world shrank to the small circle of her and him.

But then he smiled, reminding her more of the shy boy who'd asked her to the Valentine's dance junior year than the self-possessed man who ran the lodge.

Kevin ran his hands down her bare arms, leaving a trail of lightning sparking across her skin, till he reached her fingers and held her hands in his. "I'd like to dance with you. Very much."

"Then take me." A fan of heat flashed across her cheeks at his arched eyebrow. "To the dance floor." She slipped both her arms around one of his and stood close. The scent of his cologne reminded her of winters spent with her parents in a cabin overlooking the ocean. It was one of her favorite memories. A time when she felt safe.

His smile didn't lose its boyish charm as he led her into the center of the dance floor with smooth slow steps.

He took enough time Anne could imagine them dancing together. But not so long anticipation turned to impatience.

Maddie talked with Kirk near the long bar and raised her glass to Anne in a toast when they made eye contact. Kevin had Maddie's approval.

In the center of the floor, under a wide crystal chandelier that stood in for a sky full of stars, he rested one arm on her hip, and held her other hand in a gentle grip.

No movement was rushed, like he savored every second. Unlike Chad—who always had somewhere important to be, who left her always trying to keep up, look pretty, be supportive—Kevin seemed to exist for her alone.

A swirl of heat built low in Anne's stomach. The high-school girl inside her wanted to rest her head against his chest, sink into his arms, and dance in a slow back-and-forth high-school sway.

But the woman inside her resisted and let herself be led by his expert feet in a graceful box step to the beats of *Lady in Red*.

Dancing with him was weightless, her body responding as if they had history. Warmth curled in her stomach and spread to her head in a dizzy kind of heat.

She took her hand from his side and ran it down the light stubble of his jaw, pulling his head toward hers, drinking in his eyes. "Thanks for giving me this dance," she whispered, afraid she'd break the spell that had them moving so perfectly together.

"I couldn't refuse." His eyes were unguarded.

"Your job?" She missed a step. If his job was all he was doing right now, she'd rather be alone. But if this moment was as real for him as it was for her, she wanted more.

"My choice. I've waited to dance with you for a long, long time." He stretched out the words as if he was speaking across time for his teenage self as well as his grown-up self.

She let her hand drift from his cheek onto his shoulder and leaned her face against his chest. His arm drew around her waist as she slid into him. "Sorry if I'm messing up your moves."

Kevin took a deep breath. "You're not messing up anything." The rumble of his voice made her skin tingle.

Messing up. All she'd seemed to be good at this afternoon was messing things up with him. Knocking over his Harley. Opening the wrong drawer and finding his Purple Heart. Asking him about his best friend—who'd died in combat. Ruining Alice's dress. Not one of her banner days. Unless the banner announced her failure.

"I'm sorry about Alice's dress. It really was an accident." Anne looked into his eyes in simple honesty, hoping that would be enough.

He let out a sigh that said Alice didn't see it as anything but an attack. "I believe you. But Alice…"

"I wish she did. It was horrible. She had a beautiful dress."

"So do you." Kevin leaned in close, his breath fanning across her neck, sending chills cascading all the way down to her toes. "Get ready."

"Ready for—?"

"This." He pressed a hand to her back, kept an arm wrapped around her waist, and swept her down into a deep dip.

Her breath caught. Then she laughed, letting one of her knees playfully ride up the side of his leg.

He held her there, suspended, his breath moving in time with hers.

She pressed her free hand against his hard chest and swallowed. The warmth of his presence flooded her, and she was suddenly desperate to erase the distance between their lips.

The song ended. And so did their moment.

He lifted her to her feet and took an unwanted step back. "Guess I've used up my Cinderella time."

No. NO. *NO.* She reclaimed the space he created. "Stay. My magic doesn't expire at midnight. My Fairy Godmother promised."

Kevin's gaze swept the room, taking in the skylights, the statues, the fountain of champagne. "Your magic is everywhere. But this isn't my reunion. Almost no one here even remembers I existed."

Anne took his hand. "Alice told me about the Dyslexia. About Gracepoint. I didn't know."

"Did she tell you they put me in special ed? Back in the temporary buildings behind the school?" He pulled his hand back. Himself back. "Maybe you shouldn't be seen with me."

She stepped into him. Her stomach crunched together so tight it crushed the butterflies trying to take flight at his touch. "Alice said you stayed at Arborhale for me."

His eyes fell. "She shouldn't have told you that."

"Is it true?" She pressed her cheek into his palm.

He nodded.

Anne's heart sputtered. "But we were just—"

"Friends?" His smile was equal parts joy and sadness. "You had so many friends, why would you notice the one boy who planned his life around yours? I've wanted you since you sat in front of me in third grade. But you were always so popular. So out of reach."

"And then I chose the wrong guy." Anne blinked back tears. Why did this feel like a breakup when they hadn't even kissed?

"And then you chose the wrong guy." Kevin smiled like she'd just given him a combination Heisman trophy for football and Nobel prize for science. "But you did everything you said in that great speech. You set me free. When I realized I couldn't have you, I let my parents take me to Gracepoint. It changed my life. Now I only have trouble reading when I'm under a lot of stress."

She'd set him free. She'd taken him for granted. She'd hurt him. And when she found something better she left. Just like Chad.

Kevin held Anne's hand a moment longer. "This isn't my reunion. Even when I was at Arborhale, we went to different high schools. But it was nice to be in yours for a few hours."

Alice hovered nearby in a slim black cocktail dress that showed off her size three figure and thirty six-inch bust line.

"I've got to go." His good-bye smile pulled at her heart so hard it ached. "I only stayed to hear you."

He let go of Anne, and left with Alice, turning the warm spot on her cheek, where he'd had his hand, cold.

Chapter 11

Anne drifted off the dance floor almost in a stupor, passing through couples and friends and old flames flaring back to life.

One dance. One stupid, perfect, amazing dance. And he'd left. With another girl. Jerk. She wanted to crack Kevin's thick skull with the David ice sculpture and its frozen-on Bermuda shorts.

Spotting the punk champagne-cart bartender, she signaled him for another wine. "Anything but a red." At future reunions red wine would be banned from the list.

He smiled and passed her a chardonnay.

She slid him a credit card. "Just open a tab."

"You're committee." He shook his head with a sardonic smile. "Keep your money."

"Won't that get you in trouble…?"

"With Kevin?" He poured her the wine and handed her the glass. "He's my boss, but after his ditch-you-on-the-dance-floor move, I doubt he'll question your tab."

Anne tightened her grip on the stem. "What's he like?"

"Kevin? Awesome. He really knows how to run this place. But he seemed a little stressed today."

Anne could add, subtract, and even multiply. And she could definitely catch a clue. If Kevin was stressed, she could guess which member of the two-person planning committee was responsible. And it wasn't Maddie.

"Thanks." She went in search of her soul-sister. Even if Maddie didn't have any more advice, drinking alone wasn't fun.

Anne found her friend lounging next to a statue of cupid, complete with ice arrow ready to fire.

She plopped down in a seat and took a sip of her wine. "Kevin left."

"At least your plan worked."

"For one dance." The thought of his touch recharged those tingles that dance had spread across her skin.

"Isn't that all you planned? You run dealerships. Do you make your business plans to get people to test drive or to buy?"

"Buy," Anne muttered.

"Then you shouldn't have stopped at the test drive."

"You're right." Anne missed his touch as soon as it left. Their bodies had moved together in a way that could only be called…chemistry. "I had more chemistry with Kevin in one dance that I did in my entire relationship with Chad." He was always taking. But dancing with Kevin felt equal. Like they'd been partners for years.

"One dance, huh?" Maddie stared at Anne.

Anne shrugged. Sipped. Fidgeted in her seat. "I'm old enough to know happily ever after is more about planning and work than starry eyes. But I can't deny how he makes me feel. And I think he feels the same."

"Then why are you sitting here talking to me?"

Anne raised her empty hands. "It's like he broke up with me when we're not even dating."

Maddie swirled her glass. "He wasn't breaking up with you. He was breaking up with the idea of being with you."

"That doesn't make any sense." Anne really wanted to let loose her inner child and stamp her foot, yell, and maybe even break something. "Why would you break up with the idea of a relationship?"

Maddie took a slow sip and watched Anne simmer.

"Because he's with Alice," Anne answered her own question.

"Alice?" Maddie laughed. "Wine's on me if she's anything more to him than a sister."

"Wine's actually on Kevin." Anne glanced at the bartender.

"I'm going to pretend like I understand that and move on. You do realize you're your own worst enemy, right?"

"How?"

"Dear Anne. For all your sweet imperfections, self-image problems, and laundry list of neurosis, did it never occur to you that your mountain man with the Superman jaw and poetic eyes has convinced himself he isn't good enough for you?"

Anne's mouth fell open. "Not good enough for me? Are you crazy?"

"No. But he is. And so are you." Before Anne could offer a rebuttal, Maddie held up her hand. "Seems to me you've been cheated."

"Cheated?" Anne tried to assess where she'd gone wrong.

"He broke up with you without there being anything to break. So he gets off easy while you're sitting here, at your own reunion, trying to figure out what went wrong when nothing went wrong. At least nothing with you."

"You're right." A simmer of irritation boiled in Anne's stomach.

"You bet she is." Kirk flipped a chair around backwards and sat straddling it and leaning forward over the back of the chair. "About what?"

Anne punched him in the shoulder. "Jerk."

"That's the second time you've called him that tonight." Maddie passed a glance between them.

"At least this time I'm not on stage." Anne shot Maddie a quick, not-interested shake of her head.

Maddie countered with a *why* raise of her eyebrows.

"I think this is my queue to leave." Anne stood and cradled her wine glass like a protective talisman. "Too much subtext."

Maddie's laugh was as light as the Chardonnay.

Anne made her way to the door. Maddie was right. Kevin was protecting himself. And that was so Kevin. She'd only been around him for one day in the last ten years. But his protective side was as pinned to his chest as a purple heart.

He was the complete opposite of Chad. Chad thought about himself first. And his loyalty was to the mirror.

Kevin defended his platoon in Iraq, and won the heart. He was still taking care of his best friend's widow. He fought for the lodge staff and had earned their loyalty.

He might not think he was worthy, but after she got hit with a cold dose of reality at Kent State's home plate, he had every trait she wanted most in a man—all wrapped up in a better-than-chocolate package.

And she was willing to fight for him.

Chapter 12

Dragging her heart on the floor behind her, Anne walked away from the reunion she spent the last three years planning.

Down the wide empty hall, the *Private Use Only* sign on the old iron elevator hung loose. Inside the gate, the twenties retro carriage was gone. Someone had taken it. Kevin. Or Alice. Or both of them. Together. The only thing on the floors above her were an old movie theater and his apartment.

If Maddie was right, she'd find them hanging out. Talking. Maybe watching a movie with a comfortable friend-zone of space between them. If she was wrong…

She stood at a crossroad shaped like an elevator. Chase the guy. Go back to the party. Chase—the odds weren't in her favor. With all their history why wouldn't Alice and Kevin be together? Reunion magic or not, if she was Alice, she'd be giving Kevin forty very unfun lashes for dancing with another woman the way he'd danced with Anne.

But if they weren't together…

Anne didn't want to lose without trying. She strummed her fingers on the brass elevator panel.

Alice wasn't exactly friendly. The way she'd reacted to their first meeting, she must've known about the Valentine's Day decision. And staining her dress didn't help.

Even if Kevin and Alice weren't together in the biblical sense, she was still more than a best friend. Kevin was the man who'd carried her through the death of her fiancé—on the back of a motorcycle.

She took a deep breath and waited for her confidence to kick in. Nothing. Another deep shoulder's-back kind of inhale. Nothing. She rolled her eyes at herself and pushed the elevator button.

If her confidence wouldn't come to her she'd just have to find it on the way or fake it.

The well-oiled gears turned with barely a hum and the carriage descended into position. She opened the gate and let herself in. The top floor required a key. But the *Mezzanine* button didn't, so she pushed it and hoped they were watching a movie, and Alice wouldn't toss her out before she had a chance to get off the elevator.

The elevator opened to a paneled hall that smelled of fresh polish. She stepped out, her heels sinking into the thick carpet, and followed a shiny brass railing onto a balcony with plush leather seats arranged in pairs, with semi-private separators. The balcony overlooked a multi-tiered floor with dining tables set with silver and while linen.

Instead of the run down old movie theater she'd expected, this place had been transformed into a posh dinner theater.

On the first row, Alice peered around the side of the end balcony seat and dropped her smile. "Are you lost?"

Anne stepped toward her. "I was looking for Kevin."

"He's gone." She leaned back in her seat, effectively dismissing Anne. "But he'll probably be in his office tomorrow."

Anne clenched one of her hands into a fist behind her back and dug her nails into her palm. Keep cool. This isn't a friendship. This is a negotiation. "What I have to say can't wait."

"It waited ten years."

Anne walked around to the front of Alice's seat and leaned against the brass railing. Alice had a large box of popcorn set between the two seats, and a computer tablet with what appeared to be a control panel for the room.

"If you want to push me off, here's your chance." Anne kept her tone civil, as if she was making a serious offer.

Alice's eyes opened wide, and her lips parted as if she was about to give a scathing retort, but she stopped—smiled. Smiled like a snake that had spotted something interesting enough not to eat. Yet. "Tempting. So tell me, assuming you don't have a death wish, why are you really here?"

Anne could try and made the words pretty, but her list was simple. "To find out what you and Kevin mean to each other. And if you're not together—"

"He's family. More than family." Alice's voice got soft. "And ever since you came here he's been all messed up."

Alice still wore her stunning black dress. To sit in a movie theater and eat popcorn—alone. If their roles were reversed, she'd probably be protective too. "School reunions twist everything up."

"I didn't go to High School. At least not a normal one." Alice adjusted a few of the controls on her screen and the lights dimmed. "I went to school on whatever base my father was assigned to."

"Military?" Anne asked.

"Marines, like Kevin…and Frank. When military find family, you stick to them. For soldiers, it's your squad. For me—it was Kevin."

"How did he get his purple heart?" Anne would love to sit and pull off her heels. But Alice hadn't offered, and if this was a test of stubborn, Alice was in for a surprise.

"His unit was pinned down on all sides." Her voice said this was a story she'd repeated before. "He volunteered to slip out and flank the enemy unit. He was shot twice in the side. But he didn't stop till he did what he had to do to get his unit out alive."

A swell of pride filled Anne's chest. Kevin kept fighting, after he'd been shot. Not many men she'd ever met would've had that kind of determination to protect what was theirs.

"When they helicoptered him to a hospital in Germany, he was angry. He wanted a field medic to patch him up so he could stay with his unit."

"Why didn't he stay in?"

"Frank died. Made Kevin promise to take care of me." Alice's voice wavered and she wiped her eyes. "Good thing I have waterproof mascara."

Anne laughed and tried not to make it obvious she knew Alice had cried.

"He really gets to you doesn't he?" She patted the seat next to her and her snake eyes softened to something human.

Anne nodded. Took the seat and a bite of popcorn. "I won't deny the chemistry. But what about you?"

Alice sat back and stared at her. "I've tried. If any man deserved my love after Frank, it's Kevin. He's done so much for me that if he asked, I'd marry him, chemistry or not. He deserves that much."

"But?" Anne hoped there was a but. A tilt-a-whirl of emotions spun in her chest, and the last thing she wanted to hear was that Alice was marrying Kevin.

"But I've seen more spark between the two of you tonight than he and I have had for years." She swallowed and played with her skirt for a moment. "And I don't want to pretend to be in love, I want that spark for myself."

Anne had never lost a Frank. And didn't want to even try to imagine Alice's pain. Or the courage it took for her to be ready to find new love.

"I had a guy I thought was my Frank. But when he finally got everything he wanted, he left me." Anne fought to keep her voice even.

"I…heard. You were together for eight years. When he left it was like someone died."

Anne couldn't stop a sarcastic laugh. "Too bad it wasn't him."

"Kevin means the world to me. I don't have any other family anymore. And I'll do whatever I have to do to protect him." Her tone was simple, her eyes clear. She didn't have to imply a threat. It was on the table. Do what she did to him before, and Alice would be waiting to bring her pain.

Anne nodded. "I don't have a crystal ball, but I won't hurt him, not on purpose. Like you said, he's the kind of man that's worth loving. And I wish I'd seen that before."

Alice's smile was full of the kind of wisdom that was backed by painful experience. "No. You don't."

Anne paused at the other woman's sincerity. "What do you mean?"

"Young love doesn't last. You might go back to it, but people rarely start and finish there. If you'd dated him when he first fell for you in school, would you really still be together now?"

A knot of realization twisted in her gut. "No. He'd probably just be some guy I dated that I met again at the reunion."

"Once you know what it's like to lose someone, you know how precious love is, and how much its worth protecting."

Alice pressed a button on her tablet and the intro music for the film started. "Kevin was supposed to watch Casablanca with me tonight, but you got him so worked up, he needed to unwind. So he's working off his stress fixing his bike."

So he was in the barn—alone. Thousands of butterflies took flight in her stomach, brushing her insides with their wings. "Thanks Alice."

"You still owe me a new dress. A good red cocktail is hard to get in this area." Alice settled back into her chair. "Now hurry if you're going to get him back in time for more dancing. He does a great Salsa."

Humphrey Boggart took the screen as Anne made her way to the elevator. This time she went down and the carriage couldn't move fast enough.

Chapter 13

Anne's heels beat out a staccato rhythm as she *click, click, clicked* across the polished wood floor of the lodge's entrance hall. The building had seemed huge only a few hours ago, but now that her whole focus was on Kevin, it felt two sizes too small. Like her lungs.

Walking past a wall covered in old photographs, she paused at the front desk and cleared her throat to get the receptionist's attention. "How can I get to the motorcycle barn?"

The tired-looking woman pointed to the door at the back of the room with her pen. "The fastest way to the cart shed is a gravel trail off the back balcony. Door's under the moose head." She scanned Anne's low neckline and high hemline—and gave a judgmental snort. "But if you're looking for Kevin, I can have him paged."

Anne pasted on her don't-care-that-you're-judging-me smile. "No thanks."

Outside, the night air bordered on hot. Without the cool lake breeze, she had no trouble telling it was summer. Still too early for the moon, but the sun had long since gone to bed. She paused at the wooden railing to watch the lodge lights play on the water.

A flicker of light from the barn made her neck tingle. Kevin.

She picked her way down a steep gravel path to the wide lawn sweeping from lodge to lakeshore. Her foot faltered, and she almost rolled her ankle. Red pumps ruled the catwalk. But not so much the gravel walk. By the time she reached the barn, a cocktail of anticipation and curiosity swirled in her chest.

She slid the door open.

In the warm yellow light of a pair of electric lanterns, Kevin knelt, shirtless, next to his bike. He wore tight work jeans that strained over his muscled thighs and heavy leather work gloves. When he saw her, he stood, dropped his wrench, and took her breath away.

As good as he looked in a tight shirt, as stunning as he looked in a tux, he was divine shirtless. Her eyes caught all the hard planes of his perfect muscled body. Either he had won the genetic lottery for a body-builder's physique, or he never touched carbs. Either way, Kevin shirtless wasn't playing fair. Not with her attraction to him, not with her heart.

And somehow the jeans and gloves made his shirtless chest even more amazing. Like he was a calendar model personally chosen for her birthday month.

"Kevin." Anne stepped toward him and stopped in puddle of light. The lantern light glittered from her earrings.

"What are you...why are you here?" His voice wavered between surprise and suspicion.

"Hoping you'll invite me in." She lifted her chin and stared into his eyes.

"Come in." He dropped his gloves onto his toolbox and pulled on a flannel shirt.

Before he could do a single button, she took a step toward him, aware of every beat of her heart. "You left."

"I had to." He sounded unsure, but his eyes stayed steady and fixed on her.

"What you did when you walked out on me wasn't fair. You can't break up with me, or even with the idea of me, when there isn't anything to break." She took another step. "Yet."

"Yet?" He tilted his head, looking at her like he was drinking her in.

She took another step. "Should I go?"

He shook his head, the way he studied her so intense she forgot to breathe.

The butterflies that lived in her stomach when he was near her settled and went still. Maybe she shouldn't have come. Maybe the weight of their high school memories were too much of a barrier to building something new.

She moistened her lips. She wanted more than one dance, more than one night with his arms around her. She wanted his kiss. Reunion night were supposed to be magic, but the magic couldn't be hers. She'd made so many mistakes with him.

He stood in silence. The lantern light dancing across his skin, highlighting the strong lines of his face. His unreadable eyes looked deep into hers.

"Do I have to ask you to kiss me?" Her words rushed over the request in an uncertain whisper.

He shook his head again, seizing the space between them in two quick strides to wrap his arms around her and pull her into his chest.

Relief flooded her and Anne relaxed into the safety of his arms, the heat of his body, the steady thump of his heart.

He leaned back just far enough to brush his lips along her jaw. His breath hit her neck and sent shivers all the way down her back. "You'll never have to ask me again." He pressed his lips against hers with desperate, breathless intensity. Like he wanted to make up for ten years of drought in a single moment.

She clung to him, running her hands beneath his shirt to grip his shoulders, her body simmering under his touch. The butterflies in her stomach erupted into flight.

When he released her to take a long breath, he stared into her eyes like she was a mirage, and he was waiting for her to disappear.

Anne ran her fingers through his hair. "Why did you stop?"

"My mistake." He smiled against her lips and moved down her neck with a series of quick nips and long kisses. Each an explosion of tingling delight. He held her bottom lip between his teeth and gently pulled. Released. Pressed his mouth to hers and left her gasping for air and more.

If she were a cat she would have purred. "Are you glad you invited me in?"

"Kissing you is even better than I ever imagined." He spoke into her ear, then worked his lips against her throat and up the curve of her jaw, till he gently, playfully bit the side of her neck.

She ran her fingernails down his back.

"You have no idea how beautiful you are, and you don't even have to try." He touched her hair, treating it like the finest silk.

"You should take a peek in my room before you tell me how much I don't have to try to look like this."

"Anne." Her name in his smooth voice set off flutters in her stomach that spiraled out into her body.

She sighed and shook her head feeling free for the first time since Chad. "This is wonderful. You're wonderful. And I have a question."

He glanced at his bike. "Want to go for a midnight ride?"

The thought of doing anything with him at midnight filled her with the most delightful ache. "Raincheck?" She tried not to sound too hopeful. She needed enough mystery to keep him coming back for more. But her desire outweighed her power to be coy.

"Definitely." He cupped her face in his hands, raised her chin, and stared into her eyes. His lips brushed hers and found spots on her nose and cheeks that hadn't gotten nearly enough attention.

"Would you go to the dance with me?" Her voice shook when she spoke. "I can't turn back time, but I want what we should've had before. Will you give me another chance?"

He paused. Stared into her eyes, straight into her soul. Stepped into her until she felt his motorcycle against her back. He dipped his head to worship her mouth all over again, gripping her sides and lifting her onto the seat, never breaking their kiss.

The heat of his body enveloped her, and she clung to his shoulders while their lips moved together—soft and hard and sometimes overwhelmingly sweet.

Her body was alive with tingles in her skin, lightning in her nerves, fire in her heart. She was dizzy and lost in him and their kiss could've lasted minutes or hours or days.

When they parted, she leaned her head against this chest and breathed in the scent of him. "Is that a yes?"

He stroked his fingers down her cheek and neck. Her pulse thrummed under his hand. "Yes. I would love to go to the dance with you."

She stared into his dark eyes. "Tonight will be how it should have been."

"Tonight will be our new beginning."

The way he said *our* made her shudder with anticipation.

He cupped her jaw in his hand and leaned over her, dropping a soft kiss at the corner of her mouth, and lifted her off the motorcycle. "Let me change."

Warmth from his touch still filled her body. She watched him disappear into the saddle closet. "You have a tux in there?" Only men in cologne commercials were this prepared.

"I changed in here earlier. I didn't want to work on my bike in my best suit. But I forgot a shirt."

Anne was more than glad he forgot his shirt tonight. Leaning against his bike she ran a hand idly over she soft leather. "What's it like to catch the wind?"

"Peaceful." His voice made her think of a clear summer's day with no hurry, no rush, no stress. "You just ride where the road takes you and let the wind wash your soul."

"Are you a poet too?"

"No." His voice altered for a moment, like he was putting on his tie. "But it's true. And I'd love to share that with you. If a Ducati girl can bring herself to ride a Harley."

Her heart twirled at the thought of riding with him on the open road. "This Ducati girl will definitely ride with her Harley guy."

He came out in his tux, looking as fresh as if he'd never changed. "Ready?"

"Oh yes." She brushed her hands across his shoulders and took his arm.

Together they left the barn and walked to their first school dance.

"You know what?" She flashed him a thousand-watt smile. "It took me a while to get here, but this time I chose the right guy."

He ran a hand through her hair and kissed her again.

The End

Dear Reader

Thank you for reading *The Right One*. This book is dedicated to my family, all of my creativity and all of my love belong to you. And was inspired by Patty, dearest mother, and the first Harley girl in my life. She taught me what is means to *catch the wind*.

This novella kicks off my upcoming *Catch the Wind* Series. Watch for Kevin and Alice's story, *The Last One*, next.

Like most writers I love to hear from my readers.

Visit with MK at authormksmith.com on Twitter @AuthorMKSmith and FB authormksmith

MK Smith, coffee connoisseur, Danish lover, full-time dreamer has a BS in Psychology, a Masters in something complicated, and loves to spend java-fueled nights weaving stories filled with quirky imperfect characters trying to survive life, friendship, and each other. Because love really does spin the world. In addition to writing contemporary romance, MK is also the author of *Serena's Fall*—an urban fantasy with attitude.

BROKEN WINGS

Alexandrea Weis

As a wildlife rehabilitator in Southeast Louisiana, Pamela Wells has dealt with her fair share of wild animals, but her reclusive life is forever changed when she meets an elusive former soldier named Daniel Phillips. Sent to Pamela's wildlife sanctuary as part of his parole requirements, Daniel and Pamela quickly clash until Daniel's troubled past unexpectedly comes to light. Daniel finds peace in Pamela's wildlife sanctuary and an unexpected kindred spirit in Pamela. But there is another vying for Pamela's affections, and Daniel may have to fight to save her and her beloved facility from being ensnared by another. Is Daniel willing to risk everything to save her?

Chapter 1

Drab gray clouds covered the expansive horizon, obliterating the warmth of the sun. Like the delicate flora of nature covered by endless miles of sidewalks in some sprawling super city, the heavens above were suppressed behind a wall of lifeless color.

Pamela Wells stood in her back door and surveyed the sulking skies above.

Spring; thoughts of the season brought to mind frolicking bunnies and brightly colored birds preparing nests for much-anticipated hatchlings. But for Pamela, the warming breezes of the change in seasons were not always a welcomed event. She sighed as she turned her eyes to the expanse of land around her and contemplated the work that lay ahead. With the coming spring, Pamela knew all of her aches would return from their winter respite.

But her pains were not limited to the constant throbbing in the various joints of her body; dark days brought an ache to her heart, as well. It was on such a day that she met Robert—Bob to his friends. The memory of Robert Patrick dressed in his expensive tailored suit and Italian designer shoes made Pamela laugh.

Lying in a hospital bed, days after a bad car accident, Bob walked into her room. He was fresh out of law school and in desperate need of clients. After reading about her accident in the newspaper, Bob hunted Pamela down and signed her on as his first client. One year later, they married in a lavish ceremony inside St. Louis Cathedral in New Orleans.

Pamela shook her head. "Eight years after that, Bob turned into a jerk," she muttered as she gazed out at the barn behind her blue and white Acadian cottage. "Well, at least I got this place in the divorce."

Out of nowhere, a wide raccoon with a slow, lumbering gait and a glint of childlike exuberance in his masked eyes wandered up to Pamela. The raccoon stopped just below the three steps to Pamela's back porch and stood on his hind haunches. He looked at her and warbled in the way a raccoon baby calls to his mother.

"Good morning, Rodney." Pamela walked down the steps to greet the animal. "How are you today?"

She rubbed behind the raccoon's silver-tipped ears. Rodney fell on his back like a lump of whale blubber and proceeded to grab her hand and direct it to the spots on his belly that needed immediate scratching.

Pamela laughed and rubbed the animal's wide stomach as Rodney wiggled with delight. The sudden screech of an owl from a nearby tree frightened the raccoon. He jumped to a standing position and eyed a tree close to the house, snorting loudly.

Pamela patted the raccoon's round bottom. "Relax, Rodney. You know Lester won't hurt you." She spied the owl up in the tree next to her bedroom window. "Lester, did you have a good night?"

The owl screeched again, opened his large brown and white checked wings and flapped vigorously on his tree branch.

"Yes, I know you're hungry, Lester. But I have got baby squirrels to feed, and then there are cages to clean before you can have your ham and eggs."

The sound of a car heading down the gravel road toward the cottage made Pamela divert her attention away from the impatient owl.

A blue open-top Jeep Wrangler with wide off-road tires appeared from out of the brush at the end of her drive. Pamela observed the car with a feeling of trepidation sweeping through her. Strangers coming down the gravel road to her sanctuary were either delivering orphaned or injured wildlife to her care or coming to deliver food and supplies to her wildlife sanctuary. But no one was ever unexpected at her facility, and uninvited strangers were never welcome. A cacophony of barking broke out from the direction of the front porch steps. The assorted stray dogs Pamela collected through the years ran to greet the car as it came to a quick stop in front of the cottage. She walked toward the front of her home and watched tentatively as the dogs surrounded the Jeep.

A tall man with thick, dark brown hair and sunglasses stood up in the cab of the Jeep and peered down at her.

"Hey there," he greeted, and then glanced at a slip of paper in his hand. "Is this Second Chance Wildlife Rehabilitation Center?"

"Yes. Is there something I can do for you?" Pamela inspected him as the dogs around the car growled in unison.

He waved to the five dogs surrounding his Jeep. "You want to call off the posse?"

"What you're doing out here?" she demanded as she tried to walk to the car, pulling Rodney along with her as he continued to cling to her leg.

The stranger removed his sunglasses. "Your facility requested a service worker to come out and help clean cages, right? I'm your service worker."

"The probation office sent you?" Pamela balked. "But they called and told me you were supposed to come next Wednesday. Today's Saturday."

"It's my day off, and my probation officer said it would be all right."

He made a move to step down from the Jeep, but the snarl of a tall, black Catahoula mix stopped him.

"Quincy," Pamela called out to the dog. "Go back to the porch." She pointed to the porch at the front of the house.

Quincy, along with the rest of his canine pack, obediently obliged and made their way slowly to the porch steps.

Pamela waited for the dogs to settle down on the shady front porch before she glanced back at her new service worker. "I'm Pamela Wells, the owner. Your probation officer told you what's expected around here? I don't tolerate drinking, cursing or—"

"Lewd or rude behavior," the man interrupted, climbing from the Jeep. "Yeah, I got the memo. Don't worry, Ms. Wells, I will be like a choir boy in church while I'm here."

"What's your name?"

"Daniel, Daniel Phillips." He hung his sunglasses on the neck of his white T-shirt. "You don't have a stable hand or someone to clean up around here?"

Pamela noticed that his round, dark brown eyes appeared almost black and there was a seductive quality to them. "I'd have to pay for help. This facility runs on a shoestring budget already." She noticed his expensive-looking leather boots. "You ever worked with wild animals before?"

Daniel snickered. "Only the human kind. I deal with a lot of wild people at work."

Pamela carefully examined his old, faded blue jeans, slender build, muscular arms, broad chest, and long legs. Probably in his early thirties, his wide forehead and chiseled jaw gave him a commanding appearance. A scar under his left eye made him appear more sinister than innocent, making Pamela suspect that this was not the first time Daniel Phillips found himself under the scrutiny of a probation officer.

She quickly checked her disconcerting thoughts. "Where do you work?"

"Pat O'Brien's in the Quarter. I'm a bartender there."

As he checked her out, Pamela found his dark eyes disturbing. She knew from experience that her slim figure and shoulder length, dirty blonde hair made her an easy target for a man's overactive imagination. But it was the way Daniel looked at her that rattled her.

He turned his eyes away from her and browsed the facility surrounding them. About a hundred yards from the rear of the house was an old battered blue barn with a few other smaller out buildings to the right of it. Located close to the barn, at the edge of the cleared property, were several tall wood-trimmed cages.

"What kind of animals do you usually get here?" Daniel kept his eyes on the trees along the edge of the clearing.

"Fox, rabbit, skunk, gray squirrel, fox squirrel, raccoon, opossum, bats, nutria, and an occasional river otter. But I have rehabbed chipmunks, beaver, a few owls, and once, a baby coyote."

Daniel turned back to her. "So is this all there is to the place?"

"Why? What did you expect?"

He shrugged. "I don't know, something like the Audubon Zoo maybe."

"This is not a zoo," she responded, indignantly. "It's a wildlife rehabilitation facility. We care for orphaned and injured wildlife and do not keep animals for display to an indifferent public." She gave the man another going over with her eyes. "What were you convicted of? I often have volunteers on the site, and I want to make sure—"

"I'm not a serial rapist, Ms. Wells," Daniel maintained in an irritated tone. "I hit a guy in the bar where I work for roughing up his date. He filed charges, and I was busted for assault and battery. My sentence was one hundred hours of community service. Satisfied?"

"Did they throw in any anger management classes with that community service?"

Daniel smiled, cockily, revealing a row of perfectly white teeth. "No, the judge didn't seem to think I needed any." He stared into her face for a moment. "So am I to call you Ms. Wells the entire time I'm here, or will Pamela be all right with you?"

"Pamela is fine. We don't stand on formality around here."

A loud sniff came from around Pamela's feet. She looked down at the ground to see Rodney standing behind her legs, staring at the stranger.

"One of the rehabilitated returned to the wild?" Daniel nodded to Rodney.

Pamela picked up the overweight ring-tailed creature from the ground. The animal cuddled against her chest and warily watched the man standing next to her.

"This is Rodney. He was rescued from a hawk when he was about two weeks old. He's over a year now, and I can't get him to leave. He thinks he is one of the dogs."

Daniel reached out to pet the raccoon, but the animal growled at him.

"He doesn't like strangers," Pamela quickly added. "All of the animals in this facility are wild. Do not pet them or try to treat them like a cute and cuddly lap dog."

"Are there any more like him?" He motioned to the raccoon nuzzling up against Pamela's neck.

"A few. You'll meet them later. For now, I'll show you to the cages that need cleaning." She started toward the row of cages located a short distance from the back of the house.

Daniel directed his attention to the blue and white wooden Acadian cottage on his right. Some shingles on the roof were cracked and were falling away, and the paint covering the wooden boards along the side of the house were bubbling up and peeling off.

"How many acres have you got here?"

"Fifteen. There are another fifty acres behind this property that belongs to one of my patrons. So the animals have a large refuge to roam far away from any humans."

"Is there any money in this sort of thing?"

Pamela stopped walking. "There is no money here if that is what you're asking. Everything is for the animals. So if you think you can steal from me, borrow equipment, or make a tidy profit from your time here, think again."

Daniel raised his hands up in submission. "Hey, don't get all bent out of shape, Pamela. I was just wondering why anyone would go to this much trouble for a bunch of stray squirrels."

Pamela rubbed her cheek against the raccoon's fluffy face. "The cages are this way."

She quickly turned and started for the cages at the end of the clearing, leaving a wide-eyed Daniel to follow her.

*****

Pamela was sitting on the back porch of her cottage feeding a three-week-old baby gray squirrel with a small syringe. The eyes of the small gray shadow were still closed, and it resembled a baby rat rather than a squirrel. Pamela delicately rubbed the animal's cheek to encourage it to continue to suckle.

"How many is that now?"

Pamela turned around and was immediately hit head on by a pair of pale blue eyes. With sharp features and long, light brown hair pulled back in a ponytail, the woman's face was round and appealing.

"Fifteen gray squirrels. Why are you keeping count, Carol?"

Carol Corbin was Pamela's accountant, manager, board member, and all around arranger of everything impossible. She was the glue that kept Pamela's little sanctuary held together.

"I thought you were going to tell everyone we have reached our limit as far as baby squirrels go," Carol said, placing her hands on her hips.

"One more won't make any difference." Pamela shrugged. "Besides, I don't have any raccoons or skunks in yet this year so I can take in more baby squirrels."

"Last year you kept saying you were going to cut back, and we ended up with twenty-two baby gray squirrels, eighteen fox squirrels, fifteen baby raccoons, ten injured bats, nine rabbits, eight baby possums, six skunks, four fox kits, and one deranged owl."

"Lester is not deranged," Pamela clarified. "He just has issues."

"He lives on ham and eggs and thinks hunting is something you watch other birds do on the National Geographic Channel. Has he ever left the tree outside of your bedroom window?"

"He's working on it," Pamela defended. "Just last week he got down on the ground and walked over to my back porch."

Carol folded her arms. "Let me guess, chocolate?"

"Rice Krispy treats, but it's a step. It's the first time he has left the tree since he got here." She gently pulled the syringe out of the mouth of the baby squirrel in her hands.

"I know you created this place as a haven for the wildlife, but you have to be realistic. The donations are not flowing in like they used to, and the budget is getting tight, real tight. You're going to have to accept the fact that we need to cut back on the number of animals we take in," Carol informed her.

Pamela refilled her syringe from the bowl of formula. "I could apply for another of those federal grants for wildlife rehabilitation. They have helped us out in the past."

Carol shook her head. "You know how much red tape and paperwork are involved with those grants. Besides, any grant could take several months to come through, and we need an influx of cash now."

Pamela placed the syringe back in the baby squirrel's mouth. "I could go to Bob. He always said he would cover us if things got tight."

Carol took a seat next to her on the porch. "You went to him last year when the air-conditioning needed to be replaced in your house."

"But he would come through if I asked him," Pamela insisted.

"How would Imelda feel about that? You two almost came to blows last year over the air conditioner."

Imelda was Carol's name for Bob's second wife, Clarissa. A social climbing court reporter, Clarissa Turner married Bob three months after Pamela's divorce was final. She was a green-eyed beauty with an affinity for designer clothes, lavish parties, and was known around town for her obsession with shoes.

"Clarissa is not as bad as you make her out to be, Carol. She cares about this place," Pamela asserted.

"Are you kidding me? The only time the woman shows any interest in this place is when she is trying to get her name in the society pages of the *Times-Picayune*. Even when she does manage to get us any publicity, she insists that all of the donations be sent to her and not directly to you. Probably so she can buy that Chinese baby she keeps talking about adopting."

Pamela pulled the syringe away from the baby squirrel and placed it back in the bowl of formula. "You know Bob doesn't want to adopt a kid. He never wanted kids."

"Then why did he divorce you? I thought you told me Bob wanted the divorce because you couldn't have children."

Pamela wrapped the baby squirrel in the towel, sitting on her lap. "Bob didn't leave me because I couldn't have children. He left because I have lupus. He could not stand the thought of having a chronically ill wife."

"Bob always was a bit of a backstabbing snake, if you ask me. I guess that's why he became such a successful attorney." She stood up and looked down at Pamela. "But you can't always depend on him to solve your financial problems, Pamie."

She rubbed the small squirrel's round, pink stomach. "There's always the settlement fund if I need money."

Carol stomped her foot. "No, the money from your accident is your nest egg. You depleted half of it when you got this place up and running. As your accountant and your friend, I cannot stand by and let you squander any more of it. That money is for when you need it. In case you get sick or …." Carol voiced faded.

The "what ifs" hung over Pamela's head like a noose ever since she was first diagnosed with her chronic disease. Robbed her of her marriage, her chance at motherhood, her health and, at times, her sanity, she secretly vowed she would never let lupus take away her one happiness—her sanctuary.

"You worry too much, Carol." Pamela stood from the porch still holding the towel in her hands. "You know I would rather have that money go to helping these animals than paying doctor bills."

"You can't go on forever, Pamie. One day you will have to slow down and hand this place over to someone who has the money and the connections to keep it going."

"Don't bring that up again, Carol. You and I both know what Bob will do to this place if he ever gets his hands on it."

"Well, if you can't keep up with the taxes and the overhead, that, or something equally disturbing, will happen," Carol warned.

"As long as Bob's name is on the mortgage, I'm stuck with him as a silent partner. Until I'm financially viable, I'll never be rid of him; you know that."

"Then let's find another patron, a richer one."

"What do you suggest I do, Carol? Sleep with the first man that flashes a blank check in my face?"

"That would be a start." She shook her head. "Honestly, if I had your package I would be out there hunting for the first man I came across with a pulse and a high credit score. You spend every day and night up to your elbows in animals. When was the last time you even went on a date?"

The tiny squirrel was squirming around inside of the towel in her hands. "Men don't want me, Carol. I'm too old and once they find out I have—"

"Forty-one is not old," Carol cut in. "Just because Bob reacted the way he did to your lupus does not mean that another man will be such a heartless wretch." She threw her hands up in the air. "Everyone has got something wrong with them. No one is perfect."

Pamela tried to force back the slow grinding tension rising from the pit of her stomach. "But everyone does judge you. I don't want a man to consider my limitations before he ever gets to know my possibilities."

Carol stood in silence before her, as Pamela watched the woman's pale blue eyes sink in resignation.

"All right." Carol waved her hand in the air. "Lecture over. But I want you to consider at least dating someone. Preferably someone rich, but I'm not picky."

"Carol you make me sound like some—"

"Who's that?" Carol interrupted as she peered out toward the cages along the edge of the cleared property.

Pamela followed her line of sight until she saw Daniel. He was naked from the waist up, hosing out cages at the other end of the clearing.

Pamela gasped. "Oh, no!"

"What is it?"

Pamela nodded in Daniel's direction. "That's the guy the parole office sent over to clean cages."

"Him? Man, we need to call them more often."

"Not funny." Pamela handed the towel with the baby squirrel inside to Carol. "The guy needs to put his shirt back on. This isn't a Chippendales nightclub. It's a family friendly facility, for God's sake!"

"Oh, please!" Carol chuckled. "That's the first fine piece of man meat I've seen since I went into the city and got trashed at Pat O'Brien's last year."

"Yeah, well, maybe you saw him." Pamela headed toward the back steps. "He works as a bartender at Pat O'Brien's."

"Oh, this morning is just getting better and better," Carol voiced.

"It won't be so good when twenty kids and their mothers pull up and see a half-naked man on my property."

"Pamela, right now it's not the mothers getting bent out of shape by the half-naked man. It's you."

Pamela stormed down the steps and across the green grass toward the row of cages.

"What do you think you are doing?" Pamela snapped.

Daniel glanced down at the scrub brush in his hand. "What does it look like I'm doing?"

Pamela's stomach did an uneasy flip as she watched the man's eyes slice into hers. She went to the side of the cage where he his white T-shirt hung and angrily yanked it off the wire cage.

"This is not some bar in the French Quarter where women throw money at you to see your bare chest. I've got a busload of children from Gracepoint School in Georgia coming today."

"I've heard of that school. They work with dyslexic kids, right?"

"I'm surprised you know that." She handed the T-shirt to him. "Put your shirt back on. The last thing the students need to see is your half-naked butt in my facility

"It's not my butt that's naked, Pamela." He threw the scrub brush on the ground and wiped his hands on his jeans. "I'm sorry. Since so many women throw money at me to see my half-naked body, I figured you wouldn't mind."

"I don't care if you parade around here buck naked, but when I have guests coming, guests who could be potential benefactors, then I do care."

Daniel took the shirt from her. Then Pamela saw the three circular scars on the man's chest and right shoulder. The scars were unmistakable to Pamela: gunshot wounds. Having worked as an EMT on the dangerous streets of New Orleans, she was well acquainted with scars of that type.

She hated being right about people, especially when her thoughts tended to emphasize the negative rather than the positive. But she felt assured that her initial instincts about Daniel Phillips were correct.

Daniel put his T-shirt on and picked up his scrub brush from the ground. "I'll try not to further offend your delicate sense of decency."

"What is that supposed to mean?"

He pointed the scrub brush at her. "Your looks and manners scream of an upper-class kind of background. Your pale skin and delicate features mean you've probably never done a hard day's work in your life. And this place?" He waved his hand around the facility surrounding them. "Only a bored housewife looking to show off her altruistic side to her posh friends would waste her days chasing flea-infested fuzz balls around a makeshift petting zoo."

"Well, at least I don't have three gunshot wounds in my chest. How did you come by those, Mr. Phillips? Protecting the patrons of your bar from mass slaughter?"

"Why you little ...." He let the words die on his lips. "You don't know anything about me, Ms. Wells. And do not even begin to think that because I have a few scars on my body that I have led a depraved—"

".9 mm I would think by the look of the entrance wounds," Pamela stated, cutting him off.

Daniel stopped and cocked his head to the side. "How did you know it was a .9 mm?"

Pamela gave him a condescending gaze with her cool gray eyes. "Every bored housewife knows the difference between—"

"Hey," a voice called behind them.

Pamela and Daniel turned to see Carol waving her hands frantically in the air.

"Do you two want to keep it down to a dull roar over here? I've got a busload of nervous mother's asking where all the shouting is coming from."

"They're here? Already?" Pamela bit her lower lip and looked back toward the house.

Carol nodded. "Yes, ma'am. Would you like me to bring the mother's out first so they can get an eyeful of our male stripper."

"Carol!" Pamela glared back at her friend. "Keep your voice down." She turned to Daniel. "I think you and I are finished here, Mr. Phillips. You can pack up and get off my property."

"Ignore her," Carol advised, sticking out her hand to Daniel. "She just has PMS; fires everybody when she's in a bad mood. I'm Carol Corbin, Pamela's accountant and second in command around here."

Daniel took her hand. "Daniel Phillips."

Carol grinned at Daniel. "Loved your beefcake display, by the way. It added a real zing to my morning." She patted Pamela on the arm. "Pamie's, too."

Daniel ran his hand through his thick, brown hair. "Really? I got the distinct impression Ms. Wells was not at all pleased with my beefcake display."

"Trust me, unless you have fur covering some unseen portion of that body of yours, she won't be interested," Carol said with a dismissive wave of her hand.

Daniel raised his dark brows. "Lesbian?"

"Worse. Frustrated, if you know what I mean," Carol confided with a wink.

"All right!" Pamela stepped in between them. "Enough." She gestured to Daniel. "You can finish out the day, Daniel."

A sudden jolt of pain gripped Pamela's elbow. She winced as she pulled her arm against her chest.

"You okay?" Carol probed.

"Just a bad day." Pamela gave Daniel one last reproach with her eyes and started for the house, still cradling her arm.

Daniel watched as the pale, slender woman slowly made her way to the blue and white cottage. "She all right?"

"She has bad days. They seem to be coming more often lately," Carol disclosed as her eyes followed Pamela. "Trying to keep this place going is taking its toll on her."

"Why doesn't she give it up?"

"This place is all she's got. It's the only thing that keeps her from completely falling apart. She tries to act brave, but the stress is wearing her down."

"Is something wrong with her?"

"The medical term for what she has is systemic lupus erythematosus. It's more commonly known as lupus."

"Lupus? I'm not sure of what that is," he admitted, furrowing his brow.

"Pamela's immune system has trouble telling the difference between her body and a foreign body, like a virus. It attacks her joints and can destroy major organs, like her kidneys, liver, lungs, and heart."

Daniel wiped his hand across his face. "I didn't know. I shouldn't have been egging her on the way I did. Will she be all right?"

"She's not broken, only bruised, Daniel. She manages with it but some days are worse than others. She doesn't like to be handled with kid gloves. The woman is a lot tougher than she looks. My father always said she was one of the toughest women he ever met."

"Your father knows Pamela?"

"Knew her; he died a long time ago," Carol corrected. "He was her partner when she worked as an EMT in New Orleans."

"She was an EMT?"

"Yep, a pretty good one, so I was told. Gave it up after the accident."

"What accident?"

"She and my dad were transporting a patient to the emergency room when they were hit by a drunk driver. Apparently, Pamela broke her ribs in the collision, but that didn't stop her from trying to save my father's life. After my father was pronounced dead at the scene, Pamela finally agreed to let the rescue workers take her to the closest hospital. Once in the emergency room, Pamela's condition quickly deteriorated. The next day she woke up in the ICU. Her broken ribs punctured her right lung, and ruptured her spleen." Carol smiled. "Like I said, she is a lot tougher than she looks. When I finished college, I offered to come out here and help her run this place. This has always been her dream. Save the world by saving one flea-infested fuzz ball at a time."

Daniel shook his head. "You heard that?"

"Me and all of the midgets scampering off of the yellow school bus heard it." She studied Daniel for a moment. "You got quite a way with words, Mr. Phillips. Where did you hone those oratory skills of yours, or do all bartenders possess such a colorful vocabulary?"

"Only the ones with Harvard educations."

"Harvard, eh? Well, there seems to be more to you than meets the eye, Mr. Phillips."

"Carol!" Pamela's voice boomed across the compound.

"Ah, my master's voice." Carol glanced back at Daniel. "I know you may think Pamela, an uptight prude, but she's one of the best people I know, and I would be disturbed to see you upsetting her any further."

Daniel smirked, playfully. "How disturbed?"

"Let's just say I got an A+ in my torture and intimidation classes at college."

"Where did you study? Fort Bragg?" Daniel went along, looking amused.

"No, University of New Orleans. Any good accounting program makes such courses compulsory for their students. Where do you think IRS agents come from?"

Carol quickly turned on her heels and headed toward the waiting school bus, leaving a bewildered Daniel Phillips to his dirty cages.

Chapter 2

Daniel stayed busy, cleaning cages and restocking them with hay and assorted scrap cloth. As he concentrated on doing his job, his eyes would wander across the clearing to the slender blonde. Pamela Wells was enlivened. Her heart-shaped face almost glowed as she talked about each and every animal. She appeared relaxed as she laughed and interacted with the children. The rigid and uptight woman no longer existed. She looked different, more approachable, more attractive even.

Daniel quickly silenced his runaway libido. He should remove the woman from his thoughts. Nothing good could come from it. But as he observed Pamela engaging the young students in front of a cage of bouncing rabbits, he reconsidered his first assessment of her. And when Pamela turned her gray eyes to him from across the clearing, Daniel felt his frustration with the woman give way to a more intriguing feeling.

"Maybe I should start over with the elusive Pamela Wells."

*****

After spending two hours showing all the animals in her faculty to the schoolchildren, and teaching them about wildlife conservation, she packed the rambunctious kids back on their bus and sent them on their way, Exhausted, Pamela settled her aching body on the green couch in her living room/office.

Scattered about the old rolltop desk in the corner and piled up on the hardwood floor were stacks of bills and wildlife magazines. Located behind the living room was a yellow kitchen with two refrigerators; one marked for human food, the other for animal food. In the breakfast area, on top of a round breakfast table, was an assortment of square plastic containers with small, circular air holes drilled into the sides and lids. Inside the containers, mounds of felt strips could be seen moving with an occasional baby squirrel head peeping out from beneath its protective coverings. On the opposite wall from the kitchen was an old television and satellite dish receiver sitting on an oak entertainment center. Next to the entertainment center was a long wooden table with a laptop computer, printer, and large wire cage on top of it. Inside the open cage, a gray squirrel sat contentedly eating a pecan.

"Louis," Pamela called to the squirrel. "I'm exhausted."

The squirrel took no notice of Pamela and continued to enjoy his nut.

A knock at the front door made Pamela reluctantly get up from her couch.

Daniel was at her door, holding up a piece of white paper. "I need you to sign off on my time sheet before I go."

She waved him into her home. "Come in. I'll just get a pen."

Daniel stepped inside and took in the cluttered living room. "I think your animals live better than you do."

Pamela ignored his comment and went over to her rolltop desk. After shuffling around papers to find a pen, she turned back to Daniel.

He pointed at Louis in his cage. "Is that another of the successfully rehabbed?"

"No, this is my baby boy, Louis." She went to the cage and gently rubbed the squirrel's head.

Louis, more interested in his nut than the affection, never stopped munching.

"He was a Katrina baby. He injured his back in a fall from a tree during the storm and could never be released. He was just one of the many victims of that storm. The kind the media didn't bother to cover." She rubbed the squirrel's head once more. Louis tilted his head slightly to the side as he ate his nut so Pamela's fingers could scratch just the right spot. "As wildlife rehabbers, we are supposed to put all animals that can't be rehabilitated to sleep, but I just couldn't do that to him. So he lives in here with me."

Daniel watched the way she handled the squirrel. "You love animals, don't you?"

"I wouldn't go to all of this trouble if I didn't. Animals are the victims of our society. We raise them in cages to feed on them, chase them out of their habitats, abuse them for their coats, and treat them as furniture in our homes. If you ask me, they are the meek, and one day—"

"The meek shall inherit the earth," Daniel added, finishing her words.

"They are living beings with emotions and souls, just like us. If the human race can't be kind to animals, then how are we going to be kind to each other?"

He took a step closer to her. "I should apologize to you for the things I said earlier. I was out of line."

"Forget about it." She moved toward him. "Let's just say we had a misunderstanding and leave it at that."

"I would like to make it up to you." Pamela eyed him suspiciously. "This house could use some work. Why don't you let me do some repairs for you? I could patch up the broken shingles on the roof and repaint the exterior for starters."

Pamela stood for a moment, trying to gauge the depth of his sincerity. "That is work I cannot apply to your community service," she finally offered.

"I don't care about that. I just want to help out a little. You look like you could use it."

Pamela took the white piece of paper out of his hand. "Thanks, but no thanks, Daniel. We can get along just fine without your charity."

Pamela carried the paper over to a nearby end table and hastily scribbled her name on it.

"Look, I know you think I'm some thug," Daniel began. "But I would like to help out here. I saw you with those kids today; the way you lit up when you showed them the animals you are helping here. I have to admit; I was wrong about you. You come across as a real snob but—"

She spun around to him. "I do not come across as a snob!"

"Yes, Pamela, you do. You try and hide the real you from everyone because you think—"

"Don't do that," she angrily cut in. "Pretend that you know me. We just met this morning. You know nothing about me."

He ran his hand through his dark hair. "I know a lot more than you think."

Pamela stubbornly folded her arms over her chest. "Okay. Let's hear it. What do you think you know about me?"

Daniel stared her down. "You're stubborn for starters. You're tougher than you look, or at least you try to be. You prefer to do everything yourself. You think no one takes you seriously because of your beauty, so you work even harder to be seen as a woman of intelligence. You're suspicious of strangers, probably a vegetarian." He playfully raised his eyebrows. "And you don't like asking for help, even when you need it."

"Congratulations, you've probably just described half of the female population in the United States."

"Not the half I've known."

"Your bedpost must be quite the conversation piece."

He smirked at her. "I can usually figure out what a woman wants from me within the first few seconds. They all have a pretty predictable set of criteria, or at least I thought so until today. But you aren't looking for anything from anybody. You only show your emotions to your animals, don't you?"

She picked up the white slip of paper from the end table. "How comforting it must be for you to know that all of your horizontal studies has afforded you the opportunity to pass judgment on me."

He took the signed form from her. "I wasn't passing judgment, just making an observation," he calmly stated as he folded the form and put it in his pocket. "I'm not an expert on women. No man will ever accomplish that feat."

She raised her chin defiantly. "In my experience, animals are safer to care about than people. My mother was one of those women who always required help from other people, especially men. She spent her entire life looking through the bottom of a vodka bottle for someone to make everything wonderful for her. The only problem was, by the time she sobered up and figured out that only she could make her life wonderful, she died.”

Daniel sighed. “How old were you when she died?”

“Thirteen.”

“What about your father?”

“My father was the one who raised me. My mother wasn’t exactly the maternal kind.”

He scanned the living room. “Is that why I don’t see any family pictures on the walls?”

“What are you, a shrink?” She went around him to the front door. “I want to thank you for coming out and helping us. If I ever need your services again, I’ll let your probation officer know.”

“You’re not getting rid of me that easily. I told you I would be back to fix up your place.”

She glared at him. “I don’t want you coming back.”

“Afraid I’ll steal the family silver?”

“Something like that, yes,” she replied as she opened the front door.

“For a woman who doesn’t like being judged, you’re sure quick to judge others.”

“One of my many, many flaws,” she asserted with a sarcastic smirk.

He walked out the door. “Perhaps you should start taking chances on people, Ms. Wells, instead of always taking chances on animals.”

“Duly noted. Thanks for coming, Mr. Phillips.” Without another thought, she slammed the door.

Pamela returned to the couch and plopped her aching body on the soft fabric. Looking over at Louis in his cage, still munching away on his pecan, she wished at that moment that she could be like her squirrel. She wanted to be left alone, unperturbed by the world around her, and able to find pleasure in the taste of a nut.

Chapter 3

Three days later, Daniel returned. The back of his Jeep was packed with roofing materials and paint. Across the roll bars on top of the Jeep was his ladder. When he pulled up in front of the blue and white Acadian cottage, there was no one around. But before he turned off the engine, the pack of stray dogs that hung out on the front porch made for his car.

Daniel sat in his Jeep, not wanting to face the snarling teeth of Pamela's overzealous four-legged burglar alarm. The pack ranged in size from a small Chiweenie to the monster Catahoula mix named Quincy.

A few minutes later, Pamela emerged from the house, gingerly carrying a towel in her hands. She stopped on the porch and spotted his Jeep.

"Guys, calm down," she called to the barking dogs.

Instantly, the pack backed away from Daniel's Jeep and headed to the porch.

Daniel climbed out of the Jeep. "I'm glad to see that the posse is always on patrol."

Pamela came down the steps to the gravel drive. "What are you doing here?"

Daniel waved to the back of his Jeep. "I told you I was going to fix up your house."

"And I told you I didn't want your help."

He went around to the back of his Jeep. "Lucky for you I'm one of those men who doesn't pay a whole lot of attention to what women tell me."

"So what? Are you are just going to ignore my wishes and fix up my house anyway?"

He pulled a roll of roofing felt out of the back of the car. "Something like that, yeah."

Carol appeared on the front porch, carrying a cup of coffee in her hands. "Couldn't stay away, huh?"

"Nope," he answered while carting the roll of felt over to the side of the house.

Pamela pointed to Daniel. "Carol, tell this man to leave. I don't want his charity."

"Well, I do," Carol admitted as she made her way to the edge of the porch. "Your house could use some work. It's beginning to look like something one of those weird animal hoarders would live in."

"Don't consider it charity," Daniel told Pamela as he walked back to the Jeep. "Consider it a donation."

"Yeah, Pamie," Carol added from the porch. "Consider it a donation."

"You two are impossible." Pamela ran back up the porch steps, still carrying the towel in her hands. "Fine, do what you like. I have babies to feed." She stormed back into the house.

Carol raised her mug of coffee to Daniel. "I think you're growing on her."

Daniel shook his head and lifted a can of paint from the back of his Jeep.

Inside, Carol found Pamela sitting on the floor of her kitchen, holding a tiny baby gray squirrel in her lap.

"You could give the guy a break," Carol proposed as she leaned against the entrance to the hallway.

"He's a bartender from New Orleans, who beats up his customers. Now why should I give him a break?"

"He also studied at Harvard."

"How do you know that?"

"He told me."

Pamela glanced up at Carol and then she snickered. "And you believed him?"

"Of course," Carol took another sip from her coffee mug. "They're not all out to get you, you know?"

Pamela returned her attention to the baby squirrel. "What are you talking about?"

"Men. You think every one of them has some ulterior motive for talking to you or doing anything for you."

"Men always have ulterior motives, Carol. That's what makes them men."

"The guy drove up here from the city, bought supplies to fix your house, and hasn't so much as asked you for a cup of coffee, let alone a date. So what's your problem with him?"

"I have a hard enough time letting people I know into my life. How do you expect me to accept a stranger just like that?"

Carol lazily pushed away from the wall. "I've got to head over to my office and get some work done." She placed her mug down on the old brown and white tiled counter in the kitchen. "Sometimes people come into your life for a reason, Pamie. Just like the animals. You always said every animal you've rehabbed changed you. People can do the same thing, but you have to let them in first so you can find out how they will change you." Carol walked over to the couch and picked up her five-gallon purse.

Carol placed her purse over her shoulder and then walked to the front door. Without looking back, she quietly exited the house.

Pamela felt her heart sink. She wished it could be that easy for her; to just accept people into her life and not give a second thought as to the consequences. But like a prophet privileged to see the future, Pamela knew exactly how any relationship with the impossible Daniel Phillips would end.

*****

After feeding all of the baby squirrels, Pamela ventured out to the front porch to look for her uncannily quiet handyman. She found him on the side of her house, frozen atop his ladder and starring into the oak tree next to her bedroom window.

She came up alongside his ladder and gazed up at him. "Is something wrong?"

He did not move but spoke very slowly out of the corner of his mouth. "There's a big owl up here staring at me like it's going to rip my eyes out."

Pamela started to climb up the ladder. "Oh, I forgot to tell you about him. That's Lester. He won't hurt you."

Lester let out an ear-splitting screech.

"Oh, Lester, hush up," Pamela scolded, waving her hand at the large brown owl.

Daniel grabbed his chest. "That thing wants to kill me."

Pamela came up right below him on the ladder. She began to stroke the owl's wing. "He's really a pussycat when you get to know him. He already ate this morning so I can guarantee he has no interest in you. That is unless you are carrying any chocolate on you."

Daniel caught his breath. "Chocolate?"

"He loves chocolate. Only comes out of the tree for it. Otherwise, he stays up here all day and all night."

Daniel rubbed his hand across his sweaty forehead. "I've been sitting up here for thirty minutes afraid to move or make a sound in case that thing went after me. Then you come out here and tell me the owl only eats chocolate." He stared down at Pamela. "What kind of place are you running here?"

"Oh, Lester eats ham and eggs, too. I only give him chocolate on special occasions."

Pamela started back down the ladder, and Daniel quickly followed. When they reached the ground, Pamela noticed the man's dark blue T-shirt was soaked through.

"Are you all right?"

He wiped his hand across his sweaty brow. "I just don't like being cornered like that." He leaned over and gripped his knees.

Pamela saw how his knuckles turned white against the dark fabric of his jeans.

She put her hand on his shoulder. "Let's go and sit down over on the porch."

Daniel stood up and took a few deep breaths.

To Pamela, the man appeared to be trying with all of his might to regain his composure. She noted his respirations and checked his pulse.

"I'm fine," he insisted, pulling his wrist away.

"You're not fine. Come on," she urged, guiding him to the front of the house.

At the porch, she shooed the dogs away to make room for them to sit. She eased Daniel down onto the step.

"I'm going inside to get you some water. Stay right here."

Nodding, Daniel rubbed his face with his hands.

Pamela ran into the house and retrieved a glass from the kitchen cabinet and filled it with water from the tap. When she returned, Daniel was standing by the porch railing. Studying him from the steps was Rodney, the raccoon. She walked over to Daniel and handed him the water. His hands were shaking as he took the glass from her.

She gestured to the raccoon. "He came to check up on you."

Daniel took a few deep gulps of the water and then motioned to the raccoon. "I thought he was debating on whether or not to attack me."

Rodney stood on his hind haunches and sniffed at Daniel. "No, he's concerned. He senses your distress. Animals can do that. They know when someone needs help."

"Maybe it's because they're wild animals. They're just more in tune with nature, or whatever you rehabbers call it," Daniel reasoned.

"Wild is only a term used to measure degrees of distance between them and us. We call something wild because we don't know it. But once you form a bond with a creature, and become part of its family, you discover it was never wild, simply afraid." He tightly gripped his glass. The beads of sweat were still forming on his upper lip and forehead, despite the cool spring morning. "Can I get you anything?"

"I'll be all right. You got anything stronger than water in your house?" He then took another long sip from the glass.

"I've got one bottle of vodka and half a bottle of cognac."

Daniel arched one eyebrow.

"I like to take a sip of cognac when I can't sleep. It helps to calm me."

"I suspect it's a good pain reliever too." He handed her the empty glass. "I saw you holding your arm the other day. Carol told me about your lupus."

Pamela took the glass from him. "Carol has a big mouth."

"She cares for you a great deal. She even threatened me with torture if I ever hurt you."

That made Pamela laugh.

"That's something you need to do more often," Daniel said, smiling.

"What?"

"Laugh. You look good when you laugh. Your eyes are not all cold and distant like they usually are."

Her smile fell away. "My eyes are not cold and distant."

He leveled his dark eyes on her. "They are when they look at me."

She rubbed her tennis shoe against a crack in the wood on the porch deck. "Yeah, well, you're a thug, remember?"

Daniel leaned to the side and playfully nudged her shoulder. "Still think I'm a thug?"

Pamela examined his face. He was a handsome man. She wondered why she never saw him as attractive before. His eyes were the only part of his features that she found unsettling. The darkness of them seemed to hint at some hidden pain behind his welcoming smile. She found it odd how you can look into a person's face a thousand times, and then suddenly, one day, you glance over and feel as though you are seeing them for the very first time.

"Perhaps you should call it a day," she suggested.

"No, I came here to help you out, and I'm fine now. I just got a little shaken up by that crazy bird of yours."

"You were more than a little shaken up, Daniel."

He moved toward the steps. "Sorry, I just overreacted. I'll get back to your roof."

Daniel quickly trotted down the steps and around the side of the house.

Pamela felt a sense of relief when Daniel disappeared from view. It wasn't that she didn't like his company; it was more that his presence unhinged her. She could never entertain the idea of allowing a man like Daniel in her life. Enough lost souls depended on her for their survival, and there was no room in her heart to try and right another.

*****

Later that morning, Pamela returned from feeding the animals in their outdoor cages to find Daniel hammering away on her roof.

Once she stepped inside the door to her home, the constant thud of the hammer seemed to reverberate throughout her house. No room was free of the overhead banging. Even Louis, the squirrel, was hidden inside his sleeping sack, trying and get away from the noise. Unable to take the intermittent hammering, Pamela walked to her hall closet and took out the Winchester rifle she kept there. She added a few extra shells to the front pocket of her jeans and checked to make sure the rifle was loaded. She eyed Louis once more and observed the array of sleeping baby squirrels in their containers on her kitchen table.

"I don't have to feed you guys for another hour, so I'm going out to check feeders."

Rifle in hand, Pamela headed out the door. As she walked down the steps of her back porch, she toyed with the idea of telling Daniel where she was going but quickly decided against it.

Pamela made her way to the open shed that housed her truck, tractor, and ATVs. She went to the larger of the two ATVs and searched under the seat for the keys. After securing her rifle, she started the vehicle and headed for the woods.

A few feet into the thick brush around her property, she discovered the old trail she used to travel to the feeders that sustained the released animals throughout the cold winters. Normally the feeders would be empty this time of year, but because of the unusually cold winter, Pamela opted to stock the feeders for another month until spring was firmly entrenched. As she maneuvered the ATV through the high shrubs and around the low tree limbs covering the trail, she continually checked for her rifle. Wild boars, indigenous to the area, were especially aggressive in the spring. Mothers with baby piglets to protect from predators could badly maim, or even kill when encountered.

After negotiating through the dense vegetation, Pamela entered a small clearing and the first of four feeders located on her property. The feeder was nothing more than an empty metal barrel with large holes drilled along the bottom rim. A mixture of corn, seeds, and nuts would be poured into the top of the barrel, and as the animals removed the food from around the bottom of the barrel, more food would filter out through the holes.

Pamela stopped next to the feeder and left the motor running as she climbed off the ATV and went over to the barrel. Lifting the heavy top of the barrel and looking inside, she could see that the barrel was still full of food. Pamela let the lid drop with a bang.

A loud rustling from the bushes off to her left distracted her. Instinctively, Pamela reached for her gun on the back of the ATV and stood, watching the brush. Then a long angry grunt came from inside the dense foliage. She lifted the rifle and aimed in the direction of the noise. Seconds later, a huge black ball of fur came barreling out of the brush directly toward her. She fired one shot above the creature's head and saw the animal immediately halt. It was a large black bear, probably female, Pamela surmised. The animal stared at her, rocking back and forth on its front feet as if debating the prudence of pursuing an attack. Then from the brush behind the bear, a small black face emerged, and then a second face popped out next to the first. Pamela stood motionless while keeping her eyes peeled on the mother black bear. The standoff seemed to go on for several agonizing minutes until the bear emitted a low, deep growl. Pamela raised the barrel of her rifle and fired.

*****

"Pamela!" Daniel's frantic scream pierced through the woods.

He ran toward the sound of the gunshots and called out again for the woman.

"Pamela, can you hear me?"

He stopped running only long enough to listen for a reply. But there was none.

Daniel ran on, figuring he must be coming closer to the origin of the two shots he heard. But as he fought his way through the brush, he could feel that familiar pang of dread tangle his gut. His heart was racing, and his breath seemed to burn like fire in his chest.

The panic, God, the panic!

He tried to think of the techniques to control the powerful flood of adrenalin in his veins, but no peaceful thoughts of sandy beaches or cool ocean breezes were going to allay the absolute terror that was raging through him.

He heard the sound of an engine idling close by. He jumped through some brush to his left and found a small clearing. There, standing next to a tall oil barrel, was Pamela.

She spun around. The rifle, still at the ready in her hands, was pointed at his chest.

"Are you insane?" She lowered her rifle. "I could have shot you!"

Daniel stopped, bent over, and tried to catch his breath. "I heard the gunshots. I thought you might be hurt ... I took off from the house to come ... and help you."

"Surprising a woman with a loaded gun was going to help me? Do what? Spend the next eighteen to twenty in prison?" Pamela spotted several small trickles of blood flowing down his arms.

She ran to his side and inspected his arms. "Daniel! You're all sliced up."

Daniel stood up and, still gasping for breath. "What in the hell are you doing out here? Why did I hear gunshots?"

Pamela never glanced up from the man's bleeding arms. "We have got to get you back to the house."

At that moment, the shaking began. It always started in his knees and worked its way up. Soon, it would reach his hands and face, and he would not be able to hide it from her this time. He eagerly scanned the brush surrounding him. There was nowhere to run and hide.

"Daniel!" Pamela's voice registered in his brain. "Daniel, are you all right?"

The panic was ripping through him, taking over his will to fight and his desire to maintain control. Daniel sank to his knees. He covered his face with his trembling hands, and then he started to hyperventilate.

Pamela pushed his hands away from his face.

"Stop it," Daniel growled beneath his breath. "Not now." His eyes burned into hers. "Not with you." He wrapped his bleeding arms around him and started to rock back and forth. "Go away, Pamela. Leave me alone," he ordered in a shaky voice.

Pamela calmly placed her hands on his face. "Daniel, I'm not leaving you. I am right here. I have to get you back to the house."

He covered his ears. "The gunfire! I can still hear the gunfire!"

Pamela ran back to the ATV and put the vehicle into gear. She pulled it right alongside Daniel. She got off the four-wheeled vehicle and went back to him.

"I need you to focus, Daniel." She placed her hand under his chin. "I want you to listen to me and do as I say. I need you to get up and get on this four-wheeler."

Daniel fought to gain control of his rapid breathing. She helped him to his feet and lifted his leg over the back of the vehicle. She then climbed on the seat in front of him and rested her rifle across her lap.

She turned back to Daniel. "Put your arms around my waist and hold on as tight as you can."

He did as she instructed. His respirations calmed, but his shaking body was now soaked through with perspiration. His sweat mixed with blood created a chill around him.

Pamela drove the ATV out of the clearing, and Daniel could feel her tension as she maneuvered the ATV through the dense woods. He did not feel her body relax until he saw the familiar blue and white cottage looming before them.

*****

"A bear? Are you sure?"

Daniel was sitting on her green couch, naked from the waist up and wrapped in a blanket. With bandages down both his forearms, along with a few minor scratches on his face, he was holding a half glass of cognac in his now steady hands.

Pamela was sitting next to him nursing her glass of orange juice and wearing her favorite robe.

"A mother bear. She came out of the brush and found me standing next to the feeder. She was probably bringing her babies to eat."

Daniel shook his head in disbelief. "A bear in Louisiana?"

"Not something we see a lot of around here, but black bears have been spotted in this area before. Not many places for them to hibernate, but she seems to have managed."

"She could have mauled you, or worse," he calmly remarked, and then he took another sip of the amber liquid from his glass.

"I shot over her head and scared her off. I'm good enough with a rifle should she have decided to charge me." She shrugged. "But I would have been raising those babies instead of her. And a couple of baby bears would simply wreak havoc on my rehab facility."

He tilted his head as he studied her. "You're a lot tougher than you look, right?"

"Yes, I am."

A few uncomfortable minutes of silence passed between them.

"Are you going to tell me what happened out there?" she finally asked.

Daniel set his glass on the coffee table. "I was a panic attack; that's all. It happens every now and then when I get stressed, or angry." He gave her a reassuring smile.

"Panic attacks, huh?" She reached over and patted his knee. "Nice try, Daniel. But I'm not some airhead blonde trying to flirt with an attractive bartender."

Daniel grinned. "Attractive?"

Pamela ignored him. "Back in the woods, you mumbled something about gunfire. You said you could still hear the gunfire." She sat back on the couch but never removed her eyes from him. "What gunfire?"

Daniel took in a deep breath. "I did two tours of duty in Iraq."

"The scars on your chest. You got those in Iraq, didn't you?"

Daniel sat back and ran his hands over his face. "We were on foot in what we thought was a pretty secure section of Baghdad. We came around a corner and walked right into an ambush. I took the first one in the leg and then the next three … well, you saw the scars."

She admired his strong profile. "When did you get out?"

"Six years ago after I was shot." He shrugged. "I traveled around the country a bit and then I went to bartending school for the fun of it. I don't sleep well, and figured if I was going to be up all night I might as well get paid for it."

"What you are describing, Daniel, is more than just—"

"It's called PTSD: post-traumatic stress disorder. That's what the army shrinks said it was."

"So you have seen someone?"

"I've seen several someones. They all say the same thing. They try to give me pills, try to hypnotize me, desensitize me, detoxify me, and demoralize me." He got up from the couch and walked to the window next to Louis's cage.

The squirrel watched as Daniel came up to him. The creature's little eyes curiously took in the stranger without showing the least bit of fear. Louis then climbed out of his cage and slowly made his way to the tall man.

Daniel warily noted the squirrel coming closer.

Pamela rose from the couch. "It's all right," she assured him. "He doesn't bite. In fact, he's quite a sweet little boy."

She took Daniel's hand and guided it to Louis. At first, Louis seemed a little nervous about the big hand approaching, but then he let Daniel touch his head. After a few seconds, Daniel was able to gently stroke the top of the squirrel's back.

"Now reach around and stroke under his chin," Pamela instructed.

Daniel was happily surprised when the little creature lifted his front paw for Daniel to rub his fuzzy white underbelly.

"Look at that. He likes it."

"Actually, it is something all squirrels do when you rub under their chins. I call it the squirrel reflex."

Louis decided that was enough attention and moved away from Daniel's hand and back into his cage.

"I've never petted a squirrel before," Daniel admitted.

"Not many people have. Do you want to feel something truly amazing?"

Pamela went to the containers housing her myriad of wildlife babies and opened one. She came back to Daniel holding a small gray and brown lump of fur in her hands.

"Hold out your hands."

Pamela placed a six-week-old baby squirrel in his hands.

The creature's eyes and ears were open, and the body was covered with a silky brown and gray fur. The little life squirmed in his hands, as tiny teeth nipped at the calluses on his palms.

Daniel looked up at Pamela. "It's so small; I feel like I might crush it."

"Would you like to feed her?"

"Are you sure?"

She gave him an encouraging smile. "I think it might be just what you need right now."

*****

Half an hour later, Pamela looked on as Daniel sat on the floor, feeding formula to his fifth baby squirrel. The man seemed to revel in the way the eager little mouths sucked at the small syringe. He carefully rubbed each and every pink tummy after feeding to aid with digestion, just as Pamela instructed. He was enthralled with the tiny creatures, studying their faces, and caressing their little feet. The joy he seemed to find made Pamela feel as if the disturbing events of the day never happened.

"No wonder you like doing this." Daniel glanced up from the squirrel in his hands. "They are so helpless and have such trust in you. They let you feed them and rub them without the slightest bit of reservation."

"Wait until they get older and can squirm and bite. Then feeding them with a syringe becomes a real challenge."

"Why do you use a syringe? I've always seen those bottles sold in stores with the kitten and puppy formulas. I thought you would be using them to feed your babies."

"Nursing bottles can cause the formula to get into the lungs. Rehabbers always use syringes to make sure the animal doesn't aspirate."

"When do they get off the formula?"

"At eight to ten weeks. I'll get them started on a selection of apples, berries, beans, and corn, along with a little sweet potato, as well as wheat bread or crackers. Once they are off formula, I will transfer them to the bigger cages outside that you were cleaning the other day. When they are able to crack a nut with their teeth, they are ready to be released."

He gazed down at the little ball of fur in his hands. "That must be hard. You must get so attached."

"To some, yes, I become very attached. Almost from the first moment you begin feeding them, you recognize traits of each baby's individual personality, no matter how alike they may appear. Most people think they are just animals and wonder how they can have different personalities. But getting to know them is just like getting to know another person. At first, you see only the outside, but with time you learn to memorize every idiosyncrasy, every inflection, every movement until one day ...." She shrugged. "They become a part of you."

"Do they ever not want to leave? I mean they have it pretty good here."

"Some hang around for a long time, like Rodney. Usually, the males stay longer than the females." She gave him a teasing grin. "But many do come back to visit me. The mothers bring their babies to me and show me their families. That makes what I do worthwhile. I guess it is their way of saying thank you."

Daniel carefully placed the small baby back in its plastic container. The tiny creature crawled over to join the rest of the litter, which was hidden underneath a mound of cloth strips. He put the lid back on the square plastic box and placed the container with the others against the wall on his left. He looked past Pamela to the window located across the room.

"It's getting late," he stated, standing from the floor. "I should get back to your roof while there's still some daylight left."

"No, you're not going back up there today."

"I'm fine now." He gave her a cocky grin. "I'm a lot tougher than I look."

"I'm sure you think you are, but I'm not letting you get back up there with all that cognac in your system."

Daniel's deep laugh filled the cramped living room with a sudden rush of warmth.

"My dear woman, I have been known to put a hell of a lot more than that away on any given night behind the bar. I'm stone cold sober."

"You drink at work?"

He took another step closer, letting his body ease right up next to hers. "I'm a bartender, drinking on the job is required."

"You don't seem like a bartender to me. You're well-educated, resourceful, and have a curious mind. I'd say there is more to you than just tending bar and getting into fights with customers."

He stared up at the ceiling, appearing to mull over her observations. Then he gave her an amusing smile. "Sorry, that about covers it for me. Drinking and fighting are what I'm best at."

"But you can replace shingles on a roof? There must be other things you're good at?"

"There are other things I can do, but I'm not necessarily good at them. Most men know how to replace shingles on a roof. A compulsion for making minor household repairs is just one of the side effects of testosterone."

Pamela broke out into a fit of laughter.

A perplexed look came over Daniel's face. "It wasn't that funny."

Pamela wiped a happy tear from the corner of her eye. "It's just that my ex-husband always said manual labor was the result of not having enough intelligence to know how to avoid it."

"Sounds like a great guy. How long were you married?"

"Eight years."

"May I ask what happened?"

Pamela waved her hand casually in the air. "When I was diagnosed with lupus things started to fall apart. Bob tried to be the dutiful husband and help me through the bad patches, but after a few years, he couldn't handle it anymore. So he asked for a divorce."

Daniel scowled. "Why on earth did you marry him?"

"We met right after I was in a pretty bad car accident. He became my attorney and handled my lawsuit against the drunk driver who hit me. We wound up spending a lot of time together. I thought he was charming, kind, and would always be there for me. I was wrong." She wrapped her arms around her. "You ever been married?"

"No. I'm not cut out for long-term relationships. Most women get sick of me and quickly move on. It's better that way. What happened today is something I never let anyone see. At times it becomes really hard hiding my PTSD from the world, but so far I have been able to keep most of my symptoms under control."

"When you can't keep it under control anymore, then what?"

"Then it will be time for me to move on. I'll find a new town, and new people, who don't know anything about me."

"Is that what you have been doing? Moving from one town to the next to try and hide your condition?"

He turned away from her and went back to the couch. He removed the blanket from his shoulders and picked up his bloody T-shirt. "It's worked pretty well for me so far."

"But you can't go on like that forever, Daniel."

He pulled the T-shirt over his head. "You don't get it, Pamela," he said with a hint of frustration in his voice. "For someone like me, there isn't a forever. Right now is about all I can handle."

She stood in silence, watching him neatly fold up the blanket and place it on her couch. He picked up the half full glass of cognac and downed the contents in one long swallow.

"If you aren't going to let me on your roof, then I better head back to the city," he grumbled as he banged the glass down on the coffee table.

"Maybe you shouldn't be driving right now. Why not wait a while longer before you get behind the wheel?"

"I'm fine." Avoiding her eyes, he hurried to the front door. "I'll come back tomorrow after lunch and finish the roof. Thanks for today, Pamela. I know what you must think of me, but I promise I will be out of your life soon." He opened the door and stepped out into the fading afternoon light.

Pamela jumped after he slammed the door. She tried to suppress the flood of emotion that was inundating her. She did not want to feel her heartstrings tug for another, not another human anyway. She could not risk letting someone in. Her experiences with the opposite sex only ended up being mistakes she regretted. Besides, a man like Daniel Phillips would only use her and move on. Reason enough to shut him out.

Chapter 4

The following afternoon, Pamela was trying to stuff a few heads of cabbage into an old refrigerator when Daniel walked into the barn.

He examined the boxes of old cantaloupes, radishes, apples, turnip greens, and other assorted fruits and vegetables scattered around the barn floor. "What's with all the boxes of food?"

She tried to rearrange some old cantaloupe in the refrigerator. "Hey. I didn't think I would see you back here again."

"I told you I would be back."

She kept her eyes focused on the contents of the refrigerator. "Yeah, well, people may say one thing, but do another."

"You'll find I'm a man of my word, Pamela." He came up to her side and waved his hand to the boxes. "So what is all this?"

Pamela snapped up some cherry tomatoes and put them in a second refrigerator. "I just made my run,"

"Your run?"

"I have a 501C non-profit organization so businesses can donate goods to my facility and write it off as a charitable donation. The grocery in Folsom saves all of their old produce for me, and I go to collect it three times a week."

Daniel picked up a soft cantaloupe. "Is this stuff edible?"

"It is to a fox, rabbit, squirrel, raccoon …." She waved her hand at him. "You get the idea."

"Yeah, I get it." He nodded as she continued to fill the refrigerators.

"The feed store in nearby Covington donates broken or torn bags of seed and deer corn, a local grade school collects old clothes for bedding, and I have a building contractor who gives me scraps of wood I use to build nest boxes." She shoved some wilted kale into the refrigerator.

"Nest boxes? Like the ones birds use?"

"Squirrels, too. I also build dens for the foxes, climbing trees for the raccoons, houses for skunks, anything an animal will need to help them adapt to being released back into the wild."

"You've got quite an operation going here."

She walked over to a box of zucchini mixed with broccoli. "Took me a while to get everything set up, but it's finally come together in the past year or two."

He started helping her unpack some of the boxes. "So how did you get into this?"

She picked up the box and stepped back to the refrigerator. "I lived in the city with my husband and a neighbor brought a baby squirrel to me." She put the box down on the floor. "I've always been an animal nut. But I knew nothing about caring for a squirrel, so I got on the Internet and learned all I could. Soon I began to connect with permitted wildlife rehabbers in the area and learned more about raising baby squirrels and other small mammals. Right after I got my wildlife rehabilitation permit from the Louisiana Wildlife and Fisheries, my husband asked for a divorce. So I moved out here and decided to pursue rehabbing full time."

Daniel stared at the woman as she stuffed some zucchini in the refrigerator.

"What happened?" he asked, pointing to the scratches on her forearm peeking out from under her long-sleeved shirt.

"Oh, one of the baby squirrels was running all over me this morning. Their nails are really sharp when they are young. I'm always getting scratched up."

"Isn't that a little dangerous for you considering your lupus?"

Pamela reached for some broccoli. "I know I should be more careful. If I have problems, I notify my doctor, and he calls something into the pharmacy for me." She rolled her eyes. "But only after he has given me a long lecture about why I should quit rehabbing."

"That would be enough to stop a lot of other people with lupus."

She shoved the broccoli into the refrigerator. "When I was first diagnosed, I didn't want to be one of those people who spent every waking moment obsessing about their condition. I decided I needed something else to occupy my mind."

Daniel glanced around the barn. "This is what you found?"

She walked over to a box of romaine lettuce. "I love what I do, and it keeps me going." She picked up the box and moved back to the refrigerator.

Daniel patted the refrigerator door. "You need another one of these."

She placed the box of romaine lettuce on the floor next to his feet. "I need two more. It's on my to-do list."

Daniel took in the six-stall horse barn.

There was a large tack room next to him, where Pamela stored several garbage tins filled with seeds and corn. The refrigerators were located outside of the tack room door. Hay was piled up in one stall and old wood planks in another. In a third stall, he discovered a selection of power tools spread out on a makeshift table. In another were several wire cages piled one on top of the other.

"What do you use this place for?"

Pamela followed his eyes around the barn. "Storage for the time being. I would like one day to take out all of the stalls and turn this place into the nursery, medical ward, and to prep food." She shrugged as she turned back to Daniel. "It's on my to-do list."

"I can only imagine what that list entails."

"You should have seen the place when I first took it over. I try to remove one thing a year from my list, but that is completely dependent on the amount of money it takes to fix whatever meltdowns may occur around here. One broken appliance, or worse, can really set me back."

Pamela finished putting the last of the romaine lettuce away and could feel Daniel's eyes on her. Either she was becoming paranoid, or she could truly sense every time the man looked at her.

She wiped her hands on the back of her jeans and started picking up the empty boxes from the floor. Daniel stepped into help.

"What do you want to do with these?"

"I take them out to the burn pile."

Daniel followed to a large pile of boxes, dead tree limbs, discarded nesting hay, and old newspapers set up close to the edge of the cleared property.

As Pamela stepped in front of the burn pile, two squirrels came running from the nearby brush to her side. Pamela bent over to speak to the squirrels. The animals darted about her feet, and around some of the boxes gathered on the ground, before heading back to the brush.

Daniel came up to her side and tossed the boxes in his arms on top of the mound of rubbish. "Does that usually happen?"

"Two of my male squirrels from last season, Moe and Larry. Sometimes come to see me."

He picked up the boxes scattered about his feet. "I thought they were supposed to be wild. Won't interacting with you teach them not to be afraid of people?"

"No, they're wild. They won't go to strangers. I'm family." Pamela threw the last of the boxes onto the burn pile. "Thanks for helping me."

"I'll bet that hurt."

She knitted her brows. "What are you talking about?"

"You hate having people help you. Must be hard enough for you to admit that you need help, let alone thank someone for helping you."

"I was being polite," she professed, raising her voice.

"Now you're getting defensive."

She opened her mouth to respond but decided against it. "I have baby squirrels to feed." She turned away, heading back toward the house.

"Can I help?"

Pamela stopped walking. "I thought you were going to work on the roof." She watched as his expression sobered. "I didn't realize. I mean you want to feed the babies?"

His dark mood instantly lifted, and he gave her a warm smile that seemed to soften the coldness in his eyes. "Yes, I know you want me to get started on the roof but ...."

"No, it's not about the roof. I'm just surprised you want to feed the babies again. Most people, especially men, aren't very interested in helping feed babies. They think it's …."

"A woman's job," Daniel said, filling in the blank.

She nodded.

He looked sheepishly at the ground. "Well, I don't think that. I really enjoyed handling the little flea-infested fuzz balls."

Pamela laughed at him. "Well, come on then. I'll even show you how to mix their formula."

Back at the house, Pamela taught Daniel how to mix powdered formula with water and yogurt in a blender. After pouring the formula into bowls, she warmed it in the microwave. She then carried the bowls to the kitchen table.

She sat in a chair next to the table as Daniel took a seat across from her. She handed him a syringe and a bowl of formula.

She waved her hand at the pile of containers between them. "Grab a container and get to it."

Daniel eagerly lifted the first baby out of the small clear plastic container. His eyes softened as he handled the tiny creature. When he put the nipple into the animal's mouth and watched it eagerly begin sucking down the formula from the syringe, he smiled.

"You really enjoy this, don't you?"

"Yes, I really do." He briefly glanced up at her. "Makes me feel like I'm doing something worthwhile. I'm not standing behind a bar mixing drinks with names like 'Demolition Brew' to serve some moron who defines having fun as getting stupid drunk in a bar every night. It's very simple with these guys. Life is about staying full, finding someone to rub your belly, and having a warm place to sleep. It makes you remember what is important in life."

"You got all that from feeding baby squirrels?"

"And being here, in your place."

Pamela reached into the closest container and picked up the baby squirrel inside. "I'm happy your time here has helped you gain a better perspective. Shame it doesn't do that for everyone."

"Most people are too afraid to look at who they are on the inside because they won't like what they find. Instead, they concentrate on their reflection in the mirror, and believe that by making themselves prettier, thinner, or younger, they will be more admired by others, and become a better person in the process. The world would be a better place without mirrors, in my opinion. It would force everyone to see who they are through the eyes of others like animals do. Imagine how much we could grow if we learned to do away with our vanity."

"When did you learn that?"

He flipped the baby in his hands gently over and started rubbing its pink belly with his fingers. "Always living on alert in Iraq taught me to scrutinize faces for the slightest hint of a possible threat. I started seeing other things in peoples' faces, like their hopes, fears, and frustrations. Before I left, I never looked at the person standing before me. I only judged people based on their clothes or the type of car they drove. When I came back, I didn't see the material things anymore, only the faces of the people. I couldn't tell you half the names of the people I went to high school with, but I could describe to you every person I've encountered since I came home from the war."

"I think I got a taste of what it must have been like for you after Katrina. Destruction and death were everywhere in the city, but I'm sure nothing like what you encountered."

Daniel stared at the squirrel in his hands. "I lost a lot of good friends over there. Most were guys I would never have associated with prior to Iraq. But fighting side by side with anyone makes you like family." He paused and his eyes seemed to darken slightly. "What haunts me to this day is the smell. I wake up sometimes in the middle of the night, smelling the odor of charred flesh and burning buildings."

"How did you adjust to being back in the states after going through all of that?"

"People who have never been there, think you get off the plane, and because you're home, everything is fine. But it's not that simple. You walk around in open public places, and you're terrified because you feel you're an easy target for a sniper. Every noise makes you jump. Every loud bang makes you want to dive for cover."

Pamela took the syringe out of the baby squirrel's mouth and started rubbing its round tummy. "How long before you felt comfortable being home again?"

He placed the baby in his hands back in its container. "I'm still waiting for that day." He snapped the lid closed on the container and then reached for another one. "I sometimes wonder if I will ever feel comfortable again." He pulled another baby out, placed the nipple into its small mouth, and laughed as the squirrel's impatient little paws wrapped around the syringe like a human baby placing its hands around a bottle.

"Any time you want to feed babies, you are more than welcome, Daniel."

"Thanks, Pamela." His bright smile dimmed a little. "I've got to work for the next few days but after that, I'll be able to return. I'll be looking forward to getting back to these guys by then."

"You're beginning to sound like me."

Daniel gazed into her eyes and grinned. "Maybe that's not such a bad thing after all."

Chapter 5

A few days later, a brooding Daniel Phillips returned to Pamela's sanctuary. His Jeep slammed into the gravel driveway, spewing rocks all around when he came to a skidding stop just before the entrance to the cottage. Pamela and Carol watched from the front porch as the tall man climbed out of his Jeep, ignoring her pack of barking dogs.

"Mornin'," he mumbled as he removed his sunglasses.

He walked directly to the side of the house.

Carol raised her mug of coffee to her lips. "Obviously not a morning person."

Pamela put her mug down on the railing. "I'll be back," she said to Carol and then quickly made her way down the steps and around the side of the house.

"God, I just love a hot mini-drama in the morning," Carol mused.

Pamela came up to Daniel, who was banging the ladder around trying to get it positioned right up next to the house.

His face was drawn, and there were dark circles under his eyes. His hair was disheveled, and a thick five o'clock shadow covered his square jaw.

"Coffee?" Pamela offered, figuring he was probably in desperate need of a caffeine boost.

"Yeah," he grumbled without looking at her. "That would be great, thanks."

"Everything all right?"

Daniel kept his focus on the house. "Just peachy."

"Peachy, huh? You look terrible, Daniel."

His dark eyes ripped her to shreds. "Thanks. That's just what I needed to hear."

She stood there for several minutes watching him as he gathered up his tools. Finally, he stopped and glowered at her. "Didn't you say something about coffee?"

"After you tell me what your problem is this morning."

Daniel threw the hammer in his hand to the ground. Lester, in the tree behind him, gave out a sudden hoot of surprise.

Daniel flinched. "Great. That's all I need today."

"Tell me what's wrong?"

He surveyed the land around him. "Do you really want to hear this, Pamela, or are you just pretending to give a damn like the rest of the world?"

"I'm not pretending, Daniel."

His eyes probed hers. "I got fired last night."

"Fired? Why?"

"The guy that I slugged a few months back for roughing up his girlfriend; you know, the one who filed charges against me? Well, he showed up at the bar last night and started ranting about why I was still working there. Security finally escorted him out of the place. After that, the manager told me to leave and not come back."

"What are you going to do?"

He shrugged, appearing unconcerned about his situation. "Get another job. Won't be as lucrative as Pat O'Brien's, but I'll manage. There are a lot of bars in the Quarter."

"I'm sorry," was all she could think to say.

Daniel gave her a weak attempt at a smile, but his eyes were still cold and menacing. "What about that coffee?"

"Coming right up. How do you want it?"

"Black."

Pamela turned to go when his voice stopped her.

"Thank you for not pretending."

She glanced back at him. "Let's just say I think of you as a very large squirrel."

Daniel's a heartfelt laughter seemed to break the tension in his face. "I think that is the nicest thing anyone has ever said to me."

Pamela walked away, and as she turned the corner to the front of the house, she discovered Carol leaning over the porch railing, obviously straining to eavesdrop on their conversation.

"Should I send you a transcript?"

Carol waved a dismissive hand. "Nah. Heard plenty enough from my spot here." Carol smiled coyly at her. "So you and the criminal are friends, eh?"

"You told him I have lupus."

"I also tell everyone that you are mentally unstable and ritually sacrifice small children out in the woods, but no one ever believes me."

"I should sacrifice you out in the woods," Pamela replied under her breath as she climbed the steps to the porch. "Why do I put up with you and all—"

The sound of a car heading down the gravel drive silenced Pamela's remonstrations. She and Carol watched as a bright red Mercedes-Benz SLK 350 roadster pulled up next to Daniel's blue Jeep. The dogs quickly rose from their respective spots on the porch and went clamoring after the car.

Pamela's shoulders drooped. "This is all I need!"

"Oh, how exciting," Carol squealed. "Imelda has decided to grace us with her presence."

The door of the Mercedes opened and a woman's long, slender leg slid out from the car.

"Pamie!" A high-pitched voice cried from inside the sleek roadster. "Can you get the dogs away from my car?"

Pamela cursed under her breath as she ran down the steps to the drive. She tried to corral a few of the dogs away from the shiny red car, but for some reason, they seemed hesitant to listen to her. Pamela could hear Carol giggling from the porch behind her.

"Go!" She clapped her hands to try and scare them away.

Every dog ran back to the porch except for Tequila, the brown Chiweenie. She just sat there staring at the car, wagging her tail, and not paying one bit of attention to Pamela. Finally, Pamela picked up the dog and carried it to the porch.

"It's all right, Clarissa." Slowly, another leg appeared from inside the car. Then a tall woman, dressed in a form-fitting red, silk shirtdress, and black Manolo Blahnik pumps, emerged into the morning sunlight. She was slender with long, dark brown hair and bright green eyes. Her face was oval, pale, and looked slightly Asian. Her petite nose, small chin, and almond-shaped eyes only seemed to add to the exotic quality of her face.

"Pamela!" Clarissa's slender arms went up to her as if begging for a hug.

"Clarissa." Pamela gave her a friendly embrace. She quickly stepped away, trying to breathe with restraint after the first whiff of the woman's heavy perfume. "What are you doing here?"

Clarissa held up her iPhone in her perfectly manicured little hands. "I came to take some pictures of all of your animals. I've got a friend over at the *Times-Picayune,* who wants some pictures of your place to put in the Sunday paper. Like a human interest thing. Since the BP oil spill, everyone has been so worried about all of the animals affected. You never know, it might help to drum up some donations for you."

"I worked the oil spill, Clarissa, and it involved mostly birds," Pamela clarified in a patronizing tone. "I try to limit myself to small mammals at this facility."

Clarissa laughed, and the dogs on the porch all stood up and looked at her like she was a large squeaky toy. "Honey, no one is gonna know one way or the other. Mammals, birds, what's the difference? As long as it is cute and fuzzy, everyone will just melt over your little critters. You can make some money in the process." She shut the car door shut and sashayed to the porch.

"Hello, Mrs. Patrick," Carol said, sounding welcoming.

"Oh, hello." Clarissa stopped halfway up the steps and gaped at Carol. "You're Beverly, right?"

"No, I'm Carol. I handle the books, and we see each other at the fundraiser every year."

"Oh, yes, silly me. I remember you, dear." She pointed at the coffee mug in Carol's hand. "Y'all got any more of that inside?"

"I'll get you a mug," Carol offered. "Cream, no sugar, right?"

"How clever of you to remember."

"How could I forget, Mrs. Patrick?" Carol headed inside.

Clarissa turned back to Pamela. "So, why don't you show me what's new around—"

Just then Rodney the raccoon emerged from around the corner of the house. He laid eyes on Clarissa and immediately began to snort and growl at her.

"I see you still haven't gotten rid of that vile creature," Clarissa muttered as her green eyes glared at Rodney. "Shouldn't you put him to sleep or somethin'? I mean havin' such vermin hangin' around can only bring diseases to your other animals. Don't they carry rabies?"

"Clarissa, you know I don't put animals to sleep unless it's absolutely necessary. Rodney is very friendly with most people and does not have rabies. He's had his shots. I just don't understand what his problem is with you."

Clarissa shot Pamela a dirty look.

"I simply meant maybe it's your perfume or something you wear that sets him off," Pamela explained. "They have a very acute sense of smell."

"Well, I think he's just—"

A round of banging from the roof stifled Clarissa's campaign against the roaming raccoon.

"What's that?"

"I have someone repairing the broken shingles on my roof," Pamela told her.

Clarissa raised her dark brows, questioningly. "Since when can you afford to have any work done on this place?" She narrowed her small eyes on Pamela. "Bob hasn't given you any more money, has he?"

Pamela could not help but grin. "No. You and Bob have been more than generous over the years."

"Then how can you afford to have your roof fixed?" She walked around to the side of the porch, her Manolo Blahnik's clicking on the wood.

"A volunteer has generously donated the materials to fix up my house," Pamela clarified.

"Volunteer!" Clarissa almost laughed. "Your volunteers are just as poor as you. Now who would pay to have—?"

Daniel rounded the corner. He was soaked through, and his thin white T-shirt clung to his muscular torso. He stopped dead in his tracks when he saw Clarissa.

"Sorry." He cleared his throat. "I just needed to get something out of my Jeep." His dark eyes volleyed back and forth between Pamela and Clarissa.

"Well, hello there!" Clarissa purred while sticking out her amply enhanced cleavage.

"Clarissa, this is Daniel." Pamela motioned to Daniel. "Daniel has been helping out around here."

"So happy to meet you, Daniel," Clarissa purred and leaned over the porch railing, offering him her hand.

Daniel took the woman's hand and gave it a brief tug.

"Daniel, Clarissa is a very generous patron of my facility." Pamela gave a fake smile and tried to implore Daniel with her eyes to play nice.

He paused for a second or two, and then Daniel turned back to Clarissa.

"Well, hello." He flashed a boyish smile that Pamela swore he kept hidden from her. "It's very nice to meet someone so interested in Pamela's little organization. You must be a woman of exceptional taste."

Clarissa became like butter in a frying pan. "Oh, I try my best to support all worthy causes," she gushed.

Pamela curtailed her snicker as Clarissa touched her face and played with the fabric of her dress.

"Clarissa came out to take some pictures of some of the animals for the newspaper," Pamela explained. "She thinks it might be a real help in getting donations for the facility."

"Really? That is so kind of her." Daniel's smile looked so fake that Pamela wondered if he was laying it on a bit too thick.

But Clarissa didn't seem to notice. "You know I could use some people in my shots. Perhaps highlight the volunteers who work so hard to keep the place goin'."

"Gee," Carol said, coming up behind the women. "I always wanted to have my picture taken for the newspaper."

Carol extended a mug of coffee to her, but Clarissa frowned at it. "I was actually thinkin' more along the lines of havin' Daniel here …," Clarissa turned back to Daniel, "… pose for a few shots, Beverly."

"It's Carol," Carol corrected.

Clarissa just waved her hand at Carol, never taking her eyes away from Daniel. "What do you think, Daniel? Up for a few pictures to help the cause?"

Daniel glanced over at Pamela and beamed. "Absolutely!"

"Wonderful!" Clarissa clapped her hands together. "Why don't you and I go over to those cages across the way and take some pictures with the animals." She pointed to the man's sweaty T-shirt. "But lose the shirt, darlin'. I think it would be so much more interestin' if you looked like you were workin' really hard."

"Nothing says a man is working hard than when he shows off his naked chest," Carol announced.

Clarissa glanced back at Carol. "I find that to be true, Constance." She took the steps from the porch to the gravel drive one at a time, and by the time her expensive black shoes hit the ground, Daniel was at her side.

Carol and Pamela looked on as the pair walked around the side of the house and toward the back of the facility.

"I hope those heels get stuck in a big pile of mud," Carol muttered beside Pamela.

"I can't believe the fate of my rehab center rests on the shoulders of a half-naked bartender."

"Well, those shoulders can definitely handle the burden." Carol clucked. "I've seen monkeys in heat more subtle than that woman. Now there's a troubled marriage."

Pamela arched an eyebrow. "What makes you say that?"

"If she's on the prowl, so is Bob. A woman never goes after another man unless the man she's got isn't man enough, if you know what I mean," Carol expounded with a wink.

"I have no idea what you're talking about."

Clarissa squealed with delight when Daniel lifted her over a large puddle.

"God, I hope I never become that desperate," Carol commented.

"I don't care how desperate she is," Pamela vented. "If I knew it would help, I would pay Daniel to sleep with that stupid woman. I will do anything to keep this place going."

"Maybe you could get a two-for-one discount. He could do Clarissa and then you."

Pamela snapped her head around and glared at Carol. "What is that supposed to mean?"

"You two seemed real cozy earlier this morning. All I'm saying is, maybe you and the gigolo should get to know each other. You know, horizontally."

Pamela rolled her eyes. "Carol, all you think about is sex!"

"Yeah, maybe. But at least I'm thinking about it." She arched an eyebrow. "Are you?"

*****

It was well into the afternoon when Clarissa's bright red Mercedes left Pamela's gravel drive and headed back to the city. Soon after she saw Clarissa's tail lights turn on the main road at the entrance to her property, she heard the hammer start up again on her roof. Pamela stood outside on her porch and fought back the urge to go running to Daniel and ask what happened between him and the insufferable woman. She decided instead to go inside her house and feed her collection of baby gray squirrels.

After settling down at the kitchen table with a bowl of formula, a knock came from her front door.

"It's open."

The door flew open, and Daniel rushed in. Shirtless and out of breath, he hurried toward her with something cupped in his hands.

"I found this when I was up on your roof, by the chimney, sealing up some leaks. It fell into my hands when I moved some of the loose tiles away." He opened his hands to reveal a tiny creature with bright brown fur.

Pamela put the baby she was feeding back in its container and analyzed the speck of life cradled in the man's long hands. She tenderly lifted the creature out of his hands and carefully inspected it.

"It's a flying squirrel. Don't get many of those unless they are trapped up in people's attics."

"Is it hurt or something? It didn't move too much when I brought it down the ladder. Do you think I could have injured it?"

She felt a sudden tug at her heart as she caught sight of the man's pained expression. "No, I'm sure you didn't injure it. Let's find out exactly what's wrong."

Pamela pulled at each of the animal's spindly little legs and ran her fingers over its soft, silky fur. Finally, she extended its feather-like tail and pressed gently on its head.

"Nothing appears to be broken. There are no cuts or blood anywhere on the fur," she told him as she turned the creature over in her hand. "Might be sick."

"Can you help it?"

Pamela gazed over at his bare chest and felt her stomach do a few nervous flips. She immediately turned her eyes back to the flying squirrel. "I can start a round of antibiotics and get some good nutrition into her."

Daniel raised his eyebrows. "Her?"

"Her," Pamela confirmed. "She's definitely not a him."

"I guess she found me irresistible, too."

Pamela got up from the floor. She went to the kitchen cabinet where she kept her medicines.

She opened the cabinet, and he gave a long whistle. "Woman, you got a lot of drugs there," he declared, taking in the row upon row of medicine bottles piled high in the cabinet.

"Always have to stay well stocked on everything I might need."

Daniel went to the next cabinet. He looked over shelves packed with the medical and nursing supplies. "What about going to a vet?

"Vets are expensive, and most don't have any experience working with wildlife. The only place I can take the animals is to LSU Veterinary School. They work with all the permitted rehabbers in the state."

"Where did you learn about all of this stuff?"

She took out a bottle from her cabinet and reached in front of him for a syringe. "You learn some from other rehabbers, but most of it is self-taught through books or the Internet. My medical background helps, too."

"I never realized there was so much to rehabbing wildlife. You're really running a hospital and a nursery for animals here, aren't you?"

She took the flying squirrel out of his hands and fed it the contents of a syringe. "Most people think that the pictures on television of people cleaning birds from the BP oil spill depict what rehabbers do. But only rehabbers know what is involved in keeping these animals going."

"Maybe someone should tell people what you do," Daniel suggested.

Pamela was acutely aware of the close proximity of his half-naked body. She quickly redirected her attention back to the animal in her hands. "Many people don't care about what we do. I have been called an animal hoarder, anti-naturist, animal abuser ... oh, all kinds of things from all kinds of people. What I, and other rehabbers, do doesn't save the world, cure cancer, or make for an interesting mini-series. Our attention-deficit-driven society does not care when you save a life; they are only interested when you destroy one."

Daniel leaned in closer to her. "Well, I care. I care very much."

"Yes, I saw just how much you cared with Clarissa today."

"I thought you wanted me to take her around your place and get some pictures for the paper. I did not realize my services included leasing myself out to entertain lonely and bored housewives."

Pamela proceeded to her hallway closet. She retrieved a plastic container with some clean felt strips inside of it. After setting the little flying squirrel on top of the felt strips, she snapped the container lid closed.

"Clarissa is a supporter of this facility, and she was obviously impressed with you. She requested you take her around, and she wanted you, not me, in the pictures." Pamela went to the kitchen table and placed the flying squirrel's container on top of it.

"You're angry," Daniel surmised, grinning. "You're mad because that silly woman wanted me in the pictures and not you."

"Well, it is my facility!"

"Then you should have said something."

"I couldn't say anything to her. I have to kiss her ass, so she keeps letting her husband give me money!"

Daniel considered her comment. "Why does Clarissa have to let her husband give you money? Why can't she just give you the money?"

"Because Clarissa is married to my ex-husband, that's why!"

Daniel started laughing. "What a twisted triangle."

"It's not funny, Daniel. I have put up with a lot from that woman. I bit my tongue today; otherwise, she would have gone running back to Bob and nagged him into cutting off my funding."

Daniel tried to contain his laughter, somewhat. "Pamela, it's very funny. You have to admit."

Pamela tossed her hand in the air. "It's no different than women who try to get child support out of ex-husbands who have moved on to greener pastures."

"I wouldn't exactly call Clarissa greener pastures. She's a pretentious bore who made it quite clear what she wanted from me. And I've been around enough women to know when they want more from me than a handshake."

Pamela marched to the front door. "I think this conversation has gone far enough."

"You're mad at me?" He followed her to the door. "She hit on me, Pamela."

"You could have jeopardized everything I have worked for." She opened the front door. "Now get out."

"You're not angry about Clarissa. You're jealous that I spent the afternoon flirting with her, aren't you?"

Pamela's jaw dropped. "Did you flirt with her?"

"I thought I was helping you."

"Get out," she shouted, pointing outside.

"No, I won't leave until we have settled this." He slapped the front door closed.

Pamela placed her hand on the doorknob, but Daniel leaned against the door so she could not open it. Pamela stood there for several minutes pulling on the doorknob.

"Are you finished?"

Pamela let go of the doorknob and stood back from him, breathing heavily. "I want you out of here. You're an arrogant, self-centered, conceited jerk."

"Now, are you finished?"

She stood before him, still breathing hard. She was furious. No one ever challenged her like that. With wild animals, she expected this kind of behavior. Asserting dominance was merely a way to establish their authority. But this was something new. How should she handle this obstinate and difficult man? Her fists curled and, without thinking, she punched Daniel in the arm.

"Ow!" He grabbed at his arm.

"Get out." She made a move to punch him again.

But Daniel was too quick for her and circled his arms around her, pinning her to his wide chest.

"No punching or kicking. Biting and scratching, however, are definitely encouraged."

Pamela stood trapped in his long arms, wiggling with all of her might to free herself. She could not stand the feel of his skin, the smell of his body, or the way his breath teased the sensitive skin along the nape of her neck.

"Let me go."

"Not yet," Daniel whispered as he lowered his head to hers. "There's something I have wanted to do to you for quite some time."

Daniel kissed her, hard on the lips. Pamela tried to scream, but his lips stifled her cries. She wanted to flay him alive, but a forgotten part of her began to have other ideas. A vibrant and all-consuming flow of electricity consumed her. Her legs felt weak, her heart raced, and her toes tingled. This was not like Bob's kisses. Pamela's defenses caved, and she began responding to him.

He let her go and took a step back. Pamela felt her eyes searching his as if wanting to know what she'd done wrong.

"I'm sorry."

Pamela studied his face for the slightest hint of what he was thinking, but her own emotions seemed to be clouding her judgment. She lowered her eyes to the floor.

"I'll go," he blurted out and then reached for the door.

"Wait, Daniel." She ran her hand along her forehead. "You were right. I was jealous of you spending time with Clarissa today. I saw her hanging all over you ...."

"So does that mean I can come back and see you again?"

She tried to frown, unsuccessfully. "You can come back and finish fixing up my house if we happen to run into—"

"Pamela, playing hard to get doesn't suit you. Next time, just nod."

She stepped up beside him, and he kissed her forehead.

"I'll be back in a few days," he assured her as he opened her door.

"I'll be here, Daniel." She watched him stroll out the door and across the porch.

He grabbed his white T-shirt, still hanging from the porch railing. "Take care of my flying squirrel for me. I'm thinking of naming her Pamela."

He bounded down the steps and climbed into his Jeep. Daniel tossed his T-shirt on the passenger's seat, put on his sunglasses, and eyed the woman standing on the porch.

"What have I done?" Pamela mumbled as he started his Jeep. "Please, let this not be another mistake."

Chapter 6

Sitting out on the front porch, enjoying an afternoon break from the animals, a familiar silver Mercedes-Benz CL 550 coupe made its way slowly down Pamela's gravel drive from the main road.

"Great, this is all I need."

The usual welcoming committee of stray dogs surrounded the car, but there was barking as a man dressed in a tailored gray suit stepped from his Mercedes. He removed a pair of expensive Vuarnet sunglasses and threw them on the seat. The dogs eagerly gathered around the man with their tails wagging, waiting for their customary pat on the head.

"Hello, Pamela."

"Hello, Bob. What brings you out on a weekday?"

Bob Patrick was a thick, muscular man with perfectly coiffed light brown hair. A long nose, round face, and a wide forehead made his pale green eyes appear to be very intense. It was a feature Pamela knew he used to his advantage in the courtroom every time he cross-examined a witness.

"I got some free time and thought I would come out and see how things were going." He made his way up the steps. "I haven't heard from you in a while," he added as he walked up to her side and tenderly kissed her cheek.

She could smell the woodsy cologne on his clothes as he approached. Bob tended to be heavy-handed with the stuff. It used to drive her out of their bedroom every morning when they were married.

"You've been feeling all right?"

"I'm fine, Bob."

"You look good." He leered at her. "But then you always look good, no matter how sick you are."

He inspected the property as if searching for something. Pamela followed his eyes and wondered what he could possibly be looking for.

"I ran into Jennifer Barons the other days at Galatoire's." His eyes came back to her. "She asked about you. I said I would pass on her best. She and Elliot divorced last year. Ted Yanosky handled it. Very nasty, according to Ted."

"Well, Jennifer was the one with all of the money," Pamela commented, not really interested in the vacuous lives of forgotten friends in the city. "Elliot told everyone he married her for her money. He wasn't a very subtle man."

"His two mistresses didn't think so either. They both testified against him at the divorce hearing, so Jennifer ended up walking away without having to pay him a dime."

Pamela studied his face. "You didn't drive all the way up here to talk about Jennifer and Elliot. I know you, Bob, and you wouldn't go to this much trouble without a reason."

"I could never pull one over on you, P.A.."

"P.A.? You haven't called me that in years."

"I've always called you P.A.," he insisted. "You're the one who hated being called Pamela Anne."

"No, Bob, I didn't hate being called Pamela Anne. I just hated the way you said it. You made my name sound like something you owned and not someone you loved." She let out a long breath. "Why are you here?"

"Clarissa told me about the handyman you have working around here. In fact, she never shut up about the guy." He rolled his eyes. "She seems to think he's a gigolo, looking for a meal ticket. I decided to come up here and check him out."

"You came all this way to check out a worker?" Pamela cracked a grin. "That's a first. You could have saved yourself the drive. He's not here, Bob."

"You can't just let any bum off the street in here, Pamela. You're a woman living alone, and you're vulnerable in this godforsaken place. You need to use your head."

"This conversation is beginning to sound like when we were married. You pestered me to quit my job as an EMT because you thought it wasn't safe."

"It wasn't safe," he barked and then turned away. "You were a woman working on the streets of New Orleans with drug dealers and pimps."

"I knew what I was dealing with better than you, Bob." She inwardly calmed her mounting anger. He'd always known how to push her buttons. "You need to stop worrying about me. I'm not your concern anymore," she coolly added.

"Pamela, you know I can't just turn off my emotions like that. I still care for you and worry about you out here all alone with only a few stray dogs to protect you. You need to be a little more selective in your choice of workers."

"I'm not your wife anymore, Bob. Please don't lecture me. The guy was sent by the probation office to do some community service. You're the one who told me to call them and get some free help out here because you were concerned I was doing too much by myself."

He blew a breath out through his clenched teeth. "The way Clarissa described him made me think I should come and check him out."

Pamela shook her head when the realization hit her. "You came out here looking for a fight, didn't you?"

"No. Why do you persist in bringing up one minor altercation that happened over ten years ago?"

"There was more than one minor altercation, Bob." She gave him a stern reproach with her eyes. "Why this sudden urge to check out my workers? You never showed an interest in anyone who volunteered out here before. Is it because Clarissa found this one so charming? Is that what's got you worried?"

"Why are you so hostile about this? I came up here to make sure you're all right, and all I get is flack for it."

Pamela clenched her fists. She couldn't let him get to her. "I'm sorry. But there is nothing to worry about as far as Daniel is concerned."

"Then just think about it. Call me when you're ready and I will run a background check on the guy. What harm could come of it?"

Pamela said nothing. She kept the fake smile on her lips.

"Oh, the other reason I came out here was to talk to you about this big benefit the Louisiana Bar Association is hosting next weekend for Gulf Oil Spill Relief. It's at the new Roosevelt Hotel in the city. There will be a lot of wealthy people attending, and I thought maybe you could pick up a few patrons. It's black tie, so you will need a nice dress." He examined her dirty blue jeans and stained T-shirt. "Do you even own a dress?" he added with a smirk.

"I'll find something to wear, don't worry."

"It's next Saturday at seven. I'll leave two tickets at the door so you can bring Carol with you."

"She would like that. Thanks, Bob."

He looked around the porch. "I'm sure you have animals to feed or something else to do." He took a step back. "I'll see you next Saturday. And please think about letting me look into this handyman of yours."

Pamela opened her mouth to protest.

Bob raised his hand, silencing her. "I know, but if you don't do it for yourself, then do it for me. I don't want to see anything happen to you, P.A.."

"I'm not your problem anymore, remember?"

He reached up and took a strand of blonde hair. "We'll never be completely free of each other. I sometimes wonder what it would have been like if we'd stayed together."

Pamela raised her chin. "You're the one that wanted out, Bob. You always worried about how you would explain my absences from all those political fundraisers you attended. You thought my disease would become more important than your career."

He let her hair fall from his fingers. "You haven't changed, have you, Pamela? Still trying to bait me with your cool condescension." He headed down the steps. "I'll see you next Saturday," he called over his shoulder.

Pamela went inside her front door, slamming it behind her. She walked over to the large wire cage by the window and took a napping Louis out of his sleeping sack and held him against her chest. The small bundle of brown and gray fur cuddled against her skin, instantly calming the swirling frustration inside of her. Holding Louis against her, she went over and sat down on her couch. Summoning every ounce of control she possessed, she pushed all of her unhappy memories back into the darkest corners of her mind and focused her concentration on the warm little squirrel nestled in her hands.

*****

The following morning, Carol sauntered in the front door. In a dark blue pantsuit, with a light touch of makeup on her round face, she was holding two Starbucks coffee cups.

"I got our usual chocolate mocha lattes."

Pamela put the last of the baby squirrels back into its container. She stretched uncomfortably, her joints aching.

"You look nice," Pamela commented as she took in Carol's outfit.

"I have to meet with a new client this morning. I thought I would stop by and deliver one of these before heading over to the office." Carol handed Pamela the large coffee cup.

Pamela noticed the bags under Carol's eyes. "Another late night with Ian."

Carol held up her grande cup of coffee. "Hence the extra shot of espresso." She took a seat on one of the stools next to the kitchen counter. "God, that man's relentless in bed."

"Carol." Pamela tried to look offended. "I have known you since you were five years old, and to hear you discuss your sex life is rather disturbing."

"Want details?"

"No." Pamela leaned on the counter across from Carol.

"But I thought you might like to live vicariously through me since you haven't dated anyone since that weirdo, Walden." She took a sip of her coffee.

"Walden was a nice guy. Just because he was a funeral director, you thought he was a weirdo. He was just what I needed after the divorce."

"He looked like a gerbil. And that laugh." Carol feigned a shiver. "It reminded me of that peacock you took in three years ago, the one that kept losing its feathers. That bird always sounded like a woman screaming for her life."

Pamela gave Carol a withering glance and then took a sip of coffee.

"Fine, I'll change the subject. Tell me what happened after I left the other day with the gigolo and the shoe hoarder," Carol demanded.

"Nothing." Pamela peered into her coffee and prayed she sounded convincing enough to avoid further questioning.

"I find that hard to believe. The slut didn't drag him to the local Motel 6 for a quickie?"

"Visually descriptive, but no." Pamela put her coffee down on the counter. "Clarissa left after she got her pictures. Then Daniel went back to work on the roof." She turned to the kitchen cabinets behind her.

"So, if nothing happened, why do you look guilty?"

Pamela spun around to her. "I hate it when you do that!"

Carol raised her dark brows, feigning innocence. "Do what?"

"Interrogate me as though I have something to hide."

"You always have something to hide. You never tell anyone what you are thinking or feeling. You keep everything bottled up inside of you."

"I don't keep things bottled up inside of me." She picked at the paper rim of the Starbucks cup.

"Pamie, one day you're gonna blow and take half the Gulf Coast with you. You keep more bull hidden away inside of you than a pregnant nun in a cloister."

"Very colorful."

"Thank you." Carol smiled, looking pleased. "So tell me, what's going on between you and Daniel?"

Pamela rocked her head back in frustration. "Nothing is going on."

"You're overreacting. Whenever you overreact, you have something to hide. If nothing were going on between you two, you would just tell me to shut up and go feed something. But you're standing there fidgeting." She grinned. "And you never fidget."

"You've been watching too many detective shows on television." Pamela watched Carol's pale blue eyes continue to stare at her. "Oh, all right. After Clarissa left, Daniel found a flying squirrel under a roof tile, near the chimney, and brought it to me."

"Interesting, but I'm assuming there's more." Carol made a rolling motion with her hand. "Let's hear the rest of it."

"He told me that Clarissa hit on him. We argued about his brazen attempt at flirting with the woman, and then he left."

"'Brazen attempt at flirting'? Boy, have you got it bad. What else?"

"Nothing." Pamela's voice cracked. "Nothing else happened. He left and now I have a flying squirrel in the kitchen." She started nervously playing with the cup of coffee in front of her.

Carol continued to stare. "What else?" she pressed.

Pamela shifted back and forth, from one foot to the other, until she could not take Carol's eyes on her any longer. "All right, he kissed me! There, happy?"

"Don't ever murder anyone; you'd snap like a dried twig under interrogation."

Carol reached for an old newspaper on the counter and started skimming the front page.

"Aren't you going to say anything?" Pamela finally questioned, unable to tolerate Carol's continued casual indifference.

"He kissed you." She never looked up from the newspaper. "That's all?"

"Isn't that enough?"

"Hardly." Carol rolled her eyes. "Let me know when he rips your clothes off and carries you to bed." She picked up her coffee and got up from the stool. "So, any other wildlife come in beside the flying squirrel?"

The sound of a car coming down the drive made the two women turn to the front door. The dogs outside started barking.

Carol put her drink on the coffee table and quickly made her way to the door. "Maybe it's Imelda back for some of your boyfriend."

Pamela regretted ever telling the young woman about Daniel.

When the two stepped outside, they saw Daniel's blue Jeep pulled up next to Carol's green Nissan Sentra.

Carol nudged Pamela with her elbow. "I bet he's come to take you to the local Motel 6."

Daniel stood in the Jeep and threw a handful of dog biscuits to the strays gathered around his car. The dogs went for the treats and let Daniel step away from his car, unscathed.

"Good looking and resourceful," Carol murmured next to Pamela. "I say jump his bones ASAP before Imelda tries to dig those Manolo Blahnik's into him."

The dogs were still crunching away on their biscuits when Daniel came bounding up the steps, grinning like a child on Christmas morning.

"I should get going," Carol blurted out before Daniel even made it onto the porch.

"Don't feel you have to rush off because of me," Daniel said, half laughing.

Carol removed her car keys out from her pocket. "I would love to hang around and watch you two drooling over each other, but I have to go into the office today and pretend to be a real accountant for a few hours."

"Carol, wait," Pamela pleaded. "I have some things to discuss with you."

Carol eyed her suspiciously. "You've got two minutes."

"Well, for starters, Bob came by yesterday and wants us to go to this big oil spill benefit in New Orleans next Saturday."

Carol shook her head. "Can't make it." She motioned to Daniel. "Take your boyfriend."

Daniel looked from Carol to Pamela. "You told her I was your boyfriend?"

"No," Pamela replied, ready to strangle Carol.

"She told me that you found a flying squirrel, and then you kissed her," Carol clarified.

"Carol!"

"What?" Carol shrugged. "You did tell me that."

"So does that make me your boyfriend?" Daniel posed, smiling.

"Technically, it makes you interested in becoming her boyfriend," Carol explained. "I don't think it actually becomes official until you two...." She grinded her hips suggestively. "You know?"

"Oh, God," Pamela whispered.

Daniel smirked. "Perhaps I should take her out on a date first."

"Absolutely! A nice dinner at some place that uses real silverware on the table," Carol proposed.

"Would you two please stop?" Pamela begged.

"Or I could pick up something and bring it here," Daniel proposed. "Since she probably won't want to leave her babies for an entire evening."

"Ah, bringing food to the lady, nice touch." Carol gave Daniel the thumbs up.

"Enough!" Pamela ushered Carol off the porch.

"Should I bring flowers and wine with the food?" Daniel questioned as Pamela pulled Carol to her green Sentra.

"Definitely," Carol shouted. "She likes Merlot and daisies!"

Pamela stood in the drive and waited as Carol's car disappeared around the bend in the road. She didn't want to turn and see Daniel on the porch, grinning at her. But she knew there was no way around the inevitable. She finally mustered up the nerve to face him but was surprised to see that Daniel wasn't there. Relieved, she walked back up the porch steps and inside her cottage door.

Daniel was standing at her kitchen table with an open container in front of him. He didn't seem to notice as she walked in the room. Instead, he was preoccupied with something cupped in his hands.

"Couldn't wait to see how my girl was doing."

She was a little mystified, at how the man's muscular body curled around the creature as he pulled his cupped hands close to his chest. His shoulders, back, and neck reflexively encircled the contents of his hand, as if to shield the helpless animal from any further harm.

"Has she been eating?"

"Not as well as I would like. She wasn't too interested in her plate of mealworms and fruit this morning."

Daniel gingerly set the groggy, brown and white squirrel back in her container and closed the lid. Putting the container back amid the pile on the table, he then turned and looked at Pamela. He smiled and slowly walked across the room to her side, then reached his hands around her back and pulled her into his arms.

"So now that I'm your boyfriend, I guess I can do this." He kissed her tenderly on the lips.

Pamela's first instinct was to slap him across the face, but then another kind of instinct took over. Her arms reached around his neck while she eased in closer.

Daniel responded by deepening his kiss. His hands traveled the length of her back and down to her round butt.

Pamela quickly pulled away, leaving Daniel confused.

"What's wrong?"

"What are we doing, Daniel?"

"I think it's called dating."

"Dating or mating? I think you have the two confused."

"No, I don't," he affirmed. "If we were mating, we wouldn't be standing in the living room."

She took another step back from him. "Perhaps we shouldn't do this. Neither one of us has a very good track record with the opposite sex. Our becoming involved might make our working relationship difficult."

"You need to stop analyzing this, Pamela. What we were as individuals is not what we will be as a couple. People change people no matter how short, or how long, a relationship lasts. Why don't we just enjoy what we have now and see what happens?" He paused and smiled at her. "Just consider me a new type of wildlife that you are eager to learn everything about."

Pamela scowled at him. "I don't end up in bed with my wildlife."

Daniel raised his dark brows. "Have you been thinking about how we would be in bed together?"

Her cheeks burned. "Perhaps you should get to work on my roof before this gets out of hand."

"Am I moving too fast for you?"

Pamela stood for a moment and considered the question. "Daniel, I think at my age moving too fast is more a necessity than a problem."

He chuckled. "You're not old, Pamela."

"I'm older than you. Perhaps, too old."

"I don't care about your age." He pulled her back into his arms. "Relationships are not right or wrong because of someone's age. We are both over twenty-one and free to choose who we want to be with."

"Even if the woman you want to be with is broken?"

He cupped his hands around her beautiful face and brought his lips within inches of hers. "You will never be broken to me."

Her eyes eagerly searched his. "I wish I could believe you."

"How can I prove it to you?"

That familiar nagging feeling of doubt rose from her gut. No man could ever prove his sincerity as far as she was concerned. Trust was a commodity she stopped investing in years ago.

She took a step back from Daniel. "The roof is waiting," she said in a firm voice.

Daniel stared into her eyes, and Pamela thought she saw a glimmer of hurt linger in his dark orbs. He smiled, and the serious mood lifted between them.

"I'll get right on it, boss lady," he cheekily replied.

*****

Later that afternoon, Pamela and Daniel were sitting on her back porch, eating sandwiches and taking a break from their work. Daniel finished the roof and was starting to strip the old paint from the outside of the house. Small flecks of blue and white paint still covered his dark hair, face, chest, and forearms. Even on his faded jeans, there were remnants of the paint.

"Sorry, I don't have anything heartier than tuna for you. I don't have any red meat in the house, and the chicken I do have, I have to keep for the animals."

Daniel held up his sandwich. "The tuna's fine, Pamela." He gazed out over the facility. "You know, with a little work this place could really be something."

"Yes, but the kind of work I need to be done costs money."

He finished chewing on his sandwich. "What else do you need, besides an overhaul of your house and the barn?"

She eyed the cages next to the barn. "I need to get a few more exterior cages built. Then I would love to add more outdoor lights so I wouldn't have to carry a flashlight with me when I check on sick animals at night. Then there are the extra faucets needed around the cages."

"I might be able to help out with the outdoor lights. I can do some basic wiring and run a line out from the barn."

"You're already doing too much. I feel like I'm taking advantage of you. I prefer to pay people for their services."

"I told you I want to do this," Daniel insisted.

She could not help but smile. "I find it's getting harder and harder to get you to accept no."

"Like I said, I rarely listen to women; especially the stubborn kind who don't like to accept help from friends."

She watched in amazement as the man gobbled down two tuna sandwiches. She waited for him to finish the last bite of his second sandwich before she brought up the subject on her mind.

"So how is the job hunting going?"

"Great." Daniel wiped the crumbs from his hands. "Got another bartending job at the Port of Call on Esplanade. It's not far from my place in the Quarter."

"Where do you live in the Quarter?"

"I rent a cottage that was converted from a carriage house. It sits across a courtyard from a house that was split up into apartments. It's small, but it's enough for me."

"I'm glad to hear that you found a job. I was worried you wouldn't find anything."

"I always land on my feet, Pamela."

She gave him a cool going over with her gray eyes. "It's not your feet I worry about."

"You don't need to worry about that, either. It's been better lately. I feel less agitated, I guess. Every time I feel myself getting tense, I remember what holding those baby squirrels feels like. Then I think about this place … and about you."

Pamela nervously cast an eye to her cheese sandwich, avoiding his penetrating gaze.

"Thinking about all of this helps me," he continued. "I've been to shrink after shrink, and none of them have been able to do in six years what you and your animals have accomplished in a few days."

She kept her eyes peeled on her sandwich. "Animals help many people overcome mental and physical problems. Horses and dolphins have been used to connect with children who are autistic. Dogs and cats visit nursing homes and hospitals to comfort the sick and elderly. Animals are trained to help individuals with chronic diseases, physical handicaps, or mental disorders. There is a long list of animals that have been utilized in some sort of program to help all kinds of people. Maybe my animals have helped you."

"Do the animals help you? Is that why you surround yourself with them?"

She put the rest of her sandwich away in a plastic bag. "They help give me something to live for, to get out of bed for."

"Have you ever thought about when you can't do this anymore? I did some research on lupus after Carol told me about your condition. It seemed pretty daunting to me."

"It's only daunting to you. For me, it's just something to live with like a limp or bad teeth. I have no one to hand this place over to if something were to happen. I have no family to speak of, and my biggest fear is that Bob will take over the facility and turn it into an elite petting zoo."

"What about hiring others to run it for you?"

"I don't have the money for that. I would need a nice sized trust fund for the sanctuary to pay a small staff. Most rehab facilities last only as long as the person who founded them. If anything were to happen to me, this place would not survive."

Daniel stretched for his glass of iced tea. "So how do we find the money to make sure your facility keeps going?"

"'We'? Are you sure you want to get involved with all of this? It's nerve-wracking as hell. It drives Carol absolutely insane."

"I can handle it. What do we do?"

"Next Saturday there is that oil spill benefit that I mentioned to Carol. My ex-husband wants me to attend so I can hob-knob with his rich friends and see if I can drum up donations."

"Yes, I remember. I'm in." He gulped back some tea.

"It's black tie."

"I do own a tux, Pamela. I'm a bartender, not a bum." He leaned back and peered into his tea. "I'll pick you up at five. We can go have a nice dinner in the city. After the benefit, I can show you where I live."

She shook her head. "This isn't a date."

"For me it is." He took another long sip of tea.

"Now I'll need to go shopping for something to wear." She cringed and added, "The idea of wasting money on some fancy cocktail dress I'll only wear once is infuriating. I'd rather be spending the money on my animals."

Daniel stood up from the porch. "Fine. I'll take you shopping later on this afternoon and buy you a dress for the benefit. I've got a change of clothes in the car. I can shower here, and we can grab some dinner after. How does that sound?"

"I wasn't asking you to buy me a dress, Daniel. I can afford to buy my own clothes."

"You'll buy something that will cover up your body and make you appear frumpy and unattractive. I'll buy you a dress that will turn heads and have every man at that benefit pulling out his checkbook to win you over." He winked at her. "I know how to dress a woman to look like a woman."

"They teach you that little trick in bartending school?"

"Yeah, in between how to mix daiquiris and martinis." He pulled Pamela to her feet. "Now, go and take care of everybody so we can make an early start of it." He handed her his empty glass and headed down the porch steps.

Pamela could not help but smile as Daniel strode away. For the first time in a long time, she was actually excited about the prospect of shopping.

Chapter 7

"Daniel, I can't wear this."

Her reflection in the department store mirror was disconcerting. The black silk cocktail dress was cut high above the knee and draped over one shoulder. The waist and skirt were fitted, accentuating every curve of Pamela's slim figure. There were tiny silver beads sewn intermittently throughout the fabric, making the dress shimmer in the dull fluorescent light of the store.

"Now that will make any man's mouth water," Daniel remarked, standing behind her at the mirror, grinning. "But we have to do something about the scratches on your arms. You look like you have been attacked by wild animals." He waved his hand over the long red scratch marks on her arms and upper chest.

"One of the drawbacks of rehabbing wild animals, I'm afraid." Pamela looked at him through the department store mirror. Her eyes traveled once more over her reflection and then she turned to him. "I can't wear this. I look like a hooker," she whispered so as not to be heard by the saleswoman standing close by.

Daniel leaned closer to her. "You look like a hot wildlife rehabber."

"But I'm supposed to look like a respectable wildlife rehabber. I run a not-for-profit charity, not a brothel."

"Pamela, when are you going to realize that certain types of men don't want to respect you, they want to sleep with you? And wearing a dress like that is how you're going to trick them into giving you money." He spun her around and started to unzip the top portion of the dress for her. "We'll take it," he proclaimed, nodding to the older saleswoman with silver hair.

Pamela looked down at the price tag hanging from the dress. "It's a fifteen-hundred-dollar dress!" she whispered in horror. "You can't buy this. It's too much money."

"I can afford it."

"How can you afford a fifteen-hundred-dollar dress?"

"I have a trust fund."

Pamela frowned at him in the mirror. "Very funny."

Daniel turned back to the saleswoman. "Now where can we find her some shoes?"

*****

Daniel and Pamela were sitting in his Jeep outside of a drive-through burger place in downtown Folsom, a small town in St. Tammany Parish. Daniel was munching on a fried fish sandwich, and Pamela was eating french fries.

The new dress and a pair of black high-heeled pumps were neatly wrapped in fancy shopping bags in the back seat.

"You shouldn't have spent so much money, Daniel."

"You need to look stunning at that party." He finished the last bite of his sandwich.

"But I feel very guilty that you spent so much." She waved at the bags in the back seat. "That must have cost you two months of tips. I don't know when I will be able to repay you."

"I don't want you to repay me. It's a gift. And I already told you, I have a trust fund."

Pamela almost choked on a french fry. "I thought you were joking. You're serious?"

"I didn't think it was worth mentioning, but you seem so concerned about my finances."

"Are you …." She stopped herself. "I mean, how does a bartender get a trust fund?"

"The trust fund is actually from my mother's estate. My brother, Josh, and I received it after her death many years ago, but my father retains control. He sends Josh and me monthly allowances, but that's about all we get."

"Your mother left you the money in a trust fund?"

"Yes, she wanted us to have money so we could live comfortably but didn't want her family fortune squandered on fast cars and loose women. Her family owned sugar cane farms. They were from New Orleans, and that's one of the reasons I came to the city. She died when I was sixteen, and I thought maybe I could get to know more about her by coming to live in the city where she grew up."

"So you're rich?"

"My mother's family was, but not anymore. All that is left of her family's fortune is what is in the trust fund, which is quite sizable. My father is the wealthy one now. He owns an import company in Bridgeport, Connecticut, where I grew up. He was grooming me to take over the business when I signed up to go to Iraq."

"What about your brother? Does he work with your father?"

"Josh is a plastic surgeon in Boston. He's married to a great woman, and they have twin girls, May and Emily. He was always the brain in the family and wanted to be a doctor for as long as I can remember."

"Are you close with your family?"

"Josh and I talk every now and then, but we were never that close growing up. He's a few years older than me, and once he left for college, I never saw much of him. I haven't spoken to my old man since coming back from Iraq." His eyes appeared distant for a moment. "He thought once I was back everything would be as it was before I left. But I wasn't the same;

none of us were after that war. He tried to understand but never did, so I left Connecticut soon after I returned home and … well, you know the rest.”

Pamela watched the darkness in his eyes fade. “You could have told me earlier about your trust fund. Then I wouldn’t have felt so guilty about your buying all those supplies for my home and my dress.” She shook her head. “Begging for money can be so degrading. People have threatened me, called me a leech, and escorted me out of their homes or businesses when I was trying to solicit funds for my facility. It’s refreshing to meet someone who just gives what he has without asking for something in return.”

“I can’t picture anyone running you out of this benefit next Saturday.” He leaned in closer to her and leered playfully. “Especially, not in that dress.” He motioned to the dress in the back seat. “I’m not as kind as you think, Pamela. Perhaps there is something I want in return for my investment.”

Pamela eased back, and the blush rose on her cheeks. She looked down at the half-eaten container of french fries still sitting in her lap. Her appetite suddenly vanished.

He leaned back in his seat, never taking his eyes off her. “I must admit I find it hard to believe a woman like you isn’t knee deep in men asking for dates.”

“Being out at the facility all day kind of limits my ability to meet people, especially men.”

“If you wanted to meet a man, you could have found a way.”

“What does that mean? If I were desperate enough, I could have picked up some farmhand at the local bar?”

“No, it means you like being alone. Most people, men and women, can’t stand being alone, and they would have gone down to the local bar and picked up some farmhand, as you put it. I don’t know, but I get a sense that you’re afraid of becoming romantically involved with any man.”

Pamela wrapped up the uneaten french fries in a paper napkin, making sure to avoid Daniel’s inquisitive stare. “I’m not afraid of men, if that is what you’re implying.”

Daniel placed his hand beneath her chin. He slowly turned her face to his. “I didn’t say you were afraid of men. It’s more like you’re afraid of what a man might make you feel. Like the way I make you feel when I kiss you.”

Pamela’s heart was thudding away. A tingle of excitement shot up from her.

Daniel traced the outline of her jaw with his fingertip. “I don’t want you to be afraid of me.”

She pushed his hand away. “Perhaps you’re the one who needs to be afraid, Daniel. You haven’t seen me ill and when you do ….” Pamela let the words slip from her lips, instantly regretting them.

Daniel eased away from her. "I don't see illness when I look at you. Your lupus is no different from my PTSD. They're just names in a medical book; they don't define us. I see the real you, Pamela. I will always only see the real you, remember that."

She looked down at her hands and kept her thoughts to herself.

"We'd better go." Daniel started the car. "We've got to get back before all those baby squirrels of yours go hungry."

*****

Daniel parked his Jeep in front of Pamela's little cottage. It was dark, but a waxing quarter moon was rising in the sky, blanketing the trees and surrounding the property with a soft glow. The dogs seemed not the least bit interested in the car and continued to snooze on the front porch.

"I thought you were in good hands with that bunch." Daniel nodded to the five sleeping canines. "Maybe I should install an alarm in this place." He glimpsed the cottage. "I'll worry about you out here alone at night."

Pamela grabbed her shopping bags and climbed out of the car. "I was just as alone and vulnerable before you came along, Daniel. I will be the same way after you have gone."

Daniel cocked his head to the side. "What makes you think I'm leaving?"

"I just don't want you to feel like you're obligated, that's all. Things change, and people move on."

"I'm not Bob, Pamela. I don't run out on people I care about when they need me."

Holding her bags close to her chest, Pamela walked around the front of the Jeep. "Is that what you are doing, Daniel? Hanging around, buying me all of these things because you think I need you?"

"No, that's not what I'm doing." He moved closer to her and rubbed his fingers along her smooth, pale cheek. "You don't have to keep me at a distance because you think I'm going to hightail it out of here as soon as you get sick. I'm not that kind of man."

"That's not the …." Pamela fought back the lump forming in her throat. "I'm not keeping you at a distance." She dashed to the front porch.

"Yes, you are. You keep everyone at a distance. Me, Carol, probably even Bob. The only ones you let in under that thick hide of yours are covered with fur and don't have any expectations."

She turned to him, jutting her chin out defiantly. "Maybe I've been burned once too often by people. Animals are safer to love because they don't lie or let you down."

"You're not the only person who has been hurt, Pamela. You will not be repeating your past mistakes if you allow yourself to open up to someone."

All the dogs on the porch sat up and nervously observed the quarreling humans.

"I suppose you're saying I should open myself to you … and then what?" She felt her anger take control. "Sleep with you so you can get a good return on your investment?"

"Now what a minute," he howled as he bounded up the steps to her side. "Don't you think for one minute that I have done all of this just to sleep with you." He motioned to the bags in her arms.

"No, not all of it," she said, putting a touch of disregard in her voice. "I'm sure there was an element of pity mixed in with your plans." She placed her hand on the doorknob. "Go back to the bar, Daniel. I'm sure there you can find women who are easier to bed and a lot more interested in your selfish acts of philanthropy."

"That's impressive." He ran his hands through his thick hair. "When you push someone away you do it with both hands. Stop trying to sling arrows at me because you don't feel you're worthy of anyone's kindness or regard."

She stood at the door, gaping at him, not sure if she should slap him or sic the dogs on him.

She felt the fight inside of her fade away. Suddenly, she was tired; tired of second-guessing people's true intentions, tired of hiding her hurt emotions, and tired of being disappointed.

"I'm not pushing you away. I just know what you will do in the end, Daniel. It's what everyone has done in my life. They walk away."

He touched his forehead to hers. "I'm not going to do that. Despite what you may think, you and I are a lot alike, Pamela."

"I'm sorry. I'm not good at this stuff. I was never very good at dating."

He wrapped his arm around her shoulders. "No one was ever good at dating. Dating was something you did in high school on weekends and after football games. You were more interested in learning about yourself rather than someone else. At this stage in our lives, I think it would be safe to call what we have a relationship."

"How is a relationship different from dating?"

He removed his arm and took a step back. "Because in a relationship, you already know who you are, and are committed to learning more about someone else."

"Let me guess; you have learned that I'm a repressed, frightened woman who finds animals safer than people, right?"

He held up his hands to her in surrender. "No, we are not going there again. Let's just say I'm still trying to figure you out."

Pamela pulled her keys out of her purse and opened the front door. She then turned to Daniel, who was still standing on the porch behind her. "Aren't you coming in?"

"I think I should head back to the city." He took a step toward her. "I start my new job tomorrow, and they have me on a tight schedule for the next few days until I get to know the bar. So it might be a while before I can get back and do some more work on the place." He kissed her cheek. "But I will definitely be back next Saturday to pick you up for our date."

"Date?"

"The benefit? I plan on making that our first formal date."

"All right, Daniel."

He made his way toward his Jeep in the bright moonlight.

"Take care of my flying squirrel," he shouted from the car. "I expect great things from my little Pamela."

Chapter 8

The next several days seemed to drag on like a boring lecture in a room with no exits. Pamela kept busy taking in four baby opossums, a litter of fox kits, and a few more baby squirrels. But the time absorbed with feeding, cleaning, and caring for the animals did not seem to help her restless mind. No matter the hour in the day, her thoughts would find their way back to Daniel. He would call her cell phone in the afternoons before his shift began at work. They would share a few brief exchanges about the monotony of their days and then he would have to go. The short phone calls only seemed to compound her growing anxiety. And as the night of the benefit drew closer, the more anxious Pamela became.

*****

Pamela was standing in front of her bedroom mirror trying to put the last touches on her makeup. Fed up, she put away her make up and gave her reflection a thorough going over. Satisfied with the results, Pamela stepped back and admired her efforts. Her makeup was subtle but enhanced her creamy white skin and deep gray eyes. The foundation added to the scratches on her arms and chest lessened their appearance. Her shoulder length blonde hair was wrapped up in a French twist that Carol helped her pin. Her dress shimmered in the light of her bedroom as it clung to her figure. Even the high heel of her shoes seemed to add a dash of sexiness to the outfit by accentuating the curve of her slender legs. She patted away the butterflies in her belly and took in a deep breath, then glanced over to her bed and examined her packed overnight bag. Several rationalizations for bringing the bag crept head, but only one reason made sense, and it was the only excuse she feared embracing.

The sound of a car coming down the drive made her stomach twist into knots. She walked to her bedroom window and looked past the tree where Lester was perched to see a black limousine making its way to her front door.

"Oh, no," she whispered as she walked quickly to her bedroom door.

Carol and a tall, redheaded young man were peering out the living room window when Pamela stepped between them.

"Is that what I think it is?"

Carol turned around and gave a low whistle. "You look great."

The lanky man beside Carol turned, and his hazel eyes almost popped out of his head. "Pamela, you look prettier than a blue ribbon at the cattle show," he pronounced in a southern accent.

"Thank you, Ian. I think."

A good bit taller than Carol, Ian's freckled complexion complimented Carol's pale skin. With kind hazel eyes, a long nose, and a dimple in the center of his chin, he was more cute than handsome.

"Looks like your boyfriend went all out." Carol thumbed the window. "He must be a hell of a bartender to be able to shell out for a limo."

"Carol, would you stop calling him my boyfriend?"

"Would you prefer I call him your gigolo?"

Ian giggled as Pamela's eyes tore into the young woman's round face.

A knock on the door made Pamela almost jump out of her skin. She wasn't ready for this. She couldn't answer the door and see Daniel standing there. She stood glued to her spot on the floor, afraid to move.

Carol quickly went to the door and opened it. There standing in the yellow glow of the setting sun was Daniel. He was dressed in a tailored double-breasted tux. His dark hair was neatly sleeked back, and he was carrying a single red rose.

"Aww! He brought you a rose." She turned to Ian. "Look, honey, you should do that."

Daniel walked in the door and handed Carol the rose. "Actually, it's for you. A thank you for taking over for an evening."

Carol took the rose and then elbowed her boyfriend.

Daniel turned and saw Pamela standing behind him.

Pamela's stomach tightened when she saw him in his tuxedo. The smell of his spicy cologne filled the air around her and made her knees go weak. She watched as his dark eyes analyzed the curves of her body. The look on the man's face made every fiber of her being burned with an unfamiliar desire.

Pamela was the first to break the silence in the room. "Daniel, you look very handsome."

"I knew that was the right dress," he murmured to her with a devilish grin.

"I feel like I should break out a Polaroid and snap pictures like it's your first prom," Carol teased.

Pamela glowered at Carol.

"Daniel." Carol shoved Ian in front of him. "This is my boyfriend, Ian Toujaque."

The two men shook hands as Carol beamed with pride.

Daniel hurried to the kitchen table, eagerly surveying the containers on top of it. "Where's my girl?"

Pamela pulled out the container with the flying squirrel in it.

"How is she doing?" he questioned.

"She's still not eating as I would like." Pamela lifted the tiny creature out of the container. "She is too docile and still pretty lethargic, but she seems to be holding her own."

"Any idea what is wrong with her?" he asked, examining the small ball of fur in her hands.

"No. I'm still not sure what we are dealing with, but I will keep an eye on her and let you know if anything changes."

Daniel took the small flying squirrel from Pamela's hands and raised it to his face. He gave the bundle of fur a careful going over.

"A man after your own heart," Carol remarked to Pamela as she watched Daniel place the flyer back in her container.

Pamela nervously eyed Daniel. "You got a limousine for the evening?"

"I only got it to take us to dinner, and then on to the benefit. I figured after, we could walk to my place in the Quarter. It isn't far from the Roosevelt Hotel."

"An evening stroll in the French Quarter, how romantic," Carol cooed and then elbowed Ian again. "How come we never do that?"

Daniel gave Ian a sympathetic smile. He then took Pamela's elbow. "Perhaps we should go before Ian starts getting bruises."

Pamela darted to the kitchen table and picked up her black shawl and purse. She hesitated for a moment as an image of the overnight bag popped into her head. She took a deep breath and decided it might look better to leave the bag on her bed; she did not want it to appear as if she were planning for anything, and definitely did not want to give him any ideas.

"I'm ready," she announced.

They walked toward the long black limousine waiting in the driveway. Daniel opened the back door and waited as Pamela made her way inside the car. Just as Daniel was about to climb in after her, a shout came from the direction of the front door.

"Wait a minute, you forgot something," Carol yelled as she ran to the limousine.

When she reached the back door of the limousine, Carol shoved the overnight bag inside.

"You forgot this," she added, winking at Pamela.

Before Pamela could respond, Carol ran quickly back inside of the house.

Daniel slid in next to her and spied the overnight bag. He said nothing but looked from the bag to Pamela, with the silliest grin on his face.

"I, ah, just packed some casual clothes and a pair of tennis shoes for after the benefit. I thought I could change at your place, and then I would be comfortable on the drive home. I don't want to drive home dressed like this in your Jeep, right?"

Daniel said nothing and continued to grin at her.

"Don't look at me like that. It's nothing. Don't read too much into it. It's just a change of clothes—"

"And a pair of tennis shoes, so you said," he interrupted. He kissed her cheek. "You look wonderful. Don't look so nervous. We are just two people going out for a pleasant evening in the city. What will be, will be."

That was what terrified Pamela. Because with every passing second in his company, she felt her body hoping for one outcome while her mind was clamoring for another.

*****

As Pamela stepped from the limousine and looked up at the gray stone façade of the Roosevelt Hotel, she wondered what awaited her inside. She would have preferred an afternoon of general dentistry to an evening of rubbing elbows with the rich and obnoxious.

The benefit for the Gulf Oil Spill Relief Program was being held in one of the grand ballrooms of the hotel. Pamela gave her name to a young brown-eyed girl seated at a table with a clipboard. She collected the two tickets waiting for her and checked her wrap plus the small overnight bag Daniel carried in from the limousine.

Decorated in shades of gold with Greek Doric columns set against the walls, the multi-tiered crystal chandeliers hanging from the ceiling shone their warm light on the gold and cream-colored carpet. Along the walls, large portraits of wildlife and industries native to the Gulf Coast, and threatened by the oil spill, were hung. To the left of the entrance, a large buffet service was already in full swing with a long line of people waiting to be served. To the right was another long line in front of a bar built to resemble a giant pirogue, complete with crab traps and nets. Dozens of white linen-covered tables were positioned in the middle of the room for the guests to sit and dine. In the back of the room, a ten-piece band played softly in front of a small white dance floor that was cordoned off with gold rope.

Pamela scanned the room and tried to find a friendly face, or at least someone she knew from her days with Bob, but no one among the black-tie crowd appeared familiar.

Daniel examined the throng of people. "What should we do first, casually mingle or go after the first rich looking person we see? You brought your business cards, right?"

She clutched her black beaded purse. "As many as I could shove into this thing."

"Good." He peered eagerly into the crowd. "Now, just follow my lead."

Daniel pulled her along until he stopped beside an older couple. They looked reserved, uptight, and, based on the number of diamonds the woman displayed on her hands and neck, very wealthy.

"Excuse me, but are you, Peter and Esther Robillard?" Daniel asked the couple as he stood before them.

"Why, yes." The older man with a gray beard extended his hand to Daniel. "Have we met?"

"I'm Daniel Phillips of the Arceneaux family from Audubon Trace. My family was in the sugar cane business—"

Esther Robillard's gasp interrupted him. She placed her hand on Daniel's arm. "I went to school with your mother. The last time I saw her was before she married that importer, Edward Phillips, and moved to Connecticut." She clapped a diamond-clad hand to her chest. "My God, you're Elizabeth's boy. I can't believe it."

"I remember my mother mentioning you." Daniel pulled Pamela alongside him. "I'd like to introduce you to a very good friend, Pamela Wells. She runs a wildlife rehabilitation center outside of the city and has worked extensively in rescuing wildlife affected by the oil disaster."

Esther and Peter Robillard shook their heads in unison.

"Such a tragedy," Esther commented. "It's good to know that there are people like you in the world helping the animals. It is a pleasure to meet you, my dear."

"People like Pamela work tirelessly to help rescue all of these wonderful creatures." Daniel's hand waved to the pictures on the wall. "And they get no financial assistance from the state or federal government. Can you believe that?"

Esther placed a caring hand on Pamela's arm. "How do you manage?"

Pamela put on her best fake smile. "I'm dependent on the donations of private citizens to help keep my facility going. I take in over three hundred animals a year. Orphaned and injured wildlife require food, formula, housing, and medical care. I have a non-profit organization that holds fundraisers every year, but I'm a one-woman operation, and it is so difficult in these economic times to get donations."

"Do you have a card?" Peter Robillard inquired.

"Yes, I do." Pamela quickly reached into her handbag, pulled out her card, and handed it to him.

Peter Robillard inspected her card. "I have a few animal-related organizations that I make a part of my annual giving program." He looked up at her with his steely blue eyes. "My accountant is named Steve Mueller with Erickson and Walters. I'm going to give him your information on Monday and have him set you up on our annual donations list."

Pamela's heart did a few happy somersaults. "Thank you. I can't tell you how much this would mean to me and to the animals I help to rehabilitate."

"Thank your young man here." Esther patted Daniel's arm. "You keep up the good work, young lady." Esther gave Pamela a wink. "We need more people like you in the world."

Pamela and Daniel said good-bye to the Robillards and headed back out into the crowd.

"I can't believe it." Pamela sounded almost giddy. "How did you know those people? And how did you know the woman went to school with your mother?"

Daniel smiled at her excitement. "I told you I have done bartending at a few social parties in the past. Well, I've learned to keep my eyes and ears open, and I try to remember everything I hear. Mrs. Esther Robillard is known for wearing her expensive diamond jewelry to every social affair. Her husband loves gin and tonics with a twist. I took a shot, and it paid off."

"But they knew your mother's family?"

"My mother's family was very wealthy and very well connected. An older couple like that was bound to have known or at least heard of them. Everybody knows everybody down here." He searched the room once more. "Ah, I think I found another person you need to meet."

Pamela eagerly surveyed the ballroom. "Who?"

"Val Easterling," Daniel declared. "And this ball of fire, I do know."

Daniel took Pamela's hand and pulled her across the room to the side of a round woman dressed in a burgundy gown with short, silver hair, and light blue eyes. When she spotted Daniel coming her way, she roared with delight.

"Daniel, is that you? Who in the hell let you in here?" She threw her arms around him.

Daniel kissed the woman's smooth, pale cheek and stood back from her. "Val Easterling, I want you to meet someone." He gently pulled Pamela to his side. "Pamela Wells is a very dear friend."

Val's blue eyes seemed to take in every inch of Pamela's figure. "Darlin', I hope you know what you're getting into with this boy. He's a handful."

Pamela grinned. "So I'm beginning to notice."

Daniel hooked a loving arm around Val's waist. "Whenever Val has parties, she always gets me to set up the bar and hire the staff. She throws the best parties in town."

Val waved a dismissive hand in the air. "I throw much better parties than this sorry affair. Lobster and cream cheese rolls for hors d'oeuvres." She frowned. "It's so eighties. You would think with all the money they sunk into this place after the storm they could have hired a better caterer." She glimpsed Daniel's face and then crinkled her brow. "What are you doing here, Daniel? I seem to remember you saying you hated these functions. Don't tell me you have grown a sudden fondness for our local flora and fauna."

"Yes, Val, I'm afraid I have found a soft spot for all the fuzzy little fur balls down here." Daniel smiled at Pamela. "You see, Pamela is a wildlife rehabber and runs a facility outside of the city. She takes in hundreds of animals a year, and she needs money to keep her place going."

Val placed her hand on her wide hip, looking like a cunning businesswoman. "How much are we talking about?"

Pamela's stomach knotted up. "My budget varies from month to month, depending on the animals I take in, vet bills, and the amount of formula—"

"Just give me a bottom line lump sum, dearie," Val said, cutting off Pamela's marketing speech.

"Five hundred a month?" Pamela mumbled, unsure of how the woman would take her offer.

Val's deep chortle matched her boisterous personality. "When asking for money always start out high and bargain your way down. Makes people in this room feel important, or at least that they're in control of the negotiations." She paused. "All right. Give me your card."

Pamela almost dropped her purse she was shaking so much. She fished the card out and handed it to Val.

"If you're a friend of this boy's," Val winked at Daniel, "then you're a good investment. I'll have my accountant call you Monday to set up the details for a monthly deposit. If you ever need more, come to me."

"I don't know how to thank you, Mrs. Easterling."

"Call me, Val; everyone does. I need to get you a few more donations for your facility. There's a man here tonight who does nothing with his money but buy wives and gamble." She looked Pamela up and down, "He has got to meet you. We'll make him shell out some dough to help your animals." She turned and explored the crowd. "There he is. Come with me." Val took Pamela's hand and started pulling her across the ballroom.

Pamela let Val Easterling lead her through the crowds with Daniel following right behind. They stopped before a tall man with dark, wavy hair and penetrating green eyes. He was dressed in a designer tuxedo, holding a tall glass filled with some pink concoction and topped with a pink umbrella. Pamela could not help but notice how the man's eyes traveled over every inch of her petite figure.

"I thought you hated these events. Shouldn't you be out on that fancy sailboat Dallas built you?" Val teased.

"I've been waiting for you to come skinny dipping with me, Valie," the man remarked, giving the woman a friendly peck on the cheek.

"That's like inviting a lion to a barbecue. Untold amounts of suffering would be sure to occur." Val turned to Pamela. "We need to help this woman. She takes care of sick wildlife in a facility outside of the city. She needs your money to keep her facility going."

"Does she need a husband, Valie?" he asked, leering at Pamela. "I'm available."

"Did your Viagra just kick in or something? Behave," Val threatened as she waved to Pamela. "Pamela Wells, meet Lance Beauvoir, of Beauvoir Scrap Metal." Val motioned to Daniel. "This is her boyfriend and my main bartender, Daniel Phillips."

Lance shook Daniel's hand. "I remember you. You do all of Val's parties."

"Yes. I remember you, and your brother as well, Mr. Beauvoir." Daniel turned to Pamela. "The Beauvoir brothers own and operate Beauvoir Scrap Metal."

"Actually, Billy, my brother, runs everything. I'm just for decoration."

"Kind of like those stuffed heads on the walls of a taxidermist's office," Val edged in.

"I wonder if I could do that with ex-wives," Lance contemplated.

"You don't have enough wall space, Lance," Val came back.

Lance gave a mischievous grin. "Wanna bet?"

"Look, Lance, I'm giving Pamela five hundred a month for all of her expenses at her wildlife facility. You want to match me?" Val Easterling quickly challenged.

Lance held up his drink. "Count me in."

Pamela felt as if she were floating on air. "Thank you, Mr. Beauvoir."

"I'll let Valie handle all of the details." Lance took Pamela's hand. "It was a pleasure meeting you, Ms. Wells."

Lance Beauvoir ambled into the crowds and disappeared behind a sea of black tuxedos.

"I know Lance's accountant," Val said beside Pamela. "I'll have him give you a call." She turned and took Pamela's hand. "I'll see you again, Pamela. In the meantime, take good care of my boy." Val Easterling gave Daniel a quick peck on the cheek and turned away.

"Oh, my God!" Pamela all but screamed. "Do you know what that money will mean?" She felt like jumping up and down. "I could add more cages, and fix up the barn the way I always wanted so I could get the babies out of my house. I could even buy a new refrigerator." She put her arms around his neck. "Thank you," she murmured against his cheek.

"I think this joyful turn of events deserves a celebration."

Pamela pulled away. "Celebration?"

Daniel reached for her hand. "Yeah, celebration."

He started leading her across the room. He stopped before the roped-off dance area. The band's playing could barely be heard above the din in the crowded room. Daniel walked around the dance floor until he found an opening between the gold ropes. He pulled Pamela out into the middle of the empty white dance floor.

He put his hand her waist. "I was hoping I would get to do this with you tonight."

She placed her arms around his shoulders as the band began to play a slow jazz tune. "I'm not very good at dancing."

"It's okay. You're in very good hands," he joked with a playful glint in his eye.

Pamela gave in to the rhythm of the sultry beat as Daniel's warmth teased her skin. His arms felt safe, and she was protected from the cares of the world that were hovering just beyond the golden ropes that stood at the end of the dance floor.

"Pamela, is that you?"

Pamela broke away and discovered Bob, standing beside the golden rope at the end of the dance floor. In a tailored black tuxedo, his light brown hair was neatly slicked back, and his pale green eyes were staring right at Pamela. Then Bob's eyes shifted to Daniel and instantly flashed with anger.

Bob hurriedly climbed over the gold rope in front of him and walked up to Daniel's side. "What in the hell are you doing here?"

Pamela's gaze veered from Bob to Daniel. "Bob, this is my date—"

"This is Bob?" Daniel bellowed, cutting her off with his raised voice.

Pamela's brow crinkled. "You know each other?"

"This is the idiot who hit me in the middle of Pat O'Brien's," Bob explained, trying to keep his voice down.

Pamela turned to Daniel. "Wait? You hit Bob? I thought you said you—"

"He's the one who filed charges against me," Daniel whispered.

Pamela turned back to Bob. "Did you start it?"

Bob appeared astonished by the allegation. "Now you think just because of what happened before I go around starting fights with indiscriminate bartenders for fun?" Bob nervously looked around at the other guests gathered on the dance floor.

Clarissa walked up to join them in the middle of the dance floor. She was wearing a form-fitting yellow satin dress with a low neckline and a high slit up the right side. Her dark hair was piled on top of her head, and a matching gold diamond tennis bracelet and necklace glistened in the light. When she stopped right in front of Daniel, it was then that Pamela first noticed her shoes. Yellow and white high heeled sandal creations with yellow straps that went all the way up her ankle. There were even little white butterflies glued on the strap across her toes.

"What's goin' on over here?" she questioned, grabbing Bob's arm. She turned to Daniel standing before her. "Well, hello there." She nodded to

Pamela. "You look really nice. What a cute dress. Did you borrow that or somethin'?"

"It was a gift," Pamela declared as she glanced over at Daniel.

"You bought it for her? Why are you buying her clothes?" Bob demanded, raising his voice.

Clarissa turned back to her husband. "Keep your voice down. You want the whole room to hear you? I thought you said she was bringin' Carol. What's Daniel doin' here?"

"You're Daniel?" Bob exclaimed. "Why have you been hanging around my ex-wife's place?"

Pamela noticed that a few of the guests were beginning to take in their floorshow.

"Perhaps we should take this outside," she suggested to the men.

Daniel was standing next to her taking in large amounts of air through his flaring nostrils. She placed her hand on his arm.

"Don't let him get to you," she whispered to him. "You are better than he is in so many ways."

Daniel's eyes connected with hers. She could instantly see the anger begin to subside. Bob, on the other hand, was red-faced and, minus a ring in his nose looked like a bull ready to charge.

Pamela grasped Daniel's hand and pulled him off the dance floor. "Please, Daniel, not here. Not in front of these people."

Daniel allowed her to lead him across the grand ballroom and out the main entrance. Bob and a stumbling Clarissa were not too far behind. Once safely out of earshot, in the corridor outside the grand ballroom, Bob lunged for Daniel. Used to handling Bob in situations like this, Pamela instantly threw herself in between the two men.

"If you throw the first punch, Bob, I'll testify that you started it out of jealousy over me."

"What is goin' on?" Clarissa griped as she finally caught up to the group. "Bob, why are you goin' after Daniel? So what if he is Pamie's date? She can go out with anyone she likes." She paused and put her hands on her hips. "You're not married to her anymore; you're married to me. It's always about her. I'm always tryin' to keep up with perfect Pamela. Well, I'm your wife now, Bob. Not her," she shouted as she pointed to Pamela.

Bob stormed over to Clarissa. His face was a deep shade of crimson and the muscles in his jaw were quivering beneath his skin.

Pamela felt Daniel's body flex beneath her hands, but Pamela did not let go of him. She knew Bob's angry tirades better than anyone. He was looking for a fight, and she needed to keep Daniel as far away from Bob as possible.

"This man hit me when I was with ...." Bob stopped screaming at his wife. His expression immediately changed, and he cast his eyes down to the floor. "I was out at a bar after work," he began again, sounding calmer than before. "I was entertaining clients when this man jumped out at me and punched me for no reason."

Pamela's eyes swerved from Bob to Daniel. "But, Daniel, you said you hit him because he was roughing up his girlfriend."

"Yes, I did." Daniel lowered his voice so only Pamela could hear him. "The woman he was with wasn't Clarissa."

Pamela instantly realized the implications. Clarissa, however, still appeared confused.

"Bobby, what is she talkin' about? I wasn't with you when this happened," Clarissa asked as she stared into her husband's face. "You just said you were with a client, so why did Pamela say you were—"

"Go back inside, Clarissa," Bob ordered.

"But Bobby."

"Go, now!"

Clarissa jumped at the sound of Bob's blaring voice. She gazed over at Pamela and Daniel.

The hurt in Clarissa's green eyes made Pamela's insides lurch with disgust. She would never have wished such heartless treatment on her or any other woman.

Clarissa put her head down and quickly did as her husband demanded. As fast as her high-heeled butterfly shoes could carry her, Clarissa scurried back to the party.

Pamela waited for Clarissa to enter the ballroom before she confronted her ex-husband. The redness in his face was gone, but his pale green eyes were still filled with an intense hatred. It was a look Pamela was all too familiar with.

"So that's it, Bob. You're having an affair, and Daniel knew about it. That's why you're angry?"

Bob pointed at Daniel. "I didn't know that he was the same guy who has been working for you until tonight. If I'd known, I would have—"

"You would have what?" Pamela demanded. "You would have come to my place and beaten him up? How long has this been going on? How long have you been cheating on Clarissa?"

"That's none of your business," he hissed.

Pamela sank against the wall behind her as she was overwhelmed with a sickening realization.

"Did you cheat on me, Bob?" Her voice peppered with anger. "Did you lie to me just like you are lying to your wife?"

Bob said nothing. He straightened his tuxedo jacket and walked back into the ballroom.

Pamela stood motionless in the corridor. "All this time I thought that at least he never cheated on me. How could I not have seen it? How could I not have known what was going on? All the late nights at the office, the business trips, the dinners with clients. He was lying to me the entire time, and I believed him. I was so stupid."

Daniel put his arm around her shoulders. "You never suspected anything?"

"No, but what really hurts is that I never felt a reason to doubt him. I must have looked like such a fool. Eight years of marriage, and I suddenly realize I never really knew the man. Who in the hell did I marry?"

"Bob is a man who cares for no one but himself. I'm sorry you found out like this." He pulled her into his arms. "If I knew he was going to be here, I would never have come."

She stood back from him. "I thought, for a while there, you two would end up on the floor, trying to kill each other."

Daniel gave her a reassuring smile. "I admit I really wanted to, but then I kept thinking about you. For the first time since Iraq, I was more concerned about someone else than myself. Perhaps I'm finally growing up."

She gently placed her hand next to his cheek. "No, you're finally letting go."

Daniel took her hand. "Let's go home."

Chapter 9

Daniel walked hand in hand with Pamela down Dauphine Street; her overnight bag casually slung over his right shoulder. The stillness surrounding them seemed to ease the frustration coursing through Pamela. The click of her heels against the sidewalk lulled her mind into a hypnotic trance.

As they strolled slowly along, they came upon a small crowd of people standing outside of one of the more opulent houses on Dauphine Street.

"Ghost tours," Daniel offered as he gestured to the group of people.

"Which house is that?" Pamela glanced up at the impressive Greek Revival home with its long rows of romantic cast iron galleries.

"It's the Gardette-Le Pretre House, better known as The Sultan's House." .

Pamela continued to stare at the long balconies. "What happened there?"

Daniel pulled her passed the crowd of people gathered in front of the home's doorway. "All the servants were hacked to pieces. The wealthy resident was found buried alive in the back garden. The murders were never solved."

"Creepy," she proposed, strolling beside him.

"Only about the first ten times you hear it. I must run into those ghost tours at least two nights a week."

Less than half a block later, Daniel stopped in front of a green wooden door. He pulled his keys from his pocket and unlocked it. With one hard shove, he forced the door open and waved Pamela inside.

The darkness of the long alley behind the door was illuminated by a single lightbulb. Daniel pushed the thick door closed with a thud and drove the bolt home. He then took her hand.

"Follow me."

He led her through the dark alley until they stepped out into a vast courtyard. The high walls were made of old red brick and covered with green vines. Along the base of the walls were flowerbeds filled with blooming red, white, and pink azaleas. In the center, a wide three-tiered red brick pond filled the courtyard with the soothing music of cascading water.

He led her past the fountain and to the back of the courtyard where a carriage house stood. In the days when horse and buggy were the only mode of transportation, carriage houses were a vital part of any wealthy French Quarter home. But with the modernization of transportation, carriage homes became apartments. The building was two stories with three sets of french doors situated on the lower floor. Two wide french doors on the second story opened onto a long balcony. The exterior, like most homes in the French Quarter, was plaster, and two gas lamps were positioned on either side of the front door. All around the base of the building was a myriad of potted plants.

"How charming." Pamela pointed to the plants.

"Yes, my landlady does all of the gardening. It's quiet and a haven from the hustle and bustle of the Quarter outside."

Daniel opened the front door to his home and stepped inside. Pamela followed behind and waited as Daniel reached around to the wall and flipped on the lights.

A cozy main living room greeted them, with a smaller dining area off to the left. The centerpiece of the living room was a massive brick fireplace that looked as old as the building. Closed off with cement, a black decorative grate sat in the hearth. A straight, open wooden staircase hugged the far right wall and ascended to a second level. She noticed there was little furniture in the place except for a beige couch, coffee table, television stand, and a desk. On the simple oak desk, a laptop computer and printer were placed next to a small pile of books. She walked over and put her wrap and purse down on the coffee table.

Daniel stepped into the dining room and set her overnight bag on the dining room table. He removed his tuxedo jacket and hung it over one of the dining chairs.

"Do you want something to drink?" He disappeared into a room off to the right of the dining room. Suddenly, a light flashed out through the doorway. "I have wine, orange juice, and some vodka."

Pamela followed the light to a very small kitchen. There was an oven with a four-burner stovetop, next to a medium-sized refrigerator, next to a sink, and everything was built into a compact array of dark green cabinets along the wall. The beige tiled counter top was filled to capacity by a mini-microwave and a coffeepot.

"This is the tiniest kitchen I have ever seen."

Daniel pulled two glasses out of a cabinet high above the sink. "I believe the term you're looking for is efficiency."

"I've read about these," she taunted as he poured two glasses of white wine. "But I never believed they actually existed."

"Then you've never lived in New York. I once rented an efficiency apartment with a bed that folded down from the wall, a hot plate, a miniature refrigerator, and a bathroom smaller than this kitchen with only two outlets in the whole apartment. I would have to unplug appliances to watch television or work on the computer."

She took the glass of wine he offered. "How long did you live in New York?"

"A year. I worked some of the big nightclubs in the city. So I slept most of the day, which was a real feat in New York. It's the noisiest place on Earth."

"After New York?" She took a sip of wine.

He picked up his glass and leaned against the counter. "Oh, let's see. There was Atlanta, Charleston, Chicago, and Miami." He took a sip from his wine.

"Where will you go next?"

"To tell you the truth, I'm done with living out of a suitcase. I want to settle down somewhere, get a dog, hang pictures on the wall."

Pamela peered into her wine. When she looked up again, Daniel was staring at her with the silliest smile on his face.

"What?"

"What if I said I want to stay in New Orleans because of you? Would I be scaring you away?"

"No, but I would think you might be moving a little fast. We hardly know each other and—"

"You either know, or you don't, Pamela. Time won't change how we feel at this moment." He put his glass of wine down on the counter and folded his arms over his chest. "Look, I can't stand here and say I'm not a one-night-stand kind of guy because I've been that kind of guy in the past and one day might be again. But right now with you, I'm not." He took in a deep breath. "Nothing has to happen tonight. We can go as fast, or as slow, as you want."

Pamela put her glass of wine down on the counter. She walked out of the kitchen. At the dining room table, she picked up her overnight bag and slipped it over her shoulder.

Daniel found her standing in the middle of the living room. He nodded in resignation and went over to pick up his keys from the coffee table.

"I'll bring you home."

"But you haven't shown me everything. I would very much like to see the upstairs."

Daniel turned to her, and the disappointment faded from his features. He threw his keys back on the coffee table and took her hand.

The second floor was nothing more than a bedroom with a small bathroom off to the side. There was a king-sized bed that took up nearly the entire room. It was neatly made with a blue comforter and an array of blue and yellow pillows.

Pamela placed the overnight bag on the bed, walked over to the pair of french doors to her left, and opened them. She stepped out on the balcony and took in the view. The sound of the fountain was blended with the dull noise of the city beyond the garden walls. The hint of music mixed with the laughter of people wafted up to the balcony. The cool night air enveloped her bare arms, and her skin tingled with surprise. She reached up and pulled the pins from her hair, letting her golden locks fall freely to her shoulders. She ran her hands through her hair, closed her eyes, and listened to the city.

Daniel's hand pressed on her bare shoulder, and she leaned her head back as his lips teased her skin.

When she looked into his eyes, she lost all her doubts. She hesitantly touched her mouth to his. He threw his arms around her and pulled her to him. Daniel picked her up while kissing her neck. Pamela laughed into his hair as he carried her to the bed. He pushed her back against the cool blue comforter.

"Are you sure?" Daniel murmured into her cheek.

She cupped his cheek. "I've never wanted anyone more than you."

He hungrily kissed her again, and Pamela became lost in his embrace.

Chapter 10

When Daniel turned off the engine of his Jeep in front of Pamela's cottage, the dogs came out to greet them, tails wagging.

"The biscuits must have worked," Daniel speculated as he patted the dogs gathering about his legs.

"They will love anyone who brings them food," Pamela admitted. "They used to attack Bob like crazy until he started bringing them ham bones. Now they greet him as if he is their long lost friend."

"Why didn't you tell me that?"

"Couldn't make it that easy for you, now could I?"

Daniel laughed and took Pamela's hand.

Before they reached the last step, the front door flew open. A panic-stricken Carol came running out the door and grabbed Pamela.

"Thank God, you're back! She started going downhill about an hour ago," she breathlessly cried out as she dragged Pamela inside.

Alarm shot through Pamela. "Who? Who started going bad?"

Pamela and Carol were halfway into the living room when Pamela saw Ian on the couch, clinging to one of the plastic containers on his lap.

"The little flying squirrel," Carol answered.

"She started rollin' around in her container, and now she is just lyin' there. She looks like she is havin' some kind of seizure," Ian reported.

Pamela ran to the couch.

"Is that my flying squirrel?" Daniel demanded, entering the room.

All eyes watched as Pamela took the creature out of her container. She inspected the small face and eyes. Then she felt along the animal's stomach.

"Her belly is tight."

Pamela felt the animal's stomach clench in a hard contraction. She checked between the squirrel's back legs to find that a small pink head was emerging. She immediately replaced the animal back in the container and put the top back on.

She turned to see all of the worried faces staring at her. "It's not a seizure. It's a contraction. Is seems little Pamela is in labor."

Daniel let out a relieved breath. Carol smiled, and Ian looked just as confused as the moment Pamela walked into the house.

"Should we boil water or somethin'?" Ian questioned.

Pamela tried not to laugh. "No, Ian. We will just let her handle everything. She'll know what to do."

Daniel put his arms around Pamela and lifted her off the floor. "So I'm gonna be a grandpa!"

"Looks like somebody had a good time last night," Carol commented.

Daniel chuckled as he put Pamela down.

"Carol, you would not believe how wonderful Daniel was last night at the party," Pamela happily told her.

"Only at the party?" Carol raised her eyebrows teasingly.

Pamela blushed, and her eyes shot to the floor.

"Wow, you rendered her speechless," Carol remarked. "You must be a real animal in bed."

Daniel grinned. "I have my moments."

Pamela punched him in the arm.

"Please tell me there is a videotape," Carol begged.

"Carol!" Pamela yelled.

"And she's back." Carol folded her arms and stared at Pamela. "So how wonderful was he at the party?"

"We have three new monthly patrons, thanks to Daniel. Two of which have committed to five hundred a month."

"A thousand a month!" Carol exclaimed. "That's the same amount Bob gives us now."

"There's an older couple Daniel introduced me to who will have their accountant contact us on Monday to talk about more funding. Can you believe this? We've been struggling for years, and Daniel comes along and in one night does more than you and I could ever have done."

Carol grinned at Daniel. "I, ah, hope she was real grateful."

"I don't kiss and tell, Carol." He took Pamela's hand. "I have to get back to the city. I've got to work this afternoon."

Pamela followed him out the front door.

"I've been thinking about what you said this morning," he stated as they walked down the porch steps.

"I said a lot this morning."

He stopped at his Jeep and glanced back to the dogs resting on the porch. "Maybe I should phone my father and tell him he's a great-grandfather to flying squirrels."

"I think he might like hearing from you."

He wrapped her in his arms. "I'll call you later tonight when I'm on break."

"I'd like that."

He kissed her lips. "Now comes the hard part."

She gave him an awkward glance. "Hard part?"

"I've got to cover the next four days to make up for taking off last night. So I won't be able to get up here for a while."

"I'll be here when you come back. I'm not going anywhere, Daniel."

He kissed her forehead. "Neither am I."

Chapter 11

Over the next four days, the accountants for the Robillards, Val Easterling, and Lance Beauvoir all called with questions and instructions for Pamela. Her small office became inundated with paperwork, and Pamela spent a great deal of time faxing forms back and forth and even taking phone calls from other potential patrons Val Easterling referred to her.

The mother flying squirrel and her three new babies were moved from the kitchen to her bedroom to allow them a quiet place away from the constant phone calls and noise of Pamela's busy office. She tried not to notice that none of the calls on her cell phone were from Daniel. He did not call that first night like he promised, but Pamela was so busy with her animals she never gave the missed phone call much thought. However, five days later, Pamela's worry was eating her alive.

"Maybe he got in a car accident heading home from here and is lying in a hospital bed unconscious," Carol proposed to Pamela as they were feeding animals in the outside cages.

Pamela frowned as she placed a food bowl inside a cage filled with baby skunks. "How on earth do you think up such things?"

"Soap operas," Carol answered with a shrug. "I watch them all the time at my office."

"That would explain a lot."

"Maybe you should just call him," Carol hinted, moving on to the next cage.

"I did call his cell phone, several times. All I got was his voicemail." She hurried to the next cage and opened the door.

Three large opossums scurried to get out of her way.

"Then you should just go to that bar where he works and ask him what is going on," Carol instructed as she filled a large bowl with a mix of dried cat food and chopped vegetables.

"What do I say to him? Ask him why he's blowing me off? Tell him I thought our night together meant something?" Pamela picked up the water bowl.

"Did it mean something to you?"

Pamela said nothing as she took in a deep breath and tried to force back her tears.

"Don't do this. Don't give up on him. I know he cares for you, Pamie. There's got to be a very good explanation for why he hasn't called you."

Pamela felt her resolve strengthening. "Maybe I should go into the city and try to find him."

"Absolutely. Why don't you go today? I've got the whole day off, and I can cover everything here for a couple of hours. You need to get to the bottom of this."

"You're right. I'll go today." Pamela exited the cage and went to the faucet to refill the water bowl.

"It will be fine, Pamie. You'll see."

*****

Two hours later, Pamela stood outside of the entrance to Port of Call. Located on Esplanade Avenue and famous for their pizzas, hamburgers, and a specialty drink called the Monsoon, Port of Call was a familiar hangout for college students across the city.

For a Thursday night, the popular eatery was pretty crowded. She walked into the small dining area and surveyed the tables filled with young diners eagerly munching on their food. To the right of the dimly lit, paneled room, she saw a small bar with a blond-haired, older man standing behind it.

"Excuse me," she called to the bartender to be heard over the mix of conversation and music. "I'm looking for Daniel Phillips. Is he in tonight?"

The older man gave Pamela a stern going over with his blue eyes. "You a friend of his?"

Pamela nodded.

"Well, if you see that ungrateful thug, tell him he's fired. I've had to fill in his last four shifts since he stopped showing up for work three days ago."

"What do you mean he didn't show up for work?" Pamela's heart trembled with worry.

"I mean no one has heard from him since he left here late Monday night. I called his cell phone, but he's not answering. You know I got him this gig, and then he goes and blows it. If you see him, you tell him never to ask me for another favor again."

Pamela really didn't hear anything else the disgruntled man said. She quickly backed away from the bar and raced out the door.

She got back in her white pick-up truck and headed across the Quarter to Dauphine Street. She drove down the street until she found the green door to Daniel's home, then she spent thirty minutes trying to find an empty parking meter.

By the time she arrived at the entrance, the thick green door was no longer closed to the street, but open. She walked through the doorway and down the dark alleyway until she emerged into the bright courtyard. She felt herself almost running to Daniel's carriage house. When she got to the french doors that served as the main entrance to his home, she started knocking on the glass. At first, she softly tapped on the glass, but then her knocking started growing louder and louder.

"Knock any harder on that glass, honey, and you'll break it."

Pamela turned in the direction of the voice to find an older woman wearing blue overalls with a straw hat on her head, gardening gloves on her hands, and a warm smile on her lovely wrinkled face.

"You lookin' for Danny boy?" Her coarse voice belied her sweet grandmotherly looks.

"Yes, I just came from the bar where he worked, and they told me—"

"He's gone, honey," she cut in. "Packed up all his stuff, the day before yesterday. He gave me three months' additional rent and left in that blue Jeep of his."

"Gone?" Pamela's heart sank. "Gone where?"

"He never said, and I never asked." The woman peered down at a potted pink azalea by her feet. She started to pull the weeds at the base of the plant.

Pamela remembered something Daniel mentioned about the potted plants around his carriage house. "You're his landlady."

The woman looked up at her with a bright pair of gray eyes. "Yes, that's me. I own the place. Name's T.J. Powell." She held out her gloved hand.

Pamela shook the woman's dirty glove. "So, he never said anything to you about where he was going, Mrs. Powell?"

"Call me T.J., and nope he never said nothin' except that he had changed his mind. Last week, he said he was goin' to be stayin' on in New Orleans for a while. I figured he had met a girl." She paused and peered into Pamela's face. "Kinda' was hopin' that boy would settle down. I saw the women he had comin' and goin' at all hours of the night around here for a while and then it all stopped." She shrugged. "Until I saw you with him last Saturday."

"You saw us?"

T.J. nodded and pointed back to the main house across the courtyard. "Apartment A is mine. I can see all the happenin's in the courtyard through my windows." She paused for a moment and stared at Pamela. "There was a man here last Sunday. He was a real fancy dresser. He came knockin' on my door askin' where Daniel lived, so I told him. Next, I heard a lot of shoutin' comin' from the courtyard. Daniel and that attorney were having a real—"

"Attorney?" Pamela edged in.

T J. laughed. "Yeah, the guy that has got his face plastered all over town. He's an ambulance chaser; even seen a few of his commercials on television."

"Did this attorney tell you his name?"

"Didn't have to ask him. I recognized him right away. It was Robert Patrick."

*****

The R.A. Patrick Law Firm was located in the P&L building on Poydras Avenue in the Central Business District of the city. Bob moved into his luxury offices right after he and Pamela married. He considered the opulent accommodations a necessity for attracting high-end clientele. As the elevator opened on the twentieth floor of the high-rise office building, Pamela couldn't help but think that Bob was right.

The vast reception area was lined with deep mahogany paneling and decorated with luxurious burgundy leather furniture. The long desk where a perky blonde was seated was also made of mahogany and sat atop a plush gold and burgundy Oriental rug.

Pamela marched right up to the blonde at the front desk and smiled sweetly. "I need to see Bob," she said through gritted teeth.

"It's after office hours, but I'm sure if you would—"

"Tell him it's Pamela," she barked, cutting the girl off.

"I'm sorry but if you would come back tomorrow—"

"Go get him!" Pamela yelled. "He never leaves the office before six."

The girl frowned and tried to look impervious to Pamela's outburst. "I'm sorry ma'am—"

"Tell him it's his ex-wife and that I want to see him right now!"

The girl stood up from her desk. "I'll go and get him." She then disappeared into the entrance to the back offices.

Less than a minute later, Bob emerged from behind the company doors.

"Pamela, I could hear you all the way back in my office. What is it?" Bob came up to her with a worried expression.

"What did you say to him?"

Bob put a concerned hand on her shoulder. "What did I say to who, honey?"

Pamela threw off his hand. "To Daniel. His landlady told me you went to his place and that you argued."

He scanned the empty reception area.

"Pamela, why don't we go back to my office and discuss this."

"No, Bob. Tell me right now. What did you say to Daniel?"

Bob cast his eyes to the Oriental rug. "I wasn't going to mention any of this to you, but I had that man checked out after the party. Fortunately, the private investigator I hired was able to get back to me right away. I went over to his house to confront him about what I found out, and he started threatening me."

"Oh, please, Bob. You expect me to believe that?"

"He's a con artist, Pamela. He has been chased out of several other states for swindling people out of money, property, jewelry, anything he could get his hands on. He uses some phony story about serving as a soldier in Iraq to lure people in and then he tells them that he needs money for surgeries or treatments for his PTSD.”

“You’re lying. He has PTSD. I know the symptoms.”

“His name may not even be Daniel Phillips, Pamela.”

Pamela studied Bob’s pale green eyes. She could never tell when he was lying to her. He was a master at hiding the truth from anyone.

“I don’t believe you,” she declared and wheeled around to the elevator.

“Did he promise to help you get money for your organization? Did he introduce you to some of his rich friends at the party?”

“Yes, but he asked them for money to help me. He never asked for any money for himself.”

Bob walked up to her, shaking his head. “You were his ace in the hole, Pamela. Can’t you see that? He was going to flaunt you around town and get all of the rich society people to shell out money for your little sanctuary. Then he was probably going to organize everything so that the money came to him and not to you.”

“I have spent the past few days on the phone with a slew of accountants. The people he introduced me to are sending me the money, not Daniel.”

“Oh, sure; that’s the way he’ll start out to make it look legit. But then he would have weeded his way into your life and eventually he would have gotten his hands on your bank accounts. I suspect he lulled you into a false sense of security. Did he sleep with you, Pamela, and promise to take care of you?”

She folded her arms but said nothing.

Bob rolled his eyes with disgust. “That’s how these guys operate. First, they get into your pants and then into your checkbook.”

Pamela reached out to slap him, but Bob was too fast for her, and he grabbed her hand. “I know you’re angry, but think about it. If he cared so much for you would he have left town?”

Pamela anxiously searched Bob’s face. She willed herself to believe that this was all a lie. Bob was a manipulative little toad and would do anything to hold on to his control over her.

She yanked her hand away. “So that’s it? You went over to his place to confront him about what this private investigator found.”

“It’s the truth, P.A.,” Bob insisted. “I can give you the investigator’s name if you want to call him.”

“I might just take you up on that, Bob.” She took a deep breath. “Did he tell you where he was going?”

“You don’t want him, Pamela. He was no good.”

“Everyone told me the same thing about you. But I married you anyway.” She headed to the elevator.

“I’m sorry, Pamela. But this guy wasn’t for you.”

She pressed the elevator call button. "That wasn't for you to decide." She turned and glowered at him. "And if you ever go behind my back again, I'll start talking to all of those snooty friends of yours. I'll tell them the truth about you and our marriage."

"I can't believe you would threaten me after everything I have done for you."

The elevator doors opened. Pamela stepped inside and hit the button for the lobby. "Don't ever interfere in my affairs again, Bob, or I will ruin you," she warned, right before the elevator doors closed.

*****

By the time Pamela made it back home, it was well after dark. Carol was waiting patiently on the couch inside watching television when Pamela walked in the door.

Carol jumped up from the couch. "Where is he?"

"He left town a few days ago," Pamela explained. "I ran into his landlady when I went to his place to look for him. She told me he packed up, gave her three months' rent, and never said a word about where he was going."

"That's it?"

Pamela felt her body begin to ache. She rubbed her hand over the back of her neck. "No, that's not everything. She told me about a man who came to see Daniel Sunday evening. An attorney she recognized from television."

"Bob?" Carol questioned, raising her eyebrows. "That sleazeball!"

"That's what I thought, and then I went to Bob's office." She paused as Carol came over to the couch and sat down next to her. "Bob told me he hired a private investigator to check Daniel out. He says Daniel is some kind of con man who was out to use my sanctuary to swindle money out of wealthy, society types. Bob thinks Daniel would have eventually taken the money from our new patrons for himself."

"And you believe him? Bob would make up anything to keep you out of another man's arms. That creep has always been jealous of you."

Pamela waved her hand at Carol. "I know that. Bob has never told the truth about anything as long as I have known him, but he knew things that Daniel disclosed to me. I can't disregard everything he said, but I can't believe it, either."

"What are you going to do?"

Pamela sagged into the couch. "Nothing," she grumbled. "I'm not going to do a thing."

"But Daniel cares about you. If you ask me, he is in love with you as much as you are with him," Carol declared, jumping up from the couch again.

"Carol, he's gone. I don't know where and I'm not about to spend money I do not have to try and find him. If he cared about me, he wouldn't have left. So all I can assume is …." A lump formed in her throat. "All I can assume is that he never really cared for me in the first place."

"None of this makes any sense. There is something else going on here. Something that Bob isn't telling you and until you find out what's going on, Pamie, you'll never be able to let him go."

Pamela forced herself up from the couch. "Whatever it is, Daniel Phillips is not my problem anymore."

Carol went to the desk and picked up her purse. "I don't believe you. That guy got to you, and you're too stubborn to admit it." Carol marched to the front door. "I have a gut feeling we haven't heard the last of that man. And my gut feelings are never wrong." Carol slammed the door behind her.

Pamela headed to the kitchen to make formula for the babies as Carol's final words repeated in her head. Pamela hoped that was the last she heard of Daniel. The sooner she could put her time with him behind her, the sooner she could get on with her life.

Chapter 12

The following morning, Pamela was sitting on her kitchen floor, feeding her baby squirrels. Every bone in her body ached. She had slept little the night before. Her thoughts kept returning to Daniel. She analyzed every word he had spoken, every smile, and every kiss, trying to determine whether or not his affection had actually been genuine. As the sunlight crept into her room at the break of day, she knew she was no closer to figuring out the truth. The sound of a car coming down the drive broke into her concentration.

She heard barking erupt from the driveway. When she stepped outside, she saw two pick-up trucks parked in front of her house. On the door of each truck was a logo of a paintbrush and the name "Al's Painting."

Pamela examined the trucks, wondering how the two men inside had gotten so lost. She waved the dogs back to the porch and approached the trucks.

"Excuse me, ma'am, but we're looking for Second Chance Wildlife Rehabilitation Center. Is this it?" a dark-skinned man inquired from the cab of the first truck.

"Yes, this is Second Chance Wildlife. I'm the owner, Pamela Wells. Can I help you guys?"

The man opened his door and climbed out of the cab. Holding a clipboard against his white overalls, stained with a plethora of colors, he peered up a Pamela.

"I'm Chip Easton, and that there's Miles." He pointed to another man getting out of the second truck. "We're from Al's Painting. We came to complete the exterior painting on your house."

"I don't understand. You came out here to paint my house?"

The man glanced down at his clipboard. "That's what it says here. Prime and paint exterior, paint on site, paid in full."

"Who paid for this?"

Chip pulled his work order from the clipboard. "I don't know, ma'am. I just get the slip with the address and instructions. If you want, you can call the office and ask Karen, our accountant, who paid the bill." He handed her a slip of white paper.

Pamela took the paper and read it over.

"So, ah." Chip eyed the house. "Where's the paint?"

"It's around the side of the house."

Chip tipped his cap to her. "We'll go ahead and get started then." He walked toward the side of the house as Miles followed behind him.

She was climbing the porch steps, reading through the work order again, when Chip poked his head around the corner.

"Ma'am, do you know you got an owl in the tree over here?"

"That's Lester. He won't hurt you."

"All righty then," Chip returned with a nod of his head.

Pamela was struck by the memory of Daniel, frozen to the ladder next to her house, afraid Lester would attack him. She thought back to his reaction and how the sweat had poured from his body. How his hands shook as he took the glass of water she had offered him.

"You can't fake things like that."

She rushed in her door, grabbed her cell phone, and dialed the paint company's office number that was printed at the top of the work order.

"Al's Paintin'," a woman's raspy voice answered after the second ring.

"Ah, yes, this is Pamela Wells at the Second Chance Wildlife Rehabilitation Center in Folsom. Two of your workers just showed up here to finish painting my house, and I was wondering if I could find out who paid for this work to be done. I mean I didn't hire the men."

"Yes, ma'am, I understand. Kind of a weird request anyway, if you ask me. Most people have us come out and get an estimate. This guy just called up, told us where to go, and paid over the phone by credit card for the entire job. No payment plan, no pay half now, half at the end. Just paid up front for the whole thing, no questions asked."

"Who paid?"

"I got the slip right here." Pamela heard her shuffling some papers around. "Daniel Phillips was the name on the credit card."

"Did he happen to say where he was or leave a phone number?"

"No, Ms. Wells, he never said nothin' else to me. I only got a business address from the man. A Phillips Exotic Imports in Bridgeport, Connecticut."

Stunned, Pamela looked down at her cell phone.

"Can I do anything else for you, Ms. Wells?"

"No," Pamela answered, coming out of her stupor. "Thank you. You've been a great help."

As she hung up with the painting company, someone knocked on Pamela's door.

When she opened it, Chip was standing there, paintbrush in hand. "Does this belong to you?" He glanced down at his leg.

There, clinging to his leg, was Rodney, the raccoon.

Pamela pried the raccoon's legs from around Chip's calf. She picked Rodney up in her arms. "He's very friendly."

"So I noticed. I had a pet raccoon as a kid. They don't bother me."

"I'll get him something to eat and then he should leave you guys alone."

Chip nodded as Pamela shut the front door.

She set a bowl of cereal on the floor in the kitchen and watched as Rodney sat down next to the bowl. He delicately picked up each and every piece of the sweet puffed corn and placed it in his mouth. After finishing he proceeded to tip the bowl over and push it around on the kitchen floor like a hockey puck.

"I thought we got rid of that one." Carol strolled in the front door, carrying two tall Starbucks cups in her hands. "You said you were going to stop feeding him."

Rodney made a hasty retreat out the open front door before it shut.

"He started molesting one of the painters, so I had to feed him. Otherwise, he'll never leave them alone."

"I know you're all gung ho about getting that extra money, but don't you think you should consult with me before hiring painters?" Carol plopped the cups on the counter next to the sink.

"It's wasn't me." Pamela picked up Rodney's empty bowl from the floor and carried it to the sink. "Daniel sent the painters."

Carol clapped her hands and shouted with glee. "I was right!"

"I called the company, and they told me it had been paid by one Daniel Phillips."

"See, he does care about you. Why would he go to such trouble to hire painters to come out and finish the job he started if he didn't care about you?"

"I wouldn't say he cared. I think he felt guilty. That's why he hired the painters."

"Guilt is good," Carol added with a nod of her head. "Guilt implies an emotional connection, and that means he can't be a con man like Bob is asserting. If he were, he wouldn't be shelling out money to fix up your house."

"I've been thinking about that." Pamela leaned her hip against the counter. "There are a lot of things Daniel said and did that make me suspicious of Bob's story."

Carol picked up her Starbucks cup from the counter. "So, are we going to do anything about it?"

"No." Pamela turned her attention back to the sink. "It's over, Carol. I was up all night wondering why he didn't come to me and tell me about his altercation with Bob, or why he felt he had to leave. I can't spend the rest of my life wondering, so the only way to get on with my life is to forget about Daniel."

"Can you really toss people out of your life that easily, Pamie? He's not some random guy. You had feelings for him. You opened up to him. You just don't delete someone like Daniel off your hard drive with a press of a button."

"It's simply a question of making myself forget about him," Pamela argued. "I can choose to forget by never allowing myself to remember."

Carol snickered. "Let me know how that works out for you, because if you ask my opinion, you're an idiot."

*****

But it wasn't that easy for Pamela to forget about Daniel. Over the course of the next three weeks, more workers showed up on her doorstep. An electrician came to the facility to wire new outdoor lights for the cages, barn, and back porch of Pamela's home. A plumber showed up to add new faucets to the four new outdoor cages that the carpenter had been hired to build. A construction crew came in and built walls, installed sheetrock, and added a new air conditioner and heating system in the barn. An appliance company delivered two new refrigerators for Pamela to place in the finished barn. Even an alarm company and a locksmith showed up to improve security in, and around, Pamela's home.

With every newly hired worker who showed up on the property, Carol would give Pamela a roll of her eyes and walk away. By the time the workmen had finished, the place was better than Pamela had ever dreamed possible. With the new cages and amenities, Pamela could take in even more animals than before.

She was exhilarated and at the same time devastated. She wanted someone with whom she could share her newfound fortune, someone to plan with and someone to partake in her joy. But at the end of the day, she only had Louis to share her thoughts with; Louis and the flying squirrel with her three babies. She decided not to relocate the mother flyer and her babies to the barn. She wanted to hold on to something of Daniel's; something he cared about and, she hoped, not forgotten.

Chapter 13

It was a few days after the last of the workmen had finally left when Bob arrived. His silver Mercedes pulled up in front of the house as Pamela watched from outside the renovated barn.

As Pamela approached Bob's car, she watched as Rodney scurried out from underneath the house and ran to her side. When she went up to greet Bob, Rodney decided to tag along.

His venomous words from their previous encounter were still ringing in her ears, and she fought to maintain her calm.

"What are you doing here, Bob?"

Bob removed his expensive sunglasses and inspected the facility. "You've been having a lot of work done around here. I guess this is because of all your new patrons, huh? I heard that Val Easterling and Lance Beauvoir have been singing your praises all over town. It must feel pretty good to have all those high-class connections."

"The renovations were made by one sponsor. Daniel hired all of the workers to fix up the place. Not something one would expect of a con man out to use me to swindle rich people, is it, Bob?"

"I know you're mad at me, and you were right, I did interfere in your affairs, but I wanted to come out and tell you that I'm sorry. I was hoping you would let me explain about what happened with Daniel and me."

She examined his pensive face, debating her next move. "All right, I'm listening."

"I did have Daniel investigated, and he does have a past, Pamela, there's no denying that. But he has only had one previous arrest for assault and those charges were eventually dropped. Apparently, the man does have some issues."

"He's not the only one," she snarled. "So why lie to me? Why hurt me like that?"

"I was jealous. Can you blame me? You know I have always cared about you and to see you with that guy dancing … well, I just couldn't take it."

"What about the incident in the bar?"

"A misunderstanding. He thought I was pushing Kay around but—"

"Kay?" she interrupted.

"My receptionist. You met her that day you came to the office."

Pamela snickered as she thought of the perky blonde she had seen at his office. "She's a little young for you, Bob."

Bob lowered his gaze. "We were having a drink after work. We got a little hammered and got into an argument. Daniel jumped in and then he hit me."

"What was the argument about?"

He shook his head. "You don't want to know."

"But I can guess. She wants you to leave Clarissa, right?"

Bob said nothing, but Pamela had already figured it all out.

"What really happened the night you went to his place?" Pamela interrogated, still leery of her ex-husband's intentions.

"I got his address from the police report filed after I pressed assault charges against him. I went over to his place and told him to stay away from you. I threatened him and said I would take away your facility if he ever went back to you again. Said I would pull out on the mortgage and cause you to default on the loan. Then the bank would be forced to repossess the property. I told him if he cared about you, he wouldn't want you to lose everything." He gave her a weak smile. "I wanted to protect you. I thought I was doing the right thing."

"So why are you telling me all of this now?" she probed, more than a little confused by his confessions.

"Clarissa left me right after the party," he mumbled, twisting away from her. "She wanted me to end my relationship with Kay, but I refused. It hadn't been working out between Clarissa and me. She was always jealous of you. Every time I would bring up your name she'd go ballistic, but after the party, she changed. She told me when she was packing her bags that she thought you were a better person than me. She said she had been wrong about you."

"I still don't understand, Bob. Why are you here?"

His eyes explored her face. "I want us to start over, Pamela. I never really stopped loving you, I just got distracted."

"Distracted?" Pamela tried not to laugh. "You've got to be kidding me. Why? Because you saw me with another man, and finally realized I don't need you anymore? Is that why you want me back Bob?"

"Pamela, don't do this." His voice instantly filled with anger. "Don't make me beg you to come back to me."

"You don't need to beg, Bob. The answer is no. I don't want you back now or ever. Do you think I could go back to a selfish snake who ran around on me and then dumped me when I needed him most?"

"You still need me. My name is on the mortgage to this property and all it would take is one call to the bank to shut your facility down."

She took a step back. Her stomach recoiled at the sight of the man. "What are you saying, if I don't go back to you, you'll take away my home?"

He put his sunglasses on, smirking at her. "Think about it, P.A.," he said, his voice suddenly cheerful. "I can give you what you want, and you can give me what I want."

"I'm still sick, Bob. What do you want me around for? Sympathy?"

"I need a wife who will look good and keep quiet. I don't need another Clarissa in my life. I can't take a chance on ending up with a woman who stands out in a crowd and embarrasses me with her stupidity and tantrums. I need people to see me with a refined and educated woman. You always made me look good."

She closed her eyes and tried to calm the flood of revulsion surging in her veins. "If I don't agree?"

"I tell the bank to remove me from your loan, and all of this," he waved his hand at her house, "will disappear." He kissed her cheek.

Pamela reflexively curled her hands into fists but did nothing.

Bob returned to his car. "Don't take too long to think about it. I'd like to put out the word that we're getting back together before Clarissa files for divorce," he added over his shoulder.

Pamela watched as Bob's silver Mercedes headed down her gravel drive. She felt sick to her stomach at the prospect of becoming Bob's trophy wife.

She was steadying herself against the house when Carol's green Nissan Sentra made its way down the drive.

When Carol saw Pamela, she ran from her car to her friend's side.

"Are you all right?" Carol asked, sounding slightly panicked.

Pamela pushed herself away from the house and stood up straight. "I'm fine. I just felt sick all of a sudden."

"Would this be the result of Bob's visit? I saw his fancy car pulling onto the road when I turned into the drive."

Pamela went to the porch steps and sat down. "Bob came over to tell me that he and Clarissa have split up."

"And that made you sick?"

"No." She paused and wiped her hand over her mouth. "Bob told me he wants me back."

Carol frowned. "Now that would make me sick."

"He said if I didn't come back he would call the bank and have his name removed from my mortgage."

"Then the bank would call the loan. What a dirtbag!" She stared at Pamela. "So what did you say?"

"No, of course! What did you think I would say?"

"I was just checking. That man has always had a strange hold on you."

"Well, not anymore!"

Carol stood by as the color returned to Pamela's face. "We're going to have to find some way to get Bob's name off that mortgage."

"I could apply to refinance," Pamela said, thinking out loud.

"You have no sustainable income. Annual donations are not income, and you have no assets to speak of. With this economy, banks are making getting loans very tough. You wouldn't stand a prayer."

Pamela placed her head in her hands. "I've got to find some way of making a lot of money quickly so I can rid myself of Bob permanently."

"What's the rush?"

Pamela gazed up at Carol. "Bob didn't exactly take no for an answer. Either I agree to go back to him, or he will shut Second Chance Wildlife Rehabilitation Center down."

Carol became alarmed. "All right, then we need to go to the bank and talk to them."

"I will go to the bank." She patted Carol's knee. "This isn't your fight."

"Yes, it is." Carol stood over her. "Why do you always insist on fighting alone? Let me help you."

Pamela stood from the steps and gave her friend a weary smile. "Allowing someone to help me is what got me into this mess."

"Daniel cares about you. Don't give up on him, Pamie."

"He's gone, Carol." Pamela headed for her front door. "He's never coming back."

*****

Early the next morning, Pamela was driving her old white Ford pickup into New Orleans to meet with her banker.

Carol had offered to find another way to save the sanctuary, but Pamela could not ask her to do that. She loved Carol and did not want to see her worry. She feared what Carol would do when confronted with the possibility of losing their little paradise. Pamela wanted to spare her from the pain of dealing with that blow, for as long as possible.

The main branch of the Gulf States Bank and Trust was located in Downtown New Orleans in a gleaming gray building on Poydras Street.

Entering the sleek glass doors, Pamela's stomach churned. The call she made to her banker the previous day was not hopeful, but he was willing to meet with her to discuss the situation. She just hoped some sort of resolution could be reached.

Stepping inside, the din of voices carried through the arched recesses and high ceiling of the modern chrome and glass lobby.

Veering to the right, Pamela came to a stop at a large desk situated right outside a maze of cubicles.

"Can I help you?" a waifish brunette with too much eyeliner inquired.

"Jacob Hart. I have an appointment. Pamela Wells."

The brunette typed something into her computer and then smiled for Pamela. "I will take you to him. " She stood from her desk. "This way."

Pamela was shown through a meandering corridor of cubicles until she came to stop in front of an office door to the side.

When the door opened, a slender man with a receding head of gray hair, smiled warmly. His frumpy black suit, blue shirt, and gray tie hung from his frame adding to the frazzled look in his small brown eyes. Pamela always thought her banker resembled someone who should be teaching schoolchildren rather than handling currency.

"Hello, Pamela," Jacob greeted as she walked into the large office.

"Thanks for seeing me on such short notice." She went to his chrome and faux wood desk. "But I really need your help."

Jacob solemnly closed the door, his mouth pressed in a pensive smile. "I know. I have to admit I wasn't surprised by your phone call." He went to his desk and had a seat. "Bob called me some time ago and warned me thing might come to this."

Pamela was taken aback. "What do you mean he warned you I would be coming?"

Folding his hands on the desk, he retained a casual but determined demeanor. "Bob told me you were in financial straits and would probably come asking for a loan. He told me your little wildlife sanctuary had fallen on tough times. He even offered to foot the bill on the loan for a while, but said you two had some differences to work out."

Pamela slowly sank into one of the chairs in front of his desk, her hands clutching her leather purse. "When exactly did he tell you these things, Jacob?"

Jacob glanced up at the ceiling. "A few weeks ago. He said you two had discussed the situation at a party."

The party. Of course, Bob would jump at the chance to use the incident from the party to his advantage.

Jacobs gaze narrowed on her. "Normally, I wouldn't listen to anything your ex-husband would say, considering you are my client and not him. But his name is on your loan, Pamela, and he has a lot of friends at this bank. Powerful friends." He patted a hand on his desk. "I tried to tell you on the phone that there is little or nothing I can do. Bob is on your loan, and with your income there is no way you can get another one without his assets."

Pamela was not deterred. "We can try, Jacob. I have other friends, other benefactors who might be willing to sign—"

He held up his hands. "You are not hearing me. Bob has made it so no one at this bank will give you the assistance you need. Bob's influence here goes way beyond anything I can interfere with."

Pamela was dumbfounded. "So you're saying he threatened you."

Jacob shook his head, wincing at her words. "Not threatened, just hinted that he could make things impossible for me here. He knows a lot of people in this city, Pamela. You are well aware of that. You were married to the man."

Pamela sagged into her chair, "I know the circles the frequents, Jacob."

"Then understand my position. My hands are tied." He sat back in his chair. "I could recommend you go to another institution and get a loan, but who's to say he won't interfere there as well." He tapped his fingers on the arm of his chair. "I don't know what to tell you, Pamela. Bob knows everyone in this town, and your chance of finding another bank he can't set his hooks into is slim at best."

"Then what do I do?" she muttered.

Jacob leaned forward in his chair, an encouraging smile on his lips. "Work some kind of arrangement out with the man. You were married to him for eight years; surely, there is some common ground you two can find." His smile widened. "Then you can keep your little sanctuary, and Bob will be appeased." He stood from his desk. "I'm sure whatever differences you two are having can be quickly alleviated."

Summarily dismissed from her banker's office like a truant teenager from the principal's office, Pamela stood outside the towering gray stone of the bank building feeling as if her entire world was crumbling.

Still clutching her purse, she glanced down Poydras street to the array of high rises that dotted the landscape. When her eyes settled on the P&L Building, a blind fury ravaged her senses.

He had put her in a stranglehold from which there seemed little chance of escape. She either gave in to Bob's demands and saved her only source of happiness, or she would be penniless and out on the street.

The faces of the animals she had rescued danced before her eyes, and then another face came into focus, a human face.

"What difference does it make who I end up," she pondered, gazing up at the cloudy sky. "My animals are all that matter and if I have to ...." She dreaded the thought.

Could she go back to Bob after everything she had learned?

Slowly the resolve she had spent years cultivating since her divorce vanished like a puff of smoke. What choice did she have? It was her sanctuary or nothing. Her animals were worth the sacrifice because they were the only ones who had been there for her no matter what.

It seemed the time had come to meet her fate. It was not the one she envisioned for herself, but it was the only one that allowed her to keep her dream alive.

*****

Fifteen minutes later, Pamela was in an elevator climbing to the twentieth floor of the P&L building. As her head swarmed with scenarios, Pamela knew the rest of her life had been irrevocably changed.

"I'd like to see Robert Patrick, please," Pamela said to a very young, redheaded girl seated behind the desk in Bob's reception area.

"Your name please, hon?"

"Tell him Pamela is here."

The redhead smirked. "Ya' gotta' last name, sweetheart?"

"Just tell him, Pamela. He's expecting me."

Less than two minutes later, Bob appeared, bounding through the main doors that led to the attorney's private offices. His face filled with apprehension. "What is it?"

She dashed up to him. "We need to talk."

Bob turned back to the girl at the front desk. "Maureen, tell Edna to hold all of my calls," he directed and placed his arm around Pamela's waist.

He showed her through the main doors and down the hall to his expansive office. Once Pamela stepped into the room, a fleck of disappointment that the lovely shades of yellow and white she had painstakingly decorated his office in had been replaced by bold brown and taupe tones. She took in the pictures and assorted comic book memorabilia on the walls. An avid collector of comic books since his grade school days, Bob had mounted and framed many of his prized pieces for display in his office. The plain square walnut desk and dark brown chairs standing in front of it sharply contrasted with the colorful comic books hanging on the walls. It reminded Pamela of Bob in a way, a cold businessman on the outside and a selfish child on the inside.

Bob saw her taking in the décor as he shut the door. "Clarissa redecorated my office soon after we got married," he explained. "The comic books I just recently added to get rid of her paintings of horses. She has a thing for horses. Even had them painted all over the walls of our dining room." He walked across the room to her side. "I felt like I was in a bad Western movie every time we had to eat in that room." He took her hand. "You're shaking. What is it, Pamela?"

Pamela swallowed her pride. "Does your offer still stand?"

Bob gave a slow, victorious smile. "You went to the bank." He strode to his desk and rested his hip against the dark wood. "Yes, my offer still stands. Marry me and I will take care of your little sanctuary forever. I will let you live your life as long as you let me live mine. We will be seen at parties together and will present a happy home front. I need a wife who is intelligent and can improve my social standing. I have political aspirations and Clarissa was a bit of a liability."

"All right. I'll agree to marry you, but I have conditions."

Bob clapped his hands triumphantly. "Whatever you want, it's yours."

"If I marry you, I get the sanctuary free and clear. You will pay off the mortgage and introduce me to more sponsors so I can keep it going. In addition, I want a trust set up for the sanctuary, a trust you will pay for. The amount is to be determined by me. In case anything happens to me, I need to know my rehabilitation center will go on."

"I'll put whatever money away for your furry creatures. Anything else?"

"You will not debate me on the time I spend at the facility, and you will not interfere in my life there. I will make the decisions for my rehab center, not you."

Bob reflected for a moment. "Fine. But you can't spend all your time at your facility, Pamela. I know you, and we will have to work out some kind of schedule."

"I am open to that. I will have to insist at least half my time be allotted to the facility. If you agree, I will tell everyone we are sharing our time between two homes."

"The doting husband supporting his wife's noble hobby." He clapped his hands. "This actually might turn out better than I had hoped."

"What are you talking about?"

He glanced back at her. "I've been debating about getting into politics, running for local office. Our getting back together couldn't come at a more perfect time. You're the wife I need by my side on an election platform. That you help wild animals will only make me look better to voters."

Pamela stood as stiff as a board in front of him. Her life was falling apart, and there was nothing she could do to save it. She fought to keep the tears from her eyes. She could never let Bob see how much this was ripping her apart.

"If you spend half your time with me, you will need help taking care of the wildlife," Bob tossed out.

She gave a curt nod. "If you agree, I'll need money to hire someone to oversee the place."

"I'll foot the bill for whatever you need," he agreed, coming toward her. "In the meantime, get things settled at the facility, and then you'll have to come and live with me. I'll get you an engagement ring before you move in to make it look good."

"I don't need—"

"We need to make this look convincing, Pamela," Bob interrupted. "Just leave all of the arrangements to me," he insisted with a snaky smile.

She bit down on her lower lip, trying with all her might not to break down.

"This must be killing you," he commented. "I know just how much you want to tell me to shove this deal, but you can't now, can you?"

She went to the office door "No matter how much it hurts to ask, I'm going to need your help to keep my facility going. I have no one else to turn to, Bob. My feelings aren't important anymore." She reached for the door handle.

"I have to know. Did you love him?"

Pamela wiped away a tear. She had never used that word before to describe her feelings for Daniel, and hearing them coming from the man she just sold her soul to made her feel lower than dirt.

She faced Bob, keeping her head held high. "Never mention him to me again, Bob. You keep your secrets, and I'll keep mine." She opened the door and quickly marched out of his office.

Chapter 14

On a breezy afternoon, Bob showed up on her doorstep, carrying a shopping bag filled to the brim with swatches of decorative wallpaper, fabric, and paint samples.

"I've been on the phone with my decorator for the past two days," he chirped as he set the bag on her coffee table. "I got several selections for you to start going through." He picked up the different colored fabric swatches and held them out to her. "I've called Linda, my decorator. She sent over these swatches for you to choose from for the house. I told her we are redoing the entire house according to your specifications. I want it to be your home, too. So do whatever you want. Spare no expense."

Pamela's eyes grew wide with surprise. "You want me to redecorate your home?"

"I thought it might be something we should do together. You like decorating before; maybe this will help ease the adjustment." He went to the bag and pulled out a long swatch of pale yellow, silky fabric. "What do you think? I saw this and thought of you. We can use it as a starting point. Refashion the house around it. I want the place to remind me of you."

Pamela stared at Bob for several seconds before she regained her composure. "I—I can't believe this. It's almost as if you're excited about this arrangement."

He smiled, beaming with pride. "I am. I never thought I would be, but after you'd left the other day, I began to think about you and me, and suddenly, I was happy. I got you back. That's all I ever wanted."

A shudder passed through her. That Bob was seeing her as some prize he had won, only added to the hardship of her burden. At least she knew her sanctuary would always be cared for, no matter what happened to her.

He reached into his trouser pocket and pulled out a small blue velvet box. "I got this today. I want to make it official as soon as possible."

Pamela took the box from his hand and opened it. Inside was a very large emerald cut diamond solitaire set in gold and surrounded on either side by two smaller similarly cut green emeralds. Pamela's heart fell to her knees when she saw the ring. She recalled the first time Bob had given her an engagement ring and how excited she had been. This time, the emotions that clouded her mind were not happy ones. Instead, she felt a numbing chill permeate her body. The cold winter of reality settled over her like an impenetrable fog. Resigning herself to her fate, Pamela took the ring from the box and placed it on the third finger of her left hand.

"I remembered your size." Bob admired the ring. "You always loved emeralds."

Like a building snow drift covering the last red rose of fall, Pamela felt her doubt being forever silenced by the steady assurance that her animals would be saved.

*****

"You have got to be kidding me!"

Carol was standing in the middle of Pamela's renovated barn, glaring at the engagement ring. Pamela had kept the ring in its blue box tucked away in her dresser drawer for the past two weeks. But as the deadline for leaving her little sanctuary for Bob's sprawling mansion loomed, she knew that, eventually, she would have to break the news to Carol. Today seemed like the right day.

"Bob? The snake Bob! You're gonna marry that sleazeball again?"

"Maybe you shouldn't call him that," Pamela suggested as she pulled her hand away from Carol.

"I don't understand. Why are you doing this? So what if Imelda packed up all her shoes and left him. You told me before that you turned him down, and now you're going to marry him? You don't have to marry him just to save this wildlife facility," Carol challenged. "We can still find the money to get Bob off the note. I can sell my place and move in here with you, that way you could take the money and pay off—"

Pamela silenced her with a wave of her hand. "I could never allow you to do that. I told you before I'll never make this place your burden. Besides, that house was left to you by your mother when she died, and I loved both your parents way too much to even consider having you do that."

"Oh, but you can go off and marry a man you detest to save your sanctuary," Carol balked. "Do you think I can honestly stand by and let you give yourself to that … that … snake?"

Pamela sighed and placed a tender hand upon Carol's shoulder. "It's not about saving this place, Carol. There are other things I need to consider now."

"What other things?"

Pamela admired the freshly painted white walls of her renovated barn. "My health for one. I can't go on running this facility on my own, and I need to make sure there will be someone to take over for me should the day come when I can't, or won't, be here to run it."

Carol came up alongside her. "But you've always said you never wanted to have Bob get control of this place. You told me you were afraid of what he would turn it into."

"I know, and he and I discussed it, and we're going to draw up papers to protect—"

"You're lying," Carol loudly maintained with a smirk. "You would never just settle with Bob over this. You're a fighter, Pamie. You've been fighting for years. Why suddenly give up now?"

"Maybe I'm tired of fighting, I'm sick, Carol. I have to face the reality of my situation. We both do."

Carol stared Pamela down. "I know. But your lupus was never a factor before."

"It is now."

Carol's eyes breezed up and down Pamela's figure. "What about Daniel? If he knew you were selling yourself to Bob, he would—"

"What? Come back?" Pamela's snort of contempt filled the air. "He didn't leave any forwarding information with any of the companies he hired. I never got a note, a text, e-mail, or even a phone call. He's gone, and I have to accept it." She gestured at Carol. "And so do you."

"You don't need to live with Bob to save this place," Carol pointed out. "We can find him. I could hire someone to track him down. I think he would want to know about what you're sacrificing, Pamie."

Pamela searched the grounds of her facility. "Perhaps it's for the best. I don't know what kind of chance we would have had. Daniel is a runner. The responsibility of a relationship would probably have scared him back on the road."

"Wondering 'what if' is worse than knowing for certain, Pamie. If Daniel knew what you were doing, he would be right by your side."

"And when I get sick? Then what?"

Carol shook her head. "He would have stayed until death do you part."

Pamela gazed up at the blue sky. "But we would not have ended there, Carol. I need to know that if something were to happen to me, someone will be there and be committed to caring for the part of me I leave behind."

Carol's brow furrowed with dismay. "You think Bob is a better man for that job than Daniel? Are you insane?"

"Bob is here, Carol," Pamela coolly stated. "Where's Daniel?"

*****

She was on edge as her white Ford pickup maneuvered the pothole-laden streets of uptown New Orleans, on her way to Bob's home. The last few interviews left her doubting she could ever find anyone to run her facility. All the candidates were too young, too inexperienced, too ignorant, or just did not have the right personality to work with wild animals. Bob told her she was being too picky and felt anyone with a clear face and a high school education could do what she did.

As she turned into Bob's driveway, she could feel her stress mounting. Her hands tightly gripped the steering wheel, and when she finally let go, her fingers were stiff. She tried to convince herself it was just her emotions running in overdrive. There was just so much to do with maintaining the facility and preparing for the move, it was wearing her down. As she got out of her beat-up truck, feeling more like a maid than a mistress of the mansion, she knew what the real problem was. Her only concern was how long she would be able to continue like this without erupting.

"Hey," Bob said as he opened the front door. "I thought I heard your piece of junk pulling into the driveway." He spied the dingy white Ford pickup parked on his lavish red brick driveway. "Next thing on the list is to get you a new car. Can't have you pulling up in that thing. What will the neighbors think? After all, you're my fiancée, not the gardener."

The house was one of the larger mansions on the block and was a classic representation of Greek Revival architecture seen throughout the older parts of the city. Four white Corinthian columns rose from the first to the third floor while a double stained-glass front door beckoned. Balconies located outside the french doors on the second and third floors added a touch of Southern elegance to the structure.

Pamela gazed at the white rocking chairs located on either side of the front porch and yearned to rest her tired body.

"You look terrible." Bob was standing in the front doorway, staring at her. "You look like you're not sleeping enough."

Sleep was becoming something of a challenge ever since making her arrangement with Bob. Pamela wished she could blame her insomnia on her lupus, but it was her mind, rather than her body, keeping her awake at night.

"I've been staying up a lot with sick animals," she lied.

"I'm glad you're getting help then. Your lupus will flare up if you don't get enough sleep, Pamela. You know that." He reached into his pocket and pulled out a key. "This is for you. It's only for the front door, but I'll get copies of the back door made, and remind me before you leave to show you how the alarm works."

Pamela took the key, and an unsettling feeling gripped her. She knew this feeling could not be attributed to her lack of sleep.

"Thanks, Bob." She dashed in the door.

"I know there is a lot for you to do at the facility, but you look like you've been to hell and back."

"I get the picture," Pamela griped. "I promise to put on makeup in the future, so I don't embarrass you."

"That's not what I meant. I just want to take care of you."

Something Daniel once said came to mind. "I guess I'm not good at being taken care of, Bob."

"That's what I always loved about you," he affirmed. "I didn't have to spend my days catering to your needs. Unlike Clarissa."

She stepped into an elegant yellow and white wallpapered entrance and then out into the foyer. Oak stairways on the left and right of the foyer curved upward from a white marble tiled floor to the second story balcony. Along the stairwell, art deco paintings clashed with the refined the grand foyer. The cold and pretentious home made Pamela long for her cluttered little Acadian cottage.

"Bob, are you sure you want to do this today? We could go through the house another time."

"No, we need to decide what goes and what stays, so the decorator can get started." Bob moved toward the stairs. "I'm having her start with our bedroom."

Pamela stopped in mid-stride. "Our bedroom?"

"Actually, it's a master double bedroom. Two master bedrooms adjoined by a single master bath, if that makes you feel any better. Clarissa read about it in a magazine when we were renovating the house."

"You and Clarissa didn't share a bedroom?" she posed, itching with curiosity.

"Clarissa liked to stay up late and watch television, and you know how much I hate that. She always complained about my late hours, so the room was supposed to be a compromise to help our marriage."

"Are there locks on the bedroom doors?"

"For the time being," he conceded. "I'm hoping one day we can do away with the locks," he added as he gently ran his fingers up and down her arm.

She pulled away from his touch. "Bob, I think you should know something about me before we go any further with this."

He gave a curt laugh. "I already know so much about you, P.A.. What else could you possibly tell me?"

She looked him in the eye. "I sleep with a gun. Come anywhere near my bedroom door and I'll use it on you." She slyly smiled. "I can make it look like an accident. Remember, you taught me how to do that."

He angrily flung his hands behind his back, narrowing his eyes on her. "You haven't changed, Pamela."

"This is an arrangement, Bob. You need an upstanding wife who will look the other way when you sleep with your office staff and be at your side when you run for office. I need a benefactor who will keep my facility going. Having sex with you is not part of our deal."

"What if I want to make it part of our deal?"

Her stomached clenched at the thought of having Bob in her bed. "You already have my soul, Bob. What good would my body do you?"

"You'll never change." He started up the stairs. "Maybe one day I can make you fall in love with me again," he remarked over his shoulder while trotting up the oak staircase.

"Not even if you started eating nuts and grew a big fuzzy tail," Pamela muttered, following him.

Bob selected one of the former guest bedrooms for Pamela's office. Emptied of furniture, the room was deocrated with dozens of swatches for wallpaper and paint.

"I figured we could take this out." He pointed to the beige carpet. "Linda selected these swatches for the room." He waved to strips of fabric taped to the wall. "She'll be here Monday afternoon to go over some ideas for furniture and color schemes. You should be here to pick out what you want."

Pamela glided up to the french windows overlooking the balcony. "I'll be here."

She spotted a towering oak next to the house. Two squirrels were running around the trunk of the tree, chasing each other.

"Oh, and we received our first social invitation as a couple," Bob excitedly informed her. "Val Easterling invited us to a party she is having at her home in the French Quarter this weekend."

She kept her eyes on the frolicking squirrels. "How do you know Mrs. Easterling?"

"I've met her at a few parties, and she is the person to know for anyone who wants to get into politics in this town. I suspect she may have heard about my political aspirations and wants to talk to me. I think our getting back together is really going to pay off, P.A."

Pamela suspected Val Easterling's motive for inviting the two of them to her party wasn't to help Bob.

"We should make an announcement party," Bob proposed." Let everyone know we are back together."

Pamela smiled as the squirrels ran down the tree and across the lawn. She turned back to Bob. "What about Clarissa? Shouldn't we wait for your divorce to be final before you start planning parties?"

"Clarissa and I had a prenuptial agreement. If she gives me any trouble in the divorce or discredits my reputation in any way, she loses any claims to her settlement. That prenup is ironclad." He looked at his watch "Don't forget the movers will be coming to your place next Wednesday to get your things. We can go over everything this weekend when I pick you up for Val's party. Make a list of what you want brought here and what the facility can keep."

Pamela just nodded, wanting to avoid any further discussion about leaving her beloved sanctuary.

"Get something nice to wear to Val's. Her parties are always black tie and I need you looking wonderful." He retrieved his wallet from his pocket and then handed her a credit card. "Use this to buy whatever you want. The sky's the limit."

Pamela took the credit card from him as a memory of Daniel taking her shopping flashed across her mind. She searched Bob's eyes and fought to find the words to tell him what she was really thinking.

"I have to get back," she voiced, instead of clearing her conscience. "I have a few more interviews this afternoon."

Chapter 15

Two hours later, Pamela parked her truck in front of her cottage feeling worn out. An afternoon of interviews to find her replacement was still ahead of her, and the prospect of selecting someone to take over her beloved sanctuary felt daunting.

She got out of the truck and greeted each of the dogs. As she made her way to the porch steps, Rodney came out from some bushes near the side of the house and said hello. She scratched behind his silver-tipped ears and gave his back a long rub. The sunlight shimmered off the diamond in Pamela's engagement ring, and Rodney reached out with his front paws to grab the shiny object.

"Oh, no, buddy." Pamela removed the ring from her finger and slipped it into her purse. "I can just see me explaining to Bob how a raccoon ate my ring."

Satisfied with his moment of attention, Rodney waddled back into the bushes. Pamela climbed the steps to her front door and went inside.

Nursing a cup of a cup of tea, she was going to enjoy a few minutes of peace with her feet curled up on the couch when the dogs started barking. A few seconds later, she heard a car.

Pamela checked the clock on the microwave and silently cursed. The first of her interviews was half an hour early. She put the tea down on the coffee table and went to the front door. Then she noticed the silence.

"That's odd. This one must be really good with animals."

She opened the door and saw a tall man hunched over in her driveway with his back to her, petting each of the dogs.

"You're pretty good with animals," she called out from her doorway.

At the sound of her voice, the man turned to greet her.

"Daniel," she gasped.

"Hello, Pamela." Daniel took a step closer to the house as all the dogs gathered around him.

She stumbled onto the porch. He was a little leaner, and with circles rimming his dark eyes, he appeared to be a wearier version of the Daniel she once knew. It was as if all of the burdens of his life were etched across his handsome face.

He climbed the porch steps. "How are you?"

"I'm fine. How are you?" She tried to sound upbeat.

He came up to her and peered into her eyes. "I'm fine," he offered with a faint smile.

"Liar." A half-smile snuck across her lips. "You look like crap."

His smile widened. "Crap does not suit you, Pamela. Why don't you say hell, but not crap." He took a step closer.

"Well, you still look like crap to me."

"You look wonderful to me," he whispered.

An uncomfortable moment of silence filled the air. There were so many things to say, but neither said a word.

Seconds ticked by and Pamela could feel the strain building. The smell of his spicy cologne encircled her, and instantly flashes of their night together invaded her thoughts. Her pulse quickened as her body yearned for him. Pamela fought to maintain control as their silence persisted.

Unable to stand it any longer, she finally asked, "What happened to you, Daniel?"

He took in a deep breath and rubbed his hands together. "The day after the party Bob came to see me."

"Your landlady told me about that," she confirmed. "I went to your place looking for you and she mentioned that Bob had been there."

Daniel ambled to the porch railing. "Yeah, T.J. said you stopped by. I dropped my bags off at my old place before I headed out here."

"So, how long are you staying in New Orleans?"

He rested his hip against the railing. "Long enough to open a new office for my father. He wants to expand his import business, and he asked me to come down here and get it going."

"Is that where you went, back home to work with your father?"

He nodded his head.

"Why? I thought you said you and your father didn't get along."

"It was part of a deal I made with him." He ran his hands through his hair. "When Bob came to my place, he told me he was going to stop giving you money unless I left town. He said he was going to have the loan called on your facility. He wanted me out of your life. I didn't want to leave, so I called my old man and asked him for the balance of my trust fund. I wanted to make sure Bob couldn't hurt you. My father agreed to transfer the money from my trust fund to me, but he made one condition: to come home and take over the business. So, I agreed. It was the only way I could make sure you would always be safe from Bob."

"You could have said something," she argued. "You could have called and told me what was going on. Asked me what I wanted to do. We could have talked about it."

He rubbed his hand across his chin. "You would have stubbornly refused my offer. You probably would have gone back to Bob and done everything in your power to make sure he was appeased."

Pamela dropped her gaze to the deck planks. "You don't know that."

He raised her chin until her eyes met his. "I know you. The only problem with my whole plan was once I was gone I believed you wouldn't need me anymore. I figured you would forget about me, and I hoped I would forget about you." Daniel removed his hand from beneath her chin.

"But then my father ordered me to pack my bags and move back to New Orleans."

"So why are you here?"

He placed his hands behind his back. "Because my father said I was an idiot ever to leave you, and he was right. I know what I did was wrong and I'm sorry I didn't call or tell you—"

"Look, Daniel, I'm not going to stand here and pretend you didn't hurt me. You did, but now things have changed." She walked back through her open front door.

Daniel followed her inside. "What's changed? I want to be with you and I hoped you would want to be with me. I thought we could talk this through."

She went over to her desk and picked up the list of interviews she scheduled for the day. "Then what, Daniel? Date? Spend a few more nights in bed and see how it goes?"

"Pamela, this is new territory for me. I want us to have a chance together."

She darted across the living room to him. "When you left, you blew any chance for us."

"At least let me help you, financially. I have the money to take care of you and—"

"I don't want your money," she roared.

"What do you mean you don't want it? When I left, Bob was about to cut you off at the knees."

She avoided his eyes and focused on the list in her hand. "Bob and I have come to an understanding."

There was silence. She raised her eyes and spied Daniel's face. His mouth was pressed into a painful grimace, and the menacing darkness was back in his eyes.

"I never thought you were the kind of woman to sell yourself to a man, even to save your facility," he growled.

"It's not like that." She ran her hand over her forehead, trying to come up with a way to keep from hurting him further. "Bob has been there for me."

Daniel cursed and threw his hands in the air. "Have you been sick?" he shouted, sounding more hurt than angry. "Why didn't you say something to me?"

"Because you weren't here, Daniel. Bob was, and he has promised to continue to be there for me. I realized after you left that I do need someone to help me. I need someone I can count on."

"You think Bob is going to be there for you? After what he did to you the first time round, how on earth can you trust him again?"

"Where in the hell were you, Daniel? When things got tough, you ran. You showed me the kind of man you are and—"

"I left to protect you!"

"Protect me! You ran off, leaving me …." She shut her mouth and turned away from him.

"Yes, I left you." His voice sounded strained. "I left, and I'm sorry. Don't throw away what we were because you think I can't make a go of a relationship. I want us to try again. I know I let you down, but I want you to give me a second chance. Can you give me that chance, Pamela?"

A wave of guilt gripped her insides. She struggled against the desire to become his again. Pamela took in a few deep breaths and turned around to face him.

"Please go," she pleaded. "We have nothing more to say to each other."

Daniel backed away. "You don't want Bob. You're just running back to something you know because you're afraid. But the safest choice is not always the right choice, Pamela. Sometimes a person has to run away to realize what they once possessed." He paused and gazed into her eyes. "I know I love you, and I came back hoping that you might love me, too." He hurried to the front door. "I hope one day you will learn that Bob can never make you happy. When you do, come and see me." He banged the door shut behind him.

Pamela sank to her knees, clutching her list to her chest. For the first time since Daniel left, she released all the emotion she locked away. She curled up on the floor and began to cry. As she lay there, blinded by her tears, something nudged against her hand. When she wiped the tears away, she beheld Louis beside her, pressing his head against her hand. Pamela dropped her list, picked up her squirrel, and cradled him in her hands. As she gently stroked his back, tears, once more, filled her eyes. Her chance at happiness with Daniel was gone, and she was about to walk away from the only thing that ever mattered to her. The loss of her animals enveloped her with an unfamiliar emptiness. Overwhelmed by her sorrow, Pamela rocked back and forth, holding her precious little Louis against her chest.

Chapter 16

"I have it on good authority that Val wants to talk to me about my political aspirations," Bob reported as his silver Mercedes-Benz came to a stop in front of an impressive gray Creole cottage located on the corner of Dumaine and Royal streets. "So don't distract her with your wildlife exploits. I know she's your patron, but this is my night to shine."

A doorman, dressed in a black tux and tall black hat, opened Pamela's car door.

"Welcome," he greeted as he helped Pamela from the car.

Pamela eyed the elegant French Quarter home. With a plastered exterior and large french windows on both the first and second story, it reminded her of Daniel's quaint carriage house. Spying the thick green wooden shutters next to each of the windows and surrounding the front door, she tried to picture the same shutters closing her heart off from him, but it wasn't working.

"Couldn't you have chosen something a little less revealing to wear?" Bob reprimanded as he took her hand and guided her toward the entrance. "I'm trying to make a good impression tonight."

Pamela glimpsed her short, fitted black cocktail dress Carol bought for her to wear. "What's wrong with this dress?"

"Politicians' wives don't dress like that. You should be covering up your body and not showing it off?"

"I don't understand. It's a cocktail dress, Bob. I think you're making too much of it."

He worriedly played with his bow tie. "Just don't bend over in that thing; otherwise, somebody is going to get a great view of your assets."

Once inside, Pamela took in the detailed plaster inlay in the ceiling and rich burgundy antique mahogany furniture as Bob shook hands with some people he knew. She noted the way he made a point of introducing Pamela as his fiancée. They were not even out of the living room when Pamela felt a gentle tug on her arm.

"There you are."

Val Easterling was standing next to her. She was covered in a swirl of deep blue silk that accentuated her round hips and added a sparkle to her light blue eyes.

"Mrs. Easterling." Bob stretched for Val's hand. "I just want to say that I look forward to hearing your views on the current political situation in the city and I feel that—"

"Who are you?" Val demanded, turning her eyes to Bob.

Bob looked nervously from Val to Pamela. "I'm Robert Patrick. Pamela is my fiancée."

Val raised her gray eyebrows in surprise. "Is she? Weren't you already married to this ambulance chaser once before, Pamela?"

Bob frowned. "Please, Mrs. Easterling, ambulance chaser is a bit—"

"Bob?" Val raised her voice to the man. "The bar is in the courtyard." She pointed to the back door. "Go get a drink. I want to have a word with your fiancée."

Val and Pamela watched as Bob reluctantly made his way outside.

Val's eyes inspected the diamond ring on Pamela's left hand. "I heard about your engagement."

"Bob and I plan on getting married as soon as his divorce is final."

"Pamela, when I saw you with my Daniel at that benefit, I thought you two looked pretty happy together. Then Daniel left the city, without so much as a good-bye to me. The next thing I heard was you were back with your ex-husband." Val placed her hands on her hips. "I remember seeing you at a few parties when you were married to Bob. I always wondered what you were doing there. You looked so out of place. Not like you didn't belong, more like you didn't want to belong. You reminded me of another young woman I used to know. She was just as confused about her place in the world as you are now. I watched her come close to making the same mistake that you're about to make."

Pamela smiled, trying to keep up her brave face. "The young woman you knew is gone. I have other responsibilities to consider now."

"Selling yourself for your rehab facility won't help the situation." She tenderly patted Pamela's arm. "I know a lot more than you think about what you're going through, so let me give you a bit of advice. Don't settle for someone you don't want when someone you do want is waiting just on the other side of that door." Val pointed to the door leading to the courtyard.

Pamela gazed from the door to Val. "I don't understand."

Val took her elbow and urged her toward the back door. "You will."

Pamela started down the hallway, but stopped and glanced back to see Val Easterling shaking hands with her other guests. Unsure of what she was referring to, Pamela faced the back door and headed outside.

The air was cool, and there was a sweet smell of jasmine hovering about the courtyard when Pamela strolled out the back door. She was about to make her way across the bricked pavement toward the bar, when a familiar voice stopped her.

"I can't believe you're going to marry that snake."

Pamela found Daniel leaning against the wall, holding a flute of champagne in his hand.

"When Val told me about your engagement I almost punched out her front window." Daniel's took in every inch of Pamela's body. He froze when he spotted the engagement ring on her left hand.

"What are you doing here?"

"Val invited me. When she found out I was back in town, she called me. She told me you and Bob were coming, and she figured this was my opportunity to win you back."

"Win me back?" Pamela almost laughed out loud. "I was never yours to win back, Daniel."

Daniel downed the contents of his flute in one long sip. Then his eyes wandered over the courtyard.

"Please go," Pamela begged. "If Bob finds you here, someone will probably end up going to jail."

"Tell me something, Pamela. Did that night mean anything to you or was it all a lie?"

Keeping her eyes on his, Pamela raised her chin slightly. "That night meant something, Daniel. I thought it meant something to you, as well. But then you disappeared."

"I can't change the past between us and I'm not about to stand here and—"

"What's he doing here?" Bob's angry voice cut in.

Pamela scrutinized Bob's red face. "Val invited him. It's her party after all. So don't make a scene."

"I think you better leave, Phillips," Bob growled. "You've hurt my fiancée enough with your lies and manipulation."

"Lies and manipulation? This coming from a man who screws around on his wife and then dumps her when she gets sick."

"Why you good for nothing …." Bob made a move toward Daniel.

Pamela jumped in front of Bob. "Don't do this. There are too many people here tonight who could hurt your political aspirations if they witness you making a scene."

"Political aspirations?" Daniel snorted. "You'll fit right in with all the other crooks in this town."

Bob lunged at Daniel. The two men slammed against the side of the house as Daniel's flute fell to the courtyard floor and smashed into a thousand shards.

"Stop it!" Pamela tried to move in between the men.

Pamela felt a pair of strong hands pull her back.

"Let me handle this," a deep voice advised.

A tall man with thick, wavy brown hair stepped in and pulled the two men apart. When Pamela caught sight of her rescuer's profile, she cringed.

"Care to take this discussion outside?" Lance Beauvoir calmly implored while frowning at Bob to Daniel.

The buzz of conversation around their little party grew quiet. Pamela's eyes darted about the courtyard to see if any of the guests appeared distracted by the tussle.

Val came up to Pamela's side. "I hoped Bob would show a bit more restraint tonight."

"You must have known what would happen if you invited Daniel," Pamela admonished.

"I invited Daniel for you, not Bob. I know of Bob's reputation as a bully, and I'd heard about his little tussle with Daniel at Pat O'Brien's. But I figured he wouldn't be foolish enough to go after Daniel with this crowd watching."

"I can't believe this." Pamela gawked as Lance pushed Daniel toward the bar while ushering Bob inside the house. "Why, Val? Why did you invite Daniel?"

Val grinned at her. "I had to do something to make you come to your senses."

Daniel was across the patio to the bar while Bob retreated into the house. Feeling that the situation was under control, Lance came up to Val's side.

"As always, you sure do put on one hell of a party, Valie." Lance wiped his hand across his forehead. "Remind me to bring a referee whistle with me next time I come to one of your shindigs." He nodded to Pamela. "You all right?"

"Yes, thank you. I'm sorry you had to get involved in all of that."

Val slapped Lance's shoulder. "Why do you think I invited Lance, anyway? Best bouncer this side of Rampart Street."

"Valie told me there might be fireworks, so I came prepared."

Pamela's cheeks burned. "So you were both in on this?"

Lance's green eyes twinkled with mischief. "Let's just say Valie and I are old hats at this sort of thing."

"What, starting fights?" Pamela pressed.

"No, interfering," Lance clarified. "I think I'll just go and join Daniel. I think we could both use a drink." He made a hasty exit to the bar.

Val motioned to the back door of her house. "You best be getting Bob out of here before he goes after Daniel's hide again. I think we've proved our point."

"Your point? What point, Val?"

Val gave her a frustrated sigh. "He may only be a bartender, Pamela, but he will make a better husband than Robert Patrick can ever hope to be."

Pamela was about to turn to go when Val reached held her arm.

"One more thing. You'll never make a good politician's wife. Bob may want a career in politics but you can tell him from me, he'll never have one if he marries you."

Pamela stared into Val's bright blue eyes. "Do you know what he will do if I tell him that?"

"Yes," Val replied with a devilish grin. "He'll let you go."

*****

In the car on the ride home, Pamela contemplated Bob's face as it waned in and out of different shades of red. His nostrils flared, and his knuckles shone white against the walnut steering wheel of his car.

"Bob, you need to calm down. You're going to have a stroke." She noted the pulsating artery in his neck.

"Don't tell me to calm down. Did you see what he did in front of Val Easterling? I'm never going to be able to get her backing now."

"Don't worry about Val. I talked to her and everything is fine. She wants to help you. She understands what happened and she told me—"

"You talked to Val about me? What? You two are such good friends now that you can talk about me while I'm fighting off your ex-boyfriends?"

Pamela rolled her eyes. "I can't talk to you when you're like this."

"Don't do that, Pamela. Don't start with that condescending gaze of yours. I'm not an idiot."

"Well, tonight you reminded me of the hot-headed idiot I was married to all those years ago. You haven't changed one bit."

"But I have changed. I have a reputation to consider now. There were important people at that party tonight who know me, who can help me. I'm not a poor drunk's son anymore, Pamela. So stop treating me like one."

"I'm not treating you any different than I've always treated you, Bob. You're still the same insecure, selfish ass you always were. You didn't have to go after Daniel like that. You could have just walked away. But no, you had to prove yourself just like you always—"

"Of course, I must prove myself," he yelled, halting her rebuke. "Do you know what people would say if I walked away from confronting that bartender? I'm a prominent attorney known all over town as a force to be reckoned with. I can't just roll over and let my reputation be destroyed."

"Reputation? Bob, you're a personal injury lawyer, with a short fuse, who settles everything with his fists. Everyone in the city knows what you are, except you."

"What I am is a well-connected and influential attorney, Pamela. I'm not some broke wildlife rehabber who has to beg people for donations to keep herself and her animals fed. You need me to keep that miserable little zoo going."

"I don't need you, Bob. I'm beginning to wonder if I ever really did."

"But you need my money." Bob turned his eyes back to the road. The tension in his body eased a little. "Let's not forget whose name is still on that mortgage of yours. Face it; you need me."

"Do I?" She hesitated as she took in his profile. "I don't know, Bob. Is having a husband who pushes everyone around and starts fights with total strangers, more important than having no husband at all?" Pamela twirled the engagement ring around her finger. "No one should marry for convenience or as a business arrangement."

"Pamela, don't do this, not now." He slapped the steering wheel. "It's been a crappy night, and I'm in no mood for your outbursts."

She stared at the road ahead of them. "Tell me something. Did you ever love me, Bob, or was I just a great catch?"

"Listen to yourself. You sound like some love-struck schoolgirl fishing for a compliment. This isn't you. You have more class than this."

"Pull over, Bob," she demanded.

"What is it? Are you going to be sick? Don't get sick in the car. I just had it detailed."

Bob pulled the car over to the side of St. Charles Avenue.

Pamela opened the car door and stepped onto the pavement. She took in a few quick deep breaths. Once she calmed down, she leaned over and glanced back at Bob.

"What's the problem? Get back in the car, Pamela."

"You want to know what the problem is, Bob? You really don't know who I am, and you have no intention of ever trying to get to know me. The sad part is, I don't think you really know who you are either." She pulled the ring off her finger and tossed it on the passenger seat.

Bob grabbed the ring. "What's this? Are you kidding me? You're just going to call the whole thing off, here, in the middle of St. Charles Avenue? You're not being rational. Get back in this car, right now!"

"Good-bye, Bob," Pamela proclaimed and slammed the car door.

She quickly hurried over to the neutral ground in the middle of St. Charles Avenue to a waiting streetcar. She boarded the streetcar and watched as Bob's silver Mercedes sped away. She took a seat on one of the old wooden benches near a window and sighed with relief. As the streetcar headed along St. Charles Avenue to the French Quarter, Pamela could not help but smile. She took in the bright full moon above and smelled the hint of magnolia in the air. She eased her body back against the bench and let the rocking motion of the long green car soothe her cares away.

Chapter 17

Pamela walked through the open green door and down the dark entrance leading to Daniel's French Quarter carriage house. As she stepped into the moonlit courtyard, she heard the sound of water trickling down the three-tiered brick fountain. All around her shadows from the azalea bushes danced eerily along the high garden walls.

"I wondered how long it would be before you showed up."

T.J. Powell was kneeling over a flowerpot in a pair of dirty blue jean overalls.

"Hello, Ms. Powell. What are you doing out here so late at night?"

"It's T.J., sweetheart. No one calls me anythin' but T.J. 'round here." The woman stood up and wiped her hands on her dirty overalls. "I sometimes come out here at night and work in my garden when I can't sleep." She grinned at Pamela. "What's your excuse?"

"I came to see Daniel."

"I told him you'd come a callin'. Said you'd been inquirin' 'bout where he'd disappeared to." She nodded to the carriage house. "He's home. He came back about an hour ago from some fancy party. Looked mad enough to spit nails. He barely said hello to me before he went inside and slammed the door."

"I think that may be my fault. There are things he needs to know. Things I haven't been able to …." Her voice faded away.

"Then you best go and talk to him. Make him listen to you. He's a good man. In my experience, good men are like peanut butter. They stick to you no matter what."

T.J. returned to the main house, leaving Pamela to make her way to Daniel's front door. Standing in front of the carriage house, she took a deep breath and gently knocked.

She counted down the seconds as she stood waiting, but Daniel never opened the door. She knocked again, but still there was no answer. Images of Daniel hiding away in his bedroom, wanting to avoid her, began to take hold in her mind. She was just about to walk away when she heard the click of the doorknob.

"Pamela?"

Daniel, covered only in a towel, was standing dripping wet in his doorway.

"I thought at first you weren't home." She directed her gaze to the garden walls not wanting to see his dark eyes staring into hers. "Then I figured perhaps you were home and just didn't want to see me."

Unexpectedly, he pulled her inside the house. Once she was safely behind the front door, he shut it and secured the deadbolt.

Daniel wiped his wet hair back from his face. "I was in the shower and heard someone at the door, but I wasn't expecting it to be you."

Her heart shattered. "You're expecting someone else. I'm sorry. I should go."

He grabbed her arm, stopping her. "No, that didn't come out the right way." He let go of her arm. "I meant I was expecting it to be T.J., not you, standing at my door in the middle of the night. How did you get here?"

"Streetcar. I made Bob pull over on the way home from the party, and I took a streetcar to Canal Street. I walked from there."

He scowled angrily. "You shouldn't have been walking around the French Quarter alone at night, Pamela. It's not safe."

She threw her purse on the couch. "I wasn't alone. I followed one of those ghost tours to your gate."

"So what happened? Did you and Bob have a fight?"

"I'm sorry he went after you like that at the party."

"I'm sure you didn't come here in the middle of the night to apologize for Bob." He glimpsed the towel wrapped around his waist. "Look, why don't you let me get some clothes on and then I can take you home."

She took in his muscular chest and her body ached with desire. Suddenly regretting her visit, she turned away. "Perhaps I shouldn't have come here." She stretched for her purse.

"No! You're not going anywhere alone in the middle of the night." He took her hand and stepped over to the couch. "Sit here while I get dressed."

With the touch of his hand, Pamela's resolve disintegrated. She put her purse down and made herself comfortable on his beige couch.

Daniel gave her one last going over with his eyes. "You all right?" he asked, thoroughly analyzing her features.

"Get dressed, Daniel," she ordered in a weary voice. "I'm fine."

Daniel trotted up the stairs. She smiled as she observed how the taught muscles in his back flexed as he made it to the top of the open stairway and turned to go into his room. She noticed he left the bedroom door open.

"Feel free to get something to drink," he called out from the bedroom.

Pamela got up from the couch and went into his efficiency kitchen. As she made her way around the kitchen she smiled to herself. She wondered how a tall man like Daniel was managing in such a cramped kitchen. She opened the refrigerator door and spotted only a carton of orange juice, eggs, a loaf of bread, and a bottle of white wine. She pulled out the orange juice and started searching the cabinets for a glass. The only ones she could find were on a high top shelf above the sink. She tried to stand on her toes and grab for a glass. Just as she was about to give up when a man's hand reached up behind her and removed a glass from the top shelf.

His face was inches from hers and she could smell his spicy cologne on his skin. His wet hair was neatly combed back, and he was wearing a white, long-sleeved shirt and a black pair of slacks. His shirt was not yet buttoned, and she caught sight of his muscular chest beneath the white fabric.

She swallowed hard and tried to remind herself to be businesslike. "Thank you." She took the glass from his hand.

"You're welcome." He placed his hands on the sink behind her, pinning her between his arms. "So tell me, why are you here?"

"I came …." She turned her face away from his, trying to collect her thoughts without having to look into his disconcerting eyes. "I came to talk to you about something," she finally got out.

"Something? That doesn't sound very good." He leaned back from her and folded his arms over his wide chest. "Should I be expecting your fiancé to come flying through the door anytime soon?"

"I don't think Bob and I are going to work out. Conflict of interest, you could say."

Daniel frowned. "Conflict of interest?"

She placed the glass on the counter next to her. "My interests conflicted with his," she added coyly. "Ever since you showed up at my house the other day I haven't—"

"You haven't been able to stop thinking of me, eh?" he interrupted, grinning.

She pushed him away. "You're impossible." She eased herself around him in the tiny kitchen and then headed for the front door.

"Admit it, Pamela." He followed her out of the kitchen. "You can't stop thinking about me just like I can't stop thinking about you. Tell me you want to be with me and then that's it. We will see where this goes."

She stopped by the couch in the living room. "See where this goes? I need more than that, Daniel. I can't just see where it goes. I can't be so cavalier in my affections."

"I'm not being cavalier. I want to be with you. I want to spend every free moment I have with you, but I need to know you want to be with me."

She shook her head. "You're talking about dating, and I'm talking about a relationship."

"What difference does it make as long as we're together?"

"It matters to me. I need to know you will be there no matter what."

He sighed and ran his hand through his wet hair. "You're talking about if you get sick." He threw his hand up. "Of course, I will be there. I want to be there for you."

"That's not it." She retrieved her purse from the couch. "You're not ready for this kind of commitment." She moved toward the front door.

Daniel came up behind her and placed his hand against the door, halting her retreat. "Pamela, talk to me."

Pamela closed her eyes for a moment. She wanted to tell him, but reason told her not to say a word. Her heart, however, was arguing for a different approach. She took a deep breath and then turned to him.

"What I need from you, Daniel, is a promise that no matter what happens to me, you will take care of my facility. It's not just me you're getting, but my world as well. Can you handle that?"

His eyes began frantically searching hers. "What's going on? You said you've been sick. How sick are you, Pamela? You're talking as if you're dying."

"I'm not dying. I want to know if you want all of me. Me and the facility. We are a packaged deal. "

"Of course, I want you … and the facility. I want all of you, Pamela."

His words settled deep in her heart, but her mind was not yet willing to give in. "This isn't going to easy. We have a lot of hurdles—?"

She never got to finish her words. Daniel pulled her into his arms and covered her mouth with his.

Pamela pulled away from his embrace. "If something happens to me, I need to know you will carry on my work. Can you promise me that?"

He pulled her close. "So that's why you were going to marry Bob, for the animals?"

She rested her head against his chest. "You were gone, and I didn't know where else to turn."

"Why didn't you just tell me this the other day when I came to see you?" he whispered against her cheek.

"I wasn't sure what you would say, and I didn't think you would want to have anything to do with me."

He held her close. "I'm such an idiot. I should never have left. But I'll make it up to you. I promise I'll always take care of you and your animals."

"I don't want you to think you owe me, Daniel," she declared, stepping back from him. "Maybe you should take some time and think about this."

"Pamela, there's nothing to think about. You're mine, and I couldn't be happier."

"But we never really got an opportunity to be together. Perhaps I will be cramping your style."

Daniel's deep, resounding laugh lifted Pamela's spirit. "Not a chance. I told you before, I want some roots. With you, and the animals, I'm finally going to be able to settle down and have a real home."

All the years of pain and conflict instantly melted away, leaving a strange sense of completeness in its wake. It was as if she'd needed to live through the heartache to appreciate the joy she now felt.

Pamela stroked up and down the front of his white shirt. "I have to admit there is something awfully compelling about you."

"Just think of me as a large, fuzzy squirrel." Then he kissed her tenderly on the lips.

Pamela pulled away from him as her thoughts became inundated with doubt. "Maybe I should call a cab and give you some time to mull this over."

"Oh, no. You're not leaving, not now. We have plans to make. We have to decide on our living arrangements and how we're going to manage traveling between your facility in Folsom and my new business in the city. Then there are plans we need to make for our wedding."

Her heart soared. "You want to marry me?"

"I'm not just marrying you; I'm marrying you and Rodney, Louis, the dogs, and all the wonderful animals you care for." His mouth hovered over hers. "From now on, we're a team."

"I can't believe this is happening, Daniel. You really want me?"

"I want all of you, Pamela." He nuzzled her cheek. "I could never stop thinking about you after I left. I wanted to call you a thousand times, but instead …."

"Instead you sent repairmen, and plumbers, and electricians. I understand, Daniel. I think this is a big step for both of us. Planning a future is a lot harder than walking away from one."

He tossed his arms around her. "Do you think you could ever love a thug?"

Pamela held his face in her hands. "As long as that thug is you."

The End

Dear Reader

I hope you enjoyed this condensed novella of Broken Wings. The full novel is available along with my other novels.

Or you can find out more about me and my books at the sites listed below.

Alexandrea Weis is an advanced practice registered nurse who was born and raised in New Orleans. Having been brought up in the motion picture industry, she learned how to tell stories from a different perspective and began writing at the age of eight. Infusing the rich tapestry of her hometown into her award-winning novels, she believes that creating vivid characters makes a story memorable. A permitted/certified wildlife rehabber with the Louisiana Wildlife and Fisheries, Weis rescues orphaned and injured wildlife. She lives with her husband and pets in New Orleans.

Website: http://www.alexandreaweis.com/

Facebook: https://www.facebook.com/pages/Alexandrea-Weis/289566081083949

Twitter: https://twitter.com/alexandreaweis

THE MISSING INGREDIENT

Nicole Zoltack

All Mindy wants to do is bake, but when a food critic gives her a great review, she wants something more and decides to write a cookbook. Only she doesn't follow recipes or use exact measurements, and considering she's dyslexic, she opts to hire the food critic's handsome twin, Gabe, to be her ghostwriter.

When you mix peanut butter and chocolate together, you get pure magic, but none of the recipes turn out as planned. If Mindy and Gabe don't figure out that missing ingredient, Mindy's dream of a cookbook might be worse than the terrible cakes Gabe's making. Maybe baking a way to his heart will be the key.

Chapter One

The scent of vanilla and cinnamon baking made my stomach growl, and I could only hope that these muffins would be half as good as they smelled. I was running behind on making desserts and—

"Have you got anything, Mindy?" Sheila Davidson asked, bursting into the kitchen. She was the only waitress on duty tonight, and instead of being flustered, she was in her glory. She loved nothing more than to be running a mile a minute, handling five hundred things at once. Even though she was forty-six, she was more like an older sister to me than a maternal figure.

"Just a second." I eased a muffin out of the pan and put it on the plate. She reached for it.

I batted her hand away. "Has to be iced." With care, I squeezed icing on top, aiming to make a pretty design, but the muffin was too hot yet, and the icing melted, and it ended up looking like a white globby mess.

"It'll do." She grabbed the plate and scampered away.

Derrick Bo, the chef, bumped his hip into mine. "You done with this here?"

"Just a sec." I grabbed up my pots and measuring pans and the hot tray—ow! Wincing, I dropped it, gloved myself with an oven mitt, picked up the tray again, and moved out of Derrick's way.

We had a routine, us two, but I had arrived to work fifteen minutes late because of an accident, and those fifteen minutes had thrown everything off. It took me two hours to get caught up, which was way better than last time, when I had never caught up at all. It wasn't my fault the highway was terrible, and I would love to be able to move closer to the restaurant, but that just wasn't an option. We worked in a small diner, and while we were making a name for ourselves, I could only afford my apartment on the rough edge of town because of how cheap it was. Which meant I had no other option than that devil-may-care highway.

Sheila popped her head back in. "We're out of cinnamon rolls, aren't we? Just double checking."

"Oh…" I glanced around, taking in the various treats, and grinned. "There's one left. Who's the lucky one to get it?"

"A real cutie." Giggling, Sheila smoothed her hair back, but it didn't matter. Her locks were red and fizzy and out of control. Always. She liked to blame it on the humidity, but there wasn't any humidity lately.

I popped the roll into the oven for a few and drizzled on some extra icing for good measure. "There."

"Thank you!" She whisked her way out of the kitchen.

A drop of icing dribbled down my thumb, and I licked it. "Yum."

I made my way to the sink and washed up.

Derrick grunted.

"What's wrong?" I dried my hands. "Need some help with your mashed potatoes?"

"No, no. You make them too runny."

"You don't mash them enough," I countered.

"You only need one can of condensed milk per five pounds!"

"A little extra makes it that much easier to mash, and a few chunks are fine, but you leave hackingly huge pieces that could choke a person."

He chuckled, the sound echoing in the small kitchen. "Yeah, yeah. Whatever."

I laughed, flashing him a smile. We always joked with each other. He had a good twenty years on me—I was twenty—and he was like a second father to me. The only father figure in my life, considering my own was a deadbeat. I didn't even know if he was still alive.

"I wanted that last cinnamon roll," he grumbled.

"Oh. Why didn't you say something?"

"I can't be selfish. And my belly appreciates some other guy consuming the unnecessary calories."

"Hey, hot, gooey, cinnamon goodness with icing on top is *not* unnecessary."

Quick as can be, I did a quick inventory of desserts. Large enough of a selection and variety to keep the last few diners happy, so I set about gathering my ingredients.

"Oh, no. If you start them now—"

"I don't have anywhere to be tonight," I assured him.

"But they take you hours to make."

"No worries. Besides, I'm using you wanting one as an excuse. I want one myself."

He grinned and rubbed his belly. If he had white hair and a beard, he would make a perfect Santa Claus. "If you insist…"

"I do."

I was just about to start measuring when Sheila dashed back in. "Mindy, you got a sec?"

"What's up?"

"Cutie who got the cinnamon roll wants to see you."

"See me?" I pointed to myself. Derrick got asked out a few times because his meals—especially his Italian dishes—were a hit, but this was the first time I had been asked to come out and see a diner.

"Go for it." Derrick grinned.

"Yeah, sure." I wiped a hand across my forehead and quickly untied my apron. It looked like a war of epic food proportions. My appearance didn't matter, and to some extent, neither did my baked goodies, only how they tasted. At least my clothes under the apron were unsoiled.

"Coming?" Sheila grabbed my arm and yanked me through the swinging door to the front of the diner.

There was only one occupied table, so I really didn't need Sheila to escort me there, but she did, acting like a proud peacock of a mama.

"Here she is!" Sheila proudly pronounced.

I raised my eyebrows at her. "Yeah. Hi. I'm Mindy. Mindy Cave." I shifted my focus from my coworker to the guy and did a double take.

Cutie? No. This guy was one of the handsomest I had ever seen with black coffee-colored hair, chocolate-colored eyes, and licorice-colored lips. His facial angles were sharp, his clothes a little more upscale than you normally would see inside a diner, with the top few buttons of his shirt undone that were making me undone…

Why wasn't he saying anything? Should I say something?

"Did you—"

"This was—" he said at the same time.

I laughed, trying to let loose some of the awkwardness. "You first."

Out of the corner of my eye, I spied Sheila slink away to a nearby table, pretending to wipe it down. She was eavesdropping. I shook my head at her, and she blinked innocently.

"Your cinnamon roll was one of the best I've ever tasted."

"Thank you." My cheeks hurt from smiling so widely. This was why I baked. To make others happy. Well, more like to make others fat so that I didn't eat all of the goodies myself and making myself fat. Evil, kinda, but it worked. I always had a hate-love relationship with the scale, but ever since I landed this gig, I actually lost a few pounds.

"What's your secret?" he asked.

"Oh. I don't have one." I shook my head.

"Your recipe, is that a secret?"

"Don't have one of those either."

His bushy eyebrows lowered over his dreamy eyes. "You don't have a recipe?"

"Nah. I wing it."

"You… wing it?"

I nodded and shrugged. "That's what I've always done. I wing it. Not two batches of any of my desserts are ever exactly the same, but I've never had any complaints so…"

Was this normal? To get so many questions after being given a compliment? I wasn't sure. If people did get desserts, they didn't wait around to talk to me, too busy, rushing to leave the diner and move on with their lives.

"Mindy you said. Is that short for something?"

"Melinda. But no one calls me that."

"How long have you been baking?"

"Since my mom first told me I was old enough to use a stove. I'm sorry. What's your name? It's weird being interrogated by a hot guy who you don't know the name of even if he does like your cooking."

Oh, wow. Open my mouth and cram in a ton of cookies to get me to stop talking. Did I really just call him hot guy to his face?

His laugh was low and easy and put me right at ease.

"My name is Alexander Avery."

The name was vaguely familiar, but I couldn't quite place it. "Nice to meet you."

"Likewise."

I stuck out my hand, and when he didn't shake it immediately, I felt like a fool, so I pulled it back, but then he reached for it.

Man, that was the most awkward handshake ever.

"Well, I just wanted to let you know that the cinnamon roll was delicious." He nodded to his polished off plate.

"Looks like you licked it clean," I joked.

Can someone please staple my mouth shut?

"Gotta say I've never done that before. Have a good night, Melinda." He nodded to me and then Sheila, dropped some money onto the table, and left.

Sheila ran right over. Ignoring her tip, she grabbed my arm. "Did he say Alexander Avery?"

"Yeah. Why?"

"He's only the most famous food critic in all of Haverford!"

Oh. Great. I just made a complete and bumbling mess of my first treat-and-greet with a food critic.

Forget stapling my mouth shut. Just trap me in a preheated oven.

Whoops.

Chapter Two

To make matters even more embarrassing, Sheila pointed to my face. "Uh…"

"What is it?" I cringed.

"You have food all over you. You're kinda… Don't worry. It's cute. Shows your passion for your work."

I threw up my hands. "Why didn't you say anything about that before I started talking to him?"

She shrugged. "I didn't notice it until now. I've gotten too used to it, I guess."

Gotten used to me looking like a hot mess of a baker? Wasn't that just icing on the cake.

Even though I almost thought it would be better not to know, I dashed to the bathroom.

Yeah, I looked terrible. I had flour all over me, icing too, and melted chocolate, cinnamon coated to my nails…

No wonder he hadn't wanted to shake my hand at first.

I could just see his review now. *Most disheveled baker in the world.* Or maybe *Dirtiest, messiest, most disorganized baker somehow makes passable desserts.*

Great. Just great.

*****

For two days, I waited to read the review, but when I didn't see it in the newspaper, I figured I majorly blown it. A review could've been huge. Well, a good one anyway. If more people came to the diner, we would all make more money, at least I hoped so. Freddie Lanier, the owner, was a great guy, and he paid us fair wages, but a bump would be so appreciated.

That night, when I was whipping up a batch of fudge—because chocolate made everything better—my best friend Jenetta Springsteen called. With my pinky, I accepted. "'lo?"

She shrieked incomprehensibly.

To say Jenetta was a little excitable at times was like saying that peanut butter and jelly was just okay.

Namely, she was always like this.

"Use your words," I reminded her.

"Did you see the article?" she asked, her words pouring out of her like oil into water.

"What article?" I turned on the heat. My stove was rather old and tended to get too hot too fast, so I hardly ever preheated pots.

"The one on the website."

So specific.

"About the diner!" she continued. "Are you gonna do it?"

"Do what?" I added some chopped pecans to the chocolate then tossed in a few whole ones too. Chocolate and nuts were almost better than cookies and frosting.

"Write it!"

I turned off the burner. No way was I gonna risk ruining fudge. "Slow down and start over."

My phone beeped.

"I just sent you the link. Check it out. I'll hold."

I put her on speaker and brought up the link. No matter how many times I tried to read it, I couldn't quite understand it. "What…"

"'Melinda Cave's desserts tantalize the senses. With a wide array of options, each one is sure to delight. The smells alone are enough to make you dying for a taste, and that taste is going to pay off. While not all of the desserts are much to look at, the delight that explodes in your mouth will make you close your eyes anyhow,'" she read. "Is that too much?"

"Yes. Too much." I sat down at my rickety chair at the small folding table that rocked back and forth. "Guess maybe I should worry more about presentation, huh?"

"Ah, don't worry about it. But listen. 'If Melinda Cave were to ever put out a cookbook, I would be the first in line to purchase one.'" I could just picture Jenetta jumping up and down. "I've been telling you for years to write one," she shouted.

I held the phone away from my ear for a long moment to let her continue without risk of losing my hearing. "Are you done?"

"Well, are you going to?"

I rubbed a worn spot on my tablecloth. It would be so nice to be able to afford new items. I paid my own ways for things and moved out as soon as I could which meant that a lot of my furniture had been sidewalk finds or from yard sales. When it came to my place, I didn't have a lot of pride in it… yet.

A cookbook would be one way for me to be able to change all that. Get a standup mixer. New cookware. Better ingredients. Maybe even a new apartment one day.

With a start, I realized Jenetta had hung up. Strange but not completely unlike her because—

Knock, knock, knock.

I grinned. "Come on in."

Jenetta opened the door. Squealing, she squeezed me tight. "I'm so happy for you! Your first food critic review!"

"Yeah, yeah." I tried to sound modest, but I was dying inside. Overall, it had been a great review, and it made me feel legit. That maybe a cookbook was a good idea, a potentially profitable one.

She trailed me into the kitchen. "Fudge?"

I giggled, feeling so happy I could burst. "I'll finish that tomorrow."

It took me no time to put the ingredients away, and then I grabbed the homemade cherry ice cream from the freezer.

"Ah, you know me well." Jenetta laughed as she got us spoons.

We sat at the table and indulged.

Jenetta closed her eyes after she swallowed the last bite. "That always hits the spot." She rubbed her flat stomach.

"How in the world are we friends?" I teased. "You and your health consciousness!"

"You should train with me. Lifting weights won't make you bulky."

"Yeah, but I don't need to lift heavy. Just a fork to my mouth."

She shook her head but giggled. Jenetta was a personal trainer at a gym, and she always looked incredible... although sometimes she did binge on one of my desserts, and then I'd hear about it. Always made me laugh.

"Not my fault if you lack self control," I murmured.

"You're gonna make everyone lack self control if you publish a cookbook. Promise me you'll consider it."

"I..." I bit my lower lip. Jenetta had it all—looks, a great body, and brains too. We went to high school together, but we had zero classes together because she had been in all of the advanced classes, so she didn't know my secret. "It's not gonna be easy."

"Why not?"

"Because. I'm dyslexic. Letters and numbers... they just... I can't make sense of them." Which was why I hadn't bothered with college. I just started my job at the diner and never looked back.

"So?" Jenetta shrugged. "Find someone to help you."

Now that was an idea...

And two weeks later, when so many people flooded the diner that I had no choice but to increase my hours to accommodate them all, I decided I wanted to go ahead with the cookbook. My dyslexia never stopped me before, so I wouldn't allow it to stop me now.

Chapter Three

Since I wanted to do this right and I had no idea how to start, I figured it was better to reach out for help. And since it had been his idea, I hoped Alexander Avery might be able to point me in the right direction. It felt strange and maybe even a little stalkerish to look him up online, but a simple email couldn't hurt, right?

To my utter shock, he emailed me back not even two minutes later, asking for my phone number.

Now who was the stalker?

Grinning so widely I had to look like a fool, and ever so grateful that he couldn't see that same grin, I emailed him my number and waited for him to call.

Which he did. Five minutes later.

"Hi, Melinda," he said, his voice a little deeper than I remembered.

"Mindy," I corrected him. "Thank you for getting back to me."

"So you're considering the cookbook. I'm glad."

"Yes. I am. Considering it, I mean." I closed my eyes and winced. I refused to be that girl who turned into a babbling, bumbling idiot because of a good-looking guy. "The problem is, I have no idea how to write a cookbook. It's more than just the recipes, and the recipes themselves aren't going to be easy to write."

"Well..." He said the word slowly, drawing it out. "My brother, Gabriel, is a ghostwriter. If you would like, I can give you his contact information, and you two can discuss the content and fees and deadlines. I'm sure he would be willing to work with you and—"

"Fees?" I asked, glancing at my electricity bill. With all of my cooking, it wasn't a cheap expense, and I had a few more bills waiting to be paid too. I didn't have any money saved up, not after I had to buy four new tires last month for my car to pass inspection. I couldn't afford to pay this Gabriel anything upfront.

"I'll email you his information. I really hope you pursue this, Mel—Mindy. If you do, do I get a signed copy?" Alexander asked.

"Sure. If you buy the copy first," I joked.

He laughed. "Deal."

Alexander hung up first, and I sighed. He emailed me the promised info a minute later, but I didn't even bother to open it. What was the point?

Well, Alexander had honestly wanted me to write the cookbook, so I was on the right track. Maybe I should at least try to write it myself, one recipe at a time. Maybe I was making a mountain out of a molehill. Maybe it would be easier than I thought it would be.

So I grabbed a pen and some paper and got out the ingredients I needed to make a vanilla cake—cake flour, baking powder, salt, sugar, margarine, water, vanilla extract, and milk.

But here was the hard part. I used measuring cups, yes, but I didn't fill them. I underfilled or overfilled and eyeballed and guesstimated all the time, and trying to convert that into numbers to mark down wasn't easy, but I did the best I could, and just over an hour later, I removed the cake from the over. I was just icing it when the doorbell rang.

"Come in," I called.

Jenetta strolled in. "Oh, no. I have the worst timing." She heaved a dramatic sigh.

I waved my icing wand at her, careful not to drip any of my homemade peanut butter buttercream frosting on the floor. "You have perfect timing." I nodded to the piece of paper containing my scribbles. "Do me a favor. Can you follow that recipe, and see how your cake turns out?"

She brightened. "For your cookbook? Yeah." Jenetta eyed the counter and the ingredients all lined up for her, including clean mixing bowls. "You left everything out on the counter for me."

"Yep. I was planning on asking you to come over and help me out. You do want the cookbook, right?"

"Yes..."

"So you'll help?" I held up clasped hands and batted my eyelashes.

She giggled, her hands covering her mouth. "You look like a mess!"

I winced, remembering how I looked when Alexander had seen me. Did his friends call him Alex? He hadn't said to call him that... Not that he and I were friends.

"I'll help this time." Jenetta wagged a finger at me. "But I can't take this kind of temptations."

"A few snacks here and there won't kill you."

"No, but I have to plan it. Save up my macros for it."

"Yeah, yeah." Jenetta calculated her food not just by calories, but also by fat and protein and carbs. She'd explained it all to me several times, but in all honesty, it went over my head.

"Can't squeeze in some today?" I asked.

"Nope. Already calculated my food. The next time you want me to test out a recipe—"

"Tomorrow."

"—Let me know so I can save up carbs and fat. Tomorrow?"

"Yeah." I handed her the paper. "Can't have a cookbook with only one recipe in it."

"True. As long as I can fit it into my macros, then fine." She glanced over my chicken scratch. "Looks easy enough."

"Good." I exhaled. I had done my best to write everything down.

While I plated out a slice of my cake, I watched Jenetta work. So far, it looked good to me. I waited until she put hers in the oven to test mine.

"Yum." I licked my lips. "You sure you don't want a bite?"

She glowered at me, hands on her hips. Somehow, she hadn't managed to explode flour all over herself like I did every time without fail. "If you're gonna keep—"

"I'll stop!"

"Good."

We talked and laughed and joked around the entire time her cake baked. She thought I should ask Alexander out. I thought she was nuts.

After her cake cooled, I reached for my icing, but Jenetta insisted. "My cake. My job. I'll finish it through."

"Technically, I made the icing so—"

"Sh." She eased the icing on and, once finished, held up her iced-covered thumb. "Oh, well." Jenetta popped it into her mouth and closed her eyes.

I was nervous as Jenetta cut a large piece. It smelled good, but would it taste good?

As it turned out, no. It didn't. I couldn't even chew my bite. I had to spit it out.

Jenetta frowned and tried a bite from my cake. She gave me thumbs up and then tried hers. She spat hers out too. "What… How did that happen?"

"I don't know," I wailed.

"I followed the recipe exactly!"

"I know you did." I glanced at the clock. Tomorrow was Saturday, so I wouldn't have to go into work until noon. "You busy tomorrow morning?"

"Nope. Saturdays are my free day. What do you need?"

"Come over first thing in the morning…"

*****

The next morning, Jenetta arrived, and we set to work. I watched her measure everything. I hovered. I practically made it myself.

But the cake still didn't turn out right.

"I just don't get it." Jenetta sighed. "I know how to make a cake. I can follow recipes. I do it all the time. I even teach recipes to my clients. Why isn't this working?"

"'Cause I'm a failure," I mumbled. I was sitting at the table, my chin in my palm, elbow on the placemat.

"You are not," she scolded. "Wanna go out shopping? I need new sneakers."

"No thanks."

"You sure?" She patted my shoulder sympathetically.

"Nah. Gotta go to the diner soon anyhow."

"All right. Chin up, Mindy. Don't get discouraged."

But I was discouraged as I closed the door behind her. I was feeling so down in the dumps I was debating gorging myself on that fudge I still had to finish.

If I couldn't do this by myself and Jenetta couldn't help me… Maybe I should talk to Alexander's brother. Maybe he would be willing to work with me and get a percentage of the royalties instead of being paid upfront. He was a ghostwriter, but had he written a cookbook before? This wouldn't be like a biography or science fiction novel or articles or whatever it was that he normally wrote.

What makes me think that he can help me if Jenetta can't?

If there was one thing having dyslexia had taught me, it was determination. When I wanted something, I saw it through, and this wouldn't be any different. I got through high school by having tutors. Gabriel would basically be another tutor. That was all.

So I called him up. One ring. Two.

"Hello?"

"Hi, is this Gabriel Avery?"

"Yes, it is. Who's this?"

"Mindy Cave."

"Ah, the baker. My brother told me about you."

I could feel myself blush.

"You want to hire me?" he asked.

"I want to discuss terms," I said slowly. I didn't want to get my hopes up, and I didn't want to get his up either.

"Over a meal?"

"Why not?" I shrugged. There should be enough time before I had to get to work.

He suggested a place that wasn't far away, and in no time at all, I was there, sitting across from him, wondering what the heck I was gonna do because if his brother had turned me into a tongue-tied mess, so would Gabriel because they looked exactly the same.

Chapter Four

"You're twins," I blurted out.

Gabriel laughed. "Yes. Alex didn't mention that?"

So he did go by Alex. *Guess we really aren't friends.*

"Nope," I said.

We ordered our food. We were at a greasy spoon, and I opted for a wrap.

He raised his eyebrows. "No burger for you?"

"I prefer to clog my arteries from desserts, not my meals."

Gabriel laughed again. "I can understand that. And speaking of desserts…"

"Royalties. I can't afford to pay you upfront. I'm sorry. I don't mean to be a bother, and I don't want to waste your—"

"It's all right. You aren't wasting my time, and honestly, my brother would kill me if I didn't help you."

I frowned and rubbed my forehead. It was never easy to ask for help, and I so desperately wanted this to work. Now that I finally was considering writing a cookbook, I was afraid of failing.

All cooks had ruined soufflés. This cookbook was my soufflé, and I refused to allow it to collapse.

"Why is he so dead set on getting my recipes?" I asked.

Gabriel ran a hand through his perfectly messy hair. They both had great hair. They were the kind of guys who would look dashing in suits or delicious in jeans. So not fair.

"He claimed that your cinnamon rolls taste just like the kind Mom used to make." He glanced away. "She died five years ago."

"Oh, I'm so sorry."

He gave me a small smile. "Thank you. Now, how do you think we can go about cooking up your cookbook?"

I groaned. "Oh, come on. You're a writer. You can't come up with something better than that?"

"Something about how your eyes sparkle like sapphires. How perfectly shaped you are, every inch of you. It's not what I would've expected from a baker."

"Because I'm not pleasantly plump?" I rolled my eyes. "And I'm not perfectly shaped. I carry a little extra weight…"

Shut up, Mindy!

"You know what, I am perfect. Every single inch."

He laughed again, and I joined in. I liked him. Him and his brother.

I cleared my throat to try to bat down the last bit of nerves. "Just please tell me your writing isn't quite so—"

"Cheesy," we said at the same time.

More laughter, so much that we didn't hear the waiter ask if we were ready for the bill.

I reached for it, but Gabriel grabbed it. "A business expense," he said.

"But I'm the one hiring you—"

"You're a potential client."

"I *am* a client."

Yes. I wanted this. I was gonna blast off, like the temp of an oven set to broil

He grinned, his lips curling only slightly at the corners. His eyes were the happiest. "All the more reason for me to pay."

"I'd rather you not pay," I said. "Not for me at least. Let's split it."

Why was I making this an issue?

Because I didn't want him to think of me as only a client. I wanted him to pay for me if it was a date. And while he was definitely a charmer—I was so far from perfect in any stretch of the imagination, perfectly shaped included—I doubted I was in his league or his brother's.

But why? I shouldn't feel that way. I should be proud of myself and all I've accomplished and all I want to accomplish yet. Why shouldn't I flirt with Gabriel? Even if it didn't go anywhere, it could still be fun.

And while money-wise, it would be better to have him pay for it, my pride wouldn't let me, so I laid down a ten on the table. "Does that cover my half?"

"More than enough." He added another ten and then handed me two ones.

"Really?" I pursed my lips.

"Really." Gabriel winked. "So, where does that leave us?"

I thought quickly. "Stop by the diner tonight. Did Alex tell you—"

"Where you work? Yes. What time?"

"Ten, if that's not too late."

"Not too late. See you then." He walked me out to my car, but I waited in the lot to watch him pull away.

Gabriel Avery and Mindy Cave. No. If he was a ghostwriter, his name wouldn't be on the cookbook, and even if his name were to be on it, his name wouldn't come first. A title! I still had to come up with a title, and the cover...

Feeling happy and content and like gooey icing, I went to work. The diner was jammed pack, which was surprising for a Saturday, but then again, we had been super busy ever since the review. A few days ago, the local newspaper had run an article, and Freddie Lanier, the owner, had done an interview on the news, so now even more people were coming.

At ten, we closed up shop. Derrick had already left, so it was only Sheila and I in the entire diner. She was wiping down the last of the tables.

"Go ahead," I said. "I'll finish up."

Sheila frowned. "I'm fine."

"I'm serious. I got this."

She put her hands on her hips. "Got no plans tonight?"

Someone knocked at the door.

"We're closed," she called.

"Actually…" I moved toward the front.

"What's going on?" She peeked out the window. "Is that—"

"His twin brother," I explained.

Her wyes widened. "Oh! Does Freddie know you're using his place to…" She wiggled her hips.

"I am not!" I swatted her with a towel.

Gabriel knocked again.

"If you'll excuse me…" I tried to slip around her.

She grabbed my wrist. "You aren't gonna give me any details?" she pouted.

"Maybe later."

Sheila winked. "You better!"

"There won't be anything to tell, though," I warned. "This isn't a date. It's work."

"Work. Right. So that's what they're calling it nowadays." Laughing, Sheila headed to the kitchen.

As soon as the back door shut, I walked to the front and unlocking the door. "Sorry about that, Gabriel. Come on in."

"Not a problem, Mindy, and call me Gabe. So…" He rubbed his hands together. "What are we up to here?"

"I thought we could maybe discuss a few things more while I bake."

"Now?"

"To get a head start for tomorrow," I explained. "Freddie's been thinking about offering desserts for carryout. He wants to expand some, and who can blame him? Your brother's review really helped us out."

Gabe followed me to the kitchen in the back. "Sounds like Freddie's gaining. I know money's a touchy subject, but are you receiving a kickback?"

"Hopefully." I shrugged. There hadn't been time to talk to Freddie about it, and I had been wishing he would be the one to broach the subject. He did pay me a fair rate for the work I had been doing, but now I was coming in early and staying late and making twice as many desserts. It wasn't greedy of me to want to be paid more since I was working more.

He wrinkled his nose. "That some of the reason why you want to write the cookbook? Or have me write it for you?"

"Not exactly. I love baking. That's my passion. Writing isn't. That's where you come in. I just need someone to fill in the blanks for me, you know?"

I whipped up several batches of cookies but didn't bother to bake them. It would take way too long. Next I mixed up some cakes and covered up those bowls as well.

"You have an… unconventional way of cooking," Gabe remarked.

I laughed as I shifted around to make room for the bowls in the fridge. "Why do you think I need your help?"

"You do it all from memory."

"Yep."

"And you don't really measure."

"Nope."

He rubbed the back of his neck. "I think I'm starting to see why you need me."

"You got it."

"I'll be honest. I've never written a cookbook before, and I kinda thought that it was a little interesting that you needed help writing one. An editor, sure, but to actually write the recipes and what goes before it…"

"You mean like how I came up with the recipe?"

"Exactly. Or any interesting tidbit or funny story. Anecdotes. That sort of thing."

"Oh, I have stories to share." I grinned and went to wipe my forehead but stopped. I probably looked terrible, and that was the last thing I wanted in front of the other Avery twin.

"I'm sure you do. How exactly do you wanna go about doing all of this?"

I closed the fridge and stared him down. "Are you sure you're all right with taking a percentage of the royalties?"

Because if I were him, I sure wouldn't be. What if Alex was wrong, and the cookbook didn't sell? It wouldn't be fair for Gabe to do so much work and receive nothing for it.

He scratched his neck and glanced away.

"I get it. Yeah." I exhaled. "How much are we talking?"

"Normally, I ask for a certain fee upfront and then bill the difference based on a per hour fee. Some projects don't take as long to write, while others require a ton of research, so each one costs—"

"How much upfront?"

"Two… One thousand."

"O-One thousand?" I squeaked. Visions of a beautiful cover with one of my cakes—no, one of my berry tarts!—on front with my name at the bottom in a beautiful cursive style font went up in flames. No way could I afford that.

But Gabe was backing up toward the entryway toward the seating section of the diner, completely oblivious to my predicament. "It's getting late. I should go. Do you want me to stop by tomorrow? Or…"

"I'll call and let you know." I tried to smile. My lips didn't move. That soufflé? I felt like it, felt like I had been deflated.

"You got it. This is gonna be a lot of fun." He flashed me a huge smile and walked away, whistling.

A fly could zoom out of my wallet. I was that broke. What the heck was I going to do? Because I really wanted this. Badly. Funny how something you never considered could suddenly become a huge goal for yourself.

I would find a way to make this work. Somehow.

I hoped.

Chapter Five

That night, I couldn't sleep. While I tossed and turned, I tried to figure out how to cut costs, but I had no way to sign a check for that kind of money. My mom had a bad habit of racking up credit card debt, so I swore I would never get one, but maybe that was gonna be my only option.

Lack of sleep had me going to my kitchen. I slaved away, baking five different kinds of muffins, cupcakes, and tarts. Fudge chilled in the freezer. Not to mention the brownies and new ice cream. Maybe it was a bit much, but I could be a bit of an overachiever.

By now, it was almost eight in the morning, so I called up Gabe.

"Hello?"

"Hi. It's me. Mindy. I was wondering if you wanted to come over?"

A strange sound came over the line. A yawn?

"Did I wake you?" I asked.

"What time is it?"

"Sorry."

"Don't sweat it. Come over to the diner?"

"No, to my place."

"Moving a little fast, aren't we?" His laugh sent a shiver up and down my spine.

"Not at all. You see, I have an evil little plan."

"I prefer evil big plans, but go ahead. Tempt me."

"That's exactly it. I'll shove so many treats down your throat that you'll grow so fat you can't make it to the bank to cash my check."

He laughed some more. "That's a terrible plan."

"Have you tried my baked goods?" I demanded. "Now come on over. Do not go to your kitchen. Do not eat breakfast. Prepare to gain love handles."

I gave him my address and hung up.

What in the world was I doing? My place wasn't clean—at all.

I scrambled around, shoving stuff under the couch or throwing it into my room. I was just tossing a pair of clean undies into my room—they must've fallen out of my basket—when the doorbell rang.

"Come in," I called before realizing it was Gabe and not Jenetta. He didn't have a key. He couldn't let himself in.

I dashed to the door and wished I had had more time to get ready. Should've showered or at least checked my appearance over in the bathroom. Too late now.

Taking a deep breath, I opened the door. "Hi." I stepped aside so he could enter, trying not to stare. He should've been a model with those cheekbones.

"Hi. Nice place."

I flushed. It was Spartan at best, had always been a stopgap for me. I wanted a better place, a bigger one. Didn't see the need to buy a house for just one person, and I didn't have a lot of pride, especially because of the area of town I lived in. It hadn't crossed my mind to be embarrassed to give Gabe my address until now, and I almost wanted to shove him right back out the door.

But while the living room—if you could call it that, the area was so small—and my bedroom—which was off limits to Gabe—weren't that impressive, the kitchen was my domain, and I waved him over. "Sit," I instructed.

Because of my mad dash to clean the apartment, I hadn't had time to finish setting the table, so I did that now. Then I cut tiny slices and grabbed tarts and cookies and made up a dessert tray for him.

"Here you go." I presented the tray to him as if I were Vanna White.

"Wow. All this for me?"

"Yep." I was too nervous to eat a bite.

Gabe dug in, eating with gusto.

I sighed. "You're supposed to enjoy your food."

"I am enjoying it."

"Don't you know how to savor it?" I reached over and broke off a small piece of nutty fudge. It tasted so good I closed my eyes and sighed, enjoying the mix of smooth chocolate and the gritty crunchiness of the nuts. "That's how you do it," I said, opening my eyes.

"Is that right?" Grinning, Gabe enjoyed a spoonful of banana strawberry ice cream. For the most part, he did seem to savor it… a little. "Wow. Your desserts are pretty impressive."

"Just pretty?" I crossed my arms, leaning back in my chair, doing my best not to glower at him.

"Yes. They taste delicious, but the presentation…"

"Is lacking." I grimaced. "It's a bad habit I've gotten into," I confessed. "With the diner, it's always such a mad rush to get everything baked, and to make sure that Derrick has the oven whenever he needs it… I know. None of my cookies are perfectly round, and I tend to just slap the icing on, but no one complains about it, and if I'm writing—if we're writing—a cookbook, does my presentation matter?"

"Maybe. Maybe not." He reached for the brownie. "Whoa. That's rich!"

"Too rich?"

He enjoyed another forkful. "No. You know what would make this better?"

"Don't say hot chocolate syrup." That would make it way too chocolaty. I knew. Tried it.

"No. I was thinking peanut butter ice cream."

"Oh! I'm out of that flavor, but that's a fantastic idea."

"Is there any dessert you don't make?"

"I'm willing to try my hand at anything. Pies, crepes, truffles, candies—"

"We can group the desserts two different ways. By main ingredients like nuts or chocolate or by type."

"Type would probably be better, but maybe we can have an index in the back about ingredients. Is that the right word? Index?"

Gabe nodded. "Good idea." He shifted forward and removed a notepad and pen from his back pocket. "How exactly are we gonna work on the recipes? Since you just wing it."

"I don't just wing it. I just know how much to put in." I shrugged. "Hard to explain."

And if my failure with Jenetta was any indication, it was hard to replicate too.

I sighed and rubbed my forehead.

"Hey..." Gabe cleared his throat. "I can't help noticing..." His gaze drifts to the hole in my tablecloth.

Great. He thought I was poor. Which I kinda was, but I needed his help and...

"I'll pay you," I blurted. The credit card. I'd apply for one today. Or tomorrow morning. I didn't have a ton of time left before I had to go to work, and I would be working until closing.

"If you don't have the money," he started quietly.

I held up my hand. "Don't," I snapped, glaring at him. I didn't need his pity.

"I was going to suggest a fundraiser," he said mildly. "You can raise the funds that way. I kinda just assumed you were planning on self publishing the cookbook, and if that's the case, you'll need money to pay for a cover in addition to me. I can do the formatting. I'll be willing to show you how to set up accounts with Amazon and Barnes and Noble and iBooks... Don't worry, Mindy. We can make this work."

"You that desperate for money yourself that you're willing to babysit a crazy baker who can't even write down her own recipes?"

"Only because she's crazy good looking." His broad grin had me shaking my head.

"Your flirting needs work."

"It only needs work when I'm nervous."

"I make you nervous?" I snorted.

Yes. Snorted. Like a pig. Yeah, because that was attractive.

Not.

He laughed. "Is that so hard to believe?"

"Yeah," I said honestly. I had had my share of boyfriends before. I wasn't high maintenance, but I was a little on the crazy side, I'd be the first to admit it, and none of them had ever been serious. "But if you are nervous, I want you out."

"Out?" He raised his eyebrows, the perfect picture of baffled.

"Yeah. Nerves have no place in the kitchen. You can't create if you're nervous."

"Cooking is your art."

"Baking," I corrected. "I don't do a lot of cooking. Pancakes for breakfast. Simple. Sandwiches for lunch. Easy. Dinner's quick too. I use my talents for making people happy. And maybe a little fatter." I held out my hands. "A side effect. More to love. That's how I look at it."

Gabe nodded, stroking his chin. "I can see that." He eyed me.

I swatted his shoulder. "I didn't mean that I was fat."

"I don't like girls who are skin and bones."

"Good, because if I have my way, girls, and guys for that matter, will be gaining weight across the town."

"Across the US," he said. "Your cookbook will be available everywhere. Think about it."

Now that would be a dream come true.

"Will you need help organizing the fundraiser?" he asked.

"That I can handle. I guess we'll put the cookbook ghostwriting on hold until after it's held."

"If that's what you want." He grinned. "But keep in touch. I would like that."

"Your gut won't," I warned.

"More to love, right?" Gabe winked. "I'll see myself out."

The entire time I cleaned up my kitchen and put the desserts away, I was grinning. Things were looking up. No way would I allow this to crash and burn. And I wouldn't have to use a credit card. Everything was falling into place.

Chapter Six

Correction. Everything *had* been falling into place. But then I left for work later than I should've. Traffic was backed up, and a car rear-ended me. No one was hurt, and the damage was minimal, so I told him not to worry about it, but, man, was my car looking worse and worse every day. Mostly cosmetic dents and it desperately needed a new paint job, but I wasn't about to waste unnecessary money on that. Maybe after money started to roll in from the cookbook.

If it sold.

If I could hire Gabe to help me with it.

If, if, if.

Luckily, because of the prep work I did last night, I wasn't too far behind when I got into work, and by the time the early dinner crowd rolled in, I was completely caught up.

For once, Freddie was in his small office, and I dashed over and knocked on his door. "Do you have a minute?" I mouthed to him since he was on the phone.

He held up a thick finger. The man ate too much but was in decent enough shape. Always looked like he was ready to jump up and run out of the room. Couldn't even keep completely still. Even now, he was drumming his fingers on his desk.

"Sounds good," he said into the phone. "I'll talk to you later." He hung up. "Mindy. What can I help you with?"

A bonus. I cleared my throat. "I was wondering if you could do me a favor."

"What's that?"

"In two weeks, on Wednesday, I'd like to host a fundraiser here."

Every Wednesday, the diner was closed. Freddie used to be open seven days a week, but getting staffing for every day combined with the low numbers we always had on Wednesday made it a no brainer.

"A fundraiser for what?" Freddie's face was a mask. His fingers stopped drumming, and his dark eyes bore into me.

"To raise money. For me. I want to write a cookbook and—"

"A cookbook?" He rubbed his chin. "I guess that's possible. How much—"

I put my hands on my hips. "Freddie..."

He grimaced. "Most places would—"

"How much revenue have I personally brought in recently?" I asked as sweet as fruit juice.

Freddie normally had a darker complexion, so when he paled, like he was now, it really showed. "In two weeks? All right. Fine. It's yours. What time?"

Oh… Um…

"All day." I nodded emphatically, as if I hadn't made that up on the spot.

Step one down. So many more to go.

*****

Jenetta was a lifesaver. I typed up a flyer, and she looked it over, and then on a whim, I emailed it to Gabe, and he edited it too. Then I went to the library, printed out a boatload, and Jenetta and I papered the town. She even put up a flyer at her gym, which I thought was hilarious but didn't dare tell her.

I worked hard on baking, and Jenetta and Sheila helped me out with the decorations, and before I knew it, the day of the fundraiser was here, and I was so sick to my stomach that I didn't think I could do it. No one would come. Or if people came, they would taste the desserts I made especially for them and choke them down or spit them out and laugh in my face as they kept their checkbooks shut and walked back out the door.

But Jenetta forced me to the diner, and I brought out the desserts, and people came. First, only a couple of the diner's repeat customers, but by the end of the night, there had been a ton of people I never saw before. I did my best to talk to everyone, made bad jokes, and even had a good time.

Not one person or even two—more like twenty—came up to me and said about time or something along those lines. They were all customers who had come to the diner for years, some even before I started working here. Originally, I had been brought on to be a backup to Derrick, a minor part-time gig, but I had brought along brownies to the interview. Freddie took one bite and hired me on the spot to be the diner's personal baker. Ever since, I'd been doing my dream job. Baking, to me, was my passion. I had discovered long ago that cooking food for meals lacked something. It wasn't something I could quite explain, but baking gave my life meaning. It was therapeutic. All I had to do was bake, and even if I was having a bad day, it would instantly turn around. I shared a connection with my creations. It was kinda magical.

This whole fundraiser was kinda magical too. Gabe showed up, and so did his twin, and when they manned the collection box, I swore I saw more women reaching for their checkbooks. I wasn't going to complain. It felt weird to have others serve my desserts, to have them rush to the kitchen to fetch more. That should be my job, but I was expected to talk and mingle and be charming.

Well, I was talking and mingling. The charming part? I was doing my best, and either the people were all super polite and were laughing at my pathetic jokes to be considerate or else I was kinda pulling that off too.

So surreal.

Afterward, when the fundraiser finally wore down and I counted up how much money had been raised, I had to sit down.

I had raised more than I ever expected—enough to make all of my dreams come true.

Chapter Seven

To celebrate, I invited the twins, Jenetta, Sheila, Derrick, and Freddie back to my place. Only the twins and Jenetta were able to make it, and my best friend knocked her hip into mine. "Double date," she mouthed to me.

I rolled my eyes. Whatever. Yeah, they were both good looking, but I was way too busy for anything like that.

We talked and laughed and watched a movie—more like we put it on but ignored it and used it as background noise. Overall, we had a blast. Alex—he finally told me to call him that—tried to take all the credit for the cookbook, and Gabe argued that he should get the credit because he was going to write the masterpiece, and Jenetta said that it was going to be a success because of me.

I just soaked it all in, unable to believe that this was my life, that I was finding a way to become a real baker. My dreams were growing, and I wanted to become the next Rachel Ray. Why not shoot for the top? Nothing was gonna stop me! My name was gonna be synonymous with the world's most decadent desserts.

*****

It didn't take long for my bubble of pure happiness to deflate, though. Here and there, Gabe and I carved out time to be able to work on nailing the recipes, and it just wasn't working. Not my guiding him to make the recipes and me writing it down, careful to be as exact as possible. Not him watching me and writing down the recipes either. Whenever someone other than me tried to replicate my recipe, it always had the same result—disaster.

Why? I couldn't say. Gabe couldn't say. None of the other guinea pigs could say. It was like I had the Midas Touch of baking, and honestly, it was more frustrating than anything.

Gabe ran a hand through his hair. He had to have some kind of force field around him that prevent flour from sticking to his skin and clothes. While he still looked like a model, I knew I had to look like a wreck. I was sweating from racing around the kitchen, and the heat blasting from the oven wasn't helping my cause either.

And when I got hot, I tended to get cranky. Seemed like Gabe was the same way. What a pair we made.

"This shouldn't be so hard," Gabe said.

"It wouldn't be if you could write down the right measurements," I snapped.

"You watched me write them down."

"Yes, but I'm dyslexic, remember? You sure you aren't too?"

"I asked you how much you used with each ingredient. And sometimes you use pinches or grab handfuls and—"

"How many chocolate chips you add aren't going to make or break a recipe," I protested.

"—You don't level off measuring cups, so sometimes you add more than a cup, or it might be a little less," he continued as if I hadn't interrupted him.

I snorted through my nose, and he laughed. I was hotter than burned chocolate. "It's not funny! Don't you want this to work?"

"Of course I do. I just want you to know it's not on my end. I happened to follow a recipe last night."

"To make, what, a cake from a box?"

Still smiling, he rolled his eyes. "I'll have you know it was cookies from a bag."

"Seriously? It's not like I'm some kind of baking guru. I don't see why you can't just replicate—"

"It's not just me though," he pointed out.

I threw my arms into the air. He was right. I *was* the only thing different. And I hovered over him and made sure he added everything just about right. It really wasn't helping that I didn't measure exactly, but the difference between my cake and his was incredible.

Incredibly awful.

His desserts would crumble, turn out dry even if not overcooked, and tasted like cardboard. No one could bake so terribly so consistently. According to Alex, one time Gabe had made a cake from scratch—a chocolate cake—and it hadn't been bad at all. Gabe could cook... except when he tried to bake like me.

"So what are you saying?" I demanded. "That I'm a baking goddess? That no one will ever be able to do what I do with measuring cups and flour? That me, the dyslexic, am a baking savant so far above everyone else?"

"You got a better idea?" he countered, his smile fading.

"That's absurd."

"You're absurd."

"Real mature." I crossed my arms. I wasn't mad at him anymore. Well, I was, but I was also mad at the situation. Nothing seemed to explain what the heck was going on. I made cookies, not potions. I created recipes, not spells. I wasn't a witch.

But maybe there was something to it.

Nah.

Suddenly, I noticed someone was standing in the kitchen doorway.

"You two bicker like an old married couple," Alex said, wagging his finger. "Sorry for just walking in, but I knocked for five minutes. Guess you two were too busy to hear." He grinned and helped himself to a piece of cake.

"Disgusting, right?" I glowered at Gabe. Yep, still mad.

"Not my fault." He glowered right back. He was mad too. Couldn't blame him for that.

Alex wrinkled his nose. "Disgusting's too kind." And he glanced from Gabe to me to Gabe again, smiling slightly.

I made a scoffing sound. "Not looking for love," I declared. "I'm trying to be a businesswoman."

"She's hired me. A client. Nothing more." Gabe shakes his head.

It kinda hurt to realize that his flirting meant nothing, but I shouldn't be surprised. He probably flirted with all the girls.

He hadn't flirted with Jenetta after the fundraiser. Yeah, but he had flirted plenty with some of the women at *the fundraiser. Maybe he had just been trying to ensure he would receive his funds.*

I rubbed my temple. Arguing with myself wasn't any more fun than arguing with Gabe.

"Any way I can help?" Alex asked.

I tilted my head to the side and nodded. "Here. I'll instruct you on how to bake no-bake cookies. So simple even a kid could do it. With adult supervision that is."

"Bake no-bake cookies." He laughed.

"Fine. Does make no-bake cookies sound better to you?" I asked.

"Yes," Gabe cut in.

"Word play or food play, which do you prefer?"

Gabe's eyebrows rose, and his grin made a reappearance. The sight of it had me smiling myself. Of course, his was a little naughty, but that was okay. I'd much rather us tease and flirt, even if it didn't mean anything. So much better than fighting.

So I hovered over Alex, doing more of the cooking than I probably should've, and the cookies didn't taste too bad this time. Not quite like when I made them, but edible at least.

Feeling hopeful, I called Jenetta over, and she followed the recipe Gabe had written up step by step.

And her replication? Terrible. Just flat out terrible. Cardboard with icing.

Gabe swallowed a bite and grimaced. "Maybe Alex, Jenetta, and I just can't bake."

"No. Jenetta bakes awesome healthy desserts all the time," I said glumly.

Jenetta nodded and brushed back her long hair. "I do."

"She's also quite modest," I added.

"Only on days that end in 'y.'" She laughed but then sighed. "I just don't get it. I really don't. Why can't we get this right?"

"We're missing something," Alex said.

"No. I watched. You all added the right ingredients. You all followed the steps. I don't do…" I frowned and rubbed the back of my neck, my gaze lifting to Gabe's. He nodded.

"Well, I'll do my best and keep working on the recipe if you don't mind?" Jenetta held up the recipe.

Gabe grinned. "Keep at it."

"Bye, everyone!" She waved and left.

Alex stood. "I should get going too. Have another review to write up. Chin up. You'll sort through this." He closed the door behind him.

I shifted toward Gabe, my chair scrapping across the kitchen floor slightly. "You don't think that I'm the missing ingredient, do you?"

"Maybe you are. Or maybe your love is. I've been watching you when you bake, and you put everything there is in you into it—your heart and soul. Everything. Little pieces of yourself."

It sounded so absurd, so crazy. I didn't have some kind of baking voodoo magic. How long should we keep trying at this before we realized that a cookbook just wasn't happening? We were wasting a ton of food.

But I didn't want to give up. I refused to quit.

Maybe my dream should change though…

Chapter Eight

It took almost a week to get ahold of every single one of the donors, but I managed, and even more miraculously, they all agreed to my new plan.

Which was great, but now that meant having to have a heart-to-heart with Gabe.

Since I figured this wasn't going to be an easy conversation, and since it was business related, I opted to set up a business lunch. It would be more professional that way. Set up boundaries.

Because I couldn't forget what Alex had said about Gabe and I acting like an old married couple. And I couldn't stop thinking about all Gabe had done for me already. And how I had wanted the cookbook to work.

And now I was going to change everything.

Alex wasn't going to be happy. Gabe definitely wasn't going to be happy.

Would I be happy? Only time would tell.

We weren't peanut butter and chocolate. We weren't that close. We should be… peanut butter and regular butter.

Although you need both to make peanut butter cookies…

I arrived at the restaurant first and got us a table. A small table for two. The other nearby small tables were filled with happy couples, and I fiddled with my straw, trying not to feel so uncomfortable.

"Hey."

With a smile that seemed to always grace my face when I would first see him, I glanced up to see Gabe. "Hi. Sit. Please."

He sat across from me, and our waitress approached, so we ordered. I rearranged my silverware and then picked at my nails, needing something to do.

"What's wrong?" he asked. "Are you discouraged? Don't be. We can figure this out. I'm sure of it."

"Gabe." I took a deep breath and exhaled through my nose. "I wish we could, but it's been taking way too much of your time, and we don't even have one recipe yet. It's not fair—"

"You paid to book my time. You have it. Just because it's slow going—"

"The cookbook is done," I said softly. "It's not happening."

He laid his hands on the table. "You're firing me?"

"Firing is a strong word." I shook my head. This wasn't going well at all.

Gabe leaned back in his seat, looking far more dejected than I would've thought he'd be, like a cookie that's crumbling into dust. "I can't believe it. Is it because of the flirting?"

"No."

"Because I'm a failure," he muttered.

"No!" I hung my head. "I almost thought you would be happy," I murmured.

"Happy? Why?"

"Because…" I shrugged. Sometimes we had argued, like that night when his twin showed up. My frustration must've made me hard to work with.

But he had gotten frustrated too. He wanted the cookbook as much as I had. And now I was taking it away. I was forcing him to give up, and he didn't strike me as the kind of guy to give up something easily. He fought and succeeded.

"And it's not a firing," I clarified. "I still need you."

Wait. That didn't come out quite right.

"I need you to write for me still," I clarified, speaking so fast that the words came out almost like one giant word. "I need you to make up flyers and pamphlets."

"For what?" His face became expressionless.

"Well…" I rubbed my throat. This was a crazy venture, treading on new ground, and I didn't know if this would fail too, but I was willing to give it a try. "I found a small place that closed, and the price to rent it isn't that bad, and I talked to the people who made donations, and they're all okay with it…"

"With what?"

"Instead of a cookbook, I'm gonna open my own bakery. It won't be easy at first, because I won't be able to hire anyone to man the front, so I'll have to bake everything and handle the money too, but eventually, maybe I can hire a high schooler, and way down the line, I'd like to be able to do deliveries too. Just local of course. And then maybe we can see about actually owning the place instead of renting. Not we. Sorry. Me. I can buy it. If I make enough money that is, and I'm rambling. I'll stop." I clamped my mouth shut but only for half a second. "What do you think? It's a terrible idea. I haven't even talked to Freddie about it. I would have to give in my notice, and—"

"Do you want to know my thoughts?" Gabe asked, his expression still unreadable.

"Only if you think it's a good idea." I couldn't pull off a smile or a teasing tone.

"It's not a good idea. It's a great idea. I'm more than willing to help you with flyers and anything else. You paid me too much for—"

"If you can also handle the printing of the flyers, that would help."

"You still overpaid me," he insisted.

"You deserve to be compensated for your time with the failed cookbook."

He grimaced. "It didn't fail, and maybe one day, we'll revisit it."

"Yeah. I could sell it directly from the bakery." I grinned, already imagining hosting a book signing there with an array of sample treats for the customers to enjoy. But what if the bakery was just another dream that was gonna blow up in my face? I doubted the cookbook would ever come to fruition. "You think I can pull this off?" I asked, wringing my hands.

"I think you have the talent and the drive to be able to."

The expression on his face… he wasn't teasing me. He was being the most serious I had ever seen him. I almost wanted him to go back to the overly flirty Gabe. I knew where I stood with him, but this Gabe? He was a stranger to me.

"So…" he said, "have you come up with a name for your bakery?"

Chapter Nine

Giving notice was the hardest thing I ever had to do. For years, I worked here. My first real job.

Freddie glanced up from his paperwork, took one look at my face, and hung his head. "How much more do you want?" he grumbled.

"It's not—"

"You deserve it. How much?"

I grimaced and rubbed the back of my neck. Was it normal to feel this way? To feel like following your dream meant leaving others in the dust? Because this move could hurt the diner, and I had been so wrapped up in myself and my wants to only just now realize that.

Freddie stroked the stubble on his chin. "What is it, Mindy?"

"I…" I took a deep breath. I wanted this. The bakery. It wouldn't fail. I had even talked to a tax person to start to figure out all of the other loose ends of being a business owner and what exactly it entailed. Some went over my head, but the guy was good at explaining things, and I was ready to get the ball moving.

Freddie had only donated the diner as a location for the fundraiser. He hadn't actually given me any funds, which was the only reason why he didn't know about this already. Derrick and Sheila already did. They were behind me. Jenetta and the twins were. I had even talked to my mom about it. She was thrilled.

I had been thrilled. Until now. At this moment.

"What's going on?" Freddie asked, the concern in his voice making me hate myself.

"Nothing's wrong." I cleared my throat. Geez, was my mouth dry. "I just… I'm giving my two weeks' notice."

"Two weeks… Is this about the cookbook?" He was grimacing, but he didn't look devastated or angry or upset, so that was a good sign.

But when he heard about my plans, would he think I was backstabbing him?

"I… No. I'm going to start a bakery. Over on Elm." I held my breath, feeling like I was waiting for the oven timer to ding so I knew when to take out a dessert. If I didn't get it out at exactly the right time, it would be ruined.

My dream would be ruined.

His grimace grew, and he rubbed his forehead. "Renting out the old fruit store?"

"Yeah. It's a good spot, I hope. Maybe not, since the fruit store closed up, but…" I closed my eyes for a second before opening them. This was a turning point for me, I could tell. I could let doubt choke my goal, or I could fight. Honestly, the amount of different stores that had tried to thrive in that location and had failed already was enough to make any prospective buyer think twice. What made me believe that I would fare any better?

But then, something inside of me shifted. I had to reach for my dreams and wrestle them to the ground and take control if I want to be the one daring to soar. And I was gonna do just that.

That mental oven timer went off, and I imagined myself pulling out the dessert. And it was perfect.

"I will make it work," I said slowly. "I'm gonna be a baker and sell my goods, and hope for the best, and… please don't hate me!"

Freddie rubbed a hand down his face and kept his hand over his mouth. His shoulders shook, and a strange noise sounded.

"Are you all right?" I asked. What if I gave him a heart attack or something?

He moved his hand, and I realized he was laughing. "Knew this would happen since you first came on. You have a real talent, Mindy. I'm gonna miss you. My waistline won't. My wife's gonna miss you too."

Sometimes Freddie took home a few desserts that were a little old or were too misshapen to serve to diners.

"Her waistline won't miss you any though." He sighed and shook his head. "Are you sure about this? I mean, I can pay you more. I'm serious. You've done so much for the diner, what with the review bringing in so many more people."

I shook my head. "I'm sorry, Freddie." I really was. "But this is something I gotta do. I gotta try." I took a deep breath. I really wanted his support. If he didn't think I could do it, I didn't know if anyone else would be able to either.

"Two bucks more an hour. And you can have three more days off a year."

"Freddie…"

"All right, five more days. An entire week. You can…" He stared at me then nodded slowly. "It's not about the money, is it?"

"No." It was about proving to myself that I, and my desserts, was worth it. The failure of the cookbook stung. I needed this to work.

Freddie rubbed the back of his neck. "Who am I kidding? My wife and I will be your first customers. If there's anything I can do to help you, let me know."

Tears stung, but I blinked them away. "I… I'll love for your help with the business side of it. The baking, that I got down, but the rest of it…"

"Of course."

*****

One day when I was trying to fix up what will be transformed into my bakery, Alex came over.

"You all right?" he asked.

I stopped washing a window, used the crook of my arm to wipe off my brow, and glared at him. "You like watching a woman work?"

"Yes." He laughed. Alex sounded so much like his twin that I wished Gabe was here. "I wanted to talk to you."

"What about?"

"Gabe."

I swallowed hard and returned to my work, putting a little more elbow grease into my efforts to wipe away the grime and make the window shine. "What about?" I repeated, feeling myself flush.

"You don't know, do you?"

"Know what?"

"What he thinks of you."

"No." A small black speck would not come off no matter how hard I scrubbed. "He's probably glad he doesn't have to see me so often. What, with the cookbook going up in smoke. Doesn't have to deal with me when I'm at my worst. I… I should probably apologize to him." I rubbed so hard the speck finally came off.

"Apologize for getting frustrated? He got just as frustrated… in more ways than one."

I glanced over my shoulder at him. "We only have a business relationship."

"Keep telling yourself that."

"It's the truth!"

"Then you're both gonna be frustrated. It's not always a bad thing."

"What isn't?" A part of me wanted him to go away, but I did want to know more about Gabe. His opinion of me mattered.

One night, when we hadn't bothered to have him test a recipe and we just enjoyed fresh-from-the-oven cookies, he told me about his ghostwriting. How he loved helping others to write their stories. How the stories became a part of him sometimes. How he wanted to one day write his own stories. Science fiction.

"Or maybe about a girl whose magical baking powers saved a kingdom," he had joked.

He had fought for my dreams, and I wanted his dream to happen too. If that meant telling everyone about him as a ghostwriter so that he can earn money to be able to feel secure enough to start following his own dreams, I would do that in a heartbeat.

"It's not always a bad thing to argue, to disagree. It pushes you to change, right? Change isn't always bad." He held out his arms. "Without you changing your dream, you never would've bought this place."

"Yes, but…"

"Life is about risks, taking chances."

"Following your heart," I murmured.

"Exactly. Just think about it." And Alex left.

I stared out my now sparkling window. Following my heart. Gabe was right. I did pour all of my heart and soul into my cooking. And that was fine. Baking was easy. I could give everything I had into it.

But to give bits and pieces of myself to someone else, that was something else altogether. It would be better to just focus on the bakery and getting my life in order.

Right?

*****

Washing the place, painting the interior and exterior, setting everything up… It took longer than those two weeks, and I was running on fumes to get by, but finally, opening day arrived.

The fruit stand had previously been a very small deli with a few tables, so there was already a glass case counter for me to showcase my baked goods. I had been baking and freezing like a freight train for the previous week so there was a ton of variety. The flyers and pamphlets Gabe had made were beautiful, and I asked had him make small signs that I could interchange on the wall behind me so customers could see what was offered that day and the price.

I hadn't been able to sleep last night, so I made extra cinnamon rolls, and right when it turned eight o'clock, I unlocked the front door. No one was waiting outside for me, and my heart sunk. Not even Mom. *Might've blown all of her money and have too much debt to afford the gas to drive.* For years, I had been pleading with her to get help, but she wouldn't listen. Sometimes, you had to let others find help themselves.

It was all right. I didn't need her. That was why I had moved out as soon as I graduated high school. Didn't want her to go into more debt because of me. I had saved up the money I accumulated from birthdays and graduations from other relatives, found my cheap apartment, got the job at the diner, and now look at me. A business owner.

A successful one? Hopefully.

Not five minutes later, Alex came by to grab a box of cinnamon rolls.

"They look perfect," he said as he peeked through the cellophane top.

"Been practicing," I confided. "Presentation and all that. Still have a ways to go, but…" I handed him his change.

"Thanks. I hope you have a wonderful opening day."

"A review wouldn't hurt," I called out as he left. Could've sworn he chuckled.

Sporadically throughout the day, more people came in, and I served them. In between, I would duck into the back and ice more cupcakes or start new batches of cookies. Whatever didn't sell today could be sold tomorrow. If certain items never sold and I didn't think they were fresh enough to sell, I'd donate them to the local food bank. Donations, my tax person said, were a really good idea.

Br-ring!

I'd probably grow to hate that bell, but I popped out from the back with a smile on my face. "Hi. Welcome to Cave Confections! Oh, hey, Jenetta!"

My best friend leaned on the countertop. "Hm… Pecan rolls or banana nut bread or cinnamon rolls or…"

"You might like the pecan-topped apple crisp cake I made."

"Oh, that does sound good!" She inhaled deeply and closed her eyes. When her eyes opened, she frowned. "But I need something kinda healthy. Got anything that'll fit the bill?"

"I made a special batch of protein brownies. I used chocolate protein powder in the batter. Not completely healthy, but that's the best I can do. Made it especially for you."

"Awesome. I'll take it." Her eyes lit up, and I giggled.

The rest of the day went fairly smoothly, and I was worn out. One more batch of cookies and I was calling it. My back and feet were killing me. It was amazing that Sheila wasn't stick thin because of all the running around she did as the main waitress at the diner.

I had just finished rolling the balls for soy nut butter cookies—specifically for those with nut allergies—when *br-ring!*

Huh. Guessed I forgot to lock the front door.

"I'm sorry. We're… Gabe. Hi." I grinned at him like a fool.

"Sorry. I know I'm too late to buy anything, but I wanted to drop by. I started a new writing gig—a biography of a guy who lives uptown, and the interviewing process took a lot longer than expected and traffic, there was an accident, and…"

"No worries. Glad you could make it. Wanna head on back? Just about to pop some cookies into the oven."

"Sure." He glanced around as he headed toward me. "The place looks great. How did your first day go?"

"Pretty good, I think," I said as we entered the cooking area. "Not sure how to gauge it, honestly. Just have to wait and see, I guess."

I grabbed a soy nut butter cookie ball and placed it on the tray. A fork pressed nicely onto it, making those nice, crisp lines that traditionally peanut butter cookies have… only the cookie ball stayed attached to the fork as I lifted it.

"What in the world?" I peeled off the dough, re-rolled it, and tried again. Same result.

"I think freezing the batter might help," Gabe suggested.

"True. Or..." I coated the fork with flour. This time, the fork didn't stick quite so badly. "I'll try the freezing next time."

"If the flour works, use it. Just a suggestion. Baking's your forte, not mine." He reached into his back pocket and removed a slip of paper. "Now, don't take this the wrong way—"

"Uh oh. One of the phrases you're not supposed to ever say to a woman. That and engaging in conversation after she says she's fine. Oh, and never ever answer if this makes my butt look big. There's just no right answer."

"But your butt never looks anything less than perfect. Just like the rest of you."

"Um. Flattery won't get you anywhere with me. I thought we established this."

"Yes, well, we aren't working together anymore, so any boundaries we might have set—which I'm not sure anything was established, but I won't quibble that point—the boundaries are irrelevant. Aren't they?"

His gaze was too piercing, and, yes, I enjoyed talking and teasing with him, and maybe could even picture us harping on each other well into our graying years, but I couldn't. Not now. Not when my business was just starting, and I needed to devote myself to it one hundred percent. It wouldn't be fair to him to start anything. It wouldn't be fair to us.

So I ignored his hopeful stare and held out my hand for the paper. "What's this?"

His face shut down, and any warmth or hope died. "I know you've been working hard on your food presentation, and I saw that there's a course for cake decorating that you might be interested."

"Oh, yes! I might even be able to write off the price of the course as a tax deduction." I practically yanked the flyer out of his hand.

"Mindy Cave. Have you turned into a businesswoman on me?"

"Yes," I said absentmindedly. "Hm... Maybe I can close up shop a little early on Tuesdays just during the length of the course. It helps that it's at night, although I think more people might drop by later in the afternoon to get desserts for that evening. I'm still trying to figure out how long my days should be, if it's worth it to be open so early in the morning for the rushing to work crowd or not. Muffins might be a huge draw then. It's a guessing game."

"You're a guessing game," I could've sworn he muttered.

"Pardon?" I asked as I returned to flattening my cookies.

"I wish you the best, Mindy. I really do."

"Hey." I put down my fork and turned to him. This sounded like good-bye.

He pointed to me and gave a slight wave. "I'll see you when I see you."

No hug. Nothing. That was it. He just left. Sure, I was covered in flour, and my hands were gunky—I had mangled the flyer in my excitement—but he couldn't have waited a minute for me to wash my hands?

I had my business. I had grand plans. I had so much. So why did I still feel like something was missing?

Chapter Ten

The days melted together, turning into weeks and then three months, and it was a crap ton of work, and I was so busy that I ended up falling asleep most nights very early so that I could get up before the crack of dawn and start baking immediately.

And I was loving it! I never went longer than thirty minutes before having another customer to serve, and several times through a day, there was even a line!

Mrs. Flower, a woman I knew from the diner, strolled up to the counter. "Is it possible to order birthday cupcakes through you? Tommy's turning five this weekend, and his party is Thomas the Tank Engine themed."

My mind raised, already thinking about how to make icing a deep enough blue color. Thank goodness for the course Gabe told me about. My cookies all were identical in shape now, every time, and my icing skills were still improving and evolving. I'd never use fondant—I just wasn't a fan—but that didn't mean I could mold buttercream frosting and force it to my bidding. "I can do that."

"Great! How much for three dozen cupcakes?"

She paid, and I started to whistle as she left. Maybe I should have a new flyer—or a banner—hung up somewhere that mentioned hiring me for parties. Summer was coming up. Graduation parties would be in full swing.

Which meant I should call Gabe.

The bells on the front door jingled, and I glanced up with my customary serving smile in place that went full bore when I saw that the customer was none other than Gabe.

But the closer he came, my smile dropped slightly. This was Alex. I could tell. Alex looked almost too perfect all the time, with his hair gelled. Gabe left his hair wilder, and I suddenly wanted to touch Gabe's hair, to fix it, because I just knew it was out of place.

Alex shook his head. "You look disappointed."

"Of course not. Don't be silly. I'm afraid I sold my last cinnamon rolls an hour ago."

"That's all right. I wanted to try something new today anyhow." He tapped his fingers on the glass, and I forced myself not to wince. It was amazing how many times I had to wipe the display throughout the day.

"I have a lot of options. Are you looking for something rich or creamy or sweet or—"

"You might want to try something new today too," he said, stroking his chin as he eyed the baked goods. "I'd try that. The last apple cinnamon strudel muffin."

"Coming right up." I grabbed a square of wax paper, seized the desired muffin, and presented it to him with flourish. "And what do you mean I need to try something new?" I asked as I accepted his bills.

"I think you know. Call him."

"I was planning on it. I need—"

"Not about work." Alex glared at me.

My cheeks grew warm. "You're not chubby, and you don't have wings," I grumbled.

He laughed, and the sound was so similar to Gabe's that my stomach churned. "I think I make a dashing cupid myself."

"He is arrogant, so you've nailed that," I joked.

"Ha, ha. See you around."

There wasn't a moment's rest after Alex left because the timer beeped. My brownie bites with molten centers were done, and then a flood of customers came in, and I didn't have time to think about what Alex had said or about his brother.

But Gabe must've been in the back of my mind because that night, I dreamed about him, his teasing, his smile, his lips…

On one hand, I felt incredibly fulfilled. I was living my dream. I was becoming a success. I still did advertising, handing out the last of the flyers Gabe had made, and word was spreading. Everything was falling into place business-wise.

And I made time for my friends too. Sheila and I have always been close, and then there's Jenetta, of course. I wasn't lonely.

I didn't need Gabe. Not in the sense that I couldn't live without him. But I still did want him in my life.

Had I pushed him away? Did he want me, or had it all been fun and games to him? Maybe he flirted with all the ladies, especially his clients, to try to keep steady jobs.

Nah. I didn't buy that. That was insecurity speaking. He wasn't like that.

Still didn't mean he liked me.

Back and forth, I debated with myself and finally came to the decision that I needed to reach out. It took me an hour to craft the letter, to make sure I didn't misspell anything and to make sure I could say what I wanted to say and it not be too mushy or over the top. And for all of my agonizing over it, the letter was kinda short:

*****

Dear Gabe,

Thank you for everything you've done for me. I know I paid you for your work, but I want to repay you again for all the laughs too. You helped me achieve my dream, and I want you to share in my happiness. We make a great team, and I'd like to continue that camaraderie to the next level. If your stomach can handle my sweets, swing on by the shop.

All the best, Mindy

*****

Maybe it was too corny and sappy. Maybe I should scrap the whole thing. Before I could change my mind, I boxed up a cupcake and drove over to Gabe's house. I knocked on the door, laid the box down on the mat on top of the envelope, and darted out of there. It was probably too early for him to be awake, and yeah, I was being cowardly, but I did have to get ready for work.

All that day and night, I jumped every time the bells chimed. Not once did Gabe walk in though.

And he didn't the next day.

Or the next.

Or the next week.

Guess that was my answer.

Chapter Eleven

Didn't matter. I was fine. So what if I was baking more than I actually needed for the bakery? Yes, I was a stress baker.

My icing skills were getting better all the time. Too bad it wasn't Halloween time that I could get away with adding blood to cookies. Or make dagger-shaped cookies. Nope. I was trying to make nice, perfect corners for graduation caps.

Which wasn't easy, especially when you spied something white fly out from beneath the back door at nine in the morning, hours before you have to get ready for opening. Kinda taking after the diner, I had one day a week that I only worked from one until five, and that was today. Tuesday.

I cleaned up the icing I squirted onto the counter from being surprised. After wiping my hands on my blue roses apron, I picked up the note.

Go to Giant. Pick up the prepaid order from customer service. Give the name Timel.

Timel? What in the world?

I should ignore this. Finish my work. Resume my life.

But I didn't really need to ice these cookies, and I was kinda curious, and it wouldn't be terrible to get away from the bakery.

So I packed away the cookies, stored the icing, and went on to Giant. Turned out that the order was a bunch of fruit—like enough for an army— and a bag of chocolate chips and one of peanut butter chips. *Okay...*

I turned to leave.

"Oh, and this too." The teenager behind the counter handed me a note.

"Thanks." I hurried to my car, stowed away the food, and opened the note after I climbed behind the wheel.

Next stop. The state store next door. Pick up the order from Timel.

Who in the world is Timel?

But I was already here...

This time, the pick up was a simple bottle of champagne, which would pair nicely with the fruit, and another note.

Bring the items to the angel statue at the park.

What in the world is all of this? It's kinda strange. Make that really strange.

But the stuff wasn't mine. I couldn't just keep it.

Just in case, I called Jenetta. "I'm going to the park."

"All right." She sounded completely unfazed.

"Because of some Timel person. Left me a few messages to pick up things and..."

"Things?"

"Yeah, fruit and chocolate and champagne and—"

"Oh, sounds like fun."

"I don't know. Don't know what to think. Kinda freaked out actually. Now Timel wants me to go to the park, but maybe I shouldn't."

"You should. You totally should. Gotta run. Have to keep my clients on their toes. Literally. Calf raises." And she hung up.

I was beginning to smell a conspiracy, but if anything did happen to me, at least Jenetta knew where I was going. Because I was freaked out but curious too.

Ten minutes later, I arrived at the park. The angel statue was old and weatherworn, but I always thought of it as majestic *because* of her flaws not *in spite of them.* As trying as my dyslexia could be, I was glad I had it. To avoid schoolwork, I had focused more on baking, and now look at me.

Here. In the park. Meeting someone I had no idea who it was. And I wasn't wearing anything special. If Timel turned out to be an axe murderer, I'd be found wearing holey jeans and an old shirt. My hair was in a messy bun, and I wasn't wearing any makeup. Definitely not my best look. In fact, even my diner cookies had to look more presentable than I did.

Since it was a random day, the emptiness of the park didn't surprise me. I spied a runner jog by and spotted a woman leading her dog away. Other than that... I twisted in a circle and halted when I spied a hint of red on the other side of the angel statue.

A blanket. A picnic basket. With two champagne flutes and a bowl and a lit candle.

And another note.

Mix some of the chips into the bowl and use the candle flame to melt them. I'll be there soon.

The bowl was ceramic, the type that absorbed the heat so it was both microwave and oven safe. Melt the chocolate and peanut butter, huh? A makeshift dessert fondue. That I could handle.

I added double the amount of chocolate chips compared to peanut butter. Would be nice to have some cream to add to the mix. A spoon to stir would be even better, but I made due, and slowly the chips began to heat.

The sound of approaching footsteps made my heart pound, and when I glanced over to see Timel, my heart felt ready to leap out of my chest.

"Timel? What does that mean?"

Gabe shrugged, smiling his reckless smile. "That it's about time we do this." He laid a tray on the blanket and arranged a beautiful bouquet of tiger lilies in the center. "You didn't strike me as a rose-kind of girl."

"I'm not."

"I think I figured you and your baking out." He nodded toward the tray.

"Oh, yeah?" This felt so fun. So freeing. Obviously Jenetta had been in on all of this. Wouldn't be surprised if she would've called me if I hadn't called her, just to make sure I went on my errands and carried this through.

Deep down, I knew, or at least hoped, that Timel was Gabe. That was the biggest reason for my fear, not that I was meeting up with a serial killer, but that my heart was in danger.

"I was right," Gabe said softly.

"About what?"

"That love is the missing ingredient."

It should've sounded cheesy. And it was cheesy. If not for his tone and the look in his eyes.

"In what recipe?" I asked, reaching over to claim and squeeze his hand.

"In the recipe of you and me." He leaned over and kissed me. So sweet. And tender. I didn't want it to end.

But the chips were melting, and the smell was divine, and I was getting hungry. I eyed his tray.

"Brownies?" The one recipe Gabe had tried more than any other to replicate.

"Cut yourself a piece while I melt the rest of this." He pulled out a small bag, which contained paper plates and plastic silverware.

Cutting into the dense brownies wasn't easy, and the piece crumbled a bit when I removed it from the tray, but the first time removing a slice of brownies was always a challenge. I popped a piece into my mouth. "Mmm."

"Good?"

"Yes. Delicious." I picked up a large crumb and fed it to Gabe.

He chewed and swallowed then sighed. "They are very good, but they don't taste at all like yours."

"Still…" I ate some more. "I like having someone bake for me."

His smile stretched from cheek to cheek. "I don't mind cooking for you if you do the baking."

"Oh, really? I think I might be able to handle that."

"And the recipe of you and me? That's a recipe I can recreate every day."

"My baker," I teased. "Baked your way to my heart."

"Think you'll still be baking when you're old and gray?"

"Think we'll still be kissing?" I countered.

"Think we'll be that married old couple my brother was talking about."

"Don't you think you're getting a little ahead of yourself?" I asked.

"Maybe. But I do know I want to date you. I don't want a business relationship with you. Sure, if you need more flyers, I'm your guy, but…"

I popped open the champagne and poured us some. Two strawberries were added, and I handed him his flute. "To us."

"A new beginning."

"A chocolaty beginning." I dipped another strawberry into the melted chocolate and fed it to him.

"A delicious beginning."

I knew right then that it didn't matter if we took things slow or fast. One day, I would introduce him to my mom. One day, one of us would pop the question. And one day, we would get married. I was going to be baking for the rest of my life, and I had no complaints about that, but the person I most wanted to bake for was sitting here right beside me.

We had our toast and enjoyed our fruit, and even though some of the fruit wasn't ripe and Gabe partially burned the chocolate fondue, it was one of the best meals of my life.

Was love the missing ingredient in our relationship? And with my cooking? Maybe not always, but in these cases, it sure had been.

Dear Readers

I hope you enjoyed reading The Missing Ingredient! One of my recurring themes in my stories is that you should never stop daring to dream. It doesn't matter if you are dyslexic or not, if you're on the thin side or not, if you're short or tall, if you're trying to do something big or huge and uncharacteristic for your gender… Dare to try. Dare to dream. Dare to reach for your goals. You might not succeed on the first try or even the second, but if you don't even try, you will always fail. Believe in self is a powerful thing.

So try and dream and reach. I promise I'll do the same.

All the best,

Nicole Zoltack

A little about me: Nicole Zoltack loves to write in many genres, especially romance, whether fantasy, paranormal, time travels or regency. She's also a freelance editor and a ghostwriter. When she's not writing about knights, superheroes, or witches, she enjoys spending time with her loving husband, three energetic young boys, and precious baby girl. She enjoys riding horses (pretending they're unicorns, of course!) and going to the PA Renaissance Faire, dressed in garb. She'll also read anything she can get her hands on. Her current favorite TV shows are The Walking Dead and Gotham.

My Book List

Magic Incarnate series: A Question of Faith, A Matter of Doubt, A Balance of Power, A Journey of Despair

Kingdom of Arnhem trilogy: Woman of Honor, Knight of Glory, Champion of Valor

Heroes of Falledge trilogy: Black Hellebore, White Hellebore, Scarlet Magi

Beyond Boundaries series: Masked Love, Starry Love

The Test of Time

Love Before Honor

Joy to the World

Bloodlust

Starving for Love

Guns and Fangs

Feel free to keep in touch!

Author newsletter: http://tinyurl.com/NZnewsletter

FB Fan Page: http://www.facebook.com/authorNicoleZoltack

Blog: http://nicolezoltack.blogspot.com/

Twitter: https://twitter.com/NicoleZoltack

SWEET SAMANTHA

Kiersten Fay

Fifteen years after high school, Samantha never thought she'd see him again, let alone discover he'd purchased the old abandoned house next door.

Samantha Fox has started her own business working as an interior designer, but in her small town, clients are few and far between. When her old high school crush, Mathew Moore, moves into the abandoned house next door and hires her, she must work to keep their relationship professional and prevent that old flame from burning her all over again.

Chapter 1

Her taste in men was about as good as her expertise in decorative Chinese artifacts. She could tell what looked pretty, what would make a room pop and a client swoon and dish out the cash, but display a sixteenth century jade vase from the Ming Dynasty next to an imitation Walmart knock off and she wouldn't see the difference. A vase was a vase. As long as it was pretty, what did the rest matter?

Well, it mattered if that vase had a giant gaping hole at the bottom that you didn't notice until you'd filled it with all that was left of your trust in the opposite sex. That was when you found yourself high and dry with a grotesque water stain on your hardwood floor...and a bouncing baby boy.

My baby isn't a baby anymore, Samantha Fox thought. Though he was not yet a man. He was in this in between stage where Sam could see visions of both the wonderful man he would become, and the pure, innocent baby he would always be to her.

Jayden had just entered the seventh grade. It was a miracle he'd passed the sixth. She suspected many of his teachers had just pushed him through. She didn't know if that was a good thing or not. He wouldn't be held back, would get to remain in the same grade as all his friends, which was important for his self-esteem, but he was starting the year at a disadvantage.

"Hey, Mom!" Jayden yelled from the bottom of the stairs. "I'm home! Do we have anything to eat?"

If she wasn't already broke, she'd *go* broke just from feeding the child. "There are leftovers from last night," she called, finishing up her latest expense report. She was going to take a hit on this job if the client asked for any more changes.

When Sam had first been introduced to her client's open layout condo with its to-die-for vaulted ceilings and grand stone fireplace, she had been dazzled by the design possibilities. Then, in her haughty voice, the owner, Anna, had declared with a negligent roll of her hand, "Make it rustic." Well, Sam's idea of *rustic* apparently varied greatly with Anna's, who had taken one look at the wood furnishings, earthy colors, and southwest inspired accents, and complained, "I said rustic, not medieval. Can we make it a little more modern?"

Yeah, if we only change everything about it! Sam hadn't said that, of course. She desperately needed to keep her first big client happy. Anna was influential among the well-to-do. One good word to her ritzy private-club friends and Sam would be booked for life. No more worrying about next month's bills and her dwindling bank account.

Anna was her *in*.

So she'd asked, "What do you have in mind?"

Anna was persistent in her "suggestions", prompting Sam to compromise her design...with disastrous results. Earth tone walls clashed with sleek contemporary furniture that sat beside the stone fireplace that had been the centerpiece of her original creation. Now it was like walking into two opposing universes that had crushed themselves together and couldn't quite fit. To Sam, it looked abhorrent.

Anna had been delighted...at first. Then came more changes: "This won't do," she'd said, pointing to the area rug that had been integral in tying the opposing aesthetic together. "That has to go," she added, indicating the brass chandelier with its modern twist that did the same. Without those two items, nothing in the room made sense!

The state-of-the-art stainless steel appliances were next on the chopping block, and the wall color came under debate. Sam had painstakingly painted every inch in an attempt to save money on labor. Now she might have to do it again.

"Think more modern," Anna had advised. "Uptown, but downtown. Comfortable yet chic. You know, rustic. I thought we'd had an understanding on this."

Modern rustic? Oxymoron?

"Don't worry," she'd replied with forced confidence. "Once it's finished, you're going to love it."

She was seriously wondering if Anna could ever be satisfied.

"Mom!" Jayden called up the stairs. "Ben's here. Can we order a pizza?"

Sam sighed. She hit save on her document, shut down her laptop, and checked her wallet. Twenty and some change. It might have been enough to feed two growing boys, if Ben, Jayden's best friend, wasn't more ravenous than her son was—an astounding feat.

Though her bank account protested, she didn't mind the boy's near-constant presence. He was a good friend for Jayden, and she sensed his home life wasn't the best. Word around town was his drunken father and bartending mother were in the middle of a nasty divorce.

Not for the first time, Sam was glad she'd never married Jayden's father; the man who thought holding a job for more than a week was considered long-term employment.

Downstairs, she peeked into the living room. Jayden and Ben had already fired up the pawn shop PlayStation and were deeply focused on a first-person sniper game.

"Do you have any homework?" she asked Jayden.

"I'll do it later."

"Hi, Mrs. Fox," Ben greeted, glancing her way with his boyish smile.

"Hello, Ben. How are you?"

"I'm good, thanks."

"Dude, I just killed you," Jayden snapped triumphantly.

"Aww, dang it." Ben turned back to the screen.

"Game off. Books out. And I mean both of you."

"Mom," Jayden groaned. "In a minute, okay?"

"No. Now. You can play when you're done with your homework."

"I don't even have a lot to do."

"Good. Then it won't take you very long."

Jayden pouted, staring her down as he did every time she asked him to do something he didn't want to. She stared right back, determined to win this little silent battle. *I invented the stare down. I can do this all day long—*

The doorbell rang.

She gave Jayden one last measured look, and then turned to answer it. Behind her back, the game resumed.

On the porch, Tammy greeted her with a big hug, as she always did. Her next-door neighbor was the touchy-feely sort, sweet, with a light southern drawl, though she'd lived in Colorado for upwards of ten years now. "Did you see?" Tammy exclaimed. "Someone finally bought the house on the other side of you."

Sam glanced to her right, and sure enough, there was a big moving truck parked at the curb. "How about that? I was starting to think it would never sell." The abandoned two-story house had been run down for years, the neglected, unruly yard plagued by high grass with patches of dandelions and other weeds that encroached on her lawn constantly. Many of the windows were cracked, or boarded up, and the ugly green paint flaked more and more with each passing summer. She was surprised the state hadn't condemned the place.

"I hope they fix it up," Sam said.

"That would certainly raise the value of the neighborhood."

Tammy's daughter, Ellie, who was in the same grade as Jayden, hurried across their connected yards. "Mom, I can't find my blue earrings. Have you seen them?"

Tammy gave Sam that *a mom's job is never done* look, then turned to her daughter. "No, honey, did you check your room?"

"Duh." Ellie rolled her eyes, then peeked around Sam into the living room. "Hi Jay's mom."

"Hi, Ellie. Go on in. They're playing some sniper game."

Ellie rushed past to stand behind the couch.

At once, Jayden and Ben sat up straighter.

"Can I play?" she asked.

"Have you ever played this game?" Ben asked.

"No, but it doesn't look all that hard."

The boys laughed, neither paying much attention to Ellie's indignant glare. Then Jayden said, "You can play winner." At that, the competition was on, Jayden and Ben hitting the controller buttons like their lives depended on it.

So much for winning the battle, Sam thought. Girl trumps homework, no matter what *Mom* had to say about it. She'd just have to make sure he finished everything before bed. "I could use a glass of wine," Sam said, inviting Tammy inside.

"You read my mind."

As Sam poured them each a glass from her bottom-shelf vintage, Tammy speculated on the neighborhood's mysterious new resident. "I bet a family's moving in. With the school so close and the park down the street, this is such a family-friendly neighborhood. Better yet, I hope it's another single mom. Then I'd finally have someone else to talk to. Not that I don't love you, hun, but I just don't get the whole interior design thing." Tammy worked as a waitress at the local diner, and as far as Sam could tell, never aspired to be anything more.

"And I just *love* hearing about every terrible table that complained about the food and then left you a bad tip."

"Speaking of, this lady last night was such a..." Tammy trailed off, staring out the kitchen window.

"What's up?" Sam followed her gaze. A black Chevy pickup truck was now parked behind the moving van. A jean-clad man in a dark shirt was prowling the high grass. His stride was confident, his gait purely masculine. He assessed the house, then the surrounding houses, turning as he did. When he was taking in her modest home, she got a better look at him....

And her breath caught.

From this distance, it was obvious he was handsome with his clever gaze and strong jaw. She might go as far as to say too handsome, but his lips were a little too severe, pressed tightly together as his short brown hair tussled with the breeze.

"You think that's the owner?" Tammy was transfixed as well.

"Could just be a mover," she replied when the man crossed the yard and opened the back of the moving van. There wasn't a lot inside. With her full year of on-the-job experience as an interior designer, she determined the belongings would fill a single room, maybe two in a stretch. And much of it looked destined for the garage. There had to be three tool chests that she could see.

"God be praised if every mover came that *hawt*. I'd be in constant upheaval." Tammy sipped her wine.

Another car rolled into the driveway, a blue sedan. Both she and Tammy leaned in for a better angle.

"Oh, there are two of them!" Tammy exclaimed. "One for each of us."

"One of what?" Ellie strolled into the kitchen.

The women jumped back as though they'd been caught doing something untoward. "We might be getting new neighbors," Tammy replied.

Ellie glanced out the window. "Who? Those two guys?" After a minute, Ellie lost interest and headed back into the living room, throwing over her shoulder, "They're probably gay."

Tammy grabbed her chest as though she'd been struck by a hard object. "Gay? No. You think? It would be just my luck. All the good ones are either gay or taken."

Sam heard Jayden ask from in the living room, "Who's gay?"

"The new neighbors," Ellie blurted airily.

Sam took a sip of wine. "All I care about is that they are nice and quiet. Whatever they do in the bedroom is none of my business."

Tammy wiggled her eyebrows. "Let's go meet them."

Chapter 2

Matthew Moore gazed up at his new investment property slash temporary office feeling the weight of his decision. *Back to small-town life.* Not that the town was all that small anymore. In the last fifteen years, it seemed to have filled in around his old neighborhood, practically doubling in size. And it wasn't exactly a decision he would have made if his mother hadn't suddenly gotten ill. It was for her that he'd returned to the pastures of his youth. Lucky for him, real estate was on the rise in this area. In a few months, he'd be able to flip this busted up old house and make three times what he'd put into it.

He took in the other houses around his. Some of them had been kept up, a couple newly painted, but most looked tired and beat. Once he was done here, theirs would all look like dog meat compared to his filet mignon. At least his neighbor's house was reasonably well kempt, or maybe it just looked that way compared to his heap. The dichotomy of the yards alone told a story. His, overgrown and teaming with critters; his neighbor's mowed short and neat.

A couple of shadows in his neighbor's front window drew his attention. Ah, small-town folk, always curious, and unanimously nosey. *I give it five minutes before they come out to make nice.*

A blue sedan pulled into his driveway. He smiled at the driver, his oldest friend and fellow troublemaker, Brent.

Brent lumbered out of his car, unfolding his six-foot frame. "Mattie! How the heck are you?"

Whereas Brent had stayed in this town after graduation, Matt had left with thoughts of better things in his future: An NFL contract to be specific. Unfortunately, a set of torn ligaments in his knee ended that dream just as it was gaining traction.

They bro-hugged, slapping each other's backs.

"This the dump you were talking about?" Brent glanced at the house.

"Won't be a dump much longer."

"I can't believe you're flipping houses. Never would have pictured it."

Neither had Matt, but once plan A had shattered along with his knee, he'd been forced to figure out a plan B, and fast. Thank god he'd had other skills. A lot of the guys on the team hadn't.

With a small loan from his mother, he'd started his own construction company in Denver, managed to build it up to a six-figure business after only a couple years. If it hadn't been for the clients, it might have been his dream job. Tired of complaints, bill dodgers, and lazy employees, he'd sold the company to his biggest competitor for a tidy profit just before the recession hit. *Lucky as a raccoon on trash day*, his mom had told him. Had he kept the business just a few months more, he might have lost everything.

As it was, he could retire if he wanted, live off his savings for the rest of his life, but that just wasn't in him. What the heck would he do with his time if he wasn't working?

Besides, flipping houses meant he could do the project his way every time. He didn't have to tick items off a client's impossible list, and then listen to their rancor every time he informed them of the price increase due to their change requests. *That's right, people. Stuff costs money.*

"Is this all you're moving?" Brent asked, investigating his moving van.

"Most of my stuff is at Mom's house. I'm just using this place as an office until I sell it."

"How's your mom doing? I heard she's sick, but I don't know what from."

"Neither do the doctors." They'd brought up the dreaded C word: cancer. But hadn't been able to find anything. "She goes in for more tests next week."

"Sorry, man. Let me know if there's anything I can do."

"Thanks, buddy. Let's just get this stuff in the house and then go grab a beer."

"Sounds like a plan. You can tell me what's been going on with you and Erika."

Matt cringed. He hadn't really told anyone about his break up with Erika yet—another reason behind his relocation.

Brent hesitated at his expression, but before he could ask the obvious, his head swiveled to the house behind Matt. "Uh, oh. Looks like the natives are stirring."

Matt followed his gaze. Two women were crossing his neighbor's lawn toward them. He checked the time on his phone. Not even five minutes.

*****

"Hi, y'all!" Tammy waved at the two men, her southern drawl thicker than Samantha had ever heard it. She followed behind, inwardly laughing at her friend's flirty saunter. When she wanted to be, Tammy was a force to be reckoned with. *Eat your hearts out boys.*

She stopped short. My, my, they were so much bigger up close. They could be linebackers with those meat racks for shoulders.

Tammy just kept right on walking, undaunted. "I'm Tammy, and this is Sam. Y'all moving in?"

"I'm Brent," the bigger one said, shaking her hand. "This is Matt. He's the owner."

"Oh, so y'all aren't together?"

Brent blinked, speechless for a moment. "Pardon?"

Sam pursed her lip to keep from laughing out loud. As far as brain to mouth filters went, Tammy's was full of holes.

"You know? As in a couple?"

"No. We're not together," Brent said, still taken aback by the assumption.

"Well, you never know these days, with the times a changing and all. Not that there's anything wrong with it. We're very open-minded around here, but a girl's got to be sure at the get go when it comes to these things."

Sam stepped in. "I'm so glad someone is finally moving in. This house had been on the market for, well, forever. I bet it was a steal."

"Very nearly," Matt said, stifling his own grin. "Is this one yours?" He said, pointing to her house.

"Home sweet home. It'll be nice to have someone finally fix *this* place up. I can't even tell you how many weeds I've had to pull, and god knows what's been living in there, and there's this smell—"

Tammy cleared her throat. "And it'll be nice finally having new neighbors. Tell me, Matt, is there a wife and kids on the way?"

Something flashed in his eyes, but Sam couldn't make it out, and she suddenly felt as though they were being rude drilling them like this.

Tammy didn't seem to notice. "I've a daughter, myself. Her name is Ellie. Sam's son is named Jayden. Teenagers, if you can believe that." She gazed up at him expectantly, like he was supposed to be awed that the two young flowers before him had teenage children.

Matt hesitated for a moment as though he wasn't sure she was done talking. "No wife. No kids," he said. "Just me. And I won't be here long. Once I renovate, I'll put it back on the market."

Sam noticed Brent did a double take at that.

"Oh, you're a house flipper? I've always been interested in that."

Tammy the liar, everyone.

"How does one get into doing something like that?"

"Well," Matt started. "You find a cheap house, you fix it up, and then you sell if for more than you paid for it."

Tammy laughed, but Sam knew she wasn't amused. "Come now, Matt, simplify it for me, would ya?"

Ellie called from the door, "Mrs. Fox, they're not letting me play!"

"Just remind them about homework," Sam hollered back.

With a wicked grin, Ellie disappeared into the house.

"Mrs. Fox?" Brent asked, eying her with new interest. "Not Samantha Fox? From Clearwater high?"

"Yeah. Did you go there too?"

He spread his arms out wide, and then pointed between himself and Matt. "Come on, you don't remember us?"

She cocked her head, trying to place their faces.

"Oh man, really? Matt was the quarter back, and I was an offensive guard. We went to one of your parties once. Wait, is this the same house?"

Her eyes went wide, zeroing in on the other man. "Matthew *Moore*?"

He nodded, looking as though he was using every cell in his brain to recall who she was. Not that he'd have a lot left to utilize.

"As I recall, you guys weren't even invited that night." Nor was the entire football team, but that hadn't stopped them, and half the school, from showing up anyway. Her parents had gone out of town for the weekend, leaving her home alone for the very first time. She'd invited a couple friends over for a movie, but word had gotten out. She still wasn't sure who had made up those flyers.

When her parents had returned, the house was trashed, and she was grounded to infinity and back.

The only redeeming element was that she'd had her first kiss that night—from none other than Matthew Moore. It had been incredible! life-altering! Like lightning had struck when their lips touched. But the next day at school, Matt had shunned her, acting as if it had never happened.

She'd been devastated.

What she thought would be her best memory had turned into the worst.

*****

Samantha Fox? Matt thought. The name did sound familiar, but for the life of him, he couldn't remember her. That party Brent mentioned was a blur too. Hadn't that night started off at a kegger?

"Well, it was great seeing you both again." Samantha smiled at them, but there was a change in her demeanor. Before, she had been what he would consider relaxed and easygoing. Shy maybe, but filled with mirth at her friend's behavior. Now she'd gone...he didn't know. Pensive?

"And good luck with your renovations." She waved, sidling back toward her front entrance.

Looking confused, Tammy followed, but she wasn't ready to give up on her new acquaintances just yet. "You know," she said, flipping around to face them. "Y'all should come over and catch up with my little Samantha here. It's amazing you guys grew up together. I'd love to hear some stories. We were just about to order pizza, what do you guys like for toppings?"

Sam's jaw dropped, but the shock was temporary. "Now, Tam, I'm sure they're busy—"

"Nonsense." Tammy waved her statement away. "Guys? Pizza? Twenty? I bet you could get all that stuff moved even before the delivery guy gets here. What do you say? I'm buying."

"Never say no when a lady offers to pay." Brent laughed. "I love peperoni." Then he went to his car, popped the trunk, and pulled out a twelve-pack of beer, handing them to Tammy. "Here, be a doll and put these on ice for us. It's my housewarming gift to Mattie."

"Booze is your gift to me."

"Oh shut up. You love it."

A cold beer with friends did sound good right now. Well, with *friend*, one overly talkative female, and another one that he couldn't quite get a read on. Matt was usually great at reading people...book reading, not so much, but people were a cinch. Brent was his same old self. Hard worker, fun-loving, give you the shirt off his back type of guy. Hadn't changed much since high school. Didn't seem much affected by his short-lived marriage to his high school sweet-heart, Becky, that ended six months after the *I do's*. Yet the man hadn't had a serious relationship since, so maybe he *had* been affected.

Tammy was clearly in need of male attention, and was one to eat it up like cake no matter who was dishing it out. He was betting little Ellie's father was no longer in the picture.

Samantha had him stumped. He was betting not for long. No doubt he'd have her figured out by the end of the night.

Chapter 3

"I can't believe you invited them over," Sam groused, wiping down the linoleum countertop with a warm soapy rag. *Ugh, is that dried jelly?* "They could be serial killers."

"Oh, pish." Tammy leaned against the counter, wearing fresh makeup, her blond hair fluffed and sprayed stiff, sipping her second glass of wine. "Serial killers don't flip houses."

"Somewhere out there is a serial killer proving you wrong right now. And two of them could be standing right out that door." She flung her rag in the general direction of Matthew Moore's house, dripping dirty water on the floor. She bent down to mop it up.

"I think they're sweet."

"You think you're going to get a date out of this." Sam stood and wrung out the rag over the sink, onto the dishes from this morning's breakfast that she hadn't been able to get to.

"Well, one of us needs one," Tammy continued. "When was the last time *you* went out?"

She opened the dishwasher, shoving dishes in haphazardly. "I go out all the time. I took Jayden to Barker's Grill the other day. We had a nice time."

"I mean dressed up, put on perfume, the guy holds the door for you kind of date. Not *here, honey, you've got schmutz on your face.*"

"I *like* wiping schmutz off my baby's face." Samantha closed the dishwasher and then began washing the sink's basin, doing her best to scrub out the nicks and scratches from the white ceramic coating. *Face it, girl, those aren't going anywhere.*

"*Oh, la, la*, the perks of motherhood. You need a *real* date. And so do I. Lo and behold, God delivers unto us two gorgeous available men. Dibs on the big guy, by the way."

"Ew, Mom. Are you creeping on the new neighbors already?" Ellie entered the kitchen, opened the fridge, and pulled out three sodas.

Tammy placed a hand on her hip. "Did those boys send you in here for those? You make them fetch their own drinks, Ellie. You start doing everything for them and they'll come to expect it all the time."

Ellie rolled her eyes and carried the sodas back into the living room with her.

"Learn from Mama, honey! These are wise words." To Sam, she muttered, "Dang, that girl gets more and more like me every day. Scares me to death. I tell you what, she is *going* to college. I don't care who I have to f—"

The doorbell rang.

"That must be the pizza," Sam said, reaching for her purse.

"Put that away. I said I'd get it, hun."

"Are you sure?" Sam always hated letting people pay for her, even it if was just *Joe's Pizza Shack*; twenty minutes or less or you get a free coupon for a half-priced pie.

"It's no problem. I just got paid yesterday."

At the door, Tammy paid the driver, took the pies in one hand, then gave a loud wolf whistle using her thumb and index finger. "Come and get it!"

Matt and Brent were in the middle of lifting a particularly heavy looking desk. Was that Mahogany? Even from this distance and in the dim twilight she could tell its decorative carved etchings were intricate. It had that antique look. Something like that would go splendidly in Anna's rustic but not rustic living room. She heard Anna's voice in her head: *That is gorgeous, Samantha, but can we make it a little more modern, and what if it was glass instead? But I love it, really.*

At some point during the move, Matt and Brent had removed their nice work shirts, both wearing dark tank tops that revealed their impressive physiques. Sam found herself mesmerized by Matt's strength, those arm muscles bulging, as he propped the desk up higher and moved with Brent toward his open front door.

Tammy snapped two fingers in her face. "Oh, yeah, you need a date, alright."

Sam grinned. "It's not a sin to look." Just to put her heart on the table, leaving it open to be smashed. She shook her head, reminding herself that she was over her ex. Had been the moment he'd cheated on her...on their wedding day...moments before the ceremony.

*****

"Be right there!" Brent grunted out as the women looked on.

Matt shored up his grip. Why had he thought this desk was a good idea. Darn thing cost an arm and a leg, and didn't go with anything he owned. Not that *anything* he owned went with anything he owned. He'd bought this desk because it was meant to be a symbol of his success. It was the type of desk bigwigs sat at when they said things like "Buy! No, sell!" And had their secretaries bring them truffle flavored coffee. Now it was a symbol of his bad knee. He'd nearly taken a tumble when he'd stepped wrong, but those women were still watching, and his ego provided an extra burst of power. He wasn't about to let Brent show him up...on his own property!

Coordinating together, with Brent going first, they shimmied up the five steps to the porch, and then listed the desk to the side to get it in the door. Once that was done, they still needed to get up one flight of stairs.

He'd decided to make the upstairs master his office. Maybe he'd get a couch so he could nap there from time to time.

"You got this, man?" Brent asked, taking the first step.

"Of course I got this. Do *you*?"

Brent chuckled, and they tilted the desk at an angle, moving one step at a time.

"So how did you remember Samantha?" Matt asked, adjusting his grip. "My mind's drawing a blank."

"I had a little crush on her, but I was dating Becky at the time." Brent huffed. "Why on earth did you need a desk this heavy?"

"Because I wanted it. So remind me, she wasn't a cheerleader was she?"

"No. She played soccer, I think. And maybe ran track. Possibly swim team, too." He paused halfway up the stairs and turned thoughtful. Then he smiled up at the ceiling. "Oh, yeah. Definitely swim team."

Matt sucked in a breath and adjusted his grip once more as he hardened his awkward stance. "This thing ain't getting any lighter."

"You should have thought about that before you bought this monstrosity."

They started up again, both showing signs of strain. Sweat beaded their foreheads. "Swim, track, and soccer? And I thought I had my hands full with only football."

"No kidding, right? She was one of those straight-A chicks, too. I remember being happy with a C."

"Yeah, me too." *I'd been happy with a D.* At least that meant he'd passed. He'd gotten through high school by the skin of his teeth. In college, his football scholarship meant that he could basically fail and still pass. Coaches pressured teachers heavily for guys like him; the "superstars" who were being actively scouted with the potential to bring the university another accolade.

"Anyway, I think she had a crush on *you*."

Matt nearly dropped his burden. He levered himself and locked his knees, the right one screaming. Up one more step. Nearly there. "What makes you say that?"

"Because you guys made out at the party I was talking about."

Bullwhip to the brain. At the same time, his knuckle hit the banister, getting pinched between it and the desk. He yelped, freeing his now bleeding finger. His body shook from the ever increasing weight. "Can you go any faster?"

"Couple more steps. Put your back into it."

"Stop gabbing and move."

Moments later, they set the desk in the corner of the master bedroom. Matt stepped into the en-suite to rinse the blood from his finger, feeling the sting. More blood pooled. He glanced around for something to wrap the wound in, but came up empty. He hadn't thought to bring toiletries, let alone a first-aid kit.

"Hello, two *moms* next door. They're bound to have band-aids," Brent said.

*****

The first thing she heard from the hallway after Tammy went to answer the door was, "You got any band-aids?"

Her mothering instincts went into overdrive. She rushed out of the kitchen still clutching the stack of paper plates she'd been about to put out. "What happened?"

Matt was holding his cupped palm under his finger to catch the blood.

"Oh, cool!" Jayden said, on his way for a slice. "Does it hurt?"

"No, little man," Matt smiled.

Ben and Ellie rushed over like it was an event.

Ellie covered her eyes and turned away. "Ew."

"Don't be such a girl," Ben nagged.

"You don't be such a *boy*," she fired back.

"Alright, everyone," Sam said. "Grab a slice, eat up, and then it's time for homework, no arguments. Matt, come with me." She headed up the stairs.

"Can we eat in the living room?" Jayden called after them.

"Fine. Just bring napkins and don't spill anything."

As they entered the upstairs bathroom, Matt said. "Sorry about this."

She turned the sink to cold, guided his hand under it, then opened the medicine cabinet. "With two rowdy boys around, I'm used to it."

"So, wait. You have *two* sons?"

"Goodness, no. I'd go mad. Just Jayden." She reached for the family-pack adhesive strips and set them on the counter. The tube of antiseptic joined them. "He and Ben are practically inseparable, though, so I might as well just claim him." After grabbing a few tissues, she shut off the water and began patting his hand dry.

"I can take it from here."

"These never go on right when you do them one handed, especially after adding the antiseptic. It's no problem." She sensed a weird tension from him then.

When she glanced up, he was gazing around the bathroom. "I think our houses are the same on the inside."

"Oh, yeah?" Deciding she'd just imagined it, she fished an adhesive strip from the box and peeled off the backing, holding it for the ready. Then, out of blind habit, she blew on his finger.

He went stiff.

"It, uh, just needs to dry a little more, or it won't stick." Now she wished she'd splurged for the name brand Band-Aids.

"Okay," Matt said, that tension back.

I can't believe I blew on his finger! Rushing now, she squeezed a dollop of antiseptic over the cut, wrapped the adhesive strip around his finger, and then, for some reason needing to truly mortify herself, patted the top of his hand. "All done."

*****

Matt felt like he'd had the wind knocked out of him, but he couldn't understand why. As she gazed up at him with that Mona Lisa smile, he felt his world tilt on its axis. Was he growing ill? Perhaps the move was taking its toll?

"You okay?" she asked, as if he were turning green right before her eyes.

He checked himself in the mirror just to be sure. Aside from a general bewildered expression, nothing was amiss. He tested his finger, feeling the pull of the foreign material hugging his cut. "Better now, thank you."

"Well, alright, then." She gathered the wrapper, fit the lid back on the antiseptic tube, and put everything away. Then she turned the water back on, retrieved a rag from under the sink, and began scrubbing the sink bowl.

"I can do that," he said, suddenly feeling bad about bleeding all over her previously clean sink.

"It's fine," she insisted, yanking the rag away when he reached for it. "You'll get your hand wet and end up needing a new band-aid after an hour. Go on downstairs and grab a slice before the kids eat it all. I'll be down in a minute."

He nodded, still feeling guilty, but she clearly didn't need, or want, his help, so he returned to the kitchen.

They had ordered two pizzas. By the time Matt got to them, one was gone and the other had two slices missing. He slipped three slices onto a paper plate, popped a beer, and joined everyone in the living room. The TV was on, and they were watching some show about an island, or people who lived on an island. Apparently everyone in the program was stoked about getting a fire started.

The kids were fanned out around the coffee table, eyes glued to the show as they absently gobbled their food. He took the end seat on the sofa where Brent and Tammy had bunkered down. Brent was in the middle of a story from his bygone years, a particularly good play he'd executed, scoring the winning touchdown for their team.

Not exactly the winning touchdown, since, as Matt recalled, they'd been up ten points, but he wasn't going to point that out. Tammy appeared awed, which he supposed was the point. Matt ignored them and studied Sam's living space. Not surprisingly, everything was neat and in order, aside from a couple of book bags taking up one corner. Pictures of her and Jayden lined the walls. Mostly Jayden: him as a baby; him riding a bike that was too big for him at the time; him hiking through a forest, or at a lake. The few that included Sam were of her hugging her son and smiling with him. It was all rather heartwarming.

He also noticed there wasn't a man in any of the pictures.

So she was a single mother.

Years ago, that would have been scandalous in this small town. It had been for *his* mother. The town never looked at her and Matt the same once his father walked away from them. Matt had been nine. Old enough to know what was happening. Not old enough to help his mother financially. And of course the bastard who'd sired him had refused to pay child support. His mother had to get a third job just to keep up with the bills. But she had never complained. Only when he was older, looking to make a family of his own did he understand the scope of her sacrifice.

"This is dumb," Ellie complained. "Let's watch something else."

"Like what?" Jayden asked, reaching for the remote.

"I don't know. Just see what else is on."

"I don't think there's anything good on right now." Ben got up and disappeared into the kitchen. By the time he returned with another slice, Ellie was advocating for a teen drama with werewolves. Or were they vampires?

"No way," Ben said. "This show is worse than the last."

Jayden handed Ben the remote. "Here. You find something." Then he left to get himself another slice as well.

"So Matt," Tammy asked. "What do you have planned for the house next door? I know a good contractor if you need one."

"Thanks, but I'm set. Most of the work I'll be doing myself. If there's anything I can't handle, Brent will help me out."

"I will?"

"Yup."

"I guess I will. But you know I didn't work in construction for years like you did."

"Yeah, too busy being a lazy, fat cat banker. I was worried I'd come home and find you as pudgy as old man Jamison."

"Lazy? No. And I'm still working on the fat cat part."

"You own a bank?" Tammy asked.

Matt could practically see the dollar signs spring into her eyes.

Brent gave her that smile he'd perfected in the eighth grade. Matt had dubbed it the Thompson jawbreaker, because when he unleashed it, all the girls within visual range would have to pick their jaws up off the floor. "I'm just a manager right now, but I plan to open my own branch at some point."

Those dollars signs spun like reels in a slot machine. Little did Tammy know that Brent was a dedicated bachelor, a sport fisherman, strictly catch and release.

"That's impressive," she said, leaning closer. "It's rare to find a man who actually has goals in life."

Brent beamed, basking in her praise.

He had to see the bait he was throwing out. Matt hoped his friend wasn't about to play with the feelings of a single mother.

"Oh, leave it here," Jayden exclaimed. "Let's watch this." It was a comedy with a bunch of nerdy scientists. Everyone seemed mollified by the selection, and ate in silence. Except for Brent and Tammy, who continued a muted conversation.

Matt tuned them out, nibbling the last of his pizza crust. He was finishing off his beer, when movement to his right caught his attention. Sam had headed into the kitchen.

His curiosity of her revved. Brent's little revelation about the two of them having kissed rocked him. He hadn't been *that* messed up that night, had he? Surely he'd remember kissing someone like her. Even if briefly. Though, to be fair, he had been a little self-absorbed at that age.

Still, if she'd been half as cute as she was upstairs, tending his wound, young Matt would have been besotted.

No. Brent had to be mistaken.

On the other hand, her drastic shift in attitude earlier after learning who he was said something. She'd gone from happily greeting the new neighbors to *nobody will notice if I slink away.*

Because of him?

One way to find out.

Chapter 4

As Samantha entered the kitchen, she frowned at the crumb-laden pizza boxes with distinctive lines marking where each slice used to exist. She shouldn't be surprised that it was gone. Hadn't she warned Matt about this very thing? But before coming down, she'd made the mistake of checking her email, and then had sat for a good five minutes. Stunned.

Anna had given her her walking papers. In a disbelieving haze she'd read words like *not a good match* and *styles don't mesh*. At the end, Anna wished her all the best. Sam didn't even know how to respond. So she didn't.

She'd taken a deep breath, bottled her crashing hopes and pushed away from the computer. Then, like a zombie, had scuffled down the stairs, seeking comfort food. Specifically greasy, hot, cheesy pizza.

But when it rains it pours, apparently.

She allowed herself one disgruntled sigh, then crossed and opened the fridge, digging for last night's leftovers; chicken and rice.

What am I going to do? She didn't have any more jobs lined up. Anna was supposed to be her *in*. Should she email her back and beg for a second chance? Lower her commission?

She didn't want to have to contact Jayden's father for the child support he was *supposed* to be sending every month, but what other choice did she have? Not that she expected Dustin to actually pay up. Not without a lengthy court proceeding that she had neither the time nor the money for.

When she closed the fridge, she was startled to see Matthew standing in the doorway. He glanced down at her Tupperware dinner, then at the empty pizza boxes. Scrubbing a hand over the back of his neck, he said, "I guess the kids snatched the last of the pizza. Sorry."

She smiled and slid the chicken and rice into the microwave. "I'm used to it. Those boys could out-eat a whale. You need a refill?" She pointed to the bottle in his loose grip.

"Sure, thanks."

She took his empty and tossed it in the trash, then retrieved a cold bottle from the fridge and handed it to him.

He saluted her with the bottle, popped the top, and took a swig as he leaned against the doorframe. While her food heated up, she refilled her wine glass, taking a quick sip and trying not to feel self-conscious. Though she didn't know why she should be. Oh, yes she did. This was Matthew Moore. Her first crush. Her first kiss. Her first heartbreak.

And he barely remembered her.

Yet she got the impression he was studying her now.

She glanced over at him. His beer hung by his side in a loose grip, all casual and relaxed. His short blond hair was slightly spiked and messy in that dashing way coined by movie stars. And he looked as though he could bench press a moose.

To block an appreciative sigh, she brought her wine to her lips.

"So, hey, did we, uh, kiss once?"

In the midst of drinking, she coughed, sending wine into all the wrong places, burning her esophagus and nose canal. Gasping over the sink, she swallowed a hard bubble of wine-tinged air. It barreled down her throat like a bowling ball headed for a strike, making her eyes sting and water.

Matt patted her on the back. "You okay?"

The microwave dinged.

She wiped tears from her eyes. "I'm fine." Her voice sounded a little hoarse, and it was painful to talk. Fumes from the wine seemed to have suffused her senses. She filled a drinking glass with water and then gulped till the burning subsided. But her eyes were blurred from the continued stinging and she accidentally set the glass awkwardly on the edge of the counter.

Crash!

Shards scattered.

"Oh, dang it!"

Tammy called from the living room, "Everything alright in there?" at the same time Jayden said, "You okay, Mom?"

"I just dropped a glass. Don't come in here. There's glass everywhere." She bent to pick up the larger pieces. So did Matt.

"You don't have to help."

"It'll go faster if I do."

Together they scooped up, swept up, and then mopped up the last of the shards.

"Thank you."

"No problem." Then he kindly retrieved her dinner from the microwave and set it on the counter. When she went to grab herself some silverware and a plate he beat her to it.

"What are you doing?"

"This is for your own safety," he said, smiling and spooning some food onto the plate. Then he slid the plate across the counter toward her. "I didn't mean to throw you off there."

"You didn't." Her tone was way too high to be believable. She cleared her throat. "You didn't throw me off. I just...you know...wrong pipe and all." She shut her mouth up by scooping some rice into it.

He swigged his beer. "So, did we?"

After swallowing, she nonchalantly asked, "You don't remember?"

He shook his head. "So it's true? Huh." He took a drink.

"It wasn't really all that memorable." *For him.*

"I find that hard to believe."

She blinked up at him, not sure she caught his meaning. Was he suggesting that he, in all his infinite glory, was unforgettable, while she was what? Chopped liver? "It was a long time ago. We were dumb kids. Why are you even bringing it up?"

"Well, we're going to be neighbors for a time. It would be good to address any lingering feelings now before it becomes an issue."

She snorted. "Lingering feelings? Ha!" Then she laughed for real.

He frowned.

"Don't worry, hot stuff," she said through a giggled breath. "I'll try not to stalk you. Goodness, the kiss really wasn't *that* good."

"I didn't mean—"

"You two sound like you're having fun in here," Tammy said as she entered the kitchen and trashed her paper plate. "Look, hun, I'd love to stay a little longer and get to know your old school buddies, but I have an early shift tomorrow and Ellie has homework to get to. Perhaps we can all go to dinner this Friday?" Without waiting for an answer, she hugged Sam and then Matt before heading out the door. "Come on Ellie, let's go." Before she left, she called back, "I'll text you!"

"Your friend is...colorful," Matt said.

Was that a dig at Tammy's flightiness? The man still thought he was God's gift.

Sam placed her dishes in the sink. "Look, I think we should all call it a night. Jayden has homework too."

"Did I somehow insult you?"

"Don't worry about it. I'm sure it's compulsory." She returned to the living room and shut off the television. "Brent, it was nice to see you again. Jayden, homework. Now. Ben, do you need a ride home?"

"Actually my mom said it would be okay if I stayed the night."

She sighed. "Very well. Get ready for bed and then I'd better see both of you hitting the books in five." She turned back to the two men, ushering them out. "Good luck with your renovations, and good night."

As she closed the door, she heard Brent's muffled voice. "Did you just get us kicked out?"

Chapter 5

The next day, Sam returned home after dropping the kids off at school, pulled into her driveway, and gasped in horror. She'd been hoping for a little quiet time before she had to start going through her old client list. It didn't look like that was going to happen—

Because Matt was yanking up her azaleas!

She jerked the car into park, shouldered the door open, and stomped toward where Matt was crouched between their two houses, pulling up roots. "What on earth do you think you're doing!?"

Matt glanced up with an arched brow. "Um. Yard work?"

"Obviously! But you're tearing up *my* yard! These are my plants."

"Pretty sure they're on my side of the property line."

"Uh, no. I don't think so. She gestured to the line she'd repeatedly made with her lawnmower, creating the demarcation between their yards. Only it wasn't there anymore.... His yard was perfectly manicured, the same length as hers. "I...well, you can clearly see that the plants are closer to my house."

He cleared his throat. "Sorry, but so is the property line."

"Huh?"

He took a large sidestep to his left, toward her house. "This is where my property ends and yours begins."

"That's...that's ridiculous. You can't have more than half of the space between us. That's not fair." Would she ever stop getting knocked around?

"I can show you the documentation, if you like." He sounded so reasonable.

"I'm going to have to insist on it." There had to be a mistake.

He stood and wiped his hands off on his jeans. She followed him inside and up the stairs. As he'd stated yesterday, the layout was the same as hers, except it was flipped, like a mirror image. He was using the master bedroom as an office, which overlooked both their back yards. That ornate desk was pushed up against the corner, paperwork littering the surface, spilling over onto the floor.

"Organize much?"

"Hey, now. There's order in the chaos." He rifled through his papers.

She glanced around. The tawny carpet was stained and worn in places, and the scent of mildew tickled her nose. "Aren't you worried about mold?"

He glanced over a piece of paper and then discarded it, continuing his search. "Nah. Had that checked out during the inspection. No major issues that won't be fixed during renovation."

Who could ever tell if there was mold with the walls painted that obnoxious mint green?

Aside from his desk, there was no other furniture in the room. Did he dedicate one of the smaller rooms as his bedroom? Curiosity poked at her.

"Well, while you try to figure out that mess, I'm going to look around, if you don't mind."

"Be my guest."

In the upstairs hall, the carpet was in even worse shape, and that mint green paint encroached here as well. The bathroom? *Oh no, not going in there if my life depended on it.* It looked like something you'd find in some backwoods rest stop…in a horror movie. The other two rooms—the ones that mirrored Jayden's room and her office—were completely bare. So then did he not sleep here? She couldn't see him bunking down on the dingy floor. She didn't blame him there. Yet she was curious.

She returned to the master bedroom. "You must be staying somewhere else while you renovate."

He crossed toward her, paperwork in hand. "I'm staying with my mother."

She took it and began reading, her heart sinking with each word. "I only have five feet of land on this side?"

"You probably have more on the other side, but you'd have to check your property survey to be sure."

"This neighborhood is generational. I can't tell Tammy that I suddenly own part of her land. It wouldn't be right."

"Even if it's been technically your land for years?"

She shoved the paper back at him. "The lines are set and have been for years. That is my land."

His eyes darted, as if he wasn't sure how to deal with this situation. She knew the law was on his side. She just hoped he could be reasonable.

She was wrong.

"No, it's not."

She glared at him. His expression hardened with a stubborn tilt to his jaw.

She couldn't help it…her lip quivered.

He blinked twice.

She turned away, appalled at herself. She hadn't cried since she was a toddler. Technically she was only on the verge, but still. She found herself down the stairs and out the door before she realized she'd even started moving, rushing past her doomed azaleas. Back in her own home, she took several calming breaths over the sink, her palms braced on either side. Was she over reacting? Maybe. But lately it seemed her life was out of her control. And she hated that. Her business was failing, she'd just been fired by her best prospective client, and Matthew Moore moved in next door and then promptly took a huge bite out of her land.

Not only that, Jayden was struggling with school worse than ever. Last night she'd caught Ben doing his homework for him.

I planted those azaleas with Jayden just after his fifth birthday.

"Look, I'm sorry."

She jumped at the sound of Matt's voice. She had left the front door open.

Hastily, she swiped her eyes and faced him. "It's fine. It's your land. Do whatever you want."

"I should have spoken to you before pulling up the bushes. I wasn't thinking. It's just that I'm the type of guy that if I see an issue I have to address it."

"Issue? What was the issue?"

"Well, first, the bushes were growing unevenly and the leaves looked sunburned. They'd do better in shade. Second, the roots were rotting because that area is in a depression where water gathers, so the soil isn't draining enough for them to breath."

She threw her hands up. "Well great! I can't even plant bushes right."

He went quiet, shifting on his feet.

She sighed. "Look, I appreciate the apology. I really do. And I'm sorry too. It was just a shock to come home after losing my job and seeing my yard getting ravaged."

"You lost your job today? I'm sorry to hear that. Where did you work?"

"I'm an interior designer. Freelance." She rolled her hand in the air. "I meant that I lost a large client. I found out last night."

"Ah, your *biggest* client." It wasn't a question.

"How did you know?"

"When I was running my construction company, I lost a *huge* client early on. I thought my business would go under."

"What did you do?"

"I didn't let it."

"Easier said than done."

"True. Most things worthwhile are."

Silence rolled in like an autumn wind.

Matt shoved his hands into his jean pockets. "The bushes might be salvageable. If you want, I can help you replant them somewhere else. They'd look great around your air conditioning unit and would block it from the street view."

"I, um." She hesitated.

He gave her the grin that sparked her adolescent crush so many years before. "It's not like you have anything better to do today."

She fought a returning grin. "I *should* be looking for clients."

"Come on. You can take a day, can't you?"

She couldn't recall the last time she'd *taken a day*. A couple years ago, maybe. What would be the harm. Besides, she always enjoyed yard work. Found it relaxing. "Yeah, okay."

Chapter 6

This was *not* relaxing.

Late August in Colorado, the weather was balmy. After deciding to help Matt move the azaleas, she'd hurried upstairs to change into a pair of functional shorts and a tank top. When she'd stepped outside, Matt's dumfounded double take sparked a bout of self-consciousness that she hadn't felt since her teens. And as they dug holes in the soil, she couldn't help but feel his eyes on her. She was both flattered and…unnerved by it. The last man who'd showed interest in her had impregnated her and left her at the altar.

It was entirely possible she was imagining Matt's interest. Not only because it seemed like wishful thinking on her part, but few men gave her a second glance once they discovered she had a son. Although she didn't like it, she understood it. She and Jayden were a package deal, and she wasn't interested in a fling. If she ever entered into another relationship, that man would have to get in good with Jayden too. Only a truly special man would put in the time.

Men like that came around once in a blue moon and were swept up by much more interesting women than she. Needless to say, she wasn't holding her breath over Matthew Moore.

Anyway, it was more likely Matt was just being nice. Neighborly.

In fact, the more she thought about it, the more she realized she was reading way too much into a simple appreciative glance.

With that thought in mind, she sat back on her heels, and said, "Ready for the first one."

"Here we go." He lifted the heavy plant and lowered the root ball into the hole, holding the whole thing upright as she covered the base in soil.

Soon they had the air conditioning unit surrounded by azaleas.

She stepped back and brushed dirt off her hands, inspecting their work. "Looks good." She faced him. "Thanks for your help."

"Any time."

Again a thick silence blew in.

"Well," she said. "You have a good rest of your day."

"Oh. Yeah, you too."

As she headed up her porch toward her front door, he said, "Hey, here's a thought."

She paused on the landing.

"How about you give me a hand with renovations?" At her apprehensive look, he added, "I'd pay you."

"Matthew, despite my buff look, I'm not all that experienced in home construction."

"I'd do all the heavy lifting. I'd just use you for painting and general clean up. And I could really use the advice of an experienced interior decorator, you know, as far as paint and fixtures go. How much would you charge for that?"

Thinking he was joking, she thought of how much she would have made off of Anna, then doubled it."

"Great. You're hired."

She went still. "Are you serious right now?"

"Do I look like a man who jokes around?" One brow raised, elbow perched on the railing, he offered her a toothy grin.

"What you look like is trouble."

His grin widened. "Think you could manage a little trouble?"

"Oh, I'll manage just fine. And I'll get paid while I do it."

*****

Matt could barely take his eyes off her as he showed her around the house. She'd peek at him from the corner of her eye every now and again as if she could feel his gaze, and he wasn't doing anything to hide it. She was gorgeous, and her smile knocked the wind out of him every time. He endeavored to make her laugh as much as possible.

Usually he worked alone and preferred it that way, but when she'd bid him good day earlier and turned to leave, his mouth had spoken before his brain could catch up. Essentially he'd hired an assistant, which he never did. It was going to eat into his profits; he couldn't bring himself to care. Especially as he trailed up the basement stairs after her. Her figure was straight out of his dreams.

Again he wondered how it was possible that he couldn't remember the aforementioned kiss from their youth. It felt like he'd lost something precious he didn't know he'd had in the first place. He suddenly resented Brent for encouraging him to chug those last few drinks that day before they'd headed over to Sam's party.

In the upstairs hall, she faced him, hands on her shapely hips. "So it looks like you've got one heck of a mess here, Matthew."

"Nothing we can't handle." He loved the way she said his full name, which was an odd thought. He'd never taken much notice of the way women said his name before.

She didn't look convinced. "Where should we start?"

He dragged his gaze from her lips. "All this carpet is going, so we're going to have to pull it up. That's the project of the day. I have a dumpster coming, but since it's not here yet, I was going to start in the kitchen instead. The garbage disposal needs to be fixed. Why don't you take care of all the little trash debris you can find around the house? There are black bags in the living room. Pile the full ones on the porch for now." He felt bad about putting her to work, but couldn't think of any other way to keep her around. And why was it so imperative he keep her around? He wasn't quite sure, but throughout his life, his gut instincts always paid off, and Samantha Fox was kicking up his instincts something fierce.

She nodded, then pretended to crack her knuckles. "Well, alright, then." When she fluttered out of the room, he scolded himself for not thinking to give her a project in the kitchen with him so that he could keep talking with her.

Tools in hand, he stuffed his big shoulders under the sink with his back to the floor and went to work. After a while, he heard her soft footsteps come nearer. He paused in his task, eyes drawn to the door she would have to pass on her way to the porch. She traipsed by with a bag stuffed to the brim. She swiveled her head to look his way and then smiled as they locked eyes.

Again the wind was knocked out of him.

When she came back, she was still smiling, but there was a faint blush on her cheeks. She ducked her head and tucked a strand of hair behind her ear before he lost sight of her.

And that was when he knew *he* was in trouble.

"Wait, you're working for him?" Tammy asked, the din of the diner making it hard for her voice to be heard over the phone's receiver. "Doing what?"

Sam transferred the cell to her other ear and then scooped out some jelly onto a slice of bread. "Grunt work mostly. Picking up trash and stuff. After lunch we're going to pull up the carpet."

Matt had wanted to take her out for lunch. Practically insisted on it. But Sam had told him she needed to check her emails and messages in case another client had tried to contact her. That was just an excuse to get away and call Tammy for her take on things. Oh, and to clean some of the grime off of her. That house was a biohazard.

She'd taken a quick shower, redressed, and then parked it in the kitchen for a PB&J and BFF consultation.

"I'm sure he hired me just to be nice. Even for grunt work, I'm not the best choice." She hesitated. "I think he's flirting with me, though."

"How so?"

"It's hard to explain. He looks at me a lot."

"That's not flirting. That's just a guy being around a hot mama like yourself. If you went out more, it wouldn't be so foreign to you."

"And when he talks to me…I don't know. It's like I'm back in high school or something. I can't stop blushing and I have a strong urge to giggle. I'm being silly, right? Tell me I'm being silly."

"When I bring the kids home from school, I'll scope out the sitch. But if you want my advice, I think you should let loose and flirt back a little. What harm would it do? If things go south, it's not like he's going to be living next to you forever. Look, I got to go. This four top is such a pain."

"Alright, see you in a few hours."

They hung up and Sam finished her lunch before heading back over to Matt's house. She found him inside, already pulling up one corner of the carpet as Megadeath's *Symphony Of Destruction* blasted through a radio that was hooked up to his phone. He didn't notice her at first, so she took a minute to admire him. He'd always been handsome, but before it had been in a boyish way. Now he was all man. His shoulders and arms bulged as he folded the carpet away from the wall with one hand and then used a box cutter to slice into the mesh underneath. She realized he was creating a small section that would be easier to carry out to the dumpster.

Flirt back? Sam hadn't flirted since…had she ever? She didn't even know where to start.

He noticed her then and gave her that lopsided grin as though he was truly glad to see her. Something in her belly warmed, growing fuzzy. "Hi," she said.

"Hi. Have a nice lunch?"

"I did. You?"

"Mm. A bit lonely."

"Well, I guess next time—" She leaned against the door, but didn't realize the frame was rotted to a dangerous degree. The wooden doorframe cracked down the middle. The door snapped free and toppled to the floor with a loud *thud*. Off balance, she nearly went with it, but caught herself at the last second.

"Oh, I'm sorry!" Mortified, her cheeks flamed.

But he was holding back a laugh. "It's alright. Both the frame and the door have to be replaced anyway."

She pointed to the small pile of carpet pieces he'd made. "I'll just get these to the dumpster, shall I?"

As she scurried away, he called in a teasing manner, "Try not to take off more of my doors on the way."

She might have been fine if that had been her only blunder. Unfortunately, somewhere between trash duty and carpet extraction, she'd flipped on her klutz switch. After taking out the last of the carpet in the living room, they'd moved on to the wide hallway. He'd asked her to help hold the stiff carpet back while he cut a section. Inexperienced, she had pulled harder than was necessary and went tumbling backwards with the carpet folding over her. As she blew a strand of hair out of her eyes, she'd caught his amusement. *Oh yeah, laugh it up, buddy.*

Later they'd been removing carpet from one of the upstairs closets when she'd felt something like a spider on her neck. With a loud screech, she had panicked, swiping at her neck and hair, chanting, "Get it off, get it off!"

Instead of laughing at her, as she'd expected, he'd come to her aid, smoothing her hair this way and that, inspecting every inch.

"I don't see anything," he'd said, his tone slightly deeper than it had been before. His breath whispered over her sensitive skin.

"Are you sure?" she'd asked, stifling a shiver.

For good measure, he'd checked her again, running his fingers through her hair and over her nape, more slowly this time. Goosebumps had formed wherever he touched. Oddly, the moment felt almost tender with his fingers gliding lightly over her skin.

Because he couldn't see her face, she had briefly closed her eyes so she could concentrate on the first skin on skin action she'd gotten from a male in so long she couldn't even remember. Like a cobra for its charmer, she had swayed slightly.

Jayden's voice booming up the stairs snapped her out of it. "Mom! You up there?"

Both she and Matt had jumped, stepping away from each other like two teens who'd just been caught by their parents.

When she answered, she'd sounded a bit breathy, but Jayden hadn't noticed. He'd been too fascinated by the prospect of exploring the house that everyone said was haunted. While she and Matt descended the stairs in silence, she could hear his *oh cool's* and *ew's* as he studied every nook and cranny.

To Matt, he asked, "Can me and Ben stay the night here?"

"Sure," Matt said with a shrug.

"No," Sam muttered, gathering her purse.

"No," Matt repeated, laying his hand out flat. "Absolutely not."

"But why?"

Matt glanced at her. "Because it would be…dangerous?"

She nodded.

He turned back to Jayden. "That's right. Because it would be dangerous."

"But, Mom," Jayden whined. "Pleeeeeease? It would be soooo cool. Mr. Moore doesn't care."

Matt gagged. "You can call me Matt."

"Please, Mom? Please? Please?"

"Mr. Moore said no."

Matt grumbled, making her grin. At length, he grinned back.

"He only said no because you made him."

"Huh. You see how that works? Besides, you should be grounded after what you and Ben did last night."

"What did they do?" Matt asked, truly curious.

"Do you want to tell Mr. Moore how you tricked your friend into doing your homework?"

Jayden frowned. So did Matt at the repeated use of his last name.

Bottom lip sticking out, Jayden said, "I didn't trick him. He was just tired of me getting everything wrong. Because I'm stupid."

It was her turn to frown. His words were like a knife to her heart. "You're not stupid, honey. You just…you have a…." she hated the word disorder. "You just learn things a little differently than other people, that's all."

"Yeah, because I'm *stupid*."

"What have I said about using that word?"

"I don't care! It's the truth!" He pushed past then, running out the door and back to the house.

Running her hands through her hair, she sighed.

*****

Rightly so, Matt had stayed out of the mother son tiff. It wasn't his place to intervene, and he wouldn't know how to even if it had been. But now Sam appeared tired and a little sad. He didn't like it.

"You okay?"

"It's just hard, you know? I'm doing the best I can, but what if my best isn't good enough? What if I'm not doing enough for his education?" There was true pain in her voice.

"I'm sure you're doing just fine. He seems like a sweet kid."

"The sweetest. I just wish it didn't feel like I was screwing everything up."

"I hope you don't mind my asking, but does he have a learning disability?"

Her eyes teared up, and she swallowed hard. At length, she nodded. "Dyslexia. It means he—"

"I'm familiar. I've never been diagnosed, but I'm pretty sure I've got it too."

"Why weren't you ever diagnosed?"

"It wasn't like it is now. People weren't aware of the problem back then."

"So how did you deal with it?

He shook his head and felt the corners of his lips turn up in self-reproach. "I didn't."

Brow furrowed, she cocked her head.

"I realized there was something wrong with me when one of our teachers, Mr. Franklyn...do you remember him?"

She nodded.

"Well, he called me up to the front of the class one day and showed everyone a paper I'd written where I'd flipped all the lowercase Bs so they looked like Ds. He thought I'd done it on purpose, like a joke, and spent the next ten minutes embarrassing me in front of everyone. After that, I got really good at convincing other people to do my homework for me."

Her features twisted in anger. "What a horrible thing to do. And to think, I used to like him." Her fists balled. "If any of Jayden's teachers did that? Well, they'd just better watch out."

He just bet she could be a little terror when it came to her son. "You know it's not your fault, right?"

Her shoulders slumped, and her whole body deflated. "There's really no one else to blame here."

He took in her crestfallen expression and felt his stomach twist. He recalled more than once crying to his own mother that he was stupid. Had she blamed herself just as Sam was doing now?

"Some of his teachers recommended a tutor, but I haven't been able to afford the cost." She covered her mouth with the tips of her fingers, almost as if unconsciously. "I'm sorry, I shouldn't be bothering you with any of this."

"No, it's fine."

"Are we done for the day? I should really go check on him."

"Sure. I'll see you later?"

She hesitated. "Are you sure you want me to work for you? I mean, after all this?" She gestured to herself, then the rest of the house.

He didn't hesitate. "Definitely."

Chapter 8

Matt walked into his childhood home and set his tools down on the coffee table. In her bedroom, his mother sat comfortably against her headboard. The TV blasted, but she wasn't paying much attention to it. She was flipping through one of her beloved murder mystery novels, but stopped as soon as he entered.

"Hi, my baby boy."

"Hi, Mom. How are you feeling?"

"Better today. The doctor called and said my triglycerides and cholesterol were a little high, but that shouldn't be the reason for my dizzy spells. I still maintain that my fainting that day was a fluke. Honestly, I was probably just dehydrated, but they want to make a big fuss over it. They want to draw more blood and they scheduled an MRI for tomorrow."

"What did they say about your diet?" He pointedly eyed the bowl on her nightstand that held a soupy mixture of green, brown, and white at the bottom.

"They said I could have ice cream."

"Every day?"

"At my age, *I* get to decide what I eat, not some glorified pill pusher."

"Not when you're sick, you don't. I'm tossing the ice cream."

She shot upright. "Don't you dare, boy! I gave you life and, by golly, I can take it away."

He crossed to sit on the edge of the bed. "I need you to take care of yourself, Mom. I'm not ready to lose you."

She reached out and grabbed his hand, her grip sure and strong. "God's angels are going to have to come down here and drag me out of this body, because I'm not going anywhere."

"I'm holding you to that."

She returned to her novel, yet he recognized that prodding look on her features that said she was just about to—

"Besides, I don't have any grandchildren yet. You need to start working on that before I kick the bucket."

He stood. "Ah, Ma! Don't start."

She slammed her book closed. "You're so *handsome*. I can't believe you haven't been able to meet a good woman. What's the problem?" She lowered her voice. "You're not…gay…are you?"

"Mom!"

"I'd love you either way! I just need to know what we're dealing with. Francine has a lovely son—"

"I'm walking away now."

✳✳✳✳✳

"My god, did he have you hauling lumber?" Tammy gawked at Sam's disheveled appearance. A far cry from how she normally looked, even after a long day at work. In place of her typical ironed slacks, she wore her cut-off shorts. Her legs were dusted with grime. Her tank top was stained with...wait, what was that? And her shoes? Well, they were unsalvageable.

"Nothing so bad as that." She combed her fingers through her hair, feeling a thin layer of grit.

After she'd tried to talk to Jayden through his tightly closed door—he wasn't having it—she had called Tammy to talk/gossip about her day. But without even a *hello*, Tammy had blurted, "Two seconds," then hung up.

A minute later, a knock sounded on her door and she had demanded all the details.

"We just cleaned the place up a little. That's it," Sam told her.

Tammy tossed out a dramatic groan. "Come on girl. You could at least lie and tell me *something* interesting happened." She locked her fists together and brought them up by her face. "A little hot monkey love on the termite-infested hardwood." She sighed dreamily.

Sam laughed. "We are two professional adults. There will be no hot monkey anything *anywhere*."

Tammy's face lit up. "So the trial period's over and you're officially hired?" Her hands clapped together. The look in her eyes predicted a burgeoning romance on the horizon.

"Tammy, nothing is—or will be—happening between Matthew and me."

"I'll be the judge of that later tonight when we meet them for dinner."

Sam's head snapped up. "Pardon?"

"Hello? Dinner. Tonight…. Friday."

"Wait. When did they agree to that?"

"They confirmed today. Well, Brent did. But he assured me Matt would be there, which means you're coming." Her hand fluttered in her direction. "I suggest you hose off."

"I don't have a babysitter for Jayden."

"No problem. Brent said we should bring the kids along. Besides, Ellie needs to apologize to Jayden. What better time to make her do it than in an environment where I can cruelly withhold her favorite dessert."

"Why does she need to apologize?"

"They got into a bit of an argument over only god knows what. Jay told Ellie she was being stupid and then Ellie fired back and went in on him about his grades. Girl knows exactly which artery to cut for maximum carnage. That's the reason I didn't come straight over to Matt's to catch all your salacious activities. I had to give her the what for."

"So that's why Jayden was moody earlier."

"He'll feel better when he can wave some chocolate lava cake in Ellie's face if she refuses to apologize."

*****

The delicious scent of seared meat suffused the restaurant's waiting area. Several people were seated, waiting for their names to be called. However, Matt and Brent were already in a corner booth that curved around the table. When Matt saw her, his face lit up and he waved them over. She scooted into the booth next to Matt with Jayden on her other side. Tammy and Ellie entered on the other side by Brent.

"Glad you could make it." Matt said, smiling down at her.

"Me too."

"Hi," Jayden said, waving at Matt.

"Jay, my man. How's it hanging?"

"'Sgood."

"And Ellie, nice to see you again."

Ellie shrugged, still upset and stubborn about that apology she'd yet to deliver. Jayden seemed to have gotten over the whole incident on the drive over, but Tammy wasn't about to let it go.

The waiter came by with some appetizers Matt and Brent had ordered beforehand: mozzarella sticks for the kids and coconut shrimp for everyone else.

"So Sam," Brent said, spooning some dipping sauce onto his plate. "How do you like being Matt's lackey? I hope he's not working you too hard."

"She's not a lackey," Matt defended.

"Oh? Then what am I?"

"The operating director of waste management."

Both Ellie and Jayden laughed out loud.

"What does that even mean?" Jayden asked.

"It means your mom is pretty important to my work."

"Are you going to decorate Matt's house too, Mom?"

"Oh, no, hun. It's not that kind of job."

"Why not?"

"Because that's not what Mr. Moore needs. He just wants to fix it up a little and then sell it right away."

"But if you decorate it, couldn't he sell it for more?"

Matt jumped in, "It couldn't be enough to offset the cost of furnishing a whole house."

"Well, not necessarily. A few months ago, I staged a house with rented furniture at a small cost to the owner. They received several offers during the open house and ended up selling for twenty grand above asking."

"But surely they would have received that without all the dazzle. It's a seller's market."

She shrugged. "Maybe."

"Nuh, uh," Jayden said. "It was because of my mom. Tell him about the other place. The one with the fish tank."

"Oh, the condo?"

Jayden had come with her on the initial consultation. He'd been fascinated by their fish tank. And for the following three weeks, he'd asked her for nothing but a fish tank of his very own and had wanted to stop at every pet store they passed by. Finally she had bought him a new video game as a distraction. The cheaper of two evils. Plus, if she'd gotten him a fish tank, even a small one, she knew she'd be the one to take care of it, and she just didn't have the time.

"The place had needed an overhaul," she told Matt. "Kind of like yours, but not quite as bad. The renovations I recommended cost them fifteen grand, and furnishing totaled about five grand, which didn't include my fee."

Matt made a whistling noise. "That's a lot of dough."

Jayden practically bounced with pride. "But tell him how much you made them."

Matt grinned at Jayden's enthusiasm.

Butterflies suddenly sprang to life in her stomach at that look. "Before the changes, they were getting lowball offers. Afterward, well, they sold for fifty over the original asking price."

"Fifty grand? Really?"

"It's true," Jayden said.

"Sounds like maybe I should think about it. Sam, could you put a couple ideas together to discuss next week?"

"I, um. Sure." She leaned closer so that only he could hear her. "You don't have to humor me."

"It wouldn't hurt to go over my options."

Their food came then. When the waiter left, Brent leaned forward and said to Jayden, "Kid. If I ever need an agent, you're hired."

When dessert came, a smug Jayden lorded it over Ellie, who sat sour-faced, arms crossed. Tammy reminded her that all she needed to do was apologize, and she could have some. She just turned up her nose.

Matt and Brent seemed amused by the scene, both curious as to what had gone down between the two youngsters. Ellie didn't hesitate to explain.

"We were playing soccer in gym class and I had the ball, and Jay tripped me."

"It was an accident."

"It was not."

"Was too."

"Then why were you laughing?"

"Because it was funny," he said, as if that should have been obvious.

"And then he called me stupid in the car—"

Sam gave him a chastising look.

"I didn't call you stupid," Jayden defended. "I said you were *acting* stupid—"

Ignoring him, Ellie continued. "And all I did was point out that I had all As and he had all Cs and that he couldn't even figure out a simple math problem when the teacher had called him up to the blackboard."

Nothing left to say, they both flopped back against the booth with their arms crossed.

"Alright," Sam intervened. "It sounds like you both owe each other an apology."

"But Mom, she—"

"No buts."

"It's better to just get it over with, little man," Brent said.

Matt nodded grimly. "Yeah, in the long run, you'll be better off. Trust me."

"Fine," Jayden said. "I'm sorry I laughed when I *accidentally* tripped you."

Ellie hesitated, still fuming. "I'm sorry, too."

Mollified, Jay handed her a clean spoon. "You want some of my dessert?"

"Okay."

Then, as if their little tiff had happened ages ago, they both dug in.

Matt and Brent both gawked.

"If only every argument could be fixed so easily with chocolate," Matt said.

"We'd hoard the stuff like gold," Brent agreed.

Tammy playfully slapped him on the arm.

When the kid's treat was gone, Jayden asked Ellie, "You want to come over for a movie?"

"Can I, Mom?"

"I'm okay with it if Sam is."

Jayden turned to her, "Can we rent a movie, Mom?"

She stifled a sigh and checked the time. It was still early in the evening, though she was exhausted from the day's work. A relaxing night at home with the kids sounded nice. "Yeah, okay. We'll stop by Redbox on the way home."

Grinning, Jayden turned to the two men. "You want to come watch a movie with us?"

Chapter 9

Jayden, Ellie, and Ben, who had somehow been informed of the impromptu movie night, lay on their stomachs on the floor, watching the latest Avengers movie. The adults took up the two couches—Matt and Sam on one, Tammy and Brent on the other—until their constant chatter brought on a chorus of *shhhhh*s from the kids, forcing them to relocate to the dining room table.

"So, Sam," Matt said, fresh beer in hand. "I heard you were on a couple of teams at Clearwater."

"He *heard*, because I told him," Brent said smugly.

She nodded. "Track, tennis, swim, and I was both a forward and a goalie on the soccer team."

Matt looked impressed. "And I thought I had a full schedule with just football."

"And parties," Brent added with a chuckle.

"Ooh. Dish!" Tammy clapped. "Give me some of the *fast times* at Clearwater High."

Sam stood to top off her glass, and Tammy's while she was at it. "I was so occupied by schoolwork and my extracurricular activities, I skipped over all the *fast times*."

"Matt and I have more than enough stories," Brent said. "Every Friday, we were either partying with the team or getting into trouble."

"Yeah," Sam said. "I remember all the gossip about your shenanigans on Monday mornings."

"Really?" Matt leaned back in his chair. "Like what?"

"Well, let's see. There was the time you guys egged our science teacher's house."

Guilt danced around the lips of both men.

"I think it was toilet paper the next year." She glanced at Matt. "I'm pretty sure when you got that old beater truck, the whole town was terrorized."

He laughed and turned to Brent. "Do you remember when we snuck into that old abandoned cement factory outside town?"

"I think I got my first kiss that night." Brent said. "Good times." He and Matt clinked glasses and then swigged.

Tammy's eyes glinted with mischief. "Oh? I thought you guys didn't swing that way."

Matt nearly spit out his drink.

Brent was more composed. "With *Nickie Taylor*, smart stuff." He cocked his head towards Matt. "Although, if I had wanted him, I could have had him."

Matt guffawed. "In your dreams, lover boy."

They punched each other playfully. Reaffirming their manliness?

"What about you, Tammy?" Brent asked. "Tell us something from your high school days."

She wagged her finger in the air. "Oh, no. No, no, no."

"Why not?"

She examined her nails. "Because I'd put you all to shame, and I wouldn't want to embarrass you like that."

Both men hooted with laughter.

Sam laughed too, but felt like the prude in the room. She hadn't done anything exciting in high school. She'd been straight-laced by the book all the way to graduation. Not that she had any regrets about that. She'd enjoyed school, still kept in touch with many of her friends and old team mates. But she had missed out on some of the more juvenile experiences that some viewed as a rite of passage. While her classmates were sneaking out at night, she'd remain home, studying. While her friends ditched class to sneak into the latest Brad Pitt flick at the Movie Plex in the next town over—so as not to get caught—she was wondering how she was going to make it to dance all the way across town when she had a track meet the same day.

She'd followed the rules, worked hard, and graduated with honors.

Then she had gone and fallen for a deadbeat. And while everyone went off to college, she was giving birth.

But she had Jayden, and she wouldn't change that for the world.

However, she'd had to pass up college in favor of a nine to five. She'd worked for other people ever since—until recently. Her interior design business was supposed to be her path to financial freedom, so she could spend more time with Jayden and provide him with the quality education he deserved. Now that path seemed like a jaunt across a rickety old rope bridge, and *financial freedom* was a dark entity at the other end laughing maniacally and wielding a machete, gearing up to slice the bridge out from under her.

"Come on," Brent goaded Tammy. "You have to give us something. We already know Sam here was a wild child, throwing parties whenever her parents went away."

Sam didn't bother correcting him.

"Oh, all right," Tammy easily relented. She tapped her chin as if in deep thought. "Ah. So there was this sleazy guy in our senior class who was spreading rumors about my friend. You know, the kind of stuff that makes guys look good and girls not so much. We warned him several times to stop, but he didn't. So, turning on the charm, we lured him out to the lake under the pretense that we were all going skinny dipping. Well, you didn't have to tell him twice. We made him get in the water first and then turn around so we could get undressed on account of our blushing modesty and all. Naturally we stole all his clothes and left him there naked as a blue jay."

Hearty laughter filled the room.

"That's terrible," Brent said, holding a stitch in his side.

"Oh? And was it terrible for us to have organized a barbecue by the lake at the same time, invited the whole school, and ensured they'd show by offering *free weenies*?" Pleased with herself, Tammy sat back. "Pun intended."

Their raucous cackling stole their breaths. When they all settled down, the guys looked thoroughly impressed by Tammy's story.

Brent told her, "I'm going to have to watch out for you, aren't I?"

"Only if you know what's good for you."

Sam smiled at their obvious flirting, till she noticed Matt was watching *her*.

"Tell me more about you. We seem to have had a lot in common in school. Why didn't we ever hang out?"

"We ran with different crowds, that's all."

"And who'd you run with?"

She gave him the names of her friends, and he returned a blank face. "You don't remember any of them, do you?" It wasn't as if Clearwater was all that populated. Her friends had definitely known *him*. Star quarterback Matthew Moore, the hottest guy on campus. They'd all laughed at her when she'd told them he'd kissed her the night of the party—and teased her even more then next day when he'd acted as if he'd never met her.

"Those names don't sound familiar to me."

"That's not surprising." It came out a little more bitter than she'd intended.

Matt cocked his head. "Why's that?"

She bit her lip, wishing she hadn't said anything. "You just weren't very interested in anyone outside of football."

"I was too. I knew lots of people who weren't on the team."

"By name? And cheerleaders don't count."

He hesitated, thinking for a moment. Then his face lit up. "Yeah, okay. There was that kid we used to cheat off of in Math." He turned to Brent. "Um, what was his name? Norman?"

Brent shrugged and shook his head. "I cheated off of Sam here. She sat to the right of me." Brent smiled sheepishly at her as if she hadn't caught him a time or two leaning just a little too close during tests.

Matt glanced between the two of them, something flashing in his eyes that Sam couldn't recognize. "Anyway, you see, I remember Norman."

Sam cleared her throat. "His name was *Nathan*. He was my partner in science one semester."

Matt's jaw shifted back and forth. "Well, there are others," he defended. "Plenty."—pause—"I don't have to prove anything. And I don't see what makes you think...wait, is this because I don't remember when we kissed?"

Sam pursed her lips while Tammy slapped a wondrous smile on her face. "You two kissed?"

Sam said, "No," at the same time Matt confirmed, "Yes."

"How would you know?" she asked. "You don't remember it."

His eyes turned teasing. "You can't deny the passion we felt for each other that night. Fireworks lit the sky."

"Again, you don't remember."

"Then I'll just have to rely on my imagination." Wolfish grin. "I have a very active imagination."

When Matthew Moore unleashed that smile, anyone of the female persuasion was helpless not to respond. Sam tried and failed to stifle the twitching of her lips. Their gazes locked, and for a moment, time seemed as though suspended, and yet the butterflies in her tummy revved a mile a minute. Tammy and Brent's flirting was easy enough to spot, but was Matt really flirting with *her*? Surely not.

"Mrs. Fox! Mrs. Fox!"

The frantic sound of Ellie's holler from the back door turned every last butterfly into lead weights. Tammy was on the same page. A mother could register the terror in their child's tone long before their brains caught up. Both she and Tammy were up and racing for Ellie.

"What's wrong?" they asked in unison.

"It's Jay! He got hurt."

"Where is he?" Sam demanded.

"Next door. We were just playing around and the door wasn't locked and we just wanted to—"

Sam didn't wait for the rest. She sprinted for Matt's house.

Chapter 10

Sam sat stiffly in the uncomfortable hospital chair, alternately wringing her fingers and worrying her nails with her teeth. *A dislocated shoulder*, Dr. Reece had declared after she'd examined Jayden, whose expression had been twisted in pain since they'd found him in Matt's hallway, crying, holding his arm, and half buried in a heap of rotted wood. Sam still hadn't gotten the whole story from any of them, but it was clear he and Ben had been horsing around on the stairs, the railing had broken, and Jayden had taken a tumble. The injury had happened when he'd tried to hook his arm around a sturdy baluster to stop his fall, which had worked only to pull the ball of his shoulder from the socket before gravity took him down. Thankfully nothing had been broken, and both Ellie and Ben were unscathed.

Matt had been amazing. Without a second glance at his damaged staircase, he'd carefully scooped Jayden up into his arms and carried him out to Sam's car. He'd even stayed with him in the back seat while Sam drove them to the ER. Now he was across the room, asking one of the attending nurses for an update.

Unfortunately, they wouldn't allow Sam in the room with Jayden while they reset his shoulder, and, of course, she was a complete mommy-mess.

Matt returned to claim the seat next to her. "They said he should be out soon." Seeing her fidgeting fingers, he reached out to take her hand in a reassuring manner. "He'll be fine. I've seen worse on the field. The good news is nothing got broken. Do you need anything? Coffee? Something from the vending machines?"

She shook her head. "I'm fine. Thank you. Actually, thank you for everything tonight. I really appreciate it."

He nodded, relaxing back in his chair, but their hands remained intertwined. It was nice, like an anchor for her frayed nerves, and it kept her from biting her abused nails any further. She expected him to pull out of her grip any moment, but he held tight. He was probably feeling obligated, since her son had been injured in his house and all, and because she was so frazzled. Jayden had never had to go to the ER before. In fact, he'd never even seen the inside of a hospital, outside of his birth. His first major injury couldn't have happened at a worst time. She was already dreading the bill.

"You don't have to stay," she told Matt, patting the hand that held hers, a kind of nonverbal permission to extricate himself.

He only squeezed tighter and smiled down at her. "I'm not going to leave you here alone."

"It's really not a problem. It's getting late and we could be waiting another couple of hours."

"I don't mind."

It was only an hour longer before Jayden was released. Arm in a sling, and eyelids droopy from the mild sedative they'd given him, he slumped in the back seat of Sam's car. They returned to the house around midnight. Tammy's lights were still on. As Sam pulled into the driveway, the entire crew emerged—Ben, Ellie, Tammy, and Brent—all looking worried.

Sam exited the car.

"Is he okay?" Ellie asked, squinting past the darkened window to see for herself.

"He's still in a little pain," Sam told her, opening the door for Jayden and helping him stand.

"I'm sorry, Jay," Ben said, frowning deeply. "I'm sorry, Mrs. Fox. I didn't mean to hurt him."

"It wasn't his fault," Jayden defended his friend, sounding a little slurred from the pain killers.

"I don't care whose fault it was, none of you should have been in Mr. Moore's house. Jayden, you *knew* you weren't allowed over there by yourself."

He tried to shrug, but winced instead. "I know."

"All of you apologize to Mr. Moore right now."

A chorus of contrite apologies stammered forth.

"And," Sam continued, finding her stride, "I think all of you should do chores every weekend for Mr. Moore for the next month to make up for the damage you caused."

Tammy nodded, "That's a right fine idea."

The three youngsters groaned, but didn't argue.

Sam faced Ben. "I take it your parents know where you are?"

"Yeah. They said I can stay the night, if that's okay."

She nodded. She certainly wasn't going to drive him home at twelve o'clock at night.

After shooing them off to bed, she thanked Matt again and apologized to both him and Brent for the trouble.

Brent just chuckled. "This is the most exciting night I've had in ages. Aside from the trip to the ER, we should do this again next week." He and Tammy shared a look that made Sam take notice. There was a spark of something forming there. Knowing Tammy, it would either build into a brush fire, or fizzle out by next week.

"So I guess I'll see you tomorrow?" Matt drew her attention back to him. Something in the way he looked at her made her shiver. Or perhaps that was the cool night air.

"If you have a long drive home, you can always stay here." A flush crept up her cheeks. "You know, on the couch."

He hesitated, glancing between her and his car as if debating her offer. "Are you sure?"

"Yes. Of course. It's the least I can do."

He nodded. "I think I'll do that then." He and Brent exchanged a glance that she couldn't decipher before Brent waved goodbye, started his car, and disappeared down the street. He probably assumed Matt was about to get lucky, but she wasn't that type of girl. Still, having him in her home, making up the couch for him, and telling him goodnight as she made her way upstairs to her bedroom was giving her tummy the warm and gooeys.

Long after she'd tucked herself into bed, she struggled with sleep, her mind drifting to the man downstairs who seemed to be occupying more and more of her thoughts.

Chapter 11

Sam was roused by the scent of breakfast food. Was she sleep-cooking? She rubbed her eyes and sat up in bed. Jayden had probably popped a few frozen waffles in the toaster...but was that coffee she smelled?

When she recalled she'd invited Matt to stay on her sofa, she nearly fell out of bed on her way to the bathroom. Brushed teeth, a quick shower, and a dash of makeup later, she inched her way downstairs, but paused on the landing when she heard Matt's voice.

"...see, this is exactly why you shouldn't compete with each other over girls. It's called the bro code. There's enough competition out there as it is." Something sizzled in a hot pan.

"Ew," Ben said. "We don't like Ellie. Right, Jay?"

Jayden seemed to hesitate in his resonance. "Uh, right. She's just our friend."

"Yeah, right. Well, listen up anyway. If it turns out you *do* like the same girl, you got to decide in advance whose going to go after her. Rock paper scissors, flip a coin if you have to, but figure it out. Then make a pledge to stick to it and be each other's wingman. That's how you keep your friendship tight."

Jayden piped up. "I shouldn't have to flip a coin this time because Ben tried to kill me."

"I did not! I didn't know the stairs would break."

"First off," Matt said, "promise me you'll never fight over a girl again. It's not worth it...unless she's the love of your life, and you better be darn sure about that. Second, Jay-man should get the first in this case, on account of the unspoken rule and all."

"What unspoken rule?" Ben whined.

"The whole girl next door thing. It's an automatic dibs situation. Sorry, Ben, but them's the rules."

Sam stepped out from behind the corner. Jayden was the only one who noticed her.

"Hi, Mom!"

Matt had been in the midst of flipping a pancake, but upon Jayden's exclamation, he jumped and his arm jerked. The pancake catapulted to the right, slapped against the wall, and then peeled away before flopping to the floor.

The boys burst into laughter.

"Oops. Samantha! Hey! Good morning." Matt coughed into his fist, and then tried to discreetly give the boys a look that said if they mentioned their conversation they were dead meat. Sam had to restrain a laugh as he retrieved the ruined pancake and trashed it.

"Good morning, everyone." She stepped forward and kissed Jayden on the forehead. "How are you feeling?" She started checking the sling, but Jayden shrugged her off as though embarrassed by her fussing.

"It doesn't hurt so much today. Matt showed me how to put the sling on myself and gave me some ice for the swelling."

Matt poured more batter into the pan. "I also gave him some Tylenol about an hour ago. I hope that's okay."

"An hour? I hope they didn't wake you up." She forgot that the boys liked to get up early on Saturdays to watch cartoons."

"It's fine. Besides, I got to get caught up on my TMNT." Teenage mutant ninja turtles. "I can't believe they have to stream Saturday morning cartoons these days. There's something inherently wrong about that. Pancake?" With a fork, he speared a pancake from the stack he'd been building, dropped it on a plate, and held it out to her.

She accepted it and then drenched it in syrup. "I don't usually have breakfast cooked for me."

"Well, I love to cook. If you want, I could come over and cook for you every morning."

Her forkful of pancake paused on the way to her mouth.

"You know, before we get to work on my house," he hedged. "We could make a thing of it."

"Sure, maybe." She glanced at Ben and Jayden's empty plates. "Are you both done eating?" When they nodded, she sent them upstairs to get ready for a long day of working for Matt. They groaned, but secretly she thought they were looking forward to it. She could already tell they looked up to him.

He turned off the stove and then plated a couple pancakes for himself. As he lathered on the syrup, he said. "So there's this thing happening in the park next weekend, a music festival or something. You want to go?"

She blinked at him, her mouth too full to respond, which was good, because her brain was struggling to come up with something.

He scratched the back of his neck. "I mean Brent is going with Tammy and Ellie, so I thought we could tag along...I mean you could, you know, tag along...and me, er, with me."

*****

Matt stuffed his mouth full of pancakes before he stammered out more nonsense. He didn't usually find it so difficult to be eloquent around beautiful women. But something about Sam just now beguiled him. Perhaps it was her sexy damp hair curling loosely around her neck and down her back, or her amused yet piercing grin, or that she seemed to smell of heaven itself. Whatever it was, he felt like a teenager trying to talk to a girl for the first time.

"You want to take me to the fall festival?" Sam said, eyeing him with a curious tilt to her head. "The annual fall festival that celebrates couples and love?"

He choked on his pancakes. "I...uh...well..."

Her eyes turned lively. Teasing.

He grinned. "We'd be there as friends, of course." He paused for a moment, wondering if he could settle for *just friends* with this woman. He had to admit there was something powerful drawing him to her. He wondered if she felt the same, or was he alone in this? "You want to go, or not? Bring Ben and Jay along."

"So you can give them more advice on chicks?"

He ducked his head, still smiling. "Heard that did you? I hope I didn't overstep."

"It was sweet." She crossed the room to pour herself a cup of coffee. With her back to him, she added, "Surprisingly, you're not a bad role model."

"What do you mean by *surprisingly*?" He inserted the proper amount of outrage into his tone.

Her resulting laugh was like trumpets heralding his first touchdown.

She returned to her seat. "Should we revisit the conversation about egging houses?"

"Touché."

Then as if his earlier words replayed in her head, she gasped. "Brent and Tammy are going to the fall festival? Together? As in they made plans already?" Matt nodded, wondering what the excitement was all about. Especially when Sam clapped her hands together and practically squealed, "Did *he* ask *her*?"

Matt shrugged. "I suppose." Then it clicked. *The annual fall festival that celebrates couples and love.* Was Tammy jumping to the same conclusion as Sam? He needed to talk to Brent and make sure he was aware of the pot he was stirring.

Sam was still grinning over what she clearly assumed was a good thing for her friend when she said, "Why don't we see how we're all feeling after this week. After we've dealt with that massive heap you call a house. If we're not too exhausted,"—she batted her eyes dramatically and brought her clamped hands beside her face—"then maybe you can take me to the festival, Mr. Moore."

Thoughts of Brent dissipated as that cheeky smile nearly knocked the wind out of him. How could she expect him to formulate a coherent response after whacking him upside the head with that smile?

Thankfully, the boys barreling down the stairs saved him.

After tidying the kitchen together, they all headed over to his place. Matt put the boys to work in the back yard, mowing the lawn and pulling weeds. He figured it would be best to keep them out of the house while he and Sam assessed the damage. As soon as he saw the rotted wood banister in the light, he knew what the problem was, and it was going to take a huge chunk out of his profits.

"Termites," he groaned, running his hands though his hair.

"Oh no," Sam said. "Is that bad?"

"Depends on the extent of the damage, but...yeah, it's bad."

She put up her pointer finger, pulled out her phone, flipped through numbers, then placed the receiver to her ear. As it rang, she explained, "This real estate agent I worked with a couple months back is married to an exterminator. She owes me a favor, so I might be able to negotiate something—ah, hi, Marge? It's Sam." She turned away to continue the conversation. By the end, the exterminator, Dan, was scheduled to stop by later in the evening, *free of charge*.

"That was amazing!" Matt said. "How did you do that?"

She beamed. "I do pro bono work sometimes to build contacts, and in this particular case, I staged a house that had been on the market for months. It sold the next day."

"See, I knew I made a good decision hiring you."

"Best decision of your life," she chirped.

He wondered if that wasn't exactly right.

Chapter 12

Tiny bubbles of excitement danced in Sam's head, dove through her heart, and bounced in her stomach like ping pong balls. She was actually giddy. She couldn't remember the last time she'd experienced such a youthful emotion. Over the last week, she was ninety-five percent sure Matt had been flirting with her. To account for wishful thinking, she lowered that number to eighty-five percent. But that was still pretty high.

As they had made their way from room to room, cleaning surfaces, scraping chipped paint off the walls, scrubbing away caked-on grime, and pulling up carpet, Matt had drilled her with questions: about her life, what she'd done after high school, about her son and subsequently her disastrous non-marriage. She didn't often reveal that particular story to people, but had found it easy to open up to Matt about her cheating, deadbeat ex.

Measuring the doorframe, Matt had absently muttered, "Poor guy."

"Wait, what?" she'd responded, facing him. "Poor *him*?"

He'd met her gaze. "Yeah. I feel sorry for the guy. He obviously didn't know it back then, but he's got to realize by now he lost the best thing that could have ever happened to him. You and that kid out there? That's the American dream." Then, as if he hadn't just ripped her heart out through her ribcage and declared, *'Spose I'll hold onto this for a bit,* he went a back to measuring.

Matt was open to her questions as well, and she'd learned that he'd nearly made it big in the world of football, but an injury took him out of the game. He'd been married too, but she hadn't wanted children, which was why he didn't have any. And as soon as his bourgeoning career fell through, she'd left him for another player.

"I would say poor her," she'd quipped, "but she probably doesn't even realize what she's lost." And, oh, had Matt liked that. His grin had been contagious, his shoulders jutting back just a bit.

After the termites had been taken care of and the damage assessed—thankfully only the wood in the front hall and banister needed to be replaced, which he'd planned on doing anyway—Matt had made the mistake of asking her opinion on paint swatches.

Instantly, she'd gone to level ten, brightly commenting, "Deep colors are trending this year, especially in rooms that get the most light. Gray tones are both neutral and rich. Teal is incredibly versatile, and would be beautiful if you plan to do hardwood floors throughout. Oh, a soft amethyst would incorporate a romantic quality and would be just delicious in the living room, however a warm wine would bring a level of elegance and sophistication..." She'd trailed off when she noticed the glazed look Matt was giving her.

He scratched the back of his neck. "I usually just paint everything white."

She cringed, trying not to choke on her next words, "That...would be...fine, too."

He laughed at her pained look. "I guess you'll just need to come with me when I buy the paint."

"You sure? You don't have to go all out. You're just going to sell the place, remember?"

"I've been doing this a long time. I'm curious if a little dazzle will make a difference."

"Well, there's no guarantee," she hedged, suddenly feeling pressure.

"From your stories, you sound like you know exactly how to bring that dream home quality. Buyers eat that stuff up."

Monday, while Jayden was at school, they went out for paint. Matt had given her full creative freedom. After some contemplation she chose a berry-wine for the living room, a soft tan tinted with a hint of yellow for the kitchen, and then a neutral warm gray throughout. The bedroom windows faced the morning sun, and the gray would work to make the rooms appear larger. When she told that to Matt, he'd just smiled at her and nodded. Then pulled out his card to pay for the haul.

Tuesday morning, Matt had a spread of coffee and doughnuts ready for when she arrived from next door. He'd figured out her favorite flavors and had gotten an entire box of powdered sugar, chocolate frosted, and glazed. When she'd thanked him, he'd teased, "For what? These are all for me." Then he had hiked the box under his arm like a football and made her chase him down. He'd gotten as far as the back door when she had carefully snatched the box from his grasp, gauged his wolfish look, and then took off in the other direction with a half giggle, half scream. She'd made it a few steps before his arms had wrapped her torso in a strong, yet gentle hold, thwarting her escape. For several heartbeats, neither of them had breathed, neither of them had moved, and their amusement had turned into something much more serious.

He'd cleared his throat and released her, and without acknowledging the moment, said, "I think I left some napkins in the car."

When he'd returned, the awkwardness was gone, his good humor back.

Wednesday, after they'd spent the entire day laying down the first coat of paint in the bedrooms, she'd caught her disheveled reflection in a window and groaned, "I think I got more paint on myself than the walls. I'm such a mess."

Matt had scanned her from hairline to heel and then dotted the tip her nose with fresh paint. "Now you're a masterpiece."

Well, this masterpiece couldn't stop smiling.

Thursday she got a little bit of a shock. The day had started business as usual: Matt greeting her with a cup of piping hot coffee, offering her a delicious pastry from wherever he'd decided to stop that morning, and then started discussing the day's itinerary. But as he'd done so, through the window, she'd spied a teal and white Oldsmobile from the greaser era pull up to the house. Matt had let out a little groan when an elderly woman stepped out of the driver's side door and marched toward the house. By the time she'd made it to the porch, Matt had already moved to open the door for her, so Sam assumed he knew this woman. *A perspective buyer, maybe?*

She'd been way off.

"Mom, what are you doing here?" Matt had asked.

"I just came to see what's keeping you so busy these days." Then her gaze had zeroed in on Sam. Keen, wrinkled eyes slowly took her in from toe to crown and back again. Sam suddenly wished she'd taken better care with her appearance. Her hair was in a messy bun to keep it out of the way while she worked and she'd still had bits of paint on her skin from the day before that had stood up against two scalding showers.

"Now I see," Mrs. Moore had said simply.

Sam still recalled the sensation of her cheeks warming.

While Matt had introduced them, she couldn't help thinking he looked a little smug. "Samantha, this is my mother, Beverly."

Sam shook Beverly's hand with care, expecting a fragile grip. Again she was wrong. The woman's handshake was healthy and firm.

"Would you like a tour of the house?" Matt had offered his mother.

"Oh, look! Coffee and doughnuts. Don't mind if I do."

"Mom," he'd warned, and Sam got the impression she wasn't allowed to have either.

"Come now. I just got my clean bill of health. The doctor said I was healthy as an ox."

"Not doughnut-healthy."

"Just some coffee then," she'd bargained, winking at Sam. After her cup was filled and she'd taken that first sip, Beverly seemed only interested in chatting with Sam, ignoring Matt's impatient sighs and crossed arms.

"Matt tells me you're an interior decorator?"

"Designer," he'd corrected, surprising Sam that he even knew there was a difference. But what was more surprising was the fact that not only had Matt mentioned her to his mother, they'd discussed her profession on some level.

"That's right. At least that's what I'm trying to do. I'm in the middle of a client slump."

"Are you? That's too bad. But you're going to be decorating this house, right?"

She'd glanced at Matt. "It's a possibility."

"Possibility? You mean Mattie hasn't made up his mind?" She'd given him a chiding look.

He'd put his hands up in defense. "I'm hiring her. I'm hiring her. I'm just getting the paperwork together."

"There's a good boy." Beverly faced her again. "And when you're done here, you can do my home."

Matt had looked about as stunned as Sam felt.

"Really?" she asked.

"Yes. I've always wanted a decorator's touch. Just never found one I like." She'd leaned in. "I like you." Then she had turned to leave just as quickly as she had arrived, calling over her shoulder. "I'll need my place baby-proofed. I expect to be having grandchildren soon."

Matt had choked on his coffee. Sam couldn't help but laugh at his bemused expression, expecting this was some kind of inside joke between him and his mother. But Matt didn't elaborate.

At the end of each day, Sam always invited Matt over for dinner. And he always accepted. He and Jayden were becoming fast friends. They would joke with each other in that guy-to-guy way, and tease her whenever possible. Sometimes Matt would even play video games with Jayden, but usually, as Jayden put it, got his butt kicked. He tried to play if off like he was letting Jayden win, but they both saw through him.

Today Sam decided Matt had definitely been flirting with her, and had no plans to stop. She wasn't just imagining it.

Instead of waiting for her to cross the short distance to his place, he'd brought coffee and breakfast to *her*. In addition, he'd had a little surprise for Jayden: a set of The Walking Dead graphic novels.

"Cool!" Jayden had exclaimed, flipping through them. He would have brought them to school with him had Sam not snatched them away for later.

After he left, Matt had noticed a bit of frosting on her lip left behind by a chocolate doughnut. Without thinking, he had reached out to swipe it away with his thumb, lingering just a bit longer than was necessary. Then he'd licked the frosting from his finger. "Mmm, you've managed to make it even sweeter."

She'd been rendered speechless by the way his gaze had held her captive, and had found it difficult to concentrate for the remainder of the day.

That evening, Matt waved goodbye, seeming reluctant to leave her. She found herself wishing he'd stay just a little longer. Every time he left to go home, the separation got more and more acute. Jayden seemed to be getting attached as well, which frightened her. Matt would be selling the house soon. After which he'd be leaving. How far would his next acquisition take him? She didn't know. But when it did, he wouldn't be coming around every day anymore, bringing her goodies and saying sweet things.

The thought pained her.

She consoled herself with the knowledge that his current project would keep him here another few months at least.

But if Jayden got too attached, Matt's leaving might be hardest on him. She knew that children with absentee fathers could develop abandonment issues. If Matt was just amusing himself with them, biding his time until his next project took him away, not only would she be devastated, Jayden would be too.

Her protective instincts flared.

She was going to have to speak with Matt. Get everything on the table and set some boundaries.

By the time Saturday rolled around, she'd completely forgotten Matt's invitation to the Fall Festival. When she opened the door for him, he held out a dozen roses. No one had ever bought her roses. Those were meant for couples. Or lovers. Not for friends. Never friends. Was it possible he wanted more?

Her hands shook as she unwrapped the stems from their plastic casing and put them in her favorite crystal vase, proudly displaying them on the dining room table for all to see. Matt merely watched her in silence as she fussed over the flowers, arranging them just so.

When she noticed him staring at her, she was reminded of the conversation she'd practiced in the bathroom mirror. But before she got any of the words out, Jayden and Ben had bounced down the stairs, greeting Matt with wide smiles.

"You guys ready to go to the festival?" he asked?

They grew excited. Jayden turned to her. "Mom, can we get a fried candy bar?"

"We'll see."

"Yes!" Jayden pumped his fist in the air, taking that as a concrete yes.

Of course, they did get their fried candy bar, courtesy of Matt, who had also gotten one for her. *When in Rome.*

While the boys were distracted, she pulled Matt aside. "Look, Matt. We need to talk."

He went tense. "Nothing good ever starts out that way."

"I really appreciate the treats and the flowers and you being so nice to Jayden, but I'm afraid he might be getting the wrong idea about us."

"And what idea is that?"

"That you want to date me, or something. Considering the situation with his father and all...I just don't want him getting confused."

Matt nodded. "Well, then I guess we should make it official."

"Huh?"

He gave her that grin that made her fall for him so many years ago. "Samantha Fox, will you go steady with me?"

"Don't joke. I'm serious."

He grabbed her hand in his. "Not joking. I would really like to keep seeing you."

She went quiet for a moment. "I...you know I can't just mess around with you. I can't have a fling. Not when Jayden is the one who would get hurt if you leave."

"I'm not going anywhere."

"You might."

He shook his head, moving in closer till their faces were inches from hers, their eyes locked. "Don't you remember what I told you? You're the American dream."

"I am?" She whispered.

He nodded. "More than that. You're *my* dream. I want you, Samantha. All of you. And I promise, if you let me, I'll give you the world."

Mini explosions in her chest palpated her heart. When their lips met, something inexplicable passed between them. Something she couldn't describe, but instantly craved more of.

As they both reluctantly pulled away, he grinned. "Ah. Now I remember you."

She laughed so hard, tears filled her eyes. Or maybe it was because she had never before been so happy.

Epilogue

Sam sat in the tiny white fold out chair, squinting as the sun glistened off a thousand beads of sweat on the balding man's head in front of her. Around them, hundreds of proud parents shifted in the seats uncomfortably, anticipating the moment their child's name would be announced. In the front five rows, capped and gowned teens waited nervously for their walk across that daunting stage. Somewhere in that throng was Jayden.

What none of them knew, besides maybe Ben, who was undoubtedly out of his place and hanging out near her son, Jayden had worked harder than any of them to get here, and Sam couldn't be prouder. Teresa, the woman sitting to her left, and Jayden's wonderful tutor for the last five years, elbowed Sam and pointed to someone in the crowd. "I think that's him! No, wait. That's a girl. Oh, there he is! No. Not him either."

On the other side of Teresa, Tammy was seeking Ellie's familiar form as well. "They're supposed to turn and wave to us so we know where they are."

Though everything seemed to be going smoothly behind the scenes, Sam was anxious to an unreasonable degree. Jayden had already graduated. The ceremony was just a formality. But her restlessness came from the worry that Jayden's father would miss his walk.

She rolled her wedding band around her finger. After that day at the fair, she and Matt had rarely been separated more than a day. They had finished the house next to hers, which had sold well above market value, in part thanks to her decorative touch. It had been bought by a young couple who, as Matt predicted, dubbed it their dream home. Not soon after that, Matt had moved in with her and they'd started working together full time, buying and renovating houses. It was everything she loved about interior design and more. She could not only decorate a home, she could plan out and alter the layout, bringing out the best in every home.

Matt had melded into her and Jayden's life almost seamlessly, as if he'd always been there. And because of their shared experiences with dyslexia, Matt always had the power to lift Jayden up when he was feeling particularly discouraged. Sam could love him for that alone, though he gave her so many more reasons.

Darn it, where is he?

As if her thoughts summoned him, she glanced back toward the parking lot, sighing with relief when she saw Matt's SUV pull into a parking space. A small army emerged: first Matt, who moved to help his spit-fire mother out of the front passenger seat. Brent stepped out from the back, holding Wendy, his and Tammy's little six year old girl. Then Matt extracted the twins from the back seat, Ava and Andrew, and fastened them into the bulky stroller before they all marched toward the section where the three women were seated.

Brent got to them first and greeted his wife with a kiss. Sam moved over so he and Tammy could sit next to each other.

"Sorry we're late," Matt said, coming up the aisle. "The twins were being a little fussy about the outfits you picked out. They kept trying to debate the necessity of the bow tie and hair ribbons."

"They're fourteen months old," Sam reminded him as she hugged Beverly hello.

"Try telling them that," he said. "They are headstrong, stubborn little things."

"Like their father." Sam smiled and kissed her silly husband before bending to say hello to her beautiful little babies, who returned her greeting with drooling grins that were a perfect blend between her and Matt.

Not a full minute after they were seated, music began to play and the ceremony began. Both Sam and Tammy cried when Ellie, the valedictorian, made her speech about the future, possibilities, and endless potential of their young lives. They cried even harder when both she and Jayden made their walks across the stage. Even little Ben's walk had them blubbering. Beverly passed around tissues from her purse, using more than one for herself. The guys tried to remain strong and stoic, but even they were getting choked up by the end.

Finally it was over and Sam was able to give Jayden a big hug, slathering him with kisses till he protested. Matt clapped him on the shoulder and told him how proud he was.

"Thanks, Dad," he said, making Matt smile every time he used the D-word, which in turn filled Sam's heart with so much joy she thought she might burst.

When Jayden walked away to join in the youthful comradery of his graduating friends nearby, Sam took Matt's hand and placed it on her belly.

"I hope you're ready for another one," she said.

His gaze snapped to hers as he took in her words. Then his smile grew ecstatic. Strong hands wrapped her waist, lifting her in a twirl as Matt hooted out his joy. Slowly, he let her slide down his body till their lips met in a kiss that promised her the world.

Dear Reader

I hope you enjoyed Sam and Matt's sweet story. If you're in the mood for something a little more spicy, check out my other novels. I write steamy sci-fi and paranormal romance novels with brooding alpha males and strong female leads.

For a sample of my other novels, visit www.kierstenfay.com, and while you're there, sign up to my newsletter for exclusive goodies and giveaways.

Other Books by Kiersten Fay

Shadow Quest Series
DEMON POSSESSION
DEMON SLAVE
DEMON RETRIBUTION
DEMON UNTAMED

Creatures of Darkness Series
A WICKED HUNGER
A WICKED NIGHT
A WICKED DESIRE

SECOND CHANCES

Walt Mussell

Kira Sakamichi is a career-driven trying to achieve success before her mother's constant interference drags her into a relationship.

So when a drive to a grudging dinner invitation to meet her mother's latest "selection" ends in accident, Kira wakes up lost in the past. As she learns more about the person she now is, she must discover the importance of the lessons her family tried to teach her. Only by understanding the importance of family can she survive.

Chapter One

Kira Sakamichi tapped the speaker setting on her phone, set it on the bathroom shelf directly above her sink, then brushed her hair back. Still looked frizzy.

"Kira-*chan*, are you there?" her mother asked.

"Ma-ma, I'm here. What were you saying?"

"I'm saying you should come over tonight. We'll have dinner. Your grandmother wants to catch up on the latest two episodes of the Taiga Drama. She wants you to watch it with her, like you used to when you were little."

A Taiga Drama. Every year NHK, Japanese PBS, put out a new historical drama that ran once a week for nearly a year. As a child, she'd watched them often with her grandmother, first on video and then weekly when Kira's parents got the Japanese-language cable channel. Her grandmother, a retired history teacher, took great joy in pointing out historical facts portrayed wrong. For Kira, she'd often dreamed of wearing the beautiful kimonos like the women in the shows.

Not any longer.

Those teenage dreams of her wearing a kimono on a raft on a lake.

The silly fears of a child.

Her phone beeped. E-mails from the office. She adjusted her bra until it stopped digging into her sides. She had to get moving. "I'll look at my schedule, Ma-ma. I really don't know."

"Schedule? What schedule? It's Friday, Kira You should take a break from that sixty-hour-a-week job of yours."

"I'm coming for dinner in less than two weeks."

"Yeah. For Thanksgiving. You act like we live in different states not different Atlanta suburbs. I'd like you here more often than that."

"Ma-ma, I said I'll try." She took a deep breath. Upsetting her mother was never a good idea. "What's the storyline?"

"What storyline?"

"On the Taiga Drama. If I make it, I want to at least sound knowledgeable."

"I don't know. Something with lots of samurai."

"That narrows it down to about seven-eight hundred years. Pretty much covers everything back to…well, at least as far as I can remember."

"I didn't raise you to be a smartass."

"No, just to be like you."

Kira checked herself in the mirror, brushing aside the hair over her right eye. *I thought I got rid of that spot already.* She grabbed more make-up.

Her phone beeped again. She glanced at the source. *Another message from the office. Must be Tanner. He's always there early on Friday.*

"So, you're coming then." More of an expectation than a question.

"I'll try." She ran her tongue across her teeth but couldn't erase that toothpaste taste. "Now why is tonight so important for me to come? You haven't pushed like this before."

"Well," her mother's pause let Kira knew she had her, "there's someone I want you to meet."

So that's it. Another one. Will she ever stop? "Ma-ma, we've talked about this before." She touched eyeliner to her eyelids. "I don't need help finding someone to date. My social life is fine."

"I've seen your Facebook page. Your social life sucks."

Kira cursed the askew black streak that now ran from one eyelid. *Damn.* Only her mother could make her screw up her eyeliner. Her mother harrumphed over the phone line. Kira imagined her with crossed arms and her patented disapproving glare. It burned into her chest even from a distance. Take a breath. Relax. Start over. "Ma-ma, I have coworkers on my page. Have to keep it tame."

"Tame? You might as well be eating early-bird dinners with your grandmother."

"Ma-ma, this is none of your business."

"You're my daughter, so this is my business. Your grandfather was right. I should have sent you to Japan for more than just summers growing up. Maybe you'd have learned to treat your elders with more respect."

"I'll repeat that to Grandma the next time I see her. She'll love it. You sent me to Saturday school. I dressed in all the right clothes, attended every festival you could find, but that was enough. I was born here. I'm an adult. Stop trying to arrange my life."

"Just think about it. Please." Her mother's care grew in her voice.

Kira's phone beeped again. *The office.* "I'll think about it, Ma-ma. I've got to go. I need to go to work. We'll talk about it later. I love you."

Silence came from the other end. Was her mother giving in for now? Maybe. "I love you, too," she said.

"*Jyaa, nee.* Bye-bye."

"*Ki o tsukete,* bye-bye."

The phone went dead. Kira wiped away the black streak, and restarted, applying a few final touches. *Always look good enough for your future job,* her father always said.

The phone rang. *Tanner.* She answered the phone and put it on speaker. "Hi, Ted."

"Hi, Kira. Everything alright? You sound flustered."

Ted Tanner. The best person on her team. She'd thought him a total pain after he'd first been hired and assigned to her team, but Kira appreciated that he never missed a deadline. Married his high school sweetheart, put himself through college, and his wife already had a second child on the way. He was loyal to his family first, but his 2:30 a.m. e-mails showed that he got his job done, whatever it took.

"Yes, Ted. Everything's fine." She grabbed her purse and keys and headed out the door to her car. A chilling wind blasted her face. "Just running behind."

"Well, management's asking when you're going to be in."

"Ted, I'm…I'm…"

"Let me guess. You're…stuck in traffic."

The perfect Atlanta excuse. Thanks, Ted. She could see his smile in her mind. "Yes, I'm stuck in traffic. I was on-line resolving some customer issues this morning, so I was delayed getting out of the house."

"How *bad* is it out there?"

"Four accidents this morning already. You know how Fridays are. Two of them on the other side and people just staring."

Ted laughed hard. "Four accidents? I think we can do with three. I'll just make 'em all along your route. However, you should at least be in your car when we make this claim."

"Agreed. Give me one second." She closed the door on her Escalade and turned the key. The engine roared to life. She waited a few seconds as the car paired with her phone. "Tanner, you there?"

"I'm here, Kira."

"Tell everyone I'm on the way and will be there as soon as I can."

"Will do. See you soon."

She cut the call and sped forward, reaching the highway without any delays. Hopefully, the rest of the route would be the same.

Time to think about what to say to her mother. She'd call her later. Tell her she couldn't make it.

Mother would be disappointed.

Maybe Kira would go.

*****

Kira sped her Escalade down McEver Road.

Her mother was going to kill her.

Her phone rang. She pressed the button.

"Kira, where are you?"

She sighed. "Ma-ma, I'm five minutes away. Ten tops. I'll be there soon."

"We ate without you. I do have it staying warm in the oven."

Kira glanced at the clock and sighed. She'd let her mother down. Again. She should never have told her she'd drop by tonight. One of these days, she would have to make it happen.

She focused on the road. Not a bad drive on a good day. A mix of straight and windy sections with a bridge over Lake Lanier just before her parents' subdivision. Nice homes as well. However, that was during the day. At night, it was just a treacherous drive.

Her phone beeped again. She glanced down, punching in the security code with her thumb as she kept one eye on the road. Another message from the office.

She scanned the contents. Short answer. Just a few words to a co-worker, and then no more.

Hit send.

Deer!

Kira veered right and slammed on the brakes. Her car hit the guardrail.

White flashed.

Airbag.

The car rumbled down the embankment.

Toward the water. No! No! No!

The car hit the water. She lurched forward then back.

Her head hit the window.

Then nothing.

Chapter Two

"Okaasan. Okaasan."

Kira shivered, shook her head, then tried to rise from the frigid water.

She was free. How? Had she been thrown from the car?

Pain throbbed in her temples. What had happened? The car had gone in the lake. She'd hit her head, then nothing else.

"Okaasan. Okaasan."

She rubbed her head harder and shivered. Bits of sunlight pierced through the clouds. Daylight? Impossible.

She was alive. Thank God.

She needed help. Needed to call mom and get dry. She patted her chest and pockets. No phone. Where was it?

No pockets.

Why was she in a kimono?

She felt around under the water, running her fingers through mud and pebbles. Her hands, her body, shook from the cold.

The phone must be in the car, but no car in sight.

Where was it?

Where was she? This wasn't Lake Lanier.

Why was it now morning?

Small hands pressed against her side. *"Okaasan. Okaasan."*

Why was she hearing a Japanese child call her 'Mother'?

Tiny hands tugged on her arm. She turned left. A little boy, maybe six or seven, in a blue kimono, tears streaming from his eyes that stared at her as if she were his only world. *"Okaasan, daijoubu?"* the little boy asked.

Shin. His name was Shin. Why did she know that?

"Yes, Shin-*chan*, I'm fine." She spoke in Japanese. Her parents tongue and one she spoke poorly, but now her own.

The little boy threw his arms around her. "You fell in the water. You gone for awhile. You scared me."

Kira hugged the boy, then stood. The water level was above her ankles. A breeze sent chills through her clothes. "Let's get out of the water. It's cold. We both need to get warm."

She strode toward dry ground, Shin's hand in hers, her feet sinking in the mud. She moved her feet to rinse her toes as she stepped on shore, then stepped into the grass to dry them.

"Kira-*san*, are you injured?"

She turned toward the voice. A young, bald man in a gray robe and a brown bib, garments like that of monk, raced toward her, blankets in hand. Likely in his late twenties, he still carried an infectious baby grin. Monks did marry. Was this her husband?

No. He wasn't. A long acquaintance, but no more than that. She would have a feeling. She would know his name, like she knew Shin's name. The man threw blankets around her and Shin.

"I am... just cold," she said through chattering teeth. "My head...hurts. I...I'm sorry. I don't remember what happened. I don't remember anything."

"Do you remember your name?"

"Kira."

"Very good. Do you remember my name?"

She looked him and up and down, searching for some recognition. "I'm sorry, but I don't."

"It's Igami." He laughed, then beamed at her. "You must have hit your head under the water. A rock maybe. I saw you fall in. You disappeared for a second, then reappeared. Let's get you and Shin back to the house. We'll get you some miso soup and maybe some hot tea." He knelt and then picked up Shin, holding him close. A good man, Igami, to keep the boy warm.

"Thank you." She rubbed her head. Definitely a bump. From the accident? From the fall? Mossy-smelling lake water dripped down her face. "My thoughts are a little foggy."

He tilted his head, his gaze focused on her. "Foggy? What do you mean 'foggy'?"

"Like the fog," she responded, pulling the blanket tighter. "Like clouds inside my head. I can't see everything."

He nodded. "I understand. It must be a phrase from where you're from. I've never heard it before." He gestured toward a large thatch house about thirty yards away. "You can explain more later. For now, get your sandals."

Sandals? "That would be good." She scanned the ground. Adult and child-size straw shoes lay near the water's edge. She slid her feet into them.

"Good," Igami said. "Let's go inside."

She turned and glanced at the water. Mist danced on its surface. The edginess she'd known from lakes since childhood remained. When she'd gone in it was Lanier. Where was she now?

That was easy. Japan. But not a Japan she knew.

She glanced at the house Igami had indicated and others nearby. Old-style houses, but they appeared recently made. Like a film set. No wires for power or anything else. Yet nothing nearby either.

A road was beyond the house, but no cars. No bicycles. Mountains in the distance. The Japanese countryside to be sure, but even here she should see something. A few passersby walked along the road, carrying baskets on the shoulders. All wore kimonos. Most wore bandanas. No jeans. No khakis. No boots. Nothing.

She looked skyward. No planes. Nothing in the sky.

Almost like she'd gone back in time.

No. That was ridiculous.

She was halfway around the world. Ridiculous was nothing compared to now.

Her wet hair and clothes clung to her frame, moving naught with her chattering teeth.

A change of clothes with hot food would be good, too.

If only she had her phone, she could call her mother. She must be worried to death. Mother would explain. Maybe there was a phone inside.

They soon reached the house. Still carrying Shin, Igami slid open the door and invited her inside. A maid rushed up to them and bowed. She and Igami exchanged a few words, and the young woman took Shin with her, dragging Kira's heart along as the boy left. Was this the bond that mothers felt watching their kids? She was Shin's mother. That was true.

But how?

"Igami-*san*, can I use the phone inside?"

"Pardon, but what is a phone?"

He doesn't know what a phone is. Impossible. "It's…it's a device. You talk to people in other cities with it."

"Fascinating." His joyous smile returned. "I have never heard of such a thing, but I would love to see it some day. Do they have that in your town, too?"

Some day? The look on his face supported it. He had no idea what a phone was. She rubbed her temple. "Igami-*san*, my head does hurt. I have a silly question."

"Yes?"

"What day is it?"

"We are in the tenth month of the fifth year of the Tensho Era." He chuckled. "I do not recall the day."

Tenth month? It's a cold October.

No, not October. If back in time, then lunar calendar. More likely November. That explained the cold. "The Tensho Era?"

Igami's face sported a somber tone. "Yes, the Tensho Era, the name given by our lord, Oda Nobunaga."

Her knees shook. *Oda Nobunaga.*

The first of three men who united Japan.

Kira, welcome to the 16th century.

Chapter Three

Kira rubbed her head, but the pain remained. Nothing made sense. How could she be here? Was she from this time? Had she dreamed the future?

Not possible. The future had been too real.

Was her life in the future dead? Had she died in the lake?

Was this reincarnation?

No, it was something else. Reincarnation went forward. She had gone back. Maybe Igami could explain it. He was a monk. Then again, how would she explain where she'd come from to him?

The pain in her head increased. Igami likely wouldn't believe her anyway.

The sound of little feet hurried toward her. "*Okaasan*, I'm hungry."

No time to think about anything for the moment. She had to focus on caring for this boy. Her son.

Later, she would have time for reflection. *Sit tight and good things will come her* mother always said, quoting the Japanese proverb.

What she wouldn't give for coffee. Was coffee even available in this part of the world yet?

"Kira-*san*," Igami said, "do you need to lie down?"

She shook her head. "I need to get Shin something to eat. Once he's fine, maybe I can rest."

"Very good. Then you should rest now. Master Aoki is visiting today. He will make lunch for Shin."

Aoki? The name sounded familiar, but she was still uncertain. "I'm sorry, Igami-*san*. Who is Master Aoki?"

"Master Aoki is the new head of my temple."

"I don't want to trouble him. I'm certain he has more important duties."

"No trouble. Before his elevation to head of the temple, Master Aoki worked in the kitchen. He has missed his time there." Igami brought his hand to his mouth, his gaze darting away as he flashed a light smile. "And his replacement is a much better cook," he said in hushed tones. "We've all gained weight since Aoki's promotion."

"I heard that." A voice called out.

A warm feeling washed over her. She must spend a lot of time in the kitchen in this time. In her world, she ordered out or had it delivered premade. Her mother would more likely approve of here than home.

Another bald man in a gray robe and brown bib, a man about twice Igami's age and on the plump side with fat cheeks, stepped into the room. His robe carried splotches of food. Rice accented the smile on his face. "Young monks like Igami have no appreciation for the subtleties of fine cuisine," he said as he strode forward. "It's about presentation as much as taste. He will learn."

She laughed softly, the newfound cheer in her heart offsetting the chill from the lake. "It's good to see you, Master Aoki."

"You must have hit your head very hard. That's the second time you've said that to me today. The first time was earlier when I arrived this morning. I agree with Igami. You should rest this afternoon, after you get out of those wet garments."

"But what about Shin? I need to look after him."

Igami shook his head. "You need to clean yourself and put on fresh clothes. Shin needs to eat. Master Aoki will take care of him. Then it is time for his lessons. I will handle that, after I see to you." He turned to Shin and clapped his hands together. "Shin-*chan*, go with Master Aoki. I will see to your mother."

Shin stood straight and bowed. "Yes, *Sensei*."

The young boy rushed to the side of the old monk, his smile large. Whatever the reason, Shin enjoyed his time with both these men.

"Master Aoki, I am indebted to you for your kindness."

"It is nothing. With the boy's father away serving Lord Oda, it is the least I can do. Now you go with Igami and I will take of young Shin."

Boy's father. Not Kira's husband. Did that mean something?

Yes, Kira. It means you're paranoid and are reading too much into things.

"Thank you."

A whiff of smoke filled Kira's nose. She leaned over to Igami. "Is something burning?" she whispered.

He smiled in her direction. "Nothing to worry. That's only the hearth. The nights are getting colder. Time to get you cleaned up."

She nodded and fell in step behind the young monk, following him down the hall. Floor hearths. She should have known. Was she expecting centralized heat? At least Igami did not mind educating her. Plus, he knew his way around the house. How often was this man here? Likely a lot.

"So what lessons does Shin have today?" she asked.

He pivoted and stared. "Perhaps I should look at your head, for you to forget that. The same as always. His kana. He still reverses the characters of "*sa*" and "*chi*," as if he's looking at them in a mirror. Other characters confuse him, too. I've never seen a boy as challenged as Shin. Confusing, since he's such a bright child. However, he is still young, and I know he will learn."

"How do you know?"

His eyes twinkled, like hazel highlights on deep brown. She could lose herself in them. "I come from a family of teachers. My parents worked wonders with children of other samurai. My father taught me everything I know." His continued gaze stirred her heart, as much as it had outside when he'd rushed out with the blankets. "I am convinced it is only a matter of time, until his skills match those of children his age."

So Shin had problems with reading and writing. Igami seemed confident. That was good. Too much to think about. She should rest. Then she would find Shin and see for herself.

Igami slid a door open and removed his slippers. Kira did the same, stepping onto the tatami. Incense welcomed her entrance, soothing the knots in head and shoulders. She belonged here, even if she didn't remember it.

Igami slid open a closet, taking out a mattress and a cover, then opened another closet and removed a fresh kimono. "Here you are."

"Is there a room where I may wash myself?" Kira cheeks grew hot. Another question. He must think her foolish.

Igami's countenance betrayed no hint of criticism. "The bath is in the room across the hall. I instructed Nene to bring a fresh undergarment for you."

Kira searched her memory. Nothing. "Who is Nene?"

"The woman who took care of Shin."

Of course. Kira bowed and went across the hall, taking the kimono with her.

She opened the door. Heat greeted her face as she entered. The bath was in the corner, light steam rising from the water. A welcome sight. She found the dry garment on a clothing stand and placed the kimono on top of it. She then removed her wet garments, setting them on another stand. She then grabbed the small wooden bucket next to the bath, pouring water over herself to clean up before soaking for a minute. The custom hadn't changed in centuries.

If only Ma-ma could see her now.

Kira took a satisfying dip, then dried herself, and got dressed, quickly returning to the room. Igami stood there waiting. He had arranged the futon for her.

He had taken care of everything.

"I'm sorry to have troubled you," she said.

"It is no trouble. The stress of Ogawa-*sama* being away for so long, fearing he may not return from battle, leaves an emptiness."

Ogawa? So that was the name of the head of this house. Kira needed to be most respectful now in her words. "He is doing his duty for Lord Oda. I know that he is happiest serving him." She bit her lip, as if to bite the lie. She knew nothing about the man. However, a samurai would always be happiest serving his lord. Ogawa would be the same.

Images floated in her mind. Wisps of a face with a hard jaw and striking eyes wafted through her thoughts. A handsome man, though a bit older than she. Kira. Married to a samurai. Ma-ma would be happy about it, especially if she'd arranged it.

But no true feeling. None that she would expect. Why?

Time to ask now. To know her place in the house.

"Igami-*san*, may I ask you something?" Was that right? If she were Ogawa's wife. Then Igami would be shocked at her deference. For now, he was just polite.

"Certainly." No betrayal of surprise.

"I really did hit my head pretty hard. How long have Ogawa and I been…?"

The sparkle in his eyes disappeared, replaced by a look of a principal who'd caught a misbehaving child. "You really don't remember your place in this house, do you?"

She clutched her chest, then rubbed her head. A mild bump. "My head still throbs. I do not remember."

He grunted. "You are his consort. You serve his wife and him."

"But my son?" More memories floated back, of the birth and his early days. Each flashback brought wisps of pain. She rubbed her head again.

Igami said nothing, instead stepping behind her. He pressed his fingers lightly on her scalp, sending pain into her head and tingling through her body. "What are you doing?"

"Just examining you. These lapses of yours, they are strange."

He's avoiding the subject. Ask again. "So my son?"

"Is his son as well." He walked back around to stand in front of her. "You were purchased from your parents, as Lady Ogawa was barren. He needed an heir. You gave him one. For now."

That explains a lot. "What do you mean for now?"

He tilted his head. "You've forgotten that as well."

"Whatever it is, yes."

"Lady Ogawa gave birth to a son three months ago."

Kira's heart clutched at her chest. The wife had a son now? Not good. No need for her. No need for Shin. In the Bible, Sarah sent Haggai and Ishmael away when Jacob was born.

Japanese history was a little different sometimes. Execution was as common as banishment.

"I've been allowed to stay?"

"When Lady Ogawa was in her eighth month, she instructed you to leave if a son was born. When one was, I thought you would soon depart."

Flashes of the birth, of a woman on her knees with a thick rope in her mouth. Had she been there for the birth of Shin's little brother? "So did I. Maybe."

"Is your memory coming back?"

"Only flashes."

"Lady Ogawa fell ill during the pregnancy. You've spent the last two months taking care of her. Your loyalty does you honor. Only in the last few days has she seen glimpses of her previous strength, which have allowed her to spend time with young Mitsuyono. And now you should rest. You will need it soon."

Mitsuyono. So that was the baby's name. Kira knelt by her futon, her head swimming. She craved to lie down, hoping she would awake from this dream. The edge in Igami's words holding her awake. "Why?"

"Because when Lady Ogawa is completely healthy, you will have to leave."

Chapter Four

"Ogawa-*sama* has returned." Igami's voice carried through the house.

Kira turned, pausing from the sweeping she was doing in the main room of the house. She'd expected Igami any minute for Shin's afternoon lessons. He was on time. "When did he arrive?"

"Last night. The forces returned from Tedorigawa." His face turned ashen. "And their battle with the Uesugi."

Kira searched her memory. She'd heard of that battle before. One of the shows she'd watched with her grandmother. The details escaped her.

Igami's face conveyed the results.

"It went poorly, didn't it?" she asked.

He glanced at the floor. "Over one thousand men died."

Yes, that was it. The battle of the Tedori River. Lord Oda relied on guns. Lord Uesugi gambled on the river and rain. When Oda's guns wouldn't spark, his men were forced to retreat.

"Have you seen Ogawa-*sama* yet?"

"I did. He visited the temple this morning with his Lady Ogawa and Mitsuyono. He gave long prayers for the men who died, donating money and requesting to honor them.

A noble request. "How is he?"

"He shows the scars of battle."

"Anything else?"

Igami glanced behind her and froze.

A looming shadow fell across her feet. The hair stood on the back of her neck.

Kira turned.

The hard-jawed older man from her visions stood before her.

Ogawa.

"If you want to know how I am, you can ask me yourself."

She hid her gaze and fell to her knees, brushing her nose lightly against the tatami mat floor. "Welcome home, Ogawa-*sama*. You've worked so hard. Can I get you anything?"

"I wish to see Shin. It has been too long. Where is he?"

Waves of relief washed over Kira and she exhaled. She'd feared what Ogawa might say, now that his wife and other son were both fine. Would he ignore Shin? Apparently not. She struggled for the words then glanced at Igami.

Igami stepped forward. "He is in the classroom. He works diligently every day."

"Does he still have…the trouble?" Ogawa asked.

Igami bowed his head. Flashes of red streaked his face. "Yes, unfortunately. However, he is doing better. He has improved his ability to distinguish between the characters of "ah" and "oh," but there is still other work to be done."

Ogawa fumed and then his face softened. "I remember "ah" and "oh" confusing me when I was young. My father called me foolish. I learned. So will Shin. Will you promise me that, Igami? No matter the sacrifice, will you promise to ensure that he learns?"

Sacrifice? The word carried an odd tone of finality. Or did Kira only imagine a difference in Ogawa's tone?

Igami's face stiffened and he bowed low. "As my father before me did, I serve any request of the house of Ogawa. My family's debt to yours. Your kindness to the temple. I am here for you."

Ogawa turned to Kira. "The same question to you. Will you promise to see that Shin learns, no matter the sacrifice?"

Again the word *sacrifice.* Again the tone. She hadn't imagined it, but it made no sense. Hopefully she would understand later. It obviously meant much to Ogawa. She bowed again. "You have my word, Ogawa-*sama.*"

"That is good to hear."

Kira straightened and studied Ogawa's face. Sweat beaded on his forehead, as he carried a great weight. Then she saw the father in his eyes. Time with his child would lighten that burden. "Shall we go see Shin?"

"Yes." The man smiled.

Kira motioned to Igami, who led the way to the classroom. They reached the entrance and Ogawa rushed into the room, his steps almost light. Kira and Igami followed.

"Father," Shin said, his face lighting up as he put his brush aside and rose from his desk. The lad ran to his father, then bowed as he got close. "Good to see you."

Ogawa brushed his hand against his eye. Was that a tear? The warrior did have a soft heart for his children. "Is there anything you would like to do?"

"Father," Shin beamed at him, "can we walk the garden?"

Ogawa rubbed his chin. "My real thought was to look in on your little brother. He may not know me well, since I left before he was born. Would you help me? We can walk in the garden then."

Shin's eyes danced like fireworks. "Yes, sir. Let's go."

Ogawa took his son's hand and they walked out of the room.

Kira listened for the footsteps that soon faded away. "It is good to see them like that," she said to Igami.

"Yes. Ogawa is a more attentive father than most samurai I have met. I worried for Shin when Mitsuyono was born, thinking he would ignore Shin. He did not." Igami paused, as if considering his words. "Still, the tear in his eye surprised me."

"You noticed it, too?" She looked into his eyes. "I thought that to be joy at seeing his son."

"Yes, there is joy in his heart. However, I have watched Ogawa-*sama* for years. My father taught him when he was a boy. Long have I looked up to him. Admired him. Revered him. He is an emotional man. Something is different however."

Different. Would that be the reason I was brought to this time? "How do you mean? How is it different?"

"Family has always mattered to Ogawa-*sama*, but it came after duty. His manner now suggests family matters most.

"I understand." *I think.* "What garden is he talking about?"

Igami rolled his eyes, but then shot her a look that warmed her toes. At some point, he would tire of her questions. Thankfully, not yet. He closed the entrance to the rest of the house, then went to the back of the room, sliding open the door. Chilly air gripped her, and she pulled her kimono tighter as she stepped onto the porch. A rock garden lay before her, with a path both through it and around it. The path led to a smaller building set up with steps and a foundation to raise it off the ground.

"A teahouse?" she said, staring at the structure.

"Yes. Ogawa-*sama* entertains there often."

She stepped onto the path. A wall to her left sheltered the teahouse from the road and added to the solemnity of garden. She looked right, seeing the lake which only yesterday she'd come out of. Wind rustled through the trees while water lapped at the shore. Moonlight illuminated a structure next to the lake with a dock that jutted into the water. A dark flat object appeared to float next to the dock, banging into with a slow, constant thud. A raft? More flashes of memory. Her and Shin at the building on the lake. The scene was quiet, as if nothing had happened.

A chill reached her back.

Nothing had happened yet.

"Igami-*san*," she said, finally looking back, "what do you think Ogawa meant when he mentioned sacrifice?"

He looked down. "I do not know. He said the word twice. He asked each of us for a promise."

She took a deep breath and held it. What would that promise entail?

Chapter Five

The next day passed without incident. Ogawa spent more time with Shin and also Mitsuyono. Kira had seen little of either.

However, she had finally met Lady Ogawa. After a few days of pushing herself, she'd grown weak again and craved rest. Kira had brought her food, but her mistress had eaten little, and had requested only modest errands.

Kira had provided all.

What must it be like for a wife to have to depend on everything from a consort.

What a reminder to Kira of her position.

Ogawa had remained the same. The mention of the promise not broached again. He neither looked her way, nor addressed her.

She knew not to ask.

Kira focused on her other duties. She worked with other servants, ensured that the house remained clean. There was little else to do.

And now with time, she walked to the lake.

At first, she'd walked the grounds, mostly to get out of the house. Then she searched intently, as if seeking a doorway back to the present. None to be found. None but the lake.

The breeze swirled over it, lapping her with the scent of forest marsh and bamboo, dropping leaves and branches on otherwise still waters. Circles grew in all directions, bringing modest waves to the shores.

No other movement showed.

Was the doorway at the bottom? Was that the only way home? Would the lake part to show her the way?

Or was she here now? Did she grow more like the woman into whom she'd found herself? What had happened to the woman whose life she'd overtaken? Had she passed? Was her spirit in the present?

She chuckled. How confused that woman must be?

Sadness gripped her heart. How would Ma-ma handle whatever had happened?

But Kira was here now. Spending her time daydreaming would solve nothing. Doing work would get her closer to the truth. She headed back to the house. Perhaps inspecting the front gate and the entrance would provide a salve for her thoughts.

As she reached the front, the clop-clop of horses announced a visitor. The gate opened. In walked an older man dressed in fine gray *kataginu*, the kimono with wing-like shoulders, and pleated pants. Full samurai garb, down to the two swords. His thin black mustache and goatee framed his mouth. The pride and bearing in plain sight for all. A horse continued to move back-and-forth in the gate opening, its reins held by another samurai who remained outside and stoic.

The older man stared at her.

Panic gripped Kira, her heart racing.

What am I waiting for?

She hit the ground immediately, bowing low. "Welcome. Welcome to the Ogawa household. How may I serve you?"

The man approached. His steps carried the weight of his authority. "Tell your master that Niwa Nagahide is here."

"Yes, sir." She bowed again, then rose, searching her memory for his name.

None.

It didn't matter. His importance reigned over anyone who glimpsed him.

She entered the house and searched for Ogawa, finding him in the sitting room, telling the boys about Ogawa family shrine. Ogawa held Mitsuyono on his lap and against his chest, while Shin made funny faces at his little brother.

Many samurai supposedly possessed the souls of a poet. Ogawa possessed the soul of a father.

He looked up at her, as if annoyed at the interruption. "Yes?"

She knelt and bowed. "Niwa-*sama* requests to see you."

He nodded, almost gently, as if he'd expected it. He rose. "Nene," he yelled.

An older woman appeared, dressed in a brown kimono with hatched lines. Her tightly pulled hair revealed gray strands. Kira had glimpsed her twice before, avoiding the name she could not recall. Like much around here that she could not recall. 'Nene' he had said. Wisps of memory drifted in Kira's mind. Did she and Nene talk? Likely not.

Nene cuddled Mitsuyono in one arm while clasping Shin's hand, then led both out of the room. Watching them leave, Ogawa walked over to Kira. "Find Igami. Tell him to bring water and finest tea to the tea house. I will greet Niwa." He paused, his gaze softening, and placed his hand on her shoulder. A show of support. *For her.* "Be strong," he said.

Kira mouth dropped open, and she closed it quickly as she nodded her assent. She may be Ogawa's consort, but his crossing of status boundaries made her head swim. This, and his request for sacrifice, what did it mean?

Kira found Igami, who was reading in the classroom. They hurried to the kitchen and put the water over the fire to boil, while they prepared trays and treats.

"Who is Niwa?" Kira asked.

"One of Oda's generals. Like Ogawa-*sama*, he was also at battle at Tedori River."

"Does he come here often? I do not recall him at all."

"Still forgetful?"

"Maybe a little."

He inhaled through his teeth. "I have never seen him here, but that does not mean anything." He paused, as if considering his words. "I am only here in the afternoon. Samurai are early risers. He could have been here many mornings. However, I do not believe he has been here."

"Why do you say that?"

"I saw Niwa once at the temple. He is a striking man. Such men are seldom forgotten."

Kira rubbed her arms, but a deep chill remained. "Then why would he be here?"

He gazed at the ceiling, then back at her. "I do not know."

Hiding the truth. "You do know. It is written on your face."

"Written on my face?" He touched his fingers to his forehead, chin, and cheeks, checking the tips. "There's ink on me?"

She laughed inside. Another colloquialism. She'd tried to hide it, but something in his manner relaxed her. "It's only a saying. It means that the truth the can be seen in the expression on your face. I know you know why he is here."

"You have strange sayings. I have never visited the district you came from, but I wonder if I would be confused if I were there."

Flashes of Atlanta floated in her mind. How would Igami handle her time? Her home? What would he think? No telling. "A lot of things are different where I'm from."

"We can discuss that later then. The water is ready." He smiled broadly, his gaze catching hers.

Later would be too long it seemed.

They carried everything out to the tea house. Kira climbed the stone steps, taking the water and tea first and setting them down. She then knelt at the entrance, bowing before she slid the door open. She then opened the door and bowed again, setting the items next to Ogawa, then   then brought the treats and set them next to the first tray. She bowed each time, asking if anything else was needed after she set the treats.

Ogawa dismissed her without a glance.

She returned to the house with Igami while listening for sounds from the teahouse.

Nothing.

They re-entered the classroom. Shin waited at his desk, glee etched on his face.

The young monk shifted his looks between her and Shin, his care etched in his expression. She knew this man, knew him well. But how well? She likely shared much time with him because of Shin. In another time, another place, would they know each other differently?

Mother, why couldn't you have brought home a guy like this? For this man, she would come home early.

"So you really have no idea why Niwa is here?" Kira studied his face for a hint.

He paused. "None."

"You look like you know something."

"Shin-*chan*," he turned away, "give us five minutes, then we will begin." He pointed Kira back out the door.

"What is it then?" Kira's heart skipped, sending twitches through her chest.

"Do not say anything for now. After the lesson, I will request permission from Ogawa-*sama* to visit my temple this afternoon after Shin's exercises with his father. I will also request your presence. I will say it's an educational tour. I will meet you later and escort the both of you. Will you come?"

"I would be honored."

"Then I will see you later. For now, I must see to Shin. Have a good afternoon."

She watched him walk to Shin, his strong shoulders and gait etched with purpose.

Taking her thoughts and wishes with him.

*****

"Shin seems to have enjoyed the tour." Kira said, as she watched her son head away with Yutani, a tall, thin teenage monk who needed to shave his head again and pop a couple of pimples. He requested Shin help him clean the room where visitors give donations.

"Nice young man, Yutani," she added, "and Shin seems to like him."

"Yes, he's good boy and good with children. He trains boys like Shin in the basics and is an older brother to them. We have many novitiates here. They are the future of the order."

"You don't look that old." She looked around, noting several children about, their haste increasing the floor squeaks. Children did start young here. Had Igami started the same way? "I thought you were the future."

"No, I may be future leadership, but children are the future lifeblood."

She bit her lip, glancing around to see if anyone was nearby. No one. It was time. "I have something I need to ask you."

"Yes?" Igami's serene look gave her no hint he would answer now. What are you hiding?"

"Hiding?" He stared at her, his eyes wide with puzzlement.

"Not telling me."

Understanding lit his face. "Ah. You and your strange phrases again.

They are confusing. It is like you have become a different person since that day you fell in the water. I cannot explain how you are changed, other than the words you use, but you are in some way new."

"What do you mean 'new'?"

"Like a child though you are an adult. Like someone from another land."

That was an excellent description. Could she tell him? Should she tell him? Would he think her mad?

Do I have a choice?

She stiffened her frame. "I am… different."

"How?" His brown eyes fixed on her, sending heat to her face. "You are almost a different person. You have the memories. Some of them. Yet, you behave as if your memories belong to another. It's as if a spirit has taken you."

Her heart beat faster. She lowered her gaze to hide the truth she knew was there. "A spirit. What do you mean? Do you think it's an evil spirit?"

"Walk with me and I'll answer your questions."

Kira dropped a step behind, and followed him to the large wooden gate at the front of the temple complex. He pointed to the entrance. "Do you see the statues?"

Kira quickened her stride to get closer the two wooden figures. Each was roughly ten-feet tall. Warlike fierce yet somehow friendly, at least to her. Imposing to all who enter with ill. Both nearly the same but with one exception. Left side male with mouth closed. Right side female with mouth open. *Kind of like my parents.* Igami sidled next to her. She glanced at him. "They look familiar."

Igami laughed. "That probably true. The artist modeled them after the ones at Todaiji in Nara. Once you see the ones at Todaiji, you never forget."

"What are they here for?"

He steepled his fingers, almost as if taking the role of a teacher. "The same as any other temple. They are protectors. The beginning and end of life. They scare away evil spirits and allow the good ones to remain. They allowed you on the grounds." He crossed him arms, then flashed the grin that weakened her knees since the day she'd risen from the lake. "The spirit within you is not evil."

"So what's left?"

"Rebirth. We believe in it, but you are truly blessed. I've yet to meet anyone who recalls a past life."

"I remember my previous life, but I'm not from the past."

Igami's mouth opened and he stared at her.

"Are you alright?" Kira asked.

He exhaled, then stared blankly into space. "For this, I need tea…and Master Aoki. Come."

"Wait," she glanced about the grounds but saw little movement, "what about Shin?"

"Shin is under capable supervision. You will see him as soon as we talk with Master Aoki. Come now."

*****

Kira sipped her tea, her thoughts wondering to Shin. Master Aoki spoke with a few monks who entered, keeping his voice low. Temple business. Likely not for outsiders. Yet, the monks glanced in her direction, more of support with eyes wide. What did they know that she did not?

Aoki closed the door, then invited her and Igami to sit at a table on the floor. "My apologies. Igami said you remember a previous life since you fell in the water, but a life not from the past."

"Yes, but I have only glimpses of the life here. The life I know is the one from the future."

Aoki crossed his arms and looked down his nose at her. "From where?"

That's a good question. How do you explain a country that doesn't yet exist?

Directionally.

"I am from a land across the great water to the east. That is where I live in my time."

"The east?" Aoki closed his eyes. Was he praying? He opened his eyes. "I see. So you live with the red-haired barbarians on the other side of the world? You are Japanese, are you not?"

Red-haired barbarians? Likely Portuguese traders. How to explain? "I am Japanese, but I live in a different land between here and the …barbarians."

"Why leave?"

A touchy subject. "My ancestors moved there for work. Sometimes you must do what you can to protect the family."

Aoki sighed. "If we had time, you could draw me a map. However, time is short. How did you get here? To this time?"

Driving home a car? Running off a highway? What would work here?

"I was riding in a car…. I mean, cart. I was trying to reach my parents' home. It was dark. Cold. The cart slid sideways and I tumbled into a lake and fell unconscious. When I woke up, I was here."

Aoki braced himself, putting hand to floor as he stood. His frame seemed to shake from an unseen force. He grabbed a sip of tea, then opened the window and stared outside, his body stiff as the cold breeze that filtered through the room.

"Woman of the future," Aoki said without turning, "have you enjoyed your time here?"

His tone was ominous. "Yes, do you think I'm leaving soon?"

"Yes, Niwa's visit to Ogawa today was no coincidence. There have been rumors about the battle at the Tedori River, questions on Ogawa's performance there."

"He…was a coward?" Kira pressed her chest as her heart pounded against the surface. It could not be true. Nothing about the man suggested any hint of fear, any hint of cowardice.

"I do not know. Either he should have died or a decision of his led to the fate of many. Yet, he survived."

"And came home."

"Yes, and because he did, he has been judged by Lord Oda. Niwa delivered the decision. His line is to die.'

Kira swallowed hard. "His line? But that would mean…"

Aoki finally turned toward her. "Yes. Him. His children, and any potential future children."

Kira's throat constricted and she struggle to breathe.

She'd come to this time to die.

Chapter Six

The walk back to the house had only been a few minutes but had felt like an hour. Darkness had fallen just before they'd started. Only the city torches provided any light on the cloudy evening.

Kira craved to hold Shin. To run away with him. To hide him. To keep him safe.

She stayed.

Several times she glanced about. Samurai were everywhere? Were they watching her? Likely not. She was of low importance. Yet all their eyes seemed on her.

At least Igami was here. His presence calmed her fears.

They soon reached Ogawa's house. She sent Shin inside, leaving her and Igami alone. She scrutinized him, yearning to have his arms wrapped around her, hold her, tell her this was all a dream.

Yet, if she did wake up, he wouldn't be there.

"So what do I do?" she asked.

Igami exhaled a low breath. "You can delay your fate in life, but escape is impossible."

She bit her lip. "What does delay do for me?"

"Time." His gaze grew soft and supportive. "Delay provides you time."

"And time gives me?"

He leaned forward, his lips almost brushing her ear. "Acceptance. Acceptance and hope."

Her blood rushed to her heart. She wanted to hold him once again.

As she had before.

Before.

She could not hold him now.

She had held him before?

Whatever they had shared, Ogawa was not aware of it. They would both be dead otherwise.

"I'll see you tomorrow," he said.

She gave a bow and watched him leave, knowing every second was precious.

Kira entered the house and began looking for Shin. She found him at Ogawa's feet, listening as Ogawa related some historic tale. A tale of honor. Shin, normally blessed with a smile, maintained a stoic face.

Like his father.

Ogawa glanced at Kira, rubbed Shin's head, then sent him along.

Oh to run to Shin and spirit him away. Yet her feet remained locked to the floor as if shackled. Do her duty.

Not that fleeing would get her anywhere.

"Kira," Ogawa began, "You do an excellent job raising our son."

She bowed. Praise from her master. There was no higher compliment. "Thank you, sir. You honor me." Are his words preparing me for something? How to respond? "Your leadership of this house is the reason he does well."

He laughed. "Were it another day, I would agree with you. Today is not that day. Sit."

Kira's shoulders stiffened. Sit? He asked her to sit, as if she were his equal? Even as Shin's mother, she remained unworthy.

To have these thoughts, I really have gone back in time and in spirit. Ma-ma would laugh.

"How may I serve you, sir?" she finally asked.

He knelt and sat back on his feet. "Have the rumors reached you?"

She wanted to say no and hope Igami was wrong. She could not lie to the man in front of her. Never had. "I…I know. Has an order been given?"

His shoulders slumped, as if the news weighed on him like a mountain. "No, not yet."

"But it will be." A question not rhetorical, but one that needed no answer.

"A meeting will be held tomorrow mid-morning. We will all need to attend. Until then, we have time to invoke our own deities and demons."

The pit in Kira's stomach pounded like a temple bell. "Your sons? Is there no chance?"

He smiled, as if to offer whatever his heart could open. "They will be reborn. I only pray that I may watch them. You do remember your promise, do you not?"

The word *sacrifice* sounded in her head, like it had before. She would honor her commitment. "Yes, I will remain faithful to you, and to my word."

He rose and knelt beside her, placing his hands on her shoulder, rubbing them as if to provide support. Could a warrior's touch really be so gentle? He leaned in, and kissed her on the cheek. "Keep your face and expression still. There is always hope. You will know when."

He rose again and left, his gait slow and dignified. A gallant man indeed.

✳✳✳✳✳

Silence pervaded the house. Was this feeling what prisoners on death row experienced? Not likely. Those people had committed a crime and needed to pay for their deeds. How about soldiers on the eve of a hopeless battle? A maid had had brought her dinner, but it had mattered not. Food offered her strength, but she possessed no desire to eat.

This would be her last night here. Her last night on earth. She closed her eyes. Only prayer mattered.

"Do you regret your decision?" Lady Ogawa's voice startled her.

Kira scrambled to her feet and bowed. Lady Ogawa only stared at her, Mitsuyono nestled in her arms, suckling at her breast. Kira's own breasts surged. Motherhood. She'd bonded immediately with Shin when she'd arrived. But not the full years. If only she could recall how the real Kira had felt all the times before now? Did her mother feel that bond?

Of course.

"My decision?" Kira bowed. "My lady, I have no regrets."

Lady Ogawa smiled. "You maintain your thoughts well. We brought you here to provide Ogawa with a child. You gave him a son when I could not."

What this woman must have endured. To be forced to deal with another woman in her house who birthed a son when she could not. "I serve the Ogawa family, including you. I take your orders as well as his."

"Yes, you do." Lady Ogawa stared down at her own child. "And when my son was born, I told you to take your son and leave. You agreed, taking Shin with you."

Images flooded back. Images of the prior Kira. "And then you fell ill after he was born. I could not desert you."

"How did you learn that? Who told you I was ill?"

Kira searched her mind. Images again flooded her mind like the lake water had flooded her face. Leaving. Running. Indecision. What had happened?

"I apologize, my lady. I do not remember." It felt like a lie. It stung like a lie. Yet, it was the truth.

"Wherever you were, you should have stayed where you were." The woman's gaze bore into her. "Maybe you would not face our fate."

Heaviness like the mountain descended on her heart. She was to be here. "I made the right decision." What reason could she tell her that Lady Ogawa could believe? What reason would convince her?

Duty. Ending shame.

"Once my parents sold me. I could not return to them, especially with a child. As I said, I serve you. This is my fate." She steeled her nerves. "I will meet it well."

Lady Ogawa eyed her up and down. Did she believe? Did it matter? No. Only now did.

"It is good you returned. You do not deserve the name I gave you."

"You gave me?"

"Ah, you have forgotten that as well, haven't you?" She grinned and held Mitsuyono tighter. "That fall in the lake did make you lose your memory. The name of 'Kira.' I gave it to you. You were like a new toy to my husband when you first arrived. Bright and shiny. *Kirakira.* I believed you to have no substance."

"What do you believe now?"

"You stayed and proved me wrong. You gave me the time to know my son. For that, I hope the next world rewards you with favor."

Kira bowed once again. Lady Ogawa nodded, then left, cradling her son.

Kira thought of her parents, who'd always been there for her. Of her promising career. Of her education.

Of her blessed life.

Maybe the next world did reward me, only I didn't realize it.

Chapter Seven

"*Okaasan*," Shin's voice cried when he saw her. "Everybody sad. Why?"

The last few hours had passed slowly. Kira had prayed, seen Shin, then sent him to his father and prayed again. Now, he was back.

What should I tell him?

"Shin-*chan*, you have to be brave. Things will be better. Trust me. Things will be better."

"Do you promise?"

Kira's lips tightened. "I promise."

She put Shin to bed, telling him she would join him soon, then brushed his hair until he fell asleep. From there, she repaired to the classroom. Would she sense Igami there? He spent so many hours there his spirit likely remained. She opened the door that led outside, and gazed across the rock garden at the teahouse. A chilling wind cut through her clothes, but it invigorated her.

She grabbed a pair of shoes and eased down the steps, turning right toward the lake. Small streams of moonlight pierced through the clouds and reflected off the water.

Kira shivered, as if icy fingers traced her spine. Death approached on her own terms. If only Igami were here to put his arms around her and keep her warm.

If only she had more than one night remaining.

Guttural voices sounded from the street. Late night revelers likely headed home.

A place she would never see again.

Mother, I hope to see you again someday and prove that you raised me right.

Her eyes grew heavy, despite the stiff wind that cut across her face. Time to retire to bed. Time to see Shin.

A rustle in the bushes drew her attention. A slender figure.

Yutani? Why would the young monk be here?

It could not be.

Whispers. Shadows. Was she hearing things?

She circled back to the house, pressing her body against the side and in in the shadows. More whispers. More rustling.

Then nothing.

The mini-house near the lake appeared dead in the distance, except for a raft that floated in front, seeming to slap against both water and the structure.

Maybe she was hearing things.

Kira exhaled and rubbed her chest. Unfortunately, the tension remained.

Of course it would. Time to face karma.

She re-entered the house and headed to her room. Shin slept silently on the futon. She rubbed his hair again, then lay down and closed her eyes.

*****

Loud noises roused Kira from her sleep. She rushed to the window and slid it open.

Smoke billowed in, the stench filling her nose and stinging her eyes. She fought to see the direction of the smoke.

The teahouse!

A fire caller yelled orders, directing others around the ends of the wall that separated the rock garden from the road. Bells and knocks sounded from the front of the house. *The door.*

She roused Shin and took him in her arms, carrying him to the front. Other servants ran about, calling out for Ogawa.

Ogawa-sama, where are you?

Kira slid open the door. A dour looking man in a dark kimono and red face to match, pressed into the house. "Where's Ogawa? His tea house is on fire."

How to answer? "We are searching for him now."

"Help the servants. Help put out the fire."

She set Shin on the porch, finding a blanket and wrapping it around him, then ran to the tea house.

She found men digging a trench, while others brought buckets.

"Is anyone inside?" Kira asked.

"We don't know," one man responded. "The fire was too high. We couldn't go in. We must keep it here. If it spreads, we could lose many houses."

More people arrived with buckets. Men formed a line between the lake and the tea house, bringing water to douse the flames. She scanned the line. Igami, Aoki, and several others from the monastery. How did they hear of the fire? News couldn't travel this fast. Did the chanters that stand on street corners to raise money for the temple pass the news to them?

Or did the family's fate have the monks already watching them, ready to serve when death came?

Rain began to fall, a light drizzle that chilled her bones further. Smiles broke out on many of the faces of the men on the bucket line. The rain could spare the rest of the houses. She wished she could bring hot drinks to the people. What could she do to help?

She ran to join the line.

Where were Ogawa and his wife?

She looked at the burning teahouse. Her throat tightened like a drying leather belt.

There.

Chapter Eight

Dawn peaked over the lake, bringing rays of warmth, yet too little to warm her frame.

The stench of smoke remained. The combination of men and rain had contained the fire. The smoldering coals provided heat and kept the attention of the officials.

Not long enough.

An official walked over to her, his face stern and eyes piercing hate. He wore a club in his belt and likely would use it.

"My name is Haseda. I am the magistrate."

She bowed. "How may I help you, Haseda-*san*?"

"You did not join your master and his wife?"

What I thought last night was true. The news struck her heart with the weight of ten rice bushels. "You found them?"

He smiled, his black teeth a mixture of grit and grift. "We did. They took the honorable way out. They will likely be reborn to their same station."

"He was an honorable man."

"Yes, he was." Haseda spat on the ground. "You could do the same. Ogawa was samurai, and deserves ceremony, but everyone is too busy for the likes of you. If not for Ogawa's position, I would strike you down now." He spat again. "Save us the trouble. You've already taken more time than you deserve. If not, I will return in two hours."

The man walked away. His disdain for her trailed in his wake. He was right. She should be dead already. Perhaps back in Lanier she already was.

So why had she traveled here?

"How are you this morning?" a familiar voice asked.

Kira jumped and turned, the surprise ebbing as a faint smile forced its way to her lips. "Igami-*san*, what a question. How do you think I'm doing?"

He sighed. "I don't know. I don't know how I would feel, other than…an attention to duty."

"Like Ogawa?" Her eyes began to tear. "They found him and his wife."

He nodded. "Yes, I heard. They committed *seppuku* and torched the tea house."

"Why?"

"To protect themselves in death."

"What about Mitsuyono?" she asked.

"Once the remains cool further, they will sift through the debris." Igami turned and looked toward the ruins. "For now, nothing."

The poor child. His only crime was the name of his father. What was society so long ago? "And the same fate awaits Shin."

"Do not despair. There is still hope. For now, rest."

"How can I rest?"

"Because you have no choice. And because Shin needs you. He sleeps in his room at the moment. Aoki is already preparing breakfast." He leaned in, his shoulder touching hers and sending waves through her frame. "Rouse the young man. Aoki and I will restore your faith."

*****

Kira ran her fingers through Shin's hair again. She could not bring herself to wake him. Did he have any understanding of what would happen today? What do children understand of death? What do they know of life? At this moment, he knew peace.

Flashes of the accident surfaced floated into her thoughts. *How quickly it can end.*

A knock sounded at the door.

"Come in."

The door slid open. Igami smiled at her and then looked at Shin, his eyes wide. "You have not awakened him?"

"I've only been here a few minutes."

"You have been thirty. You need to wake him. Now."

She pushed again his frame. "Shin-*chan*, wake up."

"*Okaasan*, do I have to?" He moved his head slowly.

"Yes," she answered.

Shin sat up and rubbed his eyes. "Good morning, Igami-*sensei*. How are you?"

"I'm well, young Shin. Why don't you go to the kitchen? I believe Master Aoki could use your help with breakfast. I need to talk with your mother

"Yes, sir." Shin rose from his futon, which Kira helped him put away, then put on his slippers and left, his steps making a slap patter as he went down the hall.

"He's still so happy," Kira said.

"Yes, have your told him anything?" Igami asked.

"Nothing. He doesn't even know what happened to his father yet. It's best he not know."

"Good. There is a dark blue kimono about his size in the kitchen. After breakfast, tell him to put it on and say you have a special day planned. Then, when you are ready, take Shin to the building on the lake."

His words struck her like the crash into the guardrail. "Am to drown us both? What if the magistrate wants to take us in?"

"Then tell him you wish to have one last view of the lake with Shin."

Really? "The magistrate will allow that?"

He stared briefly, as if in disbelief he had to explain. "Shin is the son of a samurai. They will accept your request. The magistrate will believe you wish to spare Shin pain, like any mother.”

“Then what?”

“Then trust me. I will meet you there.”

Her heart swelled. Igami had a plan. “You can save us?”

“Not us.” He dropped his gaze. “Just Shin.”

That was the plan. To save Shin, she would have to die.

By drowning myself.

“Is this the only way?”

“Yes.”

Water. Her greatest fear. “What do we do now?”

“We eat,” Igami said, trying to look cheerful. “Master Aoki waits for us, too. As much as I make comments about his cooking, he does do some dishes very well. This meal should be good.”

Given how my stomach feels, I’ll probably puke.

*****

Igami had not been wrong. Master Aoki had done a wonderful job with breakfast. Else maybe the realization one is eating one’s last meal makes one enjoy the simple flavors of life.

“How is it?” Master Aoki asked

“You put your heart into it, Master Aoki,” Kira said.

His gaze flitted back between her and Igami. “Put my heart into it?”

Another confusing phrase. “It was the best breakfast I’ve ever eaten.”

He bowed low. “At your service.” He glanced up from his bow, a tear forming at the edge of eyes. “I will miss you,” he whispered.

Kira smiled, knowing it was the last time she would see him.

A bell sounded from the front door.

The magistrate. Must be time.

“Shin-*chan*,” Kira took a deep breath, “we’re going to the lake.”

“For swimming? It’s too cold.”

“I just want to walk around for a few minutes. Let me answer the door, then we will walk down there.”

“It’s cold.”

“Yes, I know.” She saw the blue kimono Igami mentioned earlier and pointed at it. “Put on that kimono. I’ll only be a few minutes.”

“I will.”

Shin ran away. Kira looked for Igami, but he was no longer around. She headed to the door, her steps slow.

The sound of pounding fists now resonated in the hall.

Better hurry.

Kira slid the door open. Haseda stood there, his face petulant. She bowed low. *Must keep him happy.* "Magistrate, welcome."

He didn't respond. No pleasantries. Kira was beneath him now. "It's time. Where is the child?"

"He is dressing to be presentable."

"Very well." His sneer showed his disdain. "Do you have any final requests?"

"I would like to take Shin to the lake and take one last view from the dock. It was a special place, particularly for my son. I will only be a few moments.

He frowned, as if keeping a simmering temper in check. Her mouth grew dry. Would he say no? Time stopped like a dammed creek

For Shin. Please

Haseda exhaled loudly. "Your request is granted. You have already required too much time. Make it quick."

Igami, it worked. "Yes, magistrate. Thank you for your kindness."

The magistrate departed, but only to remove himself from the grounds. Kira knew he would watch. She headed to kitchen.

Shine waited with a smile. "I'm ready."

"Good. Let's head to the lake."

Kira held Shin's hand as the two of them went outside and headed to the boathouse. A brisk noisy wind blew against her. It might be the best thing. The wind would hide Shin's cries.

The walk down to the lake took only a few minutes. Each step felt like the anchor she knew she would soon carry.

She reached the boathouse. A raft, tied to the dock that jutted out from the house, bobbed on the water. *What I saw last night was real.* An anchor lay on the raft, its rope tied to a pole near the edge. Everything set. Could she go through with this?

Shin squeezed her hand. She turned and looked into his eyes. *I have to for his sake.*

They entered the boat house from the side door.

"Igami-*sensei*," Shin said. "Is this a lesson?"

Igami knelt and brought his finger to his lips. "Young Shin, please. Say nothing. Very important."

Shin looked at Kira, his mouth open. "*Okaasan*, what is it?"

"Shin-*chan*, I need you to be quiet. Can you do that for me?"

He nodded his head. "Yes."

"Good." She looked at Igami. "What next?"

Igami went to the corner of the room and picked up a child-sized straw figure. The figure had a blue kimono, similar to Shin's, and a mask on its face. A switch?

"That thing will work?" she asked.

He inhaled and licked his lips, as if he words might stick in his mouth

"It is our hope. The magistrate likely watches from a distance. He expects you to do your duty."

"*Okaasan*, what duty? Are you going somewhere? Where's Father?" Shin stared at her. Tears formed at the edge of his eyes.

"Shin-*chan*," Kira bit her lip, "I need you to be brave. Can you be brave for me?"

He wiped his eyes with his sleeve. "Yes."

"I have to leave. Igami-*sensei* will take care of you. You need to do everything he says."

"Where's Father?"

She exhaled slowly. "Father had to leave, too."

He rubbed his fingers in his eyes. "Will I see him soon?"

"Yes, I promise."

Tears flowed from Shin's eyes. Was there any way she could change this?

Kira hugged him and kissed his cheek.

Flashes of flight. Her and Shin trying to run. Of the magistrate catching them.

Killing them both.

That's why she was here. The previous Kira had run, costing Shin his life.

Kira needed to follow through, to save Shin.

"Why are you going? Is it cause of Father? Cause of the battle?"

Kira sighed. He knew more than she'd expected.

"Yes, it's because to the battle. Father followed the will of Lord Oda. Now I must do the same."

"And me?"

She shook her head. "Your duty is to stay with Igami-*sensei*. He is your new father."

"Where will we go?"

Igami knelt and grabbed Shin's shoulders. "I will tell you in time."

"Where?"

Igami dried Shin's tears with the back of his hand. "Do not worry. For now, I want you to sit and pray. We will pray for a while. Can you do that for me?"

Shin nodded and went to one corner of the boathouse. What was he thinking? His father was dead. His mother about to die, at least the woman he knew as his mother. How did a child adjust to that?

"Any advice, Igami-*san*?" Kira still hoped for a potential change.

"Acceptance and prayer will work for you, too."

"How do you accept?"

"Swallow water, I have heard. Less air. Less time."

"Anything else?"

He pulled a string from under his robe. "You will tie this string to your wrist and to the straw Shin. You can make it move this way. The doll is weighted, so the wind will not blow it away. There is a spike in his foot, so it can look like Shin is standing on the raft. You will then set the straw Shin next to you. Then, unmoor the raft and push yourself out. Tie the anchor to your foot, then—"

"I understand the rest." Put Shin on her lap, push the anchor off the boat, and go in with it. She would sink.

Shin would be safe.

She gazed into Igami's eyes one last time, stepped forward, and pressed her lips against his. He held her tight, tasting of honey and forever. At least she would know his lips before she died.

Shin rushed forward and hugged her again. "*Okaasan*, I don't want you to go."

"I have to…for you."

"How about Lord Oda?"

"I'm following the orders of a braver man. Your father. Promise me you'll stay quiet. Your father is watching you. I'll be watching you. Always listen to Igami-*sensei*."

"I will."

Kira said one more goodbye than bowed to both of them. Time to go. She tied the fake Shin to her arm and held it against her, left through a second door that went to the dock, shutting it closed on her life here.

Kira reached the raft and set up the straw figure as instructed. She unwound the rope from the moor, then used a pole to push herself away, making sure to occasionally pull the string. It worked as Igami had said.

She looked back at the house. A tiny kimono-clad figure stood near where the teahouse had once been.

The magistrate.

Could he see her? He made no move. Gave no orders. Hopefully the plan had worked.

She drifted, minute-by-minute, a few feet by a few feet.

The wind whipped off the surface, bringing the scent of pine and sludge. Waiting sucked.

Prayer Igami has said.

She tied the anchor to her feet, put the doll in her lap, and said a prayer.

She looked again at the magistrate. At least she thought it was him. No action near the boathouse. That was proof enough.

Swallow the water Igami had said.

She took a breath, held the doll tight with one arm, and pushed the anchor off the side. Her body jerked downward. Her head struck the raft.

Reality faded into nothing.

<h1 style="text-align:center">Chapter Nine</h1>

Kira moved her head from side-to-side against her pillow. Her throbbing temple weighed on her like a brick,

"Unnh," she said.

"She's coming around," a woman's voice said.

Scents of cleaning agents filled her nose, mixed with perfume, sweat, and sterile linens. Footsteps drew nearer and familiar touches grasped each of her hands.

I'm alive. I'm alive.

Kira opened her eyes. Ma-ma and Pa-pa were on each side of her, both smiling wide.

She was home. Back in her own time.

"Where am I?"

"You're at the hospital," the unknown woman's voice said. An attractive 30-something woman of medium height with short brown hair and an obvious baby bump approached and looked at Kira over glasses perched on the end of her nose. "I'm Dr. Sanchez." You're a very lucky woman."

"What happened?"

"Your car plowed through a guardrail and plunged into Lake Lanier. You've been mostly unconscious since rescuers pulled you out last night. Sometimes, you'd mumble a few things and then go back to sleep. What do you remember?"

Kira sighed. "I don't remember anything after the air bag deployed and I rolled. What did I say?"

The doctor made a few notes on her chart. "I don't know. I didn't understand a word of it. According to your mother, you were speaking Japanese."

Kira turned to her mother. "You were here all the time? What did I say?"

Her mother squeezed her hand again. "Yes, I never left your side. But, it was difficult to watch you. Difficult to hear. You were speaking formal. Respectful." Her eyes sparkled. "Not used to that from you."

Yes, Ma-ma. Glad your sarcasm is back. "What did I say?"

"Something about children, battle, and sacrifice. You also talked writing. I didn't understand everything." She smiled at her. "No matter though. You're awake. Your father and I can rest now."

She squeezed her parent's hands again, afraid to let go. How close had she come to losing them? Or they her? Would they understand what she'd been through. She didn't understand yet.

The doctor took more vitals. "Ms. Sakamichi, you seem to be doing better, but I do recommend you rest. As for your parents," the doctor smiled,

"I recommend they, especially your mother, get something to eat. I don't want them so tired they faint."

The doctor left the room. Both her parents pulled chairs next to the edge of her bed. Both had circles under their eyes.

"You've all been waiting up with me?" Kira asked

Ma-ma pulled her chair closer. "Of course."

"Pa-pa, have you slept?"

"I have. The chair here is comfortable." He patted her hand then kissed her forehead. "Good to see you awake."

"I'm sorry to have worried you."

"The doctor said you would be fine when you woke up," Pa-pa said. "You kept mumbling. We knew it would be soon."

She turned back to her mother. "Have you even changed your clothes?"

"I gave your father a list of things to bring me from the house. A friend of mine met him there and helped him find everything."

"Why?"

"Your father's a man He'd still be looking for things."

"That was nice of your friend."

"She was happy to do it. She's the one with the son I wanted you to meet. Nice young man. He brought his mother to the hospital."

Kira's heart fluttered. "He's here? The man you wanted to set me up with is here? How could you do that?"

"You didn't object."

"Ma-ma, I was unconscious."

"Like I said, you didn't object."

She shook her head. "I must look horrible. Can I see a mirror?"

Ma-ma pulled out a compact from her purse. Kira popped it open. "Uggh."

"What's the problem?"

"Ma-ma, I have dark streaks on my eyes and cheeks. You thought this was fine?"

"You look beautiful."

Kira gritted her teeth and looked at the mirror again. "Oh well, there is one bright spot. After seeing me like this, he'll never want to see me again."

"Well," her mother started, "you'll see him at least one more time."

Kira's breath caught in her throat. "Why?"

"He went out to get coffee for your father and I. Should be back any minute."

A knock sounded from the outside. "Hello, anyone here?" a man's voice asked.

"We're here," her mother said.

A man walked in carrying a tray of Starbucks coffees. Beautiful soft eyes, rugged shoulders, and bald. Kira's mouth dropped.

Igami?

"You know my name?" the man asked.

"I…I don't think I said anything."

His smile grew wider. "You mouthed the word 'Igami' like you knew me." He handed the coffee to her parents. "Though I guess your mother or father might have mentioned my name."

"We didn't mention anything." Kira's mother turned to her. "His mother and I are childhood friends. However, it has been a long time since we've seen other. Too long. You wouldn't know the name."

"I don't know," Kira said. "Maybe I met you once before." Her face grew flushed. She would never be able to explain.

"What is it?" Igami asked.

"Oh nothing." Kira shook her head. "I guess I wasn't expecting…"

"You weren't expecting someone your mother is trying to set you up with to show up in the hospital."

"It's nothing against you. I just…look horrible."

He laughed again. "You look fine to me, especially given what you been through. As for me," he ran his hand over his head, "I normally have hair." He held out his hand. "My name is Stephen. Nice to meet you."

"Kira." She took his hand. His touch was light yet firm.

And familiar.

"So why don't you have hair?"

"I lost a bet on the Michigan-Ohio State football game." His gaze rose as he paused. "This is the result. It will grow back."

Images of the Igami she left floated in her mind. "It's not too bad now."

"Your father and I are going for a walk," Ma-ma said. "I haven't left the room much. Be back soon." She kissed Kira's forehead. "You're in good hands."

Kira shook her head. Leaving her here alone with a man she just met. Ma-ma was nuts.

Stephen pulled up a chair and sat near. "I'm glad to see you're okay."

She stared at him. "You don't even know me."

"Yes, I know."

"You could have at least brought me coffee."

"You weren't awake when I left. Didn't know you'd want some. I haven't drunk from mine yet. You can have it."

"No thanks. I'll deal without it for now. But when my parents return, could you?"

"I'll be happy to. If I get you some, will you tell me more about that dream you were having?"

Kira glanced toward the ceiling. How much could she tell him? It felt so real. No one would believe her. She pressed her hands against the bed and struggled to put herself into a sitting position. Jabs of pain pinged her temples. She would endure.

"It's probably not good to push yourself yet," he said.

"I need to move. On second thought, can I take a sip of your coffee?"

He handed it to her. "It's yours, but I actually did take a few sips."

"I just survived a plunge into a lake. I'm sure I can handle it."

"So what was the dream?"

She paused. Where to begin? "I dreamed I was back in time, sometime around the 16th century, and I was a consort to one of Nobunaga's samurai. I had a child who had difficulty learning his characters. A Buddhist monk in the dream worked with my child to help him overcome it.

"Very detailed for a dream. And fascinating."

"Why is it fascinating?"

"I work with children with dyslexia. My specialty is in using foreign languages. Most people familiar with dyslexia know that Greek is sometimes used to help children deal with their challenges. However, Japanese and Chinese are used as well. The characters are visual, stimulating, and fun for the kids."

A guy who smiles about helping children. Not bad. "How did you get interested in this?"

"I come from a long line of educators. Every generation, at least one member of my family is in education, even going back a few centuries in Japan."

"They were always teachers?"

He laughed. "If you go back far enough, they were Buddhist monks like in your dream."

I'm not surprised. "So every generation, someone in the family became a monk?"

"For a while, yes. Mostly kids following in their parents' footsteps."

"Sounds great. I'd love to hear about it."

"No," he smiled. "You don't want to take that chance I've been told I get too excited when I talk about my family history and that I can't shut up."

Kira tried to push herself up further. "Well, I'll take that chance. I do clean up well."

"Once you're out, I'd love to meet up with you. I'll keep it down to one story."

"Make it the best one, please."

"I will. One of my ancestors helped fake the deaths of two children in order to save their lives. The children were then brought up in different monasteries to hide their parentage. One child supposedly had reading difficulties, but grew up to a teacher himself."

"Sounds wonderful. I can't wait to hear it."

Epilogue

Saturday night had not come quick enough.

The doctor had released Kira two days later, wanting to keep Kira for observation. Ma-ma had moved in for a few days to ensure Kira was okay, fussing over her and driving her crazy. She'd let up when Kira had given the news she'd craved.

She'd made a date with Stephen.

The joy on Ma-ma's face had been sweet.

Stephen had taken her to Atoneta's, her now new favorite Italian restaurant. When Stephen had mentioned Italian, Kira had imagined romantic as opposed to the family crowd that was actually there. The garlic and spice scents had made her mouth water before she'd taken her seat. The pasta and rolls had guaranteed her return.

She hadn't wanted the night to end. Unfortunately, she still tired easily. Had since she'd come home from the hospital.

"How was everything?" Stephen asked, as they stopped at her door.

"It was wonderful."

"Sure you don't want to Lake Lanier Christmas lights tour tonight?"

An apprehensive tingle flowed across her skin. She did want to go. She just wasn't ready for Lanier. "How about next weekend? Maybe I'll be ready for Lanier by then.

Stephen smiled wide. "I can't wait."

She leaned forward and kissed him, his soft lips teasing hers. The feelings from Japan rushed back like a wave.

"If I didn't tell you before," she said, "your family story was amazing. Your relative sounds brave."

"Thank you" he said. "I look forward to seeing you again."

Her entire body warmed and she kissed him again. "Me, too."

"Before I leave though, I do have one question."

"What's that?"

Stephen's lips pressed into a thin line. "You never did tell me why there was a large lump of straw in your car."

Kira smiled. "One day. Soon."

The End

Dear Reader

Thank you for purchasing this anthology. I hope you enjoyed this story and all of the stories in here.

A few notes on the story. The modern characters are presented in western convention of first name first if a complete name is used. So Kira is the first name and Sakamichi is the last name. In the historical portion of the story, it is last name first per Japanese convention. This means, when samurai Niwa Nagahide appears, it is last name Niwa and first name Nagahide. I tried to write it in such a way so that it wouldn't be confusing to anyone unfamiliar with Japanese culture.

Shifting from culture to geography, the lake in the historical portion of this work, though unnamed in the book, is Lake Hamano. It was within the Oda Nobunaga's domain at the time of the story.

As for the history, I hope readers enjoyed hearing about The Battle of the Tedori River. In my study of Japanese history, I've always been fascinated by this particular clash. Beginning in the latter half of the 16th century, Japan was united by three individuals: Oda Nobunaga, Toyotomi Hideyoshi, and Tokugawa Ieyasu. (Last name first for all three per Japanese convention.) Nobunaga began the process, uniting roughly half of the country before his assassination in 1582 by one of his own generals, a man who tried to take over. Hideyoshi, another of Nobunaga's generals, avenged Nobunaga and rose to power. Hideyoshi conquered the rest of the country, but his son was too young to rule when Hideyoshi died in 1598. Ieyasu eventually usurped power, establishing a family succession that lasted until the 19th century.

So why does that make this battle of interest?

In November 1577, the forces of Oda Nobunaga met the forces of another warlord, Uesugi Kenshin, at the Tedori River. Nobunaga's forces, armed with guns and superior numbers, figured to overwhelm Kenshin's forces. However, rain and the river negated Nobunaga's advantage in arms and Kenshin's army routed Nobunaga's, a group that included both Hideyoshi and Ieyasu, though Hideyoshi may not have been there when the battle actually occurred. (Niwa Nagahide, the samurai in this story who informs Ogawa of his death sentence, was also at the battle.)

For reasons no one knows, Kenshin's forces allowed Nobunaga's to retreat. Given the hatred of Nobunaga by his rivals, any other warlord would have pressed the advantage against Nobunaga in hopes of eliminating him. However, Kenshin, who supposedly respected Nobunaga, chose not to do so. I've always wondered what would have happened in Kenshin had pursued. Even if he hadn't eliminated Nobunaga or his successors, he could have weakened him to the point where someone else might have ruled Japan.

Whoever ruled, it would not have been Kenshin. The warlord died in 1578, either from illness or possibly the most famous ninja assassination in history. With no confirmed successor, the Uesugi clan warred internally, eventually ceding much territory to the forces of Nobunaga who continued their expansion and domination.

Acknowledgements

Thank you to Lindi Peterson and Ciara Knight for asking me to participate in this wonderful project.

Thank you to Lindi Peterson and Kayla Tocco for their review of the manuscript and suggested changes.

Thank you to Mr. Jason Kinsey of the Arrowsmith School in Toronto for his comments on the usage of Japanese and Chinese characters in working with children with dyslexia.

Thank you to Officer Tom Carreiro for his assistance in the mechanics of auto accidents.

Thank you to the unnamed hostess at Atoneta's who confirmed for me what a Saturday night crowd is like. (We always do take out.)

Please note that any mistakes are the fault of the author.

Lastly, thank you to my wife, Motoyo, for putting up with me for over two decades and driving around Lake Lanier with me to figure out the best place to stage an accident.

Walt Mussell lives in the Atlanta area with his wife and two sons. He works for a well-known corporation and writes in his spare time. Walt primarily writes historicals, with a particular focus on Japan, an interest he gained in the four years he lived there.

Outside of writing, his favorite activity is trying to keep up with his kids. As they are both teenagers, this is proving more difficult each day.

Visit his website "Daddy Needs Decaf" at http://waltmussell.blogspot.com

Follow on Twitter at @wmussell

Follow on Facebook at https://www.facebook.com/Walt-Mussell-Author-1542458799362115/

Other Title by Walt Mussell
A Crash of Lives (*Hot Cocoa for the Heart* Christmas anthology)

Fanfiction from the *Body Movers* world of Kindle Worlds
Body Movers: Revenge is a Body Best Served Cold (The Wesley Tales Book 1)
Body Movers: The Good, The Bad and The Body (The Wesley Tales Book 2)
Body Movers: Even Bodies Fall From Trees (Yokohama Book 1)

THANK YOU!

This fundraising project was a collaborative effort, and would not have been possible without the tireless work of so many wonderful and caring people.

Of the many individuals who gave so much to this project, we would like to personally thank Sherrilyn Kenyon for the heartfelt foreword she contributed, and her assistant Kim Daniel for all of her help. Also, a special thank you to Ms. Kenyon and Dabel Brothers for donating a percentage of the proceeds of the Limited Edition Dark-Hunter Coloring Book Volume 02. We offer our deepest gratitude to the generous authors, cover artist, Airicka Phoenix, and formatter, Rene Folsom, who gave their time and talents for this project. To Ciara Knight for coordinating the project without the benefit of a time machine, and MK Smith for editing in mountainside thunderstorms. To Amber Garcia for holding everything together behind the scenes. And to Gracepoint and their stellar staff—Joy Wood, Susan Spruill, Karla Bowling, and Angie Fowler—for their kind help in bringing this dream of a project to fruition.

One hundred percent of the proceeds from the sale of LOVE & GRACE will be donated to GRACEPOINT – a school for the dyslexic learner.

GRACEPOINT, all the parents, and especially the students would like to thank you, the reader, for your generosity. By purchasing this boxed set, you will provide much needed funding for Gracepoint and its mission to educate dyslexic students.

If you'd like to offer an additional contribution to the school, please click here:
http://www.gracepointschool.org/donate-online/